★

"The absolute master . . . the craftsman so many of us look to for guidance. . . . ASSUMED IDENTITY is one of the most skillful jobs I've ever experienced."
—**Andrew Vachss**

★

"Fast . . . vivid . . . solid entertainment."
—*New Smyrna Beach Observer* (FL)

★

"Manages to mix successfully an intricate plot with exotic locales, a considerable amount of action, and solid characters." —*Baltimore Sun*

★

"What a terrific book! Characterization, plotting, structuring, pacing, all done to perfection."
—**J.C. Pollock, author of *Mission M.I.A.***

★

ALSO BY DAVID MORRELL

*Published by
WARNER BOOKS

*Limited edition with illustrations. Donald M. Grant,
Publisher, Hampton Falls, New Hampshire.

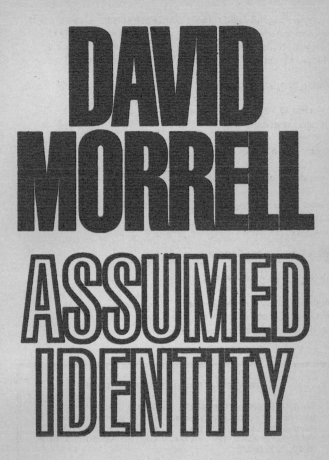

DAVID MORRELL

ASSUMED IDENTITY

WARNER
VISION
BOOKS

A Time Warner Company

WARNER BOOKS EDITION

Copyright © 1993 by David Morrell
All rights reserved.

Warner Vision is a trademark of Warner Books, Inc.

Cover design by Jackie Merri Meyer

Warner Books, Inc.
1271 Avenue of the Americas
New York, NY 10020

 A Time Warner Company

Printed in the United States of America

Originally published in hardcover by Warner Books.
First International Paperback Printing: March, 1994
First Printed in Paperback: September, 1994

10 9 8 7 6 5 4 3 2 1

To Martin E. Wingate (d. 1986),
"the rock,"
a good friend and a special teacher

No mask like open truth to cover lies,
As to go naked is the best disguise.

—William Congreve
The Double Dealer

And, after all, what is a lie?
'Tis but the truth in masquerade . . .

—Lord Byron
Don Juan

PROLOGUE

■ ■ ■

MEXICO, 1562

Less than forty years after the Spanish conquerers arrived in the New World, the systematic extermination of the natives was well under way. Much of the genocide required no effort, inasmuch as diseases to which the Europeans had become accustomed—smallpox, measles, mumps, and influenza, for example—did not exist in the New World and hence had a rapid effect on the natives, who had no immunity to them. Those who did not die from disease (perhaps as few as 10 percent of the original population survived) were beaten into submission and forced into slavery. Villages were destroyed, the inhabitants herded into labor camps. Every effort, especially torture, was used to compel the survivors to abandon their culture and convert to that of their European dominators.

In Mexico's southeastern extreme, the Yucatán Peninsula, a Franciscan missionary whose name was Diego de Landa reacted with shock to the evidence of snake worship and human sacrifice within the Mayan faith. Determined to eradicate these pagan barbarities, Landa organized the destruction of temples, statues, frescoes, any object with religious connotations—and in so doing, he not only separated the Maya from symbols of their beliefs but prevented modern historians from discovering the clues they needed to decipher the remaining hieroglyphs that described the lost ancient ways.

Landa's greatest triumph of destruction occurred at the village of Maní, where he exposed a secret library of Mayan books. These irreplaceable texts—bound like thin, small accordions and known as codices—"contained nothing in which there was not to be seen superstitions and lies of the devil," Landa reported to his superiors. "We burned them all."

We burned them all.

A present-day lover of antiquity exhales with despair at the self-righteous, narrow-minded confidence in those words. Book burners throughout time have shared Landa's purse-lipped, squinty-eyed, jut-jawed, absolute belief in his correctness. But Landa was deceived.

In several ways.

The codices contained historical and philosophical truths in addition to what Landa called lies.

And not all the codices were destroyed. Three of them—salvaged by Spaniards in charge of the burning and smuggled home to Europe as souvenirs—were eventually uncovered in private collections and recognized for their incalculable value.

Known as the Dresden Codex, the Codex Tro-Cortesianus, and the Codex Persianus, they are owned by libraries in Dresden, Madrid, and Paris. A fourth—known as the Grolier Codex and located in Mexico City—has been declared by one expert a fake and is currently under investigation.

But rumors persist that there is a fifth, that it is authentic, that it has more truths than any other, especially *one* truth, a *crucial* truth.

A modern observer wonders how Friar de Landa would react if he could be summoned from Hell and made to witness the bloodbath comparable in intensity, if not in magnitude, to the one Landa caused in the 1500s, the bloodbath that could have been avoided if Landa had never begun his inquisition or else if he had been the professional he claimed to be and had actually accomplished his hateful job. Maní, the name of the village where Landa found and destroyed the codices, is the Mayan word for "it is finished."

But it wasn't finished at all.

ONE

1

"Now I realize you all want to hear about human sacrifice," the professor said, allowing just the right mischievous glint in his eyes, signaling to his students that to study history didn't mean they had to suppress their sense of humor. Each time he taught this course—and he'd been doing so for thirty years—he always began with the same comment, and he always got the reaction he wanted, a collective chuckle, the students glancing at one another in approval and sitting more comfortably.

"Virgins having their hearts cut out," the professor continued, "or being thrown off cliffs into wells—that sort of thing." He gestured dismissively, as if he was so familiar with the details of human sacrifice that the subject bored him. Again his eyes glinted mischievously, and the students chuckled louder. His name was Stephen Mill. He was fifty-eight, short and slender, with receding gray hair, a thin salt-and-pepper mustache, square-framed, wire-rimmed bifocals, and a brown wool suit that gave off the scent of pipe smoke. Liked and respected by both colleagues and students, he was beginning

3

the last seventy minutes of his life, and if it was any consolation, at least he would die doing what he most enjoyed, talking about his life's obsession.

"Actually, the Maya didn't have much interest in sacrificing virgins," Professor Mill added. "Most of the skeletons we've retrieved from the sacred wells—they're called cenotes, by the way; you might as well begin learning the proper terms—belong to males, and most of *those* had been children."

The students made faces of disgust.

"The Maya did cut out hearts, of course," Professor Mill said. "But that's the most boring part of the ritual."

Several students frowned and mouthed "boring?" to one another.

"What the Maya would do is capture an enemy, strip him, paint him blue, take him to the top of a pyramid, break his back but not kill him—not yet at least; the temporary objective was to paralyze him—then cut out his heart, and *now* he'd die, but not before the high priest was able to raise the victim's pulsing heart for everyone to see. The heart and the blood dripping from it were smeared onto the faces of gods carved into the walls at the top of the temple. It's been theorized that the high priest may also have consumed the heart. But this much we know for certain: The victim's corpse was subsequently hurled down the steps of the pyramid. There a priest cut off the victim's skin and danced in it. Those who'd witnessed the ceremony chopped the corpse into pieces and barbecued it."

The students swallowed uncomfortably, as if they felt sick.

"But we'll get to the dull stuff later in the term," Professor Mill said, and the students laughed again, this time with relief. "As you know, this is a multidiscipline course." He switched tones with expert ease, deepening his voice, abandoning his guise as an entertainer, becoming a lecturer. "Some of you are here from art history. Others are ethnologists and archaeologists. Our purpose is to examine Mayan hieroglyphics, to learn to read them, and to use the knowledge we obtain to reconstruct Mayan culture. Please turn to page seventy-nine of Charles Gallenkamp's *Maya: The Riddle and Rediscovery of a Lost Civilization*."

The students obeyed and immediately frowned at a bewildering diagram that looked like a totem pole with two descending columns of distorted, grimacing faces flanked by lines, dots, and squiggles. Someone groaned.

"Yes, I realize the challenge is daunting," Professor Mill said. "You're telling yourselves that you can't possibly learn to read that maze of apparently meaningless symbols. But I assure you, you *will* be able to read it and many others like it. You'll be able to put sounds to those glyphs, to read them as if they were sentences." He paused for dramatic effect, then straightened. "To speak the ancient Mayan language." He shook his head with wonder. "You understand now what I meant. Stories about human sacrifice are dull. This"—he pointed toward the hieroglyphs in Gallenkamp's book—"this is the true excitement." He directed a keen gaze toward each of his twenty students. "And since we have to start somewhere, let's start as we did when we were children, by making lines and dots. You'll note that many of the columns of glyphs— which depict a date, by the way—look like this." Grabbing a piece of chalk, Professor Mill drew hurried marks on the blackboard.

"Each dot has a value of one. A line—or what we call a bar—signifies five. Thus the first group I drew equals four, the second equals eight, the third is twelve, and the fourth . . . Well, why should *I* do all the talking?" Professor Mill drew his right index finger down his list of students. "Mr. Hogan, please tell me the value of . . ."

"Sixteen?" a tentative male voice responded.

"Excellent, Mr. Hogan. You see how easy it is? You're

already learning to read Mayan symbols. But if you put all the numbers on those glyphs together, the date they depict wouldn't make any sense to you. Because the Maya used a different calendar than we do. Their calendar was almost as accurate as our own. It was also considerably more complicated. So, as our first step in understanding Mayan civilization, we'll have to understand their concept of time. For our next class, read chapters one and two in *A Forest of Kings: The Untold Story of the Ancient Maya* by Linda Schele and David Friedel. Meanwhile, I'll summarize what you'll be reading."

And so Professor Mill continued, taking obvious delight in his subject matter. With less than twenty minutes remaining in his life, he was enjoying every second. He concluded the class with a joke that he always used at this point in the course, elicited another anticipated chuckle, answered a few questions from students who lingered, then packed his books, notes, syllabus, and list of students into his briefcase.

His office was a five-minute stroll from the classroom building. Professor Mill breathed deeply, with satisfaction, as he walked. It was a bright, clear, pleasant day. All in all, he felt splendid (less than fifteen minutes to live now), and his delight with how he'd performed in class was enhanced by his anticipation of what he would do next, of the appointment he'd made for after class, of the visitor he expected.

The office was in a drab brick building, but the bleak surroundings had no effect on Professor Mill's sense of well-being and eagerness. Indeed, he felt so full of energy that he passed students at the elevator and walked rapidly up the two flights of stairs to the dimly lit corridor halfway along which he had his office. After unlocking the door (ten minutes to go) and setting his briefcase on his desk, he turned to walk down to the faculty lounge but paused, then smiled when he saw his visitor appear at the open doorway.

"I was just going for some coffee," Professor Mill said. "Would you care for some?"

"Thanks but no." The visitor nodded in greeting and entered. "My stomach and coffee don't get along anymore. I have heartburn all the time. I think I'm developing an ulcer."

The visitor was a distinguished-looking man in his middle

thirties. His neatly trimmed hair, custom-made white shirt, striped silk tie, hand-tailored double-breasted suit, and thin-soled calfskin shoes were in keeping with his occupation as a highly paid corporate executive.

"Ulcers come from stress. You'd better slow down." Professor Mill shook hands with him.

"Stress and speed are part of my job description. If I start worrying about my health, I'll find myself out of work." The visitor sat.

"You need a vacation."

"Soon. They keep promising me soon."

"So what have you got for me?" Professor Mill asked.

"More glyphs to be translated."

"How many?"

The visitor shrugged. "Five pages." He frowned as a group of students went by in the corridor. "I'd prefer to keep this confidential."

"Of course." Professor Mill got up, shut the door, and returned to his desk. "Mayan pages or contemporary pages?"

The visitor looked puzzled, then realized. "Right, I keep forgetting Mayan pages are bigger. No, contemporary pages. Eight-by-ten photographs. I assume the fee we negotiated the last time is still acceptable."

"Fifty thousand dollars? *Very* acceptable. As long as I'm not rushed, " Professor Mill said.

"You won't be. You can have a month, the same as before. The same terms of payment—half now, half when you're finished. The same conditions pertain. You may not make copies of the pages. You may not reveal what you are doing or discuss your translation with anyone."

"Don't worry. I won't, and I haven't," Professor Mill said, "although there's nothing so interesting in the translation that anybody except you and me and your employer would care. No matter. You pay me so well that I'd be insane to break the terms of the agreement and jeopardize my future relationship with you. I have a sabbatical next year, and the money you've generously paid me will allow me to devote the entire year to studying the Hieroglyphic Stairway in the Mayan ruins at Copán in Honduras."

"It's too hot down there for me," the visitor said.

"When I'm at the ruins, I'm too excited to think about the weather. May I see the pages?"

"By all means." The visitor reached into an alligator-skin briefcase, pulling out a large manila envelope.

With less than a minute to live, Professor Mill took the envelope, opened it, and removed five photographs that showed numerous rows of hieroglyphs. He shifted books to the side of his desk and arranged the photographs so that the rows of glyphs were vertical.

"All part of the same text?"

"I have no idea," the visitor said. "All I was told was to make the delivery."

"They appear to be." Professor Mill picked up a magnifying glass and leaned close to the photographs, studying the details of the glyphs. Sweat beaded on his brow. He shook his head. "I shouldn't have run up those stairs."

"Excuse me?" the visitor asked.

"Nothing. Just talking to myself. Does it feel warm in here?"

"A little."

Professor Mill took off his suit coat and resumed his inspection of the photographs. Fifteen seconds to live. "Well, leave them with me, and . . ."

"Yes?"

"I . . ."

"What?" the visitor asked.

"Don't feel so good. My hands . . ."

"What about them?"

"Numb," Professor Mill said. "My . . ."

"What?"

"Face. Hot."

Professor Mill abruptly gasped, clutched his chest, stiffened, and slumped, sagging backward in his creaky swivel chair, his mouth open, his head drooping. He shivered and stopped moving.

The small office seemed to contract as the visitor stood. "Professor Mill?" He felt for a pulse at a wrist and then the neck. "Professor Mill?" He removed rubber gloves from his briefcase, put them on, then used his right hand to collect the photographs and slide them into the manila envelope, which he held steady with his left hand. Cautiously, he used the left hand to peel off the glove on his right hand, and vice versa, in each case making sure that he didn't touch any area that had touched the photographs. He dropped the gloves into another manila envelope, sealed it, and put both envelopes into his briefcase.

When the visitor opened the door, none of the students or faculty passing in the corridor paid much attention to him. An amateur might have walked away, but the visitor knew that excitement could prime memories, that someone would eventually remember seeing a well-dressed man come out of the office. He didn't want to create a mystery. He was well aware that the best deception was a version of the truth. So he walked rapidly to the secretary's office, entered it in distress, and told the secretary, "Hurry. Phone nine one one. Professor Mill. I was visiting . . . I think he just had a heart attack."

2

GUATAMALA CITY

Despite his thirty-six-hour journey and his sixty-four years, Nicholas Petrovich Bartenev fidgeted with energy. He and his wife had flown from Leningrad—

Correction, he thought. St. Petersburg. Now that communism has collapsed, they've abolished Lenin.

—to Frankfurt to Dallas to here, by invitation of the new Guatemalan government, and indeed if it hadn't been for the Cold War's end, this journey would not have been possible. Guatemala had only recently, after forty years, resumed diplomatic relations with Russia, and the all-important Russian exit visas, which for so long had been impossible to obtain, had been issued with astonishing efficiency. For most of his life, Bartenev had one consuming dream—to travel to Guatemala, not because he was eager to leave Russia but rather because Guatemala obsessed him. But he'd persistently, repeatedly been denied permission, and all of a sudden it was merely a matter of filling out some government forms and coming back a few days later to get the necessary travel papers. Bartenev couldn't believe his good fortune. He feared that all of this would turn out to be a cruel hoax, that he'd be refused permission to enter Guatemala, that he'd be deported back to Russia.

The jet—a stretch 727 owned by American Airlines . . . American! For a Russian citizen to be a passenger on a jet labeled *American* would have been unthinkable not many years ago—descended through clouds, past mountains, toward a city sprawled in a valley. The time was 8:15 in the evening. Sunset cast a crimson glow across the valley. Guatemala City's lights gleamed. Bartenev gazed spellbound out his window, his heart pounding with the eagerness of a child.

Beside him, his wife clasped his hand. He turned to study her beautiful wrinkled face, and she didn't need to say anything to communicate the pleasure she felt because he would soon fulfill his dream. From the age of eighteen, from the first time he'd seen photographs of the Mayan ruins at Tikal in Guatemala, he had felt an eerie identification with the now-almost-vanished people who had built them. He felt as if he had been there, as if he had been one of the Maya, as if his strength and sweat had helped erect the great pyramids and temples. And he had become fascinated with the hieroglyphs.

All these years later, without ever having set foot on a Mayan ruin, without ever having climbed a pyramid, without ever having stared face-to-face at the hook-nosed, high-cheeked, slope-browed visages of the Maya in the hieroglyphs, he was one of the top five Mayan epigraphers in the world (perhaps the top of the top, if he believed his wife's flattery), and soon—not tonight, of course, but tomorrow perhaps or certainly the day after—he'd have managed yet another flight, this one to a primitive airstrip, and have accomplished the difficult journey through the jungle to Tikal, to his life's preoccupation, to the center of his world, to the ruins.

To the hieroglyphs.

His heartbeat increased as the jet touched down. The sun was lower behind the western mountains. The darkness thickened, pierced by the glint of lights from the airport's terminal. Nervous with anticipation, Bartenev unbuckled his seat belt, picked up his briefcase, and followed his wife and other passengers along the aisle. A frustrating minute seemed to take much longer before the aircraft's hatch was opened. He squinted past the passengers ahead of him and saw the murky silhouettes of buildings. As he and his wife descended stairs to the airport's tarmac, he breathed the thin, dry, cool mountain air and felt his body tense with excitement.

The moment he entered the terminal, however, he saw several uniformed government officials waiting for him, and he knew that something was wrong. They were somber, pensive, brooding. Bartenev feared that his premonition had been justified, that he was about to be refused permission to enter the country.

Instead, a flustered, thin-lipped man in a dark suit stepped away from them, nervously approaching. "Professor Bartenev?"

"Yes."

They spoke in Spanish. Bartenev's compulsive interest in Guatemala and the Mayan ruins throughout Mesoamerica had prompted him to acquire a facility in the local language, since much of the scholarship being done on the hieroglyphs was published in Spanish.

"My name is Hector Gonzales. From the National Archaeological Museum here."

"Yes, I've received your letters." As they shook hands, Bartenev couldn't help noticing how Gonzales guided him toward the government officials. "This is my wife, Elana."

"I'm very pleased to meet you, Mrs. Bartenev. If you'll please come through this door. . . ."

Abruptly Bartenev noticed stern soldiers holding automatic rifles. He cringed, reminded of Leningrad during the worst of the Cold War. "Is something wrong? Is there something you haven't told me, something I should know?"

"Nothing," Gonzales said too quickly. "A problem with your accommodations. A scheduling difficulty. Nothing serious. Come this way. Through this door and down this hallway. Hurry, or we'll be late."

"Late?" Bartenev shook his head as he and his wife were rushed along the corridor. "Late for what? And our luggage? What about—?"

"It's being taken care of. Your luggage will be brought to your hotel. You don't need to go through immigration and customs."

They passed through another door, into the night, onto a parking lot, where a Jeep filled with armed soldiers waited in front of a black limousine, behind which there was another Jeep filled with armed soldiers.

"I demand to know what is going on," Bartenev said. "In your letters, you claimed that I would feel welcome here. Instead, I feel like a prisoner."

"Professor Bartenev, you must understand that Guatemala is a troubled country. There is always much political uneasiness here. These soldiers are for your protection."

"Why would I need—?"

"Please get in the car, and we can discuss it."

The moment an escort shut the door on Bartenev, his wife, Gonzales, and two government officials, Bartenev again demanded, "Why would I need protection?"

The limousine, flanked by the Jeeps, sped away.

"As I told you, politics. For many years, Guatemala has been ruled by right-wing extremists." Gonzales glanced uneasily at the government officials, as if he suspected that they would not approve of his vocabulary. "Recently, moderates have come into power. The new government is the reason that your country now is permitted to have diplomatic relations with ours. It also explains why you were invited here. A visit from a Russian academician emphasizes the goodwill that the Guatemalan government wants with your country. You were an ideal man to invite because you are not a politician and because your expertise relates to Guatemalan history."

"The way you speak . . ." Bartenev hesitated. "It makes me think you work less for the National Archaeological Museum than you do for the government. What is the name of the dynasty that ruled Tikal?"

Gonzales didn't answer.

"In what century did Tikal reach its zenith of power?"

Gonzales didn't answer.

Bartenev scoffed.

"You are in danger," Gonzales said.

"What?"

"The right-wing extremists strongly disapprove of your visit," Gonzales explained tensely. "Despite the collapse of communism in Russia, these extremists see your visit as the beginning of a corrupting influence that will make this country Marxist. The previous government used death squads to enforce its rule. Those death squads are still in existence. There have been threats against your life."

Bartenev stared, despair spreading through him. His wife asked what Gonzales was saying to him. Grateful that she didn't understand Spanish, Bartenev told her that someone had forgotten to make a reservation for them at the hotel, that their host was embarrassed about the oversight, and that the mistake was being corrected.

He scowled at Gonzales. "What are you saying to me? That I have to leave? I refuse. Oh, I will send my wife to safety. But I did not come all this way only to leave before I see my dream. I'm too old. I will probably not have this chance again. And I'm too close. I will go the *rest* of the way."

"You are not being asked to leave," Gonzales said. "That would be almost as ruinous a political act as if someone attempted to kill you."

Bartenev felt blood drain from his face.

Gonzales said, "But we must be extremely careful. Cautious. We are asking you not to go out in public in the city. Your hotel will be guarded. We will transport you to Tikal as quickly as possible. And then we request that after a prudent length of time—a day, or at the most two—you feign illness and return to your home."

"A day?" Bartenev had difficulty breathing. "Perhaps two? So little time after so many years of waiting for . . ."

"Professor Bartenev, we have to deal with political realities."

Politics, Bartenev thought, and wanted to curse. But like Gonzales, he was accustomed to dealing with such obscene realities, and he analyzed the problem with desperate speed. He was out of Russia, free to go anywhere—that was the important factor. There were numerous other major Mayan ruins. Palenque in Mexico, for example. He'd always been fond of photographs of it. It wasn't Tikal. It didn't have the emotional and professional attraction that Tikal had for him, but it was accessible. His wife could accompany him there. They would be safe there. If the Guatemalan government refused to pay for further expenses, that wouldn't matter—because Bartenev had a secret source of funds about which he hadn't told even his wife.

Indeed, secrecy had been part of the business arrangement when the well-dressed, fair-haired American had arrived at Bartenev's office at St. Petersburg State University. The American had shown him several photographs of Mayan glyphs. He had asked in perfect Russian how much Bartenev would charge to translate the glyphs and keep the assignment confidential. "If the glyphs are interesting, I won't charge anything," Bartenev had answered, impressed by the foreigner's command of the language. But the American had insisted on paying. In fact, his fee had been astonishingly generous: fifty thousand dollars. "To ensure your silence," the American had said. "I've converted some of it to rubles." He gave Bartenev the equivalent of ten thousand dollars in Russian currency. The remainder, he explained, would be placed in a Swiss bank account. Perhaps one day Bartenev would be free to travel, in which case the money could easily be obtained. Failing that, couriers could be arranged to transport prudent amounts into St. Petersburg for him, amounts that wouldn't be so large that the authorities would ask questions about their source. Since that visit, the American had come two more times, in each case with more photographs of Mayan glyphs and with the same fee. Until now, the money had not been as important to Bartenev as the fascinating, although puzzling, message (like a riddle within a code) that the glyphs revealed.

But now the money was *very* important, and Bartenev bitterly meant to get full value from it.

"Yes," he told Gonzales. "Political realities. I will leave whenever you want, whenever I have served your purpose."

Gonzales seemed to relax. But only for a moment. Abruptly the limousine arrived at a hotel, the steel-and-glass modern design of which was jarringly un-Hispanic. The soldiers escorted Bartenev and his wife quickly through the lobby, into an elevator, and to the twelfth floor. Gonzales came with them while a government official spoke to a clerk at the check-in desk.

The phone was ringing as Gonzales unlocked the door, turned on a light, and guided Bartenev and his wife into the suite. Actually, there were two phones, one on a table next to a sofa, the other on a bar.

Gonzales locked the door behind them. The phone kept ringing. As Bartenev stepped toward the one by the sofa, Gonzales said, "No, let me answer it." He chose the closer phone, the one on the bar. "Hello." He turned on a lamp. "Why do you wish to speak with him?" He stared at Bartenev. "Just a moment." He placed a hand over the telephone's mouthpiece. "It's a man who claims to be a journalist. Perhaps it would be wise to give an interview. Good public relations. I'll listen on this phone while you use that one."

Bartenev pivoted toward the phone on the table beside the sofa. "Hello," he said, casting a shadow against the window.

"Go to hell, you goddamned Russian."

As the window shattered inward, Bartenev's wife screamed. Bartenev did not. The bullet that struck his skull and mushroomed within it killed him instantly. The bullet burst out the back of his head, spraying blood across the flying glass.

3

HOUSTON, TEXAS

The space shuttle *Atlantis* was on the second day of its current mission—a no-problem launch, an all-systems-go performance so far—and Albert Delaney felt bored. He wished that something would happen, anything to break his tedious routine. Not that he wanted excitement exactly, because he associated that word with a crisis. The last thing NASA needed was more foul-ups and bad publicity, and at all costs, another *Challenger* disaster had to be avoided. One more like that and NASA would probably be out of business, which meant that Albert Delaney would be out of a job, and Albert Delaney preferred boredom any day to being unemployed. Still, if anybody had told him when he'd been accepted by NASA that his enthusiasm for what he assumed would be a glamorous career would all too quickly change to tedium, he'd have been incredulous. The trouble was that NASA prechecked the details of a mission so often, testing and retesting, going over every variable, trying to anticipate every contingency, that by the time the mission occurred, it was anticlimactic. No, Albert Delaney didn't want excitement, but he certainly wouldn't have minded an occasional positive surprise.

A man of medium height and weight, with average features, in that cusp of life where he'd stopped being young but wasn't yet middle-aged, he'd noticed that more and more he'd been feeling dissatisfied, unfulfilled. His existence was ordinary. Predictable. He hadn't yet reached the stage of his syndrome where he was tempted to cheat on his wife. Nonetheless, he was afraid that what Thoreau had called "quiet desperation" might drive him to do something stupid and he'd get more excitement than he'd bargained for by ruining his marriage. Still, if he didn't find some purpose, something to interest him, he didn't know if he could rely on his common sense.

Part of his problem, Albert Delaney decided, was that his office was at the periphery of NASA headquarters. Away from the mission-control center, he didn't have the sense of accomplishment and nervous energy that he imagined everyone felt there. Plus, even *he* had to admit that being an expert in cartography, geography, and meteorology (maps, land, and weather, as he sometimes put it bluntly) seemed awfully dull compared to space exploration. It wasn't as if he got the chance to examine photographs of newly discovered rings around Saturn or moons near Jupiter or active volcanoes on Venus. No, what he got to do was look at photographs of areas on earth, sections that he'd looked at dozens of times before.

It didn't help that the conclusions of the research he was doing had already been determined. Did photographs from space show that the alarming haze around the earth was becoming worse? Did high-altitude images indicate that the South American rain forest continued to dwindle due to slash-and-burn farming practices? Were the oceans becoming so polluted that evidence of the damage could be seen from three hundred miles up? Yes. Yes. Yes. You didn't need to be a rocket scientist to come up with those conclusions. But NASA wanted more than conclusions. It wanted specifics, and even though the photographs that Albert Delaney examined would eventually be sent to other government agencies, it was his job to make the preliminary examination, just in case there was something unique in them, so that NASA could get the publicity.

The shuttle's current mission was to deploy a weather satellite over the Caribbean Sea and perform various weather-related observations and experiments, as well as transmit photographs. The photograph currently in front of Delaney showed a portion of Mexico's Yucatán Peninsula. For several years, a blight had been attacking the palm trees in that area, and one of Delaney's jobs was to determine how far the blight had spread, something that could easily be seen in the photographs since the sick, denuded trees created a distinct bleak pattern. The theory was that substantial loss of vegetation in the Yucatán would disturb the oxygen/carbon-dioxide ratio in the area and affect weather patterns just as the disappearance of Brazil's rain forest did. By measuring the area of blight and factoring that information with temperature and wind variations in the Caribbean, it might be possible to predict the creation of tropical storms and the direction of hurricanes.

The blight had definitely spread much farther than photographs of the Yucatán taken last year indicated. Delaney placed a transparent scale-model map over the photograph, aligned topographical features, recorded measurements, and continued to another photograph. Perhaps it was his need for a break in his routine. Perhaps it was his need to be surprised. For whatever reason, he found that he was examining the photographs far more diligently than usual, paying attention to matters that weren't related to the palm-tree blight.

Abruptly something troubled him, a subconsciously noticed detail, a sense that something was out of place. He set down the photograph he was examining and went back to the one he'd just completed. Frowning, he concentrated. Yes, he thought. There. At once he felt a stimulating flow of adrenaline, a warming in his stomach. That small area in the bottom left corner of the photograph. Those shadows among the denuded palm trees. What were those shadows doing there?

The shadows formed almost perfect triangles and squares. But triangles and squares did not exist in nature. More, those shadows could be made only by sunlight that struck and was blocked by objects above the ground. Large objects. Tall objects. Normally, shadows didn't pose a mystery. Hills made them all the time. But these shadows were in the Yucatán's northern lowlands. The descriptive name said it all: lowlands. There *weren't* any hills in that region. Even if there were, the shadows they cast would have been amorphous. But these were *symmetrical*. And they occupied a comparatively wide area. Delaney made quick calculations. Thirty square kilometers? In the middle of an otherwise dramatically flat section of the Yucatán rain forest? What the hell was going on?

4

"For our final report, something old discovered by something new. Computer-enhanced photographs received from the space shuttle *Atlantis* have revealed what appears to be a large area of unsuspected Mayan ruins in a remote section of Mexico's Yucatán Peninsula. The rain forest in that region is so dense and inaccessible that it could take months before a preliminary assessment of the ruins can be completed, but a spokesperson for the Mexican government indicated that the apparent scope of the ruins suggests that they have the potential to rival the pyramids, palaces, and temples at legendary Chichén Itzá. To paraphrase F. Scott Fitzgerald, and so we move on—into the past. This is Dan Rather. For CBS News, good evening."

5

THE VIRGIN ISLANDS

The visitor noted that several more artifacts—figurines, ceramics, and masks—had been added to the collection. All were authentic, expensive, and illegally obtained examples of ancient Mayan craftsmanship. "The woman disappeared."

"*What?*" The old man, who'd been distracted as he attached an intravenous line to a needle in his arm, snapped his head up. "*Disappeared?* You assured me that wasn't possible."

"I believed it wasn't," the fair-haired man said. His tone

was somber. "She was being paid so well and treated so lavishly that I thought it highly unlikely she would want to leave."

The old man glowered, his thin body rigid with fury. Seated in a leather chair in the main cabin of his two-hundred-foot-long yacht, flanked by displays of his current passion, Mayan art, he stretched his gaunt frame to its maximum. His gaze intensified by his glasses, his pinched expression emphasized by his thick white hair, he dominated the cabin, even though he wasn't tall. "Human nature. Damn it, that's always been your problem. You're excellent when it comes to tactics. But your emotional range is so limited that you don't understand. . . ."

"She was lonely," the pleasant-faced man said. "I anticipated that possibility. My people were watching her in case she attempted to do something foolish. Her maid, her butler, her chauffeur, the doorman at her condominium building in Manhattan—all of them worked for me. Every exit from that building was constantly watched. On those rare occasions when she had permission to leave it, she was followed."

"And yet," the old man rasped, his nostrils flaring with angry sarcasm, "she managed to disappear." His white hair contrasted with the pewter tint of his skin, which in turn was emphasized by the gray of his robe, the left sleeve of which was rolled up to admit the intravenous tube leading into his arm. "You. I blame *you*." He pointed his bony right index finger. "Everything depends on her. *How in God's name did this happen?*"

The well-dressed man gestured in frustration. "I don't know. My people don't know. It happened last night. Between two A.M., when the maid last saw her, and noon, when the maid decided to check on her, the woman managed to get out of the condo and the building. We have no idea how. When I learned what had happened, I decided I'd better report to you in person rather than use the telephone. I caught the first available flight." He gestured toward the starboard windows of the cabin and the numerous other yachts in St. Thomas's hotel-rimmed, sunset-tinted harbor.

The old man squinted. "Willingness to face blame. I respect that. It's rare for a sociopath to have character. *Does she have access to her bank account?*"

"No. Since she was provided with all the comforts she wanted, she had no need to spend money. Hence she didn't realize that the bank statements she was shown, the ones that indicated her salary deposits, were for an account that required me to cosign for withdrawals. The money's inaccessible to her."

"Jewelry?"

"She took it all. The diamond necklace alone is worth four hundred thousand dollars. In theory. But of course, the stones aren't genuine. Still, there are only certain establishments in the New York area that would have the resources to buy such an item, if it weren't a copy. And since she doesn't know it's a copy, she'll have to go to them. My people are watching those establishments."

The old man frowned. "Assuming she's able to obtain money—and I suspect she will, given the ingenuity she showed in escaping your people—where would she go? What can she do?"

"She'd be a fool to go back to her former patterns. She has to assume that we'll watch her relatives, her friends, and her previous business associates, that we'll tap their phones, et cetera. If she's smart—and she's proven she is—she'll go to ground. The last thing she wants is trouble from us."

"Us?"

"From you."

The old man gestured with a wrinkled hand, his eyes harsh with disapproval yet glinting with superiority. "Human nature. You still haven't learned the lesson. If loneliness made her run, the one thing she *won't* do is go to ground. She'll want companionship. She'll want the security and satisfaction of a life that *she* creates, not one that's forced upon her. She won't trade one cage for another."

"Then what will . . .?"

The old man stared at his intravenous line and brooded. "She'll get help."

"From?"

"There are only two reasons for someone to help someone else," the old man said. "Money and love. We can't possibly anticipate who would work for her. But I wonder if she would trust a stranger who is loyal to her only for money. I suspect that someone in her position would prefer to depend on love, or at least friendship. Who in her background has the skills to help her?''

''As I told you, her family, friends, and former contacts are under surveillance.''

''No. Look deeper. She wouldn't have fled unless she had a plan. Somewhere there's someone who knows about this sort of thing and whom *she* knows she can ask for help. Someone who isn't obvious. Someone she trusts.''

''I'll get started immediately.''

''You've disappointed me,'' the old man said. ''Your success in Chicago and Guatemala was so encouraging that I'd arranged a reward for you. Now, I'm afraid, I'll have to withhold it.''

An intercom buzzed on a table beside the old man's chair. He pressed a button. ''I told you not to interrupt me.''

''Sheik Hazim is returning your telephone call, Professor,'' a female voice said.

''Of course. I'll speak to him.'' The old man rested his hand on the telephone beside the intercom. But before he picked it up, he told his visitor, his voice stern and flinty, ''Don't disappoint me again.'' He adjusted the flow of red liquid that drained from an intravenous bottle into his arm—blood treated with hormones from unborn lambs. ''Find the bitch before she ruins everything. If Delgado discovers she's loose, if he discovers she's out of control, he'll go after her and possibly us.''

''I can deal with Delgado.''

''Of that, I have no doubt. Without Delgado, however, I can't do business. I can't get access to the ruins. And *that* would make me very unhappy. You do not want to be near me when I am unhappy.''

''No, sir.''

''Get out.''

Two

■ ■ ■

1

CANCÚN, MEXICO

All the hotels were shaped like Mayan temples, a row of terraced pyramids along the four-lane highway dividing the sandbar that until twenty-five years ago had been uninhabited. Buchanan ignored them and the redbrick sidewalk along which he concentrated to walk with deceptive calm. As twilight thickened into night, what he paid attention to were the disturbing proximity of tourists before and behind him, the threatening rumble and glare of traffic passing him on the right, and the ominous shadows among the palm trees that flanked the hotels on his left.

Something was wrong. Every instinct and intuition warned him. His stomach felt rigid. He tried to tell himself that he was merely experiencing the equivalent of stage fright. But his experience of too many dangerous missions had taught him the hard way to pay attention to the visceral warning signals that alerted him when something wasn't as it should be.

But what? Buchanan strained to analyze. Your preparation was thorough. Your bait for the target is perfect. Why in God's name are you so nervous?

Burnout? Too many assignments? Too many identities? Too many high-wire juggling acts?

No, Buchanan mentally insisted. I know what I'm doing. After eight years, after having survived this long, I recognize the difference between nerves and . . .

Relax. You're on top of things. Give yourself a break. It's hot. It's muggy. You're under stress. You've done this a hundred times before. Your plan is solid. The bottom line is quit second-guessing. Get control of your doubts, and do your job.

Sure, Buchanan thought. But he wasn't convinced. Maintaining his deceptively leisurely pace in spite of the pressure in his chest, he shifted leftward, relieved to escape the threatening traffic. Past the equally threatening shadows of the dense, colorfully flowered shrubs that lined the driveway, he proceeded warily up the curving entrance toward the glistening Mayan-temple shape of Club Internacional.

2

Buchanan's appointment was for 9:30, but he took care to arrive ten minutes early in order to survey the meeting place and verify that nothing about the site had changed that might jeopardize the rendezvous. For the past three evenings, he'd visited this hotel exactly at this time, and on each occasion he'd satisfied himself that the location was perfect.

The problem was that *this* night wasn't those other nights. A plan that existed perfectly on paper had to match the "real world," and the real world had a dangerous habit of changing from day to day. A fire might have damaged the building. Or the site might be so unusually crowded that a discreet, nonetheless damning, conversation could be easily overheard. An exit might be blocked. There were too many variables. If anything disturbed him, Buchanan would disguise his concern and drift back into the night. Then by prior agreement, when his contact arrived at 9:30 and didn't see Buchanan, the contact would know that the circumstance wasn't ideal, a euphemism for "get your ass out of here," that the meeting had been postponed until eight tomorrow morning at breakfast at another hotel, and of course Buchanan had arranged a further backup plan in case that second meeting, too, was postponed. Because Buchanan had to assure his contact that every precaution was being considered, that the safety of the contact was Buchanan's primary consideration.

So Buchanan strolled past the two Mexican porters at the entrance to Club Internacional. Inside the lobby, he eased beyond a group of jovial American tourists on their way to Cancún's Hard Rock Cafe and tried not to breathe the perfumed, acrid odor of insecticide that the hotel periodically sprayed along its corridors to discourage the area's considerable population of cockroaches. Buchanan wondered which the guests hated more—the offending spray or the ubiquitous insects that after a while seemed as commonplace as the area's numerous lizards. While a maid unobtrusively swept up dead insects, Buchanan hesitated at the rear of the lobby just long enough to notice a Japanese guest coming through a door beside the gift shop on the left. That door, Buchanan knew, led to balconies, rooms, and stairwells to the beach. One of many exits. In working order. So far so good.

To his right, he proceeded along a short hallway and came to steps that went down to a restaurant. As on previous nights, the restaurant was moderately busy, just enough for Buchanan and his contact to be inconspicuous but not so busy that they'd be surrounded by potential eavesdroppers.

Again, so far so good. Perhaps I'm wrong, Buchanan thought. Perhaps everything's going to be fine.

Don't kid yourself, a warning voice insisted.

Hey, I'm not about to cancel a meeting just because I've got a case of nerves.

He felt briefly reassured when a Mexican waiter came over and agreed to sit him at the table he requested. That table was ideally situated in the far right corner, away from the other diners, near the exit to the hotel's gardens. Buchanan chose a chair that put his back to the wall and gave him a view of the stairs leading down to the restaurant. The air conditioning cooled his sweat. He glanced at his watch: 9:25. His contact would be here in five minutes. Pretending to study a menu, he tried to seem calm.

At once, pulse increasing, he noticed two men appear at the top of the stairs that led to the restaurant.

But Buchanan had expected to meet only *one* man.

Both were Hispanic. Both wore beige linen suits that were stylishly wrinkled, their yellow silk shirts open to their breastbones. Each had a gold Rolex watch, as well as several gold neck chains and bracelets. Each was thin, in his thirties, with chiseled, narrow, severe features and thick, dark, slicked-back hair gathered in a ponytail. Their hooded eyes were as dark as their hair, and like their hair, their eyes glinted. Predator's eyes. Hawk's eyes. Merciless eyes. The men were *gemelos,* twins, and as they descended toward the restaurant, they braced their shoulders, puffed out their chests, and exuded confidence, the world at their command.

Buchanan tried to look relaxed while he intensified his awareness. The men immediately headed in his direction. Their foot soldiers would have given them his description, Buchanan knew. More, there would have been surreptitious photographs taken of him. He dreaded being photographed.

As the twins reached his table, Buchanan stood to shake hands with them. He deliberately hadn't worn a jacket, wanting them to see that he wasn't armed. They would note that his navy shirt was tucked under his belt rather than hanging loose and possibly concealing a pistol. They would also note that his shirt was somewhat tight, sufficiently so that if he were hiding a tape recorder or a transmitting device, the outline would be obvious. Of course, state-of-the-art transmitters were so miniaturized that one could easily be disguised as a button on his shirt, just as a small handgun could be secured above his ankle, beneath his pants. Not that Buchanan would need a handgun at this proximity. The ballpoint pen in his shirt pocket could be equally lethal. Nonetheless, Buchanan knew that these hawk-eyed men would appreciate his gesture of apparent openness. At the same time, he took for granted that, despite their display of confidence, they would maintain the wariness that had kept them alive this long.

They greeted him in English.

Buchanan replied in Spanish, "Thank you for meeting me." He used *ustedes,* the formal word for "you."

"*De nada,*" the first man said, and gestured for Buchanan to sit.

Both glanced around the restaurant, seemed satisfied by the meeting place, and sat as well. No doubt, Buchanan thought, they'd ordered subordinates to check the restaurant's suitability before they'd arrived. Presumably, they also had stationed guards inconspicuously outside the hotel and in the corridor that led to the restaurant. As a further precaution, they took napkins from the table, spread them on their laps, and made a smooth, practiced motion with their right hands that told Buchanan they'd slid a pistol beneath each napkin.

Finally settled, they studied him.

"You have *cojones*," the first twin said.

"*Gracias*."

"And the luck of a fool," the second twin said. "We could have dealt with you permanently at any time."

"*Claro que sí*," Buchanan said. "Of course. But I hoped that you would listen to reason. I have confidence in the business opportunity I came to offer you."

"Our business is already satisfying," the first twin said.

"So what makes you think that you can make our business even *more* satisfying?" The second twin squinted.

Buchanan spoke softly. "Because you know how satisfying my own business has become. I take for granted that I'm reasoning with disciplined businessmen. Professionals. The proof is that you didn't respond to my efforts by . . . as you put it . . . dealing with me permanently. You saw how . . ."

Buchanan coughed discreetly in warning and cocked his head to the left.

Their waiter approached and gave them menus. He compared his two Hispanic guests to the solitary *norteamericano* and obviously decided that since Cancún was Mexico's most popular resort for Americans, he would give Buchanan the most attention. "Would you like a drink, *señores*?"

"Tequila for me. *Y para mis compadres?*" Buchanan turned to them.

"The same," the first twin said. "Bring lime and salt."

"Make it doubles for everyone," the second twin said.

As the waiter departed, the first twin scowled, leaned over the table, almost touching Buchanan, and whispered hoarsely, "No more bullshit, Señor Potter"—the first time he'd used Buchanan's pseudonym. "What do you want from us? This is your one and only chance." He reached toward the napkin that covered his lap and patted his pistol. "Give us a reason not to kill you."

3

The briefing had been at a safe site in Fairfax, Virginia, an apartment on the second story of a sprawling complex into which Buchanan could easily blend. He had rented it under his then pseudonym of Brian MacDonald. He had a driver's license, a passport, a birth certificate, and several credit cards in that name, as well as a detailed fictional background for that temporary identity. His telephone bills indicated that he phoned a number in Philadelphia every Sunday evening, and if anyone investigating Brian MacDonald had called that number, a cheery female receptionist would have answered, "Golden Years Retirement Home." That establishment did in fact exist, a profitable cover organization for Buchanan's employers, and its records indicated that a Mrs. MacDonald, Brian's "mother," was in residence. She wasn't in her room at the moment, but she'd be pleased to return a call, and soon an elderly woman who worked for Buchanan's employers *would* return the call, the destination of which would of course be traced, the conversation recorded.

Buchanan's fictitious occupation at that time, three months earlier, had been that of a computer programmer. He had an interest in and talent for computers, so that part of his assumed identity was easy to establish. He worked at home, he told anyone who happened to ask, and the powerful IBM in his apartment, supplied by his employers, validated his claim. As a further proof of his bogus identity, each Thursday he sent backup computer disks via Federal Express to New Age Technology in Boston, another profitable cover organization for Buchanan's employers, but to maintain the skills of his true occupation, each evening for three hours he exercised at the local Gold's Gym.

Mostly he waited, trying to be patient, maintaining discipline, eager to do his real work. So when an executive from New Age Technology at last phoned, announced that he'd be in Fairfax on business, and wondered if he could pay a visit, Buchanan thought, *Soon.* Soon I'll be useful. Soon I won't be bored.

His controller knocked on the door on schedule. That was 4:00 P.M. on a Friday, and when Buchanan-MacDonald glanced through the door's security eye, then let him in, the short, gaunt man in a rumpled suit placed his briefcase on the living room's coffee table, waited for Buchanan-MacDonald to close and bolt the entrance, then studied his surroundings and asked, "Which would you prefer? To go for a walk or stay here?"

"The apartment's clean."

"Good." The hollow-cheeked controller opened his briefcase. "I need your driver's license, your passport, your birth certificate, your credit cards, all of your documents for Brian MacDonald. Here are the release forms for you to sign, and here's my signed receipt."

Buchanan complied.

"Now here are your further documents," the thin-lipped controller continued, "and the acceptance form for you to sign. Your new name is Edward Potter. You used to be employed as a . . . Well, it's all in this file. Every detail of your new background. Knowing how retentive your memory is, I assume that as usual you'll be able to absorb the information by the time I come back to retrieve the file tomorrow morning. What's wrong?"

"What took you so long to get in touch with me?" Buchanan asked. "It's been two months."

"After your last assignment, we wanted you to disappear for a while. Also, we thought we'd have a use for you as Brian MacDonald. Now that scenario's been discarded. We've got a much more interesting project for you. I think you'll be pleased. It's as important as it is risky. It'll give you quite a rush."

"Tell me about it."

His controller studied him. "I sometimes forget how intense field operatives can be, how anxious they are to . . . But then, of course, that's why you're field operatives. Because . . ."

"Because? I've asked myself that many times. What's the answer?"

"I should have thought that was obvious. You enjoy being someone else."

"Yes. Exactly. So indulge me. Pretend I'm a Method actor. What's my new character's motivation?"

4

In the restaurant in Cancún's Club Internacional, Buchanan showed no fear when the first twin threatened him. Instead, he replied matter-of-factly, "Give you a reason not to kill me? I can give you several million of them."

"We have many millions as it is," the first twin said. "What makes you think a few more would make us risk trusting you?"

"Human nature. No matter how much money a person has, it's never enough. Besides," Buchanan said, "I didn't offer a *few* million. I offered *several*."

"Hard to spend in prison. Impossible to spend in the grave," the second twin said. "The practical response to your offer is to eliminate your interference. We resent a competitor, and we have no need for a partner."

In the background, the drone of conversing diners muffled their exchange.

"That's just the point," Buchanan said, still showing no apprehension. "I don't want to be your competitor, and you do need a partner."

The second twin bristled. "You have the nerve to tell us what we need. Your eggs are truly hard-boiled."

"But they can be cracked," the first twin growled.

"Definitely," Buchanan said. "I knew the danger when I set up shop here."

"Not only here, but in Mérida, Acapulco, and Puerto Vallarta," the second twin said angrily.

"Plus a few other resorts where you apparently don't know I've established contacts."

The first twin's eyes narrowed, emphasizing their hawklike intensity. "You have the impudence to brag to our faces."

"No." Buchanan shook his head emphatically. "I'm not bragging. I'm being candid. I hope you'll appreciate my honesty. I assure you, I'm not being disrespectful."

The twins considered his apology, frowned at each other, nodded with sullen reluctance, and leaned back in their chairs.

"But by your own admission, you've been extremely industrious," the second twin said. "And at *our* expense."

"How else could I have attracted your attention?" Buchanan spread his hands deferentially. "Consider the risk *I* took, a *norteamericano*, suddenly conducting business not only in Mexico but in your backyard, in your country's resorts, especially here in Cancún. Even with my special knowledge, I had no idea who to approach. Fernandez, I suspected you," Buchanan told the first man. "But I had no idea you had a twin, and to tell the truth"—Buchanan switched his attention to the second man—"I don't know which of you is Fernandez. When you entered this restaurant, I confess I was stunned. *Gemelos*. Twins. That explains so much. It was never clear to me how Fernandez could be in two places, Mérida and Acapulco, for example, at one time."

The first man twisted his thin lips in what passed for a grin. "That was our intention. To cause confusion." Abruptly he sobered. "But how did you know that even one of us had the first name of Fernandez?" He spoke with increasing speed and ferocity. "What is this special information to which you refer? When our subordinates paid you our courtesy of warning you to stop interfering with our business, *why did you ask for this meeting and give our subordinates the names on this sheet of paper?*"

To demonstrate, the first twin reached into his wrinkled linen suit coat and produced a folded page. He slapped it onto the table. "The names on this paper are some of our most trusted associates."

"Well"—Buchanan shrugged—"that just goes to show."

"Show *what*?"

"How mistaken you can be about trusted associates."

"Fucker of your mother, what are you talking about?" the second twin demanded.

So the bait really worked, Buchanan thought. I'm in. I've got their attention. Hell, they wouldn't have both shown up if they weren't afraid. That list of names spooked them more than I hoped.

"What am I talking about?" Buchanan said. "I'm talking

about why you should trust me instead of those bastards. I used to belong to the . . ."

Again, Buchanan coughed in warning.

The twins stiffened as their waiter returned, carrying a tray from which he set onto the table a plate of sliced limes, a bowl of salt, a small spoon, and six shot glasses filled with amber tequila.

"*Gracias*," Buchanan said. "Give us ten minutes before we order dinner."

He used the tiny metal spoon to place salt on his left hand, on the web of skin between his thumb and first finger. "*Salud*," he told the twins. He licked the salt from his hand, quickly swallowed the contents of one of the glasses, and as quickly bit into a slice of lime. The sour juice of the lime spurted over his tongue, mixing with the sweet taste of the tequila and the bitterness of the salt, the various flavors combining perfectly. His mouth puckered slightly. His eyes almost watered.

"Never mind drinking to *our* health. Just worry about yours," the first twin said.

"I'm not worried," Buchanan said. "I think we're going to have a productive relationship." He watched them lick salt, swallow tequila, and chew on wedges of lime.

Immediately they placed more salt on their hands and waited for him to do the same.

As Buchanan complied, it occurred to him that his was one of the few occupations in which the consumption of alcohol was a mandatory requirement. His opponents wouldn't trust anyone who didn't drink with them, the implication being that an abstainer had something to hide. So it was necessary to consume quantities of alcohol, for the purpose of gaining trust from those opponents. By vigilant practice, Buchanan had learned the limit of his tolerance for alcohol, just as he'd learned how to pretend believably that he'd exceeded that tolerance and to convince his opponents that he was drunk and hence saying the truth.

The narrow-faced twins each raised their second glass of tequila, clearly expecting Buchanan to do the same. Their dark eyes glowed with the anticipation that he would soon lose control and reveal a weakness.

"You were saying," the first twin said, "that you sus-

pect the loyalty of our associates because you used to belong
to . . ."

5

"The Drug Enforcement Administration," Buchanan's controller had told him three months earlier. They'd sat opposite
each other in the living room of the safe-site apartment in the
sprawling complex in Fairfax, Virginia. Between them, on the
coffee table, the gray-haired controller had spread documents,
the details of Buchanan's new identity, what was known in the
trade as his legend. "You have to convince your targets that
you used to be a special agent for the DEA."

Buchanan, who was already assuming the characteristics of
Edward Potter, deciding how the man would dress and what
foods he preferred, pressed the tips of his fingers together
almost prayerlike and raised them meditatively to his chin.
"Keep talking."

"You wanted to know your character's motivation? Well,
basically he's sick of seeing the war against drug dealers turn
into a joke. He thinks the government hasn't provided sufficient
funds to prove that it's serious about fighting the war. He's
disgusted with CIA interference whenever the DEA gets close
to the really big dealers. According to your new character,
those big dealers are on the CIA payroll, supplying information
about the politics in the volatile Third World countries from
which they get their product. So naturally, the CIA clamps
down on the DEA whenever one of the Agency's informants
steps in shit."

"Well, that part won't be hard to fake. The CIA does have
the biggest Third World dealers on its payroll," Buchanan
said.

"Absolutely. However, that's about to change. Those Third
World dealers have become too smug. The information they've
been supplying isn't worth squat. They think they can take the
Agency's money, do virtually nothing in return, and in effect
give the Agency the finger. Apparently, they didn't learn from
our invasion of Panama."

"Of course not," Buchanan said. "After we grabbed Noriega, other dealers took his place. Nothing changed, except children starved to death because of the economic embargo."

"Good. You're beginning to sound like your new personality," Buchanan-Potter's controller said.

"Hey, I lost friends in the Panama invasion. At the start, I believed the invasion was necessary. But when I saw the pathetic follow-up—*why doesn't the American government do things all the way*?—I wanted to vomit."

"Even better. You're convincing me, and I know you're acting, so obviously you've got a damned fine chance of convincing your targets."

"But I'm not acting."

"Buchanan, give it a rest, okay? We've got a lot of details to cover. So save your Method-acting techniques until later."

"Don't call me Buchanan. My name is Edward Potter."

"Sure, right, Edward. Maybe it'll give you further motivation to know that your assignment is intended to compensate for the halfhearted follow-up to what happened in Panama. Your ultimate objective is to scare the living bejesus out of the Agency's Third World drug-lord informants who still make jokes about the American lives lost in the useless invasion of Panama."

"No. That's Buchanan's motivation. I don't want to hear that. I don't want my mind to be contaminated. Just tell me about Edward Potter. What's *his* motivation?"

The pallid controller lowered his head, shook it, and sighed. "I have to tell you, Buchanan—"

"Potter."

"—sometimes you worry me. Sometimes I think you absorb yourself too much in your assumed identities."

"But you're not risking your ass if I forget who the hell I'm supposed to be. So don't fool with my life. From now on, talk to me with the assumption that I'm Edward Potter."

Again the controller sighed. "Whatever you want, Edward. Your wife divorced you because you were too devoted to your job and not enough to her and your two sons. She remarried. Because of the numerous threats you've received from drug dealers, she asked for and was granted a court order that forbids you to come anywhere near her and your children without prior approval from her and without guarantees of safety. Her new husband earns two hundred thousand a year as an owner of several health spas. *You,* by comparison, earn a paltry forty thousand—or rather, *used* to earn that amount—a salary that's especially humiliating in contrast with the millions earned by the scum you arrested and saw released on bail and eventually plea-bargained to a short-term sentence in a minimum-security prison. You're convinced that if you'd accepted the bribes you were offered, your wife would have been satisfied with a new house, et cetera, and wouldn't have left you. When everything you believed in collapsed, you got pissed. You decided that by God, if you couldn't beat the drug lords, you'd join them. You'd show your fucking wife that you could earn a hundred times as much as her faggot new husband. *Your* dick was bigger than his."

"Yes," Buchanan-Potter said. "My dick *is* bigger."

The controller stared. "Amazing."

Buchanan-Potter's cheek muscles hardened. "So how do I get even?"

6

"You used to be an agent for the Drug Enforcement Administration?" In the restaurant in Cancún's Club Internacional, the first Hispanic twin spoke softly yet with paradoxical force. Shocked, he and his brother jerked back in their chairs.

"Take it easy," Buchanan said. "I'm on *your* side now."

"Certainly," the second twin said derisively. "By all means. Of course."

"And you truly expect us to believe this?" the first twin demanded. "To accept that you're a defector and to trust you?"

"It's not as if I haven't made a gesture of good faith," Buchanan said. "That folded sheet of paper beneath your hand. If you put pressure on the Bahamian bank officials you hire to launder money, you'll find that the supposedly loyal associates I mentioned on that list all have secret offshore bank accounts. Now I realize that graft is a way of life down here. But I think you'll agree that the amounts your supposedly loyal associates put away for a rainy day are considerably higher than payoffs and kickbacks alone would explain.''

The second twin squinted. "Assuming for the moment that your information is correct . . .''

"Oh, it is. That goes without saying. After all, I'm guaranteeing it with the best collateral imaginable.''

"And what is that?'' The first twin tapped his fingers on the table.

"My life. If I'm lying about those bank accounts—and it won't be hard for you to discover if I am—you'll have me killed.''

"But in the meantime, perhaps you'll be able to accomplish whatever you intend and drop out of sight before we can get our hands on you.'' The second twin squinted more severely.

"What could I possibly accomplish?'' Buchanan gestured. "Until you investigate the men on that list and decide if my information is valuable, you won't let me into your confidence. You won't do business with me.''

"We might not do business with you even if you're telling the truth.'' The first twin kept tapping his fingers on the table.

"There's always that possibility.'' Buchanan shrugged. "But the way I see it, I'm taking all the risks and you're taking none. Certainly there's nothing risky about your meeting me here—at a mutually agreeable, neutral place—for drinks and dinner. At the worst, you've been inconvenienced. From *my* point of view, however, at the worst, I get dead.''

Without looking at each other, the twins seemed to reach a mutual conclusion.

"*Exactamente.*'' The second twin turned toward the half-filled restaurant, caught their waiter's attention, pointed toward the glasses on their table, held up two fingers, and then waved his hand in a circle, indicating he wanted another round of tequila, doubles for everyone. Seeing the waiter nod, he pivoted toward Buchanan. "You interrupted before I could finish my earlier question.''

"*Perdón.* So ask it now.''

"Assuming you're telling the truth about these offshore bank accounts, how do you explain the considerable amounts you claim our associates have hidden from us? What is the source of those funds? They must be bribes from drug-enforcement officers for supplying information. The only other explanation would be that they're stealing a portion of our merchandise or else the money we collect, and I assure you we can account for every kilo we send to the United States and every dollar we get back.''

Buchanan shook his head. ''Bribes alone won't explain the tremendous sums in these offshore accounts. As you're aware, drug-enforcement officers have never been known for being overly generous with their bribes. Their budget's stretched too thin. But as it happens, you're wrong about having protected yourselves against theft. Your men are running an extremely sophisticated skim operation.''

''*What?*'' The second twin looked stunned. ''*No es posible.*''

''It's not only possible. It's a fact.''

''I'm telling you, we'd know!''

''Not this way. Not the way they're doing it. They're using rogue DEA officers to help them skim. How many shipments did you lose last year? An approximate percentage. Ten percent?''

''More or less,'' the first twin said. ''It's inevitable that some of our shipments will be discovered. Couriers get nervous and make mistakes. Or DEA officers happen to be at the right place at the right time. We expect a certain percentage of losses. It goes with the business.''

''But what if some of those couriers weren't as nervous as they pretended?'' Buchanan asked. ''And what if those DEA officers had advance warning to be at the right place at the right time? And what if those couriers and DEA officers were in business for themselves?''

As the waiter brought the second round of drinks, the group became silent. The moment the waiter departed, they assessed the restaurant's customers, assured themselves that no one was close enough to overhear, then faced one another, raising glasses, going through the ritual of consuming salt, tequila, and lime.

''Finish what you were saying.'' The first twin clearly hoped that the alcohol would affect Buchanan's judgment and reveal a weakness.

''Their system's quite clever.'' Buchanan set down the slice of lime from which he'd chewed. "The rogue agents from the DEA have to satisfy their superiors that they're doing their job. So they surrender a portion of what they confiscate. Then the government brags about how it's winning the war on drugs, and the American television networks report the latest victory on the evening news. But what the government doesn't know, and of course the American public, is that other shipments were confiscated and that *those* shipments were sold to American drug dealers. The money from those sales—millions—is divided between the rogue DEA officers and the trusted associates you've put in charge of sending the shipments. As far as you're concerned, those shipments have been accounted for. By your own admission, you expect those losses. As long as you receive your usual profit, why would you think you were being cheated?"

Both twins glowered.

"*How do you know this?*" the second twin rasped.

"Because, as I told you, I used to belong to the DEA. I wasn't on the take. I was one of the good guys. That's how I thought of myself, dummy that I was. I did my job. But I'm not blind. I saw what was going on. The thing is, drug enforcement is the same as any other police work. You don't turn against your fellow officers. If you do, they have ways to make your life a nightmare. So I had to keep quiet. And then . . ."

Scowling, Buchanan gulped his further glass of tequila.

"Yes? And then?" The second twin leaned toward him.

"That's none of your business."

"With respect, given our reason for meeting here, it's very much our business."

"I had personal problems," Buchanan said.

"Don't we all? We're men of the world. We understand personal problems only too well. There's no need to be defensive. Unburden yourself. It's good for the soul. What problems could have . . .?"

"I prefer not to talk about it." Buchanan made his elbow slip off the table, as if the tequila had started to work on him. "I've told you what I came to say. You know how to reach me. Use your contacts to investigate your associates' offshore bank accounts. When you find out I was telling the truth, I hope you'll decide that the three of us can cooperate."

With heart-stopping recognition, Buchanan glanced toward the stairs that led down to the restaurant and noticed a man, an American, in company with a Hispanic woman who wore a revealing dress and too much makeup, approach a waiter and ask for a table. The American was in his forties, tall, with extremely broad shoulders and a bulky chest, his sandy hair trimmed upward in a brush cut. His ample stomach protruded against his too-small green T-shirt and hung over the waist on his low-slung jeans. He wore sneakers and puffed on a cigarette as he gave orders to the waiter.

Oh, Jesus, Buchanan thought. His mind raced. *How am I going to—?*

The first twin shook his head. "Too many things about you trouble us."

Desperate to avoid the man who'd entered the restaurant, Buchanan concentrated on his targets.

"Crawford!" a booming voice called.

Buchanan ignored it. "What exactly troubles you?"

"Crawford! By Jesus, long time no see!" The booming voice cracked crustily and became a smoker's cough.

Buchanan continued to direct his attention straight toward his targets.

"Crawford!" the voice boomed louder. "Have you gone deaf? Don't you hear me? Where by Jesus did you get to after Iraq?" The voice was made more conspicuous because of its heavy, drawling Texas accent. "When they flew us to Germany and we touched down in Frankfurt, I wanted to buy you a drink to celebrate gettin' out of that Arab hellhole. But one minute you was there in the terminal with all them officials greetin' us and reporters aimin' their cameras. The next minute you dropped out of sight like one of our broken drill bits down a dry well."

The drawling voice boomed so close that Buchanan couldn't possibly pretend to ignore it. He shifted his gaze from his fidgeting targets toward the looming sun-and-alcohol-reddened face of the beefy American.

"I beg your pardon?" Buchanan asked.

"Crawford. Don't you recognize your ol' buddy? This is Big Bob Bailey talkin' to you. Come on, you can't have forgotten *me*. We was prisoners together in Kuwait City and Baghdad. Jesus, who'd have ever figured that nutcase would actually believe he could get away with invadin' Kuwait? I've worked my share of tough jobs, but when those Iraqi tanks pulled onto our drillin' site, I don't mind admittin' I was so shittin' scared I . . ."

Buchanan shook his head in confusion.

"Crawford, have you got post-trauma whatever the hell the shrinks who talked to me in Germany called it? Have you been drinkin' more than *I* have? This is Big Bob Bailey speakin' to you. We and a bunch of other American oil workers was held hostages together."

"I'm pleased to meet you, Bob," Buchanan said. "But apparently you've confused me with someone else."

The twins watched Buchanan intensely.

"Give me a break. Your name is Crawford," the beefy American said. "Jim Crawford."

"Nope. Sorry. My name's Ed Potter."

"But—"

"Honestly, I'm not Jim Crawford. I'm Ed Potter, and I've never seen you before. Whoever Jim Crawford is, I must resemble him."

"More than resemble, and that's a damned fact."

"But you're mistaken. I'm not him."

The twins watched Buchanan with greater intensity.

"Well, I'll be a . . ." The American looked uneasy, his sun-and-alcohol-reddened face becoming redder with embarrassment. "Sorry, pal. I would have sworn . . . I must have been partyin' too much. Here, let me make up for interruptin' and buy you and your friends a drink. Honest to God, I didn't mean to bother you." The American backed off, staggering slightly as he retreated.

"No problem," Buchanan said.

7

But it *was* a problem. A *big* problem. One of the nightmares Buchanan dreaded was the risk that a contact from a previous assignment would wander into a present one. Twice in Buchanan's career, fellow specialists had happened to enter locations (a pub in London, a café in Paris) where Buchanan was using false identities to recruit informants who might help him infiltrate terrorist networks. In each case, Buchanan had noticed the subtle look of recognition in his fellow operative's eyes. Briefly, Buchanan had felt nervous. However, his counterpart—obeying an absolute rule of tradecraft—had ignored Buchanan and soon, when it seemed natural, had left the location.

But while Buchanan could count on the tact of a professional, there was no way to guard against the spontaneity of a civilian whom he'd encountered on another mission, a civilian who had no idea of Buchanan's true occupation. The beefy American—now retreating in confusion to a table where his female escort waited—had indeed known Buchanan in Kuwait City as well as in Baghdad, and Buchanan's name at that time had indeed been Jim Crawford. Prior to the Allied counterstrike, Buchanan had been inserted at night via a high-altitude, low-opening parachute drop into Kuwait to reconnoiter Iraqi defenses. Buchanan had buried his jump equipment in the desert, then hiked through the dark toward the lights of Kuwait City. He wore civilian clothes—a soiled work shirt and jeans—and carried documents that identified him as an American oil worker from Oklahoma. If stopped, his cover story would be that he'd gone into hiding when the Iraqis invaded. His scraggly beard, unkempt hair, and haggard appearance would reinforce that story. For three weeks, aided by Allied sympathizers, he was able to use a small two-way radio to broadcast important information to his superiors, but prior to his extraction by submarine, an Iraqi patrol had discovered him on the way to the beach.

It wasn't any wonder that Big Bob Bailey shook his head in confusion as he joined his female escort at a table in the restaurant. After all, Buchanan had spent a month with Bailey and other captive oil workers, first in the confinement of a demolished Kuwait City hotel, then in one of several trucks that transported the Americans from Kuwait to Iraq, and finally in a warehouse in Baghdad.

Saddam Hussein eventually set free the Americans "as a Christmas present to the United States." They were flown via Iraqi Airlines to various destinations, one of which was

Frankfurt, Germany. Big Bob Bailey sat next to Buchanan during the latter flight. Big Bob Bailey chattered endlessly, with nervous relief, about how when they touched down he intended to get good and drunk with his good ol' pal Jim Crawford. But when they entered the terminal, Jim Crawford disappeared among the crowd, shielded by plainclothes Special Operations personnel who hurried Buchanan to a safe site and intensely debriefed him.

That had been twelve assignments ago, however, and Big Bob Bailey had become just another vaguely remembered contact to whom Buchanan had played one of his numerous roles.

Big Bob Bailey. Damn it, he was from another life. From several lives past. Iraq's invasion of Kuwait was ancient history. Big Bob Bailey was just a minor character in . . .

But at the moment, Big Bob Bailey was very much a major character in *this* life, Buchanan thought in dismay.

And Big Bob Bailey wouldn't stop looking over at Buchanan, all the while squinting and shaking his head as if he wasn't just confused now but angry, convinced that Buchanan *was* Jim Crawford and insulted because Buchanan wouldn't admit it.

Jesus, Buchanan thought, he looks pissed off enough that he might come over again! If he does, my cover will be absolutely destroyed. These two Mexican drug distributors didn't stay alive this long by being idiots. Check their eyes. They're already wondering what's going on. I've got to . . .

"I guess it's a variation on an old joke," he told the first twin. "South of the border, all Americans look alike, sometimes even to each other."

"Yes," the first twin replied.

"Very amusing," the second twin said flatly.

"But he certainly attracted attention to us," Buchanan continued.

"I think the sooner we get out of here, the better," the second twin said. "Especially before that man comes back here, which I suspect he's about to do."

"Fine with me. Let's go." Buchanan stood to walk toward the stairs that led up from the restaurant.

"No, *this* way," the second twin said. He touched Buchanan's arm and gestured toward the rear entrance, a sliding glass door that gave access to the hotel's night-shrouded gardens.

"Good idea," Buchanan said. "It's faster. Less conspicuous." He signaled the waiter that he'd left money on the table and turned toward the glass door.

As Buchanan stepped from the restaurant into the humid, fragrant gardens, as he heard the glass door being slid shut behind him, he noticed that the twins had positioned themselves on either side of him. He noticed as well that they held the napkins beneath which each had earlier concealed a pistol in his lap, and the napkins didn't look empty. Finally, he noticed a piece of the night step from between tall bushes to the left of the door, bushes that would have given the bodyguard a hidden view through the glass while Buchanan spoke with the twins.

The bodyguard was Hispanic, unusually tall and large-boned.

Like the twins, he held a pistol. Hard to tell in the shadows, but it looked like a 9-mm Beretta equipped with a sound suppressor.

And imitating the expression on his employers' faces, the bodyguard scowled.

8

"Who the fuck *are* you?" the first twin demanded, jabbing Buchanan's chest.

"Hey, what are you—?" Buchanan tried to object.

"We're too close to the windows of the restaurant. Someone inside will see," the second twin cautioned his brother. "We need to go down to the beach."

"Yes," the first twin said. "The beach. The fucking beach."

"*Todavia no*. Not yet," the bodyguard warned. He unhooked a hand-held metal detector from his belt and quickly but thoroughly scanned it over Buchanan.

The metal detector beeped three times.

"His belt buckle. His keys. A pen," the bodyguard said,

not needing to explain that the buckle might conceal a knife, that the keys and pen could be used as weapons.

"Take off your belt," the first twin ordered Buchanan. "Drop your keys and the pen on the ground."

"What's wrong? I don't understand," Buchanan insisted.

The second twin showed his pistol, a 9-mm Browning. "Do what you're told."

The bodyguard jabbed his Beretta into Buchanan's left kidney. "*Rapido. Ahora.* Now."

Buchanan complied, removing his belt, dropping it along with his keys and his pen.

The first twin snatched them up.

The second twin shoved Buchanan away from the restaurant toward the gardens.

The bodyguard kept the Beretta low, inconspicuous, and followed.

9

The gardens were spacious, filled with flowering shrubs, trickling pools, and meandering paths. Here and there, small lights of various colors projected from the ground, illuminating the walkways, tinting the shrubs, reflecting off the pools. Nonetheless, compared to the glare from the windows of the towering hotel, the garden was cloaked in darkness. Anyone who happened to look out would see merely the vague, moving shadows of four men out for a stroll, Buchanan thought. Certainly an observer wouldn't be able to see that three of the men held pistols by their sides. Not that it mattered. If anyone did see the weapons and felt compelled to phone the police, whatever was going to happen would have ended by the time the police arrived.

As Buchanan proceeded along a walkway toward the splash of waves on the beach, he assessed his options. One was to take advantage of the garden's darkness, overpower his captors, and escape, using the shrubs for cover in case any of his captors survived his attack and started shooting. Or at least Buchanan could *attempt* to escape. The problem was that his captors would be anticipating the likelihood of his using the darkness. They'd be primed for a sudden movement, and as soon as he made one, he'd be shot. The sound suppressor on the body-guard's Beretta would prevent anyone in the hotel from hearing the weapon's report. By the time Buchanan's corpse was discovered, the three Hispanics would be far from the area.

That wasn't the only problem, Buchanan thought. If he did manage to catch the Hispanics by surprise, the darkness that initially helped him might then work against him. All he needed to do was collide with an unseen object as he fought with his captors. If he lost his balance . . .

But a further problem—and the one to which Buchanan gave the most importance—was that the Hispanics might be threatening him merely to test him. After all, he couldn't expect the twins to believe his cover story simply because his manner of presenting it was confident and convincing. They'd need all sorts of proof about his authenticity. *All* sorts. Every detail of his fictitious background would bear up under investigation. Buchanan's controllers had made sure of that. A female opera-tive was posing as Ed Potter's ex-wife. A male operative was posing as her new husband. Each had a well-documented ficti-tious background, and each had been coached about what to say if anyone asked questions. Certain members of the DEA were prepared to claim that they'd known Ed Potter when he was an agent. In addition, the details of Ed Potter's DEA career had been planted in a dossier in government computers.

But perhaps Buchanan's opponents would take the solidity of his cover story for granted. Then what other way did they have to verify his authenticity? The more Buchanan thought about it, the more the issue became, Were the twins truly furious or only pretending to be? Would the twins suspect his credibility just because a drunken American had claimed to have known him as Jim Crawford, or was it more likely that the twins would take advantage of the drunken American's claim and use it as a pretense for intimidating Buchanan, for trying their best to frighten him, for doing their damnedest to find a weakness in his confidence?

Layers within layers. Nothing was ever self-evident, Bu-chanan thought in turmoil as his captors nudged him along a path toward the muted lights of an outdoor bar at the edge of the beach.

The bar had a sloping thatched roof supported by wooden pillars. There weren't any walls. Bamboo tables and chairs surrounded the oval counter, giving several groups of drinkers a view of white-capped waves in the darkness. Sections of the hotel bordered the gardens, so that the only way for Buchanan and his captors to get to the beach was to pass near the bar.

"Do not expect those people to help you," the first twin murmured on Buchanan's right as they neared the bar. "If you make a commotion, we will shoot you in front of them. They do not matter to us."

"They are drunk, and we are in shadows. As witnesses, they are useless," the second twin added on Buchanan's left.

"And they cannot see my pistol. I have covered it with my jacket. But be assured I am aiming it at your spine," the bodyguard said behind Buchanan.

"Hey, let's lighten up, okay? I'm missing something here. Why all this talk about shooting?" Buchanan asked. "I wish the three of you would relax and tell me what's going on. I came to you in good faith. I wasn't armed. I'm not a threat to you. But all of a sudden, you—"

"Shut up while we pass the people in the bar," the first twin murmured in Spanish.

"Or the next words you speak will be your last," the second twin said. "*Entiende?* Understand?"

"Your logic is overwhelming," Buchanan said.

A few tourists glanced up from their margaritas as Buchanan and the others walked by. Then one of the tourists finished telling a joke, and everybody at that table laughed.

The nearby outburst in reaction to the joke was so loud and unexpected that it made the twins flinch and jerk their heads toward the noise. Presumably, the bodyguard was also surprised. There wasn't any way for Buchanan to know for certain. Still, the odds were in his favor. He could have done it then. He could have taken advantage of the distraction, smashed the side of his hands against the larynx of each twin, kicked backward with his left foot angled sideways to break the bodyguard's knee, and spun to snap the wrist that held the Beretta. He could have done all that in less than two seconds. The light from the bar made him able to see clearly enough that he wouldn't have had to worry about the accuracy of his blows. The agonizing damage to the throats of the twins would have prevented them from breathing. In their panic to fill their lungs with air, they would not have had time to think about shooting Buchanan, not before he'd finished the bodyguard and swung back to finish them. That would have taken another second or two. All told, four seconds, max, and Buchanan would have been safe.

But as confident as he was of success, Buchanan didn't do it. Because his safety wasn't the point. If all he cared about was his safety, he wouldn't have accepted this mission in the first place. The mission. *That* was the point. As the laughter of the tourists subsided, as the twins and their bodyguard regained their discipline, as Buchanan and his captors finished passing the bar and reached the murky beach, Buchanan told himself, How would you have explained it to your superiors? I can imagine the expression on their faces if you told them the mission failed because you got so nervous you killed your contacts. Your career would be over. This isn't the first time someone's aimed a pistol at you. You know damned well that on this assignment it would have happened sooner or later. These guys aren't dummies. Plus, they'll never trust you until they learn if you can handle stress. So let them find out. Be cool. Play out the role.

But what would Ed Potter do? Buchanan wondered. Wouldn't a corrupt ex-DEA officer try to escape if he thought the drug distributors from whom he was taking business had decided that killing him was less risky and less trouble than becoming partners with him?

Maybe, Buchanan thought. Ed Potter *might* try to run. After all, he isn't me. He doesn't have my training. But if I behave the way Ed Potter truly would, there's a good chance I'll get myself killed. I've got to modify the character. Right now, my audience is testing me for weakness.

But by God, they won't find any.

Club Internacional had a sidewalk that ran parallel to the beach. The stars were brilliant, although the moon had not yet risen. A cool breeze came off the ocean out of the darkness. Hearing the distant echo of more laughter from the bar, which was shielded from him by a row of tall shrubs and a waist-high wall, Buchanan paused at the edge of the sidewalk.

"All right," he said. "Here's the beach. It's nice. Real nice. Now would you put those guns away and tell me what in God's name this is all about? I haven't done anything to—"

10

"God's name?" the first twin asked, and shoved Buchanan off the sidewalk onto the sand. "Yes, a name. *Many* names. *That's* what this is all about. Ed Potter. Jim Crawford."

Buchanan felt his shoes sink into the sand and spun to face the twins as well as their bodyguard, where they stood slightly above him on the sidewalk. "Hey, just because some drunk thinks he knows me? Haven't *you* ever been mistaken for—?"

"The only person I have ever been mistaken for is my brother," the second twin said. "I do not believe in coincidence. I do not believe that in the middle of a conversation about my business and my safety, I can ignore anyone—drunk or not—who interrupts to tell me the man I am speaking to is not the man he claims to be."

"Come on! That drunk admitted he was wrong!" Buchanan insisted.

"*But he did not look convinced,*" the first twin snapped.

Two murky silhouettes approached along the beach. Buchanan and his antagonists became silent. The Hispanics stiffened, wary. Then the silhouettes walked near enough for Buchanan to see a man and a woman—American, early twenties—holding hands. The couple seemed oblivious to their surroundings, conscious only of each other. They passed and disappeared into the darkness farther along the beach.

"We can't stay here," the second twin said. "Other people will come. We're still too close to the hotel, especially to the bar."

"But I want this matter settled," the first twin said. "I want it settled *now*."

The bodyguard scanned the beach and pointed. "*Por allí.* Over there."

Buchanan looked. Near the white-capped waves, he saw, were the distinctive outlines of several *palapa* sun shelters. Each small structure had a slanted circular top made from palm fronds and held up by a seven-foot-tall wooden post. Plastic tables and chairs, as white as the caps on the waves, were distributed among them.

"Yes," the first twin said. "Over there."

The Hispanic stepped from the concrete onto the sand and shoved Buchanan hard enough that Ed Potter could not have resisted the thrust, so Buchanan allowed himself to stumble backward.

"Move! Damn you and your mother, move!" the first twin said.

Continuing to stumble, Buchanan turned toward the deserted shelters. Immediately the Hispanic shoved him again, and Buchanan lurched, concentrating to maintain his balance, his shoes slipping in the sand.

The effect of adrenaline made his stomach seem on fire. He wondered if he'd been right not to defend himself earlier. Things had not yet gotten out of control. But the first twin was working himself into a rage. The insults and shoves were occurring more forcefully, more often, and Buchanan had to ask himself, Is this an act? Or is it for real?

If he's acting, I'll fail the test by ignoring some of those insults. If this guy shoves me any harder, if I don't anticipate and absorb the impact, he'll knock me down. He'll dismiss me as unworthy of respect if I don't make a pretense of resisting.

But how much resistance can I show and still be Ed Potter? And how much resistance is enough to satisfy the twin without truly making him angry?

And—

The question kept nagging at Buchanan.

What if this is for real?

As Buchanan reached a shelter, the first twin shoved him again, knocking him across a plastic table.

Buchanan straightened and spun. "Now that's enough! Don't shove me again! If you've got questions, *ask* them. I'll explain whatever's bothering you! I can settle this misunderstanding! But damn it, keep your hands off me!"

"Keep my hands off you?" The first twin stepped close to

Buchanan, grabbed Buchanan's shirt and twisted it with his fist, then raised the shirt so that Buchanan felt suspended by it. "What I'd like to do is shove my hand down your throat and pull out your guts."

Buchanan smelled the tequila on his breath.

Abruptly the twin released his grip on Buchanan's shirt.

Buchanan allowed himself to topple, sprawling again across the table, this time on his back instead of his chest. It took all his discipline to restrain himself from retaliating. He kept reminding himself, The mission. You can't jeopardize the mission. You can't fight back until you're certain he intends to kill you. So far, all he's done is shove, insult, and threaten you. Those aren't good enough reasons for you to abort the mission by responding with deadly force.

Surrounded by darkness, glimpsing the lights of the hotel beyond the twins and their bodyguard, Buchanan stared up at the first twin, who grabbed him again, jerked him to his feet, and thrust him into a chair. Buchanan's spine banged against the plastic. Waves splashed behind him.

"You promise that you can explain? Then do so. By all means, explain. It will be amusing to hear"—the twin suddenly pressed the muzzle of his 9-mm Browning pistol against Buchanan's forehead—"how you intend to settle what you call this misunderstanding."

That almost made the difference. Buchanan's pulse quickened. His muscles compacted. Inhaling, he prepared to—

But the twin hasn't cocked the pistol, Buchanan noticed, and the Browning doesn't have a sound suppressor. If he intends to kill me, isn't it more likely that he'd want to avoid causing a commotion? He'd use the bodyguard's Beretta, which does have a sound suppressor, so he wouldn't attract a crowd from the bar.

It's still possible that this is an act.

Sweating, mustering resolve, Buchanan watched the second twin approach.

The man stopped beside his brother and peered down. Even in the gloom, his eyes were vividly hawklike. "Listen carefully," he told Buchanan. "We are going to talk about names. But not the name that the drunken American called you in the restaurant. Not Jim Crawford, or at least not only Jim Crawford. And not just Ed Potter. Other names. *Many* other names. In fact, so many that I find it impossible to remember them all." He pulled a folded piece of paper from his suit coat. "You gave us a list of names of our associates whom you claim betrayed us. Well, I have a different list, one with other names." He unfolded the paper and aimed a penlight at it so he could read. "John Block. Richard Davis. Paul Higgins. Andrew Macintosh. Henry Davenport. Walter Newton. Michael Galer. William Hanover. Stuart Malik."

Oh, shit, Buchanan thought.

The second twin stopped reading, scowled at the sheet of paper, shook his head, and sighed. "There are several other names. But those will do for purposes of illustration." He refolded the piece of paper, returned it to his suit-coat pocket, and at once thrust the penlight close to Buchanan's face, aiming it into Buchanan's right eye.

Buchanan jerked his face away to avoid the light.

But the bodyguard had shifted behind Buchanan and abruptly slammed his hands against the sides of Buchanan's head, making Buchanan's ears ring. The sudden, stunning pressure of the hands was like a vise. Buchanan tried, but he couldn't turn his face away. He couldn't avoid the blinding glare of the slender beam of light aimed into his eye. He reached up to grab the bodyguard's smallest fingers and snap them in order to make the bodyguard release his grip.

But Buchanan froze in midgesture as the first twin cocked the Browning, the muzzle of which was now pressed against Buchanan's left temple. Christ, Buchanan thought, he just might do it.

"*Bueno. Muy bueno,*" the first twin said. "Don't make trouble."

The penlight kept glaring at Buchanan's eye. He blinked repeatedly, then scrunched his eyelid shut, but he could still see the light through the eyelid's thin skin. He scrunched the eyelid shut tighter. A rough hand grabbed the side of his face, clawing at the eyelid, forcing it up. The light again glared. Buchanan's eyeball suddenly felt hot, dry, and swollen. The light felt like a bright, hot needle that threatened to lance his eyeball as if it were a festering boil. Buchanan needed all his self-control not to struggle, not to attempt to break away from the hands that bound him—because he knew without doubt that if he struggled again, the first twin would blow his brains out.

"Bueno," the first twin repeated. *"Muy bueno. Excelente.* Now, if you wish to live, you will tell us what all of those names that my brother read to you have in common. Think well before you answer." He nudged the muzzle of the Browning harder against Buchanan's temple. "I cannot respect, do business with, or tolerate a liar. The names. What is their secret?"

Buchanan swallowed. His voice was hoarse. "They're all me."

11

Except for the splash of the waves and the pounding of Buchanan's heart, the night became silent. Then, in the distance, laughter echoing from the hotel's outside bar broke the quiet. The twins and the bodyguard seemed frozen. At once they moved, the first twin lowering his pistol, the second twin releasing his grip on Buchanan's right eyelid, then shutting off the penlight, the bodyguard removing his viselike hands from the sides of Buchanan's head.

The first twin studied Buchanan. "I did not expect the truth." He sat on a chair near Buchanan, placing his Browning on the table so its muzzle was pointed at Buchanan, leaving his hand on the weapon. "I asked you earlier. I'll ask you again. Who *are* you?"

"Ed Potter." Buchanan closed his right eyelid, massaging it, still seeing the painful glare from the penlight.

"And not John Block? Or Richard Davis? Or Paul Higgins?" the first twin asked.

"Or Jim Crawford?" the second twin insisted.

"I never *heard* of Jim Crawford," Buchanan said. "I don't know what the hell that drunk in the restaurant was talking about. But as far as John Block, Richard Davis, and Paul Higgins are concerned, they're . . . How did you find out about my aliases?"

"You do not have the right to ask questions." The first twin tapped the barrel of his pistol on the table. "Why did you assume those names?"

"I'm not a fool," Buchanan said. His right eye watered. He kept it closed and squinted at his captors with his remaining functional eye. "You expect me to come to Mexico, start smuggling drugs north and weapons south, and use my real name? I'd use a false name if I was dealing drugs in the United States. Here in Mexico, where a *yanquí* is conspicuous, I had all the more reason to use a false name."

The second twin turned his penlight on and off as if in warning. "A false name is understandable."

"But so *many* false names?" The first twin persisted in tapping the side of his pistol on the table.

"Look, I told you I was doing business in more places than Cancún," Buchanan said. "I have bases in Mérida, Acapulco, Puerto Vallarta, several resorts I haven't mentioned."

"But you will," the second twin said. "You will." His voice thickened with emotion. "The names. I want to hear about these names."

Buchanan slowly opened his right eye. The glare from the penlight was still seared upon his vision. If his gambit didn't work, they would try to kill him. There'd be a fight (if he was lucky and had the opportunity to try to defend himself), but he didn't have much chance of surviving a struggle against three men while his vision was impaired.

"Answer!" the second twin barked.

"I take it as a given that when an American does illegal business in a foreign country, natives of that country have to be recruited," Buchanan said. "Those natives can go places and do things that the American wouldn't dare to without the risk of being conspicuous. The local authorities have to be bribed. The drugs need to be picked up from the suppliers. The weapons need to be delivered to those suppliers. There's no way *I'm* going to try to bribe the Mexican police. Even as bribable as they are, they might decide to make an example of a gringo and stick me in jail for a hundred years. I'd just as soon someone else took the risk of picking up the drugs and delivering the weapons, especially when it comes to dealing with those crazy bastards in the Medellín cartel. Let's face it—

Mexico's so poor, there are plenty of young men who are glad to risk their lives if I pay them what they think is a fortune but what to me is nothing. Of course, I need recruits in every resort where I do business, and while I'm in those resorts, I need a cover story to account for my presence. A tourist attracts attention if he comes back every three weeks. But a businessman doesn't, and one of the most commonplace American businessmen at Mexican resorts is a time-share condominium salesman. American tourists don't trust Mexican salesmen to lease them real estate. But they'll trust an American. Under assumed names in all the resorts where I have a base, I've convinced the authorities that I'm legitimate. Naturally, I use a different name in each resort, and I have false documents in that name. But here's the trick. If my Mexican recruits in each resort get picked up by the police or questioned by suppliers who have turned against me, my recruits don't know the assumed name I'm using. They don't know where I live or where I do business. Except on terms of my own choosing, they have no way to get in touch with me or to lead the police or a drug supplier to me. The name by which each recruit knows me is also assumed, but of course I don't need identification papers for those other names."

The first twin leaned forward, his hand on his pistol. "Keep talking."

"Each of the characters I pretend to be has a particular style of clothes, a preference for different foods, an individual way about him. One might slouch. Another might stand rigidly straight, as if he used to be in the military. Another might have a slight stutter. Still another might comb his hair straight back. Or have spectacles. Or wear a baseball cap. There's always something about the character that's memorable. That way, if the police start asking questions about a man with a certain name and certain mannerisms, it'll be difficult to find that man because the mannerisms are as false as the name. I mentioned after that drunken American confused me with someone else back at the restaurant—his mistake is a variation of an old saying that all foreigners look the same to Americans. Well, that saying can be turned around. Most Americans resemble one another as far as Mexicans are concerned. We weigh too much. We're clumsy. We've got too much money, and we're not very generous with it. We're loud. We're rude. So any American who has easy-to-describe individual characteristics will be remembered by my recruits, and if they're forced to give that description—'he has spectacles and always wears a baseball cap'—to an enemy, all I have to do is assume a different set of characteristics, blend with other Americans, and become invisible.''

Buchanan watched the twins, wondering, Are they buying it?

The first twin frowned. "Since you use so many false names, how do we know that Ed Potter is your true identity?"

"What motive would I have for lying? I had to tell you my real name or else you wouldn't be able to investigate my background and satisfy yourselves that I'm not a threat to you."

Buchanan waited, hoping that he'd overcome their misgivings. He'd followed a rule of deep-cover operations. If someone challenges you to the point that you're about to be exposed, the best defense was the truth—or rather, a version of the truth, a special slant on it that doesn't compromise the mission and yet sounds so authentic that it defeats skepticism. In this case, Buchanan had established a cover, as he'd explained to the twins, but then he had yet another cover, that of Ed Potter. The latter cover was intended to manipulate the twins into accepting him as a partner. But the false names he used as a time-share condominium salesman in various resorts, and the further false names that he used with his recruits, had not been intended as a way to impress the twins and demonstrate that he would be an asset to them. Rather, those false identities had been a way for Buchanan to protect himself against the Mexican government and, equally important, to prevent the Mexican authorities from tracing his illegal activities to a covert branch of the United States military. The last thing Buchanan's controllers wanted was an international incident. Indeed, even if Buchanan was arrested while he was posing as Edward Potter, his activities could still not be traced to his controllers. Because he had yet another cover. He would deny to the authorities that he had ever belonged to the DEA, and in the meantime, his controllers would remove or erase all the supporting details for that assumed identity. Buchanan would claim that he had invented the DEA story in order to infiltrate the drug distribution system. He would insist—and there would be supporting details for this cover also—that he was a free-lance journalist who wanted to write an exposé about the Mexican drug connection. If the Mexican authorities tried to investigate beyond that cover, they would find nothing that linked Buchanan to U.S. Special Operations.

"Perhaps," the first twin said. "Perhaps we can work together."

"Perhaps?" Buchanan asked. "*Madre de Dios,* what do I have to do to convince you?"

"First we will investigate your background."

"By all means," Buchanan said.

"Then we will determine if some of our associates have betrayed us as you claim."

"No problem." Buchanan's chest flooded with triumph. I've turned it around, he thought. Five minutes ago, they were ready to kill me, and I was trying to decide if I'd have to kill them. But I did the right thing. I kept my cool. I talked my way out of it. The mission hasn't been jeopardized.

"You will stay with us while we verify your credentials," the second twin said.

"Stay with you?"

"Do you have a problem with that?" the first twin asked.

"Not really," Buchanan said. "Except that making me a prisoner is a poor way to begin a partnership."

"Did I say anything about making you a prisoner?" The second twin smiled. "You will be our guest. Every comfort will be given to you."

Buchanan forced himself to return the smile. "Sounds fine with me. I could use a taste of the lifestyle I want to become accustomed to."

"But there *is* one other matter," the first twin said.

"Oh? What's that?" Buchanan inwardly tensed.

The second twin turned on his penlight and flicked its glare past Buchanan's right eye. "The drunken American in the restaurant. You will need to prove to our satisfaction that you were not in Kuwait and Iraq at the time he claims he spent time with you there."

"For Christ sake, are you still fixated on that drunk? I don't understand how I'm supposed to—"

12

"Crawford!" a man's voice boomed from the darkness near the hotel's bar. The voice was deep, crusty from cigarettes, thick from alcohol.

"What's that?" the first twin quickly asked.

Oh no, Buchanan thought. Oh, Jesus, no. Not when I've almost undone the damage from the first time.

"Crawford!" Big Bob Bailey yelled again. "Is that you flashin' that light over there?" A hulking silhouette lurched from the hotel's gardens, a beefy man who'd had too much to drink and now had trouble walking in the sand. "Yes, *you*, damn it! I mean *you*, Crawford! You and them spics you're talkin' with under that fancy beach umbrella or whatever the hell it is." He stumbled closer, breathing heavily. "You son of a bitch, I want a straight answer! I want to know why you're lyin' to me! 'Cause you and me *both* know your name's Jim Crawford! We both know we was prisoners in Kuwait and Iraq! So why won't you admit it? How come you made a fool of me? You think I'm not good enough to drink with you and your spic pals or somethin'?"

"I don't like the feel of this," the first twin said.

"Something's wrong," the second twin said.

"*Very* wrong." The first twin snapped his gaze away from Big Bob Bailey's awkwardly approaching shadow and riveted it upon Buchanan. "You're trouble. You Americans have an expression. 'Better safe than sorry.' "

"Come on, he's just a drunk!" Buchanan said.

"Crawford!" Big Bob Bailey yelled.

I don't have another choice, Buchanan thought.

"Shoot him," the first twin told the bodyguard.

(I've got to—!)

"I'm talkin' to you!" Big Bob Bailey stumbled. "Crawford! By Jesus, answer me!"

"Shoot them both," the second twin told the bodyguard.

But Buchanan was already in motion, lunging from the plastic chair, diving toward the left, toward the first twin and the Browning pistol he'd set on the table, his hand spread over it.

Behind Buchanan, the bodyguard fired. With the sound suppressor on the barrel, the guard's Beretta made a muffled pop. The bullet missed the back of Buchanan's head.

However, it didn't miss Buchanan entirely. As he rose and lunged, his right shoulder appeared where his head had been, and the bullet sliced, burning, through the muscle at the side of that shoulder. Before the bodyguard could shoot a second time, Buchanan had collided with the first twin, toppling him over his chair, simultaneously grabbing for the first twin's weapon. But the first twin would not let go of it.

"Shoot!" the second twin told the bodyguard.

"I can't! I might hit your brother!"

"Crawford, what the hell's goin' on?" Big Bob Bailey yelled.

Rolling in the sand, Buchanan strained to keep the first twin close to him as he fought for a grip on the pistol.

"Move closer!" the second twin told the bodyguard. "I'll shine my light!"

Buchanan's shoulder throbbed. Blood streamed from the wound, slicking the first twin and himself, making it hard for Buchanan to keep a grasp on the twin and use him as a shield. As he rolled, sand scraped into his wound. If he'd been standing, the blood would have streaked down his arm to his hand, causing it to become so slippery that his fingers wouldn't be able to wrench the pistol from the first twin's hand. But he was prone, and his hand stayed dry as he struggled in the sand. He sensed the bodyguard and the second twin rushing toward him. He heard Big Bob Bailey again yell, "Crawford!" And all at once, the first twin fired his pistol. Unlike the bodyguard's weapon, the twin's Browning did not have a sound suppressor. Its report was shockingly loud. The bodyguard and the second twin cursed, scrambling to get out of the line of fire. Buchanan's ears—already ringing from when the bodyguard had slammed his hands against the sides of Buchanan's head—now rang louder from the proximity of the shot. Buchanan's right eye still retained a harsh afterimage from the glare of the penlight that the second twin had aimed at the eye. Relying more on touch than on sight, Buchanan rolled and struggled with the first twin to get control of the pistol. His shoulder ached and began to stiffen.

The first twin fired the pistol again. As much as Buchanan could tell, the bullet went straight up, bursting through the palm fronds at the top of the shelter. But Buchanan's already compromised vision was assaulted by the pistol's muzzle flash. "Jesus!" he heard Big Bob Bailey yell. Despite the ringing in his ears, he also heard distant exclamations from the hotel's outside bar. He sensed the bodyguard and the second twin surging toward him once more, and suddenly he managed to grab the first twin's right thumb, twisting it, yanking it backward.

The thumb snapped at the middle joint with a sound that was soft, gristly, not so much a crack as a crunch. The first twin screamed and reflexively loosened his hold on the pistol, needing to relax his hand, to reduce the stress on his thumb. In that instant, Buchanan wrested the pistol away and rolled, sand sticking to his bloody shoulder. The bodyguard fired. As Buchanan kept rolling, the bullet struck next to him, and Buchanan shot four times in rapid succession. His vision was still sufficiently impaired that he had to rely on other senses—the touch of sand that the bodyguard scattered while he rushed closer to Buchanan, the sound of the muffled pop from the bodyguard's sound-suppressed Beretta—to help him estimate the bodyguard's position. Three of Buchanan's bullets struck the bodyguard, knocking him backward. Buchanan immediately twisted, aiming to his left, firing twice, hitting the second twin in the stomach and the chest. Blood spurting from between his unbuttoned silk shirt, the target doubled over and fell.

But the bodyguard was still on his feet, Buchanan realized. The man had been hit three times and yet seemed only dazed. Buchanan abruptly understood that all three bullets had struck the bodyguard's chest and that the Hispanic had seemed so unusually large-boned because the bodyguard was wearing a concealed bullet-resistant vest. As the bodyguard straightened and aimed yet again, Buchanan shot him in the throat, the left eye, and the forehead. Even then, he feared that the bodyguard might spastically squeeze off a shot. Buchanan tensed, desperate to squirm backward. But instead of firing, the bodyguard rose as if trying to balance on his tiptoes, leaned back as if balancing now on his heels, and toppled across the table. At the same time, Buchanan felt thrashing to his right, twisted onto his side, and shot the first twin through his left temple. Blood, bone, and brain—hot and sticky—spattered over Buchanan's face.

The first twin shuddered, dying.

Buchanan, in turn, inhaled deeply and trembled, overwhelmed by adrenaline. The repeated shots from the unsilenced Browning had intensified the agony of the ringing in his head. Due to years of habit, he'd mentally counted each shot as he'd pulled the trigger. Four toward the bodyguard. Two toward the second twin. Three more toward the bodyguard. One toward the first twin. Earlier, the first twin had fired twice. That made twelve all told. Buchanan hadn't worried about using all his ammunition because he knew that the Browning was capable of holding thirteen rounds in the magazine and one in the chamber. Normally, he wouldn't have needed to shoot so many times, but in the darkness, he couldn't guarantee precision. But now his remaining bullets would not be enough if the shots had attracted the twins' other bodyguards. In a rush, Buchanan crouched behind the table, aiming toward the gloom of the beach, the glow of the lights at the outdoor bar, and the gleam of the lights at the hotel. A loud, nervous crowd had gathered on the sidewalk that flanked the beach. Several men were pointing in Buchanan's direction. He didn't see any armed men rushing toward him. Quickly he made sure that the bodyguard and the first twin were dead. While stopped at the first twin, he searched the body, retrieving his belt, his keys, and his pen. He didn't want anything associated with him to remain on the scene. In a greater rush, he checked the second twin, groped inside his suit coat, and pulled out the list of names—Buchanan's pseudonyms—that the second twin had read to him. He left the other list, the names of supposedly disloyal associates that he'd given the twins. The authorities would investigate those names and try to implicate them in these killings.

Or so Buchanan hoped. He wanted to accomplish at least *some* of what he'd been sent here to do, to inflict as much damage on the drug distribution network as he could. If only this mission hadn't gone to hell, if only . . . .

Buchanan suddenly froze. *Big Bob Bailey*. Where *was* he? What had happened to—?

"Crawford?" an unsteady voice murmured from the darkness.

Buchanan strained his vision to study the night, his eyes now less impaired by the glare of the penlight and the strobelike flash of the shots.

"Crawford?" Bailey's voice sounded oddly muffled.

Then Buchanan realized—Bailey had been stumbling toward this table the last time Buchanan had seen him. When the shooting started, Bailey must have dropped to the beach. His voice was muffled because he was pressed, facedown, against the sand.

"Jesus Christ, man, are you all right?" Bailey murmured. "Who's doin' all the shootin'?"

Buchanan saw him now, a dark shape hugging the beach. He shifted his gaze toward the crowd on the sidewalk near the hotel's outdoor bar. The crowd was larger, louder, although still afraid to come anywhere near where guns had been fired. He didn't see any bodyguards or policemen rushing in his direction. They will, though. Soon, he thought. I don't have much time. I have to get out of here.

The pain in his shoulder worsened. The wound swelled, throbbing more fiercely. Urgent, he used an unbloody section of his shirt to wipe his fingerprints from where he'd touched the top of the table and the sides of a chair. He couldn't do anything about the prints he'd left on the glasses in the restaurant, but maybe the table would have been cleared by now, the glasses taken to the kitchen and washed.

Hurry.

As he started to swing toward the first twin, wipe fingerprints from the pistol, and leave it in the twin's hand, he heard Bailey's voice become stronger.

"Crawford? Were you hit?"

Shut up! Buchanan thought.

Near the hotel's bar, the crowd was becoming aggressive. The glow from the hotel was sufficient to reveal two uniformed policemen who sprinted off the sidewalk onto the sand. Buchanan finished wiping the pistol clean of fingerprints and forced it into the first twin's fingers. He pivoted, stayed low, and ran, making sure he kept his right shoulder close to the splashing waves. That shoulder and, indeed, his entire right side were covered with blood. He wanted the blood to fall into the water so that the police couldn't track him by following splotches of his blood in the sand.

"*Alto!*" a man's gruff voice ordered. "Halt!"

Buchanan raced harder, staying low, charging parallel to the waves, hoping the night would so envelop him that he'd make a poor target.

"*ALTO!*" the gruff voice demanded with greater force.

Buchanan sprinted as fast as he could. His back muscles rippled with chills as he tensed in dread of the bullet that would—

"Hey, what do you think you're—? What are you shovin' me for? I didn't do nothin'!" Big Bob Bailey objected with drunken indignation.

The police had grabbed the first person they came to.

Despite his pain and his desperation, Buchanan couldn't help grinning. Bailey, you turned out not to be completely useless, after all.

THREE

1

BALTIMORE, MARYLAND

Pushing a squeaky cart along a dark, drizzly downtown alley, the woman dressed as a bag lady felt exhausted. She hadn't slept in almost forty-eight hours, and that period of time (as well as several days before it) had been filled with constant dread. Indeed, for months, since she'd first met Alistair Drummond and had agreed to his proposal, she'd never been free from apprehension.

The assignment had seemed simple enough, and certainly the fee she earned was considerable, her accommodations lavish. As a bonus, she seldom had to perform. Mostly, all she had to do was stay in the Manhattan condominium with its splendid view of Central Park and let servants take care of her, occasionally deigning to accept a telephone call but making it short, pretending to be hoarse because of a throat problem that she claimed her doctor had diagnosed as polyps and that might require surgery. Rarely, she went out in public, always at night, always in a limousine, always wearing gems, a fur, and an exquisite evening gown, always with protective, handsome escorts. Those outings were usually to the Metropolitan Opera or to a charity benefit, and she stayed just long enough to ensure that her presence was noticed, that she'd be mentioned in a society column. She permitted no contact with her character's former friends or former husband. She was, as she'd indicated in a rare magazine interview, beginning a period of self-assessment that required isolation in order for her to commence the second act of her life. Her performance was one of her best. No one thought her behavior unusual. After all, genius was subject to eccentricities.

But she was terrified. The accumulation of fear had been gradual. At first, she had attributed her unease to stage fright, to becoming accustomed to a new role, to convincing an unfamiliar audience, and of course, to satisfying Alistair Drummond. The latter particularly unnerved her. Drummond's gaze was so intense that she suspected he wore spectacles not to improve his vision but, rather, to magnify the cold glint in his eyes. He exuded such authority that he dominated a room, regardless of how crowded it was or how many other notables were present. No one knew for certain how old he was, except that he was definitely over eighty, but everyone agreed that he looked more like an eerie sixty. Numerous face-lifts, combined with a macrobiotic diet, massive amounts of vitamins, and weekly infusions of hormones, seemed to have stopped the evidence of his advancing age. The contrast between his tightened face and his wizened hands troubled her.

He preferred to be called professor, although he had never taught and his doctorate was only honorary, the result of a new art museum that bore his name and that he'd had constructed as a gift to a prestigious but financially embattled Ivy League university. One of the conditions of her employment had been that the "professor" would have access to her at all times and that she would appear in public with him whenever he dictated. As vain as he was rich, he cackled whenever he read his name—in company with hers—in the society columns, especially if the columnist called him professor. The sound of his brittle, crusty laughter chilled her.

But as frightening as she eventually found Alistair Drummond, even more frightening was his personal assistant, a pleasant-faced, fair-haired, well-dressed man whom she knew only as Raymond. His face never changed expression. It always bore the same cheery countenance, regardless of whether he helped Drummond inject himself with hormones, looked at her in a low-cut evening gown, watched a weather report on television, or was sent on an assignment. Drummond was careful never to discuss the specifics of his business transactions while she was present, but she took for granted that anyone who had accumulated so much wealth and power, not to mention worldwide notoriety, by definition had to be ruthless, and she always imagined that the assignments Drummond gave to Raymond would have repugnant consequences. Not that Raymond gave any indication. Raymond always looked as cheery when he left as when he returned.

What had made her uneasiness turn into dread was the day she realized that she wasn't merely pretending to be in seclusion—she was a prisoner. It was unprofessional of her, she admitted, to have wanted to break character and take an unescorted afternoon walk in Central Park, perhaps go over to the Metropolitan Museum of Art. The moment the thought occurred to her, she repressed it. Nonetheless, briefly she'd felt liberated, and subsequently she'd felt frustrated. I can't, she thought. I made an agreement. I accepted a fee—a *large* fee—in exchange for taking on a role. I can't break the bargain. But what if . . .?

That tantalizing question had made her impatient with her narrow world. Except for a few sanctioned outings and an occasional performance on the telephone, she spent most of each day exercising, reading, watching videotapes, listening to music, eating, and . . . It had sounded like a vacation until she was forced to do it. Her days had become longer and longer. As much as Alistair Drummond and his assistant made her uneasy, she almost welcomed their visits. Although the two men were frightening, at least they were a change. So she had asked herself, What if I did break character? What if I did go out for an afternoon walk in Central Park? She had no intention of actually doing so, but she wondered what would happen if . . . A bodyguard had suddenly appeared at the end of the corridor outside her unit and had prevented her from getting on the elevator.

She was an experienced observer of audiences. She'd known from the start—the first time she was allowed from the condominium, escorted into Drummond's limousine—that the building was being watched: a flower seller across the street, a hot dog vendor on the corner, no doubt the building's doorman, and no doubt someone like an indigent at the rear exit from the building. But she had assumed that these sentries were there to prevent her character's former acquaintances from arriving unexpectedly and catching her unprepared. At once, now, she had realized that the building was under watch to keep her *in* as much as to keep others out, and that had made her world even smaller, and that had made her even more tense; Drummond had made her more tense; Raymond had made her more tense.

When will I be able to get out of here? she'd wondered. When will the performance end? Or *will* it end?

One evening as she put on her diamond necklace—which Drummond had told her would be her bonus when the assignment was completed—she'd impulsively scraped the necklace's largest stone across a glass of water. The stone had not made a scratch. Which meant that the stone was not a diamond. Which meant that the necklace, her bonus, was worthless.

So what else was . . .? She examined the bank statement she was sent each month. A gesture of good faith from Drummond, each statement showed that Drummond had, as he had promised, deposited her monthly fee. Since all her necessities were provided, she had no need to use that money, Drummond had explained. Thus, when her assignment was over, she'd be able to withdraw the entire enormous sum.

The bank statement had an account number. She knew that

she didn't dare use the telephone in her condominium (it presumably was tapped), so she had waited for the rare opportunity when she was allowed to leave the condominium during the day, and when the bank would be open. It had given her enormous pleasure that during a pause in the political luncheon's program of speakers, she had whispered to Alistair Drummond, who had brought her, that she needed to go to the ladies' room. Taut-faced, Drummond had nodded his permission, gesturing with a wrinkled hand for a bodyguard to accompany her.

She had leaned close, pressing a breast against him. "No, I don't want your permission," she had whispered. "What I want is fifty cents. That's what it costs to get into the toilets here."

"Don't say 'toilets.' " Drummond had pursed his lips in disapproval of her vulgarity.

"I'll call them rose bowls if you want. I still need fifty cents. Plus two dollars for the attendant with the towels. I wouldn't have to ask you if you'd give me some actual money once in a while."

"All your needs are taken care of."

"Sure. Except when I have to go to the ladies' room—excuse me, the rose bowl." She pressed her breast harder against his bony arm.

Drummond turned toward Raymond, who was beside him. "Escort her. Give her what she asks."

So she and Raymond had proceeded through the crowd, ignoring the stares of celebrity worshipers. Raymond had discreetly given her the small sum of money she had requested, and the moment she had entered the powder room part of the ladies' room, she had veered toward a pay phone, inserted coins, pressed the numbers for the bank into which Drummond deposited her fee, and asked for Accounting. Several society women who sat on velvet chairs before mirrors and freshened their makeup turned in recognition of someone so famous. She nodded with an imperious "Do you mind? Can I have some privacy?" look. Conditioned to pretend not to be impressed, the society matrons shrugged and resumed applying lipstick to their drooping lips.

"Accounting," a nasally male voice said.

"Please check this number." She dictated it.

"One moment. . . . Yes, I have that account on my computer screen."

"What is the balance?"

The nasally voice told her. The sum was correct.

"Are there any restrictions?"

"One. For withdrawals, a second signature is required."

"Whose?"

Raymond's, she learned, and that was when she knew that Drummond didn't intend for her to get out of this role alive.

It took several weeks of preparations, of calculations, of watching and biding her time. No one suspected. She was sure of that. She made herself seem so contented that it was one of the best performances of her career. Last night, after going to her bedroom at midnight, after keeping her eyes shut when the maid looked in on her at two, she had waited until four to make sure that the maid was asleep. She had quickly dressed, putting on her sneakers and gray hooded exercise suit. She had stuffed her purse with the necklace, bracelets, and earrings that Drummond had promised her, the jewelry that she now knew was fake. She had to take them because she wanted Drummond to think that she still believed the diamonds and other gems to be real and that she would try to sell them. His men would waste time questioning the dealers she was most likely to approach. She had a small amount of money—what she'd been given for the attendant in the ladies' room, a few dollars that she'd stolen in isolated dimes and quarters from her maid's purse while her maid was distracted by a task in another room, twenty-five dollars that she'd brought with her the first day she'd started this assignment. It wouldn't take her far. She needed more. A great deal more.

Her first task had been to leave the condominium. As soon as she'd realized that she was a prisoner, she'd automatically assumed that the door would be rigged to sound an alarm and warn her guards if she tried to escape in the night. The alarm was one of the reasons she had waited several weeks before leaving. It had taken her that long, whenever the maid wasn't watching, to check the walls behind furniture and paintings and find the alarm's hidden switch. Last night, she had turned it off behind the liquor cabinet, silently unlocked the door and opened it, then peered left down the corridor. the guard who watched the elevator could not be seen. He usually sat in a chair just around the corner. At four in the morning, there was a strong possibility he'd be drowsing, relying on the sound of the elevator to make him become alert.

But she had no intention of using the elevator. Rather, she left her door slightly ajar—she didn't dare close it all the way and risk making an avoidable noise—then turned to the right, walking softly along the carpet toward the fire door. That door wasn't guarded on this floor, but in the lobby, the exit from the stairwell was. With painstaking care, she eased the fire door open, closed it as carefully behind her, and exhaled, wiping sweat from her hands. That had been the part she most dreaded, that she'd make a noise when she opened the fire door and would alert the guard. The rest, for a time, would be easy.

She hurried down the cold, shadowy stairwell, the rubber soles on her sneakers making almost no sound. Forty stories later, energized rather than fatigued, she reached the lobby door but didn't stop, continuing instead to the basement. As she made her way through dusty storage areas and the noisy furnace area, passing a clutter of pipes and circuit breakers, she feared that a custodian would confront her, but no one seemed on duty, and eventually she found stairs that led to a rear exit from the building, an exit that was far enough from the conventional exit that anyone watching the other exit wouldn't notice someone leaving the basement.

Still cautious, she turned off the light near the door before she opened it, so that no illumination would spill out and reveal her. Then she was in an alley, feeling the chill of late October, hurrying along. She wished that she'd been able to bring a coat, but all the coats in her character's closet had been expensive, designed to be worn with evening clothes. There'd been nothing as inconspicuous as a windbreaker. No matter. She was free. But for how long? Fear and urgency gave her warmth.

Without her wig, special makeup, and facial-altering devices, she no longer resembled her character. But even though the public wouldn't recognize her, Alistair Drummond had a photograph of her original appearance. So she didn't dare use a taxi. The driver, if questioned, would remember picking her up at this hour and in this vicinity, especially since she was Hispanic. The driver would also remember where he'd dropped her off. That destination would be a safe distance from where she intended to go. It would not reveal anything that put her in danger. Nonetheless, she considered it better if she permitted Drummond no leads whatsoever, false or true, and instead just seemed to vanish. Besides, given the little money she had, she didn't dare waste it on a taxi.

So she ran, to all appearance an early-morning jogger on the nearly deserted streets. She went hunting, skirting Central Park, trying to look like an easy target. Finally, two kids with knives emerged from shadows. She broke both their arms and took the fourteen dollars she found on them. By dawn, her exercise clothes dark with sweat, she rested in a twenty-four-hour hamburger joint in Times Square. There she sacrificed part of her meager funds on several steaming cups of coffee and a breakfast of scrambled eggs, hash browns, sausage, and English muffins. Not the sort of breakfast she usually ate and certainly not recommended by the American Heart Association, but given the frantic, furtive day she expected to have, she needed all the calories and carbohydrates her stomach would hold.

She sacrificed more of her meager funds to go to a theater that showed movies around the clock. The only woman present, she knew that she'd attract predators in the almost-deserted seats at seven in the morning. She wanted to. When the movie ended and she left the theater, she carried fifty more dollars, money that she'd taken from three men whom she'd knocked unconscious, using her elbow, when each—a half hour apart— had sat next to her and tried to molest her.

By then, a few cut-rate clothing stores were open, and she bought a plain wool cap, a pair of wool gloves, and an insulated black nylon jacket that blended with her gray exercise clothes. She tucked her hair beneath her cap, and with her slightly baggy exercise clothes hiding her voluptuous breasts and hips, she appeared overweight and androgynous. Her costume was almost perfect. Except that her clothes were new (and she remedied that by dragging her cap, gloves, and jacket in the gutter), she looked like most of the other street people.

Next, it was time to pick her spot among the hucksters

beginning to set up shop on the curb along Broadway. It took two hours, a watchful eye for the police or anyone else who showed undue interest in her, and several prudent shifts of location, but she finally used her powers of performance to sell all of her jewelry to tourists, amassing $215.

That gave her enough to travel—not enough to fly, of course (which she wouldn't have done anyhow because the airports would be among the first places that Drummond's men would check), but certainly enough to take a train, and a bus would be even cheaper. Plus, the way she was dressed, she thought she'd be more invisible on a bus, so she ate a hamburger while she walked to the junkie-infested Port Authority Bus Terminal, and by noon she was on her way to Baltimore.

Why Baltimore? Why not? she thought. It was close enough that a ticket there wouldn't use all her money. At the same time, it was comfortably far. She had no previous associations with Baltimore. It was simply a random selection, impossible for Drummond to predict, although if he eliminated the cities with which she'd been associated and if he arbitrarily chose the remaining big cities within a certain radius from Manhattan, he might make a lucky guess. Nothing was guaranteed. She had to be careful.

En route to Baltimore, while she studied the other passengers to determine whether any was a threat, she had ample opportunity to think about her options. She didn't dare fall back into old patterns. Her family and friends were a danger to her. Drummond's men would be watching them. She had to construct a new persona, one unrelated to any character she'd assumed before. She had to make new friends and create new relatives. As far as employment was concerned, she would do whatever was most tolerable, as long as it wasn't anything she'd done previously. She had to make a complete break with the past. Getting the proper documents for a new false identity wasn't a problem. She was an expert.

But as she considered her existential condition, she wondered if she was prepared to make the sacrifice. She *liked* the person she'd been before she met Alistair Drummond. She wanted to be that person again. Had she been foolish? Had she misjudged Drummond's intention? Perhaps she should have been patient and continued to live in luxury.

Until you served your purpose and your performance was no longer necessary.

And then?

Remember, the gems were fake, and there was no way you were ever going to get the money Drummond claimed to be paying you. The only explanation for the way he rigged that bank account was that he planned to have you killed and take back the money.

But why would he want me killed?

To hide something.

What, though?

The bus arrived in Baltimore at nine in the evening. A cold drizzle made the downtown area bleak. She found a cheap place to eat—more caffeine, calories, and carbohydrates, not to mention grease (she rationalized that the fat might help insulate her from the cold). She didn't want to waste her remaining money on a hotel room—even a cheap one would be disastrous to her reserves. For a time, she roamed the back streets, hoping that someone would accost her. But the man who grabbed her and whose collarbone she broke had only fifty cents in his pocket.

She was tired, cold, wet, and depressed. She needed to rest. She needed a place where she'd feel reasonably safe, where she could think and sleep. When she found a shopping cart in an alley, she decided on her next role. After wiping dirt on her face, she threw trash into the cart. With her shoulders slumped and with an assumed crazy, empty look in her eyes, she pushed the cart, wheels squeaking, through the drizzle, a bag lady on her way to a shelter for the homeless that she had just passed.

What am I going to do? she thought. The confidence she'd felt when escaping had drained from her. The rigors of her new life weighed upon her imagination. Damn it, I *liked* who I was. I want to be her again.

How? To do that, you've got to beat Drummond, and he's too powerful to be beaten.

Is he? Why did he hire me? Why did he want me to put on that performance? What's his secret? What's he hiding? If I can find *that* out, maybe he *can* be beaten.

One thing's sure. Without money and resources, you need help.

But who can I ask? I don't dare turn to my friends and family. They're a trap. Besides, they haven't the faintest idea of what to do, of what this involves.

So what about the people you trained with?

No, they're a matter of public record. Drummond can use his influence to learn who they are. They'll be watched in case I approach them—as much a liability as my family and friends.

The drizzle increased to a downpour. Her soaked clothes drooped and clung to her. In the gloom, she felt every bit the spiritless bag lady she pretended to be.

There's got to be *someone*.

The cart she pushed kept squeaking.

You can't be that alone! she wanted to scream.

Face it. The only person you could trust to help you would have to be someone so anonymous, so chameleonlike, so invisible, without a trace or a record that it would be like he'd never existed. And he'd have to be damned good at staying alive.

He? Why would it have to be a man?

But she suddenly knew, and as she reached the entrance to the shelter for the homeless, a man in a black suit with a white ministerial collar stepped out.

"Come, sister. It's not a fit night to be out."

Playing her role, she resisted.

"Please, sister. It's warm inside. There's food. A place to sleep."

She resisted less stubbornly.

"You'll be safe, I promise. And I'll store your cart. I'll protect your goods."

That did it. Like a child, she allowed herself to be led, and as she left the gloom of the night, as she entered the brightly lit shelter, she smelled coffee, stale doughnuts, boiled potatoes, but it might as well have been a banquet. She'd found sanctuary, and as she shuffled toward a crowded wooden bench, she mentally repeated the name of the man whom she had decided to ask for help. The name filled her mind like a mantra. The problem was that he probably no longer used that name. He was constantly in flux. Officially, he didn't exist. So how on earth could she get in touch with a man as formless and shifting as the wind? Where in hell would he be?

2

Until 1967, Cancún was a small, sleepy town on the northeastern coast of Mexico's Yucatán Peninsula. That year, the Mexican government—seeking a way to boost the country's weak economy—decided to promote tourism more energetically than ever. But instead of improving an existing resort, the government chose to create a world-class holiday center where there was nothing. Various requirements such as suitable location and weather were programmed into a computer, and the computer announced that the new resort would be built on a narrow sandbar in a remote area of the Mexican Caribbean. Construction began in 1968. A modern sewage-disposal system was installed, as well as a dependable water-purification system and a reliable power plant. A four-lane highway was built down the middle of the sandbar. Palm trees were planted next to the highway. Hotels designed to resemble ancient Mayan pyramids were constructed along the ocean side of the island, while nightclubs and restaurants were built along the inner lagoon. Eventually, several million tourists came each year to what had once been nothing but a sandbar.

Cancún's sandbar had the shape of the number 7. It was twelve miles long, a quarter mile wide, and linked to the mainland by a bridge at each end. Club Internacional—where Buchanan had shot the three Hispanics—was located at the middle of the top of the 7, and as Buchanan raced away from it through the darkness along the wave-lapped beach, he ignored the other hotels that glistened on his left and tried to decide what he would do when he reached the bridge at the northern end of the sandbar. The two policemen who'd arrived at the scene of the killings would use two-way radios to contact their counterparts on the mainland. Those other policemen would block the bridges and question all Americans who attempted to leave. No matter how much effort it took, the police would respond promptly and thoroughly. Cancún prided itself on appearing safe for tourists. A multiple murder demanded an absolute response. To reassure tourists, a quick arrest was mandatory.

Under other circumstances, Buchanan would not have hesitated to veer from the beach, pass between hotels, reach the redbrick sidewalk along the highway, and stroll across the bridge, where he would agreeably answer the questions of the police. But he didn't dare show himself. With his wounded shoulder and his blood-drenched clothes, he'd attract so much attention that he'd be arrested at once. He had to find another way out of the area, and as the beach curved, angling to the left toward the looming shadow of the bridge, he stared toward the glimmer of hotels across the channel that separated the sandbar from the mainland, and he decided he would have to swim.

Unexpectedly, he felt light-headed. Alarming him, his legs bent. His heart beat too fast, and he had trouble catching his breath. The effects of adrenaline, he tried to assure himself. It didn't help that he'd drunk four ounces of tequila before fighting for his life and then racing down the beach. But adrenaline and he were old friends, and it had never made him light-headed. Similarly, his profession was such that on several occasions he'd been forced into action after his deep-cover identity required him to gain a contact's trust by drinking with him. On none of those occasions, however, had the combination of exertion and alcohol made him light-headed. A little sick to his stomach, yes, but never light-headed. All the same, he definitely felt dizzy now, and sick to his stomach as well, and he had to admit the truth—although his shoulder wound was superficial, he must be losing more blood than he'd realized. If he didn't stop the bleeding, he risked fainting. Or worse.

Trained as a paramedic, Buchanan knew that the preferred way to stop bleeding was by using a pressure bandage. But he didn't have the necessary first-aid equipment. The alternative was to use a method that at one time had been recommended but had now fallen out of favor—applying a tourniquet. The disadvantage of a tourniquet was that it cut off the flow of blood not only to the wound but also to the rest of a limb, in this case Buchanan's right arm. If the tourniquet were applied too tightly or not relaxed at frequent, regular intervals, the victim risked damaging tissue to the point where gangrene resulted.

But he didn't have another option. Sirens wailing, lights flashing, emergency vehicles stopped on the bridge. As Buchanan paused at the edge of the channel between the sandbar and the mainland, he glanced warily toward the darkness behind him and neither saw nor heard an indication that he was being pursued. He *would* be, though. Soon. Hurriedly, he reached inside his pants pocket and pulled out the folded belt that the second twin had taken from him and that Buchanan had retrieved after shooting the man. The belt was made from woven strips of leather, so there wasn't any need for eyelets. The prong on the buckle could slide between strands of leather anywhere along the belt. Buchanan hitched the belt around his swollen right shoulder, above the wound, and cinched it securely, tugging at the free end with his left hand while he bent his right arm painfully upward and with sweating effort used his trembling right fingers to push the buckle's prong through the leather. His legs wobbled. His vision blackened. He feared that he would pass out. But at once, his vision returned to normal, and with tremendous effort, he compelled his legs to move. Already he sensed, without being able to see the effect clearly, that the flow of blood had lessened significantly. He didn't feel as light-headed. The trade-off was that his right arm now felt disturbingly prickly and cold.

Concerned that his blue canvas deck shoes would slip off his feet when filled with water, he removed them, tied their laces together, and wound the laces tightly around his right wrist. Then he took out the list of his pseudonyms that he'd removed from the second twin's corpse. After tearing the sheet into tiny pieces, he quickly waded into the darkness of the channel, the surprisingly warm water soaking his knees, his thighs, and his abdomen. As white-capped waves struck his chest, he pushed his feet off the sandy bottom and surged outward. A strong current tugged at him. In small amounts, he released the bits of torn paper. Even if someone managed impossibly to find all the pieces, the water would have turned the paper into mush.

Relying on the kick of his muscular legs to give him momentum, he turned so his right side was below him, allowed his wounded right arm to rest, and used his left arm to stroke sideways through the water, adding to the power of his legs. The shoes attached to his right wrist created drag and held him back. Determined, he kicked harder.

The mouth of the channel was a hundred yards wide. As Buchanan pulled with his left arm and thrust with his legs, the water soaked the belt around his right shoulder, stretched the leather, and caused the tourniquet to loosen, decreasing the pressure above his wound. His right arm—no longer cold and prickly—now felt warm and sensitive to the tug of the current. Salt in the water made his wound sting.

Maybe the salt will disinfect it, he thought. But then he smelled the film of oil and gasoline on the water, left by the numerous powerboats that used the channel, and he realized that the water would contaminate his wound, not disinfect it.

He realized something else—the loose tourniquet meant that his wound would be bleeding again. Blood might attract . . .

He swam with greater urgency, knowing that barracuda were often seen among the area's numerous reefs, knowing as well that sharks were sometimes reported to have swum up the channel and into the lagoon between the island and the shore. He had no idea how large the sharks had been or whether they were the type that attacked swimmers, but if there were predators in the water, the blood could attract them from quite a distance.

He kicked. His foot touched something. A piece of wood perhaps. Or a clump of drifting seaweed. But it might be . . .

He thrust himself faster, his foot again touching whatever was behind him.

He was a quarter of the way across the channel, far enough into it that he felt small, swallowed by the night. Abruptly, he heard the drone of a motor to his left and frowned in that direction. The drone became a roar. He saw the lights of a swiftly approaching powerboat. It came from the lagoon, sped beneath the bridge, and hurried through the channel toward the ocean. A police boat? Buchanan wondered, and strained to get out of its way. As he kicked, he again felt something behind him. He weakened from further loss of blood. Staring frantically toward the approaching boat, he suddenly recognized the silhouette revealed by its lights. The vessel didn't belong to the police. It was a cabin cruiser. Through its windows, he saw several men and women drinking and laughing.

But the vessel was still a threat. It kept speeding toward him. Halfway across the channel, feeling the vibration of the cruiser's engines through the water, so close that within a few seconds he would either be seen by someone on board or else struck, Buchanan took a deep breath and submerged, veering downward, forced to use his injured arm to help him gain more speed, to avoid the passing hull and the spinning propellers.

The rumble of the cruiser's powerful engines assaulted Buchanan's eardrums. As he dove farther, deeper, the shoes attached to his right wrist impeded the already-awkward motion of his injured arm. He heard the cruiser's rumble pass over him.

The moment it diminished, he arched fiercely upward, feeling light-headed again, desperate to breathe. Beneath him, something brushed past his feet. Hurry, he told himself. The decreasing pressure against his ears alerted him that he was almost to the surface. His lungs seemed on fire. Any second now, he anticipated, his face would be exposed to the night. He'd be able to open his mouth and—

Whack! His skull struck something large and solid. The impact was so unexpected, so painful, so stunning that Buchanan breathed reflexively, inhaling water, coughing, gagging. He might have briefly passed out. He didn't know. What he did know was that he inhaled more water, that he fought to reach the surface. He grazed past the object he'd struck, burst into the open, and greedily filled his lungs, all the while struggling not to vomit.

What had—?

His head felt squeezed by swelling pain. In agony, desperate to get his bearings, he found himself facing the receding stern of the brightly lit cabin cruiser. Ominous, a long, low shadow stalked the cruiser. The object must have been what Buchanan had struck. But he didn't understand what—

And then he did. A dinghy. The cruiser's towing it. I had no way of knowing about—

Something brushed past his legs again. Startled into action, ignoring the pain in his shoulder and now in his skull, Buchanan twisted onto his stomach and swam without regard for his wounded shoulder, using both arms, kicking with both legs, striking whatever it was that bumped past his feet. The opposite shore, the gleaming hotels past the beach, grew rapidly closer. As Buchanan stroked deeply with his left hand, his fingers suddenly touched sand. He was into the shallows. Standing, he lunged toward the beach, his knees plunging through the waves. Behind him, something splashed, and as he reached the shore, he spun toward the gloom of the channel, seeing the phosphorescent wake that something in the water had made. Or perhaps it was only his imagination.

Like hell.

Breathing heavily from pain, he wanted to slump onto the sand, to rest, but he heard the blaring rise and fall of more police sirens, and he knew that he didn't dare remain in the open, even in the darkness, so he mustered discipline, drew from the depths of his resolve, and turned his back to the bridge, staggering away from the channel, proceeding along the curve of the beach, studying the glow at the rear of the various hotels.

3

Here, as at Club Internacional, the beach was deserted, tourists preferring to go to bed early or else to party at Cancún's many night spots. Buchanan chose a hotel that didn't have an outdoor bar behind it and trudged from the sand. Remaining in the shadows, he found a lounge chair beneath a palm tree and slumped. There were other chairs, but what had attracted him to this particular chair was that a guest had left a towel on it.

He slipped the belt from the top of his right shoulder, pressed the folded towel over his wound, and looped the belt several times over the towel, securing it tightly, attempting to make a pressure bandage. Although the towel became wet and dark in places, it seemed to reduce his loss of blood. For how long, he couldn't tell. Right now, all he wanted to do was rest.

But there was too much to do.

He unlooped the laces that attached his deck shoes to his

right wrist. The canvas of his shoes was pliant because of the water. It shouldn't have been difficult putting them on his feet. But doing so and lacing them were among the hardest tasks he'd ever attempted.

His skull throbbed from its impact against the dinghy. The sharp pain remained as severe. Gingerly raising his left hand to his wet hair, he touched a gash and felt a large area of swelling. The water in his hair prevented him from determining if the gash was bleeding and, if so, how much.

At the same time, the salt in the water had severely aggravated the pain in his wounded right shoulder. That injury, too, was swollen. It pulsed against the pressure bandage. In addition, disturbingly, the fingers of Buchanan's right hand trembled.

He told himself that the trembling must be the result of the trauma to his shoulder or of the struggle with the first twin and his subsequent swim across the channel. Relief after stress. Something like that. Hey, when you exercise with weights, he reminded himself, your hands sometimes shake afterward. Sure.

But only his right hand trembled, not both of them, and the fingers seemed to have a will of their own. He couldn't help worrying that something serious was wrong.

Move. You're acting like you've never been in a firefight before.

With effort, he stepped closer to the back of the hotel, leaving the shadows of the beach, moving warily onto concrete, passing more palm trees, approaching muted lights around a small oval swimming pool.

The pool, surrounded by tropical bushes and patio furniture, was deserted. Staying close to the cover of shrubs, Buchanan reached the first dim overhead light, where he noticed that his wet shoes left prints on the concrete. He noticed as well that his shirt and pants still dripped water. What interested him most, though, was that the blood on his clothes had been rinsed away. A small blessing in a night of disasters. As soon as his shirt and pants dried, they wouldn't attract attention. But the blood on the towel strapped to his shoulder would certainly make people look twice.

He needed something to loop over his shoulder and conceal

the towel. A jacket would be ideal, but the only way he could think to get one was by breaking into a room, and that was out of the question. Oh, he could pick a lock with ease if he had the equipment, which in this case he didn't, but only amateurs smashed windows and caused a disruption, which in this case he'd be forced to do.

So what *are* you going to do?

The pain from his injured skull aggravated the pain in his wounded shoulder. The combination was excruciating. Again he felt dizzy.

While he still had strength, he had to hurry.

He veered to the left toward a tunnel. Concrete stairs led up to the right toward the rooms on the upper floors. But his interest was directed inside the tunnel toward stairs on the left that went down. He couldn't imagine that a hotel with as impressive a design as this would be crude enough to lodge tourists below ground. So the only reason the hotel would have rooms down there would be for storage and maintenance.

He squinted at his digital Seiko watch, the sort of timepiece he'd decided an ex-DEA officer would wear. It was still functioning after his swim, and when he pressed a button on the side, the LED display showed 11:09. This late, he doubted that the maintenance staff would still be working. He listened carefully for any voices or footsteps that might echo up the stairwell. Hearing none, he started down.

His rubber-soled deck shoes made almost no sound on the stairs. At a platform, the stairs reversed direction and took him to a dimly illuminated corridor. It smelled moldy and damp. The odor would be a further reason for workers not to remain down here. Peering cautiously from the bottom of the stairwell, seeing no one at either end of the corridor, he stepped from cover, proceeded arbitrarily to the right, came to a metal door, listened, heard no sound behind it, and turned the knob. It was locked.

He continued to another door, and this time after he listened and tried the knob, he exhaled as the knob moved. Slowly pushing the door open, he groped along the inside wall, found a light switch, and flicked it on, relaxing when he saw that the room was unoccupied. The light bulb that dangled from the ceiling was as sickly a yellow as those in the corridor. The room was lined with metal shelves upon which tools and boxes had been stored. A small rusted metal desk was wedged in one corner, and on the desk—

—despite his pain, Buchanan felt a surge of excitement—

—sat a black rotary telephone.

He shut the door, locked it, and picked up the phone. His heart pounded as he heard a tone. He quickly dialed a number.

A man answered. Buchanan's case officer. To be near Buchanan at this phase of the mission, he'd rented an apartment in the mainland part of Cancún. Normally, he and Buchanan communicated by means of coded messages left at prearranged dead-drop locations on a predetermined schedule. Rarely, because of the risk of electronic eavesdropping, did they speak on the telephone, and only then between preselected pay phones. Never, while Buchanan was under deep cover, had they met. Buchanan had access to a protective backup team if he suspected he was in danger, but given the paranoia of the men he'd arranged to meet tonight, it had been decided that the benefit of the backup team's presence in and around Club Internacional would be offset by the danger that the drug distributors and *their* backup team would sense they were being watched. After all, the mission had been progressing according to plan. There'd been no reason to suspect that the meeting would not go smoothly. Until Big Bob Bailey showed up. Now Buchanan didn't have to worry about jeopardizing his cover if he phoned his case officer. What worse could happen? Buchanan's contacts were dead. The mission was blown.

What worse could happen? Oh, something worse could happen, all right. The Mexican police could capture him, and his superiors could be implicated in three murders. He had to disappear.

"Yes," Buchanan's case officer said.

"Is that you, Paul?"

"I'm sorry. No one by that name lives here."

"You mean this isn't . . .?" Buchanan gave a telephone number.

"You're not even close."

"Sorry."

Buchanan hung up and rubbed his throbbing forehead. The

number he'd given his controller was a coded message for which an expanded translation would be that the mission had to be aborted, that an absolute disaster had occurred, that he'd been injured, was on the run, and had to be extracted from the area as soon as possible. By prior agreement, his case officer would try to rendezvous with Buchanan ninety minutes after Buchanan's call. The rendezvous location was on the mainland in downtown Cancún, outside a cantina near the intersection of Tulum and Coba avenues. But every plan had to allow for contingencies, had to have numerous alternate agendas. So if Buchanan didn't make the rendezvous, his case officer would try again at eight tomorrow morning outside a coffee shop on Uxmal Avenue, and if Buchanan still did not arrive, the case officer would try once more at noon outside a pharmacy on Yaxchilan Avenue. If that third contact failed to happen, Buchanan's case officer would return to his apartment and wait for Buchanan to get in touch with him. Forty-eight hours later, if the case officer still hadn't heard from Buchanan, he would assume a worst-possibility scenario and get out of the country, lest he too become a liability. A delicate investigation would be set into motion to learn what had happened to Buchanan.

Ninety minutes from now, Buchanan thought. I have to get to that cantina. But spasms in his right hand distracted him. He stared down and saw the fingers of his right hand—and only those fingers, not those on his left hand—twitching again. They seemed not to belong to him. They seemed controlled by a force that wasn't his. He didn't understand. Had the bullet that slashed his shoulder injured the nerves that led down to his fingers?

He suddenly had trouble concentrating. The pain in his skull increased. His bullet wound throbbed. He felt something warm and wet seep from the towel that formed a pressure bandage over his wound. He didn't need to look to know that the towel, held in place by his belt, was becoming saturated and starting to leak.

His vision became alarmingly hazy. At once, it cleared as he tensed, hearing footsteps beyond the door.

The footsteps echoed slowly, hesitantly, along the concrete corridor, increasing in volume. They stopped outside the door.

Buchanan sweated, frowning when he saw and heard the doorknob being turned. As a matter of course, he had locked the door after he'd entered the room. Even so, whoever was out there presumably worked for the hotel and might have a key. Someone out there pushed at the door. When it wouldn't open, the person shoved harder, then rammed what probably was a shoulder against it. No effect.

"Who is in this room?" a gruff male voice demanded in Spanish. Knuckles rapped on the door. "Answer me." A fist pounded. "What are you doing in there?"

If he's got a key, now is when he'll use it, Buchanan thought. But what made him come down here and check this particular room? The hesitant footsteps I heard along the corridor . . . the man seemed almost to be looking for something.

Or following something?

As Buchanan shifted quietly toward the side of the door where he could shut off the light and grab the man if he used a key to enter, he glanced down and realized that the man had indeed been following something. Buchanan's drenched clothes had dripped on the concrete, making a trail.

Buchanan listened nervously for the metallic scrape of a key that the man would shove into the lock. Instead, what Buchanan heard was more pounding, another indignant "What are you doing in there?" and sudden silence.

Maybe he doesn't have a key. Or else he's afraid to use it.

Abruptly the footsteps retreated, clattering along the corridor, diminishing up the stairway.

I've got to get out of here before he has time to come back with help, Buchanan thought. He freed the lock, opened the door, checked the dim corridor, and was just about to leave when he noticed what seemed like rags on one of the shelves. The rags were actually a rumpled, soiled cotton work jacket and a battered, stained baseball cap from which the patch had been torn. He grabbed them. After using the jacket to wipe his fingerprints from everything he'd touched, he hurried along the corridor and up the staircase, seeing the wet trail he'd made.

The trail didn't matter now. All that did was getting away from the hotel before the worker came back with help. They'll probably call the police about a prowler. The police will be so frantic to arrest a suspect for the three killings that they might decide this incident is related. They'll focus their search in this area.

Buchanan swung toward where the shadowy beach would eventually take him near downtown Cancún. Heading north, he ran midway between the white-capped waves and the gleaming hotels. A fragrant sea breeze cooled the sweat on his brow and cleared the utility room's foul smell from his nostrils. The breeze had sufficient strength that it might even dry his wet clothes.

But abruptly he stumbled, losing his balance enough that he almost fell. It wouldn't have worried him so much if he had tripped over an unseen object. However, he had stumbled for the worst reason he could imagine. Because he was weaker. His wound pulsed, soaking the towel with blood. His skull throbbed from the sharpest headache of his life.

Wedged between his right arm and his side, he had the rumpled cotton work jacket and the stained baseball cap. Gingerly, he set the cap on his head. The cap was battered enough that it might attract attention, but without it, the blood that it hid would certainly attract a lot more attention. Breathing with effort, he draped the soiled work jacket over his right shoulder, hiding the bloodstained towel strapped over his wound. Now he could take the chance of showing himself in public. But as he pushed a button on his watch and looked at the digital time display, he discovered to his shock that almost an hour had passed since he'd phoned his case officer. That's impossible! I left the utility room just a little while ago.

You think.

Pal, you must be having blackouts.

Buchanan's thoughts became more urgent. He would have to veer between hotels and get a taxi on the thruway. Otherwise, he'd never be able to reach the rendezvous site in time to meet his case officer. Unsteady, he left the beach.

He'd been right about one thing at least—the breeze from the sea had dried his clothes sufficiently that they didn't stick to him.

But the breeze no longer had any effect on the sweat that dripped from his brow.

4

"Jesus," Buchanan's case officer said, "that wound needs stitches. Take off your cap. Let me look at . . . Yeah, oh, man, that gash on your skull needs stitches, too."

They were stopped at an abandoned gas station on Highway 180, thirty kilometers west of Cancún. After taking a taxi into the downtown part of the city, Buchanan had waited no more than half a minute at the rendezvous site before his case officer stopped a rented Ford Taurus in front of the busy cantina and Buchanan got in.

The case officer was in his fifties, slightly balding, slightly overweight. His clothes—sandals, a lemon-colored Polo shirt, and lime-colored shorts—matched his cover as a tourist. He and Buchanan hadn't worked together before. Buchanan knew him only as Wade, which Buchanan assumed was neither his real name nor his usual cover name.

After Buchanan explained, Wade exhaled. "Shit. It's completely unsalvageable. Damn it to hell. God. . . . Okay, let's think a minute." He tapped his fingers on the steering wheel. "Let's make sure we . . . The police'll be watching the airport in town and probably the one on Cozumel. That leaves us the next closest option."

"Mérida," Buchanan said.

Wade increased speed as he drove from Cancún. "That's assuming our best move is to get you out of the country. Maybe you ought to hole up somewhere. Go to ground. Hey, all the police have is a description that fits a lot of Americans. It's not like they have a photograph. Or fingerprints. You said you took care of that."

Buchanan nodded, feeling nauseous. "Except for the glasses I drank from in the restaurant. I couldn't do anything about them. The odds are they were taken to the kitchen and washed before the police thought to check them." Buchanan raised his uninjured left arm and wiped increasing sweat from his brow. "The *real* problem is, everybody in the restaurant heard Bailey call me Crawford, and me insist that I was Ed Potter. So the police have a name that Mexican emigration officers can watch for at airports.''

"That doesn't bother me," Wade said. "I brought an alternate passport and tourist card for you. Another pseudonym."

"Good. But the police also have Bailey himself. They'll insist he help one of their artists prepare a sketch, and once copies of that sketch are faxed to every airport and every emigration officer, anybody who resembles the sketch will be stopped when he turns in his tourist card and pays his exit fee. I have to get out of the country before that sketch is distributed. Plus . . ." Buchanan stared at the fingers of his right hand. They were twitching again, an unwilled motion, as if they weren't a part of him. His wounded arm seemed on fire. Blood soaked the towel strapped to his arm. "I need a doctor."

Wade glanced in his rearview mirror. "I don't see any headlights behind us." He peered ahead along the narrow forest-lined highway. "This deserted gas station is as good a place as any." He pulled off the road, got out, took something from the backseat, and came around to Buchanan's side of the car.

But after he opened Buchanan's door, exposed Buchanan's injuries, and aimed a narrow-beamed flashlight at them, he muttered, "No shit you need a doctor. You need stitches."

"I can't depend on somebody local not to notify the police about a gunshot wound," Buchanan said.

"No problem," Wade replied. "I have contact with an American doctor in the area. He's worked for us before. We can trust him."

"But I can't waste time going to him." Buchanan's voice was raspy, his mouth dry. "The police will soon have that sketch ready. I have to reach Mérida. I have to get on a plane out of Mexico. Hell, Florida's just a couple of hours away by jet. When I said I need a doctor, I meant *stateside*. The quicker I'm out of here, the quicker I can . . ."

"You'll bleed to death before then," Wade said. "Didn't you hear me? I said you need *stitches*. At the least. I don't know about the gash in your head, but the wound in your arm—it's hard to tell with so much blood—it looks infected."

"The way it feels, it probably is." Buchanan struggled to rouse himself. "What's that you set on the ground?"

"A first aid kit."

"Why didn't you say so?"

"Hey, what you've got wrong with you is more than any first aid kit's going to help."

"I keep forgetting. You're a civilian. One of those guys from the Agency."

Wade straightened, defensive. "You don't expect me to reply to that, do you? Besides, what difference does it make?"

"Just open the kit," Buchanan said. "Let's see what you've got. Good. *My* people prepared it. Pay attention. Do what I tell you. We've got to get the bleeding stopped. We have to clean the wounds."

"We? Come on, I don't know anything about this. I haven't been trained to—"

"*I* have." Buchanan tried to stop his mind from swirling. "Take that rubber tube and tie it above the wound in my shoulder. For five minutes, a tourniquet won't do much damage. Meanwhile . . ." Buchanan tore open a packet and dumped out several gauze sponges.

Wade finished tying the rubber tube around Buchanan's exposed shoulder. The bleeding lessened dramatically.

"That plastic container of rubbing alcohol," Buchanan said. "Pour some of it onto those gauze sponges and start wiping the blood away from the bullet wound." It seemed to Buchanan that his voice came from far away. Fighting to remain alert, he pried a syringe from a slot in a block of protective Styrofoam and squinted at the label, satisfying himself that the contents was an antibiotic. "Use a clean sponge and wipe some of that alcohol on the upper muscle of my right arm."

Wade did what he was told, then quickly resumed cleaning the bullet wound.

Buchanan injected the antibiotic into his right arm. As soon as he withdrew the needle, the fingers of his right hand started jerking again. Clumsily, he returned the syringe to the slot in the Styrofoam block.

"There," Wade said. "I finished cleaning the edges of the wound."

"Now pour that hydrogen peroxide into it," Buchanan said.

"Pour?" Wade asked. "That'll hurt like—"

"Nothing compared to dying from blood poisoning. The wound *has* to be disinfected. *Do it*."

Wade unscrewed the top from the hydrogen peroxide, pursed his lips, and poured what amounted to several tablespoons of the clear liquid into the long slash of the wound.

In the glow from the flashlight propped on the seat, Buchanan saw the liquid enter the slash. He saw his flesh and blood begin to bubble, like boiling acid. The pain suddenly hit him, even worse than the pain he'd already been feeling. It gnawed. It stabbed. It burned.

His vision doubled. He wavered.

"Buchanan?" Wade sounded alarmed.

"Do it again," Buchanan said.

"You can't be serious."

"Do it again. *I've got to be sure the wound's clean*."

Wade poured. The wound bubbled, its edges turning white, clots of blood welling out. Sweat slicked Buchanan's face.

"And some on the gash on my head," Buchanan murmured.

This time, Wade surprised Buchanan by complying without objection. Good, Buchanan thought through his pain. You're tougher than I expected, Wade. You're going to need to be when you hear what you have to do next.

The hydrogen peroxide felt as if it had eaten through Buchanan's skull and into his brain.

He shuddered. "Fine. Now you see that tube in the first aid kit? That's a triple-antibiotic ointment. Squeeze some on the gash on my head and a lot more into my bullet wound."

Wade's movements became more confident.

Buchanan felt the tourniquet digging into his right shoulder. Apart from the agony of the wound, the arm seemed swollen and had no sensation. "Almost done," Buchanan told Wade. "There's only one more thing you have to do."

"One more? What's that?"

"You were right. I need stitches."

"What are you talking about?"

"I want you to sew me up."

"Sew you—? Jesus Christ."

"Listen to me. Without stitches, once that tourniquet's released, I'll hemorrhage. There's a sterile surgical needle and thread in that foil pouch. Wash your hands with rubbing alcohol, open the pouch, and *sew me up*."

"But I've never done anything like—"

"It isn't complicated," Buchanan said. "I don't give a damn about neatness, and I'll tell you how to tie the knots. *But it has to be done*. If I could reach that far around my shoulder, I'd do it myself."

"The pain," Wade objected. "I'll be so clumsy . . . You need anesthetic."

"Even if we had some, I couldn't risk using it. I have to stay alert. There's so little time. While we drive to Mérida, you have to coach me about the identity you're giving me to get out of the country."

"Buchanan, you look as if you're ready to pass out as it is."

"You son of a bitch, don't ever do that to me again."

"Do what? What are you—?"

"You called me Buchanan. I forgot about Buchanan. I don't know who Buchanan is. On this assignment, my name's Ed Potter. If I respond to the name Buchanan, I could get myself killed. From now on . . . No, I'm wrong. I'm not Ed Potter anymore. I'm . . . Tell me who I am. What's my new identity? What's my background? What do I do for a living? Am I married? Talk to me, damn it, while you sew me up."

Cursing, insulting, commanding, Buchanan forced Wade to use the curved surgical needle and stitch the bullet wound shut. With each thrust of the needle, Buchanan gritted his teeth harder, until his jaw ached and he feared that his teeth would crack. The only thing that kept him from losing consciousness was his desperate need to acquire his new persona. He was Victor Grant, he learned. From Fort Lauderdale, Florida. He customized cabin cruisers and yachts, specializing in installing audiovisual electronics. He'd been in Cancún to speak with a client. If he had to, he could give the client's name and local address. The client, cooperating with Buchanan's employers, would vouch for Victor Grant.

"Okay," Wade said. "It looks like hell, but I think it'll hold."

"Smear antibiotic cream on a thick gauze pad. Press the bandage onto the stitches. Secure the pad with a wraparound bandage, several layers, and wrap the bandage with tape." Buchanan sweated from pain, his muscles rigid. "Good," he said. "Now release the tourniquet."

He felt a surge of blood into his arm. As the numbness

lessened, his flesh prickling, the already severe pain became worse. But he didn't care about that. He could handle pain. Pain was temporary. But if the stitches didn't hold and he hemorrhaged, he didn't need to worry about remembering his new identity or about getting to the Mérida airport before a police sketch of him was faxed there or about being questioned by an emigration officer at the airport. None of those worries would matter. Because by then he'd have bled to death.

For a long minute, he stared at the bandage. No blood seeped through it. "Okay, let's move."

"Just in time," Wade said. "I see headlights coming behind us." He shut the first aid kit, slammed Buchanan's door, ran around to get in the driver's side, and veered onto the road before the headlights came near.

Buchanan tilted his head back, breathing hoarsely. His mouth was terribly dry. "Have you got any water?"

"Sorry. I didn't think to bring any."

"Great."

"Maybe there'll be a place open where we can buy some."

"Sure."

Buchanan stared ahead through the windshield, watching the glare of the car's headlights pierce the night. He kept repeating to himself that his name was Victor Grant. From Fort Lauderdale. A customizer of pleasure boats. Electronics. Divorced. No children. The tropical forest crowded each side of the narrow road. On occasion, he glimpsed machete-scarred trees from which chicle had been drained to make chewing gum. On occasion, too, he saw groups of thatched huts, aware that the inhabitants were Maya, with the broad features, high cheekbones, and folded eyelids of their ancestors who had built the great monuments at Chichén Itzá and other ancient cities now turned to ruin in the Yucatán Peninsula. Rarely, he saw a dim light through the open door of a hut and a family sleeping in various hammocks, the hammocks helping them to stay cool and to keep them safe from reptiles prowling in the night, for Yucatán meant "place of snakes." Mostly what he noticed was that every time the car approached a group of thatched huts, evidently a village, a sign at the side of the road read, *TOPE*—"slow down"—and then, no matter how slowly Wade drove, the car lurched over a traffic bump in the road and jolted

Buchanan enough that his head jerked off the back of the seat, brutally intensifying the pain in his skull and in his shoulder. His right hand again became spastic. Away from the sea, the humidity on the peninsula felt smothering. But the air was so still, so laden with bugs that the car's windows had to be closed. Victor Grant. Fort Lauderdale. Pleasure boats. Electronics.

He passed out.

5

Despite a ground mist that obscured the illumination from the moon and stars, Balam-Acab had little difficulty moving through the rain forest at night. Part of his skill was due to his having been born in this region. After thirty years, he was thoroughly at home in the jungle. Nonetheless, the jungle was a living thing, ever shifting, and another reason that Balam-Acab knew his way so well through the crowding trees and drooping vines was the feel of stones beneath his thin sandals. After all, he had made this particular journey many times. Habit was in his favor.

In the dark, he let the flat, worn stones guide his footsteps. During the day, the pattern of the stones would not be evident to an inexperienced observer. Trees thrust up among them. Bushes concealed them. But Balam-Acab knew that a thousand years ago, the stones would have formed an uninterrupted path that the ancients had called a *sacbe*: "white road." The name was not strictly accurate, inasmuch as the large flat stones were more gray than white, but even in its dilapidated condition, the walkway was impressive.

How much more so would it have been during the time of the ancients, before the Spanish conquerers, when Balam-Acab's ancestors had ruled this land? There had been a time when Mayan roads had crisscrossed the Yucatán. Trees had been cut, swaths hacked through the jungle. In the cleared section, stones had been placed, forming a level that was two to four feet above the ground. Then rubble had been spread over the stones, to fill the gaps between them, and finally the stones and rubble had been covered with a concrete made from burned, powdered limestone mixed with gravel and water.

Indeed, the path that Balam-Acab followed had once been a smooth road almost sixteen feet wide and sixty miles long. But since the extermination of so many of his ancestors, there had been no one to attend to the road, to care for and repair it. Centuries of rain had dissolved the concrete and washed away the rubble, exposing the stones, causing them to shift, as did the area's numerous earthquakes and the sprouting vegetation. Now only someone as aware of the old ways and as attuned to the spirit of the forest as Balam-Acab was could follow the path so skillfully in the misty darkness.

Stepping from stone to stone, veering around unseen trees, sensing and stooping to avoid vines, alert for the slightest unsteadiness underfoot, Balam-Acab maintained perfect balance. He *had* to, for if he fell, he couldn't use his arms to grab for support. His arms were already occupied, carrying a precious bowl wrapped in a soft, protective blanket. He hugged it to his chest. Given the circumstances, he didn't dare take the risk of packing the bowl in his knapsack along with his other important objects. Too often, the knapsack was squeezed against a branch or a tree. The objects within the knapsack were unbreakable. Not so the bowl.

The humidity in the underbrush added to the sweat that slicked Balam-Acab's face and stuck his cotton shirt and pants to his body. He wasn't tall—only five foot three, typical for the males of his tribe. Although sinewy, he was thin, partly from the exertion of living in the jungle, partly from the meager diet provided by his village's farms. His hair was straight and black, cut short to keep it free from insects and prevent it from becoming entangled in the jungle. Because of the isolation of this region and because the Spanish conquerers had disdained to have children with the Maya, Balam-Acab's facial features bore the same genetic traits as his ancestors when Mayan culture was at its zenith centuries before. His head was round, his face broad, his cheekbones pronounced. His thick lower lip had a dramatic downward curve. His eyes were dark, with the shape of an almond. His eyelids had a Mongolian fold.

Balam-Acab knew that he resembled his ancestors because

he had seen engravings of them. He knew how his ancestors had lived because his father had told him what *his* father had told him what *his* father had told him, as far back as the tribe had been in existence. He knew how to perform the ritual he intended because as the ruler and shaman of the village he had been taught by his predecessor, who revealed to him the sacred mysteries that had been passed on to *him* just as they'd been passed on to *his* predecessor and that dated back to 13.0.0.0.0. 4 *Ahau* 8 *Cumku,* the beginning of time.

The direction of the stones changed, curving toward the left. With perfect balance, Balam-Acab squeezed between more trees, stooped beneath more vines, and felt the pressure of the stones beneath his thin sandals, following the curve. He had nearly reached his destination. Although his progress had been almost silent, he now had to be even *more* silent. He had to creep with the soundless grace of a stalking jaguar, for he would soon reach the edge of the jungle, and beyond, in the newly created clearing, there would be guards.

Abruptly Balam-Acab smelled them, their tobacco smoke, their gun oil. Nostrils widening, he paused to study the darkness and judge distance as well as direction. In a moment, he proceeded, forced to leave the ancient hidden pathway and veer farther left. Since the new conquerers had arrived to chop down the trees and dynamite the rocky surface, to smooth the land and build an airstrip, Balam-Acab had known that the disaster predicted by the ancients was about to occur. Just as the *first* conquerers had been predicted, these had as well, for time was circular, Balam-Acab knew. It turned and went around, and each period of time had a god in charge of it.

In this case, the thunder of the dynamite reminded him of the thunder of the fanged rain god, Chac. But it also reminded him of the rumble of the area's numerous earthquakes that always signified when the god of the Underworld, who was also the god of darkness, was angry. And when that god was angry, he caused pain. What Balam-Acab had not yet been able to decide was whether the new conquerers would make the god of the Underworld and of darkness furious or whether the new conquerers were the *result* of that god's already excessive fury, a punishment for Balam-Acab and his people.

All he could be certain of was that placating rituals were

demanded, prayers and sacrifices, lest the prediction in the ancient *Chronicles of Chilam Balam* again come true. One of the signs, the sickness that was killing the palm trees, had *already* come true.

> *On that day, dust claims the earth.*
> *On that day, a blight covers the earth.*
> *On that day, a cloud hangs low.*
> *On that day, a mountain soars.*
> *On that day, a strong man clutches the land.*
> *On that day, things collapse into ruin.*

Balam-Acab was fearful of the sentries, but he was also hopeful of succeeding in his mission. After all, if the gods did not want to be placated, if they were truly furious, they would have punished him before now. They would never have allowed him to get this far. Only someone favored by the gods could have walked through the darkness and not been bitten by any of the area's numerous swarming serpents. In the daylight, he could see and avoid the snakes or else make noises and scare them away. But walking silently and blindly at night? No. Impossible. Without the protection of the gods, he should have stepped not on stones but on death.

At once the density of the darkness changed. The mist seemed less thick. Balam-Acab had reached the edge of the jungle. Hunkering, inhaling the fecund odors of the forest in contrast to the rancid sweat smell of the sentries, he focused on the night, and suddenly, as if an unfelt breeze had swept across the clearing, the fog dissipated. Unexpectedly able now to see the illumination from the moon and stars, he felt as if night had turned into day. At the same time, he had the eerie certainty that when he crept from the jungle into the clearing, the sentries would not be able to see him. From their point of view, the fog would still exist. It would envelop him. It would make him invisible.

But he wasn't a fool. When he stepped from the jungle, he stayed low, close to the ground, trying not to reveal his silhouette as he hurried forward. In the now-evident light from the moon and stars, he could see and was disturbed by the extent of the work that the invaders had accomplished in the mere two days since he had last been here. A vast new section of forest had been leveled, exposing more brush-covered mounds and hillocks. Without the trees to obscure the skyline, the murky contours of considerably higher breaks in the terrain were also evident. Balam-Acab thought of them as mountains, but none of them was the mountain predicted as one of the signs of the end of the world in the ancient *Chronicles of Chilam Balam*.

No, *these* mountains were part of the spirit of the universe. Granted, they weren't natural. After all, this part of the Yucatán was called the flatlands. Mounds, hillocks, and certainly mountains did not exist. They had all been built here by human beings, by Balam-Acab's Mayan ancestors, more than a thousand years ago. Although the brush that covered them camouflaged their steps, portals, statuary, and engravings, Balam-Acab knew that the elevations were palaces, pyramids, and temples. The reason they were part of the spirit of the universe was that the ancients who had built them knew how the Underworld, the Middleworld, and the glorious arch of the heavens were linked. The ancients had used their knowledge of the secrets of the passing sun to determine the exact places where monuments in honor of the gods needed to be situated, and in so doing, they focused the energy of both the Underworld and heavenly gods toward the Middleworld and this sacred precinct.

Wary of the armed intruders, Balam-Acab came to the tallest mountain. The excavators had been quick to clear the vegetation from the level ground, but whenever they came to an elevated area, they had left it undisturbed, presumably intending to return and violate it later. He studied the shadowy bushes and saplings that had somehow found places to root between the huge square stone blocks that formed this consecrated edifice. If the bushes and saplings weren't present, Balam-Acab knew that what looked like a mountain would actually reveal itself to be an enormous terraced pyramid, and that at the top there would be a temple dedicated to the god Kukulcan, the meaning of whose name was "plumed serpent."

Indeed, the weathered stone image of a serpent's gigantic head—mouth open, teeth about to strike—projected from the bushes at the bottom of the pyramid. Even in the dark, the serpent's head was manifest. It was one of several that flanked the stairs that ascended through the terraces on each side of the pyramid. Heart swelling, reassured that he had managed to get this far unmolested, becoming more convinced that the gods favored his mission, Balam-Acab held the blanket-covered bowl protectively to his chest and began the slow, painstaking ascent to the top.

Each step was as high as his knee, and the stairway was angled steeply. During daylight, the arduous climb could be dizzying, not to mention precarious, because the bushes, saplings, and centuries of rain had broken the steps and shifted the stones. He needed all his strength and concentration not to lose his balance in the dark, step on a loose rock, and fall. He didn't care about his own safety. Otherwise, he wouldn't have risked being bitten by snakes or shot by sentries in order to come here. What he *did* care about were the precious objects in his knapsack and in particular the blanket-wrapped sacred bowl he clutched to his chest. He didn't dare fall and break the bowl. That would be inexcusable. That for certain would prompt the fury of the gods.

As he climbed, his knees aching, his body drenched with sweat, Balam-Acab mentally counted. It was the only way he could measure his progress, for the bushes and saplings above him prevented him from distinguishing the outline of the square temple at the otherwise-pointed top of the pyramid. Ten, eleven, twelve . . . One hundred and four, one hundred and . . . He strained to breathe. Two hundred and eighty-nine. Two hundred and . . . Soon, he thought. By now he could see the top against the stars. Three hundred and . . . At last, his heart pounding, he reached the flat surface in front of the temple.

Three hundred and sixty-five. That sacred number represented the number of days in the solar year and had been calculated by Balam-Acab's ancestors long before the Spanish conquerers first came to the Yucatán in the 1500s. Other sacred numbers had been incorporated into the pyramid—the twenty terraces, for example, which signified the units of twenty days into which the ancients had divided their shorter 260-day ceremonial year. Similarly, there originally had been fifty-two stone images of serpents along the top of the temple, for time revolved in a fifty-two-year circle.

Circles were very much in Balam-Acab's thoughts as he gently set down the blanket, unwrapped it, and exposed the precious bowl. It didn't look remarkable. As wide as the distance from his thumb to his elbow, as thick as his thumb, it was old, yes, obviously very old, but it had no brilliant colors, just a dull, dark interior coating, and an outsider might have called it ugly.

Circles, Balam-Acab kept thinking. No longer impeded by his need to protect the bowl, he moved swiftly, taking off his knapsack, removing an obsidian knife, a long cord stitched with thorns, and strips of paper made from the bark of a fig tree. Quickly he removed his sweat-soaked shirt, exposing his gaunt chest to the god of the night.

Circles, cycles, revolutions. Balam-Acab positioned himself so that he stood at the entrance to the temple, facing east, toward where the sun each day began its cycle, toward the direction of the symbol of rebirth. From this high vantage point, he could see far around the pyramid. Even in the dark, he detected the obvious large area that the invaders had denuded of trees. More, he could distinguish the gray area that marked the airstrip a quarter mile to his right. He could see the numerous large tents that the invaders had erected and the log buildings that they were constructing from the fallen trees. He saw several camp fires that he hadn't been able to notice from the jungle, armed guards casting shadows. Soon more airplanes would arrive with more conquerers and more machinery. More gigantic helicopters would bring more heavy vehicles. The area would become more desecrated. Already a road was being bulldozed through the jungle. Something had to be done to stop them.

Cycles. Revolutions. Balam-Acab's father had told him that his name had a special history in the village. Centuries before, when the conquerers had first arrived, Balam-Acab's namesake had led a band of warriors that attempted to repulse the Spanish from the Yucatán. The struggle had persisted for several years until Balam-Acab's namesake was captured and hacked into pieces, then burned. But the glory of the rebel persisted beyond his death, indeed until the present generation, and Balam-Acab was proud to bear the name.

But burdened, as well. It wasn't a coincidence that he'd been given this name instead of another. History moved in circles, just as periodically the Maya had again revolted against their oppressors. Stripped of their culture, yoked into slavery, the Maya had rebelled during the 1600s, again in the 1800s, and most recently in the early part of this century. Each time, they had been fiercely defeated. Many were forced to retreat to the remotest parts of the jungle in order to avoid retribution and the terrible sicknesses brought by the outsiders.

And now the outsiders had come again. Balam-Acab knew that if they weren't stopped, his village would be destroyed. Circles, cycles, revolutions. He was here to make a sacrifice to the gods, to ask for their wisdom, to pray for their counsel. He needed to be guided. His namesake had no doubt conducted this same ritual during the 1500s. Uncontaminated, it would be repeated.

He raised his obsidian knife. Its black volcanic glass—"the fingernail of the lightning bolt"—was sharpened to a stilet-tolike point. He raised it to the underside of his outstretched tongue, struggling to ignore the pain as he thrust upward, piercing. The only way he could manage the task was by clamping his teeth against his tongue to hold it in place so that the exposed slippery flesh could not resist the blade. Blood gushed from his tongue, drenching his hand. He trembled from shock.

Nonetheless, he continued thrusting upward. Only when the obsidian point came completely through his tongue and scraped along his upper teeth did he remove it. Tears welled from his eyes. He stifled the urge to moan. Continuing to clamp his tongue with his teeth, he lowered the knife and raised the cord stitched with thorns. As his ancestors had done, he shoved the cord through the hole in his tongue and began to pull upward. Sweat burst from his face, no longer from humidity and exertion but from agony. The first thorn in the cord reached the hole in his tongue. Although it snagged, he pulled it through. Blood ran down the cord. He persisted in pulling, forcing another thorn through his tongue. And another. Blood cascaded down the cord and soaked the strips of paper where the bottom of the cord rested in the precious bowl.

Inside the temple behind him, there were images of Balam-Acab's ancestors performing this ritual. In some cases, the king had impaled his penis, then thrust the cord of thorns through that organ instead of his tongue. But whatever part of the body was used, the objective was the same—through pain and blood, to achieve a vision state, to communicate with the Otherworld, to understand what the gods advised and indeed demanded.

Weakened, Balam-Acab sank to his knees, as if he worshiped the blood-soaked strips of paper in the bowl. As soon as the cord of thorns had been pulled completely through his tongue, he would place it in the bowl with the strips of paper. He would add more paper and a ball of copal incense. Then he would use matches—the only adulteration of the rite that he permitted—and set fire to his offering, adding more paper as necessary, the flames boiling and eventually burning his blood.

His mind swirled. He wavered, struggling to maintain a delirious balance between consciousness and collapse, for his ancestors would not have performed this rite without assistance, whereas he would have to rouse himself and proceed alone through the jungle back to the village.

He thought that the gods began to speak to him. He heard them, at the edge of hearing. He felt them, felt their presence, felt—

The tremor spread through him. But it wasn't a tremor caused by shock or pain. The tremor came from outside him, through the stones upon which he knelt, through the pyramid upon which he conducted his ritual, through the earth beneath which lay the god of darkness, to whom he appealed.

The tremor was caused by the shock wave from dynamite as a crew continued their devastation despite the night. The rumble sounded like a moan from a restive god.

He raised a book of matches, struck one, and dropped it onto the strips of paper that lay above his blood in the sacred bowl.

Circles.

Again time had turned.

This holy place was being defiled.

The conquerers had to be conquered.

FOUR

1

When Buchanan wakened, he was soaked with sweat, his lips so parched that he knew he had a fever. He swallowed several aspirins from the first aid kit, almost gagging, forcing them down his dry throat. By then, it was after dawn. He and Wade were in Mérida, 322 kilometers west of Cancún, near the Gulf of Mexico side of the Yucatán Peninsula. Unlike Cancún, Mérida evoked an old-world feeling, its great mansions dating from the turn of the century. Indeed, the city had once been called the Paris of the Western World, for in former, richer times, millionaire merchants had deliberately tried to make Mérida like Paris, where they often went on vacation. The city still retained much of its European charm, but Buchanan was too delirious to care about the tree-lined avenues and the horse-drawn carriages. "What time is it?" he asked, too listless to peer at his watch.

"Eight o'clock." Wade parked near a not-yet-open market. "Will you be okay if I leave you alone for a while?"

"Where are you going?"

Wade answered, but Buchanan didn't hear what he said, his mind drifting, sinking.

When he wakened again, Wade was unlocking the Ford, getting in. "I'm sorry I took so long."

So long? Buchanan thought. "What do you mean?" His vision was bleary. His tongue felt swollen. "What time is it now?"

"Almost nine. Most stores still aren't open. But I managed

to get you some bottled water.'' Wade untwisted a cap from a bottle of Evian and tilted it toward Buchanan's parched lips.

Buchanan's mouth seemed like a dry sponge, absorbing most of the water. Some trickled down his chin. Frustrated, he tried again and this time managed to swallow. "Give me more of those aspirins.'' His throat sounded as if it were wedged with stones.

"Still feverish?''

Buchanan nodded, grimacing. "And this bitch of a headache won't stop.''

"Hold out your hand. I'll give you the aspirins.''

Buchanan's left hand felt weak, and his right hand suddenly became spastic again. "Better put them in my mouth.''

Wade frowned.

Buchanan swallowed the aspirins with more water.

"You have to keep your strength up. You can't survive on just water,'' Wade said. "I brought doughnuts, milk, and coffee.''

"I don't think my stomach would tolerate the doughnuts.''

"You're scaring me,'' Wade said. "We should have gone to the doctor I know in Cancún.''

"We've been over this,'' Buchanan murmured. "I have to get out of the country before the police sketch is circulated.''

"Well, what about orange juice? At least try the orange juice I brought.''

"Yes,'' Buchanan murmured. "The orange juice.''

He managed three swallows.

"I found a woman unpacking boxes, getting ready for when the market opens,'' Wade said. "She sold me this straw hat. It'll hide the gash on your head. Also I bought this serape. You can drape it over the bandage on your arm when you pass through emigration.''

"Good,'' Buchanan said weakly.

"Before that, I phoned several airlines. For a change, you're in luck. Aeroméxico has a seat available on a flight to Miami.''

Buchanan inwardly brightened. Soon, he thought. Soon I'll be out of the country. I can sleep when I'm on the plane. Wade can phone ahead and have a team waiting to take me to a clinic.

"There is a problem, though,'' Wade said.

"Problem?" Buchanan frowned.

"The flight doesn't leave until twelve-fifty."

"Until? But that's . . . what? . . . four hours from now."

"It was the first flight I could get. Another one left earlier for Houston. It had a seat, but it also made a stop en route."

"What do I care about a stop? Why didn't you book me on it?"

"Because the stop was back in Cozumel, and the man I spoke to said you had to get off the plane and then reboard."

Shit, Buchanan thought. Cozumel, near Cancún, was one of the airports he needed to avoid. If he had to leave the plane and pass through a checkpoint, a guard might . . .

"All right, the twelve-fifty flight to Miami," Buchanan said.

"At the airport, I can't buy your ticket for you. It draws attention. Besides, the clerk will want to see Victor Grant's passport. Very few people give somebody else their passport, and certainly not when they're about to leave the country. If the police have told the attendants to be on the lookout for anybody who acts suspiciously, that might be enough for them to wait for you to arrive and question you."

"Question both of us." Buchanan fought to focus his vision. "You made your point. I'll buy the ticket." He peered out the window, seeing traffic increase, frowning at the pedestrians crowding past the Ford. "Right now, I think we'd better drive around town. I get nervous staying parked like this."

"Right."

As Wade steered into a break in traffic, Buchanan used his trembling right hand to reach behind him and pull a waterproof plastic pouch from his back pocket. "Here's Ed Potter's ID and passport. Whatever pseudonym I'm using, I always carry his documents. There's no way of predicting when they might come in handy."

Wade took the plastic pouch. "I can't give you an official receipt. I don't have any with me."

"Screw the receipt. Just give me Victor Grant's documents."

Wade handed him a brown leather passport folder.

As Buchanan took it, he felt Ed Potter drain from him and Victor Grant seep into his consciousness. Weak and far from alert, he nonetheless responded to habit and began to imagine traits (Italian food, Dixieland jazz) for his new character. At the same time, he opened the folder and examined its contents.

"Don't worry. Everything's there," Wade said. "Including the tourist card."

"But I do worry." Buchanan searched through the documents. "That's how I've stayed alive this long. I never take anyone's word for . . . Yes. Okay, the tourist card and everything else is here. Where's that aspirin bottle?"

"Don't tell me you've still got a headache." Wade looked troubled.

"And it's getting worse." Buchanan didn't trust his trembling right hand. Raising his left hand, which felt wooden, he put more aspirins in his mouth and swallowed more orange juice.

"You're sure you want to do this?"

"Want to? No. Have to? Definitely. Okay," Buchanan said, "let's go through the drill. I left plenty of loose ends in Cancún." Breathing was an effort. He fought for energy. "Here are my keys. When you get back to Cancún, close up my timeshare condominium office. You know who I rented it from. Call him. Tell him I've gone out of business. Tell him he can keep the remainder of the rent, that you'll send him the keys as soon as you pick up my belongings."

"Right."

"Do the same thing about my apartment. Erase me. You know the places I used in Acapulco, Puerto Vallarta, and the other resorts. Erase me from all of them." Buchanan's head throbbed. "What else? Can you think of—?"

"Yes." As Wade drove along the Paseo de Mayo, Mérida's main thoroughfare, Buchanan ignored the grass-covered island that separated the several lanes of traffic on each side, anxious for Wade to continue.

"The contacts you recruited in each area," Wade said. "They'll wonder what happened to you. They'll start asking questions. You have to be erased from their lives, too."

Of course, Buchanan thought. Why didn't I think of that? I'm more light-headed than I guessed. I have to concentrate harder. "Do you remember the dead-drop locations I was using to pass each of them messages?"

Wade nodded. "I'll leave each contact a note, some excuse about problems with the police, along with a final payoff that's generous enough to encourage them to keep their mouths shut."

Buchanan brooded. "Is that it, then? Is that everything? There's always something else, a final detail."

"If there is, I don't know what—"

"Luggage. When I buy my ticket, if I don't have a bag, I'll attract attention."

Wade steered off the Paseo de Mayo, stopping on a side street. The stores were now open.

"I don't have the strength to carry anything heavy. Make sure the suitcase has rollers." Buchanan told Wade his sizes. "I'll need underwear, socks, T-shirts . . ."

"Yes, the usual." Wade got out of the Ford. "I can handle it, Buchanan. I've done this before."

"You son of a bitch."

"What?"

"I told you, don't call me Buchanan. *I'm Victor Grant.*"

"Right, Victor," Wade said dryly. "I wouldn't want you to forget who you were." He started to close the door, then paused. "Hey, while you're practicing your lines—that is, when you're not calling me names—why don't you try eating some of those doughnuts, so you're not so weak that you fall on your face when you get to the airport."

Buchanan watched the slightly bald, slightly overweight man in the lemon-colored Polo shirt disappear into the crowd. Then he locked the doors, tilted his head back, and felt his right hand tremble. At once his whole body shivered. The fever, he thought. It's really getting to me. I'm losing control. Wade's my lifeline. What am I doing? Don't make him mad.

Buchanan's shoes nudged the bag of doughnuts on the floor. The thought of eating made him nauseous. As did the pain in his shoulder. And in his skull. He shuddered. Just a few more hours, he told himself. Hang on. All you have to do is get through the airport. He forced himself to drink more orange juice. The acidic sweetness made his stomach queasy. Victor Grant, he told himself, concentrating, struggling to chew on a doughnut. Victor Grant. Divorced. Fort Lau-

derdale. Customizes pleasure boats. Installs electronics.
Victor . . .

He jerked as Wade unlocked the driver's door and put a
suitcase in the back.

"You look terrible," Wade said. "I brought a toilet kit: a
razor and shaving soap, toothpaste . . ."

2

They drove to a wooded park that had a public washroom.
Wade bolted the door and stood behind Buchanan, holding him
steady while Buchanan hunched over the sink, trembling, doing
his best to shave. He tried to comb his blood-matted hair but
didn't have much success, deciding that he'd definitely have
to use the straw hat that Wade had bought for him. He used
bottled water to brush his teeth, feeling marginally better now
that he was partially cleaned up. His shirt and pants, which the
sea had cleaned sufficiently of blood to stop people from staring
at him last night, were unacceptably soiled and wrinkled in the
daylight. He changed into a fresh shirt and pair of pants that
Wade had bought, and after they left the washroom, Buchanan
crammed the dirty clothes into the suitcase in the Ford's backseat. Associating his Seiko watch with the now-defunct character of Ed Potter, he traded it for Wade's Timex, anything to
get the feel of a new identity.

By then, it was eleven o'clock.

"Traveling time," Wade said.

In contrast with the large picturesque city, the airport was
surprisingly small and drab. Wade managed to find a parking
space in the lot in front of the low terminal. "I'll carry your
suitcase to the entrance. After that . . ."

"I understand."

As they walked toward the entrance, Buchanan glanced casually around, studying the area. No one seemed to be paying
attention to him. He concentrated on walking in a straight line,
not wavering, not betraying his weakness. At the sidewalk in
front of the doors, he shook hands with Wade. "Thanks. I
know I was a little grumpy a couple of times. I . . ."

"Forget it. This isn't a popularity contest." Wade continued to grip Buchanan's right hand. "Something's wrong with your fingers. They're jerking."

"It's not a problem."

Wade frowned. "Sure. I'll be seeing you, Victor." He emphasized the pseudonym. "Have a good flight."

"I'm counting on it."

Buchanan made sure that the serape was hitched firmly to his right shoulder, hiding his wound. He gripped the pull strap on the suitcase and entered the terminal.

3

Several impressions struck him simultaneously. The terminal was stark, hot, tiny, and crowded. Everyone, except for the few Anglos, seemed in slow motion. As one of those few Anglos, Buchanan attracted attention, Mexican travelers studying him as he inched through the claustrophobia-producing crowd. He sweated as much as they did, feeling faint, wishing the terminal was air-conditioned. At least I'll have a reason for looking sick, he thought, trying to muster confidence. He stood in a frustrating line at the Aeroméxico ticket counter. It took him thirty minutes before he faced an attractive female attendant. Using Spanish, he told her what he needed. For a moment, his heart lurched when she appeared not to know anything about a reservation for Victor Grant, but then she found the name on her computer screen and with painstaking care made an impression of his credit card, asked him to sign the voucher, and peeled off his receipt.

"*Gracias*." Hurry, Buchanan thought. His legs were losing their strength.

With even greater care, she tapped keys on the computer and waited for the printer, which also seemed in slow motion, to dislodge the ticket.

But at last Buchanan had it, saying "*Gracias*" again, turning away, pulling the suitcase, inching again through the crowd, this time toward the X-ray machine and the metal detector at the security checkpoint. He felt as if he struggled through a nightmare in which he stood in mud and tried to walk. His vision dimmed for a moment. Then a sudden surge of adrenaline gave him energy. With effort, he used his left hand to lift the suitcase onto the X-ray machine's conveyor belt and proceeded through the metal detector, so off balance that he almost bumped against one of its posts. The detector made no sound. Relieved that the security officers showed no interest in him, Buchanan took his suitcase from the opposite end of the conveyor belt, set it with effort on the floor, and patiently worked his way forward through the crowd. The heat intensified his headache. Whenever someone bumped against his right shoulder, he needed all his discipline not to show how much pain the impact caused him.

Almost there, he thought. Two more checkpoints and I'm through. He stood in a line to pass through a customs inspection. Mexico was lax about many things but not about trying to stop ancient artifacts from being smuggled out of the country.

The haggard customs agent pointed at Buchanan's suitcase. "*Abralo.* Open it." He didn't look happy.

Buchanan complied, his muscles in agony.

The agent pawed through Buchanan's clothes, glowered when he didn't find anything suspicious, then gestured dismissively.

Buchanan moved onward. Only one more checkpoint, he thought. Emigration. All I have to do is hand in my tourist card, then pay the fifteen-dollar exit fee.

And hope that the emigration officer doesn't have a police sketch of me.

As Buchanan moved tensely through the crowd, he heard a slight commotion behind him. Turning, he saw a tall American shove his way past an Hispanic woman and three children. The American had a salt-and-pepper beard. He wore a gaudy, red-and-yellow-splotched shirt. He held a gym bag and muttered to himself, continuing to push ahead, causing a ripple in the crowd.

The ripple spread toward Buchanan. Trapped by people on every side, he couldn't avoid it. All he could do was brace himself as a man was nudged against another man, who in turn was nudged against Buchanan. Buchanan's legs were so weak that he depended on the people around him to keep him steady, but when the ripple struck him, he suddenly found that the person ahead of him had moved forward. Shoved against his back, Buchanan felt his knees bend and reached ahead to grab for someone to steady him. But at that moment, another ripple in the crowd nudged against his left shoulder. He fell, his mind so dazed that everything seemed a slow blur. When his right shoulder struck the concrete floor, the pain that soared from his wound changed his impression, however, and made everything fast and sharply focused. Sweat from his forehead spattered the concrete. He almost screamed from the impact against his wound.

He struggled to stand, not daring to attract attention. As he came to his feet and adjusted the serape over his wound, he peered ahead through the crowd and noticed that officers at the emigration checkpoint seemed not to have cared about what had happened, concentrating only on collecting tourist cards and exit fees.

He came closer to the checkpoint, breathing easier when he didn't see a police sketch on the counter. But the terminal was so stifling that sweat oozed from his body, slicking his chest and his arms, beading on his palms.

He wiped his left hand on his slacks, then reached in his shirt pocket and gave the officer a yellow card and the fifteen-dollar exit fee. The officer barely looked at him as he took the card and the money. At once, though, the officer paid more attention, squinted, frowned, and raised his hand. *"Pasaporte, por favor."*

Why? Buchanan thought in dismay. He didn't compare my face to a sketch. Hell, I don't even see a sketch that he can refer to. If there is a sketch, it's back in the emigration office. But after looking at so many faces, surely the officer can't have a clear memory of the sketch. Why on earth is he stopping me?

Buchanan used his left hand to surrender the passport. The officer opened it, compared the photograph to Buchanan's face, read the personal information, and frowned again at Buchanan. *"Señor Grant, venga conmigo.* Come with me."

Buchanan tried to look respectfully puzzled. *"Por que?"* he asked. "Why? Is something wrong?"

The officer squinted harder and pointed toward Buchanan's right shoulder. Buchanan looked and showed no reaction, despite his shock.

Crimson soaked his serape. What he'd thought was sweat was actually blood trickling down his arm, dripping from his fingers. Jesus, he thought, when I fell on my shoulder, I must have opened the stitches.

The officer gestured toward a door. "*Venga conmigo. Usted necesita un medico*. You need a doctor."

"*Es nada. No es importante*," Buchanan said. "It's nothing. A small injury. The bandage needs to be changed. I'll fix it in the bathroom and still have time to catch my plane."

The officer placed his right hand on his holstered pistol and repeated, this time sternly, "Come with me *now*."

Buchanan obeyed, walking with the officer toward a door, trying to look relaxed, as if it were perfectly natural to have blood streaming from his shoulder. He had no hope of fleeing, certain that he'd be stopped before he could push his way through the crowd and reach an exit from the terminal. All he could do was try to bluff his way out, but he doubted that the explanation he was concocting would satisfy the officer after the officer got a look at the wound on his shoulder. There'd be questions. Plenty of questions. And perhaps the police sketch would have arrived by then, if it hadn't already. For sure, he would not be on the 12:50 flight to Miami. So close, he thought.

4

Unlike the United States, where a suspect is presumed to be innocent until proven guilty, Mexico bases its laws on the Napoleonic Code, in which a suspect is guilty until proven innocent. Prisoners are not warned that they have a right to remain silent or told that if they cannot afford an attorney, one will be provided. There is no habeas corpus, no right to a speedy trial. In Mexico, such notions are ludicrous. A prisoner has no rights.

Buchanan shared a mildewed, flea-infested, leaky-roofed, pocked-concrete cell that was twenty feet long and fifteen feet wide with twenty other foully clothed prisoners in what amounted to the tank for thieves and drunkards. To avoid bumping into anyone and causing an argument, Buchanan made sure he stayed in one place with his back to the wall. While the others took up every space on the floor, sleeping on soiled straw, he sank down the wall until he dozed with his head on his knees. He waited as long as he could before using the open hole in a corner that was the toilet. Mostly, despite his light-headedness, he struggled to remain on guard against an attack. As the only *yanquí*, he was an obvious target, and although his watch and wallet had been taken from him, his clothes and in particular his shoes were better than those of any other prisoner—hard to resist.

As it happened, a great deal of time Buchanan wasn't in the cell, and the attacks didn't come from his fellow prisoners but from his guards. Escorted from the cell to an interrogation room, he was pushed, tripped, and shoved down stairs. While being questioned, he was prodded by batons and beaten with rubber hoses, always in places where clothes would hide the bruises, never around the face or skull. Why his interrogators retained this degree of fastidiousness, Buchanan didn't know. Perhaps because he was a U.S. citizen and fears about political consequences made them feel slightly constrained. They nonetheless still managed to injure his skull when it struck concrete after they knocked over the wooden chair to which they had tied him. The pain—added to the pain from the gash he'd received when he'd struck the dinghy while swimming across the channel at Cancún—made him nauseous and created a worrisome double vision. If a doctor hadn't redressed and restitched his wounded shoulder at Mérida's jail, he probably would have died from infection and loss of blood, although of course the doctor had been supplied not out of compassion but simply for the practical reason that a dead man couldn't answer questions. Buchanan had encountered this logic before and knew that if the interrogators received the answers they wanted, they would feel no further necessity to provide him with medical courtesies.

That was one reason—the least important—for his refusal to tell his interrogators what they wanted. *The* reason, of course, was that to confess would have been a violation of professional conduct. In refusing to talk, Buchanan had three advantages. First, his interrogators were employing clumsy, brutal methods, which were easier to resist than the precise application of electrical shock combined with such inhibition-reducing drugs as sodium amytal. Second, because he was already weakened by the injury to his head and the wound in his shoulder, he had a tendency to pass out quickly while being tortured, his body supplying a kind of natural anesthesia.

And third, he had a script to follow, a role to play, a scenario that gave him a way to behave. The primary rule was that if captured, he could never admit the truth. Oh, he could use portions of the truth to concoct a believable lie. But the whole truth was out of the question. For Buchanan to say that, yes, he'd killed the three Mexicans, but they were drug dealers, after all, and besides he was working under cover for a covert branch of the U.S. military would have temporarily saved his life. However, that life would not have been worth much. As an object lesson to the United States for interfering in Mexican affairs, he might have been forced to serve a lengthy sentence in a Mexican prison, and given the severity of Mexican prisons, especially for *yanquis*, that sentence in all probability would have been the same as a death sentence. Or if Mexico released him to the United States as a gesture of goodwill (in exchange for favors), his superiors would make his life a nightmare because he had violated his pact with them.

5

"Victor Grant," an overweight, bearded interrogator with slicked-back dark hair said to Buchanan in a small, plain room that had only a bench upon which the interrogator sat and a chair upon which Buchanan was tied. The round-faced, perspiring interrogator made "Victor Grant" sound as if the name were a synonym for diarrhea.

"That's right." Buchanan's throat was so dry that his voice cracked, his body so dehydrated that he'd long ago stopped sweating. One of the tight loops of the rope cut into his stitched, wounded shoulder.

"Speak Spanish, damn you!"

"But I don't *know* Spanish." Buchanan breathed. "At least, not very well." He tried to swallow. "Just a few words." Ignorance about Spanish was one of the characteristics he'd chosen for this persona. That way, he could always pretend that he didn't know what he was being asked.

"*Cabrón*, you spoke Spanish to the emigration officer at the airport in Mérida!"

"Yes. That's true." Buchanan's head drooped. "A couple of simple phrases. What I call 'survival Spanish.' "

"Survival?" a deep-voiced guard asked behind him, then grabbed Buchanan's hair and jerked his head up. "If you do not want your hair pulled out, you will survive by speaking Spanish."

"*Un poco*." Buchanan exhaled. "A little. That's all I know."

"*Why did you kill those three men in Cancún?*"

"What are you talking about? I didn't kill anyone."

The overweight interrogator, his uniform stained with sweat, pushed himself up from the bench, his stomach wobbling, and plodded close to Buchanan, then shoved a police sketch in front of his face. The sketch was the same that the emigration officer at Mérida's airport had noticed beside a fax machine on a desk in the room to which he had taken Buchanan to find out why he was bleeding.

"Does this drawing look familiar to you?" the interrogator growled. "*Ciertamente*, it does to me. *Dios*, *sí*. It reminds me of *you*. We have a witness, a fellow *yanquí* in fact, who saw you kill three men in Cancún."

"I told you I don't know what you're talking about." Buchanan glared. "That drawing looks like me and a couple of hundred thousand other Americans." Buchanan rested his hoarse voice. "It could be anybody." He breathed. "I admit I was in Cancún a couple of days ago." He licked his dry lips. "But I don't know anything about any murders."

"You lie!" The interrogator raised a section of rubber hose and whacked Buchanan across the stomach.

Buchanan groaned but couldn't double over because of the ropes that bound him to the back of the chair. If he hadn't seen the overweight man clumsily start to swing the hose, he wouldn't have been able to harden his stomach enough to minimize the pain. Pretending that the blow had been worse than it was, he snapped his eyes shut and jerked his head back.

"Don't insult me!" the interrogator shouted. "Admit it! You *lie*."

"No," Buchanan murmured. "Your witness is lying." He trembled. "If there *is* a witness. How could there be? I didn't kill anybody. I don't know anything about . . ."

Each time the interrogator struck him, it gave Buchanan a chance to steal opportunities, to wince, to breathe deeply and rest. Because the police had already taken his watch and wallet, he didn't have anything with which to try to bribe them. Not that he thought a bribe would have worked in this case. Indeed, if he did try to bribe them, under the circumstances his gesture would be the same as an admission of guilt. His only course of action was to play his role, to insist indignantly that he was innocent.

The interrogator held up Buchanan's passport, repeating with the same contemptuous tone, "Victor Grant."

"Yes."

"Even your passport photograph resembles this sketch."

"That sketch is worthless," Buchanan said. "It looks like a ten-year-old did it."

The interrogator tapped the rubber hose against the bandage that covered the wound on Buchanan's shoulder. "What is your occupation?"

Wincing, Buchanan told him the cover story.

The interrogator tapped harder against the wound. "And what were you doing in Mexico?"

Wincing more severely, Buchanan gave the name of the client he supposedly had come here to see. He felt his wound swell under the bandage. Every time the interrogator tapped it, the injury's painful pressure increased, as if it might explode.

"Then you claim you were here on business, not pleasure?"

"Hey, it's always a pleasure to be in Mexico, isn't it?" Buchanan squinted toward the rubber hose that the interrogator tapped even harder against his wound. From pain, his consciousness swirled. He would soon pass out again.

"Then why didn't you have a business visa?"

Buchanan tasted stomach acid. "Because I only found out

a couple of days ahead of time that my client wanted me to come down here. Getting a business visa takes time. I got a tourist card instead. It's a whole lot easier."

The interrogator jammed the tip of the hose beneath Buchanan's chin. "You entered Mexico illegally." He stared deeply into Buchanan's eyes, then released the hose so Buchanan could speak.

Buchanan's voice thickened, affected by the swelling in his throat that the hose had caused. "First you accuse me of killing three men." Breathing became more difficult. "Now you blame me for failing to have a business visa. What's next? Are you going to charge me with pissing on your floor? Because that's what I'm going to have to do if I'm not allowed to use a bathroom soon."

The man behind Buchanan yanked his hair again, forcing tears from Buchanan's eyes. "You do not seem to believe that this is serious."

"Not true. Take my word, I think this is *very* serious."

"But you do not act afraid."

"Oh, I'm afraid. In fact, I'm terrified."

The interrogator glowered with satisfaction.

"But because I haven't done what you claim I did, I'm also furious." Buchanan forced himself to continue. "I've had enough of this." Each word was an effort. "I want to see a lawyer."

The interrogator stared in disbelief, then bellowed with laughter, his huge stomach heaving. "Lawyer?"

The guard behind Buchanan laughed as well.

"*Un jurisconsulto?*" the interrogator asked with derision. "*Que tu necesitas está un sacerdote.*" He whacked the rubber hose across Buchanan's shins. "What do you think about that?"

"I told you, I hardly know any Spanish."

"What I said is, you don't need a lawyer, you need a priest. Because all that will help you now, Victor Grant, is prayers."

"I'm a U.S. citizen. I have a right to . . ." Buchanan couldn't help it. His bladder was swollen beyond tolerance. He had to let go.

Urinating in his pants, he felt the hot liquid stream over the seat of the chair and dribble onto the floor.

"*Cochino!* Pig!" The interrogator whacked Buchanan's wounded shoulder.

Any second now, Buchanan thought. Dear God, let me faint.

The interrogator grabbed Buchanan's shirt and yanked him forward, overturning the chair, toppling him to the floor.

Buchanan's face struck the concrete. He heard the interrogator shout in Spanish to someone about bringing rags, about forcing the gringo to clean up his filth. But Buchanan doubted he'd be conscious by the time the rags arrived. Still, although his vision dimmed, it didn't do so quickly enough to prevent him from seeing with shock that his urine was tinted red. They broke something inside me. I'm pissing blood.

"You know what I think, gringo?" the interrogator asked.

Buchanan wasn't capable of responding.

"I think you are involved with drugs. I think that you and the men you killed had an argument about drug money. I think . . ."

The interrogator's voice dimmed, echoing. Buchanan fainted.

6

He found himself sitting upright once more, still tied to the chair. It took several moments for his vision to focus, for his mind to become alert. Pain definitely helped him sharpen his consciousness. He had no way of knowing how long he'd been out. The room had no windows. The fat interrogator seemed to be wearing the same sweaty uniform. But Buchanan noticed that the blood-tinted urine had disappeared from the floor. Not even a damp spot. Considerable time must have passed, he concluded. Then he noticed something else—that his pants remained wet. Hell, all they did was move me to a different room. They're trying to screw with my mind.

"We have brought a friend to see you."

"Good." Buchanan's voice broke. He fought not to lose his strength. "My client can vouch for me. We can clear up this mistake."

"Client? Did I say anything about a client?" The interrogator opened the door.

A man, an American, stood flanked by guards in a dim hallway. The man was tall, with broad shoulders and a bulky chest, his sandy hair in a brush cut. He wore sneakers, jeans, and a too-small green T-shirt, the same clothes he'd been wearing when he'd come into the restaurant at Club Internacional in Cancún. The clothes were rumpled, and the man looked exhausted, his face still red but less from sun and alcohol than from strain. He hadn't shaved. Big Bob Bailey.

Yeah, I bet you're sorry now that you didn't stay away from me at the restaurant, Buchanan thought.

The interrogator gestured sharply, and the guards nudged Bailey into the room, guiding him with a firm hand on each of his elbows. He walked unsteadily.

Sure, they've been questioning you since they caught you on the beach, Buchanan thought. They've been pumping you for every speck of information they can get, and the pressure they put on you encourages you to stick to your story. If they get what they want, they'll apologize and treat you royally to make certain you don't change your mind.

The guards stopped Bailey directly in front of Buchanan.

The interrogator used the tip of the rubber hose to raise Buchanan's face. "Is this the man you saw in Cancún?"

Bailey hesitated.

"Answer," the interrogator said.

"I . . ." Bailey drew a shaky hand across his brush cut. "It could be the man." He stank of cigarettes. His voice was gravelly.

"*Could be?*" The interrogator scowled and showed him the police sketch. "When you helped the artist prepare this sketch, I am told that you were definite in your description."

"Well, yeah, but . . ."

"*But?*"

Bailey cleared his throat. "I'd been drinkin'. My judgment might have been clouded."

"And are you sober now?"

"I wish I wasn't, but yeah, I'm sober."

"Then your judgment should be improved. Is this the man

you saw shoot the three other men on the beach behind the hotel?''

"Wait a minute," Bailey said. "I didn't see anybody shoot nobody. What I told the police in Cancún was I saw a friend of mine with three Mexicans. I followed 'em from the restaurant to the beach. It was dark. There were shots. I dove for cover. I don't know who shot who, but my friend survived and ran away."

"It is logical to assume that the man who survived the shooting is responsible for the deaths of the others."

"I don't know." Bailey pawed at the back of his neck. "An American court might not buy that logic."

"This is *Mexico*," the interrogator said. "*Is this the man you saw run away?*"

Bailey squinted toward Buchanan. "He's wearin' different clothes. His hair's got blood in it. His face is dirty. His lips are scabbed. He hasn't shaved, and he generally looks like shit. But yeah, he looks like my friend."

"*Looks like?*" The interrogator scowled. "Surely you can be more positive, Señor Bailey. After all, the sooner we get this settled, the sooner you can go back to your hotel room."

"Okay." Bailey squinted harder. "Yeah, I think he's my friend."

"He's wrong," Buchanan said. "I never saw this man in my life."

"He claims he knew you in Kuwait and Iraq," the interrogator said. "During the Gulf War."

"Oh, sure. Yeah, right." The pain in Buchanan's abdomen worsened. He bit his lip, then struggled to continue. "And then he just happened to bump into me in Cancún. Hey, I was never in Kuwait or Iraq, and I can prove it. All you have to do is look at the stamps on my passport. I bet this guy doesn't even know my name."

"Jim Crawford," Bailey said with sudden anger. "Except you lied to me. You told me your name was Ed Potter."

"Jim Crawford?" Buchanan grimaced at the interrogator. "Ed Potter? Get real. Does this guy know my name's Victor Grant? Show him my passport. From the sound of things—he admitted as much—he was so drunk, I'm surprised he doesn't claim he saw Elvis Presley. I'm not whoever he thinks I am, and I don't know *anything* about three men who were murdered."

"In Cancún," the interrogator said, "my brothers on the police force are investigating Ed Potter. Assuming that you did not lie when you gave Señor Bailey that name, you will have left some evidence in the area. You had to stay somewhere. You had to store your clothes. You had to sleep. We will find that place. There will be people who saw you at that place. We will bring those people here, and they will identify you as Ed Potter, proving that Señor Bailey is right." The interrogator shook the piece of rubber hose in front of Buchanan's face. "And then you will explain not only why you shot those three men but why you carry a passport with a different name, why you use so *many* names."

"Yeah. Like Jim Crawford," Bailey said. "In Kuwait."

The interrogator looked extremely satisfied now that Bailey was cooperating again.

Throughout, Buchanan showed no reaction except pain-aggravated anger. But his thoughts, despite his excruciating headache, were urgent. He worked to calculate how protected he was. He'd used the mail to negotiate for and to pay the rent on his office. The only times he'd spoken to the landlord had been on the telephone. The same methods had been employed with regard to his apartment in downtown Cancún. Recommended trade craft. So far so good. It was also to Buchanan's advantage that the police would take quite a while to contact every hotel manager and landlord in Cancún. Still, eventually they would, and although Buchanan's landlords couldn't describe him, they would tell the police that they recognized the name Ed Potter, and the police would question people who frequented the area where Ed Potter worked and lived. Eventually, someone would be brought here who would agree with Big Bob Bailey's claim that the man who called himself Victor Grant looked very much like Ed Potter, and things would get very sticky after that.

"Let them," Buchanan said. "They can waste all the time they want investigating Ed Potter, whoever he is. I'm not worried. *Because I'm not that man.*" Pain gnawed at his abdomen. He had to relieve his bladder once more, and he feared that his urine would be an even darker red. "The trouble is, while they're wasting their time, I'm getting the hell beat out of me." He shuddered. "And it's not going to stop—because I swear to God I won't confess to something I didn't do." He glared at the beefy, nervous Texan. "What did this cop say your name is? Bailey? Is that what—?"

Bailey looked exasperated. "Crawford, you know damned well my name's—"

"Stop calling me Crawford. Stop calling me Potter. You've made a terrible mistake, and if you don't get your memory straight . . ."

Buchanan couldn't restrain his bladder any longer. Indeed, he didn't want to. He'd suddenly decided on a new tactic. He released his abdominal muscles, urine dribbling onto the floor, and he didn't need to look down to know that the liquid was bloody.

Because Bailey turned pale, raised a hand to his mouth, and mumbled, "Holy . . . Look at . . . He's . . . It's . . ."

"Yeah, Bailey, take a good look. They worked me over until they broke something inside me." Buchanan was almost breathless. He had to fight to muster the strength for every word. "What happens if they kill me before they find out you made a mistake?"

Bailey turned paler.

"Kill you? That is ridiculous," the interrogator interrupted. "Obviously, you have suffered other injuries besides those to your shoulder and your head. I did not know this. I realize now that you need further medical attention. As soon as Señor Bailey signs this document, identifying you as the man he saw run from the three victims, he can leave, and I can send for a doctor."

The interrogator thrust a pen and a typed statement toward Bailey.

"Yeah, go ahead and sign it," Buchanan murmured hoarsely. "And then pray to God that the police realize there's been a mistake . . . before they beat me worse . . . before I hemorrhage so bad I . . ." Buchanan breathed. "Because if they kill me, you're next."

"What?" Bailey frowned. "What are you talkin' about?"

"Don't be dense, Bailey. Think about it. You're the one who'll be blamed. We're talking about the death of an American citizen in a Mexican jail. Do you think this cop will admit to what happened? My corpse will disappear. There'll be no record of my arrest. And the only person who can say different is you.''

Bailey suddenly looked with suspicion toward the interrogator.

The interrogator grasped Bailey's arm. "The prisoner is obviously delirious. We must allow him to rest. While you sign this document in the outer office, I will see that he gets medical attention.''

Hesitant, Bailey allowed the interrogator to turn him toward the door.

"Sure," Buchanan said. "Medical attention. What he means is another whack with that rubber hose because I made you realize how much trouble *you're* in. Think, Bailey. You admitted you were drunk. Why won't you admit that there's every chance I'm not the man you saw in Cancún?''

"I have had enough of this.'' The interrogator jabbed Buchanan's injured shoulder. "Any fool can see that you are guilty. How do you explain this bullet wound?''

Writhing in pain against the pressure of the ropes that bound him to the chair, Buchanan spoke through gritted teeth. "It's not a bullet wound.''

"But the doctor said—''

"How would *he* know what caused it? He didn't do tests to look for gunpowder in the wound. All he did was restitch it.'' Buchanan grimaced. "I got this injury and the one on my skull in a boating accident.'' Light-headedness again overcame him. He feared he'd pass out before he could finish. "I fell off my client's yacht as we left port. My skull hit the hull. . . . One of the propellers cut my shoulder. . . . Lucky I didn't get killed.''

"This is a fantasy,'' the interrogator said.

"Right.'' Buchanan swallowed. "Prove it. Prove I'm lying. For God's sake, do what I've been begging you to do. Bring my client here. Ask him if he knows me. Ask if he can explain how I hurt myself.''

"Yeah, maybe that ain't a bad idea,'' Bailey said.

"*What?*'' The interrogator jerked toward the beefy Texan. "Are you telling me that the description you gave in Cancún, that the drawing on this police sketch—*which you helped prepare*—does not match the prisoner? Are you telling me that the identification you made five minutes ago . . . ?''

''All I said was he *looks* like the man I saw.'' Pensive, Bailey rubbed a callused large fist against his beard-stubbled chin. ''Now I ain't so sure. My memory's fadin'. I need time to think. This is pretty serious business.''

''Anybody can make a mistake,'' Buchanan said. ''Your word against mine. That's all this is until we get my client to vouch for me.''

Bailey narrowed his eyes toward the bloody urine on the floor. ''I ain't signin' nothin' till this man's client proves I'm right or wrong.''

Jubilant despite his pain, Buchanan managed to squeeze out a few more words. ''Charles Maxwell. His yacht's moored near the Columbus dock in Cancún.''

With that, Buchanan gave in to the dizziness that insisted. He'd done everything possible. Drifting, he heard the interrogator and Big Bob Bailey exchanging angry words.

7

He was taken back to his cell. Staggering across it, trying not to bump into the other prisoners and cause an incident, he noticed that many of the faces scowling at him were different from those who had scowled at him when he'd first arrived, however long ago that was. His weary guess was that new drunks had replaced those who'd sobered but that the thieves and other predators had been left here until somebody got motivated enough to take the trouble to put them on trial. He knew that in his weakened condition it wouldn't be long before the predators moved against him, so he found a space against a wall and sat, straining to remain awake, staring in response to their stares, hiding his pain, calculating how best to defend himself. He didn't realize right away that two guards had unlocked the cell and were gesturing for him to come out.

They didn't take him toward the interrogation room, however. Instead they took him in the opposite direction, toward a section of the jail that he hadn't seen.

What now? Is this when I disappear?

The guards opened a door, and Buchanan blinked in confusion. He'd expected the interrogator, but what he faced was a sink, a toilet, and a shower stall. He was told to strip, bathe, shave, and put on the white cotton shirt and pants that were stacked on a chair along with a pair of cheap rubber sandals. Confused, he obeyed, the lukewarm water not only making him feel welcomely clean but bolstering his meager energy. The guards stood watch. Later, as Buchanan finished dressing, another guard came in and set a tray upon the sink. Buchanan was astonished. The tray held a plate of refried beans and tortillas, the first food that he had received since he'd been brought here. Weakness and pain had stifled his appetite, but he didn't need any encouragement to grab something else that was on the tray. A bottle of purified water. In a rush, he broke the seal, unscrewed the cap, and swallowed several large mouthfuls. Not too much. You'll get sick.

He studied the food, the aroma of which both attracted and repelled him. The food might be contaminated, he thought, the shower and the fresh clothes a trick to make him ignore his suspicion and eat. But I have to take the risk. Even if my stomach doesn't want it, I've got to force myself to eat.

Again he reminded himself, Not too much at once. It took him a long time to chew and swallow the first mouthful of beans. When his stomach didn't revolt, he was encouraged to drink more water and bite off a piece of tortilla.

He never was able to finish the meal. Holding his spoon in his right hand, he almost dropped it because his fingers began to twitch again, alarmingly. When he switched the spoon to his left hand but before he could raise more food, another guard arrived, and the four of them, looking somber, took him past his crowded cell, toward the interrogation rooms. Why? Buchanan thought. Why would they let me clean up and give me something to eat if they're planning to give me another session with the rubber hose? That doesn't make sense. Unless . . .

The guards escorted him into a room that Buchanan had never seen, a dingy, cluttered office in which the interrogator sat stiffly behind his desk and faced a stern, pinch-lipped American who sat with equal stiffness across from him. When Buchanan appeared, each man directed a narrow gaze at him, and Buchanan's hidden elation at the hope that he might be released turned into abrupt suspicion.

The American was in his middle forties, of middle height and weight, with a pointed chin, a slender nose, and thick dark eyebrows that contrasted with his thinning sun-bleached hair. He was deeply tanned and wore an expensive tropical-blend blue suit with a red-striped silk tie and a gleaming white shirt that not only accentuated his tan but seemed to reflect it. He wore a Harvard ring, a Piaget watch, and Cole-Haan shoes. Distinguished. Impressive. A man to have on your side.

The trouble was that Buchanan had no idea who the man was. He didn't dare assume that the interrogator had responded to his demand and contacted his alibi, Charles Maxwell. The emergency alibi had been established hastily. Normally, every detail of a plan was checked many times, but in this case, Buchanan didn't know what on earth Maxwell looked like. It was reasonable to assume that Maxwell, having been contacted, would come here to support Buchanan's claims. But what if the interrogator had found an American to impersonate Maxwell? What if the interrogator wanted to trick Buchanan into pretending to know the American and thus prove that Buchanan was lying about his alibi?

The American stood expectantly.

Buchanan had to react. He couldn't just keep peering blankly. If this really was Maxwell, the interrogator would expect Buchanan to show grateful recognition. But what if this *wasn't* Maxwell?

The interrogator withdrew his chin into the numerous folds of his neck.

Buchanan sighed, approached the American, placed an unsteady hand on his shoulder, and said, "I was getting worried. It's so good to see . . ."

To see whom? Buchanan let the sentence dangle. He might have been referring to his relief at seeing his friend and client, Charles "Chuck" Maxwell, or he might have been saying that he was delighted to see another American.

"Thank God you're here," Buchanan added, another statement that could apply either to Maxwell or to a fellow American whom Buchanan didn't know. He slumped on a chair beside the battered desk. Tension increased his pain.

"I came as soon as I heard," the American said.

Although the statement implied a strong relationship between the American and Buchanan, it still wasn't forthright enough for Buchanan to treat him as Charles Maxwell. Come on, give me a clue. Let me know who you are.

The American continued, "And what I heard alarmed me. But I must say, Mr. Grant, you appear in better condition than I expected."

Mr. Grant? Buchanan thought.

This man definitely wasn't Charles Maxwell. So who *was* he?

"Yeah, this is a regular country club." The severity of Buchanan's headache made his temples throb.

"I'm sure it's been frightful," the American said. His voice was deep and mellifluous, slightly affected. "But all of that is finished now." He shook hands. "I'm Garson Woodfield. From the American embassy. Your friend Robert Bailey telephoned us."

The interrogator glowered.

"Bailey isn't a friend," Buchanan emphasized. "The first time I met him was here. But he's got some delusion that he saw me in Cancún and knew me before in Kuwait. He's the reason I'm in this mess."

Woodfield shrugged. "Well, apparently he's trying to make amends. He also telephoned Charles Maxwell."

"A client of mine," Buchanan said. "I was hoping he'd show up."

"Indeed, Mr. Maxwell has a great deal of influence, as you're aware, but under the circumstances, he thought it would be *more* influential if he contacted the ambassador and requested that we solve this problem through *official* channels." Woodfield peered closely at Buchanan's face. "Those abrasions on your lips. The bruise on your chin." He turned pensively toward the interrogator. "This man has been beaten."

The interrogator looked insulted. "Beaten? Nonsense. When he came here, he was so unsteady from his injuries that he fell down some stairs."

Woodfield turned to Buchanan, obviously expecting a heated denial.

"I got dizzy," Buchanan said. "I lost my grip on the stairwell railing."

Woodfield looked surprised by Buchanan's response. For his part, the interrogator looked astonished.

"Have they threatened you into lying about what happened to you here?" Woodfield asked.

"They certainly haven't been gentle," Buchanan said, "but they haven't threatened me into lying."

The interrogator looked even more astonished.

"But Robert Bailey claims he saw you tied to a chair," Woodfield said.

Buchanan nodded.

"And struck by a rubber hose," Woodfield said.

Buchanan nodded again.

"And passing bloody urine."

"True." Buchanan clutched his abdomen and winced, a reaction that he normally would not have permitted.

"You realize that if you've been brutalized, there are a number of diplomatic measures I can use to try to obtain your release."

Buchanan didn't like Woodfield's "try to" qualification. He decided to continue following his instincts. "The blood in my urine is from my accident when I fell off Chuck Maxwell's boat. As for the rest of it"—Buchanan breathed—"hey, this officer thinks I killed three men. From his point of view, what he did to me, trying to get me to confess, that was understandable. What I'm angry about is that he wouldn't let me prove I was innocent. He wouldn't call my client."

"All of that's been taken care of," Woodfield said. "I have a statement"—he pulled it from his briefcase—"indicating that Mr. Grant here was with Mr. Maxwell on his yacht when the murders occurred. Obviously," he told the interrogator, "you have the wrong man."

"It is not obvious to me." The interrogator's numerous chins shook with indignation. "I have a witness who puts this man at the scene of the murders."

"But surely you don't take Mr. Bailey's word over a statement by someone as distinguished as Mr. Maxwell," Woodfield said.

The interrogator's eyes gleamed fiercely. "This is Mexico. Everyone is equal."

"Yes," Woodfield said. "The same as in the United States." He turned to Buchanan. "Mr. Maxwell asked me to deliver this note." He pulled it from his briefcase and handed it to Buchanan. "Meanwhile," he told the interrogator, "I need to use your facilities."

The interrogator looked confused.

"A bathroom," Woodfield said. "A rest room."

"Ah," the interrogator said. "A toilet. *Sí.*" He hefted his enormous body from the chair, opened the office door, and directed a guard to escort Mr. Woodfield to *el sanitario*.

As Woodfield left, Buchanan read the note.

Vic,
Sorry I couldn't be there in person. I'll show up if I have to, but let's exhaust other options first. Check the contents of the camera bag Woodfield brought with him. If you think what's inside will be effective, give it a try. I hope to see you stateside soon.

Chuck

Buchanan glanced down toward the briefcase beside Woodfield's chair, noticing the gray nylon camera bag.

Meanwhile, the interrogator shut the office door and frowned at Buchanan, his voice rumbling, his ample stomach quivering. He was obviously interested in the contents of the note. "You lied about being beaten. *Por qué?*" He came closer. "Why?"

Buchanan shrugged. "Simple. I want you and me to be friends."

"Why?" The interrogator stepped even closer.

"Because I won't get out of here without your cooperation. Oh, Woodfield can cause you a lot of trouble from your superiors and from politicians. But I still might not be released until a judge makes a ruling, and in the meantime, I'm at your mercy." Buchanan paused, trying to look defeated. "Sometimes terrible accidents happen in a jail. Sometimes a prisoner can die before a judge has time to see him.''

The interrogator studied Buchanan intensely.

Buchanan pointed toward the camera bag. ''May I?''

The interrogator nodded.

Buchanan set the bag on his lap. ''I'm innocent,'' he said. ''Obviously, Bailey is confused about what he saw. My passport proves I'm not the man he thinks I am. My client says I wasn't at the scene of the crime. But you've invested a great deal of time and effort in this investigation. In your place, I'd hate to think that I'd wasted my energy. The government doesn't pay you enough for all the trouble you have to go through.'' Buchanan opened the camera bag and set it on the desk.

He and the interrogator stared at the contents. The bag was filled with neat piles of used hundred-dollar American bills. As Buchanan removed one of the stacks and leafed through it, the interrogator's mouth hung open.

''I'm only guessing,'' Buchanan said, ''but this seems to be fifty thousand dollars.'' He returned the stack to the others in the bag. ''Don't misunderstand. I'm not rich. I work hard, the same as you, and I certainly don't have this kind of money. It belongs to my client. He's loaning it to me to help me pay my legal expenses.'' Buchanan grimaced. ''But I don't see why a lawyer should get it when I'm innocent and he won't have to earn his fee to get me released. He definitely won't have to work as long and hard as I will to pay the money back or as long as *you* would to receive this much.'' Buchanan sighed from pain and frowned toward the door. ''Woodfield will be coming back any second. Why don't you do both of us a favor, take the money, and let me out of here?''

The interrogator tapped his fingers on the battered table.

''I swear to you. I didn't kill anybody,'' Buchanan said.

The door swung slowly open. The interrogator shielded the camera bag with his massive body, shut the bag, and with a remarkably fluid motion for so huge a man, he set the bag out of sight behind the desk as he scrunched his wide hips into his creaking chair.

Woodfield entered.

"To pursue this matter any further would be a mockery of justice," the interrogator said. "Señor Grant, your passport and belongings will be returned. You are free."

8

"You look like you need a doctor," Woodfield said.

They walked from the jail, across a dusty street, and toward a black sedan parked beneath a palm tree.

"I know an excellent physician in Mérida," Woodfield said. "I'll drive you there as quickly as possible."

"No," Buchanan said.

"But . . ."

"No," Buchanan repeated. He waited for a fenderless pickup truck to go by, then continued toward the car. After having been in the jail for so long, his eyes hurt from the glare of the sun, adding to his headache. "What I want is to get out of Mexico."

"The longer you wait to see a doctor . . ."

Buchanan reached the car and pivoted toward Woodfield. He didn't know how much the diplomat had been told. Probably nothing. One of Buchanan's rules was never to volunteer information. Another rule was don't break character. "I'll see a doctor when I feel safe. I still can't believe I'm out of jail. I *won't* believe it until I'm on a plane to Miami. That jerk might change his mind and rearrest me."

Woodfield put Buchanan's suitcase into the back of the car. "I doubt there's any danger of that."

"No danger to *you*," Buchanan said. "The best thing you can do is drive me to the airport, get me on a plane, then phone Charles Maxwell. Tell him I asked him to arrange for someone to meet me and to take me to a hospital."

"You're certain you'll be all right until then?"

"I'll have to be," Buchanan said. He was worried that the police in Cancún would still be investigating his previous identity. Eventually, they'd find Ed Potter's office and apartment. They'd find people who'd seen Ed Potter and who'd agree that the police sketch looked like Ed Potter. A policeman might decide to corroborate Big Bob Bailey's story by having those people take a look at Victor Grant.

He *had* to get out of Mexico.

"I'll telephone the airport and see if I can get you a seat on the next flight," Woodfield said.

"Good." Buchanan automatically scanned the street, the pedestrians, the noisy traffic. He tensed, noticing a woman in the background, among the crowd on the sidewalk beyond Woodfield. She was American. Late twenties. A redhead. Attractive. Tall. Nice figure. She wore beige slacks and a yellow blouse. But Buchanan didn't notice her because of her nationality or her hair color or her features. Indeed he couldn't get a look at her face. Because she had a camera raised to it. She stood at the curb, motionless among the passing Mexicans, taking photographs of him.

"Just a minute," Buchanan told Woodfield. He started toward her, but the moment she saw him approaching, she lowered the camera, turned, and walked away, disappearing around a corner. The oppressive sun intensified his headache. Festering pressure in his wound made him weaker. Dizziness halted him.

"What's the matter?" Woodfield asked.

Buchanan didn't answer.

"You looked as if you were about to go somewhere," Woodfield said.

Buchanan frowned toward the corner, then turned toward the car. "Yeah, with you." He opened the passenger door. "Hurry. Find a phone. Get me on a flight to Miami."

All the way to the airport, Buchanan brooded about the red-haired woman. Why had she been taking photographs of him? Was she just a tourist and he merely happened to be in the foreground of a shot of a scenic building? Maybe. But if so, why had she walked away when he started toward her? Coincidence? Buchanan couldn't afford to accept that explanation. Too much had gone wrong. And nothing was ever simple. There was always a deeper level. Then if she wasn't just a tourist, what *was* she? Again he asked himself, Why was she taking pictures of me? The lack of an answer disturbed him as much as the threatening implications. He had only one consolation. At least, when she'd lowered the camera, turning to walk away, he'd gotten a good look at her face.

And he would remember it.

9

ACAPULCO, MEXICO

Among the many yachts in the resort's famous bay, one in particular attracted Esteban Delgado's attention. It was brilliant white against the gleaming green-blue of the Pacific. It was approximately two hundred feet long, he judged, comparing its length to familiar landmarks. It had three decks and a helicopter secured to the top. It was sculpted so that the decks curved like a hunting knife down to the point of the bow. Behind the decks, at the stern, a large sunning area—designed to allow voyeurs to peer down unobserved from the upper windows of the looming decks—was terribly familiar. If Delgado hadn't known for certain, if his assistant hadn't given him verified information less than an hour ago, Delgado would have sworn that the distinctive yacht didn't just resemble the source of his sleepless nights and his ulcerated stomach but was in fact the very yacht, owned by his enemy, that figured so prominently in his nightmares. It didn't matter that *this* yacht was called *Full House*, whereas the yacht he dreaded was called *Poseidon*, for Delgado felt sufficiently persecuted to have reached the stage of paranoia where he suspected that the yacht's name had been altered in order to surprise him. But Delgado's assistant had been emphatic in his assurance that as of noon today, the *Poseidon*, with Delgado's enemy aboard, had been en route from the Virgin Islands to Miami.

Nonetheless, Delgado kept staring from the floor-to-ceiling window of his mansion. He ignored the music, laughter, and motion of the party around the pool on the terrace below him. He ignored the women, so many beautiful women. He ignored the flowering shrubs and trees that flanked the expensive pink vacation homes similar to his, carved into the slope below him. Instead, he focused his gaze beyond the Costera Miguel Aleman boulevard that rimmed the bay, past the deluxe hotels and the spectacular beach. The yacht alone occupied him. The yacht and the yacht it resembled and the secret that Delgado's enemy used to control him.

Abruptly something distracted him. It wasn't unexpected, although it was certainly long anticipated, a dark limousine reflecting sunlight, coming into view on the slope's curving road, veering through the gates, past the guards. He brooded, squinting, hot despite the room's powerful air conditioning. His surname had always been coincidentally appropriate for him, inasmuch as Delgado meant "thin," and even as a boy he'd been tall and slender, but lately he had heard whispered, concerned remarks about his appearance, about how much weight he had recently lost and how his carefully tailored suits now looked loose on him. His associates suspected that his weight loss was due to disease (AIDS, it was rumored), but they were wrong.

It was due to torment.

A knock at the door interrupted his distraction and jerked him back to full awareness. "What is it?" he asked, betraying no hint of tension in his voice.

A bodyguard replied huskily beyond the door, "Your guest has arrived, Señor Delgado."

Wiping his clammy hands on a towel at the bar, assuming the confident demeanor of the second most powerful man in Mexico's government, he announced, "Show him in."

The door was opened, a stern bodyguard admitting a slightly short, balding, uncomfortable-looking man who was in his late forties and wore a modest, rumpled business suit. He carried a well-used briefcase, adjusted his spectacles, and looked even more uncomfortable as the bodyguard shut the door behind him.

"Professor Guerrero, I'm so pleased that you could join me." Delgado crossed the room and shook hands with him. "Welcome. How was the flight from the capital?"

"Uneventful, thank heavens." The professor wiped his sweaty forehead with a handkerchief. "I've never been comfortable flying. At least I managed to distract myself by catching up on some paperwork."

"You work too hard. Let me offer you a drink."

"Thank you, Minister, but no. I'm not used to drinking this early in the afternoon. I'm afraid I . . ."

"Nonsense. What would you like? Tequila? Beer? Rum? I have some excellent rum."

Professor Guerrero studied Delgado and relented, swayed by the power of the man who had summoned him. Delgado's official title was Minister of the Interior, but that influential position on the president's cabinet didn't indicate his even greater influence as the president's closest friend and adviser. Delgado and the president had grown up together in Mexico City. They'd both been classmates in law school at Mexico's National University. Delgado had directed the president's election campaign, and it was widely understood that the president had chosen Delgado to be his successor.

But all of that—and especially the chance to acquire the fortune in bribes and kickbacks that was the president's due— would be snatched from him, Delgado knew, if he didn't do what he was ordered, for in that case his blackmailer would reveal Delgado's secret and destroy him. At all costs, that had to be prevented.

"Very well," Professor Guerrero said. "If you insist. Rum with Coke."

"I believe I'll join you." As Delgado mixed the drinks, making a show of what a man of the people he was by not sending for a servant, he nodded toward the music and laughter drifting up from the poolside party on the terrace below. "Later, we can join the festivities. I'm sure you wouldn't mind getting out of your business clothes and into a bathing suit. And I'm *very* sure that you wouldn't object to meeting some beautiful women."

Professor Guerrero glanced self-consciously toward his wedding ring. "Actually, I've never been much for parties."

"You need to relax." Delgado set the moisture-beaded drinks on a glass-and-chrome table, then gestured for Guerrero to sit in a plush chair across from him. "You work too much."

The professor sat stiffly. "Unfortunately, our funding isn't large enough to allow me to hire more staff and reduce my responsibilities." He didn't need to explain that he was the director of Mexico's National Institute of Archaeology and History.

"Then perhaps additional funding can be arranged. I notice you haven't touched your drink."

Reluctant, Guerrero took a sip.

"Good. *Salud*." Delgado sipped from his own. At once, his expression became somber. "I was troubled by your letter. Why didn't you simply pick up the telephone and call me about the matter? It's more efficient, more personal." He silently added, And less official. Bureaucratic letters, not to mention the inevitable file copies made from them, were part of the public record, and Delgado preferred that as few of his concerns as possible be part of the public record.

"I tried several times to talk to you about it," Guerrero insisted. "You weren't in your office. I left messages. You didn't return them."

Delgado looked disapproving. "I had several urgent problems that demanded immediate attention. At the first opportunity, I intended to return your calls. You need to be patient."

"I've *tried* to be patient." The professor wiped his forehead, agitated. "But what's happening at the new find in the Yucatán is inexcusable. It has to be *stopped*."

"Professor Drummond assures me—"

"He is *not* a professor. His doctoral degree is honorary, and he has never taught at a university," Guerrero objected. "Even if he did have proper credentials, I don't understand why you have permitted an archaeological find of this importance to be investigated exclusively by Americans. This is *our* heritage, not theirs! And I don't understand the secrecy. Two of my researchers tried to visit but weren't allowed to enter the area. It's been sealed."

Delgado leaned forward, his expression harsh. "Professor Drummond has spared no expense to hire the best archaeologists available."

"The best experts in Mayan culture are citizens of this country and work in my institute."

"But you yourself admitted that your funds aren't as ample as you would like," Delgado said, an edge in his voice. "Think of Professor Drummond's generous financial contribution as a way of making your own funds go further. Your researchers were denied permission to enter the site because the staff there is working so hard that they don't have time to be distracted by social obligations to visitors. And the area has been sealed off to guarantee that the site isn't plundered by the usual thieves who steal irreplaceable artifacts from newly discovered ruins. It's all easily explainable. There's no secrecy.''

Guerrero became more agitated. ''My institute—''

Delgado held up a hand. '' 'Your' institute?''

Guerrero quickly corrected himself. ''The National Institute of Archaeology and History,'' he said breathlessly, ''should have the sole right to determine how the site should be excavated and who should be permitted to do it. *I do not understand why regulations and procedure have been violated.*''

''Professor, your innocence troubles me.''

''What?''

''Alistair Drummond has been a generous patron of our country's arts. He has contributed millions of dollars to constructing museums and providing scholarships for aspiring artists. Need I remind you that Drummond Enterprises sponsored the recent worldwide tour of the most extensive collection of Mexican art ever assembled? Need I also remind you the international respect that collection received has been an incalculable boost to our public relations? Tourists are now arriving in ever greater numbers, not just to visit our resorts but to appreciate our heritage. When Professor Drummond offered his financial and technical assistance to excavate the ruins, he added that he would consider it a favor if his offer was accepted. It was politically expedient to give him that favor because the favor was in *our* favor. Financially, we come out ahead. I strongly suspect that his team will finish the job long before your own understaffed group would have. As a consequence, tourists can begin going there sooner. Tourists,'' Delgado repeated. ''Revenue. Jobs for the natives. The development of an otherwise useless section of the Yucatán.''

''Revenue?'' Professor Guerrero bristled. ''Is that all our heritage means to you? Tourists? Money?''

Delgado sighed. ''Please. It's too pleasant an afternoon to argue. I came here to relax and thought that you might appreciate the chance to relax, as well. I have a few telephone calls to make. Why don't you go out by the pool, enjoy the view, perhaps introduce yourself to some young ladies—or not, whatever you prefer—and then later we can renew this conversation over dinner, when we've had the chance to calm ourselves.''

"I don't see how admiring the view is going to make me change my mind about—"

Delgado interrupted. "We can continue this conversation later." He motioned for Guerrero to stand, guided him toward the door, opened it, and told one of his bodyguards, "Escort Professor Guerrero around the property. Show him the gardens. Take him to the reception at the pool. Make sure all his needs are satisfied. Professor"—Delgado shook hands with him—"I'll join you in an hour."

Before Guerrero had a chance to reply, Delgado eased him out of the room and shut the door.

At once, his smile dissolved. His features hardened as he reached for the telephone on the bar. He'd done his best. He'd tried to do this in an agreeable, diplomatic fashion. Without being insultingly blatant, he'd offered every bribe he could imagine. Uselessly. Very well, other methods were now required. If Professor Guerrero didn't cooperate, he would discover that he was no longer the director of the National Institute of Archaeology and History. The new director, whom Delgado had selected and who was already obligated to Delgado for various favors, would see no problem about allowing Alistair Drummond's archaeological team to continue excavating the recently discovered Mayan ruins. Delgado was certain about the new director's compliance because that compliance would be a condition of the new director's appointment. And if Professor Guerrero persisted in being disagreeable, if he attempted to create a political scandal, he would have to be killed in a tragic hit-and-run car accident.

How could anyone so educated be so stupid? Delgado wondered with fury as he picked up the telephone. He didn't dial, however, for a light began to flash on the phone's multiline console, indicating that a call was coming through on an alternate number. Normally, Delgado would have let a servant answer the call by using one of the many extensions throughout the estate, but this particular line was so private that it didn't have extensions. Only this phone was attached to it, and very few people knew that Delgado could be reached on this line. Its number was entrusted only to special associates, who had instructions to use it only for matters of utmost importance.

Under the circumstances, Delgado could think of only one

such matter and he immediately jabbed the button where the light was flashing. "Arrow," he said, using the code word that identified him. "What is it?"

Amid long-distance static, a gruff voice—which Delgado recognized as belonging to a trusted aide—responded with the code word "Quiver. It's about the woman."

Delgado felt pressure in his chest. "Is your line secure?"

"I wouldn't have called unless it was."

Delgado's phone system was inspected daily for taps, just as his estate was inspected for electronic eavesdropping devices. In addition, a small monitor next to the phone measured the voltage on the line. Any variance from the norm would indicate that someone had patched into the line after the telephone system had been inspected.

"What about the woman?" Delgado asked tensely.

"I don't think Drummond controls her any longer. Her security has been removed."

"For God sake, speak clearly. I don't understand."

"You told us to watch her. But we can't get close because Drummond has his own people watching her. One of his operatives pretending to be homeless sits in a cardboard box and watches the rear of her building. Various vendors, one selling hot dogs, another T-shirts and umbrellas, watch the entrance from the park across the street. At night, they're replaced by other operatives pretending to be indigents. The building's doorman is on Drummond's payroll. The doorman has an assistant who keeps watch in case the doorman is distracted. The woman's servants work for Drummond, as well."

"I already know that!" Delgado said. "Why are you—?"

"They're not on duty any longer."

Delgado exhaled sharply.

"At first, we thought that Drummond had arranged for other surveillance," the aide continued. "But we were wrong. The doorman no longer has an assistant. The woman's servants left the building this morning and didn't return. The operatives outside the building have not been replaced."

Next to the air-conditioning duct, Delgado sweated. A crush of conflicting implications made him feel paralyzed. "She must have taken a trip."

"No," the aide said. "My team would have seen her leave.

Besides, on previous occasions when she did take a trip, her servants went with her. Today, they left alone. Yesterday morning, there was an unusual flurry of activity, Drummond's men going in and out, especially his assistant.''

"If she hasn't taken a trip, if she's still in the building, why has the security team been removed?"

"I don't believe she's still in the building."

"Make sense!" Delgado said.

"I think she broke her agreement with Drummond. I think she felt threatened. I think she managed to escape, probably the night before last. That explains the flurry of activity the next morning. The security team isn't needed at the building, so they've been reassigned to join the search for her. The servants aren't needed, either, so they've been dismissed."

"God have mercy." Delgado sweated more profusely. "If she's broken her bargain, if she talks, I . . . Find her."

"We're trying," the aide promised. "But after this much time, the trail is cold. We're reviewing her background, trying to determine where she would go to hide and who she might ask for help. If Drummond's men locate the woman, I'm certain that Drummond will send his assistant to bring her to him."

"Yes. Without her, Drummond has less power over me. He'll do everything possible to get her back."

But what if she goes to the authorities? Delgado wondered, frantic. What if she talks in order to save herself?

No, Delgado thought. Until she's absolutely forced to, she won't trust the authorities. She'll be too afraid that Drummond controls them, that they'll release her to him, that he'll punish her for talking. I've still got some time. But eventually, when she doesn't see another way, she *will* talk. She knows the price is so great that Drummond won't stop hunting her. She can't run forever.

Delgado's aide had continued speaking.

"What?" Delgado demanded.

"I asked you, if we find her or if Drummond's men lead us to her, what do you want us to do?"

"I'll decide that when the moment comes."

Delgado set down the phone. No matter how thoroughly his estate had been checked for hidden microphones and how well his telephone system had been examined for taps, he wasn't about to say anything more on this topic in this fashion. The conversation had not been incriminating, but it would certainly raise questions if the wrong people heard a recording of it. Delgado didn't want to raise even more questions and indeed supply the answers by providing the full instructions that his aide requested. For Delgado had forcefully decided what needed to be done. By all means. To soothe his ulcerated stomach. To dispel his nightmares and allow him to sleep.

If his men located the woman, he wanted them to kill her. And then kill Drummond.

FIVE
...

1

MIAMI, FLORIDA

The man's voice echoed metallically from the airport's public-address system. "Mr. Victor Grant. Mr. Victor Grant. Please go to a courtesy telephone."

Buchanan had just arrived at Miami International, and as he blended with the Aeroméxico passengers leaving the immigration/customs area, he wondered if Woodfield had gotten the message through to Maxwell and how the rendezvous would be arranged. Amid the noise and congestion of the terminal, he barely heard the announcement and waited for it to be repeated, making sure before he walked across to a white phone marked AIRPORT mounted on a wall near a row of pay phones. There wasn't any way to dial. When he picked it up, he heard a buzz, then another as a phone rang at another station. A woman answered, and when he explained that he was Victor Grant, she told him that his party would be waiting for him at the information counter.

Buchanan thanked her and replaced the phone, then analyzed the rendezvous tactic. A surveillance team is watching the courtesy telephones, he concluded. After Victor Grant's name was called, they waited for a man to go to one of the phones. The team has either studied a photograph of me or been given a description. In any case, now they've identified me, and they'll hang back to see if anyone is following me while I go to the information counter.

But as pleased as Buchanan was about the care of the rendez-vous procedure and as delighted as he was to have escaped the authorities in Mexico, to be back in the United States, he was also troubled. His controllers obviously thought that the situation remained delicate. Otherwise, they wouldn't have involved so many operatives in making contact with him.

At a modest pace, giving the surveillance team ample chance to watch the crowd (besides, he was in too much pain to walk any faster), Buchanan pulled his suitcase and proceeded toward the information counter. A pleasant, athletic-looking, casually dressed man in his thirties emerged from the commotion of passengers. He held out his hand, smiled, and said, "Hello, Vic. It's good to see you. How are you feeling? How was the flight?"

Buchanan shook hands with him. "Fine."

"Great. The van's right this way. Here, I'll take your bag."

The man, who had brown hair, blue eyes, and sun-leathered skin, touched Buchanan's elbow and guided him toward an exit. Buchanan went along, although he didn't feel comfortable since he hadn't received some kind of identification code. When the man said, "By the way, both Charles Maxwell and Wade want us to phone and let them know you're okay," Buchanan relaxed. Several people knew about his claimed rela-tionship with Charles Maxwell, but only his controllers knew that Buchanan's case officer in Cancún had used the pseudonym of Wade.

Across from the terminal, in the airport's crowded parking ramp, the man unlocked a gray van, the side of which was stenciled with white: BON VOYAGE, INC., PLEASURE CRAFTS REFITTED, REMODELED. Until then, they'd been making small talk, but now Buchanan became silent, waiting for the man to give him directions, to let him know if it was safe to speak candidly and to tell him what scenario he was supposed to follow.

As the man drove from the parking ramp, he pressed a button on what looked like a portable radio mounted under the dash. "Okay. The jammer's on. It's safe to talk. I'll give you the quick version and fill in the fine points later. I'm Jack Doyle. Used to be a SEAL. Took a hit in Panama, had to resign, and started a business, outfitting pleasure boats in Fort Lauderdale. All of that's true. Now this is where you come in. From time to time, I do favors for people I used to work for. In this case, they've asked me to give you a cover. You're supposed to be an employee of mine. Your controllers supplied all the necessary background documentation, Social Security, taxes, that sort of thing. As Victor Grant, you used to be in the SEALs as well, so it was natural that I'd treat you like more than just a hired hand. You live in an apartment above my office. You're a loner. You travel around a lot, doing jobs for me. If my neighbors get asked about you, it won't be surprising that they're not familiar with you. Any questions?"

"How long have you employed me?"

"Three months."

"How much do I earn?"

"Thirty thousand a year."

"In that case, I'd like a raise."

Doyle laughed. "Good. A sense of humor. We'll get along."

"Sure," Buchanan said. "But we'll get along even better if you stop at that gas station up ahead."

"Oh?"

"Otherwise I'll be pissing blood inside your van."

"Jesus."

Doyle quickly turned off the freeway toward a gas station. When Buchanan came out of the men's room, Doyle was leaving a pay phone. "I called one of our team who's acting as communications relay at the airport. He's positive no one followed you."

Buchanan slumped against the van, his face cold with sweat. "You'd better get me to a . . ."

2

The doctor stood beside Buchanan's bed, read Buchanan's chart, listened to his heart and respiration, checked his intravenous bottle, then took off his bifocals and scratched his salt-and-pepper beard. "You have an amazing constitution, Mr. Grant. Normally, I don't see anybody as banged up as you unless they've been in a serious car accident." He paused. "Or . . ."

He never finished his statement, but Buchanan was certain that what the doctor meant to add was "combat," just as Buchanan was certain that Doyle would never have brought him here unless the small hospital had affiliations with his controllers. In all likelihood, the doctor had once been a military physician.

"I have the results of your X rays and other tests," the doctor continued. "Your wound is infected, as you guessed. But now that I've redressed and resutured it and started you on antibiotics, it ought to heal with reasonable speed and without complication. Your temperature is already coming down."

"Which means—given how serious you look—the bad news is my internal bleeding," Buchanan said.

The doctor hesitated. "Actually, that bleeding seems more serious than it is. No doubt, it must have been quite a shock when you discovered blood in your urine. I'm sure you've been worried about a ruptured organ. The reassuring truth is that the bleeding is caused by a small broken blood vessel in your bladder. Surgery isn't necessary. If you rest, if you don't indulge in strenuous activity, the bleeding will stop and the vessel will heal fairly soon. It sometimes occurs among obsessive joggers, for example. If they take a few weeks off, they're able to jog again."

"Then what is it?" The doctor's somber expression made Buchanan more uneasy. "What's wrong?"

"The injury to your skull, Mr. Grant. And the periodic tremors in your right hand."

Buchanan's chest felt icy. "I thought the tremors were

caused by shock to the nerves because of the wound in my shoulder. When the wound heals, I assumed . . .''

The doctor squinted, concerned. "Shock. Nerves. You're partially correct. The problem does involve the nerves. But not in the way you imagine. Mr. Grant, to repeat, you have an amazing constitution. Your skull has been fractured. You've suffered a concussion. That accounts for your dizziness and blurred vision. Frankly, given the bruise I saw on the CAT scan of your brain, I'm amazed that you were able to stay on your feet, let alone *think* on your feet. You must have remarkable endurance, not to mention determination.''

"It's called adrenaline, Doctor.'' Buchanan's voice dropped. "You're telling me I have neurologic damage?''

"That's my opinion.''

"Then what happens now? An operation?''

"Not without a *second* opinion,'' the doctor said. "I'd have to consult with a specialist.''

Restraining an inward tremor, appalled by the notion of willingly being rendered unconscious, Buchanan said, "I'm asking for *your* opinion, Doctor.''

"Have you been sleeping for an unusual amount of time?''

"Sleeping?'' Buchanan almost laughed but resisted the impulse because he knew that the laugh would sound hysterical. "I've been too busy to sleep.''

"Have you vomited?''

"No.''

"Have you experienced any unusual physical aberrations, apart from the dizziness, blurred vision, and tremors in your right hand?''

"No.''

"Your answers are encouraging. I'd like to consult with a specialist in neurology. It may be that surgery isn't required.''

"And if it isn't?'' Buchanan asked rigidly. "What's my risk?''

"I try not to deal with an hypothesis. First, we'll watch you carefully, wait until tomorrow morning, do another CAT scan, and see if the bruise on your brain has reduced in size.''

"Best case,'' Buchanan said. "Suppose the bruise shrinks. Suppose I don't need an operation.''

"The best case is the worst case,'' the doctor said. "Damaged brain cells do not regenerate. I'd make very certain that I was never struck on my skull again.''

3

The one-story house was in a suburb of Fort Lauderdale called Plantation, its plain design disguised by abundant shrubs and flowers. Someone obviously took loving care of the property. Buchanan wondered if Doyle made a hobby of landscaping. Their conversation during the drive from the hospital to Doyle's home indicated that the recession had affected Doyle's business and he was hardly in a position to afford a gardener. But after Doyle parked in a carport and led Buchanan through the side screen door into the house, it quickly became obvious who was taking care of the grounds.

Doyle had a wife. Buchanan hadn't been sure, inasmuch as Doyle didn't wear a wedding ring, and Buchanan seldom asked personal questions. But now he faced an energetic, pixyish woman a little younger than Doyle, maybe thirty. She had happy eyes, cheerleader freckles, and an engaging, spontaneous smile. Buchanan couldn't tell what color her hair was because she had it wrapped in a black-and-red-checkered handkerchief. She wore a white cotton apron, and her hands were covered with flour from a ball of dough that she was kneading on a butcher-board counter.

''Oh, my,'' she said with a pleasant southern accent (Louisiana, Buchanan thought), ''I didn't think you'd be here this soon.'' Appealingly flustered, she touched her face and left a flour print on her freckles. ''The house is a mess. I haven't had time to—''

''The house looks fine, Cindy. Really,'' Doyle said. ''Traffic wasn't as bad as I figured. That's why we're early. Sorry.''

Cindy chuckled. ''Might as well look on the bright side. Now I don't have to wear myself out rushing to clean the house.''

Her smile was infectious. Buchanan returned it.

Doyle gestured toward him. ''Cindy, this is my friend I told you about. Vic Grant. I used to know him in the service. He's been working for me the past three months.''

"Pleased to meet you.'' Cindy held out her hand. Then she remembered the flour on it, blushed, and started to retract the hand.   .

"No, that's okay,'' Buchanan said. "I like the feel of flour.'' He shook hands with her.

"Classy guy,'' she told her husband.

"Hey, all my friends are classy.''

"Tell me another one.'' She studied Buchanan, pointing at the thick bandage around his skull. "I've got another black-and-red handkerchief that'll sure look better than that.''

Buchanan grinned. "I'm not supposed to take this off for a while. It doesn't do much good. It's not like a cast or anything. But it reminds me to be careful of my head.''

"Fractured skull, Jack told me.''

Buchanan nodded, his head still aching.

He expected her to ask him how he'd injured it. That would be a natural, logical next statement, and he was preparing to repeat his lie about falling off a boat, but she surprised him, suddenly switching topics, gesturing toward the dough on the counter. "I'm making you a pie. I hope you like key lime.''

He hid his puzzlement and told her, "I seldom taste home-made pie. I'm sure anything you cook would be wonderful.''

"Jack, I like this guy better and better.''

"I'll show you to the guest room,'' Doyle said.

"Anything you need, just ask,'' Cindy added.

"Hey, I bet everything is fine,'' Buchanan said. "I really appreciate your taking me in like this. I don't have a family or anything, and the doctor thought it would be better if . . .''

"Shush,'' Cindy said. "For the next few days, *we're* your family.''

As Doyle led Buchanan from the kitchen toward a sunlit hallway, Buchanan glanced back toward Cindy, still puzzled about why she hadn't asked him the obvious question about what had happened to his skull.

By now, she had turned from him and resumed kneading the ball of dough on the butcher-board counter. Buchanan noticed that she had flour handprints on the trim hips of her jeans. Then he noticed something else. A snub-nosed .38 revolver was mounted to a bracket beneath the wall phone next to the screen door, and Buchanan knew that Jack Doyle would never have chosen that type of weapon for himself. Doyle would have considered it a toy, preferring a semiautomatic 9-mm or a .45. No, the snub-nosed revolver was for Cindy, and Buchanan was willing to bet that she knew how to use it.

Was the gun there as a precaution against burglars? Buchanan wondered. Had Doyle's experience with the SEALs made him extra security-conscious in civilian life? As Buchanan followed Doyle down the hallway, he remembered Doyle's comment about sometimes doing favors for people he used to work for, and immediately he decided that the revolver wasn't the only weapon he'd find around the house and that Doyle intended the weapons to be a protection for Cindy against the possible consequences of some of those favors.

"Well, here it is." Doyle led Buchanan into a pleasant, homey bedroom with lace curtains, an antique rocking chair, and an Oriental carpet on a hardwood floor. "The bathroom's through there. You don't have to share it. We've got our own. No tub, though. Just a shower."

"No problem," Buchanan said. "I prefer a shower."

Doyle set Buchanan's bag on a polished bench at the foot of the bed. "That's about it for now, I guess. Unpack. Have a nap. There's plenty of books on that shelf. Or watch TV." He pointed toward a small set on a bureau in the corner. "Make like the place is yours. I'll come back and let you know when lunch is ready."

"Thanks."

Doyle didn't leave, though. He looked preoccupied.

"What's the matter?" Buchanan asked.

"I don't know your real background, and it isn't right for me to know it, but I figure, considering the people who asked me to give you cover, we must be brothers of a sort. I appreciate your thanks. It isn't necessary, though."

"I understand."

Doyle hesitated. "I've been following the rules. I haven't asked you any questions. All I need to know I assume I've been told. But there is one thing. What happened and why you're here . . . If you're able to . . . Is there any danger to Cindy?''

Buchanan suddenly liked this man very much. "No. To the best of my knowledge, there isn't any danger to Cindy.''

The muscles in Doyle's cheeks relaxed. "Good. She doesn't know anything about the favors I do. When I was in the SEALs, she never knew where I was being sent or how long I'd be gone. Never asked a single question. Took everything on faith. Never even asked why I wanted her to learn how to shoot or why I've got guns mounted around the house.''

"Like the revolver beneath the phone on the wall in the kitchen?'' Buchanan asked.

"Yeah, I saw you noticed it. And like this one.'' Doyle raised the cover from the side of the bed and showed Buchanan a 9-mm Colt in a holster attached to the bed frame. "Just in case. You ought to know about it. I don't care what happens to me, but Cindy . . . Well, she's a damned fine woman. I don't deserve her. And *she* doesn't deserve any trouble I bring home.''

"She's safe, Jack.''

"Good,'' Doyle repeated.

4

The muffled ringing of a phone wakened him. Buchanan became alert immediately, and that encouraged him. His survival instincts were still functioning. He glanced from the bed toward the end table, didn't see a phone, then gazed toward the closed door of the guest room, beyond which he again heard the phone, its ring muted by distance, presumably down the hall in the kitchen. He heard a murky voice, female, Cindy's. Then he heard Jack. The conversation was brief. The house became silent again.

Buchanan glanced at his watch, surprised that it showed half-past noon, that what had felt like a fifteen-minute nap had lasted almost two hours. The doctor had warned him about sleeping more than usual. Past noon? He frowned. Lunch should be ready by now, and he wondered why Cindy or Jack hadn't roused him. He stretched his arms, testing the stiffness in his shoulder where his wound had been restitched, then put on his shoes and stood from the bed.

He heard a soft rap on the door.

"Vic?" Cindy whispered.

"It's all right. I'm up." Buchanan opened the door.

"Lunch is ready." She smiled engagingly.

Buchanan noticed that she'd removed her flour-dusted apron but still wore the red-and-black-checkered handkerchief on her head. Her hair must need fixing and she didn't have time, he thought as he followed her along the sunny hallway into the kitchen.

"The pie's for supper. We don't eat big meals at lunch," she explained. "Jack's a fanatic about his cholesterol. I hope you like simple food."

A steaming bowl of vegetable soup had been set at each place, along with a tuna sandwich flanked by a plate of sliced celery, carrots, cauliflower, and tomatoes.

"The bread's whole wheat," she added, "but I can give you white if you . . ."

"No, whole wheat's fine," Buchanan said, and noticed that Doyle, who was already sitting at the table, seemed preoccupied by the tip of his fork.

"Did you have a good nap?" Cindy asked.

"Fine," Buchanan said, and took a chair only after she did, waiting until she dipped her spoon into the soup before he started to eat. "Delicious."

"Try the raw cauliflower." Cindy pointed. "It's supposed to help purify your system."

"Well, mine could definitely stand some purifying," Buchanan joked, and wondered why Doyle hadn't spoken or eaten yet. Obviously, something was bothering him. Buchanan decided to prompt him. "I bet I'd still be asleep if I hadn't heard the phone."

"Oh, I was afraid that might have happened," Cindy said.

"Yeah." Doyle finally spoke. "You know how I've got the office phone rigged so if someone calls there and we're out, the call is relayed to here?"

Buchanan nodded, as if that information was obvious to him,

trying to maintain the fiction in front of Cindy that he'd worked for her husband these past three months.

"Well, that was someone calling the office to talk to you," Doyle said. "A man. I told him you wouldn't be available for a while. He said he'd call back."

Buchanan tried hard not to show his concern. "It was probably someone I did a job for. Maybe he's got questions about a piece of equipment I installed. Did he leave his name?"

Doyle somberly shook his head.

"Then it mustn't have been very important." Buchanan tried to sound casual.

"That's what I thought," Doyle said. "By the way, after lunch I ought to go down to the office. I need to check on a couple of things. If you're feeling all right, you want to keep me company?"

"Jack, he's supposed to be resting, not working," Cindy said.

Buchanan chewed and swallowed. "Not to worry. Sure. My nap did a world of good. I'll drive along with you."

"Great." Doyle finally started to eat, then paused, frowning toward Cindy. "You'll be all right while we're gone?"

"Why wouldn't I be?" Cindy's smile was forced.

"The soup's excellent," Doyle said.

"So glad you like it." Cindy's smile became even more forced.

5

"Something's wrong," Buchanan said.

Doyle didn't respond, just stared straight ahead and pretended to concentrate on traffic.

Buchanan decided to push it. "Your wife's so good-natured, I get the sense she's working at it. Working hard. She doesn't ask questions, but she picks up overtones—about that phone call, for example. If her smile got any harder, her face would have cracked. She doesn't believe for a minute that you and I are friends. Oh, she tries to pretend, but the truth is, I make her nervous, and at lunch she finally wasn't able to hide it anymore. If she gets any *more* nervous, I might have to leave."

Doyle kept staring ahead, driving over bridges that spanned canals along which pleasure boats were moored next to palm trees and expensive homes. The sunlight was fierce. Doyle seemed to squint less from the sun and more from the topic, however, as he put on dark glasses.

Buchanan let him alone then, eased the pressure, allowing Doyle to respond at his own pace. Even so, Doyle took so long to reply that Buchanan began to think that he never would unless Buchanan prompted him again.

That wasn't necessary.

"You're not the problem," Doyle said, his voice tight. "How I wish life could be that simple. Cindy's glad to have you at the house. Really. She wants you to stay as long as necessary. When it comes to the favors I do, her nerves are incredible. I remember once . . . I was stationed at Coronado, California. . . . Cindy and I lived off base. I said good-bye to her in the morning, drove to work, and suddenly my team was put on alert. No communications to anyone off base. So naturally I couldn't tell her I was being airlifted out. I could imagine what she'd be feeling when I didn't come home that night. The confusion. The worry. No emotional preparation for what might be the last time we saw each other." Doyle's voice hardened. He glanced toward Buchanan. "I was away for six months." Buchanan noted that Doyle didn't say where he'd been sent, and Buchanan would never have asked. He let Doyle continue.

"I found out later that a reporter had managed to discover that I was a SEAL and Cindy was my wife," Doyle said. "The reporter showed up at our apartment and wanted her to tell him where I'd been sent. Well, at that point, Cindy still didn't know I was gone, let alone to where, which of course—the where part—she never would have known anyhow. But someone not as strong as Cindy couldn't have helped being surprised to find a reporter blurting questions at her and telling her I'd been sent on a mission. The natural response would have been for her to show her surprise, admit I was a SEAL, and ask him how much danger I was in. Not Cindy, though. She stonewalled him and claimed she didn't know what he was talking about. Other reporters showed up, and she stonewalled them as well. Her answer was always the same: 'I don't know what you're talking about.' Amazing. She never phoned the base, wanting to know what was happening to me. She just acted as if everything was normal, and Monday through Friday she went to her job as a receptionist for an insurance company, and when I finally got back, she gave me a long, deep kiss and said she'd missed me. Not 'Where were you?' just that she'd missed me. I left on plenty of missions, and I never for a second doubted that she was faithful to me, either.''

Buchanan nodded, but he couldn't help wondering, If Cindy wasn't nervous because of his presence, what was the source of the tension he sensed?

"Cindy has cancer," Doyle said.

Buchanan stared.

"Leukemia." Doyle's voice became more strained. "That's why she wears that kerchief on her head. To hide her scalp. The chemotherapy has made her bald."

Buchanan's chest felt numb. He understood now why Cindy's cheeks seemed to glow, why her skin seemed translucent. The chemicals she was taking—combined with the attrition caused by the disease—gave her skin a noncorporeal, ethereal quality.

"She just got out of the hospital yesterday after one of her three-day treatments," Doyle said. "All that fuss about the food at lunch today. Hell, it was all she could do to eat it. And the pie she was making . . . The chemotherapy does something to her sense of taste. She can't bear sweets. While you were napping, she threw up."

"Christ," Buchanan said.

"She's determined to make you feel at home," Doyle said.

"You've got trouble enough without . . . Why didn't you turn this assignment down? Surely my controllers could have found someone else to give me cover."

"Apparently, they couldn't," Doyle said. "Otherwise, they wouldn't have asked me."

"Did you tell them about . . .?"

"Yes," Doyle said bitterly. "That didn't stop them from asking me. No matter how much she suspects, Cindy can't ever be told that this is an assignment. All the same, she knows it is. I'm positive of that, just as I'm positive that she's determined to do this properly. It gives her something to think about besides . . ."

"What do her doctors say?" Buchanan asked.

Doyle steered onto a highway along a beach. He didn't answer.

"Is her treatment doing what it's supposed to?" Buchanan persisted.

Doyle spoke thickly, "You mean, is she going to make it?"

". . . Yeah, I guess that's what I mean."

"I don't know." Doyle exhaled. "Her doctors are encouraging but noncommittal. One week, she's better. The next week, she's worse. The next week . . . It's a roller coaster. But if I had to give a yes-or-no answer . . . Yes, I think she's dying. That's why I asked if what we're doing puts her in danger. I'm afraid she's got so little time left. I couldn't stand it if something else killed her even sooner. I'd go out of my mind."

6

"Who do you think phoned your house? Who asked for Victor Grant?"

Doyle—who'd been silent for the past five minutes, brooding, preoccupied about his wife—now turned toward Buchanan. "I'll tell you who it wasn't. Your controllers. They told me they'd contact you by phoning either at eight in the morning, three in the afternoon, or ten at night. A man would ask to speak to me. He'd say that his name was Roger Winslow, and he'd suggest a time to meet at my office to talk about customizing a boat. That would mean you were supposed to go to a rendezvous an hour before the time they mentioned. A wholesale marine-parts supplier I use. It's always busy. No one would notice if you were given a message via brush contact from someone passing you."

Buchanan debated. "So if it wasn't my controllers who phoned . . . The only other people who know I claim to be Victor Grant and work in Fort Lauderdale customizing pleasure boats are the Mexican police."

Doyle shook his head. "The man I spoke to didn't have a Spanish accent."

"What about the man from the American embassy?" Buchanan asked.

"Could be. He might be phoning to make sure you'd arrived safely. He'd have access to the same information—place of employment, et cetera—that you gave the Mexican police."

"Yeah, maybe it was him," Buchanan said, hoping. But he couldn't avoid the suspicion that he wasn't safe, that things were about to get worse.

"Since you're supposed to be working for me and living above my office," Doyle said, "you'd better see what the place looks like."

Doyle turned off Ocean Boulevard, taking a side street across from the beach. Past tourist shops, he parked beside a drab two-story cinder-block building in a row of similar buildings, all of which were built along a canal, the dock of which was lined with boats under repair.

"I've got a machine shop in back," Doyle said. "Sometimes my clients bring their boats here. Mostly, though, I go to them."

"What about your secretary?" Buchanan asked, uneasy. "She'll know I haven't been working for you."

"I don't have one. Until three months ago, Cindy did the office work. But then she got too sick to . . . That's why she can make herself believe you came to work for me after she stayed home."

As Buchanan walked toward the building, he squinted from the sun and smelled a salt-laden breeze from the ocean. A young woman wearing a bikini drove by on a motorcycle and stared at his head.

Buchanan gingerly touched the bandage around his skull, realizing how conspicuous it made him. He felt vulnerable, his head aching from the glare of the sun, while Doyle unlocked the building's entrance, a door stenciled BON VOYAGE, INC. Inside, after Doyle shut off the time-delay switch on the intrusion detector, Buchanan surveyed the office. It was a long, narrow room with photographs of yachts and cabin cruisers on the walls, displays of nautical instruments on shelves, and miniaturized interiors of various pleasure craft on tables. The models showed the ways in which electronic instruments could be installed without taking up undue room on a crowded vessel.

"You got a letter," Doyle said as he sorted through the mail.

Buchanan took it from him, careful not to break character by expressing surprise that anyone would have written to him under his new pseudonym. This office was a logical place for someone investigating him to conceal a bug, and unless Doyle assured him that it was safe to talk here, Buchanan didn't intend to say anything that Victor Grant wouldn't, just as he assumed that Doyle wouldn't say anything inconsistent with their cover story.

The letter was addressed to him in scrawled handwriting. Its return address was in Providence, Rhode Island. Buchanan tore open the flap and read two pages of the same scrawled handwriting.

"Who's it from?" Doyle asked.

"My mother." Buchanan shook his head with admiration. His efficient controllers had taken great care to give him supporting details for his new identity.

"How is she?" Doyle asked.

"Good. Except her arthritis is acting up again."

The phone rang.

7

Buchanan frowned.

"Relax," Doyle said. "This is a business, remember. And to tell the truth, I could *use* some business."

The phone rang again. Doyle picked it up, said, "Bon Voyage, Inc.," then frowned as Buchanan had.

He placed his hand across the mouthpiece and told Buchanan, "I was wrong. It's that guy again asking to speak to you. What do you want me to say?"

"Better let *me* say it. I'm curious who he is." Uneasy, Buchanan took the phone. "Victor Grant here."

The deep, crusty voice was instantly recognizable. "Your name ain't Victor Grant."

Heart pounding, Buchanan repressed his alarm and tried to

sound puzzled. "What? Who *is* this? My boss said somebody wanted to speak to . . . Wait a minute. Is this . . .? Are you the guy in Mexico who . . .?"

"Bailey. Big Bob Bailey. Damn it, Crawford, don't get on my nerves. You'd still be in jail if I hadn't called the American embassy. The least you can do is be grateful."

"Grateful? I wouldn't have been *in* jail if you hadn't mis-identified me. How many times do I have to say it? My name isn't Crawford. It's Victor Grant."

"Sure, just like it was Ed Potter. I don't know what kind of scam you're runnin', but it looks to me like you got more names than the phone book, and if you want to keep usin' them, you're gonna have to pay a subscriber fee."

"Subscriber fee? What are you talking about?"

"After what happened in Kuwait, I'm not crazy about wor-kin' in the Mideast oil fields anymore," Bailey said. "State-side, the big companies are shuttin' down wells instead of drillin'. I'm too old to be a wildcatter. So I guess I'll have to rely on my buddies. Like you, Crawford. For the sake of when we were prisoners together, can you spare a hundred thousand dollars?"

"A hundred . . .? Have you been drinking?"

"You betcha."

"You're out of your mind. One last time, and listen care-fully. My name isn't Crawford. My name isn't Potter. My name's Victor Grant, and I don't know what you're talking about. Get lost."

Buchanan broke the connection.

8

Doyle stared at him. "How bad?"

Buchanan's cheek muscles hardened. "I'm not sure. I'll know in a minute." He kept his hand on the phone.

But it took only ten seconds before the phone rang again.

Buchanan scowled and let it ring three more times before he picked it up. "Bon Voyage, Inc."

"Crawford, don't kid yourself that you can get rid of me

that easy," Bailey said. "I'm stubborn. You can fool the Mexican police, and you can fool the American embassy, but take my word, you can't fool me. I know your real name ain't Grant. I know your real name ain't Potter. And all of a sudden, I'm beginnin' to wonder if your real name is even Crawford. Who *are* you, buddy? It ought to be worth a lousy hundred thousand to keep me from finding out."

"I've run out of patience," Buchanan said. "Stop bothering me."

"Hey, you don't know what being bothered is."

"I mean it. Leave me alone, or I'll call the police."

"Yeah, the police might be a good idea," Bailey said. "Maybe *they* can figure out what's goin' on and who you are. Go ahead. Prove you're an innocent, upstandin' citizen. Call the cops. I'd love to talk to them about those three spic drug dealers you shot in Mexico and why you're usin' so many different names."

"What do I have to do to convince—?"

"Buddy, you don't have to convince me of anything. All you have to do is pay me the hundred thousand bucks. After that, you can call yourself Napoleon for all I care."

"You haven't listened to a word I've—"

"The only words I want to hear are 'Here's your money.' Crawford or whoever the hell you are, if you don't get with the program soon, I swear to God I'll phone the cops myself."

"Where are you?"

"You don't really expect me to answer that. When you've got the hundred thousand—and I want it by tomorrow—*then* I'll let you know where I am."

"We have to meet. I can prove you're wrong."

"And just how are you gonna do that, buddy? Cross your heart and hope to die?" Bailey laughed, and this time, it was *he* who slammed down the phone.

9

Buchanan's head throbbed. He turned to Doyle. "Yeah, it's bad."

He had to keep reminding himself that Bailey or somebody else might have planted a microphone in the office. So far, he hadn't said anything incriminating. Whatever explanation he gave Doyle, it had to be consistent with Victor Grant's innocent viewpoint. "That jerk who caused me so much trouble in Mexico. He thinks I shot three drug dealers down there. Now he's trying to blackmail me. Otherwise, he says he'll call the cops."

Doyle played his part. "Let him try. I don't think the local cops care what happens in Mexico, and since you didn't do anything wrong, he'll look like a fool. Then you can have him charged with extortion."

"It's not that easy."

"Why?"

Buchanan's wound cramped as he suddenly thought of something. The phone had rung just after Buchanan and Doyle entered the office. Was that merely a coincidence? Jesus.

Buchanan hurried to the front door, yanked it open, and glanced tensely both ways along the street. A woman was carrying groceries toward a cabin cruiser. A car passed. A jogger went by. Two boat mechanics unloaded a crate from the back of a truck. A kid on a bicycle squinted at the bandage around Buchanan's head.

Buchanan pulled it off and continued staring along the street. His head pounded from the fierce sunlight. There! On the left. At the far end. Near the beach. A big man with strong shoulders and a brush cut—Bailey—was standing outside a phone booth, peering in Buchanan's direction.

Bailey raised his muscular right arm in greeting when he saw Buchanan notice him. Then, as Buchanan started up the street toward him, Bailey grinned—even at a distance, his smile was obvious—got in a dusty car, and drove away.

10

"Cindy?" Doyle hurried into the house.

The kitchen was deserted.

"Cindy?"

No answer.

Doyle turned to Buchanan. "The door was locked. Her car's still here. Where would she go on foot? Why would—? Cindy?" Doyle hurried deeper into the house.

Buchanan stayed in the kitchen, frowning out a side window toward the driveway and the street.

"Cindy?" he heard from a room down the hall.

At once Doyle's voice softened. "Are you . . . ? I'm sorry I woke you, honey. I didn't know you were sleeping. When I found the door locked, I worried that something might have . . ."

Doyle's voice softened even more, and Buchanan couldn't hear it. Uneasy, he waited, continuing to stare outside.

When Doyle came back to the kitchen, he leaned against the refrigerator and rubbed his haggard cheeks.

"Is she all right?" Buchanan asked.

Doyle shook his head. "After we left, she threw up her lunch. She felt so weak she had to lie down. She's been sleeping all afternoon."

"Did any strangers phone her or come around and bother her?"

"No."

"Then why was the house locked?"

Doyle looked confused by the question. "Well, obviously so she'd feel safe while she was napping."

"Sure," Buchanan said. "But when you got here, you were surprised to find the door locked. You assumed she'd gone somewhere, which means she's not in the habit of locking the door while she's home." Buchanan walked toward him. "And *that* means the reason she locked the door is *I'm* here. She senses I brought trouble. And she's right. I did bring trouble. I don't belong here. You can't worry about me while you're worried about—"

The ringing of the phone seemed extra loud.

Doyle flinched.

Buchanan gestured for him to pick it up. "This is *your* house. If I answer, it'll seem unusual. We have to pretend everything's normal. Hurry, before Cindy—"

Doyle grabbed the phone. "Hello? . . . Who *is* this? What

do you want him for? . . . Listen, you son of a bitch. My wife might have answered. If you bother her, if—"

It's going to pieces quickly, Buchanan thought. We're almost to the point where anybody listening to a recording of what we said would have to wonder if I'm really the man I claim to be. He motioned sharply for Doyle to be quiet and wrested the phone from him. "I told you to stop."

"Crawford, your buddy sounds as if he's losin' it," Bailey said. "I guess that's because his wife is sick, huh? Too bad. A nice-lookin' gal like that."

Yeah, you did your homework, Buchanan thought. You've been watching. You must have flown to Miami right after I did. You drove to Fort Lauderdale and staked out where I'm supposed to be working. You found out where the man who pretends to employ me lives. You waited for me to get out of the hospital, and if I didn't show up for work, that would prove I wasn't who I claimed to be. Then you could really make trouble.

"A hundred thousand dollars. Tomorrow, Crawford. If you don't think I'm serious, you're in for a surprise. Because, believe me, I *will* call the cops."

At once, Buchanan heard the dial tone.

Pensive, he set down the phone.

Doyle's face was crimson. "Don't ever yank a phone out of my hand."

"Jack, honey?"

They spun.

Cindy wavered at the entrance to the kitchen. She gripped the doorjamb. Her skin was pale. The black-and-red handkerchief had slipped, exposing her hairless scalp. "Who was that? Who were you yelling at?"

Doyle's throat made a sound as if he was being choked. He crossed the room and held her.

11

The Intracoastal Waterway stretches along the eastern United States from Trenton, New Jersey, to Brownsville, Texas. An inland shipping route composed of linked rivers, canals, lagoons, bays, and sounds, it runs parallel to the Atlantic Ocean and is protected from the severity of the ocean's waves and weather by buffering strips of land. In the North, it is used mostly by commercial vessels, but in the South, particularly in Florida, the waterway's major traffic is composed of pleasure craft, and one of its most attractive sections is at Fort Lauderdale.

At 8:00 A.M., Buchanan parked Doyle's van at the side of Bon Voyage, Inc., and unlocked the building. The previous night, he had driven to a shopping mall, where he used a pay phone in a bar to get in touch with his controllers. Now, as the sun's heat strengthened, he carried several boxes of electronic components to a powerboat that Doyle kept moored at the dock behind the office. Buchanan's wounded shoulder throbbed and his injured head felt caught in a vise due to exertion, forcing him to make several trips. But at last he had the boxes safely stowed, and after locking the building, he unmoored the boat and drove it from the canal into the long expanse of the waterway.

Restaurants, hotels, and condominium buildings flanked it on each side. So did many luxurious homes whose spacious grounds were landscaped with shrubs and palm trees. No matter what type of building had been built along each shore, however, docks and boats were constant. Following Doyle's instructions, Buchanan headed south, admired a three-masted sailboat that passed him going the opposite way, and studied a mural of dolphins that someone had painted along the concrete buttress of a bridge. He pretended to enjoy the breeze and the bracing salt smell of the water. At no time did he stare behind him to see if he was being followed. It was essential that he appear to be innocent, untutored in such matters, and that he not seem preoccupied by Bailey's threats. Bailey had phoned twice more, at midnight and at 2:00 A.M., in each case waking Cindy. Furious, Doyle had disconnected the phones, the fierce look in his eyes disturbing. The more Buchanan thought about it, the more he realized that Bailey wasn't his only problem.

Continuing south in accordance with Doyle's instructions, Buchanan passed beneath more bridges, pretending to admire other buildings and boats, and finally steered to the east, toward an exclusive area of docks called Pier 66. It took him a while to find the right section, but at last he came abreast of a one-hundred-foot dark-wood yacht called *Clementine*, where two men and a woman stood from deck chairs and peered down at him from the stern. One of the men was tall and trim, with severe features and short graying hair. In his fifties, he wore white slacks and a monogrammed green silk shirt. The second man was younger, in his forties, less tall, less expensively dressed, and more muscular. The woman, a blonde, was in her thirties and gorgeous. She wore a short blue terry-cloth robe that was open and revealed a stunningly filled red bikini, the glossy color of which matched her lipstick.

The tall man, obviously in charge, asked, "Are you from . . .?"

"Bon Voyage, Inc.," Buchanan answered. He removed his Ray-Ban sunglasses and his Miami Dolphins cap so they could have a better look at him. "I've got the equipment you ordered. I was told this was a good time to install it."

"Bring it aboard," the tall man said. He gestured for the younger, muscular man—evidently a bodyguard—to help.

Buchanan threw up bow and stern lines so the powerboat could be held steady, a thick rubber rim along its gunwales preventing the boat from scratching the yacht. Then he handed the boxes to the bodyguard, all the while ignoring his light-headedness and the pain in his wounded shoulder, taking care to maintain his balance as the powerboat tilted slightly. The bodyguard dropped a rope ladder. When Buchanan climbed on deck, he tried not to look at the woman.

"Where does the equipment go?"

"Through here," the bodyguard said. He pointed toward a cabin in the stern, and this time he didn't bother to help Buchanan carry the boxes.

Inside the compartment, which had mahogany walls, antique furnishings, and a baby grand piano, Buchanan stacked the boxes, watched the muscular man close the entrance, noticed that the draperies were already closed, and waited. He didn't know how they wanted to do this.

"Captain," the tall, severe man said.

So it would be formal.

"Colonel." Buchanan saluted.

"This is Major Putnam." The tall man gestured toward the muscular man pretending to be a bodyguard. "And this is Captain Weller." He gestured toward the woman, who had closed her robe the instant she was out of sight from anyone observing the yacht.

"Major. Captain." Buchanan saluted them both.

"Now what the hell is going on?" the colonel demanded. "These past few days have been an administrative nightmare, a political mine field. Langley is having a fit about the screwup in Cancún. Your exposure to the Mexican authorities and our embassy down there could have jeopardized, not to mention exposed, everything."

"Sir, I assumed you'd been informed about what happened in Mexico. When I was in the hospital, I was debriefed."

"By the Agency. I prefer to get my information not from civilians but from one of my own."

It took ninety minutes. Periodically, Buchanan was interrupted and asked to expand on a detail. As his report became more current, his debriefers became more somber.

"A hundred thousand dollars," the colonel said.

"I assume it wouldn't satisfy him," Buchanan said. "Once he got me to pay and incriminate myself, he'd keep coming back for more and more."

"Bailey's on a fishing expedition," the muscular man, Major Putnam, said. "Unless you pay, he's got nothing."

The colonel studied Buchanan. "Is that what you think, Captain?"

"Bailey's crude, but he isn't a fool, sir. He's caught me playing three different identities. He *knows* there's something not right about me, even though he can't prove it. So he's testing me to see if I'll panic and give him the proof he needs."

"Well, obviously you're not going to panic," Major Putnam said. "He's wasting his time."

The gorgeous woman, Captain Weller, finally spoke. "But Bailey can still play hell with the operation if he decides to make good on his threat and talk to reporters and the police."

Buchanan gestured. "True. The police have got problems enough right here without bothering themselves about killings in Mexico. But multiple identities might be sexy enough to attract their attention, and if they decide I'm a drug dealer, if they call in the DEA and the FBI . . .''

"Your cover documents are perfect," the colonel said. "Hell, your passport came directly from the State Department. So did all the others. And each of your files is erased after you discard that identity. The DEA and the FBI wouldn't learn squat. As far as the records are concerned, there's no way to tie Jim Crawford and Ed Potter to Victor Grant."

"Still," the woman persisted, "Captain Buchanan would be exposed to considerable official attention and, in effect, taken out of duty."

The colonel tapped his fingers together. "I agree. So the question is, What do we do with our inconvenient Mr. Bailey? It's an admission of guilt to pay him. But if the captain ignores him and Bailey calls the authorities, the FBI might put the captain under surveillance."

"The stakes are important enough," the woman said, "we have to consider the possibility . . ."

The colonel looked puzzled. "Say what's on your mind."

"Should Bailey be terminated?"

The cabin became silent.

The muscular man finally spoke. "I'd be reluctant to advise sanctioning it. After all, termination can cause more problems than it solves. For one thing, we don't know if Bailey has someone working with him. If he does, the threat won't go away with Bailey's death. In fact, it'll get worse because the accomplice could use Bailey's death as an additional means with which to try to interest the police."

"If. Damn it, if," the colonel said impatiently. "We don't have enough information. Major, I want our people to do a thorough background check on Bailey. I want to know who we're dealing with. Also, I want the local hotels and boarding-houses checked. Find out where he's staying. Put him under surveillance. Maybe he *doesn't* have an accomplice. In that case, if he persists in causing trouble . . ."

They waited.

". . . termination might not be out of the question," the colonel said.

Again the cabin became silent.

"Sir, with respect, a background check on Bailey will take a lot of time," Buchanan said. "So will establishing surveillance on him. But there *isn't* time. Bailey said he wants his money today. He was emphatic about that. I assume he's rushing things to prevent me from having the opportunity to move against him. However we deal with him, it has to be done by tonight."

They looked uncomfortable.

"And there's another problem," Buchanan said.

The colonel looked even more uncomfortable. "Oh?"

"Jack Doyle."

"You have reservations about him?"

"I'm sure he was a damned fine soldier," Buchanan said.

"He was," the colonel said. "And the contract work he's done for us has been equally impressive."

"Well, he's not the same man," Buchanan said. "His wife has cancer. She isn't responding to treatment. She's probably going to die."

"Die?" The colonel's face tightened. "I read about her illness in the file, but there was nothing about an imminent fatality."

"It probably *isn't* imminent," Buchanan said. "But Doyle's extremely protective of her. Understandably. He's under a great deal of stress. He thinks Bailey is a threat to her. He . . . Let's put it this way. I believe Doyle will lose control sufficiently to attack him if Bailey keeps phoning the house and putting on pressure and disturbing Doyle's wife, especially if Bailey comes near the house. I have to get out of Fort Lauderdale, far away from Jack Doyle and his wife. Because if Doyle does attack Bailey, it won't be planned, and it won't be tidy. The attack will be absolute, and it won't be something we could cover up. God only knows what the authorities would learn about Doyle's background and his contract work for you as they prepared to go to trial."

"Shit," the muscular man said.

"That's what I've been thinking," Buchanan said. "I landed in a real mess. I think Victor Grant ought to move on."

"But wouldn't that be the same as an admission of guilt?" the woman asked. "Wouldn't that make Bailey all the more determined to hound you?"

"He'd have to find me first. And after I disappeared, after I assumed a new identity, he'd never be able to."

"That still leaves Jack Doyle," the major said. "Bailey could come back and put pressure on Doyle."

"Doyle's story then becomes that he doesn't know anything about me, except that I'm an old military friend who showed up three months ago and asked for work. Doyle complains to the police about Bailey's harassment. Finally, Doyle and his wife take a trip—courtesy of some former friends—to a vacation spot that has an excellent cancer treatment facility."

"Possibly," the colonel said, pensively tapping his fingers on the sides of his chair. "That's certainly one option that we'll consider." He glanced at his watch. "We'll discuss it thoroughly. For now, you'd better leave. If someone's watching the yacht, it'll seem unusual that all of us are inside this long." He glanced at the woman in the bathing suit and the man who might have been a bodyguard. "It's important to maintain cover."

"But what about Bailey?" Buchanan asked.

"We'll give you our decision later."

"Sir, there isn't much time."

"We know that, Captain." The colonel looked irritated. "I said we'll get back to you."

"But in the meanwhile, what do I do?"

"Isn't it obvious? Whatever you think Victor Grant would do."

The answer was vague and slippery. Buchanan suddenly felt apprehensive.

12

Favoring his wounded right arm, Buchanan climbed down the rope ladder into the powerboat. The moment he'd emerged from the shadowy cabin into the glaring sunlight, his head had started pounding again. He put on his cap and sunglasses while the two men and the woman peered down at him, the latter again opening her blue terry-cloth robe to reveal the stunningly filled red bikini of the rich enchantress she was portraying.

"Just send us the bill," the colonel said.

"Yes, sir. Thanks." Buchanan caught the bow and stern lines that the major tossed to him. Then he started the powerboat's engine and steered away from the yacht.

Tension cramped his muscles.

Jesus, he thought. They don't know what to do. I need a decision, and they didn't give me one. I can't act without orders. But if I don't hear from them by tonight, how am I going to stall Bailey?

Preoccupied, Buchanan drove past a dock on one side and a palm-tree-shaded mansion on the other, approaching the end of a canal, about to reenter the expanse of the waterway. Abruptly the problem of Bailey became more immediate. Buchanan's veins swelled from sudden pressure, for ahead, on his left, near a channel marker, Bailey sat in a powerboat similar to Buchanan's, its engine off, the boat motionless except for the bobbing caused by the wake of passing vessels. He wore an orange FORT LAUDERDALE IS THE GREATEST BEACH IN THE WORLD T-shirt and was leaning back in the seat behind the wheel, his canvas shoes up on the console, one beefy arm spread out as if he was relaxing on a sofa, while with his other hand he smoked a cigarette.

Buchanan eased back on the throttle.

Bailey drew his hand across his brush cut, smiled, and tossed his cigarette into the water.

Buchanan eased farther back on the throttle, noticing the camera with the telephoto lens that was slung around Bailey's massive neck. Buchanan's instructions had been to do exactly what Victor Grant would do, and right now, he decided, Victor Grant wasn't going to ignore this son of a bitch.

He steered toward Bailey, pulled the throttle back all the way, felt the bow sink, floated next to Bailey, and grabbed the side of his boat.

"How ya doin', Crawford?"

"How many times do I have to tell you? *My name isn't Crawford.*"

Bailey pulled the pop tab on a can of Blue Ribbon. "Yeah, I'm beginnin' to think you're right about that. It's probably somethin' else besides Crawford. Sure as hell, though, it ain't Victor Grant."

"Look, I've done everything I can to prove it to you. That's my limit. I've run out of patience. I want you to quit following me. I want you to quit—"

"Almost forgot. Pardon me for bein' rude. I got another beer if you'd like—"

"Shove it up your ass."

"Now is that any way to talk to an ol' buddy? Not to mention a business associate?"

"Give it a rest! I never saw you before you showed up in that jail in Mexico."

"Well, that's where you're wrong." Bailey lowered his shoes from the powerboat's console and straightened behind the wheel. "I've got a product to sell, and you're gonna buy it. When you joined those folks on that yacht, I figured you meant to get the hundred thousand from them, but you didn't carry anythin' off. Time's flyin'. You better find that money someplace. 'Cause after midnight tonight, I . . . By the way, that gal on the yacht is some looker, ain't she? Through this big lens on my camera, I could see her so close . . . What's that phone commercial? 'Reach out and touch someone'? I got some real good pictures of her, those two guys, and you on the deck. Nice and clear. Photography's a hobby of mine. Matter of fact, I got some pictures here in this envelope—"

"I'm not interested."

"Oh, but I guarantee you'll find these pictures *real* interestin'. I have to confess I didn't take 'em, though. Had 'em lifted off a tape and then cleaned up. But if you didn't know the difference, you'd swear—"

"What are you talking about?"

"*Just look at the damned pictures, Crawford.*"

Hesitant, Buchanan accepted the manila envelope. Chest tight, he was preoccupied by the threat of the pictures that Bailey had taken of him with the colonel, the major, and the captain. The officers weren't public figures. Bailey wouldn't know who they were. But if Bailey gave the pictures to the police and someone got curious about who was on that yacht, if the colonel was identified, the consequences would be disastrous. Somehow, Buchanan had to get his hands on the film.

But as he withdrew the photographs—eight-by-ten black-and-white glossies—as he sorted through them, he suddenly realized that he had much more to worry about than the pictures Bailey had taken of him with the colonel on the yacht. *Much* more. Because the photographs he now examined depicted a scene from December of 1990 in Frankfurt, Germany. They'd been lifted from a television news tape. They showed American hostages, newly released from Iraq, arriving at the Frankfurt airport. And there, in long shots and close-ups, was Big Bob Bailey getting off the plane with . . .

"A mighty good likeness of you, Crawford," Bailey said. "I've got copies of the original tape, so nobody can say the pictures have been fooled with. If you piss me off by not payin' up, I swear to God I'm gonna send 'em to the cops, along with the Mexican police sketch for Ed Potter and those bottom photographs of Victor Grant."

Photos of Victor Grant? Buchanan asked himself with puzzled alarm. He shuffled to the bottom of the pile and felt his chest turn cold as he stared at three photographs of him outside the Mexican prison, where he talked to Garson Woodfield of the American embassy.

"Another good likeness," Bailey said. "In case you miss the point, that guy from the embassy had to be in the picture so there'd be an absolutely straight-arrow witness to identify you as Victor Grant. I've got you as three different people, Crawford. Got you good."

Stalling for time while he thought, Buchanan kept staring at the pictures. The ones in Mexico. How had—? At once, Buchanan remembered. While he'd been talking to Woodfield across from the Mexican prison, he'd noticed a woman in the background, among the crowd on the sidewalk beyond Woodfield. She'd been American. Late twenties. A redhead. Attractive. Tall. Nice figure. Wearing beige slacks and a yellow blouse. But the reason he'd noticed her hadn't been her appearance.

She'd been aiming a camera at him.

Buchanan peered up from the photographs, and there wasn't any question now that Bailey had an accomplice. Possibly more than one. Dealing with him would be extremely complicated. I have to warn the colonel.

"Keep those pictures. I've got plenty like them in a real safe place, along with the negatives," Bailey said. "Plus, I've also got copies of the TV news tape from Germany. Hey, it isn't often I'm on television. A buddy taped me and made me a present of it. I never thought it would be worth anythin'." Bailey leaned forward. "Admit it, Crawford, you're screwed. Stop actin' innocent. Accept the penalty for gettin' caught. Pay the hundred thousand dollars. I won't even ask you why all the names. That's *your* business. *My* business is gettin' paid."

Buchanan suddenly noticed: Throughout their conversation, Bailey had kept his face angled to the left, as if he had a stiff neck, forcing Buchanan to shift his boat and angle his own face a similar way in order to confront Bailey eye-to-eye.

Stiff neck?

Buchanan spun toward the concrete dock across from him, and there—between two moored sailboats—was the redhead, a camera in front of her face, taking pictures of Bailey and him. Her clothes weren't the same. This time, they were sneakers, jeans, and a denim shirt, but even though her face was obscured by the camera, there was no mistaking that athletic figure and that long, dramatic flame-red hair.

"So you noticed my friend." Bailey exhaled from his cigarette. "I guess it's obvious that gettin' rid of me won't solve your problem. She's got plenty of pictures of you and me, and if anythin' happens to me—which you better hope doesn't happen, not even an accident, like me gettin' drunk and fallin' down a flight of stairs and breakin' my neck—those pictures'll be sent to the cops. Plus, she helped me make copies of the pictures you're holdin', and she also took pictures of you with them folks on that yacht. It might be interestin' to find out who they are."

The red-haired woman lowered the camera and stared across the water toward them. Definitely the same person, Buchanan thought. Strong forehead. Excellent cheekbones. Sensuous lips and chin. She reminded him of a cover model for a fashion magazine. But from the stern way she watched him, Buchanan guessed that a fashion photographer would have a hell of a hard time to get her to smile.

"Crawford, you had plenty to say until now. What's the matter?" Bailey asked. "Cat got your tongue? Or maybe you can't think of any more bullshit. Pay attention. *I want my money.*"

Buchanan hesitated, then made a choice. "When and where?"

"Stay close to your buddy's phone. I'll call his place at eight-thirty tonight and give you directions."

13

It was dark outside. Buchanan kept the guest room's light off as he packed, relying on the slight illumination from the hallway. After he finished and made sure that he hadn't left anything behind, he considered taking the 9-mm pistol from the holster attached to the side of the bed but decided against it. If there was trouble, the police might trace the gun to Doyle, and Buchanan didn't want to involve him any more than Doyle already was.

Leaving the guest room, Buchanan almost turned left toward the lights in the kitchen but changed his mind and instead turned right toward a door farther along the dimly lit hallway. He knocked, received no answer, noticed that the door was slightly ajar, and decided to take a chance. Pushing the door farther open, he knocked again. "Cindy?"

". . . What is it?" her weary voice asked from the darkness.

Buchanan entered, crossed the murky room, and knelt beside the bed, able to see her shadowy contour under the sheets but not her face. "I missed you at supper."

"Tired," she whispered. "The casserole . . .?"

"Was excellent. You didn't need to use up your energy making it. Jack and I could have eaten takeout."

"Not in *my* home." Cindy managed to emphasize the word despite her fatigue.

"Well," Buchanan said, "I just wanted to let you know I appreciate it and to thank you for everything."

She moved slowly, evidently turning toward him. "You sound as if . . . Are you leaving?"

"I have to."

She tried to sit up but couldn't. "I hope not because of me."

"What would make you think that?"

"Because people feel self-conscious about me being sick. It's hard to be around . . ."

"I don't feel that way," Buchanan said. "It's just that I have things to do. It's time for me to move on and do them."

She didn't reply.

"Cindy?"

"I sort of hoped you'd stay so you could be company for Jack." She inhaled in a way that made Buchanan suspect she was crying. "Seems like most of the time I'm either in the hospital or here in bed. I'm not afraid for me, but I feel so sorry for Jack."

"He loves you very much."

"Sure."

"He told me that several times. He told me how proud he was of you, the way you put up with being married to him when he was in the service and how you stonewalled those reporters."

She chuckled slightly, then sniffled. "Yeah, I was tough. The good times. Except Jack was gone so much then, and now that we're together . . ."

"Right. You just said it. You're together. And you don't need me around to make a crowd. In a few minutes, I'll be on my way."

"Take my car."

Buchanan cocked his head in surprise.

"I get the feeling you'll be needing it." She touched his hand. "*I* sure won't. I haven't driven it since before I was in the hospital this last time. Take it. Please."

"I'll get it back to you when I'm settled."

"There isn't any rush, believe me."

"Cindy?"

"Yes?"

"I'm sorry."

"Yeah. Me, too."

Buchanan leaned down and kissed her gently on the cheek, his lips salty from her tears. "Take care."

"I always tried to. Didn't do me any good, though. *You* take care."

"I'll have to." He stood from beside the bed. "Maybe sometime I'll be back this way."

She didn't respond.

"I'd better let you get some sleep." Buchanan touched her cheek, then backed from the room and closed the door.

14

Doyle sat, playing solitaire at the kitchen table. He didn't look up when Buchanan entered the room. "I overheard."

"And?"

"Thanks. Friends mean a lot. These days, she doesn't have too many. Most of them ran when they found out how sick she was. They didn't know enough to say what you just did to Cindy."

"What was that?"

" 'I'm sorry.' " Doyle looked up from the cards. "Cindy's right. I think it's a good idea to take her car instead of my van. Less conspicuous. When you're done with it, just let me know where to pick it up. And this is another good idea." Doyle reached under the table, where there must have been a bracket—because when his hand reappeared, it held a Beretta 9-mm pistol.

Buchanan glanced toward the windows. The blinds were pulled, so no one outside could see the weapon. But he was still wary of possible hidden microphones. Instead of talking, he shook his head in refusal.

Doyle mouthed, WHY NOT?

Buchanan picked up a notepad on the counter and wrote: WHAT IF I HAD TO DUMP IT?

Doyle took the pen and wrote on the notepad: I TOOK IT FROM A DEAD SOLDIER IN PANAMA. IT CAN'T BE LINKED TO ME.

Buchanan studied Doyle, then nodded. He removed the magazine to make sure it was loaded, reinserted the magazine, worked the slide back and forth to chamber a round, lowered the hammer, then stuck the weapon beneath his belt, at his spine, and covered it by putting on a dark brown nylon windbreaker that he'd borrowed from Doyle.

Doyle assessed the effect. "Fits you perfect."

Buchanan glanced toward the clock on the stove: 8:25. Bailey was due to call in five minutes. Doyle shrugged as if to say, Be patient. Self-conscious because the kitchen might be bugged, neither man spoke. Doyle ripped up the sheet of paper, burned the pieces in a saucer, and washed the ashes down the sink, more for something to do, it seemed, than for the sake of destroying an incriminating object. Then he returned to his game of solitaire, appearing to understand that Buchanan needed to focus his mind and not clutter it with small talk.

Eight-thirty. Buchanan kept staring toward the phone. Five minutes passed. Then ten. His head began to throb. At last, at quarter to nine, the phone rang.

Buchanan grabbed it before the noise could wake Cindy.

"There's a minimall near you on Pine Island Road. A couple of blocks from Sunrise Boulevard," Bailey's crusty voice said.

"I know the place. I've driven past it."

"Go over to the pizza joint. Stand to the right of the entrance. Be there at nine. Come alone."

Before Buchanan could acknowledge the message, Bailey hung up.

Buchanan frowned and turned to Doyle. "Got to run an errand."

"The keys to the car are in that drawer."

"Thanks." Buchanan shook his hand.

That was all the sentiment Buchanan could allow. He took the keys, lifted his suitcase, grabbed a small red picnic cooler off the counter, and nodded as Doyle opened the door for him.

Ninety seconds later, he was driving away.

15

The small red picnic cooler contained an apple and two bologna sandwiches on a white plastic tray. A lower tray contained ice cubes. Beneath that tray was a hundred thousand dollars in hundred-dollar bills. In the dark, driving, Buchanan glanced toward the cooler on the seat beside him. Then he checked for headlights in his rearview mirror to see if he was being followed.

He'd received the cooler and the money in it that afternoon while he was parked at a stoplight on his way back to Doyle's. The money was in response to a call that he'd made from a pay phone immediately after returning from his conversation with Bailey. The colonel had told Buchanan to wait at the Bon Voyage office until three o'clock and, when he drove away, to leave his passenger window open. At the stoplight, a motorcyclist had paused, pushed the cooler through the open window, and driven on.

Now, his pulse quickening, Buchanan parked at the crowded minimall on Pine Island Road. Beneath hissing sodium lights, he carried the picnic cooler to the pizza shop and stood to the right of the entrance. Customers went in and out. A delivery boy drove hurriedly away. Scanning the night, Buchanan waited. This time, Bailey made contact exactly when he'd said he would.

"Is your name Grant?" a voice asked.

Buchanan turned toward the open door to the pizza shop, seeing a gangly, pimply-faced young man wearing a white apron streaked with sauce.

"That's right."

"A guy just called inside. Said he was a friend of yours. Said you'd give me five bucks if I relayed a message."

"My friend was right." Buchanan gave the kid the five dollars. "What's the message?"

"He said you're supposed to meet him in twenty minutes in the lobby of the Tower Hotel."

Buchanan squinted. "The Tower Hotel? Where's that?"

"The east end of Broward Boulevard. Near Victoria Park Road."

Buchanan nodded and walked quickly toward his car, realizing what was ahead of him. Bailey—afraid that he'd be in danger when he showed himself to get the money—intended to shunt Buchanan to various places throughout the city, carefully watching each potential meeting site for any indication that Buchanan had not come alone.

Bailey's instincts were good, Buchanan thought as he checked a map in his car and steered from the minimall, heading toward his next destination. The truth was, Buchanan did have a team keeping track of him. Their mission was to follow

Bailey after the money was handed over and to try to find where he was keeping the videotape, the photographs, and the negatives, especially the ones depicting Buchanan on the yacht with the colonel, the major, and the captain. The colonel had been very emphatic about that point when he'd hastily returned Buchanan's phone call. The images of Buchanan with the colonel had to be destroyed.

As Buchanan headed east on Broward Boulevard, he again glanced in his rearview mirror to see if he was being followed. He looked for Bailey, not the team that was keeping track of him, for there was no way he could spot the team, he knew. They had a way to follow him and later Bailey that permitted them to stay far back, out of visual contact, and that method was the reason Bailey's protective tactic, no matter how shrewd, wouldn't work. Bailey would never see the team at any of the potential rendezvous sites. He could never possibly detect the team as they followed him after he received the money. No matter what evasion procedures he attempted, he would not be able to elude them.

Because they didn't need to keep him in sight. All they had to do was study an audiovisual monitor and follow the homing signals they received from a battery-powered location transmitter concealed within the plastic bottom of the small picnic cooler that contained the money.

Friday-night traffic was dense. Amid gleaming headlights, Buchanan reached the glass-and-steel Tower Hotel two minutes ahead of schedule. Telling the parking attendant that he would probably need the car right away, he darted inside the plush lobby and found his jeans, nylon jacket, and picnic cooler being sternly assessed by a group of men and women wearing tuxedos and glittering evening gowns. Sure, Buchanan thought. There's a reception going on. Bailey found out and took advantage of it. He wants me and especially anyone following me to be conspicuous.

Used to being *in*conspicuous, Buchanan felt self-conscious as he waited in the lobby. He looked for Bailey among the guests, not expecting to find him, wondering how Bailey would contact him this time. The clock behind the check-in counter showed twenty after nine, exactly when Buchanan was supposed to . . .

"Mr. Grant?" a uniformed bellhop asked.

Buchanan had noticed the short middle-aged man moving from guest to guest in the lobby, speaking softly to each. "That's right."

"A friend of yours left this envelope for you."

Finding a deserted corner, Buchanan ripped it open.

At quarter to ten, be at the entrance to Shirttail Charlie's restaurant on . . .

16

Three stops later, at eleven o'clock, Buchanan arrived at the Riverside Hotel on Las Olas, a street that seemed the local equivalent of Beverly Hills' Rodeo Drive. From information in the terra-cotta-floored lobby, he learned that the hotel had been built in 1936, a date that was very old by Fort Lauderdale standards. A few decades before, this area had been wilderness. The wicker furniture and coral fireplaces exuded a sense of history, no matter how recent.

Buchanan had a chance to learn these facts and notice these details because Bailey didn't contact him on schedule. By twenty after eleven, Bailey still hadn't been in touch. The lobby was deserted.

"Mr. Grant?"

Buchanan looked up from where he sat on a rattan chair near glass patio doors, a location he'd chosen because it allowed him to be observed from outside. A woman behind the small reception counter was speaking to him, her eyebrows raised.

"Yes."

"I have a phone call for you."

Buchanan carried the picnic cooler to the counter and took the phone from the receptionist.

"Go out the rear door, cross the street, and walk through the gate, then past the swimming pool." Bailey's curt instructions were followed by the sudden hum of the dial tone.

Buchanan handed the telephone back to the receptionist, thanked her, and used the rear exit. Outside, he saw the gate across the street and a walkway through a small murky park beside the swimming pool, although the swimming pool itself was deserted, its lights off.

Moving closer, enveloped by the shadows of palm trees, he expected Bailey's voice to drift from the darkness, to give him instructions to leave the money on a barely visible poolside table and continue to stroll as if he hadn't been contacted.

The only lights were ahead, from occasional arc lamps along the canal, as well as from a cabin cruiser and a houseboat moored there. He heard an engine rumbling. Then he heard a man call, "Mr. Grant? Is that you over there, Mr. Grant?"

Buchanan continued forward, away from the swimming pool, toward the canal. He immediately realized that the rumbling engine belonged to a water taxi that was temporarily docked, bow-first, between the cabin cruiser and the houseboat. The water taxi was yellow, twenty feet long, with poles along the gunwales supporting a yellow-and-green-striped canvas roof. In daylight, the roof would shade passengers from the glare and heat of the sun. But at night, it shut out the little illumination that the arc lamps along the canal provided and prevented Buchanan from seeing who was in there.

Certainly there were passengers. At least fifteen. Their shadowy outlines were evident. But Buchanan had no way to identify them. The canvas roof muffled what they said to one another, although their slurred rhythms made him suspect they were on a Friday-night round of parties and bars.

"That's right. My name is Grant," Buchanan said to the driver, who sat at controls in front of the passengers.

"Well, your friend's already aboard. I wondered if you were going to show up. I was just about to leave."

Buchanan strained to see through the darkness beneath the water taxi's roof, then stepped onto the gangplank that extended from the canal to the bow. With his right hand, he gripped a rope railing for balance while he held the picnic cooler in his left and climbed down a few steps into the taxi. Passengers in their early twenties, dressed casually but expensively for an evening out, sat on benches along each side.

The stern remained shrouded by darkness.

"How much do I owe you?" Buchanan asked the driver.

"Your friend already paid for you."

"How generous."

"Back here, Vic," a crusty voice called from the gloomy stern.

As the driver retracted the gangplank, Buchanan made his way past a group of young men on his left and stopped at the stern, his eyes now sufficiently adjusted to the darkness to see Bailey slouched on a bench.

Bailey waved a beefy hand. "How ya doin', buddy?"

Buchanan sat and placed the picnic cooler between them.

"You didn't need to bring your lunch," Bailey said.

Buchanan just stared at him as the driver backed the water taxi from between the cabin cruiser and the houseboat, then increased speed along the canal. Slick, Buchanan thought. I'm separated from my backup team. They couldn't have gotten to the water taxi in time, and certainly they couldn't have hurried on board without making Bailey suspicious.

Now that Buchanan's eyes had become even more accustomed to the darkness, the glow from condominiums, restaurants, and boats along the canal seemed to increase in brightness. But Buchanan was interested in the spectacle only because the illumination allowed him to see the cellular telephone that Bailey folded and placed in a pouch attached to his belt.

"Handy things," Bailey said. "You can call anybody from anywhere."

"Like from a car to a pizza parlor. Or from a water taxi to a hotel lobby."

"You got it," Bailey said. "Makes it easy to keep in touch while I'm on the go or hangin' around to see if extra company's comin'." Bailey lowered his voice and gestured toward the cooler. "No joke. That better not be your lunch, and it better all be here."

The other passengers on the boat were talking loudly, obscuring what Bailey and Buchanan said.

"There's no more where that came from," Buchanan murmured.

Bailey raised his bulky shoulders. "Hey, I'm not greedy. All I need is a little help with my expenses, a little reward for my trouble."

"I went through a lot of effort to get what's in this cooler," Buchanan said. "I won't go through it again."

"I don't expect you to."

"That definitely eases my mind."

The water taxi arrived at a restaurant/tavern, where a sign on the dock read, PAUL'S-ON-THE-RIVER. The stylish building was long and low, its rear section almost completely glass, separated by segments of white stucco. Inside, a band played. Beyond the large windows, customers danced. Others strolled outside, carrying drinks, or sat at tables amid flowering bushes near palm trees.

The taxi's driver set down the gangplank. Four passengers got up unsteadily to go ashore.

At once Bailey stood and clutched the picnic cooler. "This is where we part company, Crawford. Almost forgot, I mean, Grant. Why don't you stay aboard, see the sights, enjoy the ride?"

"Why not?" Buchanan said.

Bailey looked very pleased with himself. "Be seein' you."

"No. You won't."

"Right," Bailey said and carried the picnic cooler off the water taxi onto the dock. He strolled across the colorfully illuminated lawn toward the music, "Moon River," and disappeared among the crowd.

17

Thirty minutes later, the water taxi brought Buchanan back to the Riverside Hotel. He wouldn't have returned there except that he needed to retrieve his suitcase from the trunk of Cindy's car. The car was parked on a quiet street next to the hotel, and after Buchanan placed the keys beneath the driver's floor mat, he carried his suitcase into the hotel, where he phoned for a taxi. When it arrived, he instructed the driver to take him to an all-night car-rental agency. As it happened, the only one that was open was at the Fort Lauderdale airport, and after Buchanan rented a car, he drove to a pay phone to contact

Doyle and tell him where to find Cindy's car. Next, he bought a twelve-pack of beer at a convenience store, drove to a shadowy, deserted street, poured every can of beer over the front seat and floor of the car, then tossed the empty cans onto the floor and drove away, keeping all the windows open lest he get sick from the odor of the beer.

By then, it was quarter after one in the morning. He headed toward the ocean, found a deserted park next to the Intra-coastal Waterway, and smashed the car through a protective barrier, making sure he left skid marks, as if the car had been out of control. He stopped the car, got out, put the automatic gearshift into drive, and pushed the car over the seawall into the water. Even as he heard it splash, he was hurrying away to disappear into the darkness. He'd left his suitcase in the car, along with his wallet in the nylon jacket he'd borrowed from Doyle. He'd kept his passport, though. He didn't want anyone to do a background check on that. When the police investigated the "accident" and hoisted the car from the water, they'd find the beer cans. The logical conclusion would be that the driver—Victor Grant, according to the ID in the wallet and the car-rental agreement in the glove compartment—had been driving while under the influence, had crashed through the barricade, and helpless because of alcohol, had drowned. When the police didn't find the body, divers and trollers would search, give up, and decide that the corpse would surface in a couple of days. When it didn't, they'd conclude that the remains had been wedged beneath a dock or had been carried by the tide out to sea. More important, Buchanan hoped that Bailey would believe the same thing. Under stress from being blackmailed, fearful that Bailey would keep coming back for more and more money, Crawford-Potter-Grant had rented a car to flee the area, had gotten drunk in the process, had lost control of the vehicle, and . . .

Maybe, Buchanan thought. It just might work. Those had been the colonel's instructions at any rate—to make Victor Grant disappear. Buchanan hadn't told Doyle and Cindy what he intended to do because he wanted them to be genuinely surprised if the police questioned them. The disappearance would break the link between Buchanan and Bailey. It would also break the link between Buchanan and what had happened in Mexico. If the Mexican authorities decided to reinvestigate Victor Grant and asked for the cooperation of the American authorities, there'd be no one to investigate.

All problems solved, Buchanan thought as he hurried from the shadowy park, then slowed his pace as he walked along a dark side street. He'd find a place to hide until morning, buy a razor, clean up in a public rest room, take a bus twenty-five miles south to Miami, use cash to buy an Amtrak ticket, and become an anonymous passenger on the train north to Washington. Now you see me, now you don't. Definitely time for a new beginning.

The only troubling detail, Buchanan thought, was how the colonel could be sure that he got his hands on all the photographs and the negatives. What if Bailey went into the first men's room he could find, locked a stall, removed the money from the cooler, and left the cooler next to the waste bin? In that case, the surveillance team wouldn't be able to trail Bailey to where he was staying and where presumably he kept the photos. Another troubling detail was the woman, the redhead who'd taken photographs of Buchanan outside the Mexican prison while he talked with the man from the American embassy, the same woman who'd also taken photographs of Buchanan with the colonel on the yacht and later with Bailey on the waterway. What if Bailey had already paid her off and never went near her again? The surveillance team couldn't find her.

So what? Buchanan decided as he walked quickly through the secluded, exclusive neighborhood, prepared to duck behind any of the numerous flowering shrubs if he saw headlights approaching. So what if Bailey did pay the woman and never went near her again? He'd have made sure he got the pictures and the negatives first. He wouldn't have confided in her. So it won't matter if the surveillance team can't locate her. It won't even matter if Bailey ditches the cooler and the surveillance team can't find the photographs and the negatives. After all, the pictures are useless to Bailey if the man he's blackmailing is dead.

18

EXPLOSION KILLS THREE

FT. LAUDERDALE—A powerful explosion shortly before midnight last night destroyed a car in the parking lot of Paul's-on-the-River restaurant, killing its occupant, identified by a remnant of his driver's license as Robert Bailey, 48, a native of Oklahoma. The explosion also killed two customers leaving the restaurant. Numerous other cars were destroyed or damaged. Charred fragments of a substantial amount of money found at the scene have prompted authorities to theorize that the explosion may have been the consequence of a recent escalating war among drug smugglers.

19

MURDER-SUICIDE

FT. LAUDERDALE—Responding to a telephone call from a frightened neighbor, police early this morning investigated gunshots at 233 Glade Street in Plantation and discovered the bodies of Jack Doyle (34) and his wife, Cindy (30), both dead from bullet wounds. It is believed that Mr. Doyle, despondent about his wife's cancer, shot her with a .38-caliber snub-nosed revolver while she slept in their bedroom, then used the same weapon on himself.

20

THE YUCATÁN PENINSULA

Struggling to concentrate amid the din of bulldozers, trucks, Jeeps, chain saws, generators, and shouting construction workers, Jenna Lane drew another line on the surveyor's map she was preparing. The map was spread out, anchored by books, on a trestle table in a twenty-by-ten-foot tent that was her office. Sweat trickled down her face and hung on the tip of her chin as she intensified her concentration and made a note beside the line she'd drawn on the map.

A shadow appeared at the open entrance to her tent. Glancing up, she saw McIntyre, the foreman of the project, silhouetted by dust raised by a passing bulldozer. He removed his Stetson, swabbed a checkered handkerchief across his sunburned, dirty, sweaty brow, and raised his voice to be heard above the racket outside. "He's coming."

Jenna frowned and glanced at her watch, the metal band of which was embedded with grit. "Already? It's only ten o'clock. He's not supposed to be here until—"

"I told you, he's coming."

Jenna set down her pencil and walked to the front of her tent, where she squinted in the direction that McIntyre pointed, east, toward the sun-fierce cobalt sky and a growing speck above the jungle. Although she couldn't hear it because of the rumble of construction equipment, she imagined the helicopter's distant drone, its gradual increase to a roar, and then as the chopper's features became distinct, she did hear it setting down on the landing pad near camp, the churning rotors adding their own distinctive, rapid *whump-whump-whump*.

Dust rose—shallow soil that had been exposed when that section of forest was cut down, stumps blasted away or uprooted by bulldozers. Drivers and construction workers momentarily stopped what they were doing and stared toward the landing pad. This wasn't one of the massive, ugly industrial helicopters that the crew had been using to lift in the vehicles and construction equipment. Rather, this was a small, sleek passenger helicopter, the kind that movie stars and sports celebrities liked to be seen in, or in this case one that could be anchored on top of a yacht and was owned by one of the richest businessmen in the world. Even from a distance, the red logo on the side of the helicopter was evident: DRUMMOND INDUSTRIES. The force of the name was such that the sight of it compelled the workmen back to their tasks, as if they feared

Drummond's anger should he think that they weren't working hard enough.

But not the guards, Jenna noticed. Constantly patrolling with their rifles, they hadn't paid attention to the helicopter. Professionals, they kept their attention riveted on the surrounding forest.

"We'd better not keep him waiting," McIntyre said.

"He doesn't wait," Jenna said. "Hell, look at him. He's already out of the chopper. He'll beat us to the main office. I hear he swims two miles every morning."

"Yeah, the old bastard's probably got more energy than both of us," McIntyre grumbled as Jenna rolled up the surveyor's map and tucked it under her arm.

They walked quickly toward the most substantial structure in camp. A one-story wooden building made from logs, it contained essential supplies—food, fuel, ammunition, dynamite—items that needed to be protected from the weather or scavenging animals, and especially from humans. The building also contained an administrative center, where McIntyre stored the project's records, kept in radio contact with his employer, and conducted daily meetings with his various subforemen.

Jenna had been right. As she and McIntyre approached the building, she saw Alistair Drummond reach it before them. His exact age wasn't known, but he was rumored to be in his early eighties, although except for his severely wrinkled hands he looked twenty years younger, his facial skin unnaturally tight from cosmetic surgery.

In fact, rumors were the essence of Drummond's notoriety. How much wealth had he amassed? How great was his influence with the premier of the People's Republic of China? What had been his part in the 1973 Arab oil embargo? What had been his part in the Iran-Contra arms scandal? In his middle years, had he really been sexually involved with Ingrid Bergman, Marlene Dietrich, and Marilyn Monroe? Much more recently, what was his relationship with his frequent companion, the great opera diva Maria Tomez? Divorced six times, spending more days each year on his jet than he did at the estates he owned in eleven nations, devoting the pharmaceutical portion of his financial empire to AIDS research, able to boast of a first-name friendship with every Russian, British, and American leader since the 1940s, Alistair Drummond exhibited a combination of outrageous success and shameless self-promotion that gave him a larger-than-life stature in an arena of world-renowned figures. The rumors and riddles about him made him a blend of contradictions, capable of being interpreted in various ways. His commitment to AIDS research, for example. Was that for humanitarian reasons or for the opportunity to earn boundless profits? Both? He was a powerful enigma, and for that reason, anyone who'd ever met him never forgot the experience, regardless if the meeting had demonstrated his calculated charm or ruthless manipulation.

Certainly *I* won't forget him, Jenna thought, and I sure as hell won't forget this job. When she'd been interviewed for the project, Drummond had assessed her honey-colored hair, her high, firm breasts, her trim, equally firm hips, and with his raspy voice that caused her nerves to quiver, he had made his employment offer sound like a sexual proposition. Perhaps it *had* been a sexual proposition; perhaps Drummond considered all the people who worked for him to be the same as prostitutes. But high-class prostitutes, Jenna thought. While Drummond was without a doubt the coldest, meanest bastard she'd ever known, he was also the most generous. Her salary for this project was the equivalent of her last ten projects combined. Deservedly. For this assignment was obscene, and if she was going to sell her professional soul, she didn't intend to do it cheaply.

As she and McIntyre entered the dirt-floored office, Jenna's gaze immediately gravitated toward Drummond, who was already surrounded by a group of crew leaders, blurting questions to them and snapping orders. He took charge so rapidly that even with his blended-wool, blue-striped English-made suit in contrast with the sweat-stained, dirt-encrusted, rumpled work clothes of the crew leaders, he seemed perfectly in place, in his element. By contrast, the fair-haired, well-dressed man standing next to Drummond appeared aloof, not at all comfortable in these primitive conditions. His name was Raymond, and the cold expression in his eyes warned Jenna not to believe that his pleasant features were an indication of his personality. She suspected that Raymond was truly in his element only when he was causing pain.

Dear God, what have I gotten myself into?

"No," Drummond told a supervisor, his voice brittle but forceful. "*No*. You understood the rules before you agreed to be hired. You signed a document binding you to certain conditions. Under no circumstances are you or any member of your crew permitted to leave camp until all the work is completed. I'm paying everyone handsomely to work seven days a week, and I expect to receive maximum value for my money. Bring women in? Nonsense. No outsiders are allowed in camp. Permission to use the two-way radio for private communications? Absolutely not. What happens down here is *my* business, and I don't want your men telling *my* business to outsiders. You know how I feel about privacy. In every way possible, this camp is sealed. Don't raise this subject again."

Drummond turned dismissively from the group and noticed Jenna and McIntyre just inside the open door. "Good, I want to see both of you." He motioned for Raymond to take the supervisors outside, then gestured for Jenna and McIntyre to approach. "Have you found it?"

Jenna and McIntyre looked away.

"I don't know why I bothered asking," Drummond said. "If you *had* found it, those idiots would have been jabbering hysterically about it. They wouldn't have been able to restrain themselves. Which means they still don't suspect," Drummond said. "Is that true?"

McIntyre cleared his throat. "Yes. That's true."

Having taken the supervisors outside, Raymond reentered the building, shut the door, and leaned against it, crossing his arms, coldly assessing Jenna. She felt his arrogant gaze upon her.

"I'm not pleased, not pleased at all," Drummond said. "I gave you all the necessary information. The job shouldn't be that difficult. You practically have step-by-step instructions. But you still haven't found it."

McIntyre mumbled something.

"What?" Drummond glared. "Damn it, man, speak up. Muttering won't trick me into thinking my ears are failing me."

"I didn't mean to . . . ."

"Don't apologize. I hate a whimperer. Maybe that's why

you haven't achieved your objective. Because you're not man enough to direct the job.''

"The instructions weren't as specific as you claim," Jenna interrupted.

"Oh?" The old man swung toward her. "At least *you* don't mutter. But I don't recall asking you for a comment."

"If I need to be asked, that would mean I'm not a very good employee, wouldn't you agree?"

"An excellent answer." Drummond studied her. "Continue."

"A vague and possibly flawed translation isn't what I'd call step-by-step instructions."

Drummond bristled. "The translation wasn't flawed. The best experts for the maximum price were hired to decipher the text."

"But even the experts don't understand all the Mayan symbols."

"And you yourself are expert enough to know that?"

"Perhaps you've forgotten."

"I forget *nothing*."

"I'm not only a surveyor," Jenna said. "I'm an *archaeological* surveyor. My expertise is mapping sites like this one, and I may not be able to translate Mayan symbols, but I know several people who can, and they're the first to admit that there's a great deal more to be accomplished in their specialty."

"Perhaps. Or perhaps you're trying to justify a poor performance. Perhaps I should hire someone else and deduct that person's fee from yours."

Panic muted Jenna's anger. Stop. Keep your opinions to yourself. Don't antagonize him.

"Work harder," Drummond said. "Quit making excuses. The translation is as perfect as it can be. And it's explicit. What we're looking for is here. But why can't you find it?"

"Topography doesn't have much variation in the Yucatán," Jenna said. "The site described in the text could be anywhere. Plus, the geology in this area isn't stable. In the thousand years since the landscape was described, earthquakes could have obliterated some of the features we're searching for."

Drummond scowled and returned his attention to McIntyre. "I don't have time for delays. The jungle has to be cleared, but your men haven't accomplished anywhere near as much as they were supposed to by now. You haven't kept up with the schedule.''

"The schedule didn't allow for sabotage," McIntyre said.

Drummond jerked his head back. "Sabotage?"

"Someone's been tampering with the bulldozers and the trucks. Dirt in the fuel tanks. Radiator hoses cut. Tires slashed.''

Drummond became livid. "*Why wasn't I told?*"

"We thought we could handle the problem without troubling you. We fixed the vehicles and posted guards around them,'' McIntyre said.

"*And?*"

"Posting guards around the vehicles meant we had to lessen the number of men watching the perimeter of the camp. The next night, a lot of our tools were stolen. Our water supply was contaminated. Our fuel-storage barrels were punctured. That's why we've got barrels stored in here. As an emergency backup. The helicopters have been working double time bringing in spare parts and replacement supplies instead of new equipment.''

"Replacing supplies isn't the answer!'' Drummond snapped. "Find whoever's causing the damage. What about those supervisors who were in here complaining? Could it be someone who wants to shut down work so he can spend a weekend getting drunk in Mérida?''

"We thought of that,'' McIntyre said. "No. The men are tired and grumpy, but they're also eager to finish the job ahead of schedule so they can get their bonus. None of them would do anything to force them to spend more time here.''

"Then who?''

"Natives,'' Jenna said. "Maya.''

Drummond looked astonished. "You're telling me a handful of ignorant Indians are capable of outthinking you and paralyzing the project?''

"There might be more of them than you think. And as for being ignorant, this is *their* backyard, not ours. They know this territory a lot better than we do.''

"Excuses.''

"I'm sure they're watching our every move from the jungle," Jenna said, "and I strongly suspect that this site has religious importance to them, that they're furious about what we're doing here."

"Superstition and nonsense. I'm amazed that you've let it interfere with the project." Drummond scowled. "But you've given me an idea. You're right. This *is* their backyard." He turned to the fair-haired, pleasant-faced, well-dressed man who leaned against the closed door. "Raymond, how would you like to go hunting?"

"I'd like that very much, Mr. Drummond."

"The captain of the guards will see that you're outfitted properly." Drummond turned to Jenna. "Where do these natives live? Have you got their village marked on the map you're preparing?"

"Village?" Jenna said. "I've had problems enough mapping the site. We're surrounded by rain forest. There aren't any trails. You don't just go wandering around out there. You'll get lost or worse. Village? We haven't seen even one native, let alone a *village*."

"And yet you're certain they're responsible?" Drummond turned to his assistant. "Raymond, find them. Stop them."

"Yes, sir." Raymond opened the door.

"But Raymond . . ."

"Yes, sir?"

"Since this is their backyard, since they know it thoroughly, I want one native able to talk. Bring him to camp for questioning. Maybe he'll know where to find what we're looking for."

As Raymond left the building, a man in a blue pilot's uniform appeared. He had a red logo—DRUMMOND INDUSTRIES—on his jacket pocket.

"Sir, there's a call for you on the helicopter radio." He was slightly out of breath.

"Have it transferred to here. McIntyre, what frequency have you been using?"

McIntyre told the pilot, who hurried away.

Drummond gestured toward the map that Jenna had braced beneath her left arm. "Let me see what you've accomplished."

Jenna spread the map across a table.

"No, no, no," Drummond said.

"What's wrong? I was thorough. I double-checked every—"

"That's exactly the problem. You were thorough. I told you specifically. I wanted a map that would look convincing to the Mexican authorities." Drummond led her out the door, gesturing toward the commotion of the site, workers clearing trees and stacking equipment.

Assaulted by harsh sunlight after the shadows of the room, Jenna shielded her eyes and directed her attention toward where Drummond pointed. As more and more trees were cut down and dragged away to be burned, as more bushes were plowed free, as what seemed to be hills became ever more distinctly pyramids, temples, and palaces, the legacy of the once-great Mayan empire, her heart pounded.

"Too much depends on this," Drummond said. "Your map can't—"

He was suddenly interrupted by a crackly, static-ridden voice on the radio.

"That's your call coming through," McIntyre said.

"Is the scrambler functioning?"

McIntyre nodded. "Just flick the switch."

"Stay here. I won't be long."

After Drummond entered the building and shut the door, leaving Jenna and McIntyre outside, Jenna shook her head, frustrated, puzzled, angry. "That son of a bitch."

"Keep your voice down," McIntyre said. "He might hear you."

McIntyre was right, Jenna realized. Even with the noise from the vehicles and the workers, she was close enough to the door that her voice might carry.

But by that same logic . . .

The door fit the crude frame loosely. It had inched open after Drummond closed it. Jenna heard occasional raspy outbursts.

". . . *Find the woman. If Delgado learns she isn't cooperating . . . ruined. Everything. Find her. Use every pressure. I don't care what you have to . . . Kill him if . . .*"

Then Jenna couldn't hear Drummond anymore, and at once she stepped farther from the door, joining McIntyre, feeling sick but trying to seem as if she was a good employee waiting patiently.

Drummond jerked the door open and stalked outside. A black pall appeared to surround him despite the sunlight that gleamed off his thick white hair and his glasses. He was about to continue verbally assaulting Jenna when he noticed something to the left and looked briefly heartened.

Following his gaze, Jenna saw Raymond wearing outdoor clothes, carrying a rifle, entering the jungle. Even at a distance, his excitement was evident.

Then Drummond's brittle, forceful voice jerked her attention back to him.

"All of this," he demanded, gesturing. "You've been far too faithful on your map, far too diligent. The Mexican authorities can't be allowed to realize how massive and important a find this is. Your map has to make it seem minor, an insignificant site that doesn't merit undue attention, something that won't be an irreplaceable loss." Drummond pointed toward the majestic temples, the hieroglyph-engraved palaces, and the great terraced pyramid where gigantic snake heads guarded the bottom of the wide, high stairs that went up each side. "Because ten days from now, I expect all of that to be leveled. Do you hear me, McIntyre?" He glared at the foreman. "You knew the orders. You understood the schedule. Use bulldozers. Use sledgehammers. Use dynamite. If you have to, use your fingernails. Ten days from now, I expect my equipment to be set up and all of this to be gone. Level it. Scatter the rubble. Truck it out. Dump it in sinkholes. Have the helicopters lift it out. I don't care how you do it. I want it gone!"

SIX

1

ALEXANDRIA, VIRGINIA

The safe site was on the third floor, yet another apartment in yet another sprawling complex into which Buchanan could easily blend. After he'd arrived in Washington from Florida, he'd used a pay phone to report to his controller, just as he'd reported at various stops along the Amtrak route. A man's voice told him to be waiting, seated, on the steps outside the Library of Congress at 3:00 P.M. Precisely at that time, a middle-aged man wearing a blue blazer and gray slacks stopped beside him and bent down to tie his right shoe. When the man departed, Buchanan concealed the small envelope that the man had slid toward him. After waiting five minutes longer, Buchanan then went into the Library of Congress, entered a men's room, and locked himself in a stall, where he opened the envelope, took out a key, and read a slip of paper that provided him with a name, some biographical information, an Alexandria address, and an apartment number. The paper and the envelope were far from ordinary. He dropped them into the water in the toilet and watched them dissolve. In the library's reference section, he used an area directory to tell him which major streets were near the Alexandria apartment, and shortly before six that evening, he got out of a taxi a few blocks from his destination, walking the rest of the way, out of habit using evasion procedures in case he was being followed.

His name was now Don Colton, he'd been informed. He was supposed to be a writer for a travel magazine that he assumed was affiliated with his controllers. Posing as a travel writer was an excellent cover, Buchanan thought, inasmuch as a travel writer by definition was on the move a great deal and hence the neighbors wouldn't consider it unusual that they never saw him. However, because Buchanan's controllers would not have had sufficient time to tailor the cover specifically to him, he automatically assumed that this identity would be temporary, an all-purpose, one-size-fits-all persona that his controllers maintained for emergencies. As Don Colton, Buchanan was in a holding pattern and would soon be sent to God-knew-where as God-knew-who.

Avoiding the elevator, he used fire stairs to get to the third floor. After all, because most people preferred elevators, there was less chance of encountering anybody on the stairs. He reached a concrete corridor with fluorescent lights along the ceiling. As he had hoped, no one was in view, the tenants having already arrived home from work. Doors to apartments flanked each side. As he walked along green heavy-duty carpeting, he heard music behind one door, voices behind another. Then he came to 327, used the key he'd been given, and entered the apartment.

He turned on the lights, scanned the combination living room–kitchen, locked the door, checked the closets, the bathroom, and the bedroom, all the while avoiding the windows, then turned off the lights, closed the draperies, and finally turned the lights back on, only then slumping on the sofa. He was safe. For now.

2

The apartment had a hotel-room feel to it, everything clean but utilitarian and impersonal. A corner of the living room had been converted into a minioffice with a desk, a word processor, a printer, and a modem. Several copies of the magazine he was supposed to work for were stacked on the coffee table, and when Buchanan examined their contents, he found articles under his pseudonym, another indication that Don Colton was an all-purpose identity. Obviously, the magazines had been prepared well in advance, not just for him but for any operative who happened to need this type of cover. Don Colton—at least *this* Don Colton—wouldn't be in the neighborhood very long.

Nonetheless, Buchanan still had to make his portrayal of Colton believable, and the first step was to familiarize himself with the articles he was supposed to have written. But halfway through the second essay—about Tahiti—he suddenly discovered that two hours had passed. He frowned. It shouldn't have taken him that long to read just a few pages. Had he fallen asleep? His headache—which had never gone away since he'd banged his skull in Cancún—worsened, and he surprised himself by no longer caring about his persona as a travel writer. Weary, he stood, went into the kitchen, which was separated from the living room by only a counter, and poured himself a drink from a bottle of bourbon that was next to the refrigerator along with bottles of gin and rum. After adding ice and water, he debated which to do first—to shower or to open one of the cans of chili he found in a cupboard. Tomorrow, he'd have to decide what to do about clean clothes. The ones he'd found in the bedroom closet were too small for him. But he couldn't leave the apartment without establishing a procedure with his employers so they'd know how to get in touch with him, and that was when the phone rang.

It startled him.

He pivoted toward the living room, staring toward the phone on a table next to the sofa. The phone rang a second time. He sipped from his bourbon, letting his nerves calm. The phone rang a third time. He *hated* phones. Squinting, he entered the living room and picked up the phone before it could ring a fourth time.

"Hello." He tried to make his voice sound neutral.

"Don!" an exuberant male voice exclaimed. "It's Alan! I wasn't sure you'd be back yet! How the hell are you?"

"Good," Buchanan said. "Fine."

"The trip went okay?"

"The last part of it."

"Yeah, your postcards mentioned you had a few problems at some earlier stops. Nothing you couldn't handle, though, right?"

"Right," Buchanan echoed.

"That's really swell. Listen, buddy, I know it's getting late, but I haven't seen you in I can't remember when. What do you say? Have you eaten yet? Do you feel like getting together?"

"No," Buchanan said, "I haven't eaten yet."

"Well, why don't I come over?"

"Yeah, why not?"

"Great, Don. Can't wait to see you. I'll be over in fifteen minutes. Think about where you want to eat."

"Someplace that's dark and not too crowded. Maybe with a piano player."

"You're reading my mind, Don, reading my mind."

"Be seeing you." Buchanan set down the phone and massaged his aching temples. The man's reference to postcards and his own reference to a piano player had been the recognition sign and countersign that the note he'd destroyed at the Library of Congress had told him to use if he was contacted. His debriefing would soon begin.

Yet another.

His temples continued to ache. He thought about washing his face but first drank his glass of bourbon.

3

Fifteen minutes later, precisely on schedule, the doorbell rang. Buchanan peered through the door's security eye and saw a fortyish, short-haired, portly man in a brown-checkered sport coat. The voice on the phone had not been familiar, so Buchanan wasn't surprised that he'd never seen this man before, assuming that the voice on the phone belonged to this man. All the same, Buchanan had hoped that one of the controllers he'd dealt with previously would show up. He'd been through too many changes.

He opened the door warily. After all, he couldn't take for granted that the man was his contact. But the man immediately allayed his suspicions by using the same cheery tone that Buchanan had heard earlier. "Don, you look fabulous. In your postcards, you didn't say you'd lost weight."

"My diet didn't agree with me. Come on in, Alan. I've been thinking, maybe we shouldn't go out to eat. I'm not in the mood for a piano player."

"Whatever." The man who'd earlier identified himself as Alan, undoubtedly a pseudonym, carried a metal briefcase into the apartment and waited while Buchanan locked the door. Then the man's demeanor changed, as if he was an actor who'd stepped out of character when he walked off a stage. His manner became businesslike. "The apartment was swept this afternoon. There aren't any bugs. How are you feeling?"

Buchanan shrugged. The truth was, he felt exhausted, but he'd been trained not to indicate weakness.

"Is your wound healing properly?" the man asked.

"The infection's gone."

"Good," the man said flatly. "What about your skull? I'm told you hit it on a—"

"Stupid accident," Buchanan said.

"The report I received mentioned a concussion."

Buchanan nodded.

"And a skull fracture," the man said.

Buchanan nodded again, the movement intensifying his headache. "A *depressed* skull fracture. A small section of bone on the inside was pushed against the brain. That's what caused the concussion. It's not like I've got a crack in the bone. It's not that serious. In Fort Lauderdale, I was kept in the hospital overnight for observation. Then the doctor let me go. He wouldn't have let me go if—"

The portly man who called himself Alan sat on the sofa but never took his gaze from Buchanan. "That's what the report says. The report also says you'll need another checkup, another CAT scan, to find out if the bruise on your brain has shrunk."

"Would I be walking around if my brain was still swollen?"

"I don't know." The man continued to assess Buchanan. "Would you? Agents from Special Operations have a can-do attitude. Problems that would slow someone else down don't seem to bother you."

"No. The mission comes first. If I think an injury impairs my ability to perform the mission, I say so."

"Commendable. And if you thought you needed some time off, you'd say that, too?"

"Of course. Nobody turns down R and R."

The man didn't say anything, just studied him.

To change the subject as much as to relieve his curiosity, Buchanan asked, "What happened in Fort Lauderdale after I left? Was the situation dealt with to everyone's satisfaction? Were the photographs—?"

The man lowered his gaze, worked the combination locks on his briefcase, and opened it. "I wouldn't know anything about that." The man pulled out a folder. "We have some paperwork to take care of."

Uneasy, Buchanan sat across from him. His instincts troubled him. It might have been the consequence of fatigue, or perhaps it was due to the aftermath of stress. For whatever reason, there was something about the man's attitude that made Buchanan uncomfortable.

And it wasn't just that the man was brusque. In his eight years of working deep cover, Buchanan had dealt with controllers of various types, some of whom had a manner that would disqualify them from a popularity contest. But being personable wasn't a requirement for the job. Being thorough was, and sometimes there wasn't time to say things politely, and it wasn't smart to establish a relationship with someone whom the odds were you would never see again.

Buchanan had learned that the hard way over the years. In his numerous assumed identities, he'd occasionally found that he felt close to someone, to Jack and Cindy Doyle, for example. As much as he guarded against that happening, nonetheless it sometimes did, and it made Buchanan feel hollow after he moved on. Thus he could readily understand if this controller didn't want to conduct the debriefing on anything but an objective, unemotional basis.

That wasn't it, though. That wasn't what made Buchanan feel uncomfortable. It was something else, and the best he could do was attribute it to his experience with Bailey, to an instinct that warned him to be extra cautious.

"Here's my signed receipt," the portly man who called himself Alan said. "Now you can give me Victor Grant's ID."

Buchanan made a snap decision then. He didn't trust this man. "I don't have it."

"What?" The man looked up from the receipt.

"I had to abandon the ID in the car when I drove it into the water in Fort Lauderdale . . . so the authorities would have a way to identify the driver after they couldn't find a body . . . so they'd decide Victor Grant was dead."

"Everything? You left *everything?*"

"Driver's license. Credit card. Social Security card. The works. I had to leave them in a wallet in a jacket so they wouldn't float away. And I had to leave *all* of them. The police would have thought it strange if all they found was a driver's license."

"But the passport, Buchanan. I'm talking about the passport. You wouldn't have left the passport. You know that's the ID we care about. Anybody with a brain can arrange to get a fake driver's license. Who cares if the cops get their hands on it? But a fake passport, a first-class fake passport, hell, better than that because the passport blank came from the State Department. If the police had an expert study that passport, there'd be all kinds of questions that the people at State couldn't answer. And then maybe the questions would come in *our* direction.''

''I had to leave it,'' Buchanan lied. The passport was, in fact, in the bedroom, in a small travel bag that he'd bought along with a toilet kit and a few spare clothes before leaving Florida. The travel bag also contained the handgun that Jack Doyle had given him. Buchanan wasn't about to tell this man about the handgun, either.

He continued, ''If the authorities did a thorough investigation of Victor Grant, they'd find out I'd been in Mexico. They'd find out I'd shown my passport down there. So they'd have to ask themselves, Where is it now? They've got my wallet. They've got my suitcase—I left it in the trunk of the car. They've got all of Victor Grant's possessions. Except they don't have his body and they don't have his passport? No way. A good detective might decide that Victor Grant faked his death, then walked away with his passport, the only identification he'd need if he wanted to get out of the country. But since I left the passport in the jacket with my wallet, the authorities have one less detail to trouble them.''

''Smart, Buchanan,'' the portly man said. ''There's just one problem.''

''Oh?''

''The police didn't find the passport.''

''What? Then it must have floated away.''

''But not the wallet?''

''Hey, the wallet was heavier. How do *I* know what happened? My orders were to make Victor Grant disappear. I did it the best way I knew how.''

The portly man stared at him.

''Has the missing passport made the cops think something's wrong?'' Buchanan asked.

The portly man stared harder. ''You'll have to sign this document saying that you couldn't surrender the passport.''

''Whatever,'' Buchanan said. He signed and returned the document, then watched the man who called himself Alan put it in his briefcase.

''The next order of business.'' With an air of efficiency combined with distaste, the portly man opened and dumped the contents of a paper bag onto the coffee table.

Buchanan looked at the sprawl of magazines, catalogs, video- and record-club solicitations, and various other forms of bulk mail. The items were addressed to several persons, Richard Dana, Robert Chambers, Craig Madden, and Brian MacDonald, the most recent pseudonyms that Buchanan had used before becoming Ed Potter in Mexico.

"Housecleaning," the portly man said.

Buchanan nodded. To appear believable in an assumed identity, he had to be equipped with more than just fake ID. Mail, for example. It wasn't natural for people never to get mail. Bills had to be paid. Letters had to be received. Magazines—lots of people subscribed to magazines. If you said your name was Brian MacDonald and you got a magazine addressed to that name, the magazine became another bit of evidence that proved you were the person you claimed to be. So, under various names, Buchanan subscribed to magazines wherever he expected to live for an extended time. But just as he created individual characteristics for each person he pretended to be, so he had to make sure that the magazines matched each character's personality. Richard Dana subscribed to *Runner's World*. Robert Chambers liked *Gourmet*. Craig Madden was a movie fanatic and received *Premiere*. Brian MacDonald enjoyed *Car and Driver*. Because magazines often sold their subscription lists to catalog companies, soon Buchanan's various characters would begin receiving catalogs about the subject in which they were supposedly interested, and this extra mail would help legitimize his characters.

Eventually, though, Buchanan would receive a new assignment and move on, discarding one identity, assuming another. In theory, the previous identity would no longer exist. Still, even though Buchanan had made arrangements to stop mail from coming to his former characters, a few items would inevitably arrive at places where his characters used to live. To avoid arousing suspicion, he always left a forwarding address with the landlords at those places. That forwarding address was known in the trade as an accommodation address, a safe, convenient mail drop, usually a private mail service owned by—but not traceable to—Buchanan's controllers.

"Is there anything here that needs to be dealt with?" the portly man who called himself Alan asked. "Some loose end that needs to be tied? We ought to know before we destroy this stuff.''

Buchanan sorted through the items.''Nope. These magazines can go. These catalogs. This circular is exactly what they call it—junk. This . . .''

He felt a chill as he lifted a postcard. ''It's addressed to Peter Lang. I haven't used that name in six years. How the hell did it get lost this long?''

''It didn't. Check the postmark. Someone mailed it from Baltimore. . . . Last week.''

''Last week?'' Buchanan felt cold. ''Who'd want to get in touch with Peter Lang after six years? Who'd remember him? Who'd care enough to . . .?''

''That's what *we* want to know,'' Alan said, his calculated gaze threatening. ''And why a postcard? Why not a letter? And what do you make of the message?''

Troubled, Buchanan studied it. The message was handwritten in black ink, the script small, the strokes thin, the lettering ornate yet precise.

A woman's handwriting. No name.

Five sentences, some of them incomplete, seeming gibberish.

But not to Buchanan. He didn't need a signature to tell him who had sent the postcard. Because she would have taken for granted that several people, especially Buchanan's employers, would have read the message by now, he admired her indirection.

4

Here's the postcard I never thought I'd send. I hope you meant your promise. The last time and place. Counting on you. PLEASE.

Buchanan read the message several times, then glanced up at the portly man, who now was squinting.

''So?'' The man squinted harder.

"It's a woman who knew me when I was Peter Lang. Someone I needed for window dressing."

"That's all?"

Buchanan shrugged.

"Who was she, Buchanan?"

"It's been so long, I don't even remember her name."

"Don't tell me your famous memory is failing you."

"I remember what's essential. She wasn't."

"Why didn't she sign her name?"

"She was a flake. That much, I recall. Maybe she thought it would be cute and mysterious if she sent an unsigned postcard."

"And yet without a name on the card, a name you claim you can't remember, you know who sent the message."

"She used to do this kind of stuff a lot. Unsigned cryptic messages. I'd find them in my bathroom, in my pajamas, in my sock drawer. I told you she was a flake. But she sure was gorgeous, and I never read any handwriting as neat and elegant as this. She was proud of that—her handwriting."

"But what does it mean?"

"Damned if I know. Maybe she was high on something when she wrote it. Or maybe she tried so hard to make the message cute that she didn't realize she was being incoherent."

The portly man squinted even harder. "Just like that, after six years, she decided to write to you."

"Must be," Buchanan said. "Because that's what happened. She didn't even think to put a return address on it. That's how spur-of-the-moment she used to act."

"What's this 'last time and place' business?"

"Beats the hell out of me."

The portly man didn't move. He just kept staring at Buchanan as if trying to make him uncomfortable enough to demonstrate a sign of weakness.

Buchanan returned his stare.

After thirty seconds, the portly man sighed and gestured for Buchanan to give back the postcard. He shoved it into the paper bag along with the magazines, catalogs, and circulars, then placed them in his metal briefcase and locked it. "We'll talk again soon, Buchanan." He stood.

"Wait a minute."

"Is something wrong?" the man asked. "Or maybe there's something you forgot to tell me?"

"Yeah. What about my new ID?"

"New ID?"

"The driver's license and credit card, all the documents for Don Colton."

The man frowned. "You must have gotten the wrong impression. You're not being issued new ID."

"What?"

"You won't need any. The rent, the phone, and the other bills are paid through one of our cover organizations by mail. There's plenty of food here, so you won't need a checkbook to go to the grocery store, and you won't need a credit card to go to a restaurant. And since we want you to stay close, you won't need ID to rent a car."

"So what about clothes? I need a credit card to replace what I abandoned in Fort Lauderdale. What's in the closet here is too small."

"There's a gray cotton sweat suit on the bedroom shelf. It's large enough to do for now. When I drive you to the hospital for your CAT scan, I'll bring you a few more things."

"That's *it*? You're leaving me without a way to prove my cover?"

"Buchanan, we don't *want* you to prove your cover. We don't want you to be in a position to *need* to prove your cover. We don't want Don Colton leaving this apartment. We don't want him wandering around the building or going to restaurants or to shopping malls and flashing ID. Don Colton's invisible. He's been living in this complex for years, and nobody knows him. He travels so much, you see. So as long as you stay in here, no one'll bother you, and for that matter, we don't want *you* bothering anybody, either. Do you get it?"

Buchanan narrowed his eyes. "Yeah, I got it."

"We don't want you even sending out for a pizza."

"I said I got it. Anyway, how *could* I order a pizza? I'm almost out of money."

"Good." The man lifted his briefcase and walked toward the door.

"I'm in limbo?"

The man kept walking. "Until we've assessed the damage control on Cancún, Mérida, and Fort Lauderdale. A while ago, you told me you'd ask for time off if you thought you needed it. You said nobody turns down R and R." The man reached the door, unlocked it, and glanced at Buchanan. "Well, now you've got some. You've been in the field quite a while. Eight years. A *very* long while. It's time for a rest."

"And what if I don't want a rest?"

The man gripped the doorknob. "It's a funny thing, Buchanan."

"What?"

"I was told you were a fanatic about assuming your identities."

"That's right."

"A real Method actor. Invented a detailed history for each of your pseudonyms. Dressed, ate, and sometimes even walked the way you decided a particular character would. Gave each of them a distinct personality."

"You're right again. Staying totally in character is what keeps me alive."

"Sure. The thing is, I was also told that you'd practically bite off the head of any controller who called you by your real name. But I just did, and in fact I've been doing it off and on since I came here. You should have been insisting that I call you Don Colton."

"There's nothing strange about that. Until I get Don Colton's ID and background, I can't become him. I don't have any personality to assume."

"Well, in that case, I'd expect you to have insisted that I call you Victor Grant."

"How could I?"

"I don't understand."

"Calling me Victor Grant is impossible. I wouldn't have responded."

"Why?"

"Because Victor Grant is dead." Abruptly Buchanan felt a further chill as he understood the significance of what he'd just said.

The man who called himself Alan understood the significance very well. "As you said, you're in limbo." He turned the knob and opened the door. "Stay put. I'll be in touch."

5

Buchanan leaned his back against the locked door and massaged the sides of his aching head. So much was wrong, he didn't know where to start analyzing.

Try starting with why you lied to him about the passport and why you didn't tell him you had a firearm.

I didn't want to lose them. I didn't trust him.

Well, you weren't wrong on that score. Whatever that conversation was, it sure wasn't a debriefing. He didn't ask you to talk about anything that you'd done. And he didn't give you new ID. He put you on ice. It was more like an interrogation, except he didn't ask you any questions that weren't about . . .

The postcard.

Buchanan went to the counter in the kitchen and poured more bourbon and water into a glass. He took a long swallow, then felt his cheek muscles harden with tension.

The postcard.

Yeah, the passport wasn't the only thing you lied about. What's the big deal? Why didn't you tell him the truth?

Because he was too damned interested.

Hey, a postcard arrives last week for a man who hasn't existed, whom you haven't been, for the past six years. That's an attention getter. Naturally, they want to know what the hell's going on. Something from one of your pasts, some threat to the operation, catching up to you. Why didn't you tell him?

Because I'm not sure. If I did know what was going on, maybe I'd have told him.

Bullshit. The truth is, you're scared.

No way.

Yes. Confused and scared. You haven't thought about her in all this time. You've *made* yourself not think about her. And now all of a sudden, bang, she's back in your head, and you don't know how to handle it. But this much is sure—you don't want *them* to have anything to do with her.

He stared at his glass of bourbon, his emotions powerful.

6

Here's the postcard I never thought I'd send.

She'd been furious the night she decided that she didn't want to see him anymore. She'd told him not to bother trying to get in touch with her again, that if she ever needed him, she'd send him a goddamned postcard.

I hope you meant your promise.

He'd told her that no matter how much time and distance was between them, all she had to do was ask, and he'd be there.

The last time and place.

He remembered the date of their breakup well because of what had been happening around them, the costumes, the music—October 31, Halloween. The time had been close to midnight, the place Café du Monde in New Orleans.

Counting on you. PLEASE.

In capital letters? She might as well have said that she was begging him.

That wasn't like her.

She was in trouble.

He continued staring at the glass of bourbon and imagined the tension she must have felt as she wrote the postcard. Maybe she had only seconds to write it, to condense it to its essentials and hope it was clear to him, even though she didn't sign her name.

She doesn't want anyone except me to know where she's going to be and when.

She's terrified.

7

The man who called himself Alan had left Buchanan's apartment, heard the scrape of the lock, and proceeded along the green heavy-duty carpet of the harshly lit, concrete hallway. He was pleased that no one happened to come out of another apartment and see him. Like Buchanan, he avoided the elevator and used the fire stairs—less chance of encountering anyone. But unlike Buchanan, who would have headed down to the street, the portly, short-haired man in the brown-checkered sport coat went up to the next landing, heard voices, waited in the stairwell until the voices were cut off by the sound of an elevator, and then walked briskly along the corridor until he reached the door to the apartment directly above Buchanan's. He knocked twice, paused, knocked twice more, heard a lock open, and was quickly admitted.

The apartment was dimly lit. He couldn't see who was present or how the unit was furnished. Nor could anyone who happened to be passing as he entered. But the moment the door was closed behind him, he heard the click of a switch, and at once the apartment's living room was filled with light. Thick, closed draperies prevented the light from being seen by anyone outside.

Five people were in the room. A tall, trim man with severe features and cropped graying hair exuded the most authority. Although he wore a plain blue business suit, he stood with military bearing and in private was never referred to by his name but always as Colonel.

The next in charge was a younger man, in his forties, less tall, more muscular. He wore tan slacks, a brown blazer. Major Putnam.

Beside him was a blonde woman in her thirties, gorgeous, her breasts bulging at her blouse. Captain Weller.

Finally, there were two plainclothes sentries, one of whom had admitted him and then relocked the door. The sentries had last seen him not long ago, just before he went down to Buchanan's apartment, so this time they didn't ask for identification. Indeed, they barely nodded to him before they redirected their attention toward the door.

The colonel, the captain, and the major didn't pay him much attention, either. After a confirming glance, they stared again at a bank of closed-circuit television screens and various black-and-white images of Buchanan's apartment. A long table supported a row of videotape machines, each of which was in operation, recording everything that occurred in each room of Buchanan's apartment. On another table, several audiotape machines were also in operation. Except for a sofa and two chairs shoved against a wall, the electronics were the room's only furnishings. It wasn't any wonder that the colonel had the lights dimmed when the hallway door was opened—he didn't want anyone to get a good look at what was in here.

The man who called himself Alan set his briefcase beside a box of doughnuts and a steaming coffee percolator on the counter between the kitchen and the living room. There weren't any ashtrays—the colonel refused to allow smoking. And there wasn't any clutter of crumpled napkins, stale food, and used Styrofoam cups—the colonel insisted on an absolutely neat control room.

"What's he been doing since I left?" Alan asked. The question was directed to anyone who would bother to answer (they didn't always). As the only civilian in the apartment, he didn't feel obligated to use military titles. Indeed, he was getting damned tired of sensing that these Special Operations types considered themselves superior to the Agency.

After a pause, the woman, Captain Weller, answered without looking at him, continuing to concentrate on the television screens. "Leaned against the door. Rubbed his skull. Appears to have a headache. Went into the kitchen. Poured another drink."

"Another?" Alan asked, disapproving.

His judgmental tone prompted the second-in-command, Major Putnam, to face him. "It means nothing out of context. Alcohol is one of his weapons. He uses it to disarm his contacts. If he doesn't maintain a tolerance for it, he's as open to attack as if he doesn't maintain his combat skills."

"I've never heard *that* one before," Alan said skeptically. "If he was strictly mine, I'd be alarmed. But then, from the start, nothing about this unit was conventional, was it?"

Now the colonel turned. "Don't condescend to us."

"I wasn't. I was making a point about control."

"The point is taken," the colonel said. "If he finishes this drink and makes another, I'll be concerned."

"Right. It's not as if we haven't got plenty of other things to be concerned about. What's your analysis of my session with him?"

A movement on one of the monitors attracted everyone's attention. Again they stared at the screen.

Buchanan carried his drink from the kitchen.

On a separate black-and-white screen, he appeared in the living room and slumped on the sofa, placing his feet on the coffee table, leaning back, rubbing the moisture-beaded glass against his brow.

"Yeah, he sure seems to have a headache," Alan said.

"Or maybe he's just tired from stress and traveling," the woman said.

"A new CAT scan will tell us what's going on in his head," Alan said.

The woman turned. "You mean, in his brain, of course. Not in his mind."

"Exactly. That's what I meant. I asked you, what's your analysis of my session with him?"

"His explanation about the passport was reasonable," the major said. "In his place, I might not have abandoned it, but perhaps that's why I'm not in his place. I don't have the talent for role-playing that he does. A water-destroyed passport, one that validated his identity without jeopardizing the passport's source, would have added credence to his character's death."

"But," Alan corrected, "the passport was never found."

"An accident of circumstance."

"Our opinions differ. But we'll leave that subject for later," Alan said. "What about the postcard?"

"Again his explanation was reasonable," the major said.

"This conversation sounds like an echo," Alan said. "I'm losing patience. If you wanted a whitewash, why did you need me here? I've got a wife and kids who wonder what I look like."

"Whitewash?" the colonel intruded, his voice like steel against flint. "*I'm* losing patience with *you*. The person we're observing on these monitors, the person you had the privilege of interrogating, is without doubt the finest deep-cover operative I've ever had the honor of directing. He has survived longer, has assumed more identities, has endured greater dangers and accomplished more critical missions than any other deep-cover specialist I've ever heard about. He is one of a kind, and it is only with the greatest regret that I am forced to consider his termination."

Ah, Alan thought, there it is. We're finally getting to it. He gestured toward the sentries. "Are you sure you want to talk about something so serious in front of——?"

"They're loyal," the colonel said.

"Just like Buchanan."

"No one's questioning Buchanan's loyalty. It wasn't his fault that he was compromised. There was absolutely no way to predict that someone he knew in Kuwait and Iraq would walk into that restaurant in Cancún while he was making his pitch to those two drug dealers. The worst nightmare of a deep-cover specialist—one identity colliding with another. And there was no way to predict that Bailey would be so damned persistent, that he'd put together evidence showing Buchanan in three different identities. Jesus, the photographs. If only the son of a bitch hadn't started taking photographs."

Especially of you and Buchanan together, Alan thought.

What the colonel said next seemed in response to the accusing look in Alan's eyes. "I admit the mistake. That's why I sent you to interrogate him. I will never again allow myself to be in direct contact with him. But as it is, the damage is done, and *your* people made mistakes, too. If there'd been time in Fort Lauderdale, I'd have brought in one of my own surveillance teams. Instead, I had to rely on . . . Your people assured me that they'd found Bailey's hotel room and confiscated all the photographs.''

"That was my information, as well," Alan said.

"The information was *wrong*. No photographs of Buchanan and myself were retrieved. And before Bailey could be interrogated, the bomb concealed in the picnic cooler was detonated.''

"Those were the orders," Alan insisted. "The location transmitter in the wall of the cooler would lead the team to Bailey when Buchanan delivered the money. Then the C-four explosive that was also in the walls of the cooler would be detonated by remote control. Bailey wouldn't be a problem anymore.''

"You're simplifying to excuse failure. The specific orders were to wait in case Bailey rendezvoused with the woman photographer who was helping him. The C-four was chosen because it was a convenient means to take care of both of them.''

"*In case* they met," Alan emphasized. "But what if Bailey. had already paid her off and wouldn't be seeing her again? Or what if Bailey took the money and abandoned the cooler?''

"Then you admit your people disobeyed orders by acting prematurely.''

Alan didn't reply.

"Well?" the colonel asked.

"The truth is, no one disobeyed. The bomb went off on its own.''

"*On its* . . . ?''

"The expert who assembled the bomb thought he'd set the remote-controlled detonator to a radio frequency that wasn't used in the area. In fact, it had to be triggered by two *different*, uncommon radio frequencies, one to arm it, one to set it off. All those boats at Fort Lauderdale. All those two-way radios. Apparently there *aren't* any uncommon frequencies down there.''

"Jesus," the colonel said. "The bomb could have gone off while Buchanan had it, before he gave the cooler to Bailey.''

"I don't know why *that* should bother you. You were just talking about the possibility of having Buchanan terminated.''

The colonel looked puzzled. Then abruptly he understood.

"Terminated *without* prejudice. What's the matter with you? Do you think I'd actually order the death of one of my men, an officer who served me faithfully for many years?"

"Whether he's faithful hasn't been proven." Alan pointed toward one of the many television screens, toward the black-and-white image of Buchanan slumped on the sofa, his eyes closed, troubled, the moisture-beaded glass of bourbon and water held to his wrinkled brow. "I'm not convinced he was truthful when I talked to him."

"About the passport?"

"I wasn't referring to the passport. The postcard. *That's* what bothers me. I think he held back. I think he lied to me."

"Why would he do that?"

"I'm not sure. But by your own admission, he'd been working under cover, in multiple identities, for an unusual amount of time. He endured a great deal of physical trauma in Mexico. His head obviously still hurts. Maybe he's about to fall apart. There are pictures of you and him that we can't locate. As well, there's a woman who saw Bailey with Buchanan and *you* with Buchanan. A lot of loose ends. If Buchanan is compromised, if he does fall apart, well, we obviously don't need another Hasenfus on our hands."

Alan was referring to an ex-Marine named Eugene Hasenfus who in 1986 was shot down while flying arms to U.S.–backed Contra rebels in Marxist Nicaragua. When questioned by Nicaraguan authorities, Hasenfus implicated the CIA and caused a political scandal that revealed a secret White House–directed war in Nicaragua. Because intermediaries had been used to hire Hasenfus, the CIA could plausibly deny any connection to him. Nonetheless, congressional and media attention directed toward the Agency had been potentially disastrous.

"Buchanan would never talk," the colonel said. "He'd never violate our security."

"That's probably what someone said about Hasenfus when he was hired."

"It'll never come to that," the colonel said. "I've made my decision. I'm putting Buchanan on inactive status. We'll ease him out slowly so he doesn't have culture shock. Or maybe he'll agree to become a trainer. But his days of deep cover are over."

"Tomorrow, when he's taken for a new CAT scan . . ."

"What are you getting at?" the colonel asked.

"I'd like to have sodium amytal administered to him and then have him questioned about that postcard," Alan said.

"No."

"But—"

"No," the colonel repeated. "He's *my* operative, and I know how he'd react if you used drug therapy to question him. He'd feel threatened, insulted, betrayed. Then we *would* have a problem. The fastest way to make a man disloyal is by *treating* him as if he's disloyal."

"Then I insist on at least keeping him under surveillance," Alan said. "There's something about him that bothers me. And I'm still bugged about that postcard."

"Keeping him under surveillance?" The colonel shrugged and turned toward the television monitors, watching the black-and-white image of Buchanan slumped on the sofa, his eyes scrunched shut as if he had a headache, the glass of bourbon against his brow. "I don't have a problem with that. After all, that's what we're already doing."

8

Caught in limbo but not realizing it, Buchanan hadn't been conscious of being called by his real name when the portly man in the brown-checkered sport coat had questioned him the previous night. But as soon as the man had drawn attention to what he'd been doing, as soon as Buchanan realized that he was suspended between identities, he became extremely self-conscious about his name. He was so thorough an impersonator that seldom in the past eight years had he thought of himself as Buchanan. To do so would have been incompatible with his various assumed identities. He didn't just pretend to be those people. He *was* those people. He had to be. The slightest weakness in his characterization could get him killed. For the most part, he'd so thoroughly expunged the name Buchanan from his awareness that if someone had attempted to test him by unexpectedly calling his name from behind him, he wouldn't have turned. Habit would not have controlled him. The name would have belonged to a stranger.

But now as the portly man who called himself Alan drove him to get his CAT scan, Buchanan inwardly squirmed whenever his escort called him by his true name, something the escort did often, apparently by intention. Buchanan felt as he had the first time he'd asked a girl to dance or the first time he'd heard his voice on a tape recorder or the first time he'd made love. The doubt and wonder of those experiences had been positive, however, whereas the self-consciousness he endured at being called Buchanan produced the negativity of fear. He felt exposed, vulnerable, threatened. *Don't call me that. If certain people find out who I really am, it'll get me killed.*

In Fairfax, Virginia, at a private medical clinic presumably controlled by Buchanan's controllers, he was again made nervous, inwardly squirming when the doctor assigned to him persistently called him by his real name.

How are you, Mr. Buchanan? Does your head still hurt, Mr. Buchanan? I have to do a few tests on you, Mr. Buchanan. Excellent responses, Mr. Buchanan. My nurse will take you downstairs for your CAT scan, Mr. Buchanan.

Christ, they didn't bother to give me even a minimal assumed identity, Buchanan thought. *Not even just a John Doe cover name. I wouldn't have needed supporting documents. An arbitrary alias for purposes of the examination would have been fine. But my real name's on the medical file the doctor's holding. I can understand that they wanted to protect the Don Colton pseudonym. But I didn't have to use it. I could have called myself anything. This way, with my name associated with the CAT scan, if anyone makes a comparison, I can be linked to* Victor Grant's *CAT scan.*

The doctor turned from examining the film. "Good news. The bruise is considerably reduced, Mr. Buchanan."

If he calls me that one more time, I'll—

"And there's no indication of neurological damage. The shaking in your right hand has stopped. I attribute that previous symptom to trauma caused by the wound to your shoulder."

"What about my headache?"

"After a concussion, a headache can persist for quite some time. It doesn't trouble me."

"Well, you're not the one with the headache."

The doctor didn't react to the attempt at humor. "I can prescribe something for the pain, if you like."

"Something with a label that says, 'Do not drive or use heavy machinery while taking this medication'?"

"That's correct."

"Thanks, but I'll stick to aspirin," Buchanan said.

"As you wish. Come back in a week—let's make it November second—and I'll reexamine you. Meanwhile, be careful. Don't bang your head again. If you have any problems, let me know."

Problems? Buchanan thought. The kind of problems I've got, you can't solve.

9

Here's the postcard I never thought I'd send.

10

"Do you want to tell me what's going on?" Buchanan asked as they drove along the Little River Turnpike from Fairfax back to Alexandria. The day was gray, a late-October drizzle speckling the windshield.

The man who called himself Alan glanced at him, then peered forward again, concentrating on traffic. He turned on the windshield wipers. "I'm not sure what you mean."

"Why have I been exposed?"

As the drizzle changed to rain, the man turned on the windshield defroster. "Exposed? What makes you think . . . ?"

Buchanan stared at him.

The man turned on the headlights.

"There's not much left," Buchanan said, "for you to toy with and avoid the question. What are you going to do next? Turn on the radio and keep switching stations, or pull over and start changing the oil?"

"What are you talking about, Buchanan?"

"That. My name. For the first time in eight years, people are using it openly. I'm deliberately being compromised. Why?"

"I told you last night. It's time for a rest."

"That doesn't justify violating basic rules."

"Hey, the doctor has a security clearance."

"It was a needless violation," Buchanan said. "He certainly didn't need to know who I was in order to assess a CAT scan. And he mentioned the wound in my shoulder, but he didn't get a look at that shoulder, and I didn't tell him about it. What else has he been told that he didn't need to know? How I got the wound?"

"Of course not."

"Sure. I bet. This isn't just a rest. I'm not just in limbo. I'm being eased out. Am I right?"

The man steered into the passing lane.

"I asked you a question. Am I being eased out?"

"Nothing lasts forever, Buchanan."

"Stop calling me that."

"What *should* I call you? Who the hell do you think you are?"

Buchanan's skull throbbed. He didn't have an answer.

"An operative with your talent and experience could do a lot of good as a trainer," Alan said.

Buchanan didn't respond.

"Did you expect to work under cover all your life?"

"I never thought about it."

"Come on," the man said. "I fail to believe that."

"I meant what I said. I literally never thought about it. I never thought beyond who I was during any given assignment. If you start planning your retirement while you're working under cover, you start making mistakes. You forget who you're supposed to be. You fall out of character. That's a great way to ensure you don't live long enough for the retirement you're not supposed to be planning."

"Well, you'd better think about it now."

Buchanan's skull ached more fiercely. "Why is this being done to me? I didn't screw up. Nothing that happened was my fault. I compensated perfectly. The operation wasn't damaged."

"Ah, but it could have been."

"That still would not have been my fault," Buchanan said.

"We're not discussing fault. We're discussing what did and didn't happen and what *almost* happened. Maybe you've become unlucky. The bottom line is you're thirty-two. In this game, that makes you a senior citizen. Eight years? Christ, it's amazing you're still alive. It's time to walk away."

"The fact that I'm still alive proves how good I am. I don't deserve . . ."

The rain increased, drumming on the car's roof. The windshield wipers flapped harder.

"Did you ever see your file?"

Despite his pain, Buchanan shook his head.

"Would you like to?"

"No."

"The psychological profile is very revealing."

"I'm not interested."

"You've got what's called a 'dissociative personality.' "

"I told you, I'm not interested."

The man changed lanes again, maintaining speed despite the rain. "I'm not a psychologist, but the file made sense to me. You don't like yourself. You do everything you can to keep from looking inward. You split away. You identify with people and objects around you. You objectify. You . . . dissociate."

Buchanan frowned ahead at the traffic obscured by the rain.

"In average society, that condition would be a liability," the man continued. "But your trainers realized what a prize they had when their computer responded to a survey by choosing your profile. In high school, you'd already demonstrated a talent—perhaps a better term is *compulsion*—for acting. At Benning and Bragg, your Special Ops commanders gave you glowing reports for your combat skills. Considering the unique slant of your personality, all that remained to qualify you was even *more* specialized training at the Farm."

"I don't want to hear any more," Buchanan said.

"You're an ideal undercover operative. It's no wonder you were able to assume multiple identities for eight years, and that your commanders thought you were capable of doing so without breaking down. Hell, yes. You'd already broken down. Working under cover was the way you healed. You hated yourself so much that you'd do anything, you'd suffer anything for the chance not to be yourself.''

Buchanan calmly reached out and grasped the man's right elbow.

"Hey," the man said.

Buchanan's middle finger found the nerve he wanted.

"*Hey*," the man repeated.

Buchanan squeezed.

The man screamed. Jerking from pain, he caused the car to swerve, its rear tires fishtailing on the wet, slick pavement. Behind and in the passing lane, other drivers swerved in startled response and blared their horns.

"Now the way this is going to work," Buchanan said, "is either you'll shut up or else you'll feel what it's like to lose control of a car doing fifty-five miles an hour."

The man's face was the color of concrete. His mouth hung open in agony. Sweat beaded his brow as he struggled to keep control of the car.

He nodded.

"Good," Buchanan said. "I knew we could reach an understanding." Releasing his grip, he sat rigidly straight and looked forward.

The man mumbled something.

"What?" Buchanan asked.

"Nothing," the man answered.

"That's what I thought."

But Buchanan knew what the man had said.

Because of your brother.

11

"What's he doing now?" the man who called himself Alan asked as he entered the apartment directly above Buchanan's.

"Nothing," the muscular man, Major Putnam, said. He sipped from a Styrofoam cup of coffee and watched the television monitors. Again he wore civilian clothes.

"Well, he must be doing *something*." Alan glanced around the apartment. The colonel and Captain Weller weren't around.

"Nope," Major Putnam said. "Nothing. When he came in, I figured he'd pour himself a drink, go to the bathroom, read a magazine, watch television, do exercises, whatever. But all he did was go over to the sofa. There he is. That's what he's been doing since you left him. Nothing."

Alan approached the row of television monitors. Massaging his right elbow where the nerve that Buchanan had pinched still troubled him, he frowned at a black-and-white image of Buchanan sitting on the sofa. "Jesus."

Buchanan sat bolt straight, motionless, his expression rigid, his intense gaze focused on a chair across from him.

"Jesus," Alan repeated. "He's catatonic. Does the colonel know about this?"

"I phoned him."

"And?"

"I'm supposed to keep watching. What did the two of you talk about? When he came in, he looked . . ."

"It's what we *didn't* talk about."

"I don't understand."

"His brother."

"Christ," the major said, "you know that's an off-limits subject."

"I wanted to test him."

"Well, you certainly got a reaction."

"Yeah, but it's not the one I wanted."

12

Buchanan was reminded of an old story about a donkey between two bales of hay. The donkey stood exactly midpoint between the bales. Each bale was the same size and had the same fragrance. With no reason to choose one bale over the other, the donkey starved to death.

The story—which could never happen in the real world because the donkey could never be exactly at midpoint and the bales could never be exactly the same—was a theoretical way to illustrate the problem of free will. The ability to choose, which most people took for granted, depended on certain conditions, and without them, a person could be motiveless, just as Buchanan found that he was now.

His brother.

Buchanan had so thoroughly worked to obliterate the memory that for the past eight years he'd managed not to be conscious of the critical event that controlled his behavior. Not once had he thought about it. On rare occasions of weakness, late at night, weary, he might sense the nightmare lurking in the darkness of his subconscious, crouching, about to spring. Then he would muster all his strength of resolve to thrust up a mental wall of denial, of refusal to accept the unacceptable.

Even now, with his defenses taken from him, with his identity exposed, unshielded, he was repulsed sufficiently that the memory was able to catch him only partially, in principle but not in detail.

His brother.

His wonderful brother.

Twelve years old.

Sweet Tommy.

Was dead.

And he had killed him.

Buchanan felt as if he were trapped by ice. He couldn't move. He sat on the sofa, and his legs, his back, his arms were numb, his entire body cold, paralyzed. He kept staring toward the chair in front of him, not seeing it, barely aware of time.

Five o'clock.

Six o'clock.

Seven o'clock.

The room was in darkness. Buchanan kept staring, seeing nothing.

Tommy was dead.

And he had killed him.

Blood.

He'd clutched Tommy's stake-impaled body, trying to tug him free.

Tommy's cheeks had been terribly pale. His breathing had sounded like bubbles. His moan had been liquid, as if he was gargling. But what he gargled hadn't been salt water. It had been . . .

Blood.

"Hurts. Hurts so bad."

"Tommy, oh, God, I'm sorry. I didn't mean to."

Push him.

Just horsing around.

Didn't think Tommy would lose his balance and fall.

Didn't know anything was down in the pit.

A construction site. A summer evening. Two brothers on an adventure.

"Hurts so bad."

"Tommy!"

"Doesn't hurt anymore."

"*Tommy!*"

So much blood.

When Buchanan was fifteen.

Still catatonic, sitting bolt straight on the sofa, staring at the darkness, Buchanan felt as if a portion of his mind were raising arms, trying to ward off the terrible memory. Although he was chilled, sweat beaded his brow. Too much, he thought. He hadn't remembered in such detail since the days and nights before Tommy's funeral and the unendurable summer that followed, the guilt-laden, seemingly endless season of grief that finally *had* ended when . . .

Buchanan's mind darted and burrowed, seeking any protection it could from the agonizing memory of Tommy's blood on his clothes, of the stake projecting from Tommy's chest.

"It's all my fault."

"No, you didn't mean to do it," Buchanan's mother had said.

"I killed him."

"It was an accident," Buchanan's mother had said.

But Buchanan hadn't believed her, and he was certain that he'd have gone insane if he hadn't found a means to protect himself from his mind. The answer turned out to be amazingly simple, wonderfully self-evident. Become someone else.

Dissociative personality. Buchanan imagined himself as his favorite sports and rock stars, as certain movie and television actors whom he idolized. He suddenly became a reader—of novels into which he could escape and become the hero with whom he so desperately wanted to identify. In high school that autumn, he discovered the drama club, subconsciously motivated by the urge to perfect the skills he would need to maintain his protective assumed identities, the personas that would allow him to escape from himself.

Then after high school, perhaps to prove himself, perhaps to punish himself, perhaps to court an early death, he'd joined the military, not just any branch, the Army, so he could enter Special Forces. The name said it all—to be special. He wanted to sacrifice himself, to atone. And one thing more—if he saw enough death, perhaps one death in particular would no longer haunt him.

As the man who called himself Alan had indicated, Buchanan's Special Operations trainers realized what a prize they had when their computer responded to a survey by choosing Buchanan's profile. A man who desperately needed to assume identities. An operative who wouldn't be wearied but, on the contrary, would flourish for long periods under deep cover.

Now they were stripping away his barriers, taking away his shields, exposing the guilt that had compelled him to become an operative and that he had managed to subdue.

Buchanan? Who the hell was Buchanan? Jim Crawford was a man he understood. So was Ed Potter. And Victor Grant. And all the others. He'd invented detailed personal backgrounds for each of them. Some of his characters were blessed (in Richard Dana's case literally, for Dana believed that he was the recipient of the grace of God as a born-again Christian). Others carried burdens (Ed Potter's wife had divorced him for a man who earned more money). Buchanan knew how each of them dressed (Robert Chambers was formal and always wore a suit and tie). He knew which kinds of music each liked (Peter Sloane was crazy about country-western), and which foods (Jim Crawford hated cauliflower), and which types of women (Victor Grant liked brunettes), and which types of movies (Craig Madden could watch *Singin' in the Rain* every night of the week), and . . .

Who the hell was Buchanan? It was significant that Buchanan and his controllers always thought of him in terms of his last name. Impersonal. Objective. After eight years of having impersonated—correction, of having *been*—hundreds of people,

Buchanan had no idea of how to impersonate himself. What were his speech mannerisms? Did he have a distinctive walk? Which types of clothes, food, music, et cetera, did he prefer? Was he religious? Did he have any hobbies? Favorite cities? What came naturally?

Christ, he hadn't been Buchanan in so long that he didn't know who Buchanan was. He *didn't want* to know who Buchanan was. The story of the donkey between the two bales of hay was *his* story. He was caught between the identity of Victor Grant, who was dead, and the identity of Don Colton, who wasn't formed. With no way to turn, with nothing to help him choose whom to be, he was paralyzed.

Self-defense made the difference—protective instincts. Sitting rigidly in the quiet, dark room, he heard a noise, the scrape of a key in the front door's lock. A portion of his mind jolted him. His body was no longer cold and numb. His lethargy drained, dispelled by adrenaline.

The doorknob creaked. As someone in the outside hallway slowly pushed the door open, the glare of fluorescent lights spilling in, Buchanan was already off the sofa. He darted to the left and disappeared into the darkness of the bedroom. He heard the flick of a switch and stepped back farther into the bedroom as light filled the living room. He heard a metallic scratch as someone removed the key from the lock. He heard a soft *thunk* as the door was gently shut. Cautious footsteps made a brushing sound as they inched across the carpet.

He tensed.

"Buchanan?" The voice was familiar. It belonged to the portly man who called himself Alan. But the voice sounded wary, troubled. "Buchanan?"

Uneasy, Buchanan didn't want to respond to that name. Nonetheless, he showed himself, careful to keep partially in the shadows of the bedroom.

Alan turned, his expression a mixture of concern and surprise.

"Don't you believe in knocking?" Buchanan asked.

"Well . . ." Alan rubbed his right hand against his brown-checkered sport coat, awkward. "I thought you might be sleeping and . . ."

"So you decided to make yourself at home until I woke up?"

"No," Alan said. "Uh, not exactly."

"Then *what* exactly?" The man was normally confident to the point of being brusque, but now he was behaving out of character.

What was going on?

"I just thought I'd check on you to make sure you were all right."

"Well, why wouldn't I be?"

"You, uh, you were upset in the car and . . ."

"Yes? And what?"

"Nothing. I just . . . I guess I made a mistake."

Buchanan stepped completely from the darkness of the bedroom. Approaching, he noticed Alan direct his gaze furtively, nervously, toward a section of the ceiling in the far-right corner.

Ah, Buchanan thought. So the place is wired—and not just with microphones.

With hidden cameras. Needle-nosed.

Yesterday when Buchanan had arrived, he'd felt relieved to have reached a haven. There'd been no reason for him to suspect the intentions of his controllers and hence no reason for him to check the apartment to see if it was bugged. Later, after last night's conversation with Alan, Buchanan had felt disturbed, preoccupied by the postcard, by the unexpected echo of one of his lives six years ago. It hadn't occurred to him to check the apartment. What would have been the point? Aside from the man who called himself Alan, there was no one to talk to and thus nothing for hidden microphones to overhear.

But video surveillance was a different matter. And far more serious, Buchanan thought. Something about me spooks them enough that they want to keep extremely close tabs on me.

But what? What would spook them?

For starters, being catatonic all afternoon and half the evening. I must have scared the hell out of whoever's watching me. They sent Alan down to see if I'd cracked up. The way Alan keeps pawing at his sport coat. After I bruised his arm this morning, he's probably deciding whether I'm disturbed enough that he'll have to draw his handgun.

Meanwhile, the cameras are transmitting every move I make. But Alan doesn't want me to know that.

Buchanan felt liberated. The sense of being on stage gave him the motivation he needed to act the part of himself.

"I knocked," Alan said. "I guess you didn't hear me. Since you're not supposed to leave the apartment, I wondered if something had happened to you." Alan seemed less nervous now that he'd come up with a believable cover story. He gestured with growing confidence. "That injury to your head. Maybe you'd hurt it again. Maybe you'd slipped in the shower or something. So I decided to let myself in and check. I debrief operatives here a lot, so I always have a key."

"I guess I ought to be flattered that you care."

"Hey, you're not the easiest guy to get along with." Alan rubbed his right elbow. "But I do my job and look after the people assigned to me."

"Listen," Buchanan said. "About what happened in the car this morning . . . I'm sorry."

Alan shrugged.

"A lot's been happening. I guess I'm having trouble getting used to not being under pressure."

Again Alan shrugged. "Understandable. Sometimes an operative still feels the pressure even when it's gone."

"Speaking of which . . ."

"What?"

"Pressure."

Buchanan felt it in his abdomen. He pointed toward the bathroom, went in, shut the door, and emptied his bladder.

He assumed that the bathroom, like the other rooms in the apartment, would have a needle-nosed camera concealed in a wall. But whether he was being observed while he urinated made no difference to him. Even if he *had* felt self-conscious, he would never have permitted himself to show it.

And even if his bladder hadn't insisted, he would still have gone into the bathroom.

As a diversion.

Because he needed time to be away from Alan. He needed time to think.

13

Here's the postcard I never thought I'd send. I hope you meant your promise. The last time and place. Counting on you. PLEASE.

Buchanan stepped from the bathroom, its toilet flushing. "Last night, you mentioned something about R and R."

Alan squinted, suspicious. "That's right."

"Well, you call this being on R and R? Being caged in here?"

"I told you, Don Colton's supposed to be invisible. If you start wandering in and out, the neighbors will think you're him, and when the next Don Colton shows up, they'll get suspicious."

"But what if I'm out of here? Me. Buchanan. A furlough. I haven't had one in eight years. Who'd notice? Who'd care?"

"Furlough?"

"Under my own name. Might do me some good to be myself for a change."

Alan cocked his head, squinting, nonetheless betraying his interest.

"Next week, I'm supposed to go back to that doctor," Buchanan said. "By then, maybe your people and the colonel will have decided what to do with me."

"I don't have the authority to make that decision alone."

"Talk with the colonel," Buchanan said.

Alan continued to look interested. "Where would you go? Since you don't have a passport, it can't be out of the country."

"I wouldn't want to leave the country, anyhow. Not that far. South. New Orleans. Two days from now is Halloween. A person can have a damned good time in New Orleans on Halloween."

"I heard that," Alan said. "In fact, I heard that a person can have a damned good time in New Orleans *any*time."

Buchanan nodded. His request would be granted.

But he wouldn't be going as himself.

No way, he thought.

He'd be stepping back six years.

He'd be reinventing himself to be the person he was *then*. A hundred lifetimes ago.

A once-happy man who liked jazz, mint juleps, and red beans with rice.

A charter pilot named Peter Lang who'd had the tragic love affair of his life.

14

Here's the postcard I never thought I'd send.

SEVEN

1

Pilots—especially when being a pilot is not their true occupation and they need to establish an assumed identity—ought to fly. Instead, Buchanan-Lang took the train to New Orleans.

That method of travel had several advantages. One was that he found it relaxing. Another was that it was private, inasmuch as he'd been able to get a sleeper compartment. Still another was that it took a while, filling the time. After all, he didn't have anything to do until Halloween the next evening. Certainly he could have spent the day sight-seeing in New Orleans. But the fact was, he was quite familiar with New Orleans, its docks, the French Quarter, the Garden District, Lake Pontchartrain, Antoine's restaurant, Preservation Hall, and most of all, the exotic cemeteries. Peter Lang had a fascination with exotic cemeteries. He visited them whenever he could. Buchanan didn't allow himself to analyze the implications.

However, the major reason for taking the train instead of flying was that there wasn't any metal-detector and X-ray security at train stations. Thus he could bring the 9-mm Beretta pistol that Jack Doyle had given him in Fort Lauderdale. It was wedged between two shirts and two changes of underwear, along with Victor Grant's passport, next to the toilet kit in the small canvas travel bag that Buchanan had been carrying with him since Florida. As his confusion about his employers and about himself continued to aggravate him, he was grateful that he'd lied about the passport and that he hadn't told anyone about the handgun. The passport and the gun gave him options. They allowed him potential freedom. That he'd never before lied to a debriefer should perhaps have troubled him. It should perhaps have warned him that he was more disturbed than he realized, that the blow to his head had been more serious than he knew. But as he sat next to the window of his locked compartment, listening to the *clack-clack-clack* of the wheels on the rails, watching the brilliant autumn colors of the Virginia countryside, he persistently rubbed his aching head and was grateful that he hadn't tried to conceal the handgun somewhere in Don Colton's apartment. If he had, the cameras would have exposed him. As it was, his story had evidently been convincing. Otherwise, his controllers wouldn't have given him money as well as ID in his real name and then have allowed him to take this brief trip.

He'd bought a paperback novel before boarding the train at Washington's Union Station, but he barely glanced at it while the train continued south. He just kept massaging his forehead, partially because of pain and partially because of concentration, while he stared out the window at intermittent towns and cities, hills and farmland.

Peter Lang. He had to remember everything about him. He had to *become* Peter Lang. Pretending to be a pilot wasn't a problem, for Buchanan *was* a pilot. It was one of several skills that he'd acquired while he was being trained. Almost without exception, the occupations he pretended to have were occupations with which his employers had arranged to give him some familiarity. In a few cases, he had genuine expertise.

But what *was* a problem was reacquiring Peter Lang's attitude, his mannerisms, his personality. Buchanan had never kept notes about his numerous characters. To document an impersonation was foolish. Such documents might eventually be used against him. On principle, a paper trail was never a good idea. So he'd been forced to rely on his memory, and there had been many assignments, especially those in which he was meeting various contacts and had to switch back and forth between identities several times during one day, when his ability to recall and adapt had been taxed to the maximum. He'd suffered the constant worry that he would switch characters unintentionally, that he would behave like character X in front of a contact when he was supposed to behave like character Y.

Peter Lang.

2

Buchanan had been in New Orleans, posing as a charter pilot who worked for an oil-exploration company, supposedly flying technicians and equipment to various sites in Central America. His actual mission, however, had been to fly plainclothes Special Forces advisers to secret airfields in the jungles of Nicaragua, where they would train Contra rebels to battle the Marxist regime. A year earlier, in 1986, when Eugene Hasenfus had been shot down over Nicaragua while attempting to drop munitions to the rebels, Hasenfus had told his captors that he assumed he had been working for the CIA. The trouble was that the United States Congress had specifically forbidden the CIA to have anything to do with Nicaragua. The resultant media exposure created a political scandal in which the CIA repeatedly denied any connection with Hasenfus. Since intermediaries had been used to hire him and since Hasenfus later repudiated his story, the CIA avoided blame, but Nicaragua continued to be a sensitive political subject, even though President Reagan had subsequently issued an executive order that overrode the congressional ban on U.S. aid to the Contras. However, the resumption of aid was not supposed to include American soldiers on Nicaraguan soil attempting to topple the Nicaraguan government. Inasmuch as blatant military interference was potentially an act of war, the soldiers Buchanan flew to Nicaragua were, like Buchanan, dressed in civilian clothes. Also like Buchanan, they had false identities and could not be traced to the U.S. military.

Because New Orleans and Miami were the two cities most associated with covert aid to the Contras, investigative journalists showed great interest in private firms that sent aircraft to Latin American countries. A plane scheduled to deliver legitimate merchandise to El Salvador, Honduras, or Costa Rica might make an unscheduled, illegal stop in Nicaragua, leaving men instead of equipment. Any journalist who could prove this unauthorized degree of U.S. military involvement would be a candidate for a Pulitzer Prize. Thus Buchanan had had to be especially careful about establishing his cover. One of his techniques had been to ask his employers to provide him with a wife, a woman who was in business with her husband, who liked to fly and could speak Spanish, who would ideally be Hispanic and who would thus not attract attention if she flew with her husband on his frequent trips to Latin America. Buchanan's intention was to deceive curious journalists into doubting that he had connections with Nicaragua. After all, they might think, who'd be callous enough to fly his wife into a war zone?

The wife his employers had supplied to him was indeed Hispanic. A spirited, attractive woman named Juana Mendez, she'd been twenty-five. Her parents were Mexicans who'd become U.S. citizens. A sergeant in Army Intelligence, she'd been raised in San Antonio, Texas, a city that Buchanan's persona, Peter Lang, claimed as his hometown as well. Buchanan had spent several weeks in San Antonio prior to his assignment in order to familiarize himself with the city, lest someone test his cover story by trying to manipulate him into saying things about San Antonio that weren't accurate. Juana's constant presence with him would make it more difficult for anyone to question him about San Antonio. If he didn't know the answer, if he hesitated, Juana would answer for him.

Being Peter Lang had been one of Buchanan's longest assignments—four months. During that time, he and Juana had lived together in a small apartment on the second story of a quaint clapboard building with ornate wrought-iron railings and a pleasant flower-filled courtyard on Dumaine Street in the

French Quarter. Both he and Juana had known the dangers of becoming emotionally involved with an undercover partner. They had tried to make their public gestures of affection strictly professional. They had done their best not to be affected by their enforced private intimacy, eating together, combining laundry, using the same bathroom, sharing the same sleeping quarters. They didn't have intercourse. They weren't that undisciplined. But they might as well have, for the effect was the same. Sexual activity was only a part—and often a small part, and sometimes *no* part—of a successful marriage. In their four months together, Buchanan and Juana portrayed their roles so well that they finally admitted awkwardly to each other that they did feel married. In the night, while he'd listened to her softly exhale in sleep, he had felt intoxicated by her smell. It reminded him of cinnamon.

Shared stress is a powerful bonder. On one occasion, during a firefight in Nicaragua, Buchanan would never have been able to reach his plane and maneuver it for a takeoff from the primitive airstrip in the jungle if Juana hadn't used an assault rifle to give him covering fire. Through the canopy of his slowly turning aircraft, he had watched Juana run from the jungle toward the passenger door he had opened. She had whirled toward bushes, fired her M-16, then raced onward. Bullets from the jungle had torn up dirt ahead of her. She had whirled and fired again. Revving the engines, he had managed to get the plane in position and then had raised his own M-16 to shoot through the open hatch and give her covering fire. Bullets had struck the side of the plane. As she lunged toward the hatch, he'd released the brakes and started across the bumpy clearing. She'd scrambled in, braced herself at the open hatch, and fired repeatedly at the jungle. When she emptied her weapon, she'd picked up his, emptying it as well. Then grabbing a seat belt so she wouldn't fall out, she had laughed as the plane bounced twice and rose abruptly, skimming treetops.

To depend on someone for your life makes you feel close to that person. Buchanan had experienced that emotion in the company of men. But that four-month assignment had been the first time he had felt it with a woman, and in the end, he was a better actor than he wanted to be, for he fell in love with her.

He shouldn't have. He struggled desperately with himself to

repress the feeling. Nonetheless, he failed. Even then, he didn't have sex with her. Despite powerful temptation, they didn't violate their professional ethics by getting physically involved. But they did break another rule, one that warned them not to confuse their roles with reality, although Buchanan didn't believe in that rule. His strength as an imposter was precisely that he *did* confuse his roles with reality. As long as he was portraying someone, that person *was* reality.

One night, while Buchanan was watching television, Juana had come in from buying groceries. The troubled look on her face had made him frown.

"Are you all right?" Concerned, he'd walked toward her. "Did something happen while you were out?"

Apparently oblivious to his question, she'd set down the bag of groceries and begun to unpack. But then he'd realized that she didn't care about the groceries. She was preoccupied by a jazz-concert handout that someone had given her on the street. She removed it from the bag, and when Buchanan saw the small *x* in the upper-right corner, he'd understood why she looked disturbed. The person who'd given her the handout must have been their contact. The small *x*, made by a felt-tip pen, was their signal to dismantle the operation.

They were being reassigned.

At that moment, Buchanan had been terribly conscious of Juana's proximity, of her oval face, of her smooth dark skin and the firm-looking outline of her breasts beneath her blouse. He'd wanted to hold her, but his discipline had been too strong.

Juana's usually cheerful voice had sounded tight with stress. "I guess I knew we'd eventually be reassigned." She'd swallowed. "Nothing lasts forever, right?"

"Right," he'd answered somberly.

"So. . . . Do you think we'll be reassigned together?"

"I don't know."

Juana had nodded, pensive.

"They almost never do."

"Yes." Juana had swallowed again.

The night before they left New Orleans, they'd taken a stroll through the French Quarter. It was Halloween, and the old part of the city had been more colorful and festive than usual. Revelers wore costumes, a great many of them depicting skeletons. The crowd danced, sang, and drank in the narrow streets. Jazz—some tunes melancholy, others joyous—reverberated through open doors, merging, swelling past the wrought-iron railings above the crowd, echoing toward the reflection of the city's lights in the sky.

Oh, when the saints . . .

Buchanan and Juana had ended their walk at Café du Monde near Jackson Square on Decatur Street. The famous open-air restaurant specialized in café au lait as well as beignets, deep-fried French pastries covered with powdered sugar. The place had been extremely crowded, many costumed partygoers wanting caffeine and starch to offset the alcohol they'd consumed before they continued their revels. Regardless, Buchanan and Juana had stood in line. The October night had been balmy with the hint of rain, a pleasant breeze coming in from the Mississippi. Finally, a waiter had guided them to a table and taken their order. They'd glanced around at the festive crowd, had felt out of place, uncomfortably subdued, and had finally discussed the subject that they'd been avoiding. Buchanan didn't recall who had raised the topic or how, but the gist had been, Is this the end, or do we continue seeing each other after this? And as Buchanan had faced the question directly, he'd suddenly realized how absurd it was. Tomorrow, Peter Lang wouldn't exist. So how could Peter Lang continue to have a relationship with his wife, who wouldn't exist tomorrow, either?

Softly, their conversation impossible to be overheard in the din of the crowd, Buchanan had told her that their characters were at an end, and Juana had looked at him as if he was speaking gibberish.

"I'm not interested in who we were," she had said. "I'm talking about *us*."

"So am I."

"No," she'd told him. "Those people don't exist. *We* do. Tomorrow, reality starts. The fantasy is over. What are we going to do?"

"I love you," he'd said.

She'd exhaled, trembling slightly. "I've been waiting for

you to say that. . . . Hoping . . . I don't know how it happened, but I feel the same. I love *you*."

"I want you to know that you'll always be special to me," Buchanan had said.

Juana had started to frown.

"I want you to know," Buchanan had continued, "that—"

Their waiter had interrupted, setting down a tray with their steaming coffee and hot sugar-covered beignets.

As the aproned man left, Juana had leaned toward Buchanan, her voice low but tense with concern. "What are you talking about?"

"—that you'll always be special to me. I'll always feel close to you. If you ever need help, if there's anything I can ever do . . ."

"Wait a minute." Juana had frowned harder, her dark eyes reflecting a light in the ceiling. "This sounds like good-bye."

". . . I'll be there. Any time. Any place. All you have to do is ask. There's nothing I wouldn't do for you."

"You bastard," she had said.

"What?"

"This isn't fair. I'm good enough to risk my life with you. I'm good enough to be used as a prop. But I'm not good enough for you to see after . . ."

"That's not what I meant," Buchanan had said.

"Then what *does* it have to do with? You're in love with me, but you're giving me the brush-off?"

"I didn't mean to fall in love. I—"

"There aren't many reasons why a man walks away from a woman he claims he loves. And right now, the only one I can think of is, he doesn't believe she's good enough for him."

"Listen to me . . ."

"It's because I'm Hispanic."

"No. Not at all. That's crazy. Please. Just listen."

"*You* listen. I could be the best thing that ever happened to you. Don't lose me."

"But tomorrow I have to."

"Have to? Why? Because of the people we work for? To hell with them. They expect me to sign up again. But I'm not planning to."

"It's got nothing to do with them," Buchanan had said.

"This is all about me. It's about what I do. We could never have a relationship after this, because I won't be the same. I'll be a stranger."

"What?"

"I'll be different."

She had stared at him, suddenly realizing the implications of what he was saying. "You'd choose your work instead of—?"

"My work is all I have."

"No," Juana had said. "You could have *me*."

Buchanan studied her. Looked down. Looked up. Bit his lip. Slowly shook his head. "You don't know me. You only know who I pretend to be."

She looked shocked.

"I'll always be your friend," Buchanan had said. "Remember that. I swear to you. If you ever need help, if you're ever in trouble, all you have to do is ask, and no matter how long it's been, no matter how far away I am, I'll—"

Juana had stood, her chair scraping harshly on the concrete floor. People had stared.

"If I ever need you, I'll send you a goddamned postcard."

Hiding tears, she had hurried from the restaurant.

And that was the last time he had spoken to her. When he returned to their apartment, she had already packed and left. Hollow, he had stayed awake all night, sitting in the dark, staring at the wall across from the bed they had shared.

Just as he stared out at the darkness beyond the window of the compartment in the speeding train.

3

He had done it again, Buchanan realized.

He'd become catatonic. Rubbing at the pain in his skull, he had the sense of coming back from far away. The compartment was dark. The night beyond the window was broken only by occasional lights from farms. How long had—?

He glanced down at the luminous dial on his pilot's watch, Peter Lang's watch, disturbed to see that the time was eight minutes after ten. He'd left Washington shortly before noon. The train would long ago have left Virginia. It would be well into North Carolina by now, perhaps into Georgia. All afternoon and most of the evening? he thought in dismay. What's happening to me?

His head throbbing, he stood, turned on the lights in the locked compartment, felt exposed by his reflection in the window, and quickly closed the curtains. The reflected haggard face had looked unfamiliar. He opened his travel bag, took three aspirins from his toilet kit, and swallowed them with water from the tiny sink in the compartment's utility washroom. While he urinated, he felt his mind drifting again, going back six years, and he concentrated to pay attention to now.

He needed to get into character. He had to rebecome Peter Lang. But he also had to be functional. He couldn't keep staring off into space. After all, the whole point of going to New Orleans, of finding out why Juana had sent the postcard, was to give himself a purpose, a sense of direction.

Juana. As much as he needed to focus on reassuming the character of Peter Lang, he had to focus on Juana. She'd be—what?—thirty-one now. He wondered if she'd kept in shape. She hadn't been tall, and she'd been thin, but her military-trained body had compensated. It had been hard and strong and magnificent. Would her thick dark hair still be as short as when he'd known her? He had wanted to run his fingers through it, to clutch it, to tug it gently. Would her dark eyes still be fiery? Would her lips still have that sensuous contour? She'd had a habit, when she'd been concentrating, of pursing those lips and sticking them out slightly, and he had wanted to stroke them as much as he'd wanted to touch her hair.

What was his true motive for going back? he wondered. Was it really just to give himself mobility?

Or had the postcard awakened something in him? He'd repressed his memories of her, just as he'd repressed so much about himself. And now . . .

Maybe I shouldn't have let her go. Maybe I should have . . .

No, he thought. The past is a trap. Leave it alone. Obviously, it's not doing you any good if it makes you catatonic. What you're feeling is a bush-league mistake. In your former lives, you left plenty of unfinished business, a lot of people whom you liked or at least whom your assumed identities liked. But you've never gone back before. Be careful.

But I didn't *love* those other people. Why did she send the postcard? What sort of trouble is she in?

Your controllers would have a fit if they knew what you were thinking.

The trouble is, I remember her so vividly.

Besides, I promised.

No, a warning voice told him. *You* didn't promise. Peter Lang did.

Exactly. And right now, that's who I am.

I meant what I said. I promised.

4

Welcoming the distraction of hunger, relieved to be in motion, Buchanan-Lang unlocked the compartment, checked the swaying corridor, saw no one, and was just about to leave when he decided that the simple lock on the compartment couldn't be trusted. He took his small travel bag—the passport and the handgun in it—with him, secured the compartment, and proceeded toward the dining car.

It was three cars away, and when he entered it, he discovered that it was almost deserted, a few passengers sipping coffee, waiters clearing dirty dishes from the tables. The overhead lights of the dining car gleamed off the windows and made the area seem extra bright, obscuring whatever was out in the darkness.

Buchanan rubbed his aching forehead and approached the nearest waiter.

The weary-looking man anticipated his question. "Sorry, sir. We're closed. Breakfast starts at six in the morning."

"I'm afraid I took a nap and overslept. I'm starved. Isn't there something you can give me so my stomach won't growl all night?" Buchanan discreetly held out a ten-dollar bill.

"Yes, sir. I understand your problem. I'll see what I can do. Perhaps a couple of cold roast beef sandwiches to take with you."

"Sounds good."

"And maybe a soda."

"A beer would be better."

"Well," a voice said behind Buchanan, "I don't have the beer. But just in case, I did plan ahead and arranged for some sandwiches."

Refusing to show that he was surprised, Buchanan made himself wait a moment before he slowly turned to face the woman whose voice he had heard. When he saw her, he was even *more* careful not to show his surprise. Because he definitely *was* surprised.

The woman had long, dramatic flame-red hair. She was tall. In her late twenties. Athletic figure. Strong forehead. Excellent cheekbones. Fashion-model features.

He knew this woman. At least, he'd seen her before. The first time, she'd worn beige slacks and a yellow blouse. That had been in Mexico. She'd been taking photographs of him outside the jail in Mérida.

The second time, she'd worn jeans and a denim shirt. That had been near Pier 66 in Fort Lauderdale. She'd been taking photographs of him while he stopped his boat next to Big Bob Bailey in the channel.

This time, she wore brown poplin slacks and a khaki safari jacket, the type with plenty of pockets, several of which had objects in them. She looked like an ad from a Land's End catalog. A camera bag was slung over her left shoulder. The camera itself dangled from a sling around her neck. The only detail that didn't fit the Land's End image was the bulging paper bag in her right hand.

With her left hand, she added ten dollars to the ten that Buchanan had already given the waiter. "Thank you." She smiled. "I didn't think my friend would ever show up. I appreciate your patience."

"No problem, ma'am." The waiter pocketed the money. "If there's anything else . . ."

"Nothing, thank you."

As the waiter went back to clearing dirty dishes from a table, the woman redirected her attention toward Buchanan. "I hope your heart wasn't set on those roast beef sandwiches he mentioned. Mine are chicken salad."

"I beg your pardon?" Buchanan asked.

"Chicken . . ."

"That's not what . . . Do we know each other?"

"You ask that after everything we've been through together?" The woman's emerald eyes twinkled.

"Lady, I'm not in the mood. I'm sure there are plenty of other guys on the train who . . ."

"Okay, if you insist, we'll play. Do we know each other?" She debated with herself. "Yes. In a manner of speaking. You could say we're acquainted, although of course we've never met." She looked amused.

"I don't want to be rude."

"It doesn't matter to me. I'm used to it."

"You've had too much to drink."

"Not a drop. But I wish I *had* been drinking. I'm bored enough from waiting here so long. On second thought . . ." She turned to the waiter. "A couple of beers sound good. Do you suppose we could still have them?"

"Certainly, ma'am. Anything else?"

"Make it *four* beers, and you may as well add those roast beef sandwiches. I have a feeling this is going to be a long night."

"Then maybe coffee . . . ?"

"No. The beers will be fine," she said. As the waiter headed away from them, she turned again toward Buchanan. "Unless you'd prefer coffee."

"What I'd prefer is to know what the hell you think you're doing," Buchanan said.

"Requesting an interview."

"What?"

"I'm a reporter."

"Congratulations. What's that got to do with me?"

"I'll make you a bet."

Buchanan shook his head. "This is absurd." He started to leave.

"No, really. I'll bet I can guess your name."

"A bet means you win or lose something. I can't see what I win or—"

"If I can't guess your name, I'll leave you alone."

Buchanan thought about it. "All right." He sighed. "Anything to get rid of you. What's my name?"

"Buchanan."

"Wrong. It's Peter Lang." Again he started to walk away.

"Prove it."

"I don't have to prove anything. I'm out of patience." Buchanan kept walking away.

She followed him. "Look, I was hoping to do this in private, but if you want to make it difficult, that's up to you. Your name isn't Peter Lang any more than it's Jim Crawford, Ed Potter, Victor Grant, and Don Colton. You did use those names, of course. And many others. But your *given* name is Buchanan. First name: Brendan. Nickname: Bren."

Muscles cramping, Buchanan stopped at the exit from the dining car. Not showing his tension, he turned, noting with relief that the tables at this end of the car were all empty. He pretended to be innocently exasperated. "What do I have to do to get rid of you?"

"Get rid of me? That's a figure of speech, I hope."

"I don't know what you're—"

She held up the bulging paper bag. "I'm hungry. I couldn't find you on the train, so I kept waiting for you to come to the dining car. Then I worried that maybe you'd brought something with you to eat. Every half hour, I had to slip the waiter ten dollars so he'd let me keep my table without ordering. Another ten minutes, the place would have been empty, and he'd have made me leave. Thank God you showed up."

"Sure," Buchanan said. "Thank God." He noticed the waiter come down the aisle toward them.

"Here are the sandwiches and the beer." The waiter handed her another paper bag.

"Thanks. How much do I owe you?" She paid him, adding a further tip.

Then Buchanan and she were alone again.

"So what do you say?" The woman's emerald eyes continued to twinkle. "At least you'll get something to eat. Since I couldn't find you in the coach seats, I assume you have a compartment. Why don't we . . . ?"

"If I really use all the names you claim I do, I must be involved in something very shady."

"I try not to make judgments."

"But what am I? In the Mafia? A secret agent? Won't you be afraid to be alone with me?"

"Who says I'm alone? Surely you don't think I'd go on this assignment without help."

"Don't tell me you're with those two guys who just finished their coffee at the other end of the car," Buchanan said. "They're leaving and not in this direction. It doesn't look to me like you're with anybody."

"Whoever it is wouldn't let you see him."

"Yeah, sure, right."

"Just as I assume that anybody following you wouldn't be obvious, either."

"Why would anybody follow *me*?" Buchanan suddenly wondered if he *was* being followed. "This is certainly the weirdest . . . Okay. I'm hungry. I get the feeling you won't let me alone. Let's eat."

He opened the door from the dining car. The *clack-clack-clack* of the wheels became louder. "I'm warning you, though."

"What?" She straightened.

"I'm not easy."

"What a coincidence." She followed.

5

Pretending not to notice her suspicion when he locked the door, Buchanan lifted the compartment's small table from the wall and secured its brace. Then he unpacked the paper bags and spread out their contents, making sure he took the roast beef sandwiches, since he didn't know what she might have put in the chicken salad sandwiches while she waited for him. He twisted off the caps on two bottles of beer.

Throughout, she remained standing. In the narrow compartment, Buchanan felt very aware of being close to her.

He handed her an open bottle of beer, bit into a sandwich, and sat on one side of the table. "You think you know my name. In fact, according to you, I've got several of them. What's yours?"

She sat across from him, brushing back a strand of red hair. Her lipstick was the same color. "Holly McCoy."

"And you say you're a reporter?" Buchanan drank from his beer, noting that she hadn't touched hers, thinking, Maybe she expects me to drink all four bottles and hopes the beer will make me less careful about what I'm saying. "For what newspaper?"

"The *Washington Post*."

"I read that paper a lot. But I don't think I've ever seen your name as a byline."

"I'm new."

"Ah."

"This will be my first major story."

"Ah."

"For the *Post*. Before that, I worked as a feature writer for the *L.A. Times*."

"Ah." Buchanan swallowed part of a sandwich. The roast beef wasn't bad—a little dry, but the mayonnaise and lettuce compensated. He sipped more of his beer. "I thought you were hungry. You're not eating." As she made herself nibble at some chicken salad, he continued. "Now what's this about an interview? And these names I'm supposed to have . . . I told you, I'm Peter Lang."

Buchanan regretted that. It had been a mistake. When the woman had confronted him in the dining car, he'd responded with the name of the role on which he was concentrating at the moment. His identities had become confused. He had no ID for Peter Lang. He had to correct the problem.

"I have a confession to make," he said. "I lied. You told me you'd leave me alone if you couldn't guess my name. So when you called me by my right name, I decided to pretend I was somebody else and hoped you'd go away."

"I didn't," she said.

"Then I might as well be honest." He set down his bottle of beer and reached in his back pocket, bringing out his wallet, showing her his driver's license. "My name *is* Buchanan. Brendan. Nickname: Bren. Although no one's called me Bren in quite a while. How did you know?"

"You're in the military."

"Right again. And I repeat, how did you know? Not that it's any of your business, but I'm a captain with Special Forces.

My home base is Fort Bragg. I'm on furlough, heading to New Orleans. Never been there before. So what? You have a thing about soldiers? Is that it?''

She tilted her head, a motion that emphasized her elegant neck. ''In a manner of speaking.''

''Well, as long as you're speaking, why don't you speak plainly?'' Buchanan said. ''Enough is enough. You still haven't told me how you know my name. I've been a good sport. What's this about?''

''Humor me. I'd like to mention some code words to you,'' she said.

''Code words? Of all the . . .'' Buchanan gestured with exasperation.

''Tell me if they mean anything to you. Task Force One Hundred and Sixty. Seaspray. The Intelligence Support Activity. Yellow Fruit.''

Jesus Christ, Buchanan thought, not showing how startled he was. ''I've never heard of them.''

''Now why don't I believe you?''

''Look, lady—''

''Relax. Enjoy the sandwiches,'' she said. ''I'll tell you a story.''

6

Operation Eagle Claw. On April 24, 1980, a U.S. military counterterrorist unit known as Delta was sent into Iran to rescue fifty-two Americans who'd been held hostage in Teheran since November of 1979. Eight helicopters, three MC-130 troop planes, and three EC-130 fuel planes were scheduled to set down at a remote area, code-named Desert One. After refueling, the helicopters would then proceed to a landing site outside Teheran. The 118-man assault team, concealed by night, would enter the city and converge on the target zone.

From the outset, however, problems afflicted the mission. En route from the U.S. aircraft carrier *Nimitz* in the Persian Gulf, one of the helicopters had to turn back because of difficulties with its rotor blades. Soon, another had to return because of a failed navigational system. At Desert One, yet another helicopter malfunctioned, this time the victim of a hydraulic leak. Because no fewer than six helicopters were required for the mission, Operation Eagle Claw had to be aborted. But as the team pulled out, one of the remaining helicopters struck one of its companion EC-130 fuel planes. The resulting explosion killed eight U.S. soldiers and critically burned five others. Flames prevented the bodies of the victims from being recovered. Secret papers and classified equipment had to be abandoned.

Humiliated and outraged, the Pentagon determined to find out what had gone wrong. Clearly, more than just mechanical failures were at fault. An exhaustive investigation concluded that various branches of the U.S. military had so competed with one another to be a part of the rescue that their efforts were dangerously counterproductive. Inefficiency, lack of preparedness, insufficient training, inadequate transportation, incomplete and unreliable information—the list of problems went on and on. It quickly became evident that if the United States was going to have an effective military antiterrorist group, that group would have to be capable of operating on its own, without needing help from outside sources, either military or civilian. Delta, the team of commandos who would have performed the hostage rescue, was assigned a permanent training base in a restricted section of Fort Bragg in North Carolina. A similar group, SEAL Team 6, was stationed at the Little Creek Naval Base in Virginia. The Joint Special Operations Command was created to supervise unconventional units in all branches of the U.S. military. A separate group, the Special Operations Division, was created to coordinate special operations exclusively within the Army.

7

As the woman talked, Buchanan finished one beer and opened another. He bunched up his sandwich wrappers, putting them in a paper bag. He stifled a yawn. "This sounds more like a history lecture than a story. Remember, I'm assigned to Fort

Bragg. I know all about the specifics of the failed hostage rescue and the establishment of Delta Force.''

"I'm sure you know much more than that," Holly McCoy said. "But let's take this one step at a time."

Buchanan shrugged. As he listened to the *clack-clack-clack* of the swaying train, he gestured for her to continue.

"One of the first problems the Special Operations Division decided to deal with was transportation," Holly said. "It had taken Delta too long to get into Iran. The aircraft hadn't been adequate to the task. Too many channels in the military had needed to be informed about where and when Delta was going. Obviously some streamlining was in order. Delta needed to get to its targets as quickly and secretly as possible and with the best means. That's why Task Force One Hundred and Sixty and Seaspray were formed."

Again Buchanan needed all his discipline not to show how startled he was by the mention of those code names. While his stomach muscles hardened, he pretended another yawn. "Sorry. I don't want you to think you're boring me. Go ahead and finish your beer."

Holly brushed back another strand of red hair, gave him an irritated look, and continued. "Task Force One Hundred and Sixty was a classified Army unit that provided aviation for Delta as well as Special Forces and the Rangers. It had the big Chinook cargo helicopters, as well as various utility choppers and gunships. Seaspray, though, was a totally off-the-books, covert Army aviation unit that bought aircraft through civilian intermediaries, secretly modified the planes with state-of-the-art equipment—motor silencers, infrared radar, rocket launchers, that sort of thing—and used the planes for small-scale secret missions. The civilian intermediaries who Seaspray used were provided by the CIA, and some of the work that Seaspray did was for another civilian agency, the Drug Enforcement Administration. That's where the trouble started, I think. Civilians and the military working together but hiding that cooperation from the Pentagon and from Congress."

Buchanan sipped more of his second beer and glanced at his watch. "It's almost midnight. If there's a point to this, I suggest you get to it—before I fall asleep."

"I doubt there's much risk of that," Holly said. "In fact, I think you're a lot more interested than you're pretending."

"Interested in you. Except I prefer my dates to be less talkative."

"Pay attention," Holly said. "The next problem for the Special Operations Division was obtaining intelligence. When the Shah fell from power in Iran in 1979, the CIA lost most of its assets there. During the Iran hostage crisis, the Agency wasn't able to furnish much reliable information about where the hostages were being held and how they were being guarded. Obviously, Delta Force needed details about the situations it would have to face. But the intelligence it received had to have a military perspective to it. So the ISA was formed. The Intelligence Support Activity."

Again Buchanan felt his muscles cramp. Jesus, he thought. Where the hell is this woman getting her information?

"ISA was another secret military unit," Holly said. "Its purpose was to send soldiers, who pretended to be civilians, into emergency situations in foreign countries—a terrorist crisis at an airport, for example. There, they conducted reconnaissance of possible Delta targets and not only provided intelligence but, if necessary, tactical support. This was something new. An operational military unit working under civilian cover and providing the sort of information that the CIA normally does. Commandos who were spies. The ISA was so unorthodox and hush-hush that most top officials in the Pentagon didn't know anything about it. In theory, it didn't exist."

Buchanan opened his third beer. He was going to close his eyes soon and pretend that the alcohol had put him to sleep.

"Pay attention," Holly repeated.

"I am. I am."

"You're going to like this part. The Special Operations Division discovered it had a problem. How was it going to keep all these secret units truly secret, even from the Pentagon, which has never been fond of unconventional tactics? The answer was to establish a security unit that itself was secret. Its code name was Yellow Fruit. Again military personnel used civilian cover. They dressed as civilians. They pretended to operate civilian businesses. But in reality, they were providing security for Seaspray, the ISA, and several other covert military units. It was Yellow Fruit's job to make sure that everything stayed hidden.''

Holly studied him, waiting for a reaction.

Buchanan set down his beer bottle. He assumed his most judicious expression. ''Fascinating.''

''Is that all you've got to say?''

''Well, the operation certainly must have succeeded,'' Buchanan said, ''assuming that what you just told me isn't a fantasy. The reason I know it succeeded is I've never heard of Yellow Fruit. Or the Intelligence Support Activity. Or Seaspray. Or Task Force One Hundred and Sixty.''

''You know, for the first time I think you might be telling the truth.''

''You're suggesting I'd lie to you?''

''In this case, maybe not. Those units were compartmentalized. Often members of one group didn't know about the other groups. For that matter, the ISA was compartmentalized within itself. Some members didn't know who their fellow members were. Plus, Seaspray and Yellow Fruit were eventually exposed and disbanded. They don't exist anymore. By those names, at least. I know that Seaspray was later temporarily reformed, using the code name Quasar Talent.''

''Then if they don't exist . . .''

''Some of them,'' Holly said. ''Others are still doing business as usual. And others have been newly created, much more secret, much more compartmentalized, much more ambitious. Scotch and Soda, for example.''

8

''Scotch and . . . ?'' Buchanan felt the back of his neck turn cold.

''That's a code name for yet another undercover military group,'' Holly said. ''It works with the Drug Enforcement Administration and the CIA to infiltrate the Central and South American drug networks and destroy them from within. But since those foreign governments haven't sanctioned the presence of plainclothes American soldiers—*armed* soldiers, using false names—on their soil, the operation is very much against the law.''

"Either you've got one hell of an imagination, or your sources must be in a mental ward," Buchanan said. "Whatever, it doesn't concern me. I don't know anything about this stuff, so why . . . ?''

"You used to work for the ISA, but six months ago you were transferred to Scotch and Soda."

Buchanan stopped breathing.

"You're one of numerous Special Operations soldiers assigned to covert duty—wearing civilian clothes but armed and carrying forged identities—who are, in effect, functioning as a military branch of the DEA and the CIA in foreign countries."

Buchanan slowly straightened. "All right, now I've had enough. That's it. What you're telling me . . . what you're accusing me of . . . is preposterous. If you said that kind of nonsense in front of the wrong people, some fool—a politician, for example—might actually believe you. And then I'd be in crap to my eyebrows. I'd be answering questions for the rest of my career. Because of a damned fantasy."

"*Is* it a fantasy?" Holly reached in her camera bag and brought out a copy of the Cancún police sketch of him, as well as copies of the photographs that Big Bob Bailey had shown Buchanan in Fort Lauderdale. "These don't look like a fantasy."

Buchanan's chest ached as he examined the police sketch and the pictures of him getting off a plane in Frankfurt, accompanied by Bailey, and of him in front of the jail in Mérida, accompanied by Garson Woodfield from the U.S. embassy. Some of the pictures were unfamiliar. They showed him on a powerboat in the channel near Pier 66 in Fort Lauderdale, stopped next to another boat, talking to Bailey. The latter photograph had been taken from shore (Buchanan recalled turning and seeing Holly lower her camera), and the angle had been chosen so that it included a Fort Lauderdale sign in the background.

For God's sake, Buchanan thought, these photographs were supposed to have been destroyed. What happened in Fort Lauderdale after I left? Didn't the team do its job?

"So?" he asked, fighting not to reveal his tension. "What are these supposed to mean?"

"You're really amazing."

"What?"

"You sit there with a straight face and . . . You'd deny anything, no matter how strong the evidence was," Holly said.

"These aren't evidence of anything. What are you talking about?"

"Come on. They show you posing as three different people."

"They show three men who look a bit like me, and whatever they're doing, it certainly doesn't look like any secret-agent stuff."

"Jim Crawford. Ed Potter. Victor Grant."

"Huey, Dewey, and Louie. Curly, Larry, and Moe. I don't know what you're talking about. And speaking of questions—which you're awfully good at coming up with but don't seem to like to answer—*I'll ask you again*. How did you know my name? How did you know I'm a soldier? How the hell did you know I'd be on this train?"

Holly shook her head. "Confidential."

"And the junk you're accusing me of isn't? Look, there's a good way to prove that you're wrong about me. A simple way. It's very easy. You know my name is Buchanan. To prove I've got nothing to hide, I even showed you my driver's license. You know I'm stationed at Fort Bragg. So check on me. All you'll find is that I'm a captain whose specialty is field training. That's all. Nothing else. Nothing dark and mysterious. No cloak-and-dagger stuff."

"I did check," Holly said. "And you're right about one thing. All I found out was what you just told me. There's plenty of paperwork about you. But you travel around so much on these mythical training exercises that I couldn't find anyone who'd actually ever met you."

"You asked the wrong people."

"*Who?* Tell me who to ask. Not that it would make a difference. I take for granted that anyone you told me to ask would by definition be part of the conspiracy."

"Lady, do you know what you sound like? The next thing you'll probably tell me is that I had something to do with the two Kennedy assassinations, not to mention Martin Luther King's."

"Don't be condescending."

"What I am is pissed off."

"Or pretending to be. I've got a feeling you're all smoke and mirrors, layers within layers. Your name. Your ID. How can I be sure that Buchanan isn't just another pseudonym?"

"For God's sake . . ."

"Let's consider Delta Force, which is classified but everybody knows about it. It isn't nearly as covert and shadowy as ISA or Scotch and Soda. The members of Delta live off base. They have average civilian apartments. They drive average civilian cars. When they get up in the morning and go to work, it's just as if they're going to any other job, except that *their* job is practicing how to blast their way into hijacked planes and rescue hostages. They wear civilian clothes. They carry civilian ID. *Fake* ID. Bogus names and backgrounds. No one who lives around them has any idea of who they really are or what they really do. In fact, most people at Fort Bragg don't have any idea, either. If members of Delta use that kind of cover, how deep would the cover be for someone who belonged to much more secret operations like ISA or Scotch and Soda?"

"You can't have it both ways, Holly. You say you want the truth, but apparently you don't intend to trust a single thing I say. What if I said I did belong to this Scotch and Soda thing? You'd probably say I was lying and actually belonged to something else."

"You're very skilled. Honestly. My compliments."

"Suppose you were right?" Buchanan asked. "Isn't it foolish of you to accuse me of being some kind of spy? What if I felt threatened? I might have tried to keep you quiet."

"I hardly think so," Holly said. "You wouldn't try to do anything to me unless you knew you could get away with it. I made sure I was protected."

"You sound awfully confident." Buchanan rubbed his aching forehead. "Did you honestly think that I'd look at those photographs, lose control, and confess? Even if I did, I could deny it later. Your word against mine. Unless . . ."

Buchanan reached for her camera bag.

"Hey," she said.

He tugged it away from where it hung on her shoulder. She tried to stop him, but he held her wrists together with his left hand while he used his right hand to open the bag. Inside there was a small tape recorder, a red light glowing, a slight hum as the recorder's wheels turned.

"My, my," he said. "I'm on 'Candid Camera.' Only in this case, it's candid audio. Naughty, naughty. It isn't nice to be deceptive."

"Right. Coming from you."

Buchanan pulled the machine out and traced a wire from it to a small microphone concealed in the latch on the outside of the bag. "What were you using? An extra-slow speed on the tape so you wouldn't have to worry about turning it over? And if you did have to turn it, you could always pretend to have to go to the bathroom?"

"You can't blame me for trying."

Buchanan shut off the machine. "For all the good it did you. I told you I've got nothing to do with this stuff you're talking about. That's all you have on the tape—my denial."

Holly shrugged, looking less confident.

"No more games." Buchanan stepped closer. "Take off your clothes."

She looked up sharply. "*What?*"

"Take off your clothes, or I'll take them off for you."

"You can't be serious!"

"Lady, when you pick up men on trains, you have to expect they might want something more than conversation. *Take off your clothes.*" Buchanan banged his fist on the table.

"Get away from me!"

Outside the compartment, someone pounded on the door.

"Impressive," Buchanan said. "Quicker than I expected."

Holly's expression was a combination of fright, relief, and bewilderment. "What do you—? Quicker than—?"

Buchanan opened the door. A tall man in his thirties—square-jawed, broad-shouldered, heavy-chested, an ex-football-player type—was about to ram his shoulder against the door. He blinked in surprise at Buchanan's sudden appearance.

"And who are you?" Buchanan asked. "The husband?"

The surly man looked past Buchanan to make sure that Holly was all right.

"Or the boyfriend? Come on," Buchanan said. "I'm running out of categories."

"An interested party."

"Then you might as well *join* the party." Buchanan opened the door wider and gestured for the man to enter. "There's no point in standing in the hall and waking the neighbors. I just hope we all fit in this tiny compartment."

His rugged features contorted with suspicion, the man slowly entered.

Buchanan felt the man's wide shoulders press against him. He managed to close the door. "It's a good thing you didn't bring company. We might run out of oxygen."

"Shut up with the jokes," the man said. "Take off her clothes? What did you think you were—?"

"Inviting you," Buchanan said.

The big man opened his mouth.

"That tape recorder's a little too obvious," Buchanan said and turned to Holly. "I figured you meant for me to find it. Then I'd feel safe to talk, nothing I couldn't deny later, your word against mine, but what I wouldn't know is that the good stuff would be transmitted by a microphone you were wearing to your partner in a nearby compartment. The only way I was going to find that microphone was by doing a strip search, so I thought I'd suggest the idea and see what happened." He turned to the man. "And here you are."

"You . . ." Holly didn't finish the curse.

"Hey, I meant what I told you. I've got nothing to do with this secret-agent stuff. But that doesn't mean I'm an idiot," Buchanan said. "Now is there anything else you want to ask me? Because it's late. I'm tired. I want to get some sleep."

"You . . ."

"Yeah, I'm probably that, too," Buchanan said.

"Come on, Holly," her companion said.

Buchanan squeezed out of the way. With difficulty, he opened the door. "Thanks for paying for the beer and sandwiches. You really know how to show a guy a good time."

Holly's eyes narrowed. "I'm staying."

"Don't be crazy," her companion said.

"I know what I'm doing," she said.

"Look, this is all very interesting," Buchanan said. "But I mean it. I'm tired."

"And *I* mean it. I'm staying."

"Fine," Buchanan said. "Anything to convince you I'm

telling the truth. You can satisfy yourself that I don't say anything incriminating in my sleep.''

"Holly, think about it," her companion said.

"I'll be fine, Ted."

"Yeah, Ted," Buchanan said. "She'll be fine. I promise I won't take off her clothes. Good night, Ted." Buchanan guided him out the door. "Stay tuned. I hope my snoring won't keep you awake."

In the swaying corridor, a white-haired elderly woman in a nightgown adjusted her spectacles and peered intensely at them from the compartment to the right.

"Sorry if we woke you, ma'am," Buchanan said. He watched Ted walk along the corridor and enter the last compartment on the right. With a wave to both him and the elderly woman, Buchanan stepped back into his compartment and closed the door.

He locked it and studied Holly. "So which position do you like? Top or bottom?"

"Don't get the wrong idea because I stayed. Ted's really very tough. If he thinks I'm not safe with you, he'll—"

"Bunks."

"What?"

"I'm talking about bunks." Buchanan reached up to grab a lever and pulled down the top one. He started to prepare the bottom one. "I don't know what you expect to accomplish by this. But I suggest we flip a coin to see who uses the bathroom first."

"Oh."

"And if you don't happen to have a toothbrush, you can use mine."

"On second thought . . ."

"You bet." Buchanan unlocked and opened the door. "Good night, Holly."

"Good night."

9

"*How did she know my real name? How did she know so many of my pseudonyms? How did she know where to find me? I* asked her those questions several times." Buchanan was in a phone booth on Loyola Avenue, not far from Union Passenger Terminal in New Orleans. The street was noisy. The October sky was hazy blue. The weather was warm and humid. But all Buchanan cared about was what he heard on the phone and whether he was being followed.

"We'll find out," his deep-voiced contact officer said. "Do whatever you were going to do. Don't change your plans. We'll get back to you. But if anything new develops, call us immediately. Just remember, the evidence she claims to have—the photographs—they aren't conclusive."

"But she's not supposed to have those photographs at all. What happened in Fort Lauderdale after I left?" Buchanan demanded. "This problem was supposed to have been taken care of."

"We thought the woman was merely a hired hand. Nobody guessed she'd be a reporter. When she didn't resurface, she didn't seem important."

"For all I know, Bailey's involved in this, too."

"No," the voice said firmly. "He isn't. Just stay calm. Enjoy your furlough. At the moment, the woman can't prove anything."

"Tell the colonel he was in one of the photographs she showed me."

"Don't worry. I'll be sure to tell him. Meanwhile, in case we need to get in touch with you, stick around your hotel room between six and eight tonight. After that, check the possible rendezvous sites we agreed on before you left."

Tense, Buchanan hung up the phone, picked up his travel bag, opened the booth's door, and stepped out.

A redheaded woman and her male companion appeared from behind trees in a nearby park.

God, Buchanan thought.

He stalked toward them. "Enough is enough. You're not going to ruin my furlough by following me."

Holly McCoy looked disappointed that she'd been spotted. "Who were you phoning? Your superior officers to tell them you'd been exposed?"

"An old friend who moved down here. Not that it's any of your business."

"Prove it. Let's go visit him."

"His girlfriend told me he had to go to Houston for an emergency sales conference."

"Convenient. What's his name?"

"Lady, I'm annoyed that I won't get to see him, and you're not making things any better by—"

"Holly. Please, call me Holly. I mean, since we nearly spent the night together, we might as well use each other's first name."

Buchanan turned to her male companion. "Whatever you're being paid, it isn't enough. After listening to her all the time, don't you just want to put a noose around your neck and put an end to it all?"

He walked away toward the entrance to the nearby post office.

"Brendan!" Holly called.

Buchanan didn't respond.

"Bren!" she called.

Buchanan kept walking.

"Hey!" she called. "What hotel are you using?"

It had been so long since anyone had used Buchanan's first name and his nickname that he didn't identify them with himself. Slowly, they registered on him. He turned. "Why should I make things easy for you? Damn it, find out for yourself."

In front of the post office, a man got out of a taxi. Buchanan ducked in and gave directions to the driver. As the taxi sped into traffic, the last thing he heard Holly shout was, "Hey!"

10

Brendan. Bren. As his first name and his nickname echoed in his consciousness, Buchanan became more aware of how long it had been since he had portrayed himself.

But this was different. Now he found himself confronted by the most complex assumption of identity that he had ever attempted. Not one identity but two. Simultaneously. Brendan Buchanan and Peter Lang. Not schizophrenia, for in that case, one identity would alternate with the other. No, *these* identities had to be multilayered, coexisting. Compatible yet separate. Balanced within the same instant.

To fulfill his purpose for coming to New Orleans, to find out why Juana had sent the postcard, to learn the trouble she was in, he had to reconstruct Peter Lang. After all, Peter Lang had made the promise to help her. Peter Lang had been in love with her. Desperate not to be himself, Buchanan wanted very much to be Peter Lang.

But Peter Lang wasn't being followed by Holly McCoy. Peter Lang hadn't worked for the Intelligence Support Activity. He wasn't now assigned to Scotch and Soda. Oh, Peter Lang had worked for a clandestine branch of Special Operations. That was true. But not these particular ones. Peter Lang wasn't under investigation by the *Washington Post*. Brendan Buchanan was, and it was Brendan Buchanan who would have to deceive and discourage Holly McCoy.

Thus Peter Lang would pretend to be Brendan Buchanan. And Brendan Buchanan . . . Well, he had to do something while he was in New Orleans. He couldn't just sit in his hotel room and show Holly that she'd made him nervous. As a consequence, he would pretend to be Peter Lang and revisit the spots he had so admired when he'd lived here six years ago.

Peter Lang would have stayed at a place he knew in the French Quarter, but in theory, Brendan Buchanan had never been to New Orleans. He didn't know the secret good places. He would choose an easier-to-book, less quaint, but first-rate hotel, something near the French Quarter but also near the Riverwalk mall and the other downtown attractions. The Holiday Inn—Crowne Plaza, tall and gleaming, seemed ideal. Having made a reservation for Brendan Buchanan, he checked in, was shown to his twelfth-floor room, waited until the bellhop had left, then locked the door and transferred his handgun and Victor Grant's passport from his travel bag to his clothes. After all, the room might be searched. The passport fit within his lightweight gray sport coat. The gun fit underneath the sport coat, behind his belt, at his spine. He didn't bother to check the view.

Two minutes after having been shown to his room, he left it, taking the fire stairs to the lobby. He scanned it to make

sure that Holly McCoy wasn't in sight, then walked outside
and got in the taxi whose driver he had told to wait for him.

"Where you gwin to now, suh?" the elderly, silver-haired,
resonant-voiced black man asked.

"Metairie Cemetery."

"Somebody die, suh?"

"All the time."

"Ain't *that* the truth, suh."

Buchanan's contact officer had told him to stay at the hotel
from six to eight this evening in case he had to be given a
message. But that was three hours from now, and Buchanan
wanted to keep moving. More important, he wanted to do what
Peter Lang would do. So he leaned back in the taxi, pretending
to admire the sights as the driver headed down Tchoupitoulas
Street, got on the 90 expressway, and merged with rushing
traffic, speeding toward Metairie Road.

The huge cemetery, established in 1873, had once been a
pre–Civil War racetrack. Like the many other old cemeteries
in New Orleans, it consisted of rows and rows of masonry
tombs. Each tomb was one hundred feet long and four tiers
high, with niches into which coffins had been slid, the entrances
sealed. The land was so flat and the Mississippi so close that
in the previous century the city's moist soil had necessitated
aboveground burial. Since then, modern drainage systems had
reduced the moisture problem. Nonetheless, tradition had been
established, and most interments were still above ground.

Peter Lang had come here often. Among the old cemeteries
he'd frequently visited, Metairie had been his favorite. His
ostensible purpose for coming had been his taste for gothic
atmosphere and his interest in history, although the actual reason had been that the nooks and crannies of the decaying
cemeteries had provided abundant locations for message dead
drops (Buchanan-Lang's then control officer had had a morbid
sense of humor). On rare occasions, a messenger had passed
him a coded note by means of brush contact, the cemeteries so
crowded with visitors and mourners that the skillful exchange
would not have been detected.

Now Buchanan-Lang came for another reason. He associated
the cemetery with Juana. She had often accompanied him on
his visits, and her interest in the old tombs had eventually

rivaled his. He particularly remembered her delight when she first came upon the miniature mausoleum built for Josie Arlington, a prominent madam in the city many years before. Josie had decided to have her tomb built from symbolic red stone and decorated with granite torches. As Buchanan-Lang reached the tomb, he could almost hear Juana's laughter. The haze in the sky had lifted. The sharp sun gleamed from deep blue, and in the sudden clarity that contrasted with the gloom of the crumbling cemetery, he imagined Juana standing next to him, her head tilted back, her smile bright, her hand on his shoulder. He wanted to hug her.

And tonight he would.

I should never have let you go. My life would have been so different.

I won't let you go a second time. I didn't know how much I needed you.

I meant what I said six years ago. I love you.

Or Peter Lang does.

But what about Buchanan-Lang? he wondered.

And what about *Buchanan*?

His skull wouldn't stop throbbing. He massaged his temples, but his headache continued to torture him.

11

SIX P.M.

Back in his hotel room, he obeyed instructions and waited in case his superiors needed to contact him. He thought about ordering a meal from room service, but his appetite was gone. He thought about watching CNN, but he had no interest. Juana. He kept anticipating his reunion with her. He kept reliving their last night together six years ago. He kept regretting his failed opportunity.

He sat in a chair, and suddenly the room was in blackness. He'd left the draperies open to appreciate the sunset. A moment ago, it seemed, the sky had been crimson. Now abruptly it and the room were dark. Confused, uneasy, he glanced at the luminous dial on his watch.

Nine-sixteen?

No. That wasn't possible. The shadows must be playing tricks on him. He wasn't seeing the dial correctly. Leaning toward a table, he turned on a light and studied his watch, disturbed to discover that the time was indeed 9:16, that three hours and sixteen minutes had passed without his being aware of them.

Dear God, he thought, that's the third time in the last three days. No. I'm wrong. It's the fourth. Jesus. Am I so preoccupied that I'm blotting out my surroundings?

He stood, went to the bathroom, then came back and paced, trying to regain his sense of motion. As he passed the telephone on the bureau near the closet, he was startled to notice that the tiny red message light was flashing.

But I didn't hear the phone ring.

Worried that his contact officer had tried to relay emergency instructions, he quickly picked up the phone and pressed zero.

After three buzzes, a woman answered. "Hotel operator."

He tried to sound calm. "This is room twelve fourteen. My message light is flashing."

"Just a moment, sir, while I . . . Yes."

Buchanan's heart pounded.

The operator said, "Holly McCoy left a message at five-forty-five. It says, 'We're staying in the same hotel. Why don't we get together later?' I can call her room if you like, sir."

"No, thank you. It won't be necessary."

Buchanan set down the phone.

His emotions were mixed. He felt relieved that he hadn't missed an urgent message that his superiors had tried to give him. He felt equally relieved that the message he did receive had been logged at 5:45. *Before* he'd returned to his room. *Before* he'd sat down and lost over three hours. At least he wasn't losing touch so deeply that a phone call had failed to rouse him.

But he also felt disturbed that Holly McCoy had managed to track him to this hotel. It wasn't just her annoying persistence that troubled him, her relentless pressure. It was something further. How had she found him? Was she so determined that she'd telephoned every one of the hundreds of hotels in the area and asked for . . . ?

When I made the reservation, I should have used a different name.

Hey, using different names is what got you into this. If Holly McCoy found out that you used an alias to register, then she'd *really* be suspicious. Besides, if you'd used an unauthorized false name to register, your superiors would have wondered what on earth you thought you were doing? You're supposed to be on R and R, not on a mission.

But that's exactly what Buchanan *was* on, a mission, and the rendezvous time was almost upon him. He had to get to Café du Monde by eleven o'clock. That was when he and Juana had arrived there six years ago.

Tonight. After making sure that his pistol was covered by his gray sport coat and securely braced behind his belt, at his spine, he opened the door, checked the hallway, locked his room, and went quickly down the fire stairs.

12

The night was eerily similar to the one six years ago. For example, as Buchanan left the hotel, he noticed that the air was balmy with the hint of rain, a pleasant breeze coming in from the Mississippi. The same as before.

He took care to make sure that Holly McCoy wasn't in sight, but as he walked along Tchoupitoulas Street, restraining his pace so he wouldn't attract attention, another parallel between tonight and six years before became disconcertingly obvious. It was Halloween. Many pedestrians he passed wore costumes, and again similar to six years before, the most popular costume seemed to be a skeleton: a black tight-fitting garment with the phosphorescent images of bones painted on it and a head mask highlighted with white, representing a skull. With so many people resembling one another, he couldn't tell if he was being followed. More, all Holly McCoy needed to do to disguise her conspicuous red hair was to wear a head mask. By contrast, on *this* night, *he* looked conspicuous, since he was one of the minority who weren't wearing a costume of some sort.

As he crossed Canal Street toward the French Quarter, he

began to hear music, faint, then distinct, the increasing throb and wail of jazz. A while ago, he'd read in a newspaper that New Orleans had instituted a noise ordinance, but tonight no one seemed to care. Street bands competed with those in bars. Dixieland, the blues—these and many other styles pulsed along the French Quarter's narrow, crowded streets as costumed revelers danced, sang, and drank in celebration of the night of the dead.

. . . gone and left me.

When the saints . . .

Buchanan tried to lose himself in the crowd. He had less than an hour before he was supposed to be at Café du Monde, and he wanted to use that hour to guarantee that his meeting with Juana would not be observed.

As he headed up Bienville Street and then along Royal Street, then up Conti to Bourbon Street, he felt frustrated by the density of the crowd. It prevented him from moving as fast as he wanted, from taking advantage of opportunities to duck into a courtyard or down a side street. Every time he attempted an evasion tactic, a group would suddenly loom in front of him, and anyone who followed would not have trouble keeping up with him while blending with the festivities. He bought a devil's mask from a sidewalk vendor and immediately found that it restricted his vision so much that he bumped into people, making him feel vulnerable and self-conscious. He took it off, glanced at his watch, and was amazed to discover how much his concentration had compressed the time. It was almost eleven. He had to get to the rendezvous site.

Soon, he thought. Soon he would put his arms around Juana. Soon he'd be able to find out why she needed him. He'd help her. He'd show her how much he loved her. He'd correct the mistake he'd made six years ago.

Who had made?

Coming down Orleans Avenue, he reached the shadows of St. Anthony's Garden. From there, he took Pirate's Alley down to Jackson Square. Its huge bronze statue of Andrew Jackson on horseback rose ghostlike from the darkness of the gardens in the locked, deserted park. Using one of the walkways that flanked the wrought-iron fence of the square, he at last reached

Decatur Street and paused in the shadows next to the square while he studied his destination.

Where he stood was surprisingly free of the congestion and noise of the rest of the French Quarter. He felt apart from things, more vulnerable. Several glances behind him gave him the assurance of being alone.

And yet he felt threatened. Again he studied his destination. At last, he stepped into view, felt as if he had reentered the world, crossed Decatur, and made his approach toward Café du Monde.

It was a large concrete building whose distinctive feature was that its walls were composed of tall, wide archways that made the restaurant open-air. During heavy rains, the interior could be protected by lowering green-and-white-striped canvas, but usually—and tonight was no exception—the only thing that separated people on the street from the restaurant's patrons were waist-high iron railings. Tonight, the same as six years ago, the place was crowded more than usual. Because of the holiday. Because of Halloween. Expectant customers, many of them in costume, stood in a line on the sidewalk, waiting to be admitted.

Buchanan strained to catch a glimpse of Juana, hoping that the crowd would have made her decide to wait outside for him. He and Juana would be able to get away from the noise and confusion. He would lovingly put his arm around her and try to find a quiet place. He would get her to tell him what terrible urgency had made her send the postcard, allowing him a second chance.

There was an addition to the restaurant. Smaller than the main section, it had a green-and-white roof supported by widely separated slender white poles that made this part of the restaurant seem even more open-air. He stared past the low metal railing toward the customers close together around small circular tables. The place rippled with constant movement. Hundreds of conversations rushed over him.

Juana. He strained harder to see her. He shifted position to view the interior of the restaurant from a different angle. He scanned the line of waiting customers.

What if she's wearing a costume? he thought. What if she's

afraid to the point that she put on a disguise? He wouldn't be able to recognize her. And she might not hurry to meet him. She might be so terrified that she had to assess everyone around him before she revealed herself.

Juana. Even if she *wasn't* wearing a costume, how could he be certain he would recognize her? Six years had passed. She might have grown her hair long. She might have . . .

And what about him? How had *his* appearance, like his identities, changed in six years? Was his hair dyed the same color? Did he weigh the same? Should he have a mustache? He couldn't remember if Peter Lang had worn a mustache. Did—?

Juana. He brushed past waiting customers and entered the restaurant, determined to find her. She had to be here. The postcard couldn't have had any other meaning. She needed to see him. She wanted his help.

"Hey, buddy, wait your turn," someone said.

"Sir, you'll have to go to the end of the line," a waiter told him.

"You don't understand. I'm supposed to meet someone, and—"

"Please, sir. The end of the line."

Juana. He backed away. His headache intensified as he scanned the crush of customers in the restaurant. Outside on the sidewalk, he rubbed his throbbing head. When a rush of people in costumes swept past him, he whirled to see if Juana might be one of them.

The knife slid into his side. Sharp. Cold. Tingly. Suddenly burning. It felt like a punch. It knocked him off balance. It made him groan. As he felt the wet heat of his gushing blood, someone screamed. People scrambled to get away from him. A man knocked against him. Fighting to stem the flow of his blood, he slipped. The iron railing appeared to rush toward him.

No! he mentally screamed. Not my head! Not again! I can't hurt my—!

EIGHT

1

CUERNAVACA, MEXICO

The black limousine and its escort cars proceeded along Insurgentes Sur freeway, forced to maintain a frustratingly moderate speed as the caravan fought the congestion of holiday traffic heading south from the smog of Mexico City. After thirty-seven miles, the limousine and its escorts reached Cuernavaca, the capital's most popular but at the same time most exclusive retreat. It was easy to understand why the rich and powerful came here each weekend. Sheltered in an attractive wooded valley, Cuernavaca had space, silence, pleasant weather, and most prized of all, clean air. Aztec rulers had built palaces here. So had Cortés. Emperor Maximilian had been especially fond of the area's gardens. These days, what important visitors from the capital valued were the luxurious hotels and the castlelike mansions.

The limousine proceeded along the stately streets of a quiet neighborhood and stopped at the large iron gate of one of the mansions. Majestic shade trees projected above the high stone wall that enclosed the spacious grounds. The uniformed driver stepped out of the limousine and approached an armed guard who stood beyond the bars of the gate and scowled at the visitor. After a brief conversation during which the driver showed the guard a document, the guard entered a wooden booth beside the gate and picked up a telephone, speaking to someone in the house. Thirty seconds later, he returned to the gate, opened it, and motioned for the driver to bring the limousine into the estate. As the escort cars attempted to follow, the guard raised his left hand to stop them. At the same time, another armed guard stepped into view to close and lock the gate.

The limousine proceeded along a shady, curved driveway, past trees, gardens, and fountains, toward the mansion. As it stopped before the stone steps at the entrance, one of the large double doors opened, and a mustached, aristocratic-looking man came out. It was a measure of his need to seem respectful that he had not sent a servant to greet this particular visitor. His name was Esteban Delgado, and his surname—which meant "thin"—was even more appropriate than when he'd met with the director of the National Institute of Archaeology and History in Acapulco a week earlier, for Delgado's body and features were now no longer merely rakishly slender but unhealthily gaunt. His aquiline face was pale, and he would almost have believed the rumors that he was seriously ill if he hadn't been acutely aware of the unbearable tension that he suffered.

At the bottom of the stairs, he forced himself to smile as the limousine's far-rear door opened and a well-dressed, fair-haired, pleasant-looking American in his middle thirties emerged from the car. The man gave the impression of exuding good nature, but Delgado wasn't fooled, for the man's smile—on the rare occasions when he did smile, and this was not one of them—had no warmth. The man's name was Raymond, and the only time Delgado had seen him smile was during a cockfight.

Raymond ignored Delgado, assessed the estate's security, then came around the limousine and opened the other door. An elderly man with thick glasses and dense white hair stepped out. He was in his eighties although, except for extremely wrinkled hands, he appeared to be in his sixties.

"Professor Drummond," Delgado said with forced brightness. "I had no idea that you planned to visit. If I had known, I would have arranged a reception in your honor."

Drummond shook Delgado's hand with authority, fixed his gaze upon him, and waited a moment before he replied in Spanish, one of his seven languages. "I happened to be in Mexico City on business and wanted to discuss something with you. Your office informed me that you were here. If you have an hour to spare . . ."

"Certainly." Delgado led Drummond and his assistant up the stairs. "It will be an honor to have you in my home." Despite the shade trees, Delgado found that he was sweating. "I'll have the servants bring some refreshments. Would you like a rum and Coke? Or perhaps . . ."

"I never drink alcoholic beverages. By all means, you have one if you wish."

"I was going to send for some lemonade."

They entered subdued light in the mansion and crossed the cool, echoing marble vestibule. A colorfully dressed teenage girl appeared at the top of the wide, curved staircase, seemed surprised that there were visitors, and abruptly obeyed Delgado's sharp gesture commanding her to go back to where she had been. At the end of a corridor, Delgado escorted Drummond and Raymond into a mahogany-paneled study that was furnished in leather and filled with hunting trophies as well as numerous rifles and shotguns in glass cabinets, many of the firearms antique. For once, Raymond's eyes displayed interest. Two servants immediately brought in refreshments and as quickly departed.

Neither Drummond nor Raymond picked up the lemonade.

Instead, Drummond leaned back in his chair, sitting imperiously straight, his long arms stretched out on the sides of the chair. His voice was brittle yet strong, his gaze direct. "I suspect your associates have already told you, but we need to compare reactions."

Delgado pretended to look confused.

"The woman, Minister. It will come as no surprise to you when I tell you that she has disappeared."

"Ah." Delgado's heart lurched, but he didn't show any reaction. "Yes. The woman. I did receive information that led me to believe she had disappeared."

"And?"

Delgado tried to make his voice stern. "What do you intend to do about it?"

"What I *am* doing, what I *have* been doing, is using all my resources to locate her. Every element of her background, every conceivable place or person where she might run for shelter and help, is being investigated."

"And yet after two weeks, you have no results."

Drummond nodded in compliment. "Your sources are excellent."

"You still haven't answered my question. What do you intend to do about this?"

"Relative to you? Nothing," Drummond answered. "Our agreement remains the same."

"I don't know why it should. You broke your part of the contract. You assured me you could control the woman. You were emphatic that she would solve my problem."

"And she did."

"Temporarily. But now that she's disappeared, the problem is the same as before."

Drummond's aged eyes narrowed. "I disagree. This disappearance cannot be traced to you."

"*Unless she talks.*"

"But she won't," Drummond said. "Because if she planned to talk, she *would* have by now. It's an obvious method by which she could try to save her life. She knows we would kill her in retribution. On principle. I believe that she remains silent out of fear and as a sign to us that if we leave her alone, she won't be a threat to us. I should say, a threat to *you*. After all, the problem is yours. I was merely doing you a favor by trying to correct it."

Delgado's pulse increased with anger. "Not a favor. A business agreement."

"I won't quibble with terminology. I came to tell you that despite her disappearance, I expect to be allowed to conduct *my* business as you agreed."

Delgado released his nervous energy by standing. "That would be very difficult. The director of the National Institute of Archaeology and History has become furious about your control of the site in the Yucatán. He is mustering government support for a full investigation."

"Discourage him," Drummond said.

"He's very determined."

Now it was Drummond's turn to rise. Despite his frail body, he dominated the study. "I need only another few weeks. I'm too close. I won't be stopped."

"Unless you fail."

"I *never* fail." Drummond bristled. "I am an unforgiving partner. If *you* fail *me*, despite the woman's disappearance, I will take steps to make you regret it."

"How? If you don't find the woman and she never talks."

"She was necessary only to protect you. To expose you, all I need is this." Drummond snapped his fingers.

In response, Raymond opened a briefcase, then handed Drummond a large envelope that contained a videotape.

Drummond gave the envelope to Delgado. "It's a copy, of course. I've been saving it as a further negotiating tactic. Be careful. Don't leave it where your wife and daughter might wonder what was on it. Or the president. You wouldn't want *him* to see it. A political scandal of this sort would threaten his administration, and needless to say, it would destroy your chances of becoming his replacement."

Delgado felt sweat trickle down his back as he clenched the videotape.

Abruptly the study's door was opened. Delgado whirled, his stomach cramping when he saw his wife step in. Intelligent, sophisticated, well-educated, she understood her role as a politician's spouse and always conducted herself perfectly. She tolerated Delgado's frequent absences and no doubt was aware of his frequent indiscretions. She was always there when he needed symbolic support at public functions. But then, she had been raised in a family of politicians. From her youth onward, she had learned the rules. She was the sister of Delgado's best friend, the president of Mexico.

"I'm sorry to disturb you, dear. I didn't realize you had company. How are you, Mr. Drummond?" she asked in perfect English. Her expensive clothes and jewelry enhanced her plain features.

"Excellent," Drummond answered in Spanish. "And yourself? I trust you are well, Señora."

"Yes, I am fine. Would you care to stay for dinner?"

"Thank you, but I'm afraid I was just about to leave. Your husband and I needed to discuss some matters. I have to fly to Europe."

"You're welcome anytime," she said. "Esteban, I'll be in the garden." She closed the door.

The room was uncomfortably silent for a moment.

"Think about it," Drummond said. "Don't be a fool and ruin everything you've worked so hard to achieve. Don't deny yourself the chance to achieve even greater things. Watch the tape, destroy it, and make the further arrangements we discussed."

Delgado did not reveal the sudden anger that blazed inside him. *You come to my home. You ignore my hospitality. You threaten me. You threaten my relationship with my wife and daughter.* His jaw ached with fury. *There will come a time when you do not have power over me.*

And then I will destroy you.

"The director of the Institute of Archaeology and History," Drummond said. "When I told you to discourage him from interfering with what I'm doing at the site, I meant eliminate him. I want him replaced by someone who knows how to compromise, who won't make trouble, who values favors."

2

NEW ORLEANS

Buchanan squirmed.

"Welcome back. How are you feeling?"

He took a moment to understand what the woman had asked him. He took another moment to answer.

". . . Sore."

"I bet." The woman chuckled. It wasn't a chuckle of derision. It communicated sympathy. Its sound was soft yet deep.

He liked it.

He took another moment for the haze to clear enough that he realized he was in a hospital bed. He didn't know what pained him more, the throbbing in his head or the burning in his right side. His skull was wrapped with bandages. His side felt stiff from bandages, as well. And stitches.

"You had me worried," the woman said.

He focused on her, expecting to see a nurse leaning over the bed or possibly, blessedly, Juana, although this woman didn't have an Hispanic accent.

As he noticed her red hair, the significance of it alarmed him. He squirmed harder.

"Relax," Holly McCoy said. "You're all right. You're going to be fine."

Like hell, he thought. Everything was wrong, *very* wrong, although his clouded thoughts prevented him from knowing precisely *how* wrong.

"Well," a man said, "I see you're coming around."

A doctor. His white coat contrasted with his black skin. He entered the room and studied the medical chart attached to the foot of the bed, finally saying, "The nurses on the night shift had to wake you periodically to test your neurological signs. Do you remember that?"

". . . No."

"Do you remember *me*?"

". . . No."

"Good. Because I didn't treat you last night when you were brought into the emergency ward. Answer my questions honestly. The first thing that comes into your mind. Understand?"

Buchanan nodded, wincing from the pain that the movement had caused.

"Do you know why you're here?"

". . . Stabbed."

"Another good answer. Do you remember where?"

". . . My side."

The doctor smiled slightly. "No. I mean where outside the hospital were you stabbed?"

". . . French Quarter. . . . Café du Monde."

"Exactly. You were assaulted on the sidewalk outside the restaurant. As soon as you're up to it, the police will want a statement from you, although I gather your friend here has already provided most of the necessary details."

Holly nodded.

My friend?

The police?

"If you're someone who likes company for his misery, you aren't alone," the doctor continued. "We had several mugging victims in the emergency ward last night, and some of them weren't as lucky as you. A few are in critical condition."

". . . Mugging?"

"I gave the police a description of the man who did it," Holly said. "Not that it helps. A pirate costume. Last night, a *lot* of people were wearing costumes." She raised a plastic cup and placed a bent straw between his lips.

The water was cool.

"You're at the LSU Medical Center," the doctor said. "Your wound required twenty stitches. But you were lucky. No major organs were injured. The blade didn't penetrate as much as it slashed."

The police? Buchanan thought. Jesus, I was carrying a gun. What if they found it? They *must* have found it. And Victor Grant's forged passport. They'll wonder what—

"You struck your head when you fell," the doctor said. "You have a concussion."

Another one?

"There doesn't appear to be any neurologic damage. Still, you might get tired of everybody asking you the same questions. . . . Like, how many fingers am I holding up?"

"Three."

"How old are you?"

"Thirty-two."

"What's your name?"

. . .

"What's your name?" the doctor repeated.

He concentrated.

Of all the questions . . .

Come on. Come on. Who am I supposed to be?

". . . Peter Lang." He exhaled.

"Nope. Wrong answer. Your wallet—which the mugger didn't manage to get, by the way—indicates that your name is . . ."

"Brendan Buchanan."

"Better," the doctor said. "Much better. So let's be clear. What's your name?"

". . . Brendan Buchanan."

"Then why did you say your name was Peter Lang?"

". . . A friend of mine. Have to tell him what happened to me."

"Ms. McCoy can make your phone calls for you. You had

me worried for a moment. I was afraid the concussion was more severe than your CAT scan indicated."

Didn't get my wallet? To know that, the police must have searched me. They *must* have found the gun.

And the passport, too! Maybe this doctor expected me to call myself Victor Grant.

A nurse had been taking his blood pressure. "One fifteen over seventy-five."

The doctor nodded with approval. "Try to open your eyes as wide as you can. I need to shine this light at your pupils. Good. Now follow the movement of my hand. Bear with me while I tap at your joints. I have to draw the end of this hammer along the bottoms of your feet. Fine. Your reflexes don't seem impaired. Your lungs sound normal. Your heartbeat is strong and regular. I'm encouraged. Try to rest. I'll be back this afternoon."

"I'll keep him company." Holly gave Buchanan another sip of water.

"As long as he rests. I don't want him talking a lot. On the other hand, I don't want him sleeping a lot, either. Not until I'm sure he's out of danger."

"I understand. I'll just be here to reassure him," Holly said.

"TLC never hurts." The doctor started to leave, then looked back. "You've certainly been having your share of injuries, Mr. Buchanan. What caused the wound to your shoulder?"

". . . Uh. It . . ."

"A boating accident," Holly said. "The edge of a propeller."

"It's a good thing you've got medical insurance," the doctor said.

3

Tense, Buchanan waited for the doctor and the nurse to leave, then slowly turned his head and stared at Holly.

She smiled engagingly. "You want more water?"

". . . What's going on?"

"You know, when I was a little girl, I couldn't decide whether to be a nurse or a reporter. Now I'm getting to be both."

Buchanan breathed with effort, his voice a gravelly whisper. "What happened? How did . . . ?"

"Save your strength. Last night, I followed you from the hotel."

"How did you know where I was staying?"

"That's confidential. Rest, I told you. I'll do the talking. I figured you had to leave the hotel sometime, so I waited across the street. There's no back exit, except for the service doors. But I didn't think you'd draw attention to yourself by making the staff wonder why you'd use a service door, so it seemed to me the best bet was the front. Mind you, I did have Ted—you remember Ted, from the train—watching the back. He and I were linked by two-way radios. When you came out, I was just one of several people wearing costumes. Otherwise, this red hair would have been a giveaway. You didn't notice when I followed you."

Buchanan breathed. "Ought to dye it."

"What?"

"Your hair. For following people. Change the color to something bland."

"Never. But I guess you've changed the color of *your* hair often enough."

He didn't respond.

Holly gave him another sip of water. "By the way, was my answer right? When the doctor asked how you got the wound to your shoulder? A boating accident? When you were Victor Grant, isn't that what you told the Mexican police?"

"I don't know what you're talking about."

"Sure."

His eyelids felt heavy.

Where does she get her information? he thought.

"Confidential," she said.

"What?"

"You asked where I got my information. That's confidential."

I did? I asked her that out loud?

He couldn't keep his eyes open.

4

The doctor pointed at the uneaten tuna sandwich. "Your lack of appetite worries me."

"Hospital food. I never liked it. I can smell all the other meals that were on the cart."

"Mr. Lang . . ."

"Buchanan."

"Right. Mr. Buchanan. I just wanted to be sure. If you want to get out of here, you're going to have to satisfy my slightest concern about your concussion. If I were you, I'd eat that meal, and then I'd ask the nurse to get me another."

Buchanan mustered the strength to reach for the sandwich.

"Here, I'll give you a hand," Holly said.

"I think the doctor wants to see if I can do it by myself."

"You're a student of human nature," the doctor said. "After you've enjoyed your meal, I want you out of bed and walking around a little. To the bathroom, for example. I need to be satisfied that your legs and the rest of you are all in working order."

"Did anyone ever tell you you're a slave driver?"

The black doctor raised his eyebrows. "You're getting better if you can make jokes. I'll be back to examine you after lunch."

The moment the doctor left, Buchanan set down the tuna sandwich. He glanced at Holly. "I don't suppose you'd eat this for me. Or dump it somewhere and make it look as if I finished everything."

"Do the manly thing and eat it yourself if you want to get out of here." Holly's emerald eyes gleamed with mischievousness.

"How do you get your eyes that color? Tinted contact lenses?"

"French eye drops. A lot of movie stars use them. The drops emphasize the color of their eyes. It's a trick I learned when I was working in Los Angeles. Come to think of it, you'd find the trick handy. For when you're altering your appearance. You wouldn't have to fool around with those tinted contact lenses you mentioned."

"Why would I want to alter my appearance?"

She sounded exasperated. "You don't give up."

"Neither do you. Last night. What happened? You didn't finish telling me."

"I followed you through the French Quarter and over to Café du Monde. By then, it was eleven o'clock. You seemed to be looking for somebody. In fact, you were looking pretty hard."

"An old friend I'd arranged to meet. The only reason I didn't want you following me was that I was getting tired of your questions."

"And here you are, listening to more of them."

"Café du Monde."

"I was watching from across the street, so I didn't see everything perfectly. You came out of the restaurant. There was a commotion, a group of costumed people going by. They acted as if they'd been drinking. Then one of them, a man dressed as a pirate, bumped into you. All of a sudden you grabbed your side and spun. A woman screamed. People were scrambling to get out of your way. You tripped over somebody. You hit your head on an iron railing. I ran toward you, but not before I noticed the guy in the pirate costume shove a knife back into his belt as he disappeared into the crowd down the street. I stayed with you, trying to stop the blood while one of the waiters in the restaurant phoned for an ambulance."

"Blood doesn't make you squeamish?"

"Hey, I can't write the end of my story if you die on me."

"And all along, I thought it was my personality that attracted you."

"Which one?"

"What?"

"Which personality? You've had so many."

Buchanan set down a remnant of the tuna sandwich. "I give up. I can't think of any way to convince you that . . ."

"You're right. There *isn't* any way to convince me. And last night made me more sure than ever. The man in the pirate costume didn't try to mug you. I just told that to the police so they wouldn't wonder about you. No, that wasn't an attempted mugging. That was an attempted *murder*." She sat straighter. "Why? Who were you meeting? What's—?"

"Holly."

"—going on that—?"

"I've got a question of my own," Buchanan said. "I had something with me. If anyone found it, I'm sure the police would have—"

"Sure," Holly said.

"—given it back or—"

"Wanted to have a very deep heart-to-heart with you about it." Holly opened her purse. "Is this what you lost?"

Inside the purse, Buchanan saw his Beretta 9-mm semiautomatic pistol. His eyes narrowed.

"You didn't drop it," Holly said. "I felt it while I was trying to stop you from bleeding. Before the police and the ambulance arrived, I managed to get it off you without being noticed."

"No big deal. I carry it for protection."

"Sure. Like when you're meeting an old friend. I don't know what the gun-concealment laws are in this state, but it's my guess you need a permit to carry this. And for certain, if you're legitimate, I know the Army wouldn't approve of you walking around armed while you're on furlough."

"Hey, a lot of people carry guns these days," Buchanan said. "That attempted mugging last night proves why."

"An attempted murder, not a mugging."

"That proves my point. Some nut gets drunk, maybe cranked up on drugs. He's wearing a pirate costume. Suddenly he thinks he's a real pirate. So he stabs somebody. The equivalent of a drive-by shooting. Only this is a walk-by stabbing."

"You expect me to believe that?"

"Look, I have no idea why he stabbed me. It's as good a theory as any," Buchanan said.

"But would the cops buy it if they'd also found the other thing you lost?"

Other . . . ? Buchanan felt suddenly cold.

"I've been waiting for you to ask me about it." After glancing at the door to make sure no one was looking in, Holly reached under the pistol and removed a passport from her purse. "The ambulance attendants had to get your jacket off so they could check the wound. I told them I was your girlfriend and hung on to the jacket. A good thing I did. For your sake." She opened the passport. "Victor Grant. My, my."

Buchanan felt even more chilled.

"Not a bad picture of you. Your hair was a little shorter. Yep, the gun along with a passport that didn't match the ID in your wallet would definitely have made the police wonder what was going on," Holly said. "For starters, they'd have suspected you were running drugs. Actually, that's not so far from the truth, given your involvement with covert operations like Scotch and Soda."

Buchanan stopped breathing.

"So?" Holly put the passport back under the gun in her purse. "You've always got so many reasonable explanations for your unusual behavior. What's your story this time?"

Buchanan pulled his salad toward him.

"Suddenly hungry? Trying to fill the time while you come up with a reason for the fake passport?"

"Holly, I . . ."

He picked up his fork.

"Can't think of one, can you?" she asked.

He put down his fork and sighed. "You don't want to mess around with this. Do yourself a favor and bow out quietly. Forget you ever saw that passport."

"Can't. I've always wanted a Pulitzer. I think this'll get me one."

"Pay attention. Let's assume for the moment that you're right." Buchanan held up a hand. "I'm not admitting anything, but let's assume. The people you'd be up against don't play by any rules you know about or can imagine. What you might get instead of a Pulitzer is a coffin."

"Is that a threat?"

"It's a hypothetical, well-intentioned warning."

"Don't you think I've protected myself? I've made copies of my research. They're with five different people I trust."

"Sure. Like your lawyer. Your editor. Your best friend."

"You've got the idea."

"All predictable," Buchanan said. "A good black-bag man could find where the research was hidden. But it's probable that no one would even bother looking. If your research was so wonderful, the story would have been published by now. You've got nothing but suspicions. All deniable. But if any-body feels threatened by that research, they might not know or care that you've left copies of the research with other people. They might just decide to get rid of you.''

"What about you?" Holly asked.

"You mean, would *I* think about getting rid of you? Don't be absurd. I've got nothing to do with any of this. I was only giving advice.''

"No. What about *you*? Don't *you* feel threatened?''

"Why on earth would I . . . ?''

"If you were on a sanctioned mission, you wouldn't be traveling under your own identity, not while you carried a passport under someone else's name. Your controllers won't like that. After what happened to you in Mexico and Florida, they'll think they've got a loose cannon. They'll wonder what in God's name you were doing with a gun and a passport that you weren't supposed to have. You've got other problems besides me. You and your controllers must have established a schedule for staying in touch. If you've missed any part of that schedule, they'll be very nervous. You'd better call them.''

"If I'm who you say I am, do you honestly think I'd call them in front of you? On an unsecured phone?''

"You'd better do something. They'll be getting impatient. And don't forget this—the longer you're out of touch with them, the more suspicious they'll be about your ability to do your work.''

Buchanan felt pressure behind his ears.

"I see your appetite improved,'' the doctor said, coming back into the room.

"Yeah, I'm almost done with my salad.''

"Well, finish your Jell-O, Mr. Lang.''

"Buchanan.''

"Then take your walk to the bathroom. After that, I might be encouraged enough to think about releasing you.''

5

Wearing sneakers, jeans, and a short-sleeved blue shirt that he'd asked Holly to buy for him to replace his bloodstained shoes and clothing, Buchanan felt trapped in the wheelchair that a nurse insisted he keep sitting in while she wheeled him from the elevator and through the hospital's crowded lobby to the main doors.

"I told you I can walk," Buchanan said.

"Until you trip and fall and sue the hospital. Once you're out those doors, you're on your own. Meanwhile, you're my responsibility."

Through the doors, amid the din of street noises, Buchanan was forced to raise a hand to his eyes, the bright sun making him squint painfully.

The nurse helped him out of the wheelchair. "You said somebody was going to meet you?"

"Right," Buchanan lied. He hadn't seen Holly for quite a while and had no idea what had happened to her. Normally, he would have felt reprieved from being pestered by her questions, but at the moment, he felt nervous. Worried. The gun and the passport. *He had to get them back.* "I'll just sit over on that bench. My friend ought to be here any minute."

"Enjoy your day, Mr. Buchanan."

"Lang."

The nurse looked strangely at him as she took the chair away.

He wondered why.

Then he realized.

His skin prickled.

What's happening to me?

The moment the nurse disappeared into the hospital, he stood. The reason he hadn't wanted to be brought down in a wheelchair was that he didn't want to leave the hospital before he had a chance to get to a pay phone.

Managing not to waver, he reentered the lobby and crossed toward a bank of telephones. His hand shook as he put coins in a slot. Thirty seconds later, he was talking to a contact officer.

"Where have you been?" the gruff voice demanded.

Keeping his own voice low, relieved that the phones on either side of him weren't being used, taking care that he wouldn't be overheard, Buchanan answered, "I've been in a hospital."

"*What?*"

"A guy tried to mug me," he lied. "I didn't see him coming. I got stabbed from behind."

"Good God. When you didn't show up at the various rendezvous points this morning, we got worried. We've had a team waiting in case you're in trouble."

"I got lucky. The wound isn't serious. Mostly, they kept me in the hospital for observation. With so many nurses coming in and out, I didn't want to risk phoning this number, especially since the hospital would automatically have a record of the number. This is the first chance I've had to call in."

"You had us sweating, buddy."

"The emergency's over. If you had people at the rendezvous sites, that means you had something you wanted me to know about. What is it?"

"About the woman reporter you met on the train. . . . Is your phone secure?"

"Yes."

"Then this is the message. Continue your furlough. Don't worry about the reporter. We're taking steps to guarantee that she's discouraged."

Buchanan's grip tightened on the phone.

"Check in at the rendezvous sites on schedule. We'll let you know if anything else develops."

"Roger," Buchanan said. Swallowing dryly, he set down the phone.

But he didn't turn away. He just kept staring at the phone.

Taking steps to guarantee that she's discouraged? What the hell did that mean?

It wasn't considered professional for him to ask to have a deliberately vague term clarified. His superiors never said more or less than they intended to. Their use of language, even when vague, was precise. "Discouraged" could mean anything from seeing that Holly lost her job . . . to attempting to bribe her . . . to discrediting her research . . . to trying to scare her off, or . . .

Buchanan didn't want to consider the possibility that Holly might be the target of ultimate discouragement.

No, he thought. They wouldn't assassinate a reporter, especially one from the *Washington Post*. That would enflame the story rather than smother it.

But reporters *have* been assassinated from time to time, he thought.

And it wouldn't look like an assassination.

As he turned from the phone, he touched the bandage on his right side, the stitches under it.

Holly—wearing a brown paisley dress that enhanced the red of her hair and the green of her eyes—was in a chair twenty feet away.

Buchanan didn't show his surprise.

She came over. "Checking in with your superiors?"

"Calling another friend."

"Why don't I believe you?"

"Listen, I want you to stay away from me," Buchanan said.

"And end a beautiful relationship? Now you're trying to hurt my feelings."

"I'm serious. You don't want to be around me. You don't want to attract attention."

"What are you talking about?"

Buchanan crossed the lobby, heading toward the hospital's gift shop.

"Hey, you're not going to get rid of me that easily." Her high heels made muffled sounds on the lobby's carpet.

"I'm trying to do you a favor," Buchanan said. "Take the strong hint. Stay clear of me."

In the gift shop, he paid for a box of superstrength Tylenol. His head wouldn't stop aching. He'd been tempted to ask the doctor to give him a prescription for something to stop the pain, but he'd known that the doctor would have been troubled enough as a consequence to want to keep him in the hospital longer. The only consolation was that the headache distracted Buchanan from the pain in his side.

Holly followed him from the gift shop. "I've got a few things to show you."

"Not interested." He stopped at a water fountain, swallowed three Tylenol, wiped water from his mouth, and headed toward the exit. "What *does* interest me is getting my belongings back."

"Not a chance."

"Holly." He pivoted sharply toward her. "Let's pretend I

am the kind of person you think I am. What do you suppose would happen to you if I told the people I work for that you had a false passport with my picture in it? How long do you think you'd get to walk around with it?''

Her emerald eyes became more intense. ''Then you didn't tell them.''

''What do you mean?''

''I wondered if you would. I doubted it. You don't want your superiors knowing you had that passport—and lost it. What did you want it for in the first place?''

''Isn't it obvious? So I'd be able to leave the country.''

''Is there something wrong with using your own passport?''

''Yeah.'' Buchanan scanned the people near the exit. ''I don't have one. I've never been issued one.''

They reached the noisy street. Again the glare of the sun stabbed his eyes. ''Where's your friend? Ted. The guy on the train. It's my guess you don't go anywhere without him.''

''He's nearby, looking out for my welfare.''

''Using a two-way radio? I won't keep talking with you unless you prove to me this conversation isn't being recorded.''

She opened her purse. ''See? No radio.''

''And my belongings aren't in there, either. Where'd you put them?''

''They're safe.''

In front of the hospital, a man and a woman got out of a taxi. Buchanan hurried to get in after they walked toward the lobby.

Holly scrambled in after him.

''This isn't a good idea,'' Buchanan said.

''Where to?'' the driver asked.

''Holiday Inn—Crowne Plaza.''

As the taxi pulled from the curb, Buchanan turned to Holly. ''This is not the game you seem to think it is. I want my belongings returned to me. Give me the key to your room. I'll get what's mine, pack your things, and check you out.''

''What makes you think I want to leave the hotel?''

Buchanan leaned close. ''Because you do not want to be seen near me. Don't ask me to be more explicit. This is as plain as I can make it.''

"You're trying to scare me again."

"You bet, and lady, I hope I'm succeeding."

6

"Close enough," Buchanan told the driver.

"But we got another two blocks, suh."

"This is fine. Take the lady for a drive. Be back on this corner in thirty minutes." Buchanan stared at Holly. "The key to your room." He held out his hand.

"You're really serious."

"The key."

Holly gave it to him. "Lighten up. Your belongings, as you call them, aren't in my room anyhow."

"Where are they? In *Ted's* room?"

She didn't answer.

"I mean it, Holly. Neither you nor your friend wants to be found with my things in their possession. It wouldn't be healthy for you."

Her face changed color slightly, paling, as if he was finally getting his message across. "What do I get in return?"

"Peace of mind."

"Not good enough," Holly said.

"What do you want?"

"The chance to keep talking with you."

"I told you, I'll be back in half an hour."

Holly studied him. "Yes. All right. They're in Ted's room."

"I don't suppose you have a key to it."

"As a matter of fact." She handed it to him. "In case I needed to get your belongings and Ted wasn't around."

"You just did a very smart thing." Buchanan got out of the taxi.

"Be careful when you pack my underwear. It's expensive. I don't want the lace torn."

Buchanan stared at her and shut the door.

7

The two blocks felt like two miles. Along the way, Buchanan unwrapped the bandage from around his skull and shoved it into a trash can. By the time he reached the Crowne Plaza, he felt light-headed, his brow filmed with sweat. His only consolation was that as he entered the softly lit lobby, escaping the hammer force of the sun, his headache felt slightly less severe.

Rather than go directly up to Ted's room and then Holly's, he decided he'd first better learn if he had any messages. He checked the lobby to see if anybody showed any interest in him.

There. In the corner on the right next to the entrance. A man, late twenties, in a blue seersucker suit. Sitting in a lounge chair. Reading a newspaper.

The well-built man was in a perfect position to see people coming into the lobby before they had a chance to notice him. The man's glance in Buchanan's direction was ever so brief but ever so intense. And like a good operative, the man gave no sign that he recognized Buchanan.

So they staked out the hotel, Buchanan thought.

But it isn't me they're looking for.

No. The person they're looking for is Holly.

Showing no indication that the man in the corner interested him, Buchanan went over to the front desk, waited while a clerk took care of a guest, and then stepped forward.

"Yes, sir?"

"Are there any messages for me? My room number's . . ."

The clerk smiled, waiting.

"My room number's . . ."

"Yes?"

" . . . Damn." Buchanan's pulse raced. "I can't remember what it is. I left my key here at the desk when I went out, so I'm afraid I can't tell you the number on it."

"No problem, sir. All you have to do is give me your name. The computer will match the name with your room number."

"Victor Grant," Buchanan said automatically.

The clerk tapped some letters on a computer keyboard, hummed, and studied the screen. He began to frown. "Sorry, sir. No one by that name is registered here."

"Victor Grant. There must be."

"No, sir."

Jesus, Buchanan suddenly realized. "Brendan Buchanan. I gave you the wrong name."

"Wrong name? What do you mean, sir?"

"I'm an actor. We're making a movie in town. My character's name is Victor Grant. I'm so used to responding to that name I . . . If I'm into my character *that* much, I ought to win an Oscar."

"What kind of movie is it, sir?"

"Did you ever see *The Big Easy*?"

"Of course, sir. I see all the films made in New Orleans."

"Well, this is the sequel."

"I have it now, sir. Brendan Buchanan. Room twelve fourteen. And no, there aren't any messages."

"Could I have my key, please?"

The clerk complied. "What other movies have you been in?"

"None. Until now, I've worked on the stage. This is my big break. Thanks."

Buchanan walked toward the elevator. He pressed the button and gazed straight ahead, waiting for the doors to open, certain that the clerk was staring toward him. Don't look back. Don't look back.

Victor Grant? You're losing it, buddy. When you left the hospital, you made the same mistake. You told the nurse you were . . .

No. That was a *different* mistake. You told the nurse you were *Peter Lang*. Now you say you're . . .

You can't even keep the names consistent.

His head ached. It wouldn't stop aching.

The doors at last opened. Inside, alone, as the elevator rose, Buchanan sagged against a wall, wiping sweat from his forehead, wondering if he was going to be sick.

Can't. I have to keep moving.

He had no intention of going to his room. The only reason he'd approached the desk clerk was that he needed to find out if he'd received any messages. The fact that at the start of the conversation he hadn't been able to recall his room number terrified him.

Two floors above his own, he got off the elevator and used the key that Holly had given him to open Ted's door. It took him less than five minutes to find the gun and Victor Grant's passport where Ted had hidden them under the mattress.

Victor Grant. Buchanan stared at the photograph in the passport. He was tempted to tear the document to pieces and burn it in the sink. That would solve one problem. There'd be one less piece of evidence linking him to a past identity. But what he'd told Holly was true. He'd hung on to the passport in case he needed to get out of the country. And the way things were developing, he might still have a need to do that.

Victor Grant.

Peter Lang.

Brendan Buchanan.

Pick one, damn it. Be consistent.

What are you here for?

Juana.

Where was she last night? Why did somebody stab me? Was somebody trying to stop me from helping . . . ?

Pay attention. What are you going to do?

Hell, who am I going to be?

Holly. He still had to deal with . . .

He looked in a closet and found a brown sport coat that Ted had left. Although Ted had broader shoulders, the garment fit Buchanan better than he expected. He shoved the passport into one of its pockets and the gun behind his belt, at the spine, making sure that the jacket covered it. When he left the room, no one noticed.

Now for Holly's room.

It was two doors down, and as Buchanan approached it, he kept thinking about the man in the seersucker suit in the lobby. If they staked out the hotel, isn't it logical that they'd put someone in Holly's room to grab her when she came in? Maybe I ought to stay out of this. Maybe the smart thing to do is keep walking toward the elevator. Let Holly check herself out of the hotel, or let Ted do it for her. Now that I've got the gun and the passport, why should I care about . . . ?

Buchanan slowed, thinking, The longer Holly waits, the greater the odds that someone *will* be in her room when she comes back.

So what? That still isn't your concern. If something happened to her, it'd be one less thing for you to worry about. One less . . .

He pivoted, knocked on her door, announced, "Hotel housekeeping," knocked again, and unlocked the door.

The room was empty. It took him even less time to pack her things than it had for him to find the gun and the passport in Ted's room. He took care only when he put her underwear into her suitcase. What Holly had said was true. It was expensive, and it did have lace. He liked the feel of it.

She would have been required to leave a credit-card number when she checked in. He found an early-checkout form on the counter beside the television, filled it out, and left it on the bed, pleased that she hadn't brought much luggage as he carried the two bags down the fire stairs and out a service exit, all the while thinking of the lace on the underwear he'd packed. It had been a long time since he'd felt intimate with a woman. Not had sex with but felt intimate with. As long as six years ago.

And Juana.

8

Exertion, combined with the glaring sun, squeezed sweat from him. The stitches in his right side, the tenderness of his wound, required him to carry one bag in his left hand, the other wedged under his left arm. Exhaust fumes from passing cars aggravated his headache and made him nauseous.

At least the taxi was waiting as promised. When the driver saw that Buchanan was having trouble with the bags, he got out. "Here, let me help, suh."

"Thanks." Buchanan gave him ten dollars, then turned his attention toward Holly and someone else sitting in the backseat.

He frowned.

While the driver carried the bags toward the trunk, Buchanan got in the backseat, next to a square-faced man who was built like a college football player gone to seed. "Well, Ted, long time no see."

From the opposite side, Holly leaned forward. "I figured he might as well travel with us instead of keep following in another taxi. We picked him up while you were gone."

"Ted, I appreciate the help with the bags."

"What help?"

"My point exactly."

"You should have asked."

"I shouldn't have needed to."

"Just like *you* didn't feel you needed to ask my permission to go into my room. I don't like the idea of someone rummaging through my stuff. And that's my jacket you're wearing."

"Very observant. So what do you think, Ted? Doesn't fit me too bad, huh? Here's your key back."

Holly tried to distract them. "Did you find what you were looking for?"

"Right away. Ted isn't very good at this."

"Hey," Ted said.

"All right, I can understand why you're angry," Holly said. "When I saw you coming, *I* should have helped with the bags. I knew you'd just been released from the hospital. I'd have gotten out to help a friend."

"Well, this guy isn't a friend," Ted said.

"Ted," Holly said in warning. She turned to Buchanan. "Look, I'm sorry. Remember, it was your idea to check me out of that hotel. If you want to go in for melodramatic gestures to try to scare me, you can't expect me to cooperate in the tactic."

"Then maybe we ought to go back so I could introduce you to the fellow waiting for you in the lobby."

Holly's eyes narrowed. "That's a joke, right?"

"He didn't look like he had a sense of humor."

"This is all bullshit," Ted said.

"Right, Ted. Bullshit," Buchanan said. "I don't care what happens to you, but until Holly and I get some issues settled, I'd just as soon she stayed in good health."

"Quit trying to scare me," Holly said.

"Where to, suh?" The driver had gotten back into the taxi and was waiting.

"That errand wore me out." Buchanan rubbed his sweaty forehead. "I came here to enjoy the sights. I think a river cruise would relax me. Why don't you take us over to Toulouse Street Wharf? It's almost two-thirty. Maybe we've still got time to get on the *Natchez*."

As the taxi pulled into traffic, Holly said, "For a man who claims he was never in New Orleans before, you certainly know a lot about the tourist attractions."

"I studied them in a guidebook."

"Right. When was that? When you were unconscious?"

9

As its calliope whistled "Way Down South in Dixie," the colorfully trimmed paddlewheeler eased away from the wharf and began its tour along the Mississippi. Hundreds of passengers crowded the railings on the three decks, enjoying the breeze off the river, studying the docks they passed, warehouses, a refinery, a War of 1812 battlefield, and a pre–Civil War plantation mansion.

While the passengers seemed to enjoy the strength of the sun, Buchanan's eyes were still sufficiently sensitive that he stayed in the shadow of a canopy at the stern. Holly sat next to him. Since most passengers were at the railing, there was little chance that their conversation would be overheard.

Holly shook her head. "I don't understand. Why a steamboat cruise?"

"Process of elimination." Buchanan sipped from one of the Cokes that he'd bought for Holly and himself when they came aboard. "I need time to think, a *place* to think." After swallowing two more Tylenol, he shut his eyes and tilted his head back.

"You should have stayed in the hospital longer."

"Too much to do," Buchanan said.

"Yeah, like watching the muddy Mississippi. Ted didn't like it when you made him stay behind with my bags."

"You said you wanted to talk. The thing is, I don't want company while we're doing it. This way, he can't follow. And pretty soon, we'll be far enough that those two-way radios you mentioned won't be able to communicate with each other. By the way, where are you hiding yours? In your purse? Or maybe . . . ?" Buchanan gestured toward the open neckline of her dress.

"Okay." Sounding discouraged, she reached inside her dress, unhooked a tiny microphone and miniature transmitter from her bra strap, and handed it to him. "You win."

"Too easy." Buchanan shut the transmitter off, feeling her body heat on the metal. "How do I know there aren't others?"

"There's only one way to be sure. But if I wouldn't let you search me in your train compartment, I'm certainly not . . ."

"What did you want to talk about?"

"For starters, who do you think tried to kill you? And please, don't give me that guff about a walk-by random stabbing."

"Who? Yes, that's the big question, isn't it?"

"One of them."

The issue had been preoccupying Buchanan since he'd wakened in the hospital. If he addressed it out loud, he'd also be distracting Holly from his role in Scotch and Soda. "Open your purse."

She did.

He didn't find a tape recorder.

"Okay, I'll tell you this much. I wasn't lying when I said I came to New Orleans to see a friend." He debated whether to continue. "A woman." He thought about it. "None of this is classified. I don't see any reason not to . . . It's been six years since I heard from her, but recently she sent me a message that she needed help. My friend is very independent. She's definitely not the type to ask for help unless the problem's serious."

"This friend, was she your lover?"

"Are you a reporter or a gossip columnist? I ought to tell you that's none of your business."

Holly waited.

Buchanan bit his lower lip. "Could have been my lover. Maybe should have been. Maybe we'd have gotten married."

"But . . . ?"

"Well, let's just say I was having some problems figuring out who I was." Past tense? Buchanan asked himself. "Anyway, I was supposed to meet her last night, eleven o'clock, at Café du Monde. She didn't show up. But that guy did with his knife.'' Leaning back in the deck chair, feeling his handgun behind his belt and against his spine, Buchanan suddenly realized that the only reason his wound hadn't been more serious was that the gun had deflected the blade. As he appreciated how close he'd come to dying, he started sweating again.

In contrast, his mouth became dry. Disturbed, he swallowed more Coke. ''Is it a coincidence that the man happened to show up and pick me as a victim while I was looking for my friend, who happened *not* to show up? I try to keep an open mind. I do my best to have healthy skepticism. But the coincidence is too hard to ignore. I have to believe that my friend and the man with the knife are connected.''

''And he was trying to stop you from helping your friend?''

''Unless you can think of a better explanation.''

''Well, one part of your logic troubles me. Since she didn't show up, you wouldn't have been able to know what she wanted, so it wouldn't have been necessary for you to be stopped.''

''Or maybe—''

Buchanan's heartbeat matched the *thump-thump-thump* of the paddlewheeler's engine.

''Maybe someone was afraid that when she didn't show up, I'd become so upset that I wouldn't stop until I found out where she was and why she needed me.'' Buchanan's voice hardened. ''If so, they were right to be afraid. Because that's exactly what's going to happen.''

10

The steamboat rounded a bend.

''At the hospital, you said you had something for me to look at.''

Holly straightened. ''Yes. But you wouldn't give me a chance.''

''Because I wanted my belongings back. Now I've got them.'' Despite his headache, Buchanan mustered strength. He had to keep playing the game. "I'll look at whatever it is you want me to see. Anything it takes to settle your suspicions. I need to help my friend. But I can't do it if you keep interfering. Ask the rest of your questions. I want to be done with this."

Holly opened her purse, studied him as if doubtful about something, then pulled three folded newspaper clippings from an envelope.

Puzzled, Buchanan took them and glanced at the date at the top of the first one. "Six days ago." He frowned.

He frowned harder when he saw that the story was datelined Fort Lauderdale.

EXPLOSION KILLS THREE

FT. LAUDERDALE—A powerful explosion shortly before midnight last night destroyed a car in the parking lot of Paul's-on-the-River restaurant, killing its occupant, identified by a remnant of his driver's license as Robert Bailey, 48, a native of Oklahoma. The explosion also killed two customers leaving the restaurant. Numerous other cars were destroyed or damaged. Charred fragments of a substantial amount of money found at the scene have prompted authorities to theorize that the explosion may have been the consequence of a recent escalating war among drug smugglers.

His heart now pounding faster than the *thump-thump-thump* of the paddlewheeler's engine, Buchanan lowered the clipping and turned to Holly. No matter what, he couldn't let her detect his reaction. His head ached even more fiercely. "All those people killed. A terrible thing. But what does this have to do with me? Why did you show it to—?"

"Are you denying that you knew Robert Bailey?"

"I don't know anything about this."

And that was certainly the truth, Buchanan thought.

He strained to look calm as dismay flooded through him.

Holly squinted. "Mostly, he called himself 'Big Bob' Bailey. Maybe that refreshes your memory."

"Never heard of him."

"Jesus, Buchanan, you are making me impatient. You and I both know he bumped into you in Cancún. I was *there*."

Buchanan felt as if he'd been jolted by electricity.

"I was watching from a corner of the restaurant," Holly said. "Club Internacional. I saw it happen. That's when all your trouble started. When Bailey stumbled into one of your lives."

Buchanan came close to revealing his shock.

"Those two drug dealers became suspicious when Bailey called you Crawford instead of Potter. They took you down to the beach. Bailey went after you. He told me later that he interrupted a fight. You shot the two drug dealers and their bodyguard. Then you ran along the beach into the night, and the police arrested Bailey, thinking he was responsible."

"You're not a reporter. You're a fiction writer. When was this supposed to have happened? I've never been to Cancún. I've never . . ."

"Not as Brendan Buchanan you haven't, but you sure as hell were there as Ed Potter. I told you I was in the *restaurant*. I saw it happen!"

How? Buchanan thought. *How did she get there? How did she know I'd be there? How did—?*

"You saw me taking pictures of you outside the jail in Mérida," Holly said. "Of course, that doesn't prove you knew Bailey, even though I saw the police bring him in to see you at the jail. But later, near Pier Sixty-six in Fort Lauderdale, you saw me photographing you and Bailey talking to each other in the channel. I already showed you the pictures I took."

"You showed me photographs, yes, and I admit one of the men did have some resemblance to me. He *wasn't* me," Buchanan said. "But he did resemble me. The thing is, I've never been to Fort Lauderdale, either."

"I believe you."

"Good."

"As Brendan Buchanan. But as Victor Grant, you very definitely have been to Fort Lauderdale."

Buchanan shook his head as if disappointed that she persisted in her delusion. "And one of the men in the photographs you showed me is Bailey?"

Holly looked exasperated.

"I don't get it," Buchanan said. "Did you know this Bailey? Were you following him? Why are you so interested in . . . ?"

"I wasn't following him. I was following *you*. And why am I interested in Bailey? *Because he worked for me*."

Buchanan felt his stomach cramp.

Two children ran by, clambering down stairs to a lower deck. Their mother hurried after them, shouting for them to be careful. Buchanan was grateful for the interruption.

"Oh, he wasn't working for me when he bumped into you in Cancún," Holly said. "But I made sure he was working for me after that. What's the word you people use? I recruited him. A thousand dollars, plus expenses. Bailey was really down on his luck. He didn't think twice before he accepted."

"That's still a lot of money for a reporter to be able . . ."

"Big story. Big expense account."

"Your editor won't be happy when your story doesn't hang together."

Holly looked furious. "Are you on another planet? Do they teach you people to deny everything no matter how obviously true it is? Or are you so out of touch with reality that you can honestly convince yourself that none of this happened, because it happened to someone else, even though that someone else is you?"

"I'm sorry about what happened to Bailey," Buchanan said. "I meant what I told you. It's a terrible thing. But you have to believe me—I had nothing to do with it."

Who did, though? Buchanan thought. How did—?

The answer was suddenly obvious.

They had plastic explosive in the walls of the cooler I gave him. When he got in his car, he must have opened the cooler to look at the money and . . .

That's all he had to do to detonate it—open the cooler.

But what if he'd opened the cooler while I was with him?

"What's the matter?" Holly asked.

" . . . Excuse me?"

"You turned pale again."

"It's just this headache."

"I thought perhaps it was because you'd glanced at the second clipping."

"Second . . . ?" Buchanan lowered his gaze toward the second of the three clippings in his hand.

MURDER-SUICIDE

FT. LAUDERDALE—Responding to a telephone call from a frightened neighbor, police early this morning investigated gunshots at 233 Glade Street in Plantation and discovered the bodies of Jack Doyle (34) and his wife, Cindy (30), both dead from bullet wounds. It is believed that Mr. Doyle, despondent about his wife's cancer, shot her with a .38-caliber snub-nosed revolver while she slept in their bedroom, then used the same weapon on himself.

Buchanan reread the story. He read it again. And then again. He stopped being aware of the motion of the steamboat, of its thumping engines, of the splashing paddlewheel. He was oblivious to the crowd at the railings, the trees along the river, and the humid breeze on his face.

He just kept staring at the piece of newspaper.

"I'm sorry," Holly said.

Buchanan took a while before he realized that she had said something. He didn't respond. He just kept staring at the clipping.

"Are you going to deny you knew him? If you're tempted to, don't," Holly said. "I took photographs of you and Jack Doyle together, just as I did of you and Bailey."

"No," Buchanan said. With tremendous effort, he lowered the clipping and turned, concentrating on Holly. His mind reeled from the implications of what he'd just read. For the first time in his long career as a deep-cover operative, he did the unthinkable.

He broke cover. "No." His unsteadiness, combined with the motion of the steamboat, made him feel as if he was about to fall from his chair. "I won't deny it. I knew Jack Doyle. And Cindy. His wife. I knew her, too. I liked her. I liked her a lot."

Holly's eyes became more intense. "Earlier, you were talking about coincidence, about how sometimes it has to be more than that, like your friend not showing up at Café du Monde but a man showing up to stab you. Well, that's how I feel about what you just read. You knew Bailey. He's dead. You also knew Jack Doyle and his wife. They're dead, too. And it all happened on the same night. What's . . . ? I just realized something."

"What?"

"The look on your face. You're a hell of a good actor. But nobody's *that* good. You really didn't know anything about Bailey and the Doyles being killed."

"That's right." Buchanan's throat was so dry that he could hardly speak. "I *didn't* know." His eyes ached as he reached for his Coke can and swallowed.

For an instant, he stubbornly suspected that he'd been tricked, that these newspaper clippings weren't genuine. But he couldn't maintain his suspicion. By hindsight, what had happened to Bailey and the Doyles felt so operationally right, so tactically logical that he didn't doubt the truth of what had happened. He'd been tricked, yes. But not by Holly.

"Or maybe there is a coincidence," she said. "Maybe Jack Doyle did just happen to kill his wife the same night Bailey died in an explosion."

"No."

"You think it was a double murder?"

"It can't be anything else."

"How can you be sure?"

Buchanan pointed at the newspaper article. " '. . . shot her with a thirty-eight-caliber snub-nosed revolver.' No way."

"I'm missing something. What's wrong with using a thirty-eight-caliber . . . ?"

"Snub-nosed revolver? This," Buchanan said. "Jack Doyle was an ex-SEAL."

"Yes. A Navy commando. I still don't . . ."

"Weapons were his business. To him, a thirty-eight-caliber snub-nosed revolver was a toy. Oh, he did have one in his house. For his wife. In case Cindy had to protect herself while he was away. But Jack had a lot of other handguns there as well, and for him, the weapon of choice was a nine-millimeter semiautomatic pistol. He loved his wife so much that I envied him. Her cancer was serious. It wasn't responding to treatment. She was probably going to die from it. But it hadn't yet reached the point where her suffering was greater than her dignity could bear. When that day came, though, if Jack decided—with Cindy's permission—to free her from her suffering, he sure as hell would not have used a weapon that he didn't respect."

"Your world's a whole lot different than mine," Holly said. "Ethics about which weapon to use for a murder-suicide."

"Jack wasn't any nut. Don't think for a minute that . . ."

"No," Holly said. "That isn't what I meant. What I did mean was exactly what I said. Your world's very different than mine. No value judgment intended. My father was an attorney. He didn't approve of guns. The first time I saw one, aside from in movies, was when I was reporting on a gang war in Los Angeles."

Buchanan waited.

"So," Holly said. "If it was a double murder, who did it? The same people who killed Bob Bailey?"

Temples throbbing, Buchanan sipped his Coke, then stared at the label. "I had nothing to do with any of it."

"You still haven't read the third newspaper clipping."

Buchanan lowered his gaze, apprehensive about what he would see.

ACCIDENT VICTIM STILL NOT FOUND

FT. LAUDERDALE—Divers continue to search for the body of Victor Grant, the presumed occupant of a rental car that last night crashed through a barrier and sank within a section of the Intracoastal Waterway south of Oakland Park Boulevard. Numerous empty beer cans in the vehicle lead authorities to suspect that Grant was intoxicated when he lost control of his car. A suitcase and a windbreaker containing a wallet with Victor Grant's identification were recovered from the car. Police suspect that the victim's body floated from an open window and became wedged between one of the numerous docks in the area.

Buchanan felt as if he had plummeted and would never hit bottom.

"The reason I didn't kick and fight when you wanted your Victor Grant passport back," Holly said, "is I've taken photographs of every page. I've got photographs of you in Fort Lauderdale. I can link you to Bailey. I can link you to Doyle. This newspaper article proves that somebody named Victor Grant was in Fort Lauderdale and disappeared the same night Bailey and Doyle were killed. You said my editor would be disappointed because my story didn't hang together. Well, it seems to me that the story hangs together beautifully."

Buchanan felt a jolt as if he *had* struck bottom.

"I'm waiting for a reaction," Holly said. "What do you think about my story now?"

"The real question is, What do I feel?"

"I don't understand."

Buchanan rubbed his aching forehead. "Why does ambition make people so stupid? Holly, the answer to the question What do I feel? is I feel terrified. And so should you. I'm a fortune-teller, did you know that? I really have a gift for predicting the future. And given what you just told me, I can guarantee that if you go any further with this story, you'll be dead by this time tomorrow."

Holly blinked.

"And," Buchanan said, his voice hoarse, "if I don't give the best performance of my life, so will I. Because the same people who killed Jack Doyle and Bob Bailey will make sure of it. Is that plain enough for you? Is that what you wanted me to say? That would make a good quote. It's too bad you can't use it."

"Of course, I can use it. I don't care if you deny it or—"

"You're not listening!"

Buchanan spoke so loudly that several people standing along the railing of the steamboat swung and stared at him.

He leaned close to Holly, his voice a raw whisper. "In your world, people are afraid of getting caught breaking the law. In *my* world, people make their own laws. If they feel threatened, they'll shoot you or drop you from a building or hit you with a car and then have a good dinner, feeling justified because they've protected themselves. You will absolutely, positively be dead by this time tomorrow if we don't find a way to convince my people that you are not a threat to them. If *I* feel terrified, you're a fool if *you* don't."

Holly studied him. "This is another act. You're just trying to trick me into backing off."

"I give up," Buchanan said. "Look out for yourself. Believe me, I intend to look after *my*self."

11

Buchanan walked into the Crowne Plaza's lobby. While he waited for the elevator, he glanced around and noticed that the man in the seersucker suit had been replaced by a man in a jogging suit. He, too, was pretending to read a newspaper. After all, there wasn't much to do that seemed natural while sitting in a lobby and watching for someone. This second man was a clone of the first: late twenties, well-built, short hair, intense eyes.

Military, Buchanan thought. The same as the first man. Civilian intelligence agencies had access to surveillance personnel of various appearances. In contrast, military surveillance operatives tended to resemble one another in terms of sex, age, body type, and hairstyle. More, they had a collected, disciplined, single-minded look about them.

Holly, he thought. They're still looking for her.

He got into the elevator, went up to the twelfth floor, and took out his key. Holly's revelations on the steamboat, combined with the pain in his side and the ache in his head, had exhausted him. Fear had exerted its effect. He needed to rest. He needed to think.

When he opened the door . . .

Three people were waiting for him. They sat in plain view, obviously not wanting to startle him and provoke a defensive reaction.

Buchanan knew each of them.

Alan, the portly man who a few days before had been Buchanan's debriefer at the apartment complex in Alexandria, Virginia, sat on the bed. In Alexandria, he'd habitually worn a brown-checkered sport coat. Here, his sport coat was again checkered, but this time the color was blue.

On the sofa, a muscular man—Major Putnam—sat next to

an attractive blond woman—Captain Weller. Buchanan had met them on the yacht in Fort Lauderdale. Each wore civilian clothes: in the major's case, a beige suit; in the captain's, a white silk blouse and blue skirt, both of which were tight and were no doubt intended to attract public attention away from the two men.

Buchanan glanced toward the right, toward the bathroom, to make sure that no one else was waiting. The closet was open, unoccupied.

He took his key from the lock, closed the door, locked it, and walked toward them. Late-afternoon sunlight filled the room.

"Captain," the major said.

Buchanan nodded and stopped five feet away.

"You don't seem surprised to see us," the major said.

"At the Farm, I had an Agency trainer who used to say, 'The only thing you ought to expect is the *un*expected.' "

"Good advice," the woman said. "I understand a mugger stabbed you."

"That I certainly *didn't* expect."

"How's the wound?"

"Healing. Where's the colonel?"

"I'm afraid he couldn't make it," Alan said.

"Well, I hope you haven't been waiting long."

"Aren't you curious how we got in?"

Buchanan shook his head.

"Captain"—the major looked displeased—"you were seen in the hotel lobby at one-forty-five. Supposedly you were going to your room. Now you've come back, but no one saw you leave in the interim. Where have you been for the past three hours?"

"Taking a steamboat ride."

"Is that before or after you checked the reporter out of her room?"

"So you know about that? After. In fact, the reporter went with me on the steamboat ride."

"*What?*" Captain Weller leaned forward, her blouse tightening against her breasts. "Weren't you informed that we were looking for her?"

"I was told you intended to discourage her. But she kept

hounding me, so I decided to do some discouraging of my own. I scared her away from the story."

"You . . . ? How did . . . ?"

"By using her arguments against her. She showed me these." Buchanan pulled the newspaper clippings from a jacket pocket and set them on the coffee table. As the major grabbed and read them, Buchanan continued, "About Bob Bailey dying in an explosion. About Jack Doyle killing his wife and then himself. Alan"—Buchanan turned to him—"you left out a few things when you told me what happened in Fort Lauderdale after I disappeared from there. Did you know about Bailey and the Doyles?"

"It didn't seem necessary to tell you."

"Why?"

"The less you knew about Bailey, the better. If you were interrogated, your confusion would be genuine. As far as the Doyles are concerned, well, we didn't want to burden you with the knowledge that a man you had worked with had killed his wife and then himself shortly after you left them."

"I convinced the reporter that what happened to the Doyles was actually a double murder."

"You what? Oh, Jesus," the major said.

"I asked her to consider a hypothetical situation," Buchanan said. "If Bailey was killed because he was blackmailing me, and if the Doyles were killed because they knew too much and might be linked to me when the divers couldn't find my body, what did that say about the further lengths certain people would go in order to keep Scotch and Soda—she mentioned it first— a secret? I don't think there's anything paler than a redhead when the blood drains from her face. She suddenly realized how much danger she was in, that writing a front-page story wasn't worth losing her life. She's in a taxi on her way to the airport, where she'll catch the first plane back to Washington. There won't be any story."

"You actually believe her?"

"Yes. I told her I'd kill her if she ever wrote the story. I believe her because I know *she* believed *me*."

The room became silent.

"She's out of it," Buchanan said.

The major and the captain looked at each other.

Come on, Buchanan thought. *Take the bait.*

"We'd want all the photographs and the negatives." Alan shifted his weight on the bed.

The major and the captain turned in his direction, as if they hadn't been aware of him until now, surprised that he'd spoken.

"That's not a problem," Buchanan said. "She's already agreed to give them to me. As a gesture of good faith"—he pulled some photographs from an inside pocket of his jacket—"these are the ones she had on her."

"You honestly think she'll stick to her bargain?" the major asked.

"She's too afraid not to."

"You certainly must have been convincing."

"That's my speciality. Being convincing."

But have I convinced *you*? Buchanan thought.

"She could make copies of the photographs and create new negatives," the major said.

"Or hold some back," the captain added. "The only way to be sure is to get rid of her."

Alan squirmed again, then stood from the bed. "I don't know." He shook his head, troubled. "Would that really solve anything? Even if she was terminated, we'd still have to worry that she had copies of her research hidden with friends. There'd be no guarantee that we could find it all. Fear can be an effective motivator. If Buchanan thinks he managed to neutralize the situation without the need for violence, maybe we ought to go along with his suggestion. After all, no matter how much we made her death seem like an accident, there would still be repercussions. Suspicions. Killing her might cause more problems than it solves."

Inwardly, Buchanan sighed. I've got him. He's agreeing. Now all I have to do is . . .

The major frowned. "I'll have to talk with the colonel."

"Of course," Alan said sarcastically. "The colonel has the final word. The Agency doesn't count in this. Only you people."

The major responded flatly, "We have as much authority as you. The colonel has to be consulted."

Shit, Buchanan thought. I only got a postponement.

He quickly tried another approach.

"I have something else for you to tell the colonel."

"Oh?"

". . . I'm resigning."

They stared.

"You were already planning to take me out of operations and use me as an instructor. Why do things halfway? Accept my resignation. If I'm out of the military, I won't be a threat to you."

"Threat? What do you mean?" the major asked.

"I think that's obvious enough. The real problem here is me."

The room seemed to shrink.

"I repeat, Captain. What do you mean?" the major asked.

"We wouldn't be in this situation if it hadn't been for what happened to me in Cancún and then in Fort Lauderdale. The operation wouldn't be threatened if I was out of the way. That wasn't a mugger who stabbed me last night. It was someone working for you."

"That's absurd," the captain said.

"Using a street weapon so it wouldn't look like a professional hit. Because of the knife, I didn't figure it out right away. No reputable assassin would ever use a blade. Compared to a bullet, it's too uncertain. For that matter, too risky, because you have to get right next to your target. But then I realized that what looked like an amateur killing would be a perfect cover for a professional one. Bailey, the Doyles, me. We'd all be dead. A suspicious coincidence, yes. But each of the deaths would be explainable without any need to drag in a conspiracy theory. And if the reporter had a car accident . . ."

Everyone became very still.

"All because of the photographs," Buchanan said. "The ones that showed you, Major, and you, Captain, and more important, the colonel with me on the yacht in Fort Lauderdale. For me to be exposed wasn't a problem. You knew I'd never implicate anyone. But for you two to have your photograph on the front page of the *Washington Post*, and in particular for the colonel to be on the front page, that's a different matter. That would lead to the exposure of all sorts of things. You don't have to worry about any of that now. The reporter isn't going to write her story. And even if I hadn't scared her off, the photograph of me with the two of you and the colonel doesn't mean anything if I can't be linked to Scotch and Soda. You don't need to go to the trouble of killing me. I'll do you all a favor and disappear."

The group seemed frozen.

Finally, the major cleared his throat, then looked awkwardly at the woman and finally Alan.

"Come on," Buchanan said. "We've got a problem. Let's discuss it."

"Captain, do you realize what you sound like?" the major asked, uneasy.

"Direct."

"Try *paranoid*."

"Fine," Buchanan said. "Nobody ordered my termination. We'll pretend it was the random act of violence you wanted it to resemble. However you want to play this. It makes no difference to me. Just so you get the point. I'll disappear. That way, you've got double protection. Holly McCoy won't write her story. I won't be around to be questioned."

"To hear you talk like this." The major frowned. "I'm glad we did decide to observe you. You've definitely been under cover too long."

"I think you'd better get some rest," Alan said. "You've just been released from the hospital. You've got to be tired."

The woman added, "Being stabbed. Injuring your head again. In your place, I'd—"

"How'd you know I hurt my head again? I didn't mention it to anybody."

"I just assumed."

"Or you heard it from the man you sent to kill me."

"Captain, you're obviously distressed. I want you—in fact, I order you—to stay in this room, to try to relax and get some sleep. We'll be back here at nine hundred hours tomorrow morning to continue this conversation. Hopefully, you'll feel less disturbed by then."

"I honestly don't blame you for trying to protect the mission," Buchanan said. "But let's not talk around the problem. Get it out in the open. Now that I've given you a better solution, you don't have to kill me."

Alan studied Buchanan with concern, then followed the major and the captain somberly out the door.

12

Buchanan's legs felt unsteady as he crossed the room and secured the lock. The strain of the conversation had intensified his headache. He shoved three Tylenol caplets into his mouth and went into the bathroom to drink a glass of water. His mouth was so dry that he drank a second glass. His reflection in the mirror showed dark patches under his eyes. I'm losing it, he thought.

In the bedroom, he awkwardly closed the draperies. His side hurt when he stretched out on the bed. The darkness was soothing.

But his mind wouldn't stop working.

Did I pull it off?

Were they convinced?

He didn't understand why he was so concerned about Holly's safety. He'd met her only a few days ago. In theory, they were antagonists. Most of his troubles were due to her interference. In fact, it could be argued that Jack and Cindy Doyle were dead because of her. But the truth was that Holly McCoy hadn't killed the Doyles. His own people had. Just as they'd killed Bailey. And they'd have killed me, too, if I'd been around when Bailey opened the cooler to look at his money.

So they waited for another chance to get me, a way that wouldn't look suspicious even to a reporter.

Holly McCoy.

Have I grown attracted to her? he wondered. There had been a time when he could have justified anything—the murder of a reporter, anything—for the sake of maintaining an operation's security. Now . . .

Yes?

Maybe I don't care about the operation any longer. Or maybe . . .

What?

Maybe I'm becoming a human being.
Yeah, but *which* human being?

13

"One more time," Alan said. "I want to be sure about this." He drove a rented Pontiac from the Crowne Plaza hotel. Major Putnam sat next to him. Captain Weller leaned forward from the back. "Do any of you know anything about an order to terminate Buchanan?"

"Absolutely not," the captain said.

"I received no such instructions," the major said.

"And *I* didn't," Alan said.

"What's this about Jack and Cindy Doyle?" the major asked. "I thought their deaths were a murder-suicide."

"So did I," the captain said. "Buchanan caught me totally off balance when he·said they were a double murder. I don't know anything about orders to terminate *them*."

"Who tried to kill Buchanan?" Alan asked.

"An attempted mugging is still the most logical explanation," the major said.

"In the middle of a crowd outside a restaurant?" Alan gripped the steering wheel harder. "A pickpocket, sure. But I never heard of a pickpocket who drew attention to himself by stabbing the guy he was trying to lift a wallet from."

"How about some weirdo who gets his kicks out of stabbing people in public?" the captain asked.

"That makes more sense." Alan turned onto Canal Street, squinting at headlights. "It's crazy, but it makes sense."

"The thing is, Buchanan believes *we* did it," the major said. "And that's just as crazy."

"But do you think he *really* believes it?" the captain asked. "He's an actor. He says things for effect. He can be very convincing."

"He certainly convinced me," Alan said.

"But why would he lie?" the major asked.

"To create a smoke screen. To confuse us and divert our attention from the reporter."

"Why?" the major repeated.

"Buchanan might be right that killing the reporter would cause more problems than it solves," Alan said. "If she's genuinely intimidated and she doesn't write the story, we've accomplished our purpose."

"If. I keep hearing a lot of ifs."

"I agree with Buchanan," the captain said. "I think it's better if we do nothing at this point and just sweat it out."

"On that score, the colonel's opinion is the only one that matters," the major said.

They drove in silence.

"We still haven't . . ." Alan scowled at the bright lights of traffic.

"What?" the captain asked.

"*Did* someone try to kill Buchanan? Not a wacko but a professional following orders. And if we didn't give the orders, who did?"

14

The rule was, if a contact didn't show up at an agreed place on schedule and if no arrangements had been made for an alternate time and place for a meeting, you returned to the rendezvous site twenty-four hours later. With luck, whatever had prevented the contact from coming to the meeting would no longer be an obstacle. But if the contact didn't show up the second time . . .

Buchanan didn't want to think about it. He made his way through the French Quarter. Crowded, narrow streets. Dixieland. The blues. Dancing on the sidewalk. Commotion. But no costumes. This time, with no masks to hide people's faces, Buchanan would have a much better chance to learn if he was being followed. Last time, he'd been conspicuous because he hadn't been wearing a costume. Now, just one of the many people in street clothes, he would have a much better chance of blending with a crowd, slipping down an alley, and evading anyone who did try to follow.

With a sense of déjà vu that made him wince from the

memory of when the knife had entered his side, he passed the shadows of Jackson Square, studied Decatur Street, and once more crossed toward Café du Monde. Again the restaurant was busy, although not as much as on Halloween. To make sure that the crowd didn't prevent him from entering, he'd taken care to arrive early, at 10:15 rather than the scheduled time of eleven when he had last been here with Juana six years ago.

He festered with impatience. Never showing it, he waited his turn and was escorted by a waiter past pillars, through the noise of the crowd, and to a seat at a small circular white-topped table surrounded by similar busy tables in a corner at the back. By chance, the table was in exactly the spot he would have chosen to give himself an effective view of the entrance.

But he wasn't satisfied. He needed something more, another way to be sure, a further guarantee, and when he saw his chance, he stood to claim a suddenly empty table near the center of the restaurant. It was here, he remembered, that he and Juana had sat six years earlier. Not this same table. He could never be positive of that. But the position was close enough, and when Juana came in, she would have no trouble finding him. Her gaze would scan the congested room, settle on the area that she associated with him, and there he would be, rising, smiling, walking toward her, eager to hold her.

He glanced at his watch: 10:40. Soon, he thought. Soon.

His headache made him sick again. When the waiter came to take his order, he asked for the specialty: café au lait and beignets. He also asked for water. That was what he really wanted. Water. The coffee and the beignets were just so he'd be allowed to sit there. The water was so he could swallow more Tylenol.

Soon.

Juana.

"*I love you,*" he had told her. "*I want you to know that you'll always be special to me. I want you to know that I'll always feel close to you. I swear to you. If you ever need help, if you're ever in trouble, all you have to do is ask, and no matter how long it's been, no matter how far away I am, I'll—*"

Buchanan blinked, realizing that the waiter was setting down the water, the coffee, and the beignets. After he swallowed the

Tylenol, he was startled when he glanced at his watch. Fifteen minutes had passed like fifteen seconds. It was almost eleven o'clock.

He kept staring toward the entrance.

Here's the postcard I never thought I'd send. I hope you meant your promise. The last time and place. Counting on you. PLEASE.

"Is something wrong, sir?"

"Excuse me?"

"You've been sitting here for half an hour and you haven't touched your coffee or the beignets."

"Half an hour?"

"Other people would like a chance to sit down."

"I'm waiting for someone."

"Even so, other people would like—"

"Bring me another round. Here's ten dollars for your trouble."

"Thank you, sir."

Buchanan stared at the entrance.

Midnight.

One o'clock. People frowned toward him, whispering.

By two o'clock, he knew that she wouldn't be coming.

What in God's name had happened to her? She needed his help. Why hadn't she let him prove he loved her?

15

He packed his bag and dropped a signed checkout form on the bed. At 3:00 A.M., no one saw him leave the hotel through a service exit. Stepping out of shadows onto Lafayette Street, he hailed a taxi.

"Where to, suh?" The driver looked wary, as if a man carrying a suitcase at 3:00 A.M. might be a threat.

"An all-night car-rental agency."

The driver debated briefly. "Hop in. It's kinda late to be takin' a trip."

"Isn't it, though."

He slumped in the backseat, thinking. It would have been easier to fly to where he needed to go. But he didn't want to wait until morning and catch the first plane to his destination. For one thing, the major, the captain, and Alan might arrive earlier than they'd said they would and intercept him. For another, because he didn't have enough cash to buy an airplane ticket, he'd need to use a credit card. But the only credit card he had was in Brendan Buchanan's name. That would leave a paper trail for the major, the captain, and Alan to follow.

This way, while he'd still have to use a credit card to rent a car, there'd be no record of where he was planning to drive. The paper trail would end right here in New Orleans. And with luck, the major, the captain, and Alan would accept that he'd decided to do what he'd told them and disappear. In a perfect world, they would consider this a reassuring gesture and not a threat. To direct their thinking, he'd written a note about his determination to disappear, had sealed the note in an envelope addressed to Alan, and had left it on the hotel room's bed, beside the signed checkout form.

"Here we are, suh."

"What?" He roused himself and looked out the taxi's side window, seeing a brightly lit car-rental office next to a gas station.

"If I was you, suh, I'd take it easy drivin'. You look beat."

"Thanks. I'll be fine."

But I'd better look more alert when I rent the car, he thought.

He paid the driver and didn't show the effort with which he carried his bag into the office, where the bright lights hurt his eyes.

A weary-looking spectacled man shoved a rental agreement across the counter. "I'll need to see your credit card and your driver's license. Initial about the insurance. Sign at the bottom."

He had to look at the credit card he'd set on the counter to see which name he was using. "Buchanan. Brendan Buchanan."

If only this headache would ease off.

Juana.

He had to find Juana.

And there was only one place he could think to start.

16

"It's been taken care of," Raymond said.

Seated at the rear of the passenger compartment of his private jet, Alistair Drummond peered up from a report he was reading. The fuselage vibrated softly as the jet streaked through the sky. "Specifics," he said.

"According to a radio message I just received," Raymond said, "last night, the director of Mexico's National Institute of Archaeology and History was killed in a car accident near the National Palace in Mexico City."

"Tragic," Drummond said. Despite his age, he didn't show the strain of having flown to a business meeting in Moscow, then to another in Riyadh in Saudi Arabia before his present transatlantic flight back to Mexico's Yucatán Peninsula, all within forty-eight hours. "Do we have evidence that Delgado was responsible?"

"The man Delgado ordered to do it is on our payroll. He'll implicate Delgado if we ask him, provided we guarantee he won't be punished."

"We?" Drummond asked.

"I meant *you*."

"Your confusion of pronouns troubles me, Raymond. I'd hate to think that you consider me an equal."

"No, sir, I don't. I won't make the mistake again."

"Has his successor been chosen?"

Raymond nodded.

"An executive favorable to our cause?"

Raymond nodded again. "And money will make him more so."

"Good," Drummond said, his voice brittle, one of the few signs of his age. "We no longer need the woman, even if we find her. The leverage she provided against Delgado isn't necessary any longer now that we have another way to put pressure on him. In all probability, Delgado will be Mexico's next president, but not if we reveal his crimes. Let him know we have proof that he ordered the death of the Institute's director, that his political future continues to depend on me.''

"Yes, sir.''

·"Then, when he becomes president, I'll have even more influence.''

"All the influence you need.''

"Never," Drummond corrected him.

"Perhaps, then, you do need the woman.''

The old man scowled, his wrinkles deepening so much that his true age began to show. "I almost lost everything because of her. When your operatives find her . . .''

"Yes, sir?''

"Make certain they kill her on sight.''

NINE

∎∎∎

1

SAN ANTONIO, TEXAS

Buchanan arrived by nightfall. He'd driven west on Route 10 from New Orleans to Baton Rouge, past numerous small towns into Texas, toward Beaumont and Houston and finally . . .

His headache, combined with the pain in his side, had forced him to rest several times along the way. At Beaumont, he'd rented a hotel room in midmorning so that he could shave and shower and sleep for a couple of hours. The hotel clerk had looked puzzled when he checked out at noon. That was no good, attracting attention like that. It wasn't any good, either, that his scarcity of cash forced him to use his credit card to rent the room. Now there was a further paper trail, although by the time Alan, the major, and the captain traced him to the hotel, he'd be long gone, and they still wouldn't know his destination. Sure, if they checked the records of his past assignments, they might guess it, but he'd had a great many assignments in the six years since he'd known Juana, and it would take them quite a while to make the connection between her, New Orleans, and San Antonio. By then, he'd be somewhere else.

He ate takeout food while he drove, hamburgers, french fries, po'boys, tacos, anything to give him fuel, washing it down with plenty of Coca-Cola, relying on the soft drink's calories and caffeine to maintain his energy. Three times, he pulled off the busy highway and napped at a rest stop. He parked the rented Taurus near the toilet facilities so that the noisy coming and going of vehicles and travelers would prevent him from sleeping too deeply, for he knew that if he did truly sleep, he wouldn't waken until the next day.

He had to keep moving. He had to get to San Antonio and begin the urgent process of finding out what had happened to Juana. Why had she failed to meet him? What trouble had caught up to her? Despite his pain and confusion, he had sufficient presence of mind to ask himself if he was overreacting. A promise made six years ago to a woman whom he hadn't seen since then. A plea for help in the form of a cryptic postcard.

Maybe the postcard didn't mean what he thought. Did it make sense for Juana to contact him after so long a time? And why him? Wasn't there anyone else whom she could ask for help?

What made *him* the logical choice?

He didn't have answers. But this much he knew for certain: Something had happened to him.

Something terrifying.

He tried to establish when it had begun. Perhaps when he'd been shot in Cancún, or when he'd injured his head while he made his escape, swimming across the channel. Perhaps when he'd been tortured in Mérida and had struck his head on the concrete floor. Or possibly later when he'd been stabbed and had *again* struck his head.

The more he considered those possibilities, he didn't think

that they were the source of his fear, however. No doubt they were contributing factors. But as he analyzed the past weeks, as he replayed his various traumas, one incident disturbed him more than any.

The trauma had not been physical. It had been mental.

It threatened his sense of identity.

Or rather, multiple identities. During the past eight years, he had been more than two hundred people. On some days, he had impersonated as many as six different people while attempting to recruit a series of contacts. During the past two weeks, he'd been confused for Jim Crawford and had identified with Peter Lang while he'd impersonated Ed Potter and Victor Grant and Don Colton and . . .

Brendan Buchanan.

That was the trouble. After disposing of Victor Grant, he'd expected to be given yet another identity. But at the Alexandria apartment, Alan had told him that there wouldn't be a new identity, that he was being transferred from field operations, that he would have to be . . .

Himself.

But who the hell was that? He hadn't been Brendan Buchanan for so long that he didn't know who on earth Brendan Buchanan was. On a superficial level, he didn't know such basics as how he liked to dress or what he liked to eat. On the deepest level, he was totally out of touch with himself. He was an actor who'd so immersed himself in his roles that when his roles were taken away from him, he became a vacuum.

His profession wasn't only what he did. It defined what he *was*. He was nothing without a role to play, and he realized now how brutally the realization had struck him that he couldn't be Brendan Buchanan for the rest of his life. Thus, to escape being Brendan Buchanan, he would become Peter Lang. He would hunt for the most important person in Peter Lang's world. And possibly in his own world, for the more he thought about it, the more he wondered how positively his life would have changed if he had stayed with Juana.

I *liked* Peter Lang, he thought.

And Peter Lang had been in love with Juana.

2

Past Houston, he used a pay phone outside a truck stop. It fascinated and disturbed him that the only person he cared about from Brendan Buchanan's world was Holly McCoy. He'd known her only a few days. She was a threat to him. And yet he had an irresistible urge to protect her, to ensure that she escaped the danger she had created for herself because she had investigated him. He thought he had convinced the major, the captain, and Alan of her intention not to pursue the story. There was a strong chance they would leave her alone. But what about the colonel? Would the colonel agree with their recommendation?

Buchanan hadn't been lying when he'd told them that Holly had flown back to Washington, and he hadn't been lying when he'd said that he'd made Holly frightened enough not to pursue the story. Still, he had to reinforce her resolve. Assuming that her phones would be tapped, he'd told her that he would use the name Mike Hamilton if he needed to leave a message on her answering machine or with someone at the *Washington Post*. As it happened, she was at the newspaper when he called there.

"How are you?"

"Wondering if I made a mistake," Holly answered.

"It wasn't a mistake, believe me."

"What about your negotiations? Did they work?"

"I don't know yet."

"Oh."

"Yes. Oh. Did you send them what you promised?"

" . . . Not yet."

"Do it."

"It's just that . . . It's such good material. I hate to . . ."

"Do it," Buchanan repeated. "Don't make them angry."

"But giving up the story makes me feel like a coward."

"There were plenty of times when I did things rather than think of myself as a coward. Now those things don't seem worth it. I have to keep on the move. The best advice I can give you is . . ." He wanted to say something reassuring but couldn't think of anything. "Stop worrying about bravery and cowardice. Follow your common sense."

He hung up, left the pay phone, got quickly into the rented Taurus, and returned to the busy highway, squinting from the painful sunlight that now was low in the west ahead of him. Even the Ray·Bans he'd bought at noon in Beaumont didn't keep the sun's glare from feeling as if a red-hot spike had been driven through each eye and into his skull.

Follow your common sense?

You're good at giving advice. You don't seem to want to take it, though.

3

Shortly after 9:00 P.M., he drove from the low, grassy, often wooded, rolling plains of eastern Texas and entered the lights of San Antonio. Six years ago, when he'd been researching the character of Peter Lang, he'd spent several weeks here so he wouldn't be ignorant about his fictional character's hometown. He'd done the usual touristy things like visiting the Alamo (its name was a Spanish word, he learned, which meant "cotton-wood tree"), as well as the restored Spanish Governor's Palace, the San Jose Mission, and La Villita, or The Little Village, a reconstructed section of the original eighteenth-century Spanish settlement. He spent a lot of time at Riverwalk, the Spanish-motif shopping area along the landscaped banks of the San Antonio River.

But he'd also spent a lot of time in the suburbs, in one of which—Castle Hills—Juana's parents had lived. Juana had used a cover name so that an enemy could not have found out who her parents were and gone to San Antonio to question them about her supposed husband. There'd been no need—and in fact it would have been disruptive—for Buchanan to meet her parents. He knew where they lived, however, and he headed straight toward their home, making a few mistakes in direction but surprising himself by how much he remembered from his previous visit there.

Juana's parents had a two-story brick-and-shingled house fronted by a well-tended lawn that had sheltering oak trees. When Buchanan parked the rented Taurus at the curb, he saw that lights were on in what he gathered was the living room. He got out of the car, locked it, and studied his reflection, which a streetlight cast on the driver's side window. His rugged face looked tired, but after he combed his hair and straightened his clothes, he at least appeared neat and respectable. He was still wearing the brown sport coat that he had taken from Ted's room back in New Orleans. Slightly too large for him, although not unbecomingly so, it had the advantage of concealing the handgun that he'd tucked behind his belt before he got out of the Taurus.

He glanced both ways along the street, out of habit watching the shadows for any sign that the house was under surveillance. If Juana was in trouble, as the postcard and her failure to meet him suggested, if she was on the run—which would explain why she hadn't shown up at Café du Monde—there was a possibility that her enemies would watch her parents in case she contacted them in person or telephoned and inadvertently revealed where she was. The Juana who'd been in the military would never have let anyone know the name and location of her parents. But a great deal could have happened in the intervening six years. She might have foolishly trusted some-one enough to give that person information that was now being used against her, although being foolish had never been one of Juana's characteristics.

Except maybe for falling in love with Peter Lang.

The street suggested no threat. There weren't any vehicles parked on this block. No one was loitering at a corner, pre-tending to wait for a bus. Lights in the other houses revealed what appeared to be normal family activity. Someone might have been hiding in bushes, of course, although in this neigh-borhood where everybody seemed to take pride, a prowler on long-term surveillance wouldn't be able to hide easily, espe-cially from the German shepherd that a man was walking on a leash along the opposite sidewalk. Still, that was assuming the man with the dog was not himself on surveillance.

Buchanan took just a few seconds to register all this. From someone else's point of view, he would have seemed merely a visitor who'd paused to comb his hair before walking up to the house. The night was mild, with the fallen-leaf fragrance of autumn. As he stopped on the brick porch and pushed a button, he heard not only the doorbell but the muted sound of a laugh track on a television sitcom. Then he heard footsteps on a hardwood floor, and a shadow appeared at the window of the front door.

A light came on above him. He saw an Hispanic woman—in her late fifties, with shoulder-length black hair and an appealing oval face—peer out at him. Her intense dark eyes suggested intelligence and perception. They reminded him of Juana, although he didn't know for sure that this woman was Juana's mother. He had never met her parents. There was no name on the mailbox or beneath the doorbell. Juana's parents might have moved during the past six years. They might even have died. When he arrived in San Antonio, Buchanan had been tempted to check a phone book to see whether they still lived at this address, but by then he was so anxious to reach the house that he hadn't wanted to waste even a minute. He would know soon enough, he'd told himself.

An amateur might have phoned from New Orleans, and if he managed to contact Juana's parents, that amateur might have tried to elicit information from them about whether Juana was in trouble. If so, he would have failed, or the information he received would have been suspect. Most people were gullible, but even a fool tended to hold back when confronted by personal questions from a stranger using a telephone, no matter how good that stranger's cover story was. A telephone was a lazy operative's way of doing research. Whenever possible, face-to-face contact was the best method of obtaining information, and when the military had transferred Buchanan for training at the CIA's Farm in Virginia, Buchanan had quickly acquired a reputation as being skilled at what was called in the trade elicitation. His instructor's favorite assignment had been to send his students into various local bars during happy hour. The students were to strike up conversations with strangers, and in the course of an hour, they had to gain the trust of those strangers to such a degree that each stranger would reveal the day, month, and year of his birth, as well as his Social Security number. Experience had proved to the instructor that such personal information was almost impossible to learn in a first-time encounter. How could you invent a casual question that would prompt someone you'd never met to blurt out his Social Security number? More than likely, your question would result in suspicion rather than information. All of the students in the class had failed—except for Buchanan.

The Hispanic woman unlocked the door and opened it, although she didn't release the security chain. Speaking through the five-inch gap in the door, she looked puzzled. "Yes?"

"Señora Mendez?"

"*Sí.*"

"*Perdone.* I know it's late. My name's Jeff Walker, and I'm a friend of your daughter." Buchanan used the Spanish he'd learned at the Defense Language Institute in Monterey, California, when he'd been preparing for his mission into Mexico. "I haven't seen her in several years, and I don't know where she lives. I'm visiting town for a couple of days, and . . . Well, I hoped that she was around. Can you tell me where to find her?"

Juana's mother studied him with suspicion. However, her suspicion seemed tempered by an appreciation that he was using Spanish. Juana had told him that while her parents were bilingual, they much preferred speaking Spanish and they felt slighted when whites whom they knew spoke Spanish forced them to speak English.

"*Conoce a mi hija?*"

"*Sí,*" Buchanan continued in Spanish. "I know your Juana. We were in the military together. I knew her when she was stationed here at Fort Sam Houston." That had been one of Juana's cover assignments. Although she had worked with Army Intelligence and was affiliated with Special Forces at Fort Bragg, her ostensible assignment had been with the Fifth Army headquarters here in San Antonio. "We got along real well. Several times, we went out together. I guess you could say . . . Well, we were close. I wish I'd kept in touch with her. But I was overseas for a while and . . . I'd sure like the chance to say hello."

Juana's mother continued to study him with suspicion. Buchanan was certain that if he hadn't been speaking Spanish and if he hadn't mentioned Fort Sam Houston, she wouldn't have listened to him this long. He needed something else to establish his credibility. "Do you still have that dog? The golden retriever? What was his name? Pepe. Yeah. Juana sure loved that dog. When she wasn't talking about baseball, she was talking about him. Said she liked to take Pepe out for a run along the river when she wasn't on duty."

The mother's suspicion began to dissolve. "No."

"I beg your pardon?"

"The dog. Pepe. He died last year."

"Oh. I'm sorry to hear that, Señora Mendez. Losing a pet can be like . . . Juana must have taken it hard."

"You say your name is Jeff Walker?"

"That's right." Buchanan made sure to stand straight, as if his character retained habits of bearing from when he'd been in the military.

"I don't remember her mentioning you."

"Well, six years is a while ago. Juana certainly told me a lot about you. The way I hear it, you make the best chicken fajitas in town."

The mother smiled slightly. "Those were always Juana's favorite." The smile became a frown. "I would remember you if I'd met you before. Why didn't Juana ever bring you to the house?"

I've got another "why," Buchanan thought with growing concern. Why so many questions? What the hell's going on?

4

Two blocks along the street, a small gray van was parked in front of a house with a FOR SALE sign on the lawn. The van had been parked there for several days, but the neighbors had not been troubled by its presence. On the contrary, they felt reassured because the van's driver, a private detective, had paid a visit to everyone who lived on that block and had explained that recent vandalism in the neighborhood had prompted a security firm with clients in the area to dispatch a guard to keep a watch on several homes in the district, particularly the vacant house, which seemed a natural target for vandals. If the neighbors had telephoned the number on the business card that they were given, a professional-sounding secretary would have told them that what the private detective had said was correct. The man did work for the firm. What the secretary would not have said, of course, was that she was speaking from an almost-empty one-room downtown office, and that the security firm had not existed two weeks ago.

The private detective's name was Duncan Bradley. He was twenty-eight years old. Tall and slim, he almost always wore sneakers and a cotton sweat suit, as if he expected at any moment to play basketball, his favorite leisure activity. He preferred so informal an outfit because it was comfortable during lengthy stakeouts, and this particular stakeout—already lengthy—promised to become even longer.

He and his partner were working twelve-hour shifts, which meant that the van, the windows of which were shielded so that no one could see in, had to be equipped with cooking facilities (a microwave) and toilet facilities (a Porta Potti). The cramped working conditions also meant that the van had needed to be customized in order to comfortably accommodate Duncan Bradley's six-foot-eight-inch frame. Thus all the seats had been removed from the back and replaced by an extralong mattress clamped to a plank and tilted upward on a fifteen-degree angle so that Duncan, who constantly lay upon it, didn't need to strain his neck by his persistent need to keep looking up.

What he looked at was the monitor for a miniature television camera that projected from the van's roof and was hidden by the cowling of a fake air vent. This camera, a version of the type used in assault helicopters, had considerable magnification ability, so it was able to show the license plate of a car parked two blocks farther along the street, a blue Ford Taurus with Louisiana license plates. This camera also had state-of-the-art night-vision capability, and thus, although the street was for the most part in shadow, Duncan had no trouble seeing the green-tinted image of a man who got out of the Taurus, combed his hair, glanced at the neighborhood as if admiring it, and then walked toward the house. The man was Caucasian, about five-eleven, in his early thirties. He was well-built but not dramatically muscular. He was dressed casually, unremarkably. His hair was of moderate length, neither long nor short.

His features were rugged but not severe, just as he was good-looking, handsome, but not in a way that attracted attention.

"This is November second," Duncan said into a tape recorder. "It's nine-thirty at night. I'm still in my surveillance vehicle down the street from the target area. A man just showed up at the house." Duncan proceeded to describe the car and its driver, including the Louisiana license number. "He's not too tall, not too short. A little of this, a little of that, not too much of one thing or another. Could be something, could be nothing. I'm monitoring audio surveillance."

Duncan lowered the tape recorder and turned up the volume on an audio receiver, then adjusted the earphones he was wearing. The receiver corresponded with several miniature microphone-transmitter units that Duncan had hidden in the phones and light switches of every room in the target house. The units were tapped into the house's electrical system and thus had a permanent source of power. They were programmed to transmit on an FM band that wasn't used in San Antonio, so the transmission wouldn't interfere with television or radio reception in the house and possibly make the occupants suspicious.

The day he'd been given this assignment, Duncan had waited until the targets were both out of the house. They'd made things easy for him by doing so after supper, when the neighborhood was dark. Followed by Duncan's partner, the targets had driven to a shopping mall, and if they'd decided to return sooner than anticipated, Duncan's partner had a cellular phone with which he could have transmitted a warning beep to the pager that Duncan wore. Of course, Duncan had not depended on the good fortune that the targets had left the house unattended while it was dark. If necessary, he could have entered the unoccupied house during daylight by posing as an employee of the lawn-care company that the targets hired to maintain their property. No neighbor would have thought it unusual for a man wearing a lawn-care uniform and carrying an insect-spray canister the size of a fire extinguisher to check the bushes at the side of the house and then to proceed intently around to the back. Duncan had invaded the house through a patio door, picking its lock in fifteen seconds, installing all the microphones within forty minutes.

In the van, dials on the receiver's console allowed him to

adjust the sound level from each transmitter. The equipment also permitted Duncan to record the sound from each transmitter onto separate tapes. He hadn't been doing much recording, however. In the two weeks since he'd had this assignment, he'd heard nothing but what seemed to be normal household conversation. If the occupants were using a private code to communicate secret information, Duncan had detected no indication of it. Phone calls had been the usual neighborhood chitchat. Dinner talk had mostly been about the husband's extremely successful car-repair business. At night, the couple watched a lot of television. They hadn't had sex as long as Duncan had been listening.

For most of this evening, Duncan had been listening to the laugh track on a string of TV situation comedies. Now, when he heard the doorbell and the husband telling the wife to answer it, he activated a bank of tape recorders and lowered the volume of the transmitter in the living room, at the same time raising the volume of the transmitter in the front hallway.

Duncan understood Spanish. It was one of the reasons that he'd been assigned to this house, and right from the start of the conversation, he felt charged. Because right from the start, the stranger, who said his name was Jeff Walker, asked about Juana Mendez. Baby, we are in business now, Duncan thought. We are finally getting some action. While he eagerly listened and adjusted dials and made sure that the tape machines were recording every word, he simultaneously pushed a button on his cellular telephone. The number he needed to call had been programmed into the phone.

"You know my daughter?" Mrs. Mendez was saying in Spanish.

The man who called himself Jeff Walker was explaining that he'd known Juana in the military, at Fort Sam Houston.

With the cellular phone pressed against his left ear, Duncan heard it buzz.

The man who called himself Jeff Walker was talking about a dog that Juana Mendez had owned. Whoever this guy was, he certainly seemed to know her.

The cellular phone buzzed a second time.

Now Jeff Walker was carrying on about how Juana had bragged about her mother's chicken fajitas.

You're laying it on a bit thick, aren't you, buddy? Duncan thought.

Abruptly someone answered the phone, a smooth male voice absorbing the cellular static. "Tucker here."

"This is Bradley. I think we've got ignition."

5

"Why didn't Juana bring me to the house?" Continuing to use Spanish, Buchanan repeated the question that Juana's mother had asked him. "You know, I wondered that myself. I think it was because she wasn't sure if you and your husband would approve."

Buchanan was taking a big chance here, but he had to do something to distract her from her suspicion. Something was wrong, and he didn't know what, but he thought if he put her on the defensive about *one* thing, she might open up about *other* things.

"Why wouldn't we approve?" Juana's mother asked. Her dark eyes flashed with barely controlled indignation. "Because you're white? That's crazy. Half my husband's employees are white. Many of Juana's high school friends were white. Juana knows we're not prejudiced."

"I'm sorry. That isn't what I meant. I didn't intend to insult you. Juana told me—in fact, she emphasized—that you didn't have any objection if she dated someone who wasn't Hispanic."

"Then why wouldn't we have approved of you?" Juana's mother's dark eyes flashed again.

"Because I'm not Catholic."

". . . Oh." The woman's voice dropped.

"Juana said you'd told her many times that was one thing you expected of her . . . that if she got serious about a man, he would have to be a Catholic . . . because you wanted to be certain that your grandchildren would be raised in the Church."

"Yes." Juana's mother swallowed. "That is true. I told her that often. Apparently, you do know her well."

In the background, a man's gruff voice interrupted. "Anita, who are you talking to? What's taking you so long?"

Juana's mother glanced down the hallway toward the entrance to the living room. "Wait here," she told Buchanan and closed the door.

Feeling exposed, Buchanan heard muffled words.

Juana's mother returned. "Please, come in."

She didn't sound happy about the invitation, though, and she didn't *look* happy as she locked the door behind them and escorted Buchanan into the living room.

It was connected via an archway to the kitchen, and immediately Buchanan smelled the lingering fragrance of oil, spices, onions, and peppers from dinner. The room had too much furniture, mostly padded chairs and various wooden tables. A crucifix hung on the wall. A short, heavy-chested, fiftyish man with pitch-black hair and darker eyes than his wife sat in a La-Z-Boy recliner. His face was round but craggy. He wore work shoes and a blue coverall that had a patch—MENDEZ MECHANICS. Buchanan remembered that Juana had told him about the six garages her father owned throughout the city. The man was smoking a cigar and holding a bottle of Corona beer.

"Who are you?" It was difficult to hear him because of the laughter from the television.

"As I told your wife, my name is . . ."

"Yes. Jeff Walker. Who *are* you?"

Buchanan frowned. "I'm sorry. I don't understand."

Juana's mother fidgeted.

"I'm a friend of your daughter," Buchanan said.

"So you claim." The man looked nervous. "When is her birthday?"

"Why on earth would . . .?"

"Just answer the question. If you're as good a friend as you say, you'll know when she has her birthday."

. . .

"Well?"

"As I recall, it's in May. The tenth." Buchanan remembered it because six years previously he and Juana had started working together in May. Under the pretense of being husband and wife in New Orleans, they'd made a big deal about her birthday on the tenth.

"Anybody could look that up in a file. Does she have any allergies?"

"Señor Mendez, what's this about? I haven't seen her in several years. It's very hard to remember if . . ."

"That's what I thought."

"But I recall she had a problem with cilantro. That always surprised me, her being allergic to an herb that's used so often in Hispanic cooking."

"Birthmarks?"

"This is . . ."

"Answer the question."

"There's a scar on the back of her right leg, up high, near her hip. She said she got it when she was a kid, climbing over a barbed-wire fence. What's next? Are you going to ask me how I saw the scar? I think I made a mistake. I think I shouldn't have come here. I think I should have gone to some of Juana's friends to see if *they* knew where I could find her."

As Buchanan turned toward the door, Juana's mother said sharply, "Pedro."

"Wait," the father said. "Please. If you're truly a friend of my daughter, stay."

Buchanan studied him, then nodded.

"I asked you those questions because . . ." Pedro seemed in turmoil. "You're the fourth friend of Juana to ask where she was in the past two weeks."

Buchanan didn't show his surprise. "The fourth . . .?"

"Is she in trouble?" Anita's voice was taut with anxiety.

"Like you, each of them was white," Pedro said. "Each was male. Each hadn't seen her in several years. But unlike you, they didn't have any personal knowledge about her. One of them claimed that he'd served with her at Fort Bragg. But Juana was *never* assigned to Fort Bragg."

That was wrong, Buchanan knew. Although Juana's cover military assignment had been at Fort Sam Houston, her actual assignment had been through Fort Bragg. But her parents would never have known that because Juana would never have broken cover to tell them. So they naturally thought that the man who had claimed to be Juana's friend was lying when he claimed that he'd known Juana at Bragg. Quite the contrary: The man was telling a version of the truth. Whoever he was, he knew

Juana's background in detail. But he had made a mistake in assuming that her parents would also know it.

Juana's father continued. "Another supposed friend claimed that he had known Juana at college here in San Antonio. When I asked which one, he looked confused. He didn't seem to know that she had transferred from Our Lady of the Lake University to St. Mary's University. Anyone who knew her well would have known that information."

Buchanan mentally agreed. Somebody had fucked up and skimmed through her file instead of reading it in detail.

"The third supposed friend," Pedro said, "claimed that, like you, he had dated her when they worked together here at Fort Sam Houston, but when we asked why we had never met him—since Juana brought most of her boyfriends to see us—he didn't have an explanation. At least, *you* did, just as you actually seem to know personal things about her. So I will ask you again . . . Jeff Walker . . . is our daughter in trouble?"

Juana's mother waited, clutching the sides of her dress.

Buchanan had a difficult, quick decision to make. Pedro was inviting him into their confidence. Or maybe Pedro was offering bait. If Buchanan admitted his true intentions, Pedro might very well suspect that Buchanan was yet another impersonator sent by Juana's enemies to find her.

He decided to take the gamble. "I think so."

Pedro exhaled as if he was finally hearing what he wanted, even though the knowledge dismayed him.

"I knew it," Juana's mother said. "What kind of trouble? Tell us. We've been worried to death about . . ."

"Anita, please, no talk about death." Pedro squinted toward Buchanan and repeated the question that his wife had asked. "What kind of trouble?"

"If I knew, I wouldn't be here," Buchanan said. "Last week, I received a message that she needed to see me. The message was vague, as if she didn't want anyone else to read it and figure out what she was telling me. But *I* could figure it out. She desperately needed help. There's a place in New Orleans that was special to us. Without mentioning it, she asked me—begged me, really—to meet her there at the same time and date we'd last been there. That would have been at eleven P.M. on Halloween. But she didn't show up that night or the night after. Obviously, something's wrong. That's why I came here. Because you were the only people I could think of to try to establish contact with her. I figured that you of all people would have some idea what was going on.''

Neither Pedro nor Anita said anything.

Buchanan gave them time.

''No,'' Anita said.

Buchanan gave them more time.

''We don't know anything,'' Anita said. ''Except that we've been worried because she hasn't been behaving normally.''

''How?''

''We haven't heard from her in nine months. Usually, even when she's on the road, she phones at least once a week. She did say she'd be away for a while. But nine months?''

''What does she do for a living?''

Pedro and Anita looked uncertain.

''You don't know?''

''It's something to do with security,'' Pedro said.

''*National* security?''

''Private security. She has her own business here in San Antonio. But that's as much as Juana told us. She never discussed specifics. She said that it wouldn't be fair to her clients. She couldn't violate their confidence.''

Good, Buchanan thought. She stayed a pro.

''All right,'' he said, ''so she hasn't been in touch in nine months. And suddenly several men who claim to be old friends of hers show up to ask if you know where they can find her. What else isn't—?''

Abruptly Buchanan noticed that Juana's parents were looking at him differently. Their gaze was harder, more wary, their need to confess their concerns about their daughter now tempered by renewed suspicion about him. The risk he'd taken had finally caught up to him. His remark about the other men who'd come looking for her had prompted Juana's parents to associate him with those men.

But he was troubled by something else. The intensity of his headache had made him temporarily relax his guard. If an enemy was trying to find Juana and if that enemy was impatient enough to send three different men to ask Juana's parents about where she could be found, might not that enemy have gone further in an effort to learn what the parents knew? Might not that enemy have . . . ?

"Excuse me. May I use your bathroom?"

Pedro's suspicion made him look surly. He nodded grudgingly. "It's down the hall. The first door on the left."

"Thank you."

Buchanan stood, feigning self-consciousness, and went along the hallway. In the bathroom, which was bright, white, and extremely ordered, he locked the door, strained to get some urine from his bladder, flushed the toilet, and turned on the sink to wash his hands.

He left the water running, silently opened the medicine cabinet, found a nail file, and used it to unscrew the wall plate to the light switch. Taking care not to touch the wires, he unscrewed the switch from its cavity in the wall and pulled it out to study what was behind.

His discovery increased the nausea that his headache caused. A miniature microphone-transmitter was attached to the wires. Because most people felt that a bathroom gave them privacy, that was the room they'd least likely suspect had a bug, hence the first room that Buchanan always checked. And because Mrs. Mendez kept this bathroom scrupulously clean, about the only place in the room where she wouldn't find a bug was behind the light switch, a spot favored by professional eavesdroppers. The phones were probably miked, as well.

Okay, Buchanan thought. Here we go.

He shut off the water, the sound of which he had hoped would conceal the noise he'd made when he unscrewed the wall plate. Now he unlocked the bathroom door and went back to the living room, where it was obvious that Juana's parents had been whispering about him.

"Pedro, I apologize," Buchanan said.

"For what?"

"When I was washing my hands in the bathroom, I must have pulled the sink plug's lever too hard. It looks like I broke it. I can't get the sink to drain. I'm sorry. I . . ."

Pedro stood, scowling, and strode toward the bathroom, his chest stuck out, his short legs moving powerfully.

Buchanan got ahead of him in the hallway and put a finger

over his own lips to indicate that he wanted Pedro not to say anything. But when Pedro didn't get the message and opened his mouth to ask what was going on, Buchanan had to put his hand firmly over Pedro's mouth and shake his head strongly from side to side, mouthing in Spanish the quiet message, *Shut up*. Pedro looked startled. *The house is bugged*, Buchanan continued mouthing.

Pedro didn't seem to understand. He struggled to remove Buchanan's hand from his mouth. Buchanan responded by pressing his left hand against the back of Pedro's head while at the same time he continued to keep his right hand over Pedro's mouth. He forced Pedro into the bathroom and bent his head down so that Pedro could see behind the light switch that Buchanan had pulled from the wall. Pedro owned a string of car-repair shops. He had to be familiar with wiring. Surely Pedro would know enough about other types of wiring to realize that the small gadget behind the light switch shouldn't be there, that the gadget was a miniature microphone-transmitter.

Pedro's eyes widened.

Comprende? Buchanan mouthed.

Pedro nodded forcefully.

Buchanan released his grip on Pedro's head and mouth.

Pedro wiped his mouth, which showed the strong impression of Buchanan's hand, glared at Buchanan, and rattled the sink plug's lever. "There. You see, it was nothing. You merely hadn't pulled the lever far enough. The water's gone now."

"At least I didn't break it," Buchanan said.

Pedro had several pens and a notepad in the top pocket of his coveralls. Quickly, Buchanan removed the pad and one of the pens. He wrote: *We can't talk in the house. Where and when can we meet? Soon.*

Pedro read the message, frowned, and wrote: *7:00 A.M. My shop at 1217 Loma Avenue.*

"I do not trust you," Pedro said abruptly.

"What?" The effect was so convincing that Buchanan took a moment before he realized that Pedro was acting.

"I want you out of my house."

"But—"

"Get out." Pedro grabbed Buchanan's arm and tugged him

along the hallway. "How much plainer can I make it? Out of my house."

"Pedro!" Anita hurried from the living room into the hallway. "What are you doing? Maybe he can help us."

"Out!" Pedro shoved Buchanan toward the front door.

Buchanan pretended to resist. "Why? I don't understand. What did I do? A couple of minutes ago, we were talking about how to help Juana. Now all of a sudden . . ."

"There is something not right about you," Pedro said. "There is something too convenient about you. I think that you are with the other men who came to look for Juana. I think that you are her enemy, not her friend. I think that I should never have spoken to you. Get out. Now. Before I call the police."

Pedro unlocked the door and yanked it open.

"You've made a mistake," Buchanan said.

"No, *you* did. And you will make a greater mistake if you ever come near my home again."

"Damn it, if you don't want my help . . ."

"I want you out!" Pedro shoved Buchanan.

Buchanan lurched outside, feeling exposed by the porch light above him. "Don't touch me again."

"Pedro!" Anita said.

"I don't know where my daughter is, but if I did, I would never tell you!" Pedro told Buchanan.

"Then go to hell."

6

"You'd better get here pronto," Duncan Bradley said into his cellular phone while he listened to the transmission from the house. "Something about the guy who showed up definitely rubbed Mendez against the grain. Mendez thinks the guy's with us. They're yelling at each other. Mendez is kicking him out."

"Almost there. Just two blocks away," Duncan's partner said through the cellular phone.

"You might as well be two *miles* away." Duncan stared at the green magnified night-vision image on his closed-circuit television screen. "I can see the dude coming off the lawn toward his car. He'll be gone before you get here."

"I told you I'm close. Can you see my headlights?"

Duncan glanced at another screen that showed the murky area behind his van. "Affirmative."

"Perfect. When he pulls away, I'll be just another car on the road," Tucker said. "He won't think anything when he sees my lights behind him."

"He's getting in his car," Duncan emphasized.

"No problem. The license number you gave me."

"What about it?"

"I accessed the Louisiana motor-vehicles computer. The Taurus belongs to a New Orleans car-rental agency."

"That doesn't tell us much," Duncan said.

"There's more. I phoned the agency. Pretended to be a state trooper. Said there'd been an accident. Wanted to know who'd rented the car."

"And?"

"Brendan Buchanan. That's the name on the rental agreement."

Tucker's headlights loomed larger on the rear-view television screen.

On the front-view screen, two blocks away, the Taurus's lights came on. The car pulled away.

With a flash, Tucker's Jeep Cherokee passed the van. Duncan pivoted his gaze from the night-vision television image and smiled toward the front windshield and the swiftly receding taillights of Tucker's Jeep.

"See, I told you," Tucker said through the cellular phone. "No sweat. I'm on him. No headlights pulling away from the curb behind him. Nothing to make him suspicious."

"Brendan Buchanan?" Duncan wondered. "Who the hell is Brendan Buchanan? And what's his connection with the woman?"

"The head office is checking on him." Tucker's taillights diminished to red specks as he followed the even-more-minute specks of the Taurus. "Meantime, I'll find out where he's staying. We'll pay him a visit. We'll find out all we need to know about Brendan Buchanan."

7

A microphone-transmitter required something to receive its broadcast. Depending on the strength of the transmitter, the receiver might be as far away as a mile. But practical considerations—static-producing electrical equipment in the area, for example—usually required that the receiver be much closer to the source. As well, it was useful for the person monitoring the reception to maintain visual surveillance on the target area. Thus the odds were, Buchanan concluded, that the receiver was in the neighborhood—possibly in a building, although in this respectable single-family-dwelling area it would have been difficult for a surveillance team to take over a house—more likely in a vehicle of some sort. But there weren't any other cars parked on the street in this block. Buchanan had noticed that when he'd arrived, and he checked again as he crossed the lawn toward his rented car.

He turned to glare at Pedro Mendez, who continued to stand on his front porch, scowling at Buchanan.

Damned good, Pedro, Buchanan thought. You missed your calling. You could have been an actor.

Pretending to be furious, Buchanan spun toward his Taurus. As he rounded it to unlock the driver's side, he glanced both ways along the street, and there it was, some kind of vehicle parked two blocks away. He hadn't noticed it before because the vehicle, small down there, was in shadows between widely spaced streetlights. The only reason he noticed it now was that the headlights of an approaching car exposed it.

I think it's time to pay somebody a visit, Buchanan thought as he started the Taurus, turned on its lights, and drove away. The headlights of the approaching car came up behind him, aggravating his headache.

Somebody wants to find Juana badly enough that they bug the house. But they still can't be sure Juana didn't get a message to her parents in a way that the microphones couldn't detect, so whoever wants to find Juana becomes impatient and sends somebody around to the house to pretend they know Juana and ask where she is. No success. They send somebody else. Nothing. So they send yet another . . .

Does that make sense? Buchanan wondered. They must have realized that three old friends coming around in two weeks would make Juana's parents suspicious. Then why would—?

Yes, Buchanan thought. If Juana *is* in touch with her parents, whoever is after her wants her to know that her parents are being watched. They want to make Juana nervous about her parents. They want to threaten her by implying a threat against her parents. They hope that'll force her to come out of hiding.

And now that I showed up, now that the surveillance unit knows there's a wild card, they might get nervous enough to stop being patient and have a long, forceful chat with Juana's parents. I have to let Pedro and Anita know they're in danger.

And what about me? Buchanan thought as he steered around a corner. Whoever's after Juana will want to talk to a stranger who suddenly shows up and asks the same questions they did.

Buchanan steered around another corner.

The headlights behind him kept following.

My, my, Buchanan thought.

8

FALLS CHURCH, VIRGINIA

The colonel had chosen a motel on the edge of town, using a pay phone to reserve a room under a pseudonym. At 11:00 P.M., after he'd used an electronic scanner to make sure that the room was free of microphones, his three associates arrived, their clothes speckled with water from the dank November rain that had greeted them at Washington National Airport following their flight from New Orleans.

All of them looked tired, even Captain Weller, who normally exuded sexual vitality. Her blond hair looked stringy, her blouse wrinkled. She took off her jacket, slumped on the motel room's sofa, and toed off her high-heeled shoes. Major Putnam and Alan had haggard red cheeks, presumably from fatigue combined with the dehydration that occurs on aircraft and the further dehydrating effect of alcohol.

"Can we get some coffee?" Captain Weller asked.

"Over there," the colonel said flatly. "The carafe on the tray beside the phone." In contrast with his visitors, the colonel looked fit and alert, standing as straight and attentively as ever. He'd shaved and showered before he'd arrived, partly to keep himself fresh, partly to appear more energized than his companions. His clothes, too, were fresh: shined Bally loafers, pressed gray slacks, a starched white shirt, a newly purchased red-striped tie, and a double-breasted blue blazer. The effect was to make his tall, trim body suggest the military, even though he did not wear military clothing.

"Oh." Captain Weller glanced toward the carafe on the tray beside the phone. She and Major Putnam, who slumped on a chair beside the television, did not wear military clothing, either. "Right. I didn't notice it when I came in."

The colonel's eyes narrowed as if to imply that she had been failing to notice a lot of things.

Alan, the only civilian in the room, loosened his rumpled tie, unbuttoned the top of his wrinkled shirt, and walked over to the coffee, pouring a cup. Everyone in the room looked surprised when he carried the cup over to Captain Weller and then returned to pour another cup, blowing steam from it, sipping. "What are we doing here? Couldn't this have waited until the morning? I'm dead on my feet, not to mention I've got a wife and kids who haven't seen me in—"

The colonel's flint-and-steel voice interrupted, "I want a thorough update. No more of your hints and guesses that you don't feel comfortable talking about because you don't trust the security of the phones."

"Hey," Alan said, "if we'd been given portable scramblers, I'd talk on phones all you wanted, but once burned, twice shy, Colonel. In this case, we need extra-tight security."

"I couldn't agree more." The colonel stood straighter. Rain pelted against the window, making the dismal room even less agreeable. "That's why I ordered you to be here right now instead of at home in bed with your wife."

Alan's expression hardened. "Ordered, Colonel?"

"Somebody tell me what's going on." The colonel's voice became more flinty. "Major, you've been unusually silent so far."

"A lot of it you already know." The major rubbed the back of his neck. "In New Orleans, we went to meet Buchanan at his hotel room. The arrangement was to be there at nine hundred hours. He didn't respond when we knocked. After we tried several times, we asked a maid to unlock the door. The day before, he'd been released from the hospital. Maybe he'd fainted or something. What we found was his room key, a signed checkout form—obviously he didn't want the hotel to start a search for him—and this note addressed to Alan."

The colonel took the note and scanned it.

"So he says he's going to do us a favor by dropping out of sight. That way, he's an invisible man, and the reporter from the *Post* can't verify her story if she pursues it."

"That seems to be the idea," the major said.

"And how do you feel about this?" The colonel scowled.

"Hell, I don't know," the major said. "This is all out of hand. Everything's so confused. Maybe he's right."

"Damn it, have you forgotten that you're an officer in the United States Army?"

The major straightened with controlled indignation. "No, sir, I definitely have not."

"Then why must I remind you that Captain Buchanan is absent without permission? *A deserter*. Our operatives can't just decide to quit and go off on their own, especially when they know as much as Buchanan does. We'd have chaos, a security nightmare. I can see I haven't been supervising you closely enough. What this assignment requires is more discipline, more—"

It was Alan's turn to interrupt. "No, what this assignment needs is for *everybody* to remember who's an officer in the United States Army." He set down his coffee cup with such force that liquid splashed over the side. "That's where this assignment went wrong in the first place, with military personnel doing work that's supposed to be done by civilians. You've been impersonating civilians so long you don't know the difference."

"By 'civilians,' you mean the Agency."

"Obviously."

"Well, if the Agency had been doing its job, it wouldn't have needed to call on *us*, would it?" the colonel said. "During the eighties, your people got so stuck on gadgets and satellites, you forgot it took operatives on-site to get the truly useful information. So after you screwed up enough times—Iran, Iraq, the old USSR—even the Soviet collapse caught you by surprise—you decided you needed a team of on-line, can-do personnel to pull your asses out of the fire. Us."

"Not *my* ass," Alan said. "I've never been a fan of gadgets. It wasn't my fault that—"

"The truth is," the colonel said, "when the Cold War ended, your people realized you'd be out of a job if you didn't find something else to do. But the trouble is, all the jobs that needed to be done, like stomping out Third World drug lords, required more risks than you wanted to take. So you asked *us* to take the risk. After all, the reason there hasn't been more success against the drug lords is you've been using the top men as informants in exchange for giving them immunity. It's kind of tough to go after people you've been chummy with. So you ask *us* to go after them and do it in such a way that they don't realize *you're* the ones who turned against them."

"Hey," Alan said, "it's not one of *my* people who suddenly thinks he's a free spirit and drops out of sight."

"Captain Buchanan wouldn't have been able to drop out of sight," the colonel said, "if *your* people had kept proper surveillance on the hotel."

"It wasn't *my* people who were put in charge of watching that hotel," Alan said. "If this had been turned over to me . . . This is a military screw up all the way. Soldiers don't have any business doing—"

"That's enough," the colonel said. "Your opinion is no longer *required*."

"But—"

"That is all." The colonel swung toward the major and the captain, who looked shocked by the sudden argument they'd witnessed. "What do we do about Buchanan?"

Captain Weller cleared her throat. "I phoned his credit-card company and claimed that he was my husband, that his card had been stolen. I expected that maybe he'd have bought a plane ticket. I was wrong. The credit-card company told me someone using his name had rented a car in New Orleans."

"And?" the colonel demanded.

"The next thing, someone using his card rented a motel room in Beaumont, Texas."

"I'm impressed, Captain. I assume our people are in Beaumont now."

"Yes. But Buchanan isn't there."

"Isn't . . .?"

"It turns out he only stayed a couple of hours. He left at noon."

"*What?*"

"Obviously, he wants to keep on the move," Captain Weller said.

"To where?"

She shook her head. "He seems to be heading west. The credit-card company promised to keep me informed."

"There's only one problem," Alan said.

They looked at him.

"The next time Buchanan surfaces with that card, the company won't only shut off his credit. It'll send the police after him. That'll be dandy, won't it? To have the police involved."

"Shit," Captain Weller said.

"And if you get your hands on him first," Alan said, "what are you going to do with him? Put him in solitary confinement? Don't you see how out of control this could get? Why don't you just let the man alone to disappear as he promised?"

Rain pelted against the window.

"Last night, you reported that he was convinced we were trying to assassinate him," the colonel said.

"Correct."

"Well, his suspicions are absurd. He's paranoid if he thinks we've turned against him. What does that say about his ability to disappear as he promised? Maybe he'll keep coming back to haunt us. And what about the reporter? She surrendered her research. But did she keep copies? Will she kill the story as she promised?"

"Whatever we decide, let's do it fast," the major said. "I've got two dozen undercover personnel in Latin America who expect me to make sure they have backup. Every minute I spend worrying about Buchanan, I run the risk that something else will go wrong. If only Buchanan had cooperated. All he had to do was stick to his cover story and become a trainer. What's wrong with being a trainer?''

"Because that isn't what he is," Alan said.

They stared at him.

"And I'm not sure Buchanan is who he is, either," Alan said.

9

The man following Buchanan became less conspicuous as they drove toward downtown San Antonio. When they reached better-lit streets, Buchanan was able to see that the man used a Jeep Cherokee, gray, a good unobtrusive color for a surveillance vehicle, especially at night. The man took care to stay back among other cars when he had the chance. It was only the first two minutes that had given him away.

It had been enough.

Buchanan pulled into a gas station, filled the tank, and went into the office to pay. When he came out, he noticed that the Jeep Cherokee was parked down the street from the gas station.

A little farther along the road, Buchanan stopped at a minimall and went into a Tex-Mex quick-service restaurant, where he ate a beef-and-bean burrito and drank a Coke while he carefully glanced out the window toward where the Jeep Cherokee was parked in the shadows at the edge of the mall. Behind the steering wheel, the driver was talking to a car phone.

The spices in the burrito made Buchanan's face warm. Or maybe he was feverish from fatigue. He didn't know. His injured side ached. I've got to get some rest, he thought, and swallowed three more Tylenol caplets.

The restaurant had an exit near the rest rooms in back. Buchanan stepped out behind the minimall and hurried along a shadowy alley in the direction of where the Jeep Cherokee was parked.

The man behind the steering wheel was too busy talking on the phone and watching the entrance to the restaurant to notice when Buchanan came up behind him on the passenger side.

The moment the man—in his late twenties, wearing a Houston Oilers jacket—set down the phone, Buchanan opened the passenger door, got in, and rammed his pistol into the man's beefy ribs.

The man groaned, his surprise aggravating his pain.

"What's your name?" Buchanan asked.

The man was too afraid to answer.

Buchanan pressed the gun harder against the man's ribs. "Your *name*."

"Frank. . . . Frank Tucker."

"Well, let's take a drive, Frank."

The man seemed paralyzed with shock.

"Drive, Frank, or I'll kill you." The threat was starkly matter-of-fact.

The man obeyed.

"That's right," Buchanan said. "Nice and easy into traffic. Keep both hands on the steering wheel."

They passed Buchanan's car. He'd parked it along with several other cars in front of the Tex-Mex restaurant, where it wouldn't be conspicuous until the lot was otherwise empty at closing time.

"What do you want?" The man's voice trembled.

"Well, for starters . . ." Buchanan used his free hand to grope beneath Frank's windbreaker. He found a holster but no weapon. "Where's the piece, Frank?"

The man's nervous gaze indicated the glove compartment.

Buchanan opened it and found a Smith & Wesson .357 Magnum revolver. "So where are the others?"

"I don't *have* any others."

"Maybe, Frank. I'll soon find out. But if you're lying, I'll blow off your right kneecap. You'll be a cripple for the rest of your life, which might be a whole lot shorter than you'd hoped. Turn into this convenience store. Swing around. Go back the way we came."

"Listen, I don't know what this is about, but I'll give you all the money I have, and—"

"Spare me the line, Frank. Careful. I told you, both hands on the steering wheel." Buchanan cocked his pistol and shoved it harder against Frank's ribs.

"Come on, man! If I hit a bump, that thing might go off."

"Then don't hit a bump," Buchanan said. "What are you? Official or private?"

"I don't know what you—"

"Who do you work for?"

"I don't work for anybody."

"Right, Frank. You just decided to amuse yourself by following me."

"I wasn't following you. I've never seen you before."

"Of course, Frank. We're just two strangers who bumped into each other and happen to be carrying guns. A coincidence. A sign of the times." Buchanan studied him. "You're not a cop. If you were, you'd have been covered by a backup team. You could be with the mob, but an Oilers jacket and a Jeep Cherokee aren't exactly their style. What are you?"

No answer.

"Frank, I'm getting bored talking to myself. If I find a PI license on you, I'll shoot *both* your kneecaps." Buchanan reached for the man's wallet.

"All right, all right." Sweat beaded Frank's trembling upper lip. "I'm a PI."

"Finally, we're getting to know each other. Tell me, Frank. Where'd you get your training? Come on. Keep up the conversation. Your training. Where did you—?"

"I learned on the job."

"That's what it looks like. On the job and from movies. Here's a tip. When there isn't much traffic, follow your target from one block over. Stay parallel to him. If you keep the same speed, you'll see him at every intersection. But the odds are, he won't notice you. Only when you *don't* see him do you go over to the street he's on. That's where you made your first mistake—by staying behind me. Your second mistake was failing to lock your doors. It should have been harder for me to get at you. Third mistake: I don't care how uncomfortable it feels on a lengthy stakeout, keep your gun in your holster, where you can reach it in a hurry. It's useless in the glove compartment if somebody's climbing into your car and pointing a gun at you."

The phone rang.

"No, Frank. Keep your hands on the steering wheel."

The phone rang a second time.

"Whoever it is can wait to talk to you," Buchanan said. "In fact, why don't we talk to him in person? Let's go back to Castle Hills."

10

On his tilted mattress in the rear of the van, Duncan Bradley kept watch on the television screen that showed the magnified area in front of the Mendez house two blocks away. Simultaneously he listened to his earphones, although the audio transmissions from the target area had stopped thirty minutes ago, shortly after the man who called himself Jeff Walker had been forced from the Mendez house. The wife had argued with the husband about what he had done, about how the stranger might have been able to help find their daughter. The husband had told her to shut up, that the stranger was obviously no different from the other imposters who had asked about Juana. They'd gone to bed in sullen silence.

While he listened, Duncan kept trying to telephone his partner. Twice now, he'd let the phone ring ten times before canceling the attempted call. Tucker's failure to answer troubled him. Granted, there might be a reasonable, nonthreatening explanation. Tucker might have followed Jeff Walker into a hotel, for example. But Duncan's unease prompted him to pick up the cellular phone yet again and press the button that would automatically dial Tucker's number.

He never had a chance to press the number, however, because movement attracted his gaze toward the second television and green-tinted night-vision images of what was going on behind the van. The movement he'd seen was Tucker's Jeep Cherokee stopping behind him. The Jeep's headlights went off. Duncan exhaled. Something must have gone wrong with Tucker's car phone. That was why he'd come back to tell him in person what he'd learned about Jeff Walker.

As the monitor showed Tucker getting out of his Jeep and approaching the rear door of the van, Duncan raised himself off the mattress, crawled on his hands and knees toward the back, heard Tucker's knock, and opened the door.

"What happened to your phone? I've been trying to—" Duncan's throat clamped shut. His mouth hung open in stunned surprise as he saw a man next to Tucker. The man must have been hiding in the Jeep. The man was Jeff Walker.

The man had a gun.

Oh, shit, Duncan thought.

11

The persistent ringing of the doorbell made Pedro Mendez angry.

For a lot of reasons. Worry about his daughter, confusion about Jeff Walker, and apprehension about the microphone in the bathroom's light-switch socket had made him so restless that it seemed he would never get to sleep. What was Jeff Walker going to tell him when they met at the garage tomorrow morning? Tense, Pedro had squirmed beneath the covers until at last, impossibly, mercifully, he'd somehow managed to doze, and now somebody was pushing that damned doorbell.

"Anita, stay in bed," he ordered as he fumbled to his feet, put on a bathrobe and slippers, grabbed a baseball bat from the closet, and stormed downstairs. Through the front door's window, he saw the shadow of a man on the murky porch. By God, if this was someone else looking for his daughter, Pedro intended to make very sure that the man explained what was going on.

But when Pedro turned on the porch light, his determination wavered when he saw that the man was Jeff Walker, who gestured impatiently for Pedro to unlock and open the door.

Pedro obeyed to a certain extent, making sure that when he inched the door open, he didn't release the security chain. "What do you—?"

"Hurry. I have to show you something." Jeff Walker pointed urgently toward the street.

Staring past him toward the darkness, Pedro noticed a small van at the curb. "What are you doing here at—?"

"Please," Jeff Walker said. "It's about Juana. It's important."

Pedro hesitated—but only for a moment. There was something about Jeff Walker that insisted on being trusted. Compelled, Pedro stifled his misgivings and opened the door.

Jeff Walker was already off the porch, moving quickly toward the van.

Pedro ran to catch up to him. "What do you want to show me? Whose van is—?"

For the third time, Pedro was interrupted, this time because Jeff Walker opened the back of the van and turned on a flashlight.

Two men—naked, their hands tied behind them by their shirt sleeves, their ankles tied by their pant legs, their mouths stuffed with their underwear—lay on the floor of the van. They were lashed together by their belts. When the light revealed them, they squirmed.

"I know it's hard to be sure under these conditions," Jeff Walker said, "but are these two of the men who came to your house and asked about Juana?"

Pedro took the flashlight and stepped closer, aiming the beam from one face to the other. "Yes. How did—?"

"They've been watching your house," Jeff Walker said.

Pedro aimed the flashlight beam toward shelves of electronic equipment along the right side of the van. A television monitor showed a green-tinted magnified image of the area in front of his house. Several tape recorders were linked to audio receivers. So it wasn't only *one* microphone that had been planted in the house, Pedro thought in dismay. The whole house must be . . . His knees felt weak. The pavement seemed to tilt.

Jeff Walker removed the gag from one of the men. "Who else was working with you? Where do I find him?"

The man had trouble speaking, his mouth dry from the absorbent cloth that had been taken from his mouth.

Pedro flinched as Jeff Walker shoved a pistol against the man's testicles and asked, "Who was the third man who came to Pedro's house?"

But as unnerved as Pedro felt, he leaned closer, desperate to learn everything he could.

"Somebody . . . somebody working for us part-time. We only used him one day. He went back to . . ." The man seemed to realize he was saying too much and shut up.

"Back to where?" Jeff Walker asked. When he didn't get an answer, he sighed. "I don't believe you are taking me seriously." He shoved the underwear back into the man's mouth, took a pair of pliers from an open tool case, and yanked out a clump of pubic hair.

The man screamed silently, tears welling from his eyes.

Pedro was shocked. At the same time, he was so afraid for Juana that a part of him wanted impatiently to grab the prisoner's head and bang it against the van's floor, anything to get answers.

Jeff Walker pivoted toward the second man, removed the underwear that gagged him, and sounded very reasonable when he said, "Now I'm sure you wouldn't want that to happen to you. After I plucked every inch of your hair, I'd use some of Pedro's matches to singe the stubble. By the time I was through, your groin would look like the neck on a well-done turkey. But I've never liked the neck. I always . . ." He made a cutting motion as if he had a knife.

The first man continued to thrash in pain.

"Where did your part-time employee go back to?" Jeff Walker asked. "Your accent isn't Texan. Where's home base for you?"

Jeff Walker brought the pliers toward the man's groin.

"Philadelphia," the man blurted.

"You're watching this house to find Juana Mendez. Why?"
Yes, Pedro thought. *Why?*

The man didn't answer.

"Pedro, go get your matches."

Pedro's angry resolve surprised him. He turned toward the house.

"Wait," the man blurted. "I don't know. That's the truth. I really don't. We were told to watch for her, to learn where she was."

"And if you saw her? If you found out where she was?" Jeff Walker demanded.

Pedro listened intensely.

The man gave no response.

"You're disappointing me," Jeff Walker said. "You need a reminder." He leaned toward the first man and used the pliers to yank out more pubic hair.

Pedro suddenly began to appreciate Jeff Walker's tactic, realizing that the pain Jeff Walker inflicted on these men wasn't physical but psychological.

The first man thrashed, his tear-streaked face contorted by another silent scream. Since the two men were lashed together, every time the first man jerked, the second man was jolted.

"Care to try again?" Jeff Walker asked the second man, whose eyes bulged with fear. "What were you supposed to do if you saw Juana or found out where she was?"

"Phone the people who hired us."

"Who are they?"

"I don't know."

"You don't know why they want her. You don't know who they are. It seems to me there's an awful lot you don't know. And it's making me angry." Jeff Walker pinched his pliers into the skin of the second man's groin.

"No," the second man pleaded.

"Who hired you?"

"They used an intermediary. I never had a name."

"But you know how to get in touch with them."

"On the phone."

"What's the number?"

"It's programmed into . . ." The second man pointed his chin toward a cellular telephone on the floor of the van. "All I had to do was press the recall button, number eight, and send."

"Do they know I came to the house?"

"Yes."

"What's your check-in code."

"Yellow Rose."

Jeff Walker picked up the phone. "I hope for your sake that you're telling the truth." He pressed the three buttons as instructed, placed the phone against his ear, and waited for someone to answer.

It took less than half a ring. Pedro was close enough to the phone to hear a seductive male voice say, "Brotherly Love Escort Service."

What Pedro heard next astonished him. Jeff Walker mimicked the second man's voice.

12

"This is Yellow Rose," Buchanan said into the phone. "That guy who came to the Mendez house tonight still worries me. Have you got anything more on him?"

The male voice lost its smoothness. "Just what I told you. His name isn't Jeff Walker. It's Brendan Buchanan. He rented the Taurus in New Orleans, and . . . Wait a minute. Something's coming in on another line." The connection was interrupted.

Buchanan waited, disturbed that these people had been able to learn his real name so fast.

The connection abruptly resumed, the voice strained. "It's a good thing you called. Be careful. Our computer man found out that Brendan Buchanan is a captain in Army Special Forces, an instructor at Fort Bragg."

Damn it, Buchanan thought.

"So I was right to be worried," Buchanan said. "Thanks for the warning. We'll be careful."

Troubled, Buchanan pressed the END button. Throughout the call, the number he'd contacted had been shown on a display at the top of the phone. Now he took a pad and pencil from the floor of the van, printed the number, tore off the sheet of paper, and put it in a shirt pocket.

He studied the second man, deciding what further questions to ask, when suddenly he heard approaching footsteps. Whirling, he saw Anita Mendez crossing the lawn toward the van. She wore a housecoat. Her face was contorted with worry, puzzlement, and fear.

"Anita," Pedro said, "go back in the house."

"I will not. This is about Juana. I'm sure of it. I want to know what it is."

As she rounded the back of the van, she stopped abruptly, startled to see the naked, bound men. "*Madre de Dios*."

"These men can help us find Juana," Pedro said. "This is necessary. Go back to the house."

Anita glared. "I'm staying."

Fatigue made Buchanan's headache worsen. "Does Juana have an office here in town?"

The interruption made Anita and Pedro look at him.

"Yes," Anita said. "At her home. Although she is seldom there."

"I don't have time to wait until morning," Buchanan said. "Can you take me there now?"

Pedro frowned. "You think she is at her home? You think she is hurt and . . ."

"No," Buchanan said. "But maybe her office records can tell me why someone in Philadelphia wants to find her."

Anita started toward the house. "I'll get dressed and take you."

"We both will," Pedro said, hurrying after her.

At once Buchanan turned to the second man where he lay bound on the floor of the van. "If Juana's home is in town, you must have other sentries watching the place."

The man didn't answer.

"The easy way or the hard way." Buchanan showed him the pliers.

"Yes, another team," the man said.

"How many men?"

"Two. The same as here."

"They alternate shifts?"

"Yes."

The tactic was flawed, Buchanan knew. Thorough surveillance wasn't possible if only one man at a time watched a target site. Suppose Juana showed up. The spotter would phone for help. But how could the spotter be sure that a team would arrive in time to trap her?

As Buchanan brooded, the shadow of a long object secured horizontally to the van's left wall attracted his attention. He shifted the flashlight's beam to see what it was.

His stomach felt cold. Seeing the object made him realize that the surveillance tactic did make sense—in an efficient, deadly way.

The object on the wall was a sniper's rifle equipped with a state-of-the-art night-vision telescopic sight. The intent of the surveillance wasn't to capture Juana. It was to kill her the minute she was spotted.

13

Juana's home was in the hills south of the city, along the western bank of the San Antonio River. They took forty-five minutes to get there, Pedro driving the van while Buchanan sat in back and guarded the captives, Anita following in the Jeep Cherokee. En route, Buchanan used the pliers again, forcing the first man to give him the telephone number that would put him in touch with the sniper who watched Juana's home.

The telephone barely made a noise before a man's gravelly voice answered, "Yellow Rose Two."

"It's Frank," Buchanan said. Trained to mimic voices, he made himself sound like the first man. "Anything doing?"

"Quiet as hell. No sign of movement here for the past two weeks. I think we're wasting our time."

"But at least we're being paid to waste it," Buchanan said. "I'm going to stay with Duncan and watch the Mendez place. Meantime, I thought I'd better tell you I'm sending a guy out there in my Jeep. That's how you'll know he belongs. He's going to pick the front lock and go in to check a few things we're beginning to think we missed, especially some stuff in her files."

"I'm not sure that's a good idea. If she's watching the house, debating whether to go in, she'll get spooked if she sees anybody."

"I agree. The thing is, it's not like I have a choice. This wasn't *my* idea. These are orders."

"Fucking typical," the sniper said. "They pay us to do a job, but they won't let us do it properly."

"Just let the guy I'm sending do *his* job when he shows up," Buchanan said.

"No sweat. Be seeing you."

Sooner than you expect, Buchanan thought as he broke the connection.

14

A little after one in the morning, Pedro warned Buchanan that they were about a mile from Juana's home.

"Close enough. Stop right here," Buchanan said.

After Anita pulled up behind them, he got out of the van, told Anita to wait with Pedro, and drove Tucker's Jeep Cherokee over a murky rise, proceeding the rest of the way along a winding, partially wooded road. His headlights revealed mist drifting in from the river. They also showed new streets and the start of construction on houses for a new subdivision.

Juana won't like that.

What you mean is, you pray to God that she's still alive so she'll be *able* not to like it.

Pedro and Anita had described the house, which for the present was one of a very few along this section of the river, so Buchanan had no trouble finding it. Wooden and single-story, on stilts in case of flooding, it reminded him more of a cabin than a house as he passed a cottonwood tree and stopped in the gravel driveway. Quaint, rustic. If Juana's dog had still been alive, Buchanan imagined how much Juana would have enjoyed running with it along the river.

. . . had still been alive.

Man, you sure are thinking about death a lot.

You bet, with a sniper watching me from God-knows-where.

Buchanan's back felt tense as he opened the screened porch and approached the main door. With the mist coming in from the river, the sniper might not have been able to recognize the car whose headlights had veered toward the house. What if he came down to investigate?

Play the scenario you described to him, Buchanan thought.

He picked the two dead-bolt locks and entered, smelling the must of a building that had not been occupied for quite a while. Feeling vulnerable even in the darkness, he shut the door, locked it, felt along the wall, and found a light switch. A lamp came on, revealing a living room that had a bookshelf, a television, a VCR, and stereo equipment but very little furniture, just a leather sofa, a coffee table, and a rocking chair. Obviously Juana hadn't spent much time here. Otherwise, she would have paid more attention to its furnishings. Also, few furnishings suggested that she seldom had company.

Buchanan proceeded across the room, noting the dust on the sofa and the coffee table, further evidence that Juana hadn't been here in some time. He glanced into the kitchen, turned on its light, and assessed its neat appearance, its minimum of appliances. Remote, austere, the place gave Buchanan a sense of loneliness. It made him feel sorry for her.

Down a hallway, the first door he came to—on the left, facing the river—was an office. When Buchanan turned on the overhead light, he saw that here, too, everything was kept to a minimum: a metal filing cabinet, a swivel chair, a wooden table upon which sat a computer, a laser printer, a modem, a telephone, a gooseneck lamp, a yellow notepad, and a jar filled with pencils and pens. Otherwise, the room was bare. No rug. No pictures. Impersonal.

He wondered what the sniper would be thinking in the misty darkness outside. How would the man react as he watched various lights come on in the house? Despite the instructions that the man had been given, would he come down to investigate?

Buchanan opened the top drawer of the filing cabinet, and immediately two things became important to him. The first was that each file had a stiff folder with hooks on each side that suspended the file rigidly on metal tracks along each side at the top of the drawer. The second was that the files were arranged alphabetically but that the files in A to the middle of D were bunched together, separated by a slight gap from the rest of the files that continued D through to L. The rigid hooks on each side of the neighboring files prevented them from expanding to fill the gap. Obviously, one of the D files had been removed. Possibly Juana had done it. Possibly an intruder who'd been searching as Buchanan was. No way to tell.

Buchanan opened the second drawer, found the files marked M through Z, and noticed a slight gap where a T file appeared to have been removed. D and T. Those were the only two apparent omissions. Buchanan thought about it as he opened the bottom drawer and discovered a Browning 9-mm semiautomatic pistol. The basic necessities, he thought.

What did Juana do for a living? Her parents had said that she was involved in private security. That kind of work would be a logical progression from what Juana had done in military intelligence. But private security could mean anything from doing risk assessments, to installing intrusion detectors, to providing physical protection. She might be a free-lance or work for a major corporation.

He shut the bottom drawer, reopened the top one, and began to read some of the files. A pattern became obvious. Juana's principal activity had been to act as a protective escort for businesswomen, female politicians and entertainers, or the wives of their male equivalents, primarily when they traveled to Spanish-speaking countries or to cities in America that had a sizable Hispanic population. The logic was clear. A protector had to blend with the local population. Because Juana was Hispanic, she would lose considerable effectiveness in an environment in which her Latin facial characteristics and skin color attracted attention. There wasn't any point in her working in Africa, the Orient, the Mideast, or northern Europe, for example. For that matter, even some of the northern United States. But Spain and Latin America were ideal for her. With that kind of travel, it wasn't any wonder that she stayed away from home for months at a time. Possibly her absence could be easily explained. Possibly she was merely on an assignment.

Then why the postcard? Why did she need my help?

Something to do with a job she was on? She might have wanted to hire me.

The notion that her interest in him would have been professional and not personal made Buchanan feel hollow—but only for a moment. He quickly reminded himself that a request for professional help would not have required so unusual and secretive a means of contacting him.

And snipers wouldn't be lying in wait to kill her.

No. Juana was in trouble, and even if she'd been away on a lengthy assignment, she wouldn't have neglected to phone her parents, certainly not for nine months in a row. Not willingly.

Something was stopping her. Either she wasn't physically

capable of doing it or else she didn't want to risk involving her parents in what had happened to her.

At the back of each file, Buchanan found itemized statements, copies of bills submitted and checks received. He learned that Juana's business had been quite successful. She'd been earning fees that ranged from $5,000 for consultations, to $10,000 for two-week escort jobs, to $100,000 for a two-month protective assignment in Argentina. A note in the file indicated that there had evidently been some shooting in the latter case. Protection was a demanding, sophisticated occupation for those who knew what it truly entailed. The best operatives were paid accordingly. Even so, Juana had been unusually successful. Buchanan made a rough estimate that she'd been earning close to half a million dollars a year.

And living this simply, paradoxically without security devices? What had she been doing with the money? Had she been saving it, investing it, planning to retire in her mid-thirties? Again, Buchanan had no way to tell. He searched the office but didn't find a bankbook, a statement from a brokerage firm, or any other sign of where she might have placed her money. Now that he thought about it, there hadn't been any mail outside or on the coffee table. Juana must have told the post office to hold it for her. Or else her parents had been picking it up. Before they'd come out here tonight, Anita had mentioned that she and Pedro sometimes drove out to inspect the place. Buchanan made a mental note to ask them about her mail, about whether she ever received statements from financial institutions.

At once the room appeared to sway, although actually it was his legs that caused the effect. They were wobbly. Exhausted, he sat in the tilt-back chair and rubbed his throbbing temples. The last time he'd slept through the night had been forty-eight hours ago, but that had been in the hospital, and even then his sleep had not been continuous, the nurses waking him intermittently to check his vital signs. Since then, he'd slept for a few hours at the motel in Beaumont, Texas, and had a few naps at freeway rest stops en route to San Antonio. The knife wound in his side ached, its stitches making him itchy. The almost-healed bullet wound in his shoulder ached as well. His eyes were gritty from lack of sleep.

The files, he thought. Whoever was concerned enough to want to find Juana and kill her would have searched her home in hopes of discovering a clue about where she was hiding. If they wanted to kill her because she knew too much about them, they would have searched for and removed any evidence that linked her with them.

A name that begins with D. Another that begins with T. Those had been the two files that were obviously missing. Of course, the files might not be missing at all. Juana might have caused the gap in the sequence of the files when she replaced two files, scrunching a group of other files together in order to make room, leaving a space where her fingers had been.

But I've got to start somewhere, Buchanan thought. I have to assume that two files *are* missing and that they're important. He leaned back in the chair, hearing it creak, thinking that the pages in the files looked like computer printouts, wondering if the files might be in the computer.

And realized that the creak he had heard had not been from the chair but from the hallway.

15

Slowly, Buchanan turned his head.

A man stood in the doorway: mid-thirties, five foot ten, 150 pounds. His hair was sandy and extremely short. His face, like his build, was thin, but not unhealthily so; something about him suggested he was a jogger. He wore cowboy boots, jeans, a saddle-shaped belt buckle, a faded denim shirt, and a jeans jacket. The latter was slightly too large for him and emphasized his thinness.

"Find what you're looking for?" The man's flat mid-Atlantic accent contrasted with his cowboy clothes.

"Not yet." Buchanan lowered his hands from where he'd been massaging his temples. "I've still got a few places to check."

I locked the door after I came in, he thought. I didn't hear anybody follow me. How did——?

This son of a bitch hasn't been watching from outside. He's been hiding somewhere in the house.

"Such as?" The man's hands stayed by his side. "What places haven't you checked?"

"The computer records."

"Well, don't let me hold you up." The man's cheeks were dark with beard stubble.

"Right." Buchanan pressed the computer's ON button.

As the computer's fan began to whir, the man said, "You look like hell, buddy."

"I've had a couple of hard days. Mostly, I need sleep."

"I'm not having any picnic, hanging around here, either. Nothing to do but wait. Where I bunked." The man pointed toward the next room down the hall. "Weird. No wonder the woman had it locked. Probably didn't want her parents to see what she had in there. At first, I thought it was body parts."

"Body parts?" Buchanan frowned.

"The stuff in that room. Belongs in a horror movie. Fucking bizarre. You mean you weren't told?"

What in God's name is he talking about? Buchanan wondered. "I guess they didn't figure I needed to know."

"Seems strange."

"The stuff in that room?"

"No. That you weren't told," the man said. "If they sent you out here to take another look for something to tell us where the target is, the first thing they'd have done was prepare you for weird shit."

"All they mentioned was the files."

"The computer's waiting."

"Right." Buchanan didn't want to take his gaze away from the assassin, but he wasn't being given a choice. If Buchanan didn't seem to care about business, the man would become more suspicious than he already seemed.

Or maybe the man's suspicion was only something that Buchanan imagined.

On the computer screen, the cursor flashed where a symbol asked the user what program was to be activated.

"What's your name?" the killer asked.

"Brian MacDonald." Buchanan immediately reverted to

ASSUMED IDENTITY

that identity, the one he'd assumed prior to becoming ex-DEA operative Ed Potter and going to Cancún, where all his recent troubles had started.

Brian MacDonald was supposed to have been a computer programmer, and in support of that identity, Buchanan had received instruction in that subject.

"Having trouble getting into the computer?" the killer asked. "It didn't give *me* any trouble when they ordered *me* to erase a couple of files. You know about that, right? They told you I erased a couple of files?"

"Yes, but those files aren't what interest me."

The cursor kept flashing next to the program-prompt sign. Juana's printed-out files had not been in a spread-sheet format but, rather, in standard prose paragraphs.

A word-processing program. But which one?

Buchanan-MacDonald typed DIR. At once the disk drive made clicking sounds, and a list of the symbols for the computer's programs appeared on the screen.

One of those symbols was WS, the abbreviation for a word-processing program known as WordStar.

Buchanan-MacDonald exited the list of the computer's programs and typed WS after the symbol that asked him what program he wanted. The computer's hard-disk drive made more clicking sounds. A list of other files appeared on the screen.

DIRECTORY OF DRIVE C:
A\ B\ C\ D\ E\ F\ G\ H\ I \
J \ K\ L\ M\ N \ O\ P\ Q\ R\
S \ T\ U\ V \ W\ X\ Y\ Z\
AUTOEXEC.BAK   .1k   AUTOEXEC.BAT   .1k

Buchanan-MacDonald knew that AUTOEXEC.BAK was a precautionary backup for AUTOEXEC.BAT, a program that allowed the computer's user to switch from one file to another. The designation .1k merely indicated the small amount of memory space that this program used. As for the alphabetical series, Juana had evidently subdivided her clients' files into subdirectories governed by the first letter of each client's last name.

Or so Buchanan guessed. At the moment, he was intensely preoccupied by the presence of the man in the doorway. The killer's breathing seemed to have become loud, strident, as if he was disturbed by something.

"Having problems?" the killer asked. "Don't you know what to do next? Do I have to show you?"

"No," Buchanan said. If he'd been alone, he would have accessed the subdirectories for *D* and *T*. But he didn't dare. If the killer had erased files in those subdirectories as he'd earlier mentioned, the man would wonder why Buchanan was interested in those same groups of names.

"But what I *want* to do next," Buchanan said, "is get something for this damned headache." Slowly, he stood, using his left hand to massage the back of his neck. "Does the woman have any aspirin around here?"

The killer stepped slightly backward. He still kept both hands at his sides, not yet fully alarmed. But Buchanan, his heart pounding, had a sense that a crisis was about to explode.

Or it might have been that the man wasn't stepping backward defensively but, rather, to let Buchanan go past him and into the bathroom.

It was extremely hard to know.

"Bufferin," the killer said. "The medicine cabinet. Top shelf."

"Great."

But the man stepped out of the way yet again as Buchanan approached him, and obviously this time he was making sure that Buchanan didn't come within an arm's length of him.

The bathroom—across from the computer room—was dusty. White walls. White floor. White shower curtain. Simple. Basic.

Buchanan had no choice except to pretend to look for the aspirins, even though his headache was the last thing he now cared about. He opened the medicine cabinet.

And heard a buzz. Surprised, he stared down at the cellular phone that he had taken from the van and attached to the left side of his belt. He'd taken that phone instead of the one in the Jeep because the Jeep's phone wasn't portable. This way, if Pedro and Anita needed to get in touch with Buchanan, they could use a second phone, a nonportable one, that was part of the surveillance van's instrument panel. Now Pedro or Anita was evidently calling him to warn him about something.

Or maybe the call was from the surveillance team's controllers in Philadelphia.

Buchanan couldn't just let it keep ringing. That would arouse even more suspicion.

But as he reached to unhook the phone from his belt, he saw motion in the hallway. The killer appeared, and now he, too, had a cellular phone. He must have gotten it from the room where he'd been hiding.

He didn't look happy.

"Funny thing," the killer said. "I never heard of Brian MacDonald. I just called Duncan's van to make sure everything about you is on the up and up, and damned if *your* phone doesn't respond to his number, which tends to suggest that your phone is actually Duncan's phone, which makes me wonder why in hell—"

While the killer talked, keeping his left hand around the cellular phone, he moved his right hand beneath his jeans jacket. As Buchanan had noticed, the jacket was slightly too large, a logical reason for which would be that the killer had a holstered handgun beneath it.

"A coincidence," Buchanan said. "You're calling Duncan while somebody else is calling me. I'll show you." He used his left hand to reach for the phone.

The killer's eyes focused on that gesture.

Simultaneously Buchanan shoved his right hand back beneath his sport coat, drawing his pistol from behind his belt.

The killer's eyes widened as he yanked his own pistol from beneath his jeans jacket.

Buchanan shot.

The bullet hit the man's chest.

Although the man was jolted backward, he still kept raising his weapon.

Buchanan's second bullet hit the man's throat.

Blood flew.

The man was jolted farther backward.

But his reflexes made his gunhand keep rising.

Buchanan's third bullet hit the man's forehead.

The impact knocked the man over. His gunhand jerked toward the ceiling. His spastic finger pulled the trigger. The pistol discharged, blowing a hole in the hallway ceiling. Plaster fell.

The man struck the hardwood floor in the computer room. He shuddered, wheezed, and stopped moving. Blood pooled around him.

Buchanan hurried toward the fallen man, aimed his pistol toward the man's head, kicked his gun away, and checked for life signs.

The man's eyes were open. The pupils were dilated. They didn't respond when Buchanan shoved his fingers toward them.

Quickly, Buchanan searched the man's clothes. All he found were a comb, coins, a handkerchief, and a wallet. He set the wallet on the table and hurried to get a small area rug that he'd seen in the living room. After rolling the body onto the rug, he pulled the rug along the hallway, through the living room, and toward a back door in the kitchen.

The oppressive night concealed him. Shivering, his skin prickling from the river's dampness, Buchanan tugged the body across a screened porch, down three steps, and toward this deserted section of the river. He eased down the bank, found a log, hunched the body over it, shoved the log into the current, and watched as the body slipped off as soon as the current grabbed the log. The two objects drifted away, at once out of sight in the darkness. Buchanan threw the area rug as far as he could into the river. He took out the man's gun, which he'd put beneath his belt, and threw it out into the river as well, obeying the rule of never keeping a weapon whose history you don't know. Finally, he took out the killer's cellular phone along with the three empty shell casings from his own semiautomatic—he'd picked them up as he left the house—and threw them toward where the gun had splashed. He stared toward nothing, took several deep breaths to calm himself, and hurried back to the house.

16

His ears rang from the roar of the gunshots. His nostrils widened from the stench of cordite and blood. Drawing his weapon had pulled the stitches in his side and strained the muscles in his injured shoulder. Tugging the body had further strained his side and shoulder. His head continued to feel as if a spike had been driven through it.

He locked the back door behind him, found another area rug, took it into the computer room, and set it over the pool of blood. Then he opened a window to clear the smells of violence. Next, he searched the man's wallet, found close to three hundred dollars in various denominations, a driver's license for Charles Duffy of Philadelphia, and a credit card for that name. Charles Duffy might be an alias. It probably was. It didn't matter. If these credentials had been good enough for the killer, they were good enough for Buchanan. He shoved the wallet into his pocket. He now had a new identity. On the unlikely chance that anybody in this remote area had heard the shots and came to investigate, everything looked normal, except for the finger-sized hole in the hallway ceiling, which by itself wouldn't arouse suspicion, although the pieces of plaster on the floor would. Buchanan picked them up and shoved them into a pocket.

With haste, he sat before the computer, glanced at the file directory on the screen—A\ B\ C\ D . . .—moved the flashing cursor from A to D, and pressed RETURN.

The disk drive made a clicking sound. A new list of files appeared on the screen, a subdirectory for all the headings under D.

	\	DARNELL	3k	DARNELL.BAK	3k
DAYTON	2k	DAYTON.BAK	2k	DIAZ	4k
DIAZ.BAK	4k	DIEGO	5k	DIEGO.BAK	5k
DOMINGUEZ	4k	DOMINGUEZ.BAK	4k	DRUMMER	5k
DRUMMOND.BAK	5k	DURAN	3k	DURAN.BAK	3k
DURANGO	5k	DURANGO.BAK	5k		

Quickly Buchanan opened the top drawer of the filing cabinet and took out the printed documents for D. The only way he could think of to learn whether someone had removed any of the files was to compare the names on the files with those in the computer's subdirectory. Even so, he didn't have much hope. The man who'd been hiding here to kill Juana had said that he'd erased some files in the computer, presumably to stop an investigator from doing what Buchanan was trying to do. Almost certainly, the computer's list would match the names on the printed files. He wouldn't be able to tell which documents were missing.

Each computer file had a companion file marked BAK, the short term for BACKUP, signifying that the computer's memory retained the previous version of a newly updated file. DARNELL. DARNELL.BAK. Comparing, Buchanan found a printed file for that name.

He continued. DAYTON. DAYTON.BAK. Check. DIAZ. DIAZ. BAK. Check. DIEGO. DIEGO.BAK. Check. He was finding printed files for every name on the computer screen. DOMINGUEZ. DOMINGUEZ.BAK. DRUMMER. DRUMMER.BAK. DURAN. DURAN.BAK. DURANGO. DURANGO.BAK. Every name was accounted for.

He leaned back, exhausted. He'd wasted his time. There'd been no point in risking his life to come here. All he'd learned was that someone was determined to kill Juana, which he'd known already.

And for that, he himself had nearly been killed.

He rubbed his swollen eyelids, glanced at the computer screen, reached to turn off the computer, but, at the final instant, stopped his trembling hand, telling himself that no matter how hopeless, he had to keep trying. Even though the subdirectory for the files that began with T would probably be as uninformative as the subdirectory for D, he couldn't ignore it.

He shifted his hand from the OFF button to the keyboard, about to switch subdirectories, when something about the image on the screen made him feel cold. He'd been aware that a detail had been troubling the edge of his consciousness, but he'd attributed his unease to apprehension and the disturbing aftermath of violence.

Now he realized what had been troubling him. His eyes had played a trick on him. DRUMMER. DRUMMER.BAK. Like hell. Drummer didn't have a backup file. The backup file was for DRUMMOND. Buchanan was certain that he hadn't seen a file for Drummond, but by now exhaustion so controlled him that he couldn't trust what he thought he was sure of. His hands shook as he sorted through the printed files. DRUMMER. DURAN. DURANGO. No Drummond.

Christ, he thought. When the killer erased the Drummond file, he hadn't thought to erase the backup file, or maybe he'd considered doing so but had been stopped because his eyes played the same trick on him that Buchanan's eyes had played, creating the impression that DRUMMOND.BAK was actually DRUMMER.BAK. The names looked so much alike.

Drummond.

Buchanan didn't know what the name signified, and when he accessed the DRUMMOND.BAK file, he found to his dismay that it was empty. Either Juana had created the file but never put information into it or else the assassin had erased it from the inside.

Buchanan accessed the subdirectory for *T,* and now that he knew what to look for, he checked the backup files rather than the primary ones, comparing the names to those on the printed *T* documents that he took from the filing cabinet.

TAMAYO.BAK. TANBERG.BAK. TAYLOR.BAK. TERRAZA. BAK. TOLSA.BAK. He was becoming more aware of the considerable number of Hispanic names. TO-MEZ.BAK. Buchanan's pulse increased.

There wasn't any Tomez in the printed files or in the primary files of the computer's subdirectory for *T.* Again Buchanan entered the file, and again he found nothing. Cursing, he wondered if Juana herself had erased the contents of the file. All Buchanan had was two last names, and if the assassin hadn't made the mistake of not deleting the backup titles, Buchanan wouldn't even have learned those names.

Frustrated, he debated what else to do, reluctantly shut off the computer, and decided to make a quick search of the house, even though he was sure that whoever wanted to kill Juana had sanitized the place.

That was when a chill swept through him as he remembered something odd that the killer had said. *"Where I bunked. Weird. No wonder the woman had it locked. Probably didn't want her parents to see what she had in there. At first, I thought it was body parts."*

17

Body parts?

There'd been so much to do that until now Buchanan hadn't had the time to find out what the killer referred to. Apprehensive, he stood, left the computer room, and walked along the short hallway toward the next room on the left. The door was open, but the light was off, so Buchanan couldn't see what was in there. When the killer had gone in to get his cellular phone, he evidently had known exactly where to find it and hadn't needed to turn on a light. Now Buchanan braced himself, noticed that the door had a dead-bolt lock, unusual for an indoor room, and groped along the inside wall to find a light switch.

When the overhead light gleamed, he blinked, not only from the sudden illumination but also because of what he saw.

The room was startling.

Body parts? Yes, Buchanan could understand why the killer had first thought that body parts were what he was looking at.

Everywhere, except for a corner where the killer had placed a mattress for himself, there were tables upon which objects that resembled noses, ears, chins, cheeks, teeth, and foreheads were laid out in front of mirrors that had lights around them. One table had nothing but hair—different colors, different styles. Wigs, Buchanan realized. And what seemed to be body parts were prosthetic devices similar to what plastic surgeons used to reconstruct damaged faces. Another table was devoted exclusively to several makeup kits.

As Buchanan entered the room, staring to the right and then the left, then straight ahead, studying each table and the various array of eerily realistic imitations of human features, he understood that in her security business Juana had become a version of what *he* was. But whereas his own specialty was creating new personalities, hers was creating new appearances.

He'd never been confident with disguises. On occasion, he would grow a mustache or a beard, or else he would put on well-made facsimiles. A few times, he had used noncorrective contact lenses that changed the color of his eyes. A few other times, he had altered the length, style, and color of his hair. As well, he always tried to make each of his identities dress differently from the others, preferring particular watches, belts, shoes, shirts, sunglasses, even ballpoint pens, anything to make each character distinctive, just as each character had a favorite food, favorite music, favorite writer, favorite . . .

But Juana had become the ultimate impersonator. If Buchanan's suspicion was correct, she hadn't only been altering her personality with each job—she had been totally altering her physical appearance, not just her clothes but her facial characteristics, her weight, her height. Buchanan found padding that would have increased Juana's bust size. He found other padding that would have made her look pregnant. He found cleverly designed sneakers that had lifts that would have made her seem taller. He found makeup cream that would even have lightened the color of her skin.

A part of him was filled with professional amazement. But another part was horrified, realizing that at Café du Monde in New Orleans, she could have been sitting right next to him while he waited for her to enter the restaurant and he would never have known how close she was. During his quest, he might have bumped into her or even spoken to her and never have been aware.

What had happened to her in the past six years? Where had she learned this stuff? For whom was he looking? She could be anybody. She could *look* like anybody. He remembered the last conversation they'd had. "You don't know me," he'd said to justify his inability to commit to her. "You only know who I pretend to be."

Well, she had outdone him, becoming the ultimate pretender. As he'd gone through the house, he'd thought it frustrating and strange that he'd found no photographs of her. He'd wanted so much to be reminded of her brown eyes, her shiny black hair, her hauntingly lovely face. Then he'd suspected that her hunters had taken the photographs so they'd be better able to memorize what she looked like. But if so, he now understood, the photographs wouldn't do them any good because there wasn't any definitive image of her. It may have been that Juana herself had removed the photographs because she no longer identified with any individual version of her appearance. Buchanan suddenly had the terrible sense that the woman he (or Peter Lang or whoever the hell he was) had fallen in love with was as insubstantial as a ghost. As himself. He felt sick. But he still had to find her.

18

He closed the window in the computer room, then used a handkerchief to wipe his fingerprints off everything he had touched. He shut off lights as he left each room, reconfirmed that he had done everything he had to, and finally shut the front door behind him, using his picks to relock the two dead-bolts. When the killer's partner arrived to begin his shift, the partner would take a while to figure out what had happened. The two area rugs that had been moved (and one of which was missing), the bullet hole in the hallway ceiling, the blood beneath the area rug that Buchanan had put in the computer room—each individually would not be obvious, but together they would eventually tell the story. The killer's partner would then waste time looking for the body. His report to his bosses would be confused, adding to the further confusion that the two snipers watching the Mendez house couldn't be found, either. The only certainty was that the people who were hunting Juana knew that a man named Brendan Buchanan had visited Juana's parents, and that made it equally certain that they would associate Brendan Buchanan with everything that had happened tonight. By morning, they'll be hunting me, he thought. No. They'll be hunting Brendan Buchanan. With luck, it'll take them a while to realize that tonight I became Charles Duffy.

Patting the wallet that he'd taken from the dead man and put in his jacket, Buchanan got into the Jeep Cherokee and backed from the driveway. His hands shook. His wounds hurt. His head throbbed. He'd come to the limit of his endurance. But he had to keep going.

A mile down the murky road, at the bottom of a misty hollow, he came to the van. Getting out of the Jeep, he kept his right hand behind his back so that he could quickly draw his weapon if there had been trouble while he was away. He saw movement in the mist, tensed, then relaxed somewhat as Anita came toward him, telling him in Spanish that Pedro was in back with the bound-and-gagged sentries.

"The phone kept ringing."

"I know," Buchanan said.

"We thought it might be you, but it didn't ring twice, stop, and then ring again as you said it would if it was you. We didn't answer."

"You did the right thing."

Buchanan studied her. She seemed nervous, yes, but not in a way that suggested she knew that someone was hiding and aiming a weapon at her. Nonetheless, he didn't fully relax until he made sure that the prisoners were as they had been and that nothing had happened to Pedro.

"Did you find Juana?" Pedro asked.

"No."

"Did you find any sign of her?"

"No," Buchanan lied.

"Then this was pointless. What are we going to do?"

"Leave me alone with these men for a minute. Sit with your wife in the Jeep," Buchanan said.

"Why?" Pedro looked suspicious. "If you're going to question them about Juana, I want to hear."

"No."

"What do you mean? I told you if this is about my daughter, I want to hear."

"Sometimes it's better to be ignorant."

"I don't understand," Pedro said.

"You will. Just leave me alone with these men."

Pedro hesitated, then somberly got out of the van.

Buchanan watched to make sure that Pedro got into the Jeep with Anita. Only then did he close the van's rear doors. The back of the van smelled from when Buchanan had allowed each man to use the Porta Potti before he drove to Juana's house. They were still naked and looked chilled.

He aimed a flashlight at one man and then the other. "You should have told me the sentry was in the house."

Terror made their eyes wide, their faces gaunt.

"Now he's dead," Buchanan said.

Their fearful expressions intensified.

"That puts the two of you in an awkward position," Buchanan said. He took out his gun and used his other hand to ungag the first man.

"I figured," the man said. "That's why you sent the man and woman away. You didn't want them to see you kill us."

Buchanan picked up a blanket from a corner of the van.

"Sure," the man said in despair. "A blanket can make a not-bad silencer."

Buchanan pulled the blanket over the man and his partner. "I wouldn't want you to get pneumonia."

"What?" The man looked surprised.

"If our positions were reversed," Buchanan said, "what would *you* do to *me*?"

The man didn't answer.

"We're alike, yet we're not," Buchanan said. "Both of us have killed. The difference is, I'm not a killer."

"I don't know what you're talking about."

"Is the distinction too subtle for you to grasp? I'll make it plain. I'm not going to kill you."

The man looked simultaneously troubled and bewildered, as if mercy was not a familiar concept.

"Provided you follow the ground rules," Buchanan said.

"What kind of . . .?"

"First of all, you're going to stay tied up until sunset," Buchanan said. "You'll be fed, given water, and allowed to use the toilet. But you'll remain in the van. Is that clear?"

The man frowned and nodded.

"Second, when you're released, you will not harm Pedro and Anita Mendez. They know nothing about me. They know nothing about their daughter. They're totally ignorant about any of this. If you torture them or use any other means to interrogate them, I'll get angry. You do not want me to be angry. If anything happens to them, I'll make your worst fears seem an understatement. You can hide. You can switch identities. It won't do you any good. I make a specialty of finding people. For the rest of your life, you'll keep looking behind you. Clear?"

The man swallowed. "Yes."

Buchanan got out of the van, left the doors open, and gestured for Pedro and Anita to come over.

Pedro started to say something in Spanish.

Buchanan stopped him. "No. We have to speak English. I want to make sure that these men understand every word."

Pedro looked confused.

"You're going to have a busy day watching them," Buchanan said. "I want you to find a place where this van won't be conspicuous. Maybe in back of one of your garages." He explained his conversation with the prisoners. "Let them go at sunset."

"But . . ."

"Don't worry," Buchanan said. "They won't bother you. In fact, they'll be leaving town. Won't you?" he asked the first man.

The first man swallowed again and nodded.

"Exactly. Now all I need is for you to tell me if you have a check-in schedule," Buchanan said. "Is there anybody you have to phone at a specific time to let your employer know there hasn't been trouble?"

"No," the man said.

"You're sure? You're negotiating for your life. Be very careful."

"We're supposed to phone only if we have a question or something to report," the man said.

"Then let's wrap this up." Buchanan's legs were rubbery from pain and fatigue. He turned to Pedro and Anita. "I need something to eat. I need a place to sleep."

"We'd be honored to have you as a guest," Anita said.

"Thanks, but I'd prefer that you don't have any idea where I am."

"We'd never tell."

"Of course not," Buchanan said, not bothering to correct her, knowing that Pedro and his wife didn't have the faintest idea of how vulnerable they would be to torture. "The less you know about any of this, the better, though. As long as these men realize you can't tell them anything, you're safe. Just keep the bargain I made. Release them at sunset. Meanwhile, on our way into town, I need to pick up my car. My bag's in the trunk."

"What happens later? After you rest?" Pedro asked.

"I'm leaving San Antonio."

"To where?"

Buchanan didn't answer.

"Are you going to Philadelphia? To find the people who hired these men? The people you spoke to on the phone?"

Buchanan still didn't answer.

"What happened at Juana's house?"

"Nothing," Buchanan said. "Pedro, drive the van while I stay in back and watch these men. Anita, follow in the Jeep."

"But what about Juana?"

"You have my word. I'll never give up."

19

THE YUCATÁN PENINSULA

McIntyre, the sunburned, leathery foreman of the demolition crew, lay feverish and helpless on a cot in the log building that his men had constructed when they'd first arrived at the site. Dense trees and shrubs had still covered the ruins back then. The ruins themselves had still been here. Sanity had still prevailed.

Now, as it took all of McIntyre's strength for him to use his good arm to wipe sweat from his brow, he wished from the depths of his soul that he had never agreed to his damnable contract with Alistair Drummond. The considerable fee—a greater sum than he'd ever received for any assignment—had been irresistible, as had the equally considerable bonus that Alistair Drummond had promised if the project was successfully completed. McIntyre had worked all over the world. In the course of his career, his nomadic existence had resulted in two divorces, in his being alienated from two women he loved and two sets of children he adored. All because of McIntyre's urge to conquer the wilderness, to put order where there was chaos. But *this* assignment had required him to destroy order and create chaos, and now he was being punished.

The earth itself seemed infuriated by the obscenity that McIntyre and his crew had caused to happen here. Or maybe it was the gods in whose honor the ruins had been constructed. An odd thought for him, McIntyre realized. After all, he had never been religious. Nonetheless, as his death approached, he found that he was increasingly thinking about ultimates. What he would once have called superstition now seemed to make perfect sense. The gods were angry because their temples and shrines had been desecrated.

Destroy the ruins, Drummond had commanded. Scatter them. His word be done. And with each dynamite blast, with each crunch of a bulldozer, with each hieroglyph-covered block of stone dumped into a sinkhole, the earth and the gods beneath had protested. Periodic tremors had shaken the camp. Their duration had lengthened. And with the increased tremors had come a further horror, myriad snakes escaping from holes and fissures in the ground, a pestilence of them, only to be controlled by spraying kerosene and scorching the earth, further despoiling it. A pall of smoke hung over the devastated ruins.

For a time, the snakes had seemed everywhere, but as the tremors had stopped, the snakes had simultaneously vanished. No longer disturbed, they'd returned to their underground nests.

Not in time, however. At least for McIntyre. The previous day, just before sunset, he had reached into a toolbox to get a wrench and felt a sharp, burning pain just above his right wrist. Compelled by fear, rushing toward the medical tent, he barely had a glimpse of the tiny snake that slithered from the toolbox and into a hole. The camp physician, an unshaven man who always seemed to have a cigarette in his mouth and whiskey on his breath, had injected McIntyre with antivenom and disinfected the puncture wounds, all the while assuring McIntyre that he'd been very lucky inasmuch as the fangs had missed the major blood vessels in his arm.

But as McIntyre had shivered from fear and shock, he hadn't felt lucky at all. For one thing, different snake toxins required different types of antivenom, but McIntyre hadn't been able to get a good enough look at the snake that had bitten him in order to identify it. For another, even if he had been given the correct antivenom, he still desperately needed emergency care in a hospital. But the nearest major hospital was in Campeche, 150

miles away. A road had not yet been built through the jungle
to allow a vehicle to leave the ruins. The only way McIntyre
could be taken to Campeche in time for the medical treatment
he urgently needed was by helicopter. But two of the camp's
helicopters were much farther away, in Vera Cruz, getting
supplies, and weren't expected back for twelve hours. The
third helicopter was in camp but disabled. That was why McIntyre had been reaching into the toolbox when the snake hidden
there bit him—he'd been helping a mechanic to fix the chopper's hydraulic system.

As he lay on a bunk in a corner of the camp's office, his
mind seemed to float while death spread slowly through his
body. Death felt suffocatingly hot, squeezing moisture from
his body, soaking his clothes. At the same time, death felt
unbearably cold, racking him with chills, making him wish
fervently for more blankets.

McIntyre's vision clouded. Sounds were muffled. The roar
of bulldozers, the blast of explosions, the din of jackhammers
seemed to come from far away instead of from the remnants
of the ruins outside his office. But the one thing he listened
for, the one sound he knew he couldn't fail to hear no matter
how far away, was the rapid *whump-whump-whump* of a helicopter, and to his despair, he still had not detected it. If the
chopper in camp wasn't fixed soon, if the other choppers didn't
return soon, he would die, and it occurred to him, making him
furious despite how weak he was, that adequate medical care
in camp was one of the conditions that Alistair Drummond had
guaranteed. Since Drummond had failed to make good on that
promise, perhaps none of the other promises would have been
fulfilled, either. The bonus, for example. Or the fee for the
job. Maybe Drummond would have all kinds of reasons for not
being able to complete the terms of the contract.

This suspicion had obviously not occurred to any of the
surviving workers. They were so eager to get out of here that
they attacked the job with relentless fury. Their impatience
filled them with greater anticipation of the reward they'd been
guaranteed. Nothing discouraged their greed, not the tremors,
not the snakes, certainly not McIntyre's impending death. They
had persisted despite efforts by Indians in the area to scare
them away. Those natives, descendents of the original Maya

who had built these monuments, had been so outraged by the obliteration of the ruins that they had sabotaged equipment, poisoned the camp's water, set booby traps, attacked sentries, and in effect waged war. Responding, calling it self-defense, the workers had hunted and killed any native they found, dumping the corpses into wells in unconscious imitation of the human sacrifice once practiced by the Maya. In this region untouched by civilization, the struggle had reminded McIntyre of what had happened four hundred years earlier when the Spaniards had invaded the region. The area was sealed. No outsider would ever know what had happened here. Certainly no outsider would be able to prove it. When the job was finished, all that would matter would be the results.

Delirious, McIntyre heard the office door open. From outside, bulldozers crunched past. Then the door was closed, and footsteps crossed the earthen floor toward this area of the office.

A gentle hand touched his brow. "You're still feverish." A woman's voice. Jenna's. "Do you feel any better?"

"No." McIntyre shivered as more sweat oozed from his body.

"Drink this water."

"Can't." He struggled to breathe. "I'll throw it up."

"Just hang on. The mechanics are working as fast as they can to fix the chopper."

"Not fast enough."

Jenna knelt beside his cot and held his left hand. McIntyre remembered how surprised he had been to learn that the camp's surveyor/cartographer was female. He'd insisted that this was no place for a woman, but she'd soon overcome his chauvinistic attitudes, proving that she could adapt to the jungle as well as any man. She was in her forties, the same as McIntyre. She had honey-colored hair, firm-looking breasts, an appealing smile, and in the three months they'd been working together, McIntyre had fallen in love with her. He had never told her. He'd been too afraid of being rejected. If she did reject him, their working relationship would have been intolerable. But as soon as the job was completed, he had intended to . . .

Stroking his left hand, Jenna leaned close, her voice interrupting his thoughts. "But I'm betting there'll be a chopper here quicker than we can repair the one we've got."

"I . . ." McIntyre's mouth was parched. "I don't know what . . ."

"Drummond will be here soon. We'll put you in his chopper to get you to a hospital."

"Drummond?"

"Don't you remember?" Jenna wiped a damp cloth across his forehead. "We talked about this when I used the radio a half hour ago."

"Radio? Half hour ago?"

"We found what Drummond wants." Jenna spoke quickly, her voice taut with excitement. "It was here all along. Right under our noses. We had the instructions from Drummond's translation, but we were too clever. We made the search too hard. We thought the instructions were using figures of speech, but all along, the text was meant to be taken literally. The god of Darkness. The god of the Underworld. The god of the Pyramid. It was so damned easy, Mac. Once your men leveled the pyramid, it was so obvious why the Maya built it where they did. We found what Drummond wants."

TEN

1

One-thirty in the afternoon. As soon as Buchanan got off the TWA flight from San Antonio, he headed toward the first row of pay phones he saw in the terminal at National Airport. He'd managed to get some sleep during the five-hour, several-stop trip. The naps, combined with the additional four hours of sleep he'd gotten the night before at a motel near San Antonio's airport, had given him back some energy, as had a carbohydrate-rich breakfast at the airport and another on the plane. His wounds still hurt. His head still ached. But he felt more alert than he had in days, adrenaline pushing him. He was traveling as Charles Duffy. He felt in control again.

A man answered Holly's phone at the *Washington Post*, explained that she was on another line, and asked who was calling.

"Mike Hamilton."

That was the name Buchanan had told Holly he would be using to contact her. He had to assume that the colonel and Alan would have her under surveillance, watching for any sign that she didn't intend to keep her agreement with them. If she seemed intent on pursuing the story, if she gave indications that she had not surrendered all of her research, there was a strong chance they would move against her. For certain, if the colonel and Alan found out that Buchanan remained in contact with her, that would be enough to arouse their suspicions to a deadly level. Even if Holly wasn't in danger, Buchanan couldn't afford to use his real name. The colonel and Alan would be searching for him.

That thought made Buchanan uneasy as he waited for Holly to come on the line. His nervousness wasn't caused by concern about his safety. Rather, he was nervous because he wondered about his motives. What did he think he was doing? You didn't just leave a top-secret undercover military operation as if you were quitting a job at Domino's Pizza. For eight years as a deep-cover operative and for three years prior to that, Buchanan had followed every order. He was a soldier. It was his job to be obedient. He'd been proud of that. Now suddenly his discipline had snapped. He'd walked away, not even toward the future but into the past, not as himself but as one of his characters.

Hey, buddy, he told himself, it's not too late. You'd better get back in line and with the program. Phone the colonel. Tell him you made a mistake but you're better now. Tell him you'll do whatever he wants. You'll be an instructor. You'll stay out of sight. Anything.

But a stronger thought insisted.

Have to find Juana.

He must have said that out loud, because a woman's voice was suddenly speaking to him on the telephone. "What? I didn't hear what you said. Mike? Is that you?"

The throaty, sensuous voice belonged to Holly.

Buchanan straightened. "Yeah, it's me." Before leaving San Antonio this morning, he'd called Holly's apartment to make certain she was in Washington, to ensure he didn't make the trip for nothing. Six-thirty in Texas had been 7:30 along the Potomac. She'd been awake and about to go to work when she'd picked up the phone rather than let her answering machine take the message. Assuming that her phone was tapped, he'd used the name Mike Hamilton and made tentative arrangements to meet her.

"Is our late lunch still on?" she now asked.

"If your schedule's free."

"Hey, for you, it's always free. I'll meet you in McPherson Square."

"Give me forty minutes."

"No rush."

"See you." Buchanan put the phone back on its hook. The conversation had gone perfectly. Sounding natural, it had nonetheless contained the words *no rush*, the code they'd chosen in New Orleans to indicate that Holly did not sense a threat. *See you* was Buchanan's equivalent message.

He picked up his small bag, turned from the phone, and joined a mass of passengers that had just gotten off another flight. Both National and Dulles airports were under constant surveillance from various government agencies. Some of the surveillance was a throwback to the Cold War. Some of it was due to a practical need to know which travelers of importance were showing up unexpectedly in the nation's capital. A lot of it had to do with the increasing conviction that Mideastern terrorists were poised to make their long-postponed assault on the United States.

Buchanan had no reason to suspect that the colonel would have operatives watching the airport in case he passed through. After all, logic suggested that Washington would be one of the places Buchanan wanted most to avoid. Besides, his paper trail would have led the colonel's operatives to San Antonio by now. Before leaving Texas, Buchanan had left his car at an office of the company from which he'd rented it. That would be the dead end of the paper trail. The colonel's people would assume that Buchanan had flown out of San Antonio, since the car-rental office was near the airport. But they would have no way of knowing that Buchanan had used Charles Duffy's name and credit card to rent the motel room and buy a plane ticket to Washington.

The only risk Buchanan took in the airport was that someone would notice him by accident, but that would happen only if he drew attention to himself, and he wasn't about to get that careless. Buchanan-Lang-Duffy-Hamilton blended skillfully with fellow travelers, exited into a drab, damp afternoon, got into a taxi, and headed toward downtown Washington. The terminal had not been a threat.

But McPherson Square would be another matter.

2

In New Orleans, before Holly had gone back to Washington, Buchanan had explained to her that if he phoned and suggested they get together, she was to choose a public place in the area. The place had to be part of her routine. ("Do nothing conspicuous.") It had to have numerous entrances. ("So we don't get trapped.") And it had to be dependable in terms of not being closed at unpredictable hours. ("I was once told to meet a man at a restaurant that had burned down the day before. Nobody on the team advising me had checked the location to make sure the rendezvous site was viable.")

In terms of those criteria, McPherson Square was ideal. The park was hardly likely to have burned down. It was as public as a restaurant but far more open, and it was only a few blocks from Holly's office, hence a natural place for her to meet someone.

Buchanan managed to reach the rendezvous area before the forty-minute deadline. Watching the newspaper building from a crowded bus stop farther along L Street, he saw Holly come out of the *Washington Post* and head down Fifteenth Street, but at the moment, he wasn't so much interested in her as he was in anyone who might be following her. He waited until she was out of his sight, waited another fifteen seconds, then strolled with other pedestrians toward the corner. There, while waiting for a traffic light, he glanced down Fifteenth Street in Holly's direction toward her destination on K Street.

She wore a London Fog raincoat, tan, an excellent neutral color when you didn't want to stand out in a crowd. A matching cap had the extra merit of concealing Holly's red hair, which she'd tucked up beneath it. The only thing conspicuous about her was the camera bag that she carried in lieu of a purse.

It was enough for Buchanan to distinguish her from other tan raincoats in the crowd. He followed slowly, glancing unobtrusively at store windows and cars, subtly scanning the area to see if Holly had anyone observing her.

Yes. A man in a brown leather jacket on the opposite side of the street.

As the man walked, he never took his gaze away from Holly. On occasion, he adjusted something in his right ear and lowered his chin toward his left chest, moving his lips.

Buchanan studied the street more intently and saw a man on the corner ahead of Holly. The man wore a business suit, held an umbrella, and glanced at his watch a couple of times as if waiting for someone. But he, too, adjusted something in his ear and did so at the same time that the first man was lowering his chin and moving his lips. Hearing aid–style audio receivers. Lapel-button miniature microphones.

But which group—the colonel's or Alan's—was tailing Holly? Were they military or civilian, from Special Operations or the Agency? As Holly reached K Street and crossed toward the park, Buchanan got a look at the backs of the men who followed her. They had narrow hips, their torsos veering upward toward broad shoulders, a distinctive build for Special Operations personnel. Their training was designed to make them limber while giving them considerable upper-body strength. Too much muscle in their legs and hips would slow them down. But muscle in the upper body didn't interfere with anything, creating only advantages. Buchanan himself had once possessed that body build, but since it would identify his background to anyone who understood these matters, he'd cut back on building up his arms and shoulders, going instead for activities that gave him stamina and agility.

Now that he had a distinctive silhouette to look for, he noticed two other men dressed in civilian clothes and with a Special Operations build. The colonel must certainly be apprehensive about her or else he wouldn't have so many men on her, Buchanan thought. The two men he'd just noticed were ahead of Holly, staking out the park. The only way they could have known to get to the park ahead of her was if they had her phones tapped and knew where and when she had arranged to meet someone named Mike Hamilton. He'd been right to be cautious.

Instead of following Holly into the park, Buchanan hung back, turned right on K Street, and went around the next block. His approach returned him to Fifteenth Street, but this time farther south, where Fifteenth intersected with I Street. From a busy entrance to the Veterans Administration Building, he looked across to the leafless trees in the park and glimpsed Holly sitting on a bench near the statue of General McPherson in the middle of the square. Pedestrians came and went, but the four broad-shouldered men had spread out through the park and were now immobile, on occasion touching an ear or lowering a chin, concentrating on Holly, then switching their attention to anyone who seemed to be approaching her.

How do I get a message to her? Buchanan thought.

Continuing along I Street, he came to a black man who held a small sign that read, I'LL WORK FOR FOOD. The man needed a haircut but had shaved. He wore plain, clean clothes. His leather shoes looked freshly shined but were worn down at the heels.

"Can you spare the price of a hamburger?" the man asked. His eyes showed subdued bitterness. Shame struggled with anger as he tried to maintain his dignity even though he was begging.

"I think I can do better than the price of a hamburger," Buchanan said.

The man's eyebrows narrowed. His expression became puzzled, with a trace of wariness.

"You want to work?" Buchanan asked.

"Look, I don't know what's on your mind, but I hope it isn't trouble. The last guy stopped told me if I wanted to work, why the hell didn't I get a job? He called me a lazy bastard and walked away. Get a job? No shit. I wouldn't be out here beggin', lettin' people call me names if I could find a job."

"How does this sound?" Buchanan asked. "Five minutes' work for a hundred dollars?"

"A hundred dollars? For that much money, I'd . . . Wait a minute. If this is about drugs or . . ."

3

At a safe-site apartment five blocks north of the *Washington Post*, the phone barely rang before the colonel stopped pacing and grabbed it off its hook. "Home Video Service."

"Looks like it's a no-show," a man's voice said. "Whoever this Mike Hamilton is, he was supposed to meet her at twenty after two. But now it's quarter to three, the drizzle's turning to rain, and she's making moves as if that park bench she's sitting on is awfully cold."

"Keep watching until she goes back to work and our man in her department can take over watching her," the colonel said.

"Maybe that's what she's doing now. Working," the man's voice said. "Just because the guy at the desk next to hers never heard her talk about anybody named Mike Hamilton, that doesn't mean Hamilton still can't be a source for a story she's working on. Hell, for that matter, he might be a friend she knew when she worked in California."

"Might be, Major? I don't like my officers to make assumptions. The tapes of the conversations don't mention California or anything else. She and Hamilton talk as if they've got some kind of relationship. But what? It's all smoke."

"Well, most people don't review their life history when they phone somebody for lunch."

"Are you being sarcastic, Major?"

"No, sir. Definitely not. I'm just trying to think out loud and analyze the problem. I'm guessing that if this meeting with

Hamilton has anything to do with us, she wouldn't be doing it in plain sight. Besides, we checked our computer records. No one named Hamilton was ever associated with our operations.''

"No one named Hamilton?" the colonel said. "Doesn't it seem relevant to you that one of our specialties is pseudonyms? Damn it, what if Hamilton isn't his real name?"

The line became silent for a moment. "Yes, sir, I get your point."

"Since she came back from New Orleans, everything she's done has been routine. Now, for the first time, she's doing something that can't be fully explained. For her sake, I hope it doesn't involve us. I want to believe what she told Buchanan, that she's given up the story. But I also want to know who the hell Mike Hamilton is."

"Colonel, you can depend on me to . . . Hold it. I'm getting a report from the surveillance team . . . Somebody's approaching the woman."

The colonel stopped moving, stopped blinking, stopped breathing. He stared at the opposite wall.

"False alarm, sir," the voice said. "It's a black guy with a sign about needing a job. He's trying to beg from everybody in the park."

The colonel exhaled and seemed to come out of a trance. "Maintain surveillance. Keep me informed. I want to know what that woman's doing every second." With force, he terminated the connection.

From a chair in the corner of the room, Alan studied him. "Why don't you give it a rest? Whatever happens will happen regardless if you're staring at the phone."

"You don't seem to take this seriously."

"Oh, I take it very seriously," Alan said. "To me, this is a sign of how out of control this operation has become. Instead of taking care of business, you're wasting all your resources worrying about Buchanan and this reporter."

"Wasting?"

"As far as I'm concerned, both problems are solved. Let Buchanan keep digging a hole to bury himself. He's gone—and I say fine. He'll act his way into oblivion. About the reporter—hey, without Buchanan she doesn't have a story. It's as simple as that. If she breaks her agreement, we'll deny everything she says, accuse her of putting her career ahead of the truth, and challenge her to produce this mysterious man she claims was God knows how many people."

"Maybe she can."

"What are you talking about?" Alan asked.

"She's the reason Buchanan walked away from us," the colonel said. "But maybe it's not just professional. He tried to protect her, after all. Maybe there's something personal between them."

Alan frowned.

"One of Buchanan's talents is changing his voice, imitating other people," the colonel said. "Hasn't it occurred to you that no matter what this guy sounds like on tape, Mike Hamilton could be Buchanan?"

4

Before Holly had returned to Washington from New Orleans, there hadn't been time for Buchanan to explain all the basics of how to behave if she thought she was being watched. The most important thing, he'd emphasized, was not to become so self-conscious that she exaggerated her movements as if putting on a show for someone. "Never do something that you wouldn't normally do. Never fail to do something that you *would* normally do."

At the moment, what Holly would normally have done would have been to stop sitting on a goddamned park bench when the drizzle turned to rain. She'd been on the bench since twenty after two, the rendezvous time she'd established with Buchanan. Now he was twenty-five minutes late, and in New Orleans he had told her that thirty minutes was the maximum time she should ever wait for him to show up. Otherwise, if she was under surveillance, she would make her observers wonder why she was lingering. That she was lingering now became even more conspicuous given the recent turn in the weather.

Holly strongly suspected that she should do the natural thing and leave right now. Buchanan had told her that if he ever failed to show up, she should return to the rendezvous area twenty-four hours later, provided he didn't get a message to her in the meantime. Returning tomorrow would be conspicuous, yes, but it was a lot less conspicuous than seeming not to have the brains to get out of the rain. There weren't many people in the park anymore; most had headed toward the shelter of buildings. She felt as if she was center stage and hoped that she seemed natural when she looked around. When she made up her mind and stood, she abruptly noticed movement to her left.

The movement had been there for about a minute. She just hadn't paid attention to it. It was so common that she took it dismally for granted. But now turning, she saw a black man with a cardboard sign that said I'LL WORK FOR FOOD approach a woman who was hurrying through the park. The black man said something to her. The woman shook her head with force and kept hurrying. The black man continued through the park. The rain had begun to streak the inked letters on his sign so that now it read, I ORK OR OOD.

Holly felt a pang of sympathy as the black man approached another hurrying pedestrian, a man this time, who strode quickly on as if the beggar were invisible. Now the black man's sign began to droop.

Oh, hell, at least one good thing will come out of this, Holly thought. She reached in her camera bag, took a dollar from her wallet, and handed it to the man as he came to her. She felt so dejected that she would have given him more, just to heighten her spirits, but she kept remembering Buchanan's instruction not to do anything unusual. A dollar at least was better than a quarter.

"Thank you, ma'am." What he said next startled her. "Mike Hamilton says you're being watched."

Holly's pulse faltered. "What?"

"You're to go over to the Fourteenth Street entrance to the Metro. Take the train to . . . Metro Center. Go out the east doors. Walk toward the . . . yes . . . the National Portrait Gallery. He'll be in touch."

Pocketing the dollar Holly had given him, the black man moved on.

Holly's instinct was to rush after him, to ask for a more

detailed explanation, to question him about how Buchanan had known she was being watched.

But her instinct was totally wrong, she knew, and she fiercely repressed it, ignoring the black man's retreat, acting as if he was an inconvenient interruption, glancing around as if still in hopes that the person she waited for would arrive. She didn't dare act immediately after speaking to the man. If so, whoever was watching her might suspect that she'd been given a message.

She waited. Five seconds. Ten seconds. Fifteen. Drops of water fell from the brim of her hat. What was the most natural thing to do? To check all around her one more time, then shake her head with annoyance and walk away.

She headed back toward work, then stopped as if she had a better thought, and changed direction, moving in the opposite direction toward the Fourteenth Street entrance to the Metro. Certainly the conflict she acted out was true to what she was feeling. Two days ago, Buchanan had scared her during their talk on the paddlewheeler in New Orleans. He had made the potential threat to her seem disturbingly vivid. Because of the story she was researching. The story about *him*. Seeing the deadly conviction in his eyes had made Holly feel cold. This man had killed. The men he worked with had killed. They didn't operate by any rules that Holly understood. A Pulitzer Prize wouldn't be any consolation to her in the grave.

But what about journalistic responsibility? What about the courage of being a professional? Holly had dodged those issues by postponing her decisions, by telling herself that if she waited for further developments, the story might get even better. She hadn't walked away from the story; she was merely letting it cook. Sure. Then why was she so terrified because Buchanan had gotten in touch with her? What did he want? If she was the reporter she'd always believed she was, she ought to be eager. Instead, she had the feeling a nightmare was starting.

Ten minutes later, amid the echoing rumble of trains behind her, she climbed the congested stairs from Metro Center, exited onto noisy, traffic-glutted G Street, and walked through the rain toward the huge Greek Revival quadrangle that housed the National Portrait Gallery. Despite the weather, the sidewalk was crowded, people hurrying. And here, too, there were indigents, wearing tattered, rain-soaked clothes, asking for quarters, food, work, whatever, or sometimes holding signs that announced their need.

One of them had a sign identical to that of the black man in the park: I'LL WORK FOR FOOD. She started to pass.

"Wait, Holly. Give me a quarter," the indigent said.

To hear him call her by name shocked her as if she'd touched an exposed electrical wire. Overwhelmed, she stopped, managed to make herself turn, and saw that the stooped man in the tattered clothes and droopy hat with grime on his face was Buchanan.

"Jesus," she said.

"Don't talk, Holly. Just give me a quarter."

She fumbled for her wallet in her camera case, obeying, liking the way he said her name.

Buchanan kept his voice low. "Drummond. Tomez. That's all I have. No first names. The sort of people who'd need protection. Find out everything you can about possible candidates. Pretend to make a pay-phone call at the gallery. Meet me at eight tonight. The Ritz-Carlton. Ask the hotel operator to connect you with Mike Hamilton's room. Have you got that? Good. Keep moving."

All the while, Buchanan held out his hand, waiting for Holly to give him the quarter. He took it, saying louder, "Thanks, ma'am. God bless you," turning to an approaching man, saying, "Can you spare a quarter, just a quarter?"

Holly kept moving as Buchanan had instructed, proceeding toward the National Portrait Gallery, hoping that she looked natural. But although she managed to keep her pace steady, her mind swirled from fear and confusion.

5

The large blue helicopter cast a streaking shadow over the dense Yucatán jungle below. In the rear compartment, Alistair Drummond's scowl became so severe that its wrinkles added years, making him look the eighty-something that he was. He'd been sitting rigidly straight, but now, with each piece of information that Raymond told him, Drummond sat even straighter. His brittle voice managed to be forceful despite the *whump-whump-whumping* roar of the aircraft's engine. *"Brendan Buchanan?"*

"An instructor for Army Special Forces, assigned to Fort Bragg. He rented a car in New Orleans and drove to San Antonio to visit the woman's parents. Our sentry there called to say that Buchanan used the name Jeff Walker when he claimed he was a friend of their daughter and asked if they knew where she was."

"Is he a friend?" Drummond squinted through his thick glasses. "Why would he use an alias? Obviously, he's hiding something. But what? What does he want with the woman?"

"We don't know," Raymond said. "But the two men assigned to watch the Mendez house are missing now. So is one of the men assigned to the target's house outside San Antonio. His partner found recent blood beneath a carpet and a bullet hole in the ceiling. It would be foolish not to make the connection between Buchanan's appearance and their *dis*appearance. If he shows up again, I've given orders to have him killed."

Drummond's ancient frame trembled. "No. Cancel that order. Find him. Follow him. Maybe he'll lead us to her. Did they work together at Fort Bragg? Learn his connection with her. He might know places to look that we haven't imagined."

6

While flying from San Antonio to Washington National, Buchanan had used an in-flight phone and Charles Duffy's telephone credit card to call several hotels in Washington, needing to make a reservation for the night. As he'd expected, the task was frustrating. Most of the good hotels in Washington were always full. He'd started at the middle of the price scale but finally decided to try the high end, reasoning that the recession's effect might have made extremely expensive hotels less popular. As it happened, Buchanan got lucky with the Ritz-Carlton. The early morning checkout of a Venezuelan group due to a political emergency at home had caused several rooms to be available. If Buchanan-Duffy had called a half hour later, the hotel clerk assured him, the rooms would have been spoken for. Buchanan was able to reserve two.

The Ritz-Carlton was among the most fashionable hotels in Washington. Filled with an amber warmth, designed to seem like an English hunt club, it had numerous European furnishings as well as British paintings from the eighteenth and nineteenth centuries, most of the artwork depicting dogs and horses. After Buchanan's brief contact with Holly near the National Portrait Gallery, he had noticed that she continued to be followed but that none of her surveillance team appeared to be interested in him. Even so, he had needed to be sure and used extensive evasion techniques involving the subway, buses, and taxis to determine if he was followed. Those techniques took two hours, and Buchanan assumed that if the surveillance team had been interested in him and had managed to stay with him, they'd have picked him up by then. So he felt reasonably protected when he checked in at the Ritz-Carlton shortly after 5:00 P.M. He showered, applied new dressing and bandages to the stitches in his knife wound, changed into dry clothes from his travel bag, ate a room-service hamburger, and lay on the bed, trying to muster his energy as well as focus his thoughts.

The latter was difficult. The last two days of constant travel had wearied him, as had his activities throughout the afternoon. Eight years earlier or even last year, he wouldn't have been this tired. But then, last year he hadn't been nursing two wounds. And he hadn't been suffering from a persistent, torturous headache. He'd been forced to buy another package of Tylenol, and he wasn't a fool—he knew that the headache could no longer be treated as a temporary problem, that it had to be related to the several injuries to his skull, that he needed medical attention. All the same, he didn't have time to worry about himself. If he went to a doctor, he'd probably end up spending the next week under hospital observation. Not only would a stay in the hospital be a threat to him, keeping him in one place while his hunters tracked him down, but it would increase the danger for someone else.

Juana. He couldn't waste time caring about himself. He'd done too much of that for too long. He needed to care about someone else. Juana. He had to find her. Had to help her.

7

The telephone rang at eight in the evening. Precisely on time. Good. Buchanan sat up in bed and reached for the phone, answering with a neutral voice. "Hello."

"Mike?" The deep, sensuous female voice was unmistakably Holly's.

"Yes. Where are you?"

"I'm using a house phone in the lobby. Do you want me to come up? What's your room number?"

"At the moment, it's three twenty-two. But I want you to go to five twelve. And Holly, you have to do it in a certain way. Take the elevator to the third floor. Then use the stairs to go up to the fifth. Anybody watching the numbers above the elevator in the lobby will assume that you didn't go any farther than the third floor."

"On my way." Tension strained her voice.

Buchanan broke the connection and pressed the button for the hotel operator, telling her, "Please, don't put through any phone calls until eight tomorrow morning."

He left the light on, picked up his travel bag, walked out of the room, put a DO NOT DISTURB sign on the door, made sure that the door was locked behind him, and headed toward the fire stairs. As he started toward the fifth floor, he heard the elevator stop behind him on the third.

Holly arrived at room 512 a minute after he did. The room was registered to Charles Duffy. It and Mike Hamilton's room had been rented using Charles Duffy's credit card. Buchanan had told the check-in clerk that Mike Hamilton would be arriving soon. After showering and changing, he'd gone back down to the lobby, waited until the clerk who'd checked him in was off on an errand, and then had checked in again with a different clerk, this time as Mike Hamilton.

When Buchanan turned from letting Holly in and relocking the door, she surprised him, dropping her camera bag and a briefcase onto a chair, putting her arms around him, holding him tightly.

She was trembling.

Buchanan wondered if she was putting on an act, trying to seem more distraught than she actually was.

"How do you stand living this way?" She spoke against his shoulder.

"What way? This is normal." He responded to her embrace.

"Normal." Her voice dropped.

"It's just stage fright." He smelled her perfume.

She stepped away, looking depressed. "Sure." As rain pelted against the window behind the closed draperies, she took off her wet London Fog hat and overcoat, then listlessly shook her hair free.

Buchanan had forgotten how red her hair was, how green her eyes.

She wore a sand-colored pantsuit, a scooped white T-shirt, and a brown belt. The outfit complemented her height and figure, the flow of her hips and breasts.

He felt attracted to her, remembered how her breasts had felt against him, and forced himself to concentrate on business.

"I wanted a room where we wouldn't be disturbed if the men following you decided to barge in," he explained. "This way, if they talk to the desk clerk, they'll think they know where you are and who you're seeing."

"That part I understand." Holly slumped on the Victorian sofa. "But what I *don't* understand is why you told me to pretend to make a call from a pay phone at the National Portrait Gallery. Who was I supposed to be talking to?"

"Mike Hamilton."

Holly ran her fingers through her hair and didn't seem to follow his logic.

"Otherwise, how were you supposed to know Mike Hamilton wanted to meet you here?"

"But . . ." She frowned. "But you'd already told me as I came out of the Metro station."

"The people following you didn't know that. Holly, you have to remember: In this business, everything's an act. You want your audience to know only what's necessary for you to maintain an illusion. Suppose I'd just let you go back to work and then had phoned you and told you to meet me here. Your phones are tapped. This hotel would have been staked out fifteen minutes after I completed the call. They'd have found out who Mike Hamilton was. Regardless of the switch in the rooms, you and I would be under interrogation right now.''

"Nothing you do is uncalculated."

"That's how I stay alive."

"Then how do I know I'm really being followed? How do I know that this business in the park and at the Metro station isn't just a charade to frighten me into cooperating with you and staying away from the story?"

"You don't. And I can't prove it to you. Correction. That's wrong. I *can* prove it to you. But the proof might get you killed."

"There. You're doing it again," Holly said. "Trying to frighten me." She crossed her arms and rubbed them as if she was cold.

"Have you eaten?" Buchanan asked.

"No."

"I'll order you something from room service."

"I don't have any appetite."

"You've got to eat something."

"Hey, fear's good for losing weight."

"How about some coffee? Or tea?"

"How about telling me what the names you gave me have to do with my story?"

"They don't," Buchanan said.

"*What?* Then why did you get in touch with me? Why did you put me through all this, being followed and passing secret messages and—?"

"Because I didn't have any choice. I need your help."

Holly jerked her head up. "You need my help? What could possibly—?"

"Drummond and Tomez. People important enough to need protection. What did you find out about them?"

"Why do you need to know?"

"It's better if you don't know anything about—"

"Bullshit," Holly said. "Since I met you on the train to New Orleans, you've been playing games with my mind. Everything has to be your way, and you're damned good at manipulating people into doing it. Well, this is one time that isn't going to happen. If you need my help, there has to be something in it for me. If it isn't about the story I was working on, what *is* it about? Maybe I can use *that* as a story. Quid pro quo, buddy. If I have to give up something, I want to get something in return."

Buchanan studied her, then feigned reluctance. "Maybe you're right."

"Jesus, you are really something. You never stop acting. I get the impression you meant to tell me all along, but this way it looks like *you're* doing *me* a favor instead of the other way around."

Buchanan slowly grinned. "I guess you're too smart for me. How about that coffee?"

"Tea. And if you're going to tell me a story, I think I feel my appetite coming back."

8

"It concerns the woman I told you about in New Orleans," Buchanan said after ordering food. "The friend who sent me a message asking for help. The one I was supposed to meet at Café du Monde. Except she didn't show up."

Holly nodded. "Your former lover."

"No. I told you we were never lovers." Buchanan brooded. "In fact, I think that's when a lot of my problems started. Because I didn't commit to her." He remembered how much he had wanted to, how much he had denied himself for the sake of duty.

Holly's face didn't change expression. But her eyes did, narrowing, assessing him.

"One of the last things I told her," Buchanan said, "was that she couldn't be in love with me because she didn't know me—she only knew who I pretended to be."

Holly's eyes narrowed more. "It certainly seems you never stop acting. For example, right now. I can't tell if this is the truth or more manipulation."

"Oh, it's the truth. Even if you don't believe it, it's the truth. This is one of the most honest things you'll ever hear from me. I want to help her because I want to be the person I was when I knew her. I want to choose to be somebody and to stay that somebody. I want to stop changing. I want to be consistent.''

"Because of all the people you impersonated?''

"I told you, I don't know anything about—''

"Don't act so defensive. I'm not trying to get you to admit to anything. You want to stop changing? Why make it so complicated? Why be somebody else? Why not be yourself?''

Buchanan didn't answer.

"You don't like yourself?''

Buchanan still didn't answer.

"This woman, what was her name?''

Buchanan hesitated. All his instincts and training warned against revealing information. He prepared to lie.

Instead he told the truth. "Juana Mendez.''

"When you knew her, I'm assuming you were on an assignment together.''

"You know what you can do with your assumptions.''

"No need to get touchy.''

"Since the first time I spoke to you, I have never revealed confidential information. Everything I've said about my background has been hypothetical, a 'what if' scenario. As far as you're concerned, I'm an instructor in military Special Operations. That's all I've ever admitted to. This has nothing to do with the story you abandoned. I want that understood.''

"As I said, no need to get touchy.''

"After you left New Orleans . . .'' He told her about his drive to San Antonio, his discovery that both Juana's and her parents' homes were under surveillance, and his search of Juana's records. He omitted all reference to the man he'd killed. "Drummond and Tomez. The files for those names were the only ones that seemed to be missing. Juana was a security specialist. I have to assume those people were clients.''

"Important enough to need protecting.'' Pensive, Holly walked toward the briefcase she'd set on a chair and opened it. "I used the reference system at the *Post*.''

"That's why I had to get in touch with you. I didn't have access to anyone else who could get the information I needed as quickly as you could.''

"You know . . ." Holly studied him. "Sometimes you might consider trying to impersonate somebody with tact."

"What?"

"I don't delude myself that you'd go to all this trouble if you didn't have something to gain. All the same, it wouldn't have hurt you if you'd also left the impression that you found me interesting."

"Oh. . . . I'm sorry."

"Apology accepted. But if you were this charming with Juana Mendez, it's no wonder things didn't work out."

"Look, I'm trying to make up for mistakes."

Holly didn't speak for a moment. "Let's see if this helps. Drummond and Tomez. I had my suspicions, but I wanted to check thoroughly before I made any conclusions."

"Drummond is *Alistair* Drummond," Buchanan said. "I more or less figured that already. The last name brings him immediately to mind. He's rich, famous, and powerful enough to fit the profile."

"Agreed. I kept checking, but he's the only Drummond I think we should consider." Holly pulled a book and several pages in a file folder out of the briefcase. "Bedtime reading. His biography and some printouts of recent stories about him. I'd have given you his *auto*biography, but it's such a public-relations whitewash that it's useless for dependable information. Certainly it doesn't show any skeletons in closets, and in Drummond's case, skeletons in closets might not be a figure of speech."

"What about Tomez?" Buchanan asked.

"That was harder. I'm a Frank Sinatra fan myself."

"What's he got to do with . . . ?"

"Jazz. Big bands. Tony Bennett. Billie Holiday. Ella Fitzgerald."

"I still don't see what . . ."

"Listened to much Puccini lately?"

Buchanan looked blank.

"Verdi? Rossini? Donizetti? Not ringing any bells? How about titles? *La Bohème. La Traviata. Lucia di Lammermoor. Carmen.*"

"Operas," Buchanan said.

"Give the man a cigar. Operas. I guess you're not a devotee."

"Well, my taste in music . . ." Buchanan hesitated. "I don't *have* any taste in music."

"Come on, everybody likes *some* kind of music."

"My characters do."

"What?"

"The people I . . . Heavy metal. Country western. Blue-grass. It's just that I never got around to impersonating anybody who liked opera."

"Buchanan, you're scaring me again."

"For the past week, I've been thinking of myself as a man named Peter Lang. *He* likes Barbra Streisand."

"You really are scaring me."

"I told you, I'm changeable." Buchanan-Lang smiled oddly. "But no one I've ever been had an interest in opera. If he had, believe me I'd be expert enough on the subject to give you a lecture. What does opera have to do with the name Tomez?"

"*Maria* Tomez," Holly said. "The name occurred to me immediately but not as strongly as Alistair Drummond. I wanted to make sure there weren't any famous or rich or power-ful people named Tomez I didn't know about." Holly took another book and file from the briefcase. "And indeed there *are* some, but they're not pertinent here. Maria Tomez—to quote from her press releases—is the most controversial, char-ismatic, and compelling mezzo-soprano in the opera world today. As far as I'm concerned, she's the only candidate for your attention."

"What makes you so sure?"

"Because for the past nine months, Alistair Drummond and Maria Tomez have, despite the difference in their ages, been an item." Holly paused for effect. "And Maria Tomez disap-peared two weeks ago."

9

Buchanan leaned forward. "*Disappeared?*"

"That's what her ex-husband claims. Don't you read the newspapers?" Holly asked.

"The past few days, I haven't exactly had time."

"Well, this morning, the ex-husband went to the New York City police department and insisted that she'd been missing for at least the past two weeks. To make sure he wasn't treated as a crank, he brought along a couple dozen newspaper and television reporters. It turned into quite a circus."

Buchanan shook his head. "But why would he think he'd be treated as a crank?"

"Because he and Maria Tomez had a very public and very nasty divorce. He's been bad-mouthing her ever since. He recently filed a lawsuit against her, claiming she lied about her financial assets when they divided their property during the divorce. He insists he has a right to ten million dollars. Naturally, the police might think she dropped out of sight to avoid him. But the ex-husband swears he honestly believes something has happened to her."

Holly gave Buchanan a page from the previous day's *Washington Post* and a photocopy of a profile in the *Post*'s Sunday magazine from five years earlier. Buchanan scanned the newspaper story and the profile. The ex-husband, Frederick Maltin, had been an agent who discovered Maria Tomez when she was twenty-two, starring in a production of *Tosca* in Mexico City. While a few male Hispanics, Placido Domingo, for example, had achieved significant careers in opera, no Hispanic female had ever had similar success. Until Maria Tomez. Indeed, despite her talent and fiery stage presence, the fact that she was Mexican had worked against her, relegating her to regional operas, mostly in South America. Traditionally, female opera stars got their training in Europe and the United States. For Tomez to have been trained in Mexico meant that she was combating a professional prejudice when she auditioned for major opera companies in the United States and Italy.

But Frederick Maltin, who had been on vacation in Mexico, had been enchanted from the moment he first heard Maria Tomez sing. He had sent flowers to her dressing room after the performance, along with his business card and his Mexico City telephone number. When he received a call the next morning, he considered it significant that the call had come so early and that it was Maria herself who called, not her representative. Which tended to suggest that she either didn't *have* a representative or else didn't have confidence that the representative would contact him at her request. Professionally speaking, she was available.

Maltin invited her to lunch. They continued their conversation after an afternoon rehearsal and later, at dinner, after an evening performance of a different opera, *Rigoletto*. As Maltin repeatedly emphasized, in those days Maria's schedule had been brutal, and he had sworn to her that if she agreed to let him represent her, he would change all that. He would make her a worldwide opera phenomenon. He would arrange it so that she performed only where and when she wanted to. Two years later, he had achieved his promise.

They married in the interim, and working relentlessly on her behalf, advising her about her clothes, her hairstyle, and her makeup, insisting that she lose weight, hiring a physical trainer to give her body definition, calling in every favor owed to him by anyone of influence in the opera world, Maltin promoted Maria Tomez as a singer in the passionate tradition of Maria Callas and Teresa Stratas. The former was Italian, the latter Greek, and Maltin's genius was in making his client's weakness her strength, in making audiences associate Maria Tomez with those divas because of a common denominator they shared, their ethnic origins. For Maria Tomez at least, it suddenly became fashionable to be Hispanic. Out of curiosity, European audiences came to hear her sing. Impressed, they stayed. Enthusiastic, they kept attending her other performances. After Frederick Maltin finished creating her public image, Maria Tomez never had any performance that wasn't a sellout.

Buchanan rubbed his throbbing forehead. "This guy Maltin sounds like a cross between Svengali and Professor Henry Higgins."

"That's why the marriage failed," Holly said. "He wouldn't stop controlling her. He supervised everything she did. He dominated so much that she felt smothered. She endured it for as long as she could. Then fifteen years after she met him, she abruptly left him. It's almost as if something inside her snapped. She retired from performing. She went into seclusion, making occasional public appearances, mostly keeping to herself."

"This started . . ." Buchanan picked up the newspaper article to jog his memory. "She divorced him six months ago, a few months after she took up with Alistair Drummond. But why would a comparatively young woman—what is she, thirty-seven now?—choose a man in his eighties?"

"Maybe Drummond makes no demands. I know that seems out of character for him. But maybe he just wants to shelter her in exchange for the pleasure of her company."

"So she went into seclusion, and now her ex-husband claims she's disappeared altogether." Buchanan frowned. "He could be wrong, or he could be lying. He's an expert in publicity, after all. He could be trying to attract so much attention that to get any peace, she'll have to deal with his claims about the property settlement."

"Or maybe something really happened to her."

"But what?" Buchanan became impatient. "And what does that have to do with Juana? Was Juana protecting her? Are they both hiding somewhere? Are they . . . ?" He was about to say *dead*, but the word stuck in his throat, making him feel choked.

Someone knocked on the door. Buchanan spun.

"Room service," a man's voice said from the hallway.

Buchanan breathed out. "Okay." He glanced toward Holly and lowered his voice. "In case this is trouble, take your camera bag and the briefcase. Hide in the closet."

Holly's brow knotted with worry.

"I think everything will be fine. It's only a precaution," Buchanan said. "Here, don't forget your coat and hat."

"I asked you before. How do you stand living this way?"

After shutting the closet, Buchanan approached the room's entrance, peering through the small lens in the door, seeing the distorted image of a man in a hotel uniform next to a room-service cart in the hallway.

Buchanan no longer had his handgun. Having traveled with it from Fort Lauderdale to Washington to New Orleans to San Antonio, he'd finally been forced to throw it down a storm drain. His trainers had emphasized—never keep a weapon that links you to a crime. Plus, the urgency of his self-imposed deadline had required him to use a commercial airline to get back to Washington, and he wasn't about to risk getting caught with a handgun in an airport.

With no other weapon but his body, Buchanan concealed his tension and opened the door. "Sorry I took so long."

"No problem." The man from room service wheeled in the cart. A minute later, he'd turned the cart into a table and set out the food.

Wary about having to compromise his hands, Buchanan signed the bill and added a 15 percent tip.

"Thanks, Mr. Duffy."

"Don't mention it."

Buchanan locked the door behind the waiter. Slowly, he relaxed and exhaled.

Holly emerged from the closet, her features strained. "I guess in your line of work, you have to distrust everybody."

"I was taught early—a person's either on the team or not."

"And if not?"

"There aren't any innocent bystanders."

"Cynical."

"Practical."

"And what about me?"

Buchanan took a long time answering. "You're not a bystander."

10

Buchanan had ordered pasta primavera for both of them. Now, instead of eating, he glanced at his watch, saw that it was ten o'clock, and went to the phone. Before leaving San Antonio, he and Pedro Mendez had chosen a pay phone near where Pedro worked. Buchanan had instructed Pedro to be waiting next to the phone at nine—ten o'clock in Washington. An enemy could not have anticipated that location and eavesdropped on the line when Buchanan called to make certain that there hadn't been any trouble after the prisoners were released.

Pedro had been told to use English if he was being pressured. To Buchanan's relief, he used Spanish.

"Any problems?"

"The men followed the agreement," Pedro said. "When I let them go, they did not harm us."

Buchanan imagined the courage that Pedro and Anita had required in order to go through with their part of the bargain.

"But I do not think they are far away," Pedro said. "I have to believe that they are nearby, watching us."

"I think so, too," Buchanan said. "I never believed them when they said they'd leave town. Don't remove the microphones from your house. Do everything as usual. The two things protecting you are that they believe you don't know anything about your daughter's whereabouts and that they need you alive and well in case Juana tries to get in touch with you. If they harm you, they're destroying a potential link with her. Pedro, I need to ask you a question. It might have something to do with Juana, but I want you to think carefully before you let me ask it. Because if it helps explain why Juana disappeared, you'll be putting yourself in danger. You'll have exactly the kind of information that whoever's trying to find Juana needs to know."

The line was silent for a moment.

"I don't have a choice," Pedro said. "If this is about my daughter, if it might help her, I must do my best to answer your question."

Buchanan's respect for Pedro kept increasing. "Does the name Maria Tomez mean anything to you? Did Juana ever mention her? Does Maria Tomez have anything to do with—?"

"Of course," Pedro said. "The singer. I don't know anything about opera, but I saw her perform. A year ago, she came to San Antonio to sing at HemisFair." Pedro referred to one of San Antonio's main attractions. The site of the 1968 world's fair, it had been converted into a cultural-athletic complex, linked to the city by a canal. "I remember because that was one of the few times Juana told us anything about her work. She was hired to do the security for the performance. In fact, she gave us front-row seats. I didn't want to go, but Anita made me, and I was surprised that I liked it. I don't remember the name of the opera. It was about students living in slums. Maria Tomez played somebody who was dying from a disease. The words were in Italian, but Spanish is close enough to Italian that I understood. Maria Tomez sang like an angel. I was stunned. But what does this have to do with Juana and

what happened to her? How would an opera singer who came
here a year ago . . . ?"

"I don't know yet. Listen carefully, Pedro. From time to
time, I'll phone your office to make sure no one's bothering
you. I'll use the name Ben Clark. Can you remember that? Ben
Clark. I'll ask about a Ford you're supposed to be repairing.
If you tell me it'll cost a lot of money to fix, I'll know you're
in trouble, and I'll get there as soon as I can to help you."

". . . Ben Clark."

"Right. Take care, Pedro."

"Jeff Walker, whoever you are, thank you."

Exactly, Buchanan thought as he set down the phone. Whoever I am.

When he turned, he saw Holly watching him.

"What's the matter? Why are you looking at me like that?"

"Ben Clark? A Ford? In this room, you're Charles Duffy.
Downstairs, you're Mike Hamilton. You mentioned something
about Peter Lang. That doesn't include . . . How the hell do
you keep it all straight?"

"Sometimes I wonder." To avoid the topic, he sat down
and started eating, not realizing how ravenous he was until the
first bite of food hit his stomach. During his phone call, the
pasta had gotten cold. It didn't matter. He couldn't get enough
of it.

Holly set down her fork. "You've been constantly on the
go since you left the hospital."

Buchanan kept eating, trying to ignore his headache.

"Don't you think it's time you slowed down?"

"Can't. As soon as we finish eating, I'll get you out of the
hotel. Then I have to take a trip."

"Where?"

"It's better if you don't know."

"You don't trust me? After I proved I want to help? You
said I was on the team."

"It's not a matter of trust. What you don't know won't hurt
you—and it won't hurt me if . . ."

"What you're trying not to say is if I'm questioned, I can't
give away your next move."

Buchanan swallowed a piece of bread and stared at her. "The
men watching you have nothing to do with what happened to

Juana. But if they see us together, they'll assume you're back on the story about *them,* and they'll do everything they can to protect themselves."

"Now you've done it." Holly shuddered.

"What?"

"Scared me again. Just when I get to feeling normal, you remind me . . ."

"Nothing is ever normal."

"Right. I keep forgetting."

11

Buchanan went with her down the fire stairs to the third-floor landing. Her instructions were to take the elevator from that floor down to the lobby. That way, to anyone watching the numbers above the elevator in the lobby, it would seem that Holly had been in Mike Hamilton's third-floor room all evening. "If anybody stops you, tell them to leave you alone or you'll call a cop. But if it gets serious, tell them a version of the truth. You're doing a story on the Maria Tomez disappearance and whether there's some connection between Tomez and Drummond. If they pressure you about Mike Hamilton, tell them he's a confidential source who works for Drummond. Tell them the man contacted you, using a false name. He's a disgruntled employee. He wants to make trouble for Drummond, but he doesn't want the trouble to be traced to him. So far, he hasn't been much use."

At the third-floor fire stairs, Buchanan motioned for Holly to wait while he checked that the corridor was safe. After peering cautiously out the door, he stepped back, his expression concerned enough to make Holly frown.

He motioned for her to follow. "We have to hurry. Two men are outside Mike Hamilton's room."

Before leaving 512, Buchanan had packed, made sure that the books and research files were in his travel bag, and filled out an early checkout form, putting it on the bed. A note explained that Mike Hamilton was checking out, too, but that as agreed all expenses were to be on Charles Duffy's credit card. "I don't want any more people looking for me than necessary. Quickly. Let's go."

He hurried with Holly down the fire stairs to the exit for the lobby. "Wait until some people get off the elevator. Go out behind them. Where do you live?"

She told him.

"I'll leave a minute after you. I'll take a taxi, and if I'm not followed, I'll have the driver go past your place. By then, your own taxi should have brought you home. Leave a light on behind an open window in front. If I see that a window's open, I'll know you're okay."

"Taxi? I brought my car."

"Then you'll get home faster. The elevator's opening. Now."

She touched his cheek. ". . . Be careful."

Buchanan felt the impression of her fingers for quite a while after she was gone.

12

"Buchanan!"

It must have been the result of fatigue.

"Buchanan!"

Or else it resulted from his conversation with Holly. Although he'd come to Washington thinking of himself as Peter Lang impersonating Charles Duffy and Mike Hamilton, he'd been distracted into talking to Holly as the core identity he'd been trying to avoid.

"Buchanan!"

So when he heard a man call his name as he walked along the rain-misted street away from the hotel, Buchanan almost turned reflexively to see who wanted him.

It was a mistake, he instantly realized, and he caught himself before he fully turned, but he did twist his head partially, and that was all the indication his hunter needed.

"Yeah, you! Buchanan!"

Buchanan kept walking, not changing his pace, not appearing to feel pressured, although he did feel pressured. A lot. Nerves quickening, he heard rapid footsteps behind him on the wet sidewalk. One person, it sounded like, but Buchanan didn't dare look to see if he was right.

The time was nearly ten-thirty. Traffic was sparse, sporadic headlights gleaming through the beads of moisture in the gloomy air. Buchanan had glanced casually from side to side when he'd left the hotel, a natural thing to do, one that allowed him to check for any sign that Holly had been detained or that anyone was outside watching him. Seeing no problem, he had turned off Massachusetts Avenue, heading south on Twenty-first Street.

Now, heart pounding, he realized that Twenty-first was a one-way street and that the traffic headed in a southern direction just as he did, which meant that all the cars approached from behind him. Unless he looked over his shoulder, he had no way to tell if a vehicle would be veering toward him. But if he did look, he would reinforce his pursuer's suspicion. Plural. Other urgent footsteps had joined the first.

"Goddamn it, Buchanan!" a different voice yelled.

The voice was directly behind him, close enough to attack.

With no other viable option, Buchanan whirled, seeing a well-built, short-haired man in his mid-twenties lurch to a sudden, defensive stop.

But not quickly enough. Buchanan struck the man's chest with the palm of his right hand. The blow was hard but controlled, calculated to knock the man off balance but not to break his ribs.

The man was jolted backward. He exhaled forcefully, a practiced reaction that helped him absorb the impact. That reaction and the resistance the man's solid chest provided told Buchanan that this wasn't a civilian. The man was military: trim hips, broad shoulders for upper-body strength. While the man briefly lost his balance, Buchanan swung his right leg hard, twisting it so that his shinbone struck along the outside of the man's left thigh. A major sensitive nerve ran down each leg in that area. If the nerve was traumatized, the victim suffered not only intense pain but temporary paralysis in the leg.

As Buchanan anticipated, before the man could retaliate from the blow to his chest, he grunted, grasped his leg, and toppled sharply. That left a second man rushing toward Buchanan, cursing, reaching beneath his windbreaker. Buchanan threw his travel bag toward him, forcing the man to zigzag while raising a hand to deflect the bag. Before the man could recover from this distraction and draw the handgun he was reaching for, Buchanan came in close, rammed the palm of his hand sharply against the bottom of the man's nose, and felt cartilage snap. The man's vision would blur. The pain would be intense. That gave Buchanan enough time to jab an elbow into the man's solar plexus and yank his pistol away as he doubled over.

Immediately Buchanan whirled, grabbed the first man, who was struggling to stand, and walloped him against a lamppost. The man's head made a *whunking* sound. Then Buchanan whirled yet again, back to the second man, who lay sprawled on the sidewalk, fighting to breathe through his broken nose, spewing blood.

If this had been combat, Buchanan would have killed them. As it was, he didn't want to make the incident even more serious than it was. If he eliminated the colonel's men, the next time their orders would be to do the same to him instead of to detain him. Or perhaps these men *had* been ordered to kill him. Otherwise, why would the second man have been drawing a weapon?

From where Buchanan had come, at the corner of Massachusetts Avenue and Twenty-first Street, a well-dressed elderly man and woman gaped in Buchanan's direction. The woman pointed a trembling arm, her outcry shrill.

Buchanan grabbed his travel bag and ran. His reaction wasn't caused only by fear that a police car would soon arrive. What sent adrenaline surging through him in even greater quantity, with greater urgency, were the two men who'd scurried around the corner in response to the woman's cry. Seeing Buchanan, they charged, and their chests were as muscled, their shoulders as broad as the men on the sidewalk.

Buchanan ran harder, the stitches in his knife wound threatening to tear open. He didn't care. He had to keep straining. Because when the second two men had seen him and raced toward him, both had reached beneath windbreakers, pulling out handguns, and there was no question now. This wasn't just a surveillance team. It was a hit team.

What had they done to Holly?

But he couldn't let himself think about that. He had to concentrate on staying alive. The first priority was to get off this damned one-way street, where the direction of traffic left him vulnerable from behind. Approaching P Street, he risked wasting time to look behind him on his left, saw an opening between two approaching cars, and darted between them, hoping that the cars would shield him, having noticed that the men were raising their weapons. A horn blared. Brakes squealed. He scrambled onto the opposite sidewalk and skidded on a slippery puddle but kept his balance, then bolted around the corner as the cars stopped shielding him and two gunshots roared, bullets shattering a window across from him.

Tightening his grip on the pistol he'd taken from the man whose nose he'd broken, Buchanan raced in a greater frenzy. The misty rain seemed thicker, the night darker. There wasn't any traffic. The rain discouraged pedestrians. Ahead, opposite, on the right, a murky street light revealed a lane that headed south, bisecting the block between Twenty-first and Twentieth. Buchanan lunged toward it, his travel bag slowing his momentum, but he couldn't ditch the bag. He couldn't give up the books and files that were in it.

Behind him, he heard curses, strident breathing, rapid footsteps. The sign for the lane read HOPKINS. Sprinting from P Street onto it, he flinched as bullets struck the corner he passed. At once, he whirled, crouched, and aimed one-handed with his elbow propped on his bent knee, controlling his trembling arm. Sweat merged with beads of mist on his brow. Leaning out from the corner, he wasn't able to see clearly enough to line up the front and rear sights of the pistol. But if he couldn't, his pursuers couldn't aim clearly, either. Judging as best as he could, he squeezed the trigger rapidly, firing three times, the shots echoing in the narrow street, assaulting his eardrums.

Nonetheless, he heard the clink of ejected cartridges striking the pavement and a groan as if he'd hit one of the men, although he had no way of knowing if any of his bullets had connected because both men dove flat on the pavement and shot in his direction, their gun muzzles flashing. A bullet blew a chunk off the corner of the building, nearly hitting Buchanan's eyes. He flinched and shot three more times toward the men, who now rolled in opposite directions, seeking cover behind parked cars.

Buchanan wasn't about to get caught outnumbered in a stationary gun battle. The moment he lost sight of the men, he ducked backward, rose, and charged toward the end of the narrow street. The gunshots had caused lights to come on in upstairs apartments. People foolishly showed their silhouettes at windows. Buchanan kept racing. He heard a distant siren grow louder. He heard a window open. He heard a shout above him. But the rapid, echoing footsteps behind him were the only sounds he cared about.

Spinning, seeing the two men appear at the entrance to the narrow street, Buchanan fired twice more. The men separated and lunged into doorways.

Buchanan zigzagged, trying to confuse their aim. A bullet tugged at his left sleeve; another forced tickling air past his right ear. But this time, he didn't hear gunshots, only eerie muffled sounds, as if hands were striking pillows. The men had put sound suppressors on their weapons, making the noise of Buchanan's own weapon seem even more explosive when he spun again and fired. More lights came on in upper apartment windows. The siren sped closer, louder. Another joined it.

Buchanan sprinted from the narrow street, racing through the misty rain across O Street, charging to the left toward Twentieth Street. Relieved to be temporarily out of the line of fire, he suddenly tensed as headlights blazed behind him. In the middle of the street, not knowing which way to dive, he had to spin, and the headlights streaked directly toward him. Brakes squealed. But the car wouldn't be able to stop soon enough. Buchanan had to leap forward, onto the hood of the car, sliding along it to absorb the impact, his face pressing against the windshield, stunned to see the unmistakable red hair of Holly McCoy behind the steering wheel.

Holly's face was contorted in a shocked, silent scream. Then a flapping windshield wiper struck the side of Buchanan's face and he snapped his head up, peering over the top of the skidding car, seeing the two gunmen appear at the exit from the narrow street. Breathing rapidly, Buchanan raised his weapon and fired along the roof of the car, unable to aim effectively but shooting four times, often enough to send the men scurrying back into the cover of the narrow street.

"Drive, Holly! Don't stop! Drive!"

The car quit skidding and increased speed. Sliding, Buchanan banged his face against the windshield. He glanced frantically over his shoulder, seeing that they'd reached Twentieth Street. A one-way heading north, it forced Holly to veer left into a break in sparse traffic. But the momentum caused Buchanan to slide sideways on his stomach, to his left, across the car's wet hood. With a travel bag in his left hand and a pistol in his right, he couldn't grab for anything. But even if his hands had been free, there wasn't anything on the slick hood to grab.

The car kept veering. He kept sliding. He anticipated his impact on the pavement. Tuck in your elbows. Roll. Keep your head up, he mentally shouted to himself. He couldn't afford another trauma to his head. And then he was slipping off the right side of the hood. Heart pounding, seeing the sideview mirror, he hooked his right elbow around it, bent his legs up under him, felt a jolt, and dangled. The sideview mirror sagged from his weight. He kept his elbow crooked around it, dangling lower, his shoes inches above the pavement. The car skidded. His shoes touched the pavement. The car slowed. When the sideview mirror snapped off, Buchanan landed hard, rolling in a puddle, the wind knocked out of him, but not before the car had stopped, its momentum throwing him forward.

He lurched to his feet. More headlights blazed toward him. He heard sirens. He thought he heard racing footsteps. Then he definitely heard Holly shout from inside the car. She pressed a button that unlocked the doors.

But instead of opening the passenger door in front, Buchanan yanked open the door in back and dove in, slamming the door behind him. Sprawling out of sight, he yelled, "Go, Holly! Move!"

13

She obeyed, squinting ahead past the flapping windshield wipers, darting her gaze toward her rearview mirror, straining to see if the sirens belonged to police cars chasing her. But the headlights behind her remained steady, and no men appeared on the sidewalk to shoot at her, and the sirens came from farther away, less intimidating.

"What happened?" she asked in dismay.

As she turned right onto Massachusetts Avenue, steered a quarter of the way around Dupont Circle, and then headed south on Connecticut Avenue, Buchanan quickly explained, all the while remaining low on the backseat, out of sight. Even though their hunters knew what type of car Holly drove, they'd be looking for a man and a woman, not a woman alone.

Holly's hands were sweaty on the steering wheel. "Are you hurt?"

"I pulled some stitches." His voice was taut. "If that's the worst, I'll be fine."

"Until the next time."

"Thank God you just happened to be driving along that street."

"There was nothing 'just happened' about it."

"What do you—?"

"When you started down Twenty-first Street and they chased you, you ran from the sidewalk and darted between two passing cars."

"Right, but how did you know about—?"

"The second car, the one that beeped at you, was mine. After the hotel's parking attendant brought it to me, I decided to drive around the block to see if I was being followed."

"Sounds like you're learning."

"And I also wanted to see if you got out of the hotel okay. I was driving toward you when I saw the fight, but you ran in front of me before I could get your attention. Then you disappeared along P Street. I was past that intersection, so I figured if I turned left onto O, I might get a glimpse of you coming from Hopkins or Twentieth Street."

"But what if I'd stayed on P Street?"

"You don't strike me as the type to run in a straight line."

"You really *are* learning," Buchanan said.

"Evasion and escape." Holly exhaled. "I missed that course when I was in journalism school."

"I didn't mean to get you involved. It was the furthest thing from my mind. I'm sorry, Holly."

"It's done. But I helped make it happen. I didn't need to

agree to meet you. I could have kept my distance. I'm a big girl. I stopped letting people control me a long time ago. Do you want the truth? I thought you wanted to meet me to tell me something that would put me back on the story. I got foolish and greedy. Now I'm paying the price."

"Then you understand." Staying low in the backseat, Buchanan spoke reluctantly. "You realize that because they caught us together, they think we're both a threat to them. It was a possibility before, but now your life really is in danger."

Holly tried to control her breathing. "I had another reason for agreeing to meet you. An even more foolish reason. It had nothing to do with the story. Deep down, I wanted to see you again. Dumb, huh?"

Except for the flapping of the windshield wipers and the drone of the engine, the car became quiet.

Holly waited.

She finally said, "Don't respond. Just let what I said hang there. Make me feel like a jerk."

"No. I . . ."

"What?"

"I'm flattered."

"You'd better say something more positive than that, or so help me, I'll stop this car and . . ."

"What I'm trying to explain is, I'm not very good at this. I'm not used to anybody caring about me." Buchanan's disembodied voice came from the darkness of the backseat. "I've never been in one place long enough to establish a relationship."

"Once."

"Yes. With Juana. That's right. Once."

"And now I'm risking my life to help you find another woman. Wonderful. Great."

"It's more complicated than that," Buchanan said.

"I don't see how . . ."

"It's not just that I was never in one place long enough to establish a relationship. I was never one *person* long enough. It isn't me who wants to find Juana. It's Peter Lang."

"Peter Lang? Didn't you say he was one of your pseudonyms?"

"Identities."

"I think I'm going to scream."

"Don't. Later. Not now. Get us out of town."

"In which direction?"

"North. Toward Manhattan."

"And what's in——?"

"Frederick Maltin. The ex-husband of Maria Tomez. There's one other thing we have to do."

"Get you a shrink."

"Don't make jokes."

"That wasn't a joke."

"Stop at a pay phone."

"I'm beginning to think *I'm* the one who needs a shrink."

14

At 1:00 A.M., between Washington and Baltimore, Holly parked at a truck stop on I-95. Buchanan got out and used a pay phone.

A man answered, "Potomac Catering."

"This is Proteus. I need to speak to the colonel."

"He isn't here right now, but I'll take a message."

"Tell him *I* got the message. Tell him there won't be any trouble. Tell him I could have killed those four men tonight. Tell him to leave me alone. Tell him to leave Holly McCoy alone. Tell him I want to disappear. Tell him my business with Holly has nothing to do with him. Tell him Holly doesn't know or care about him."

"You sure have a lot to tell him."

"Just make certain *you* do."

Buchanan hung up, knowing that the number of the pay phone would automatically have shown itself on a screen on the "catering service's" automatic-trace phone. If the colonel wouldn't accept Buchanan's attempt at a truce, a team of men would soon converge on this area.

Buchanan hurried back into the car, this time in the front. "I did my best. Let's go."

As she pulled out into traffic, he reached for his travel bag. The effort made him wince.

He took off his pants.

"Hey, what do you think you're doing?" Holly asked.

His legs were bare.

"Changing my clothes. I'm soaked." In the flash of passing headlights, he squinted at the waist of his pants. "And bleeding. I was right. Some stitches did open up." He took a tube of antibiotic cream and a roll of bandages from his travel bag, then started to work on his side. "You know what I could use?"

"A normal life?"

"Some coffee and sandwiches."

"Sure. A picnic."

15

The colonel frowned and set down the phone. In the safe-site apartment five blocks north of the *Washington Post*, Alan—who'd been watching the colonel while listening on an extension—set down his phone as well.

The only sound was the faint drone of a car that went by outside.

"Do you want my advice?" Alan asked.

"No." The colonel's narrow face looked haggard from strain and fatigue.

"Well, I'll give it to you anyhow." Alan's portly cheeks were emphasized by whisker shadow. "Buchanan's waving you off. He's asking for a truce. Agree to it. You've got nothing to win and everything to lose."

"That's your opinion, is it?" the colonel asked dryly. "I'm not used to taking advice from civilians, especially when they don't understand the serious nature of Buchanan's offense. A soldier can't be allowed just to walk away from his unit, certainly not Buchanan. He knows too much. I told you before, his behavior makes him a security risk. We're talking about chaos."

"And gun battles in the street aren't chaos? This has nothing to do with principle or security. It's about pride. I was afraid of what would happen when the military became involved in civilian intelligence operations. You don't like taking advice from civilians? Well, maybe you ought to read the Constitution. Because taking advice is exactly what you're supposed to do. Without the Agency's oversight on this, you'd be autonomous. You'd love that, wouldn't you? Your own private army to do with as you want. Your own private wars."

"Get out of here," the colonel said. "You're always grumbling about never seeing your wife and kids. Go home."

"And give you control? No damned way. I'm staying with you until this issue is resolved," Alan said.

"Then you're in for a long, hard ride."

"It doesn't need to be. All you have to do is leave Buchanan alone."

"I can't! Not as long as he's with that reporter."

"But Buchanan says that his business with the reporter has nothing to do with you."

"*And you believe that?*"

"He's not a fool. I was talking about gains and losses. He has nothing to gain if he turns against you, and everything to lose. But if you hunt him, he'll turn against you out of spite, and frankly, Colonel, he's the last person I'd want to be my enemy."

ELEVEN

1

Buchanan woke to a throbbing headache aggravated by banging metal and a roaring engine. He roused himself and blinked through the windshield at where a sanitation crew was emptying cans and throwing bags of refuse into the back of a garbage truck. He glanced at his watch: 8:00 A.M. Holly was driving north on Madison Avenue in New York City.

"You should have wakened me." Buchanan shielded his eyes from the hazy sunshine.

"So you could keep me company? No. You obviously needed the rest. Besides, I didn't mind the quiet. It gave me a chance to think."

"About what?"

"I realized I can't go back. Not until we find a way to convince them this has nothing to do with them. I have to keep moving forward."

"But there's only so far you can keep going until you drop. I'm not the only one who needed rest."

"I took your advice," Holly said.

"I don't remember giving . . ."

"Last night, I asked you how you'd managed to drive all the way from New Orleans to San Antonio, as tired as you must have been after having been wounded. You said you'd napped at rest stops along the way. So whenever I had to stop to go to the bathroom, I locked the car doors and closed my eyes. You're right. People make so much noise slamming their car doors, it's hard to sleep more than a few minutes."

"You certainly don't look like you've been up most of the night."

"The miracle of cosmetics. Thanks to sinks and mirrors at rest stops. If we're going to pull this off, by the way, you need a shave."

Buchanan rubbed his jaw, reached into his travel bag, pulled a safety razor from a pouch, and began to scrape it along his beard-stubbled cheeks.

"Ouch," Holly said. "Doesn't that hurt?"

"You get used to it. A lot of times on assignments, this was the only way to try to keep clean."

He waited uneasily, hoping that she wouldn't take advantage of the reference and ask him questions about those assignments.

Instead, she passed the test and merely concentrated on her driving.

"Have we got any coffee left?" he asked.

"We drank it all. But now that you mention it . . ."

She pulled over to a curb, parked with the motor running, ran into a coffee shop, and returned in a minute with two Styrofoam cups of coffee and four Danish.

"You're a good provider."

"And you'd better keep being a good teacher," Holly said. "The Sherry-Netherland's one block over on Fifth. It was mentioned in yesterday's article in the *Post*. How do you want to do this?"

"First, we find a parking garage that has space."

"Easier said than done."

"Then we look for somebody watching Frederick Maltin's apartment."

"Why would someone be watching—?"

"To tie up an unfortunate loose end. I don't think he was expected to be as big a problem as he's become, going to reporters, drawing attention to Maria Tomez's disappearance. My guess is, whoever's responsible will want to take care of that."

2

The Sherry-Netherland was diagonally across from the Plaza Hotel on Fifth Avenue. Immediately across from it were the Grand Army Plaza and an entrance to Central Park. Despite the upscale address, so many people came and went, lounged and loitered in the area that it wasn't difficult for Buchanan and Holly to portray a convincing version of two tourists when they arrived an hour later. It was cool but pleasant for early November. They strolled around the block, admired buildings, checked out the entrance to the park, and effectively scouted the busy area.

"Somebody could be watching from neighboring buildings, of course," Buchanan said as he took a photograph of a skyscraper, using Holly's camera. "But it doesn't look like anybody in the crowd is doing that."

They sat on a bench near the gold-gilded statue of William Tecumseh Sherman.

"What now?" Holly asked.

"Time for you to do some role-playing. But I'm afraid it's a tough one."

"Oh?"

"You're going to have to impersonate a reporter."

She jammed her elbow into his ribs.

"Hey, Jesus, watch it," Buchanan said. "That came close to where I was stabbed."

"I might stab you myself if you keep acting that way."

Buchanan laughed. "You brought your reporter's ID, I hope."

"Always. It's in my camera bag."

"Well, I just became your assistant. Call me . . . Who was that guy who tagged along with you in New Orleans?"

"Ted."

"Right. Call me Ted. We're about to pay a professional visit to Mr. Maltin. You'd better let your assistant carry the camera bag."

"You know, you don't do that often enough."

"Carry your bag?"

"No. A moment ago, you were smiling."

They waited for the light, crossed at Fifty-ninth Street, and headed north along crowded Fifth Avenue toward the canopied entrance to the Sherry-Netherland. Nodding to the uniformed doorman who was getting a taxi for a well-dressed elderly woman, Buchanan pushed the revolving door and entered ahead of Holly to check out the lobby.

Gentle lights gave it a golden hue. Colorful flowers stood in a vase on a side table. Ahead, on the right, a short corridor led to elevators. On the left, across from the corridor, the reception counter was next to a newspaper-and-magazine shop. A uniformed clerk stood in the lobby, another behind the counter. A middle-aged spectacled woman straightened things next to the cash register at the magazine shop.

No sign of a threat, Buchanan decided as he waited for Holly to come out of the revolving door and join him.

"Yes, sir?" The clerk in the lobby stepped forward.

Typically, the clerk singled out the male of a couple. But because Buchanan was supposed to be Holly's assistant, he straightened the camera bag around his shoulder and turned to her, his eyebrows raised, waiting for her to answer.

Holly immediately assumed her role. "I'm a reporter." She held out her press ID.

The clerk glanced at the card, his inspection cursory, probably paying attention to the newspaper's name and little else, Buchanan hoped. Holly hadn't volunteered her own name, and with luck, the clerk wouldn't have noticed it on the card.

"I'm here to see Mr. Maltin." Holly put the press card away.

"Did you have an appointment?"

"No. But if he's free, I'd appreciate ten minutes of his time."

"One moment." The clerk walked over to the counter and picked up a phone, pressing numbers. "Mr. Maltin, there's a reporter from the *Washington Post* to see you. A lady with a photographer. . . . Yes, sir, I'll tell them." The clerk set down the phone. "Mr. Maltin doesn't wish to be disturbed."

"But yesterday, he couldn't get enough of reporters."

"All I know is, he doesn't wish to be disturbed."

"Please call him back."

"I'm afraid I—"

"Really, it's important. I have information about his missing wife."

The clerk hesitated.

"He'll be very unhappy if he finds out you didn't give him the message."

The clerk's gaze darkened. "One moment." He walked back to the desk, picked up the phone, pressed numbers, and this time spoke with his back turned so that Holly and Buchanan couldn't hear what he said. When the clerk pivoted in their direction and set down the phone, he looked irritated. "Mr. Maltin will see you. Come with me."

They followed the clerk toward a row of elevators, and after they got in, the clerk stared straight ahead, pressing the button for the thirtieth floor. Sure, Buchanan thought. This way, he guarantees that we get off where we're supposed to be going.

At the thirtieth floor, the clerk waited until Holly rang the bell for Frederick Maltin's apartment. Only when Maltin opened the door, glowered at Holly and Buchanan, and gestured grudgingly for them to enter did the clerk step back into the elevator.

Buchanan and Holly walked past Maltin, who shut the apartment door impatiently and strode toward the middle of a spacious room.

Spacious was an understatement. The high rectangular room was large enough to hold at least four standard rooms. The wall to the left and the long one directly ahead were a panorama of windows that began at thigh level and went all the way to the ceiling, continuing around the room, giving a spectacular view of Fifth Avenue to the south and Central Park directly across. The furniture, tastefully arranged, was antique. Buchanan had the impression of polished wood and crystal, of expensive fabrics and Oriental rugs, of authentic-looking Cubist paintings. A gleaming grand piano stood in a corner, next to a display of what appeared to be museum-quality ceramics. It wasn't any wonder that Fredrick Maltin had complained about the financial terms of his divorce from Maria Tomez. He was obviously used to luxury.

"I don't know what information you think you have about my ex-wife, but it isn't pertinent any longer because I just heard from her."

Buchanan needed all his discipline not to start asking questions. The scenario made this Holly's show. She had to carry it.

She did. "Then you must be relieved."

"Of course. Very much." Frederick Maltin was a man of medium height and weight, in his middle forties, with a moderate amount of hair and a moderate amount of gray in it. As for the rest of his characteristics, there was nothing medium or moderate about him. His dainty, thin-soled, polished black shoes and meticulously pressed, blended-wool, double-breasted blue suit were obviously foreign, custom-designed, and hand-sewn. His brilliant white shirt and subtle striped tie had contrasting textures of premium silk. It was impossible for Buchanan not to pay attention to Maltin's diamond cuff links as the man made a show of impatience by checking the time on his diamond-studded Cartier watch. He had a sapphire ring on the small finger of his left hand. All told, it probably cost him twenty thousand dollars to get dressed in the morning.

"The hotel clerk said you needed ten minutes with me, but I can't spare even that much time," Maltin continued. His voice was reedy, imperious.

"But surely you're eager to tell the press the good news,"

Holly said. "Yesterday, there was so much commotion about your insistence that something had happened to her. You'll want everyone to know it was a false alarm."

"Well, yes," Maltin said, "of course. I hadn't . . . You're right. It's important for you and other reporters to inform her fans that she hasn't been harmed."

Holly sounded puzzled. "The way you say that . . . It's as if you haven't called the media yet."

"I . . . The news just reached me. I'm still adjusting. I'm so relieved, you see." Maltin removed a burgundy silk handkerchief from the breast pocket of his suit and wiped his brow.

Yeah, you look relieved all to hell, Buchanan thought.

"I haven't had time to compose myself. To make plans."

"What did your ex-wife tell you?" Holly asked. "Where has she been for the past two weeks?"

Maltin looked blank. "Away. She told me where, but she doesn't want me to reveal the precise location. She wants to stay away a while longer. To rest. After this misunderstanding, reporters will swarm all over her if they get the opportunity."

"Well, can't you give us a general idea of where she is?"

"France. But that's all I intend to reveal."

"Did she explain why she dropped out of sight?"

"She wanted to take a trip. In my impatience about these unfortunate legal matters, I made the mistake of assuming that because I couldn't contact her, something disastrous must have happened to her."

As Buchanan surveyed the room again, he smelled the faint odor of cigarette smoke, but there weren't any ashtrays in this fastidiously maintained room. Nor was there any odor of cigarette smoke on Maltin's clothes. Buchanan was always amazed that smokers didn't realize how pervasive the odor of their habit was. In this case, cigarette smoke from a distant area of the spacious apartment drifted in this direction. And Buchanan had the strong conviction that Frederick Maltin not only didn't smoke but also didn't approve of anyone smoking in his presence, certainly not in his apartment.

"I'll make a confession," Maltin said. "I overreacted because Maria wouldn't respond to my telephone calls. When she sold her apartment a few weeks ago and seemed to vanish,

I was outraged that she had ignored me, that she hadn't consulted with me. She used to consult with me about everything. I couldn't imagine she'd be that independent, even though we were divorced. So my pride insisted she must have been the victim of foul play. Ridiculous of me."

"Yes," Buchanan said, the first time he'd spoken. "Do you mind if I use your bathroom?"

"Indeed I do. Very much."

"But this is an emergency. I have to go."

Buchanan walked across the room, heading toward a door at the far end.

"Wait. What do you think you're doing?" Maltin exclaimed in outrage. "You can't . . . Stop right there. You stop where you are!"

"But I told you, I need a bathroom." Buchanan opened the door, entering a tastefully, expensively decorated hallway.

Maltin charged after him. "If you don't stop, I'll call the police!"

Buchanan kept on. The cigarette smoke was stronger. It seemed to come from . . .

He opened a door on his left, revealing an oak-furnished study from which cigarette smoke drifted. A surprised man straightened from where he'd been leaning his hips against a large polished desk. He was in his middle thirties, wore an average suit, had hair in slight need of a trim, needed a touch-up on his shoes, held a cigarette, and generally looked like the sort of person whom Frederick Maltin would prefer to avoid.

"Sorry," Buchanan said. "I thought this was the bathroom."

"No problem," the man said.

A handgun, its butt forward, bulged beneath the left side of the man's suit. To draw the weapon, he would have to use his right hand, but his right hand held the cigarette. The man leaned forward as if to flick ashes into a wastebasket. What he did instead was drop the cigarette into the wastebasket and grab for his weapon.

Not soon enough. Buchanan didn't want gunshots to alarm anyone in the building. Clutching the strap of the camera bag, he turned as if to leave. And kept turning. Gaining momentum, he swung the bag hard and fast. The bag collided with the side of the man's jaw. It hit with a loud, sharp *whack*. The man arched sideways. His eyes rolled up in his head. Blood flew out of his mouth. With a groan, he landed on an Oriental carpet, skidded, and slammed his skull against the bottom of a shelf of leather-bound books. He breathed but otherwise didn't move.

"Jesus Christ." Frederick Maltin had rushed along the hallway and now gaped in shock at the man on the floor. "Jesus Christ, what have you done?"

"I think he didn't want me to use the bathroom."

"Oh, Jesus Christ."

"Yeah, I get the idea. But Jesus isn't going to help you."

Buchanan drew his own gun, which made Maltin gasp and Holly, behind him, flinch. Approaching the man on the floor, Buchanan aimed the weapon at the man's head while he took the man's .357 revolver away. Then he checked the man's pulse, turned the man's head so that he wouldn't choke from the blood in his mouth, and straightened, shaking his head. "Sorry about the blood on the carpet, Fred. You ought to be careful about the people you hang around with. Or, rather . . ." Buchanan noticed a satchel on the desk and opened it. "Or, rather, the people you do business with. How much money is in this satchel? It sure is a lot of hundred-dollar bills. Banded in five-thousand-dollar units." Buchanan took them out and made stacks. "What would you estimate? Let's see. One hundred thousand. Two hundred thousand. Hard to squeeze all of it in there, and heavy to lug around, but yeah, I'd say that what we've got here, all told, is a million dollars."

Maltin's mouth hung open. His face had turned pale.

Behind him, in the corridor, Holly looked stunned, not only by the money but by what she was witnessing.

"Fred, get down on your knees."

Maltin trembled. "Why?"

"Just do it. Here." Buchanan went past Maltin, over to Holly, and gave her the revolver. "If Fred tries to stand up, shoot him." With a baleful stare toward Maltin, Buchanan went into the corridor.

"But where are you going?" Holly asked.

"To make sure we're alone."

3

Working cautiously, ready with his pistol, Buchanan proceeded from room to room, searching everywhere. Just because he'd found one man, that didn't mean there wouldn't be others hiding in other sections of the apartment.

But he found no one. Relieved, he walked back into the study, again examined the man on the floor, satisfied himself that the man's life signs were steady, tied his hands with his belt, and turned to Maltin, whose face was beading with sweat that he couldn't wipe away fast enough. Indeed, Maltin's burgundy handkerchief was soaked.

"Sit down, Fred. You look as if you're going to faint. Is there anything we can get you? A glass of water? Some brandy? Make yourself at home."

Maltin's face was the color of concrete. Sweating more profusely, he nodded with a trace of desperation. "Over there. In the top desk drawer."

Buchanan opened the drawer and made a *tsking* sound. "Fred, I'm disappointed in you. You mean to tell me you're a candy sniffer? Naughty, naughty, Fred. Haven't you ever heard of just saying no?"

Buchanan took a vial of white powder from the drawer and set it on the desk. "But hey, the privacy of your home, an informed adult, blah, blah. Help yourself."

Maltin glared at him, then pulled the top from the vial and inhaled cocaine up one nostril, then the other.

"You got a little on your lip there, Fred."

Maltin wiped it off and licked his finger.

"That's it. Don't be wasteful. Now are you comfy, Fred? Are you ready for some conversation?"

"You son of a bitch."

Buchanan slapped him so hard that Maltin didn't have time to blink before his head was snapped sideways and specks of white powder flew out of his nose. The slap filled the room like the crack of a whip. It left a raw, welting red handprint on Maltin's cheek.

Holly raised a startled hand to her mouth.

Buchanan slapped Maltin's other cheek, using even more force, snapping Maltin's head in the other direction.

Maltin wept uncontrollably. "Please, don't kill me." He wailed, his eyes scrunched pathetically, tears welling out of them. "Please."

"You're not paying attention," Buchanan said. "I want conversation. This satchel. This money, Fred. No one carries around this much cash for anything that's legal. What is it? A payoff? Were you already thinking about how to get it to an offshore bank so you wouldn't have to pay taxes on it? I mean, paying taxes on a payoff, that doesn't seem reasonable, does it? So what were you being paid off for, Fred? It had to do with your ex-wife, right? You drew attention to her, and somebody didn't like that. So you were told to shut up, and the inducement was . . . Well, you had a choice. A bullet in the brain or a million bucks in the bank. But you're no dummy. Hell, for a million bucks, you'd sell out anybody. It doesn't matter if Maria Tomez is in trouble. She divorced you, so let the bitch take care of herself. Right, Fred? Pay attention, Fred. Tell me I'm right, or I'll slap you till your head's turned around."

Buchanan raised his hand as if to swing, and Maltin cringed. "Please, no, don't, no, please."

"Don't mumble, Fred. The money's a payoff, and we got here while it was happening. The deal was, you were supposed to call off the media, and since we were insisting, you decided to interrupt the proceedings and handle us. Except you hadn't worked out your routine yet. But by noon, when you called the reporters you spoke to yesterday, your act would have been perfect. Right, Fred? *Right?*" Buchanan feinted his hand at him.

Maltin swallowed tears, blubbered, and nodded.

"Now just so this isn't a one-way conversation, I've got a question for you, Fred. Are you ready?"

Maltin struggled to breathe.

"Who paid you off?"

Maltin didn't answer.

"Fred, I'm talking to you."

Maltin bit his lip and didn't answer.

Buchanan sighed, telling Holly, "I'm afraid you'd better leave us alone. You don't want to see this."

"Drummond," Maltin whimpered.

"What, Fred? You're mumbling again. Speak up."

"Alistair Drummond."

"My, my," Buchanan said. "Your ex-wife's new companion. And why would Alistair Drummond pay you a million dollars to keep you from telling the media you can't find her?"

"I . . ."

"You can tell me, Fred."

"I don't know."

"Come on, don't disappoint me, Fred. You were doing so well. Why would Drummond pay you off? Think about it. Make a wild guess."

"I tell you, I don't know!"

"Have you ever had any bones broken, Fred?" Buchanan reached for the little finger on Maltin's right hand.

"No! I'm telling the truth!" Maltin yanked his hand away. "Don't touch me, you bastard! Leave me alone! I mean it! I'm telling the truth! I don't know *anything*!"

"For the last time, Fred, I'm asking you to make a wild guess."

"*Nothing* about Maria has made any sense since she left me and went on that cruise with Drummond nine months ago."

"Cruise, Fred? Exactly what cruise are we talking about?"

"Off Acapulco. Drummond has a two-hundred-foot yacht. He told her she could relax on board while the divorce was being settled. She may have hated me as a husband, but she relied on me as a manager. After that cruise, though, she wouldn't speak to me about anything. She canceled business meetings with me. She wouldn't take my telephone calls. The few times I saw her in public, at the Met or at charity events, Drummond's bodyguards wouldn't let me near her. Damn it, by not dealing with me, she's costing me money! A lot of money!"

"Relax, Fred. The million dollars you were paid to stop bothering her will keep you in cocaine for a while. But do you want some advice? If I were you, I'd use the money to travel. Light and fast and far away. Because I have a very strong feeling that when this is over, whatever it's about, Alistair

Drummond intends to guarantee that you keep quiet, to make sure you don't come back for more money, to give you a jolt of cocaine that'll take you right out of this world, if you get my meaning. In fact, I'm surprised he hasn't done it already. My guess is he didn't want it to happen so soon after you were making speeches in front of those reporters. Too coincidental. Too suspicious. But it *will* happen, Fred. So I suggest you liquidate, haul ass, change your name, and dig a deep hole. Bury yourself. Because they'll be coming.''

Maltin's face contorted.

"Be seeing you, Fred."

"But . . .?" Maltin gestured toward the unconscious man on the floor. "What about . . .?"

"The way I see it, you have two options. Think up a good story or be gone by the time he wakes up. Got to run, Fred."

4

"Lord, I've never seen anything like that," Holly said.

They had emerged from the Sherry-Netherland, turned right off Fifth Avenue, and were walking along Central Park South. Traffic blared while tourists waited to get on horse-drawn carriages.

"Keep a slower pace," Buchanan said. The sunlight aggravated his headache. "We don't want to look as if we're running away from anything."

"And we're not?" Holly whispered nervously. "You broke a man's jaw. You assaulted Maltin. He'll have called the police the second we left his apartment."

"No," Buchanan said. "He'll be packing."

"How can you be sure? Every time I hear a police siren—"

"Because if *you've* never seen anything like what just happened, Maltin hadn't, either. If he called the police, he would also have called hotel security, but no one tried to stop us when we left." Buchanan guided Holly into the Seventh Avenue entrance to Central Park. A cool November breeze tugged at his hair.

"Why are we going into—?"

"Backtracking. We'll turn right at this path up ahead and head back the way we came. To find out if we're being followed by anyone connected with the guy in Maltin's apartment. Besides, there aren't many people in the park. We can talk without being overheard. Maltin was terrified."

"No kidding. I felt terrified myself. I got the feeling you were out of control. Jesus, you were going to break his fingers."

"No. I knew I wouldn't have to. But you and Maltin believed I would. The performance was successful."

"Don't you do anything without calculation?"

"Would you have preferred that I *did* break his fingers? Come on, Holly. What I did back there was the equivalent of doing an interview."

"Not like any interview *I* ever conducted."

Buchanan glanced behind him, then scanned the trees and bushes on either side of them.

"I don't mean just the threats," Holly said. "Why didn't you keep questioning him? How do you know he was telling the truth?"

"His eyes," Buchanan said.

"*Your* eyes looked as if you were a maniac."

"I'm good with them. I practice with them a lot. They're the key to being an operative. If somebody believes my eyes, they'll believe everything else."

"Then how can you be so sure about *Maltin's* eyes? Maybe *he* was pretending."

"No. It takes one to know one. Maltin's a single-role person. A shit who crumbles as soon as his power is taken away. It's no wonder Maria Tomez divorced him. He told me everything I needed to hear. I could have cross-examined him, but that would have wasted time. I already know what we have to do next."

"What?"

They left the park and entered the din of traffic at the Avenue of the Americas exit.

"Be practical. Check into a hotel," Buchanan said. "Get some food and rest. Do some research."

"And after that?"

"Find Alistair Drummond's yacht."

5

After using a subway and three taxis to make sure that they weren't being followed, they ended in the general area where they had started, managing to find a vacancy at the Dorset, a softly carpeted, darkly paneled hotel on Fifty-fourth Street between the Avenue of the Americas and Fifth Avenue. There, they brought Holly's car from the parking garage and left it with the hotel's attendant, then registered as Mr. and Mrs. Charles Duffy and went to their room on the twenty-first floor. Buchanan felt reassured that the room was near the elevators and the fire stairs. They were in so public an area that it was unlikely anything threatening would happen. More, the location gave Buchanan and Holly access to several close escape routes.

They ordered room service: coffee, tea, salads, steaks, baked potatoes, French bread, plenty of vegetables, ice cream. While waiting for the food, Holly showered. Then Buchanan did. When he came out of the bathroom, wearing a white robe supplied by the hotel, Holly—also wearing a robe—was using a hotel hair dryer.

She turned it off. "Sit down. Pull your robe down to your waist."

"What?"

"I want to check your stitches."

His back tingled as her fingers touched his skin.

She circled the almost-healed bullet wound in his right shoulder, then moved her fingers lower, inspecting the knife wound. "You did pull a few stitches. Here." She took antibiotic cream and bandages from his travel bag. "There doesn't seem to be any infection. Hold still while I—"

"Ouch."

"Some tough guy you are." She laughed.

"How do you know I'm not acting? How do you know I'm not trying to get your sympathy?"

"You test people by checking their eyes. I have other ways."

"Oh?"

She ran her fingers up to his shoulders, turned him, and kissed him.

The kiss was long. Gentle. A slight parting of the lips. A tentative probing of the tongue. Subtle. Sensual.

Buchanan hesitated.

Despite his protective instincts, he put his hands behind her, holding her, feeling her well-toned back beneath her robe.

Her breath was sweet as she exhaled with pleasure and pulled slowly away. "Yep. You definitely want sympathy."

Now it was Buchanan's turn to laugh.

He reached to kiss her again.

And was interrupted by a knock on the door.

"Room service," a man said from outside in the corridor.

"You're corrupting me," Holly said.

"What do you mean?"

"I'm beginning to think your habits are normal. Here." She reached beneath the pillow. "Doesn't everybody need this when room service arrives? Tuck this into the pocket of your robe." She handed him his pistol.

6

It was sunset when Buchanan wakened, dusk thickening behind the closed draperies. He stretched and enjoyed the feeling of having had a good meal, of having slept naked beneath smooth sheets, of having Holly's body next to him. She wore her robe. He'd discarded his own after making love. Exhaustion had been like a narcotic that made them stretch out and doze. She attracted him: her humor, her sensuous features, her tall, slender, athletic grace. But he had always made a point of never allowing his personal life to interfere with his work, of never becoming physically and emotionally involved with anyone on an assignment. It clouded your judgment. It . . .

Hell, you never had any personal life. There wasn't any *you* to have it. All you had were the identities you assumed.

And that's why you're here right now. That's what brought you this far. Because you kept that rule of being uninvolved when you worked with Juana, no matter how much you wanted her, and now you're searching for her, trying to make amends.

Are you going to make the same mistake again, this time with Holly?

What's wrong with me? he thought. Searching for one woman while I'm becoming attracted to another?

Get your mind straight.

He got out of bed, put on his robe, and walked over to a chair, next to which he stacked the books and files that Holly had given him. Setting a lamp on the floor where it wouldn't cast much light and wake Holly, he leaned back in the chair and began to read.

Two hours later, Holly raised her head, rubbed her eyes, and looked over at him.

"Hi." She smiled, lovely even after having just wakened.

"Hi."

"How are you?"

"Feeling as if I've just seen a ghost."

"I don't understand."

"This material you gave me. I think I know what's going on. I don't spook easily, but this makes me cold."

Holly sat up straight. "What are you talking about?"

"The photographs in these books. There's something about . . ."

Holly got out of bed, tied her robe, and came over quickly. "Show me." She pulled a chair next to his, then peered at the book in his lap. "What photographs?"

"This biography of Maria Tomez. I still have a lot to read, but one thing that's clear is that Frederick Maltin didn't just discover her and manage her. In a very real sense, he created her."

Holly looked curious, waiting for him to continue.

"I've never seen her perform," Buchanan said, "but from what I gather, Maria Tomez sings not just well but passionately. That's her reputation, a fiery, passionate diva. An opera critic wouldn't ever go this far, but to put it bluntly, Maria Tomez is . . ."

"Sexy," Holly said.

"That's the word. But look at these early photographs."

Buchanan turned pages in the book. "This is Maria Tomez at the beginning of her career. Before Frederick Maltin. When she was singing in Mexico and South America and none of the major critics was paying attention to her."

Buchanan placed his index finger on a photograph of a young, short, overweight, dark-skinned woman with an insecure look in her eyes, a broad nose, an unbecoming hairstyle, pudgy cheeks, and slightly crooked teeth.

"All that hair piled on top of her head," Holly said. "And the way her oversized costume hung on her, as if she was trying to hide the weight."

"The early reviews are unanimous about the quality of her voice, but it's obvious that the critics are holding back, trying to be kind, talking about her awkward stage presence," Buchanan said. "What they're really saying is that she's too frumpy to be treated seriously as a stage performer."

"Sexist but true," Holly said. "The big money goes to the women with a great voice *and* magnetism."

"The night Maltin saw her performing *Tosca* in Mexico City, Maria Tomez wasn't even scheduled. She was the understudy who had to step in when the production's star got sick."

"I wonder what Maltin saw in her."

"Someone to dominate. Someone to sculpt and shape. If Maltin had heard her perform under other circumstances, he wouldn't have associated her with a sexy role like Tosca. But once he did, he took advantage of the possibilities. According to this biography, no one had ever shown so much interest in her. Her career was going nowhere. What did she have to lose? She turned herself over to him. She gave him absolute obedience."

"And?"

"Look at these next few photographs. What do you notice?"

"Well, she's progressively thinner. And her costumes take advantage of that." Holly picked up the book to examine the photographs more closely. "Obviously her hairstyle's been changed. Instead of being piled on top of her head, it's now swept back. It's long and thick. It's loose and curled. There's a kind of wild abandon to it."

"As if a breeze is blowing it," Buchanan said. "As if she's

on a cliff and the sea is crashing below her. What's the word? Tempestuous? That's what I noticed, too. The hairstyle has a passionate look to it. Now check *this* photograph.''

Holly did and shook her head. "I don't know what . . .'' At once, Holly pointed. "Her nose. It's been narrowed and straightened.''

"And check *this* photograph taken three months later.''

"This time, I really don't get it,'' Holly said.

"She's smiling.''

"Right.''

"Is she smiling in the previous one?''

"No.''

"And in the one before that?''

"She's not smiling there, either, but in this first picture she is, and . . . Oh, my God,'' Holly said, "the teeth. They aren't the same. They're crooked at the start, and now . . . She's had them straightened and capped.''

"Or Frederick Maltin did,'' Buchanan said. "He promised her that within two years he'd have her career turned around. What none of the publicity mentions is how much physical alteration was necessary. In the next photograph, three months further along, her eyebrows are different. In the photograph after that, it looks as if something chemical or surgical has been done to her hair to raise the scalp line, to give her more forehead, to help proportion the rest of the face.''

"And all the while, she's been losing weight,'' Holly said with excitement. "Her wardrobe's been getting more stylish. The designs made her look taller. She's wearing expensive necklaces and earrings that glint and look good to the camera. *Those* changes attract the most attention, so the other, gradual, step-by-step changes become less noticeable. They're subtle and equally important, but done over a long enough period, they don't make anybody realize the degree to which she's been reconstructed.''

"Her fame was still growing,'' Buchanan said. "She wasn't under the same close scrutiny then that she would be in her prime, so a lot of the changes wouldn't have been noticed as she moved from opera house to opera house in various countries. Still, look at these later photographs, after she'd become a sensation. The changes continued. Here. Am I wrong, or has she had cosmetic surgery around her eyes to make them seem more intense? In *this* photograph, have her earlobes been shortened? There's something about them that's different and makes her face look more proportioned."

"Not only that, but her breasts seem higher," Holly said. "Possibly some kind of surgery there, as well. Her waist seems longer. This is amazing. At first, it just seems that she's maturing and glowing from her success. But I think you're right. She was being sculpted and shaped. Frederick Maltin created her."

"Once her body matched the passionate roles that Maltin wanted her to play, the critics paid more attention to her voice," Buchanan said. "She became an overnight sensation that took two years and who knows how many visits to dentists and surgeons. And all of a sudden, she wasn't awkward on stage—because she wasn't self-conscious about her appearance anymore. She'd been made beautiful, and she loved being adored. The more her audiences applauded, the better she improved her stage technique to encourage their applause. Her voice blossomed. She became rich. Or rather, she and Maltin became rich. Part of the deal was that she'd marry him. Not that I think Maltin cared about having sex with her. My guess is, he wanted to control her finances, and he could do that better as her husband in addition to being her manager. For fifteen years, he controlled her. Maybe he threatened to reveal the true story behind her success, to release before-and-after pictures, that sort of thing. Then one day at the start of this year, it became too much. She finally left him. She and Drummond met at a charity benefit in Monaco. They struck up a friendship. Drummond became her escort. Maybe he seemed safe to her. After all, he was old enough to be her grandfather. He was thousands of times richer. He probably didn't want sex. In fact, on the surface, there wasn't anything she could give him that he needed or didn't already have. So she kept seeing him, but the gossip photographers wouldn't leave them alone, and Drummond offered her a chance to get away from the public eye, to relax and regroup, to keep her picture out of the magazines, not to mention to be out of touch from the jerk she was divorcing. Drummond flew her to his yacht off the western coast of Mexico. A vacation in her home country. She stayed on board three weeks, flew back to New York, bought an apartment, retired from singing, and in effect, like Garbo, told the world that she wanted to be left alone.''

"Now months later, she disappears." Holly frowned. "And your friend who sometimes provided security for her disappears as well. What happened two weeks ago? What's going on?"

"I don't think it happened two weeks ago."

Holly didn't move for a moment. Then she straightened.

"I think it happened on the yacht," Buchanan said.

"*What* happened? I still don't—"

"The photocopies of the recent articles you gave me don't reproduce the pictures very well. But this page from yesterday's *Washington Post* has clear photographs. A shot of Maltin at his news conference. A recent shot of Maria Tomez during one of her infrequent public appearances. Dark glasses. Concealing hat."

"Tell me what you're getting at."

"It looks like Maria Tomez had some work done on her jawline. It's just a little different. And the ridges on her collarbone are a little different," Buchanan said.

"A nose job's one thing," Holly said. "But changing a jawline? Altering ridges on a collarbone? That's major reconstructive work."

"Exactly," Buchanan said. "This last photograph. I don't think it's Maria Tomez. The more I look at it . . . the more I'm sure it's Juana impersonating her."

7

"*But how is such a thing possible?*" Sounding frustrated, Holly drove rapidly along the busy expressway. Headlights blazed in the opposite lanes. "Sure, Montgomery had a double in the Second World War. Movie stars use doubles all the time. These days, theatrical makeup is so realistic that actors can believably change their appearance. But Montgomery wasn't showing up at society charity benefits. As far as the movies go, cameras can play a lot of tricks. This is different. We're talking about a critically acclaimed opera singer. I don't care how good the makeup was, no one could imitate that once-in-a-generation voice.''

"But Juana didn't have to," Buchanan said, still frozen by the implications of what he'd discovered.

Holly steered quickly around a truck and drove faster.

"The newspaper articles are emphatic," Buchanan said. "Maria Tomez retired from performing after she finished the cruise on Drummond's yacht. She went into seclusion in New York, except for brief public appearances, none of which involved singing. In some of these articles, she complains about having had pneumonia, about recurring laryngitis. The reporters note that her voice was hoarse. Since that's the one thing Juana couldn't have faked, she removed the problem by pretending to have problems with her voice. Otherwise, both women are Hispanics, with the same general build and facial characteristics. Maria Tomez kept changing her appearance in gradual ways, after all, so if Juana didn't look absolutely like her, it wouldn't have attracted attention. It would have been just another case of how Maria Tomez continued to change. As long as Juana's special makeup guaranteed that the similarities far outnumbered the differences. How many people know Maria Tomez intimately? Her ex-husband, whom she refused to see. Her other business contacts, whom she shut out after she retired. Her entourage, which she apparently changed after the cruise. Alistair Drummond, who continued to see her after the cruise and accepted her as Maria Tomez. We're talking about a woman who guarded her privacy to begin with. All Juana had to do was take a few phone calls from time to time, complain about a cold, appear briefly in public, get her picture in the paper, and no one would suspect that she wasn't the person she pretended to be.''

"Except you.'' Holly steered around another vehicle, squinting from the glare of headlights. "*You* suspected.''

"Because I had a reason to suspect. Because I'd seen the makeup room in Juana's house. Because I became more struck by Juana's resemblance to Maria Tomez as I looked at the photographs. Juana was on my mind, so I made the connection. What she did was brilliant. I can't get over what a genius she was at impersonating. I could never have done the equivalent.''

"The question is, Why?" Holly said. "Why did Juana impersonate her?"

"One common denominator is Alistair Drummond. The retirement, the need for seclusion, came after the cruise on Drummond's yacht. Drummond accepted Juana as Maria Tomez, and it was someone working for Drummond who paid Frederick Maltin to stop talking to reporters about his ex-wife. The disappearance . . . I think I understand," Buchanan said quickly.

The tone in his voice made Holly shiver. "What?"

"There were *two* disappearances."

"*Two?*"

"It wasn't Maria Tomez but *Juana* who disappeared a few weeks ago. Drummond's doing his damnedest to find her. *Why?* Because if I'm right, nine months ago Maria Tomez never got off Drummond's yacht. That was Juana, and Drummond doesn't want anyone to know about the switch."

Holly clenched the steering wheel. "What in God's name happened on that yacht?"

8

La Guardia Airport. To get there, they'd used Holly's car rather than a taxi because, after checking out of the Dorset, they didn't want to attract attention by leaving her car in the hotel's garage for an indefinite period. At the airport's parking ramp, however, it wasn't unusual for cars to be left for quite a while.

They'd been forced to rush. They had needed luck with reservations and traffic. Nonetheless, they'd managed to get two tickets on the last flight out of La Guardia for Miami, and although they got to the boarding gate with only seconds to spare, that didn't matter. The point was, they were on the plane.

During the flight, both were too tense to sleep. They had no appetite. Still, they ate the lasagna the airline served, needing to maintain their strength.

"Your itinerary. Cancún, Mérida, and Fort Lauderdale," Holly said.

"I've never admitted to being in any of those places," Buchanan told her.

"But the rest aren't in doubt. Washington, New Orleans, San Antonio, Washington again, New York, now Miami and points south. All in two weeks. Hanging around with you could be exhausting. And this is normal for you."

"Better get used to it."

"I think I'd like that."

Back at the Dorset, Buchanan had wondered if the home port for Drummond's yacht would be the same as the city where Drummond's corporate headquarters were located. Knowing that all large vessels were required to file a float plan indicating the length and itinerary of an intended voyage, he had phoned the Coast Guard in San Francisco. However, the officer on duty told him that the yacht was based somewhere else—they didn't have a float plan for it. Buchanan had then phoned the National Association of Insurance Underwriters at its main offices in Long Beach, California. Eight P.M. eastern time had been 5:00 P.M. Pacific time. He made contact just before the office closed.

"My name's Albert Drake." He pretended to be agitated. "My brother, Rick, works on . . . God, I can't remember. . . . The *Poseidon*. That's it." Buchanan knew the name from the research Holly had given him. "Alistair Drummond owns it. A two-hundred-foot yacht. But Rick didn't leave an itinerary. Our mother's had a stroke. I have to get in touch with him, but I don't know how else . . . The Coast Guard suggested . . ."

Large vessels require such large amounts of insurance that the underwriters for the insurance companies insist on knowing where those vessels are at all times. As soon as Drummond's yacht reached a new berth, its captain was obligated to report his location to the insurance officials.

9

KEY WEST

After arriving in Miami past midnight, Buchanan and Holly used Charles Duffy's credit card to rent a car and began the

150-mile drive south along the Florida Keys. During the trip, they stopped for takeout coffee and alternated driving while the other dozed, mercury-vapor lights along the extensive forty-two bridges of the Overseas Highway hurting their eyes and adding to their fatigue.

It was just before dawn when they arrived at their destination, the southernmost community in the continental United States. Key West, only four miles long and one and a half miles wide, had a permanent population of almost thirty thousand. One of the last bastions of the counterculture in America, the sand-and-coral island remained synonymous with the unorthodox lifestyle of Hemingway, who had once lived there and whose home—with its numerous cats supposedly descended from the novelist's original pets—was a National Historic Landmark. The town's atmosphere and architecture were an exotic blend of Bahamian, West Indian, and Cuban influences. It was known for its deep-sea fishing and its tropical foods. There was a U.S. naval air station. John James Audubon once had been in residence, also Harry Truman. The singer-novelist Jimmy Buffet was its most famous current spokesman.

But there was only one thing in Key West that Buchanan cared about, and after he and Holly caught a few more hours of sleep at a cheap motel that accepted cash in advance (he was getting nervous about using Charles Duffy's credit card), they cleaned up, ate, then got down to business. An hour's stroll around the crowded harbor, where they bought sandals, short-sleeved pullovers, and cutoff jeans so they wouldn't be conspicuous, gave Buchanan ample chance to pose seemingly casual questions to vendors and fishermen. Soon he and Holly were able to stand on the wharf, lean forward against the railing, breathe the humid, tangy salt air, and study their target.

Drummond's yacht, gleaming white against the green-blue of the Gulf of Mexico, was anchored a hundred yards offshore. Two hundred feet long, with three decks and a helicopter pad on the top (the chopper had taken off a few days earlier, heading south, Buchanan had been told by a fisherman), the yacht should have inspired awe, but instead it made Buchanan feel cold despite the eighty-five-degree temperature. The sleekly styled profile seemed threatening, like the curved tip of a massive hunting knife. The large sunning area at the stern, with windows providing a view from the upper decks, made Buchanan think of voyeurs and exhibitionists. Regardless of its resplendent white exterior, the yacht appeared cloaked in a black pall of gloom.

"Sometimes," Holly said, "when you're deep in thought, your eyes and face change. You look like a stranger."

"How?"

"Solemn. Troubled."

"Just so we understand each other, this has nothing to do with Maria Tomez," Buchanan said. "I want to know what happened to her, yes. But more than anything, I want to know what happened to Juana." He turned his attention from the yacht and focused on Holly, who concentrated on his gaze, confused. "A lot of this doesn't make sense to me. What I feel about you, for example. But I have to settle old accounts before I start new ones. After this is over, you and I can talk about what we have."

Her red hair blowing in the wind, Holly thought about what he had said, then nodded. "I never assumed there were any guarantees. I never planned this. I got swept along. Fine. We understand each other. First things first. So now that we've found the yacht, what do we do?"

"You noticed the way I spoke to the fishermen and vendors in the area? A little conversation combined with a few well-chosen questions. The technique is called elicitation. It's the equivalent of what you'd call doing an interview. But the difference is that *your* subjects almost always know they're being interviewed, whereas *my* subjects must never know. Sometimes, if they realize they're being pumped for information, their reaction can be lethal."

Holly listened attentively.

"I thought you might be offended because I'm telling you how to do an interview," Buchanan said.

"This whole thing's been a learning experience. Why should it stop now?"

"Good," Buchanan said. "Okay, elicitation." He told her about his training, how he'd been required to practice by going into bars and striking up conversations with strangers, getting them to reveal such intimate data as their Social Security numbers and their birth dates, not only month but year.

"How did you manage that?" Holly asked. "I'd have thought you were snooping."

"I'd sit next to my target, have a few drinks, make small talk, comment on the television program that was showing above the bar, and at one point say that I'd learned something interesting today. The response, of course, would be, 'What?' I'd pull out my wallet and show him my forged Social Security card. 'These numbers all mean something,' I'd say. 'I thought they were assigned sequentially, but if you break down each group, you see that the numbers tell all kinds of things like when and where I was born. See, this number means I came from Pittsburgh, and this group of numbers was assigned to whoever was born in 1960, and this number here tells which month, and . . . Here, I'll show you. What's your number? I'll bet you a dollar I can tell you where and when you were born.' "

Holly shook her head in amazement. "Is that really true?"

"That I was trained that way?"

"No. About the Social Security number."

"What's yours? Let's see if I can tell you when and where you were born."

Holly laughed. "It works. You make up a place and date, and to show how wrong you are, the person you're interviewing tells you the information you want. Slick."

"Elicitation," Buchanan repeated. "The art of extracting information without allowing your target to realize that you're extracting it. It's a standard method used by operatives trying to obtain military, political, and industrial secrets. It usually happens in bars, and the targets are usually assistants, secretaries, officers of lower rank, the kind of people who might feel frustrated in their positions and don't mind talking about their problems at work, provided they're stimulated with proper subtlety. A few drinks. A show of interest. One piece of information leads to another. It usually takes time, several meetings, but sometimes it can be done quickly, and in this case, it has to be because I have to find out what's happened to Juana. If she's still alive . . ." Buchanan's voice tightened. "If she's still alive, I have to get the pressure off her."

Holly studied him. "What do we do?"

"What *you* have to do is be just what you are: sexy and desirable."

Holly looked puzzled.

"While we've been talking, a launch from Drummond's yacht has been coming toward shore. Three crew members are on board."

Squinting from sunlight off the water, Holly followed Buchanan's gaze.

"We'll watch where they go," Buchanan said. "Maybe they're in town on an errand. But maybe this is their day off. If they go into a bar, I'll . . ."

10

"Damn it, I didn't want to drive all this way in the first place," Buchanan said. "What's in it for me? Every time I turn around, you're winking at some young stud with a bulge in his shorts."

"Keep your voice down," Holly said.

"Harry warned me about you. He said to watch you every second. He said you'd screw any male old enough to get an erection, the younger the better."

"Keep your voice down," Holly said more strongly.

"I notice you don't deny it. You just don't want anybody to know the truth."

"Stop it," Holly warned. "You're embarrassing me."

They were in the Coral Reef Bar, sitting in a corner that had fishing nets on one wall and a stuffed marlin on the other. The small circular table had a cloth with wavy lines and numbers that made it look like a nautical chart. The ceiling lights were chandeliers that resembled the rudder wheel on a ship.

Buchanan slumped in a captain's chair and swallowed half a glass of beer. "Keep my voice down. That's all you say. I'll make you a deal. I'll keep my voice down if you keep your pants on. Waiter, two more beers."

"I'm not thirsty," Holly said.

"Did I say I was ordering for you? Waiter! I've changed my mind. Make it a bourbon on the rocks."

"You already had two at the other place. Two beers here and . . . Dave, it's only noon, for God's sake."

"Just shut up, okay?" Buchanan slammed the table. "I'll drink when I want to. If you'd stop jumping into bed with every—"

"Sir," a voice said, "you're disturbing the other customers."

"Tough shit."

"Sir," the man said, a *big* man, blond, with a brush cut and muscles straining at his T-shirt, "if you don't keep your voice down, I'm going to have to ask you to leave."

"Ask all you want, pal, but I'm staying right here." Buchanan swallowed the rest of his beer and yelled to the waiter, "Where's that bourbon?"

People were staring.

"Dave," Holly said.

Buchanan slammed the table again. "I told you, shut the fuck up!"

"Okay," the big man said. "Let's go, buddy."

"Hey!" Buchanan objected as the big man grabbed him. "What the—?" Jerked to his feet, pretending to stagger, Buchanan fell against the table, upsetting glasses. "Jesus, watch my arm. You're breaking it."

"I'd like to, buddy."

As the big man twisted Buchanan's arm behind his back and guided him toward the exit, Buchanan glared backward toward Holly. "What are you waiting for? Let's go."

Holly didn't answer.

"I said, let's go!"

Holly still didn't answer. She flinched as Buchanan kept shouting from outside the bar. Slowly, she raised her beer glass to her lips, sipped, squinted at her trembling hand, lowered the glass, and wiped at her eyes.

"Are you all right?"

Holly looked up at a good-looking, tanned, slender man in his twenties who wore a white uniform.

She didn't answer.

"Hey, I really don't mean to bother you," the man said. "You've had enough of that already. But you do look a little shook up. If there's anything I can do . . . Can I buy you another drink?''

Holly wiped at her eyes again, straightening, trying to look dignified. She directed her gaze, frightened, toward the door. "Please."

"Another beer for the lady."

"And . . ."

"What?"

"I'm . . . I'd really appreciate it if you could make sure he doesn't hurt me when I leave."

11

Buchanan leaned against the railing on the dock. Surrounded by the activity of tourists and fishermen, he wouldn't be noticed as he watched the launch cutting through the green-blue water, passing cabin cruisers and fishing boats, returning to the three-decked, two-hundred-foot-long gleaming white yacht that was anchored beyond the other vessels, a hundred yards offshore. The overhead sun was now behind him, so he didn't have to squint from the reflection of sunlight off the Gulf of Mexico. He had no trouble seeing that among the three crew members returning to the yacht, a gorgeous redheaded woman was chatting agreeably with them, one of the crew members allowing her to put her hand on the wheel of the launch's controls.

As they boarded the yacht, Buchanan nodded, glanced around to make sure he wasn't being watched, and strolled away. Or seemed to. The fact is that as he wandered along the Key West dock, he persistently, subtly studied the yacht, pretending to take pictures of the town, using the telephoto lens on Holly's camera as a telescope. After all, Holly might get in trouble over there, although she'd been adamant that she was able to take care of herself. Even so, if she came out onto one of the decks and looked agitated, he had told her he would get to her as fast as he could.

Near five o'clock, the launch left the yacht again, coming toward shore: the same three crew members and Holly. She got out on the dock, kissed one of the men on the cheek, ruffled another's hair, hugged the third, and walked with apparent contentment into town.

Buchanan reached their small, shadowy motel room a minute before she did. Worry made the time seem longer.

"How did it go?" he asked with concern as she came in.

She took off her sandals and sat on the bed, looking exhausted. "They sure had trouble keeping their hands to themselves. I had to stay on the move. I feel like I've been running a marathon."

"Do you want a drink of water? How about some of this fruit I bought?"

"Yeah, some fruit would be nice. An orange or . . . Great." She sipped from the Perrier he brought her. "Is this what you call a debriefing?"

"Yes. If this was business."

"Isn't it? You make the agent you've recruited feel comfortable and wanted. Then you . . ."

"Hey, not everything I do is calculated."

"Oh?" Holly studied him for a moment. "Good. In that case, the yacht. There are fifteen crew members. They take turns coming ashore. They think Drummond's—to quote one of the crew members—a domineering asshole. He scares them. While he's aboard. But when the cat's away, the mice play, sometimes bringing women aboard. To show off the yacht and get even with Drummond for the way he abuses them."

Buchanan set a pencil and a notepad on the dingy table. "Draw a diagram for the layout of each room on each deck. I need to know where everything is, where and when the crew eat and sleep, every detail you can think of. I know you're tired, Holly. I'm sorry, but this is going to take a while."

12

It wasn't difficult getting a wet suit. There were plenty of dive shops in Key West. The water was warm enough that Buchanan normally wouldn't have needed to rent the insulating suit, but the stitches in his side made this an abnormal situation. He needed to protect the healing knife wound. He wanted to minimize the amount of blood that would dissolve from the scabs around the stitches and disperse through the water. As in Cancún, when he'd escaped the police by swimming across the channel from the island to the mainland, he worried about sharks and barracuda. Back then, of course, it had been blood from a bullet wound that had worried him, but the difference was the same. At least this time he'd been able to prepare, although another element from the Cancún swim continued to trouble him—his headache.

His skull wouldn't stop throbbing. He felt as if his nerves were leather cords being stretched to the snapping point. But he couldn't let the pain distract him. He had to keep going, swimming through the 3:00 A.M. water, his black wet suit blending with the night. He kept his arms loose at his sides, moving his feet gently, stroking with his fins, trying anxiously not to make noise or create whitecaps in the water. He kept his face down as much as possible, even though he had blackened it before leaving shore so that it wouldn't contrast with the dark water. The stars glistened. A quarter moon was beginning to rise. That would be enough light for him as he eased closer to the yacht.

Then he touched the anchor chain. Peering up, he heard no footsteps or voices. Although the wet suit made the water feel even warmer than it was, he shivered involuntarily, his testicles receding toward his groin. He squinted back toward the lights of Key West, thought of Holly waiting for him, mustered his resolve, took off his mask and flippers, tied them to the chain, and began to climb. The effort strained his shoulder and his side. But he had to keep moving. Slowly, soundlessly, he pulled himself up the chain until he reached where it went into the hull. The hole was too small for him to enter, but it and the bulky chain gave him places to wedge his mesh rubber slippers while he fought for balance, reached up, and grasped the edge of the bow. Drawing himself up, he peered over the edge, saw no one, looked for intrusion detectors, saw no evidence of them either, and squirmed over the railing onto the softly lit deck.

As he scurried for cover beneath an exterior stairway, he knew he'd left a trail of water, but that couldn't be avoided.

Fortunately, most of the water had drained from his wet suit while he'd climbed. Soon the remainder would stop trickling out. Until then, he had to take advantage of the time he had.

A few windows were lit on the decks that loomed above him. The stairways, corridors, and walkways had lights as well. But they glowed, separate enough and weakly enough that there were abundant shadows into which Buchanan could creep. The mesh rubber slippers that he'd worn beneath his fins had ridges along the soles that gave them traction. He left almost no water as he made his way softly along a walkway, into a corridor, and up a stairwell.

He followed Holly's instructions. Her description of the yacht's layout had been detailed. So had her assessment of the crew, who evidently were unmotivated when the master wasn't there to intimidate them. Buchanan listened intently, heard no one, emerged from the stairwell, and crept along a corridor on the middle deck, passing doors on each side. Only one door attracted him—at the end on the right. Holly had said that was the one area the crew hadn't shown her.

"Off limits," they'd told her.

"Why?" she had asked.

"We don't know. It's always locked," had been the answer.

The door was situated between the door to Drummond's sleeping quarters on the right and the door to the yacht's reception area, a large, luxuriously appointed room that occupied a third of this level and had windows that looked down on the sun deck at the stern.

"Well, you must have *some* idea what's in there," Holly had said to the crew members.

"None. We were told we'd lose our jobs if we ever tried to get in."

The door had two double-bolt locks. Buchanan removed two short metal prongs from a pocket of the wet suit. He'd finished picking the first lock when he heard footsteps on the stairway at the opposite end of the corridor. Fighting to keep his hands steady, he worked the pins in the second lock.

The footsteps came lower, closer.

Buchanan didn't dare look in that direction. He had to keep concentrating on the lock, manipulating the metal prongs.

The footsteps were almost to the bottom.

Buchanan turned the knob, slipped into the murky room, and closed the door. He held his breath, pressed an ear against the bulkhead, and listened. After thirty seconds, still not having heard any sound from the corridor, he found a light switch, flicked it, and blinked from the sudden illumination.

What he saw made him frown. In this narrow room, which was connected by a locked door to Alistair Drummond's sleeping quarters, there were several rows of television monitors and videotape recorders.

Buchanan turned down the sound controls, then activated the monitors. In a moment, the glowing screens revealed numerous rooms and sections of decks. On one screen, he watched two crewmen in the control room. On another screen, he saw two other crew members watching television. On a third screen, he saw a half-dozen crew members sleeping on bunks. On a fourth, he saw a man—presumably the captain—sleeping in a room that he had to himself. On other screens, Buchanan saw numerous empty bedrooms. Those dark rooms and the others in which people slept appeared in a green tint, an indication that a night-vision lens was being used on the hidden cameras that monitored those areas. The monitors that showed exterior sections of the yacht were also tinted green. Presumably, the cameras would automatically convert to a normal lens when the indoor lights were on or during daylight.

So Alistair Drummond likes to eavesdrop on his guests, Buchanan thought. The old man goes into his bedroom, locks his door, unlocks the door to this adjacent room, and comes in here to see what his crew is doing when he isn't around—more important, to see what his guests are up to: undressing, relieving themselves, fucking, doing drugs, whatever. And all of it can be recorded for repeated viewing enjoyment.

Buchanan directed his attention to a locked metal cabinet. After picking its lock, he opened the cabinet and found row upon row of labeled videotapes. August 5, 1988. October 10, 1989. February 18, 1990. Buchanan glanced quickly over them, noting that they were arranged sequentially. At least a hundred. Alistair Drummond's greatest hits.

The cruise Buchanan wanted to know about had occurred

during February. He found a tape for that month, put it into a
player, and pressed the ON button, making sure that the sound
was off. The video quality was remarkably clear, even when the
images had a greenish tint. The cruise had been well attended.
Various shots of numerous locations showed guests in their
most intimate, revealing, compromising positions. Oral sex and
sodomy were especially popular. Buchanan eventually counted
thirteen men and twelve women. The men—in middle age—
had an overbearing manner, as if addicted to wielding power.
The women were attractive, well dressed, and treated as if they
were hookers. All the men and women were Hispanic.

Buchanan noticed an earplug and inserted it into the television monitor. After adjusting the sound, he was able to hear
what was on the tape. As he concentrated to translate the
Spanish voices, he realized from comments they made that the
women were indeed hookers and that the men were high-rank-
ing members of the Mexican government. At once he realized
something else. These tapes weren't intended merely for Drummond's voyeuristic pleasure.

Blackmail crossed Buchanan's mind at the same time he
reacted with shock to the sight of Maria Tomez on the screen.
At least, he believed it was Maria Tomez. Thinking about
doubles, he couldn't be sure. He needed to study the image
carefully before he was convinced that it was definitely Maria
Tomez and not Juana impersonating her. The night-vision lens
tinted the image green. It showed what appeared to be the sun
deck at the rear of the yacht. The angle was from above,
downward, as if the camera had been hidden in an upper wall
or beneath an elevated walkway. A digital display indicated
that the time the tape had been made was 1:37 A.M. The sound
track was somewhat crackly. Nonetheless, Buchanan was able
to hear distant party music, a woman laughing faintly.

Maria Tomez, wearing an elegant low-cut evening gown,
leaned against the stern's railing, her back to the camera, apparently watching the wake of the ship. A man spoke to her in
Spanish, and she turned. A tall, slender, thin-faced, hawk-
nosed Hispanic male wearing a dinner jacket stepped into view.
He spoke again. This time, Maria Tomez answered. The quality
of the sound became better, presumably because Drummond
had used a remote control to adjust the directional microphone

hidden on the sun deck. "No, I'm not cold," Maria Tomez said in Spanish.

The camera zoomed in as the man approached her.

13

"My God," Holly said. She watched the tape and felt sick. "Jesus."

Dismayed, Buchanan had made a copy of the tape and then sealed the copy in a plastic bag that he'd found in the room. Otherwise, he had left everything the way he had found it. Muscles rigid from tension, he had locked the door behind him and crept down to the main deck. His head had continued to ache all the while he'd climbed down the anchor chain, retrieved his mask and fins from where he'd tied them, and swam back to shore, this time on his back, keeping the tape above water.

The tape ended, and Holly continued to stare at the screen in disgust. "God damn him to hell."

What she had seen on a video player that Buchanan had rented when he returned to the motel was the rape and murder of Maria Tomez. Or possibly the sequence was in the reverse—murder and then rape, if it was possible to rape—as opposed to violate—a corpse. *Rape* implied overcoming someone's will, whereas a corpse couldn't object to anything, and perhaps the latter was what the tall, slender, hawk-nosed man had liked, an absolute lack of resistance.

The man had approached Maria Tomez, asking again if she felt cold. He'd put his arm around her with the pretense of warming her. Maria Tomez had taken his arm away. The man had persisted, and Maria Tomez had begun to struggle. "Now, now," the man had said drunkenly, "you must not be cold to *me*. I forbid it." He had chuckled, pinning her with his arms, kissing her face and neck, trying to kiss the tops of her breasts while she squirmed and twisted her face from side to side and tried to push him away. "Be warm," he had said in Spanish. "Be warm. *I* am warm. Can you feel it?" He had chuckled again. When she shoved at him, he had laughed and shaken her. When she slapped his face, he had punched her. She had spat at him. "*Puta*," he had said and struck her with an uppercut that jolted her up, and then back, then down. As she toppled, he grabbed for her, his fingers catching the top of her gown, ripping, exposing her breasts. As the back of her skull hit the deck, he lunged and kept ripping, exposing her stomach, her groin, her thighs, her knees. He tore off her lacy underwear. For a moment, he paused. The camera showed Maria Tomez motionless, naked on her back on the deck, her dress spread out on either side like broken wings. The man's paralysis lasted another second. Abruptly he opened his belt, dropped his pants, and fell upon her. His breathing was rapid and hoarse. His buttocks kept pumping. Then he moaned and slumped and chuckled. "Now do you feel warm?" She didn't answer. He nudged her. She didn't move. He slapped her again. When she still didn't move, he groped to his knees, grasped her face, squeezed her cheeks, twisted her head from side to side, and breathed more hoarsely. Urgently he stood, buckled his pants, glanced furtively around, lifted Maria Tomez to her feet.

And with an expression that combined fear with disgust, he threw her overboard.

As Holly continued to stare in dismay at the static-filled screen, Buchanan stepped past her to shut off the VCR and the television. Only then did Holly move. She lowered her gaze and shook her head. Buchanan slumped in a chair.

"Was she dead?" Holly asked quietly. "When he dropped her into the water?"

"I don't know." Buchanan hesitated. "He might have broken her neck when he hit her. She might have suffered a fatal concussion when her skull struck the deck. He might have smothered her while he was on top of her. But she might also have been in shock, catatonic, still alive when he threw her into the water. The son of a bitch didn't even take the trouble to make sure. He didn't care if she was alive. All he cared about was himself. He'd used her. Then he threw her away. Like a sack of garbage."

The room was dark. They sat in silence for quite a while.

"So what happened next?" Holly asked bitterly. "What do you figure?"

"The man who killed her probably thought he could convince people that she fell off the yacht. He was drunk, of course, and that would have affected his judgment in several ways. Either he would have had the false confidence to report having seen her fall or else a part of his mind would have warned him to go to his cabin, sober up, and seem as confused as everybody else when Maria Tomez was reported missing. Then he could have plausibly suggested that perhaps she'd been drinking, had lost her balance, and fallen over the railing.''

"Except that Alistair Drummond knew the truth," Holly said.

Buchanan nodded. "He'd watched everything on the monitor in his private video-surveillance room. And a tape of a rape/homicide is so much more useful than oral sex, sodomy, and drug use when you want to blackmail a member of the Mexican government. Drummond must have been delighted. I imagine him going to her murderer, revealing what's on the tape, and arranging a cover-up in exchange for certain favors. The initial stage wouldn't have been difficult. All Drummond needed to do was order his pilot to fly the yacht's helicopter to the mainland. Then Drummond could have told his guests that Maria Tomez had left the cruise early. They'd have no reason to suspect differently.''

"After that, though," Holly said.

"Yes, after that," Buchanan said. "Drummond must have felt inspired when he thought of Juana. Perhaps Maria Tomez had told him about the clever way she had of avoiding tedious social events by using Juana to double for her. Perhaps Drummond found out another way. For certain, though, he did find out. He needn't have told Juana anything incriminating. All he had to do was explain that Maria Tomez wanted absolute privacy and offer Juana an irresistible amount of money to impersonate Maria Tomez for an extended period of time.''

"So complicated and yet so simple," Holly said. "If I weren't so disgusted, I'd call it brilliant.''

"But what does Drummond want from the person he's blackmailing?" Buchanan said. "Obviously not money. Drummond's so rich, it's hard to imagine that money alone would motivate him, especially the comparatively small amount that even a wealthy Mexican politician could give him. You're a reporter. Do you recognize the man on the tape?''

Holly shook her head. "Mexico isn't my specialty. I wouldn't know one of its politicians from another."

"But we can find out." Buchanan stood.

"How?"

"We're going back to Miami." His voice was like flint against steel. "Then we're flying to Mexico City."

14

'This is Buttercup." Clutching the phone, speaking urgently, the husky-voiced woman used the code name she'd been assigned.

On the other end of the line, a man's sleep-thickened voice was tinged with annoyance. "What time is . . . ? Lord, it's almost five in the morning. I got to bed only an hour ago."

"I'm sorry. This was the first chance I had to call."

"They've been looking everywhere for you." The man had said his name was Alan, although he was probably using a pseudonym.

"That's what I was afraid of. Is it safe to talk?"

"This call is being relayed from another phone," Alan said. "The two phones are linked by scramblers. Why are you calling me? I told you it had to be an emergency."

"I'm with Leprechaun." The woman used the code name they'd agreed upon.

"Yes. I assumed."

"You have to understand. He's been telling the truth. What he's doing has no involvement with . . ." She tactfully didn't mention Scotch and Soda.

"I assumed that as well. I believe he genuinely wants out. It's his superiors who need reassurance."

"But *how*?"

"It's a little late to ask that," Alan said. "You're part of the problem, after all. If you'd stayed away from him . . ."

"But in Washington, he came to *me*."

"Same difference. You're together. Guilt by association. His superiors believe that the two of you reneged on your bargain not to publicize their activities."

"This has nothing to do with their activities. How do I get that across to . . . ? Should I phone them? Give me a number to call and . . ."

"No," Alan said sharply. "You'll only make things worse. They can instantly trace any call you make. You'd be guiding them to you."

"Then what do I do?"

"Sever ties with Leprechaun," Alan said. "Go to ground. Wait until I tell you it's safe to reappear."

"But that could take *months*."

"True."

"Damn it, I wish I'd never listened to you. When you approached me, I should have told you I wasn't interested."

"Ah, but you couldn't," Alan said. "The story was too good to ignore."

"And now it might get me killed."

"Not if you're careful. Not if you stop making mistakes. There's still a way to salvage things."

"You son of a bitch," she said. "You're still thinking of the story."

"I'm thinking of approaching another journalist who might be interested in telling *your* story. That would draw so much attention to you that they wouldn't dare make a move to have you eliminated. I could bring you in. The two of us could still get what we want."

"What *you* want. All *I* want is a normal life. Whatever that is. Lord, I'm not sure anymore."

"You should have thought of that before you accepted my information," Alan said. "But I repeat, if you're careful, if you do what I tell you, I think I can eventually bring you in safely. For now, go to ground. Assume another identity."

"And what about Leprechaun?"

Alan didn't answer.

"I asked you, what about Leprechaun?" Holly said.

"Sometimes we can't get everything we want."

"What are you talking about?"

"I never wanted this to happen. Really. I'd hoped that . . . He's a soldier. He'd understand more than you. Sometimes there are . . ."

"What?"

"Casualties."

As Holly turned from staring at the phone in the booth down the lane from her room in the Key West motel, she saw a man's shadow next to ferns in the predawn gray. In the numerous palm trees, birds began to chirp.

"I can't talk anymore," Holly said into the phone.

"Trouble?" Alan asked.

"Let's just say I didn't win the Publisher's Clearing House Sweepstakes."

Holly set down the phone.

Buchanan stepped out of the shadows. Despite a predawn breeze off the ocean, the air was humid.

"I thought you were taking back the wet-suit gear," Holly said.

"I was. I paid the motel clerk to return it for me when the dive shop opens." Buchanan stopped before her. "Who were you calling?"

She glanced away from him.

"At least you're not trying to lie," Buchanan said. "And at least you had brains enough not to make the call from the motel room, where there'd be a record on the bill. Not that it matters. The area's so small that automatic tracing equipment will tell our hunters we're in Key West."

"No," Holly said. "The number I called is private. Your people wouldn't know about it."

"So *you* say. In my business, I don't take anything for granted unless I do it myself. *All* phones are suspect. It must have been really important for you to make the call."

"I did it for us."

"Oh?"

"I was trying to get us out of at least part of the mess we're in," Holly said.

"What part is that? Right now, it seems we've got plenty of mess to go around."

Holly bit her lip. "Shouldn't we talk about this when we're back in our room?"

"And give you time to think up believable answers? No, I think we ought to keep talking." Buchanan grasped her arm. "Exactly what part of the mess were you trying to get us out of?"

He guided her along the lane. The sky was less gray. The breeze was stronger. Birds scattered into the sky.

"All right, I've been wanting to tell you since we were in New York," Holly said. "God, I'm so relieved to . . . At the start, the reason I knew you were in Cancún, the reason I was able to get to Club Internacional ahead of time and watch you talk to those two . . ." She almost said "drug distributors," then looked around the shadowy lane and chose other language, wary of being too specific before she reached their room. ". . . businessmen. The reason I . . ."

"Someone in my unit set me up." Buchanan opened the squeaky door to their room.

Holly spun in surprise. "You knew that?"

"It was the only explanation that made sense. Someone on the inside. No one else could have known where I'd be. The same person who told you about Yellow Fruit, Seaspray, the Intelligence Support Activity, and Scotch and Soda. That information could have come only from one of my superiors."

Still grasping Holly's arm, Buchanan led her into the room, turned on the light, closed the door, locked it, and guided her to the bed. He set her down firmly. "Who?" he asked.

Holly fidgeted.

"*Who?*"

"What will you do? Beat it out of me?"

"No." Buchanan studied her. "Cut my losses." He put his toilet kit into his travel bag, glanced around the room to make sure that he hadn't forgotten anything, and walked toward the door. "There are buses that'll take you back to Miami."

"Wait."

Buchanan kept walking.

"Wait. I don't know his real name. I only know him as Alan."

Buchanan paused. "Medium height. Chubby face. Short brown hair. Early forties."

"Yes. That's him."

"I know him. He was my controller a while ago. He's with the . . ."

The hesitation seemed to be a test for Holly. She decided to fill in the gap. "The Agency."

Buchanan seemed reassured by her candor. He walked toward the bed. "Keep talking."

"He was very straightforward about what he wanted. He doesn't approve of the military's involvement in civilian intelligence operations. American servicemen, armed, in civilian clothes, using false ID, conducting Agency operations in foreign countries. It's bad enough to have a civilian caught as a spy. But a member of Army Special Forces? On active duty? Pretending to be a civilian? On a strike team intended to topple unfriendly foreign governments or engage in an unsanctioned private war against major drug dealers? If the public realized how out of control the relationship between the CIA and the military had become, Congress would be forced into a major investigation of American intelligence tactics. The Agency is under enough pressure as it is. One more controversy and it might be replaced by an intelligence bureau with stricter limits. That's what Alan's afraid of. So he came to me and gave me certain information, insisting that he never be named, that he be cited only as a reliable government source. To make my story look less like a setup, he didn't tell me everything. He gave me just enough hints that my work in checking them out and linking them would provide me with evidence to maintain the fiction that I'd come up with the story on my own. . . . Why are you looking at me like that?"

"It doesn't make sense. If Alan was afraid that exposing the Agency's use of unauthorized military action would threaten the Agency, why the hell would he give you the story? It's exactly what he doesn't want."

"No." Holly shook her head. "He was very specific about that, and I agreed. You and *only* you were to be the object lesson."

"Oh, Christ," Buchanan said.

"The idea was that I'd expose you as a single example of the dangerous use of the military in civilian intelligence operations. The government wouldn't have any more information than what was in my story. I'd testify that I didn't know anything further. The congressional investigation would eventually end. But the message would be clear. If the CIA was using military strike teams, it had better stop, or else the

Agency and certain Special Operations units would be severely limited, if not disbanded. Careers would be destroyed.''

"Sure." Buchanan's voice was strained. "And in the meantime, you'd be a journalist celebrity. And Alan would have the shop back in his control."

"That was the idea," Holly said.

"Politics." Buchanan made the word sound like a curse.

"But it's not the idea any longer."

"What are you talking about?"

"That's why I phoned Alan," Holly said. "To cancel my agreement with him. I told him I wanted out. I told him I wanted to talk to your superiors, to assure them that what we're doing isn't related to them, that you aren't a risk to them and neither am I."

"You honestly expected he'd go along? No hard feelings? Nice try? We can't win 'em all? That sort of thing? Jesus."

"Alan told me he was sorry things got out of hand."

"I bet."

"We're still being hunted. He suggested I distance myself from you while he figures out a way to bring me in."

"Damned good advice." Buchanan squinted. "Distance yourself."

"No," Holly said. "I won't let you go."

"Just how the hell do you think you're going to stop me?"

"Follow."

"Lots of luck. What is it with you? You still think I'm a front-page story?"

No answer.

"Then maybe you figure it's safer to stay with me and run from them than to try to do it by yourself."

Still no answer.

"Look, I don't have time to guess what you're thinking. I've got to get out of Key West before your phone call brings a hit team down here."

"You."

"What?" Buchanan frowned.

"You," Holly said. "That's why I want to go with you."

"Make sense."

"I can't make it any plainer. I want to be with you. It's not just because I feel safe with you, although I do. It's . . . I didn't expect you to be what you are. I didn't expect to feel attracted to you. I didn't expect that I'd get so used to being with you that my stomach cramps at the thought of you going away."

"Now who's playing a role?"

"I'm telling the truth! I got *used* to you. And as long as we're spreading blame around, don't forget you're the one who came to me the second time. I wouldn't be in danger if you hadn't decided to use me. Hell, in Washington I saved your life. That ought to prove something."

"Yeah, and I'm so wonderful that you fell in love with me."

She started to say something.

"Save your energy," Buchanan said. "You're going to get your wish."

Holly's eyes widened in surprise.

"I can't leave you behind," Buchanan said. "I just realized I made a mistake. I told you where I was going."

"Yes. Mexico City," Holly said.

"Because of Juana, I can't change my plans. I swore I'd help her if she ever needed me, and I intend to keep that promise. Which means I can't let you wander around until you're caught and you tell them where I've gone and what I'm doing. Pack. I want to get off this island before they get here."

Holly breathed out. "Thanks."

"Don't thank me. This isn't a favor. As soon as I think you're no longer a risk to me, I'm cutting you loose. But in the meantime, Holly, pay attention. Take this advice. Do not force me to treat you as an enemy."

15

THE YUCATÁN PENINSULA

A pall of smoke clung to the massive clearing. As construction proceeded, the crackle of gunshots punctuated the roar of bulldozers, cranes, and other heavy machinery. So did the crackle of flames, the source of the smoke that filled the area. Trees were being burned back, the clearing widened, anything to reduce the cover from which natives—descendants of the original Maya—persisted in their attacks on the construction crew and the equipment. The scattered stones of the leveled ruins of once-magnificent towering pyramids and temples still lay among the towers that had replaced them, these made of steel. Occasionally the earth tremored, but the workers and guards no longer paid attention. As with the snakes, the smoke, and the gunshots, those who labored here had become used to anything. The job mattered. Completing it. Being paid. Escaping.

Alistair Drummond did that to a person, Jenna thought as she obeyed his orders, completing the archaeological survey map that would show that the ruins were not as impressive as photographs from space had led scholars to expect. A few minor structures. Numerous scattered stones, the result of earthquakes. Pathetic remnants of a formerly great culture. With one exception. The Mayan ball court. For reasons unexplained—perhaps because one intact structure might lend credence to his story—Drummond had insisted that the ball court, a distance from the area of demolition and construction, be spared. There, on its grassy rectangular surface flanked by stone terraces upon which royal spectators had nodded approval, teams of men wearing leather armor had played a game in which they attempted to throw a punishing globe the size and weight of a medicine ball through a vertical hoop on either side of the court. The stakes of the game had been ultimate: life or death. Perhaps that was why Drummond had spared it—because the ball court represented his cruelty, his pursuit of a goal at any cost.

He and Raymond had arrived the day before yesterday, brazenly, in Drummond Enterprises' large blue helicopter, as if he had nothing to hide as he took charge of the final stages of the operation. "You've done well," he'd told Jenna. "You'll get an extra bonus."

Jenna had muttered acquiescence, mentally screaming, All I want is to get out of here with my sanity. Her coworker, her friend, her potential lover, the project's foreman, McIntyre, had died from a snakebite, a half hour before Drummond's helicopter had arrived. Jenna had prayed for the helicopter to arrive sooner so that Mac could be flown to a hospital, but the moment she had seen Drummond's determined, wizened face as the old man strode toward her through the smoke, she had realized that Drummond would never have agreed to waste the resources of the helicopter to take a dying man from the camp. "He'll be dead before he gets to the hospital. We don't have time. Make him as comfortable as possible," Drummond would have said. As it was, what he did say was, "Bury him where the natives can't get to him. No, I've changed my mind. Burn him. Burn them all."

"All" were the natives who'd been exterminated in their attempts to stop the desecration of their sacred land. Jenna had been certain she was going insane when she realized that a massacre had taken place. She'd known of tribes that were exterminated in South America, in the depths of the Amazon rain forest. But it had never occurred to her that portions of Mexico were equally remote and that communication with the outside could be so minimal that no one "in the world" would have any idea of what was happening here. By the time word leaked out, there'd be no evidence of the atrocity. And who was going to talk? The workers? By acquiescing to the slaughter, by accepting obscenely huge bonuses, they were implicated in the slaughter. Only a fool would break the silence.

Now, standing in the camp's log-walled office, remembering how Mac had writhed feverishly on a cot in the corner, she listened numbly to final commands from Drummond about the charts she had prepared.

"Above all"—Drummond's aged voice was filled with phlegm—"the extent of the true discovery must be made to dwarf the archaeological ones. There'll be photographs, of course. But your charts will be given primary attention."

At that moment, the door opened, and Raymond came in, wearing jungle clothing, holding a rifle, his face sooted from smoke, his shirt crimson with blood. "If there are more, *I* can't find them."

"But a different kind of enemy might be coming here. I think he's hunting us," Drummond said.

Raymond straightened, challenged. "Who?"

"A dead man."

Raymond furrowed his brow.

"Charles Duffy," Drummond said. "Do you recognize the—?"

"Yes, he was hired to watch the target's home in San Antonio. To deal with her if she arrived. He disappeared from the house three nights ago."

"He's no longer missing," Drummond said. "His body washed up on a bank of the San Antonio River. He'd been shot. The authorities say he had no identification. One of the men you hired was able to get a look at the body in the morgue, however, and has no doubt that it's Duffy. But Mr. Duffy is remarkable," Drummond continued. "While dead, he used his credit card to fly from San Antonio to Washington, D.C. He stayed at the Ritz-Carlton. For a portion of the next day, he stayed at the Dorset Hotel in Manhattan. After that, he and a companion flew to Miami, where they rented a car."

Raymond brooded. "I don't understand the Washington connection, but the Dorset isn't far from the target's apartment in Manhattan."

"And from the ex-husband. He was paid a visit by a man and a woman the day before yesterday. They interrupted the agreed-upon payment to him."

"Maltin knows nothing," Raymond said. "All you paid him for was to stop attracting attention to the target's disappearance."

"Nothing?" Drummond looked furious. "Maltin knew it was I who paid him. That's what the man and woman learned from him. The woman so far hasn't been identified, although she has red hair and she claimed to work for the *Washington Post*, but the man's description matches that of the same man who interfered with surveillance on the home of the target's parents."

"Buchanan?" Raymond scowled.

"Yes. Buchanan. Now think. What's the Miami connection?" Drummond snapped.

"The yacht. It's south of there. In Key West."

"Exactly," Drummond said. "The captain reports that three crew members brought a woman aboard yesterday afternoon. A woman with red hair."

"She must have been helping Buchanan. Checking ways to sneak aboard."

Drummond nodded. "I have to assume he knows something about the tape. And I have to assume that he'll keep coming closer. Intercept him. Kill him."

"But where would I find him?"

"Isn't it obvious? What's the next link in the chain?"

"Delgado."

"Yes. Mexico City. I just received word from my contacts at Miami International Airport that a man calling himself Charles Duffy bought two airline tickets to Mexico City. The helicopter will have you there by this afternoon."

TWELVE

1

MEXICO CITY

The unregulated exhaust from countless smoke-belching factories and ill-maintained automobiles burning leaded fuel was trapped by a thermal inversion above the mountain-surrounded metropolis and made the air in the largest and fastest-growing city in the world virtually unbreathable. Buchanan's throat felt scratchy. He began to cough as soon as he and Holly got tourist cards and left Juárez International Airport. His eyes burned from the haze—so dense that if not for its acrid smell and biting taste it might have been thought to be mist. The air conditioner in the taxi they hired wasn't working. Nonetheless, he and Holly closed their windows. Better to swelter inside the cab than to breathe the noxious atmosphere outside.

It was 9:15. They'd managed to drive from Key West to Miami in time to catch an 8:00 A.M. United flight to Mexico City. Because of a time-zone change backward, the duration of the flight had actually been two hours and fifteen minutes, and after eating a cheese-and-onion omelet supplied by the airline, Buchanan had been able to doze. For too long now, his schedule had been erratic. His exhaustion worsened. His headache continued to torture him.

So did the bitterness he felt toward Holly. Against his instincts, he had actually begun to trust her. As she'd pointed out to him, she *had* saved his life, and in other ways she'd been of considerable help. But he needed to keep reminding himself that she was a reporter. In the stress of his search for Juana, he'd already indirectly revealed too much about his past. More, it made him angry to think that this woman whom he had allowed to get close to him had been sent by Alan to destroy him.

For her part, Holly remained silent, as if understanding that anything she said would be misinterpreted, as if knowing that her presence would be tolerated only if she didn't draw his attention to her.

"The National Palace," Buchanan told the cabdriver in Spanish, and the words were similar enough to English that Holly understood, although she didn't ask why they were going to a palace instead of to a hotel. Or maybe the National Palace *was* a hotel. She didn't know. She'd never been to Mexico City before. As it turned out, their destination was neither a hotel nor a palace but Mexico's center of government.

Even in the dense haze of pollution, the site was impressive. Amid congested traffic, an immense square was flanked by massive buildings, two of which were cathedrals. The National Palace itself was renowned for its arches, pillars, and patios.

After leaving the taxi, Buchanan and Holly passed through a crowd and entered the National Palace's vestibule, where large colorful murals lined the main staircase and the first-floor corridors. The murals, by Diego Rivera, conveyed the sprawling history of Mexico from the era of the Aztecs and Maya, to the invasion by the Spaniards, to the mixture of races, the numerous revolutions, and ultimately an idealized future in which Mexican peasants worked happily and coexisted gloriously with nature. Given the pollution outside, that idealized future was obviously a long way off.

Buchanan stopped only a moment to assess the murals. He'd become more intense, more driven, as if he was controlled by a terrible premonition and didn't dare waste even a second. In a noisy, echoing corridor, he spoke to a guide and was directed toward a door down the hall. There, in a gift shop, Buchanan ignored books and artifacts on sale, scanning the walls, seeing photographs of what were obviously government officials, some in groups, others alone. He studied several of the photographs, as did Holly, although she risked a sideways glance toward him that revealed his alarmingly rigid cheek muscles and a strong, furious pulse in his neck and temple. His dark eyes seemed to blaze. He pointed at a photograph, the image catching Holly's attention as well: a tall, slender, thin-faced, hawk-nosed Hispanic male in his early forties. The man had a mustache, wore an expensive suit, and exuded arrogance.

"Yes," Holly said.

Buchanan turned to a young female clerk and pointed toward the photograph. *"Este hombre. Cómo se llama, por favor?"*

"Quien? Ah, sí. Esteban Delgado. El Ministro de Asuntos Interiores."

"Gracias," Buchanan said. As he bought a book, he asked the clerk more questions, and five minutes later, when he and Holly left the gift shop, Buchanan had learned that the man who'd raped and murdered Maria Tomez was "not just the Minister of the Interior. He's the second most powerful man in Mexico. Next in line to be president. According to the clerk, that's common knowledge," Buchanan said. "In Mexico, when the outgoing president chooses his replacement, the election is mostly a formality."

Surprised that he'd broken his silence toward her, Holly took advantage of the opportunity, hoping that his anger toward her had softened. "Unless somebody's got a videotape of him that's so disgusting it would totally destroy his career, not to mention put him in prison."

"Or get him executed." Buchanan rubbed his pained forehead. "A man like Delgado would give anything not to have that tape made public. The question is what, though? What does Drummond want?"

"And what happened to Juana Mendez?"

Buchanan's gaze was intense. "Yes. That's finally what this is about. Juana."

The word stung, as did its implication: not you.

"Don't just tolerate me," Holly said. "Don't just keep me along because you're afraid I'll turn against you. I'm not your enemy. Please. Use me. Let me help."

2

"My name is Ted Riley," Buchanan said in Spanish. With Holly, he stood in a carpeted, paneled office, the door of which was labeled MINISTRO DE ASUNTOS INTERIORES. Minister of the Interior. A bespectacled gray-haired secretary nodded and waited.

"I'm the interpreter for Señorita McCoy." Buchanan gestured toward Holly. "As you can see from her credentials, she is a reporter for the *Washington Post*. She is in Mexico City for a limited time, doing interviews with important government officials—to learn their opinions about how the United States could improve its relations with your country. If at all possible, could Señor Delgado spare a few moments to speak with her? It would be greatly appreciated."

The secretary looked sympathetic, spreading her hands in a gesture of regret. "Señor Delgado is not expected in the office for the rest of the week."

Buchanan sighed in frustration. "Perhaps he would meet us if we travel to where he is. Señorita McCoy's newspaper considers his opinions to be of particular importance. It is widely known that he is likely to be the next president."

The secretary looked pleased by Buchanan's recognition that she was associated with future greatness.

Buchanan continued. "And I am certain that Señor Delgado would benefit from complimentary remarks about him in the newspaper that the President of the United States reads every morning. It would be a fine opportunity for the minister to make some constructive comments that would prepare the United States government for his views when he becomes president."

The secretary debated, assessed Holly, and nodded. "One moment, please."

She entered another office, shut the door, and left Buchanan and Holly to glance at each other. Numerous footsteps clattered past in the hallway. In rows of offices, voices murmured.

The secretary returned. "Señor Delgado is at his home in Cuernavaca, an hour's drive south of here. I will give you directions. He invites you to be his guests for lunch."

3

"Can I ask you something?"

Holly waited for a reply, but Buchanan ignored her, staring straight ahead as he drove their rented car south along the Insurgentes Sur freeway.

"Sure, what did I expect?" Holly said. "You haven't been communicative since . . . Never mind. We'll skip that topic. What I want to ask is, how do you do it?"

Again Buchanan didn't reply.

"At Delgado's office," Holly said. "That secretary could just as easily have told us to get lost. Somehow you manipulated her into phoning Delgado. I've been trying to figure out how. It wasn't what you said exactly. It . . ."

"I get in someone else's mind."

Holly frowned at him. "And the CIA taught you how to do this?"

Buchanan's voice hardened. "Now you're being a reporter again."

"Will you stop being so defensive? How many times do I have to tell you? I'm on *your* side. I'm not out to destroy you. I . . ."

"Let's just say I had training along the line." Buchanan clutched the steering wheel and continued to stare at the busy highway. "Being a deep-cover operative isn't just having false documents and a believable cover story. To assume an identity, I have to transmit the absolute conviction that I am who I claim to be. That means believing it absolutely myself. When I spoke to that secretary, I *was* Ted Riley, and something in me went out to her. Went into her mind. Stroked her into believing in me. Remember we talked about elicitation? It isn't merely asking subtle questions. It's enveloping someone in an attitude and emotionally drawing them toward you.''

"It sounds like hypnotism."

"That's how I made my mistake with you." Buchanan's tone changed, becoming bitter.

Holly tensed.

"I stopped concentrating on controlling you," Buchanan said.

"I still don't understand."

"I stopped acting," Buchanan said. "For a while with you, I had an unusual experience. I stopped impersonating. Without realizing it, I became somebody I'd forgotten about. Myself. I related to you as . . . me." He sounded more bitter.

"Maybe that's why I became attracted to you," Holly said.

Buchanan scoffed. "I've been plenty of people better than myself. In fact, I'm the only identity I don't like."

"So now you're avoiding yourself by being—who did you say you once were? Peter Lang? . . . searching for Juana?''

"No," Buchanan said. "Since I met you, Peter Lang has become less and less important. Juana matters to me because . . . In Key West, I told you I couldn't decide anything about my future until I settled my past." He finally looked at her. "I'm not a fool. I know I can't go back six years and God knows how many identities and start up where I left off with her. It's like . . . For a very long time I've been pretending, acting, switching from role to role, and I've known people I couldn't allow myself to care about in those roles. A lot of those people needed help that I couldn't go back and give them. A lot of those people died, but I couldn't go back and mourn for them. Most of my life's been a series of boxes unrelated to one another. I've got to connect them. I want to become . . ."

Holly waited.

"A human being," Buchanan said. "That's why I'm pissed at you. Because I let my guard down, and you betrayed me."

"No," Holly said, touching his right hand on the steering wheel. "Not anymore. I swear to God—I'm not a threat."

4

After the noise and pollution of Mexico City, Cuernavaca's peace and clean air were especially welcome. The sky was clear, the sun bright, making the valley resplendent. In an exclusive subdivision, Buchanan followed the directions he'd been given and found the street he wanted, coming to a high stone wall within which a large iron gate provided a glimpse of gardens, shade trees, and a Spanish-style mansion. A roof of red tile glinted in the sun.

Buchanan kept driving.

"But isn't that where we're supposed to go?" Holly asked.

"Yes."

"Then why . . . ?"

"I haven't decided about a couple of things."

"Such as?"

"Maybe it's time to cut you loose."

Holly looked startled.

"Anything might happen. I don't want you involved," Buchanan said.

"I *am* involved."

"Don't you think you're going to extremes to get a story?"

"The only extreme I care about is what I have to do to prove myself to you. Delgado's expecting a female reporter. Without me, you won't get in. Hey, you established a cover. You claim you're my interpreter. Be consistent."

"Be consistent?" Buchanan tapped his fingers on the steering wheel. "Yeah. For a change."

He turned the car around.

An armed guard stood behind the bars of the gate.

Buchanan got out of the car, approached the man, showed Holly's press card, and explained in Spanish that he and Señorita McCoy were expected. With a scowl, the guard stepped into a wooden booth to the right of the gate and spoke into a telephone. Meanwhile, another armed guard watched Buchanan intently. The first guard returned, his expression as surly as before. Buchanan's muscles compacted. He wondered if something had gone wrong. But the guard unlocked the gate, opened it, and motioned for Buchanan to get back in his car.

Buchanan drove along a shady, curved driveway, past trees, gardens, and fountains, toward the three-story mansion. Simultaneously, he glanced in his rearview mirror, noting that the guard had relocked the gate. He noted as well that other armed guards patrolled the interior of the wall.

"I feel a lot more nervous than when I went on Drummond's yacht," Holly said. "Don't *you* ever feel—?"

"Each time."

"Then why on earth do you keep doing it?"

"I don't have a choice."

"In this case, maybe. But other times . . ."

"No choice," Buchanan repeated. "When you're in the military, you follow orders."

"Not now, you're not. Besides, you didn't have to join the military."

"Wrong," Buchanan said, thinking of the need he'd felt to punish himself for killing his brother. He urgently crushed the thought, disturbed that he'd allowed himself to be distracted. Juana. He had to pay attention. Instead of Tommy, he had to keep thinking of Juana.

"In fact, I don't think I've *ever* felt this nervous," Holly said.

"Stage fright. Try to relax. This is just a walk-through," Buchanan said. "I need to check Delgado's security. Your performance shouldn't be difficult. Just conduct an interview. You're perfectly safe. Which is a hell of a lot more than Delgado will be when I figure out how to get to him."

Concealing his intensity, Buchanan parked in front of the mansion. When he got out of the car, he noticed other guards, not to mention groundskeepers who seemed more interested in visitors than in their duties. There were closed-circuit television cameras, wires in the panes of the windows, metal boxes among the shrubbery—intrusion detectors.

I might have to find another place, Buchanan thought.

Subduing his emotions, he introduced Holly and himself to a servant who came out to greet them and escort them into a cool, shadowy, echoing marble vestibule. They passed a wide, curved staircase and proceeded along a hallway to a mahogany-paneled study that smelled of wax and polish. Furnished in leather, it was filled with hunting trophies as well as numerous rifles and shotguns in glinting glass cabinets.

Although Buchanan had never met him, Delgado was instantly recognizable as he stood from behind his desk, more hawk-nosed and more arrogant-looking than he appeared on the videotape and in photographs. But he also seemed pale and thinner, his cheeks gaunt, as if he might be ill.

"Welcome," he said.

Buchanan vividly remembered the images that showed Delgado raping and murdering Maria Tomez. As soon as he had the information he needed, Buchanan planned to kill him.

Delgado came closer, his English impressive, although his syntax was somewhat stilted. "It is always a pleasure to speak with members of the American press, especially when they work for so distinguished a periodical as the *Washington Post*. Señorita . . . ? Forgive me. I have forgotten the name that my secretary . . ."

"Holly McCoy. And this is my interpreter, Ted Riley."

Delgado shook hands with them. "Good." He ignored Buchanan and kept his attention on Holly, obviously intrigued by her beauty. "Since I speak English, we will not need your interpreter."

"I'm also the photographer," Buchanan said.

Delgado gestured dismissively. "There will be an opportunity for photographs later. Señorita McCoy, may I offer you a drink before lunch? Perhaps wine?"

"Thank you, but it's a little too early for . . ."

"Sure," Buchanan said. "Wine would be nice." There hadn't been time to teach Holly not to turn down an offer to drink with a target. Refusing alcohol stifled the target's urge to be companionable. It made the target suspect that you had a reason not to want to relax your inhibitions.

"On second thought, yes," Holly said. "Since we're having lunch."

"White or red?"

"White, please."

"Chardonnay?"

"Fine."

"The same for me," Buchanan said.

Delgado continued ignoring him and turned to the servant, who had remained at the door. "*Lo haga, Carlos*. Do it."

"*Sí, Señor Delgado*."

The white-coated servant stepped back and disappeared along the hallway.

"Sit down, please." Delgado led Holly toward one of the padded leather chairs.

Buchanan followed, noticing a man on a patio beyond the glass doors that led to the study. The man was an American in his middle thirties, well-dressed, fair-haired, pleasant-looking.

Noticing Buchanan's interest in him, the man nodded and smiled, his expression boyish.

Delgado was saying, "I know Americans like to keep to a busy schedule, so if you have a few questions you would like to ask before lunch, by all means do so."

The man came in from the patio.

"Ah, Raymond," Delgado said. "Have you finished your stroll? Come in. I have some guests I would like you to meet. Señorita McCoy from the *Washington Post*."

Raymond nodded with respect and went over to Holly. "My pleasure." He shook hands with her.

Something about the handshake made her frown.

Raymond turned and approached Buchanan. "How do you do? Mr . . . ?"

"Riley. Ted."

They shook hands.

At once Buchanan felt a stinging sensation in his right palm. It burned.

His hand went numb.

Alarmed, he looked over at Holly, who was staring in dismay at *her* right palm.

"How long does it take?" Delgado asked.

"It's what we call a two-stepper," Raymond said. As he took off a ring and placed it in a small jeweler's box, he smiled again, his blue eyes bottomless and cold.

Holly sank to her knees.

Buchanan's right arm lost all sensation.

Holly toppled to the floor.

Buchanan's chest felt tight. His heart pounded. He sprawled. Desperate, he fought to stand up.

Couldn't.

Couldn't do anything.

His body felt numb. His limbs wouldn't move. From head to foot, he was powerless.

Staring above him, frantic, helpless, he saw Delgado smirk.

The blue-eyed American peered down, his empty smile chilling. "The drug comes from the Yucatán Peninsula. It's the Mayan equivalent of curare. Hundreds of years ago, the natives used it to paralyze their victims so they wouldn't struggle when their hearts were cut out."

Unable to turn his head, unable to get a glimpse of Holly, Buchanan heard her gasp, trying to breathe.

"Don't *you* try to struggle," Raymond said. "Your lungs might not bear the strain."

5

The helicopter thundered across the sky. Its *whump-whump-whumping* roar vibrated through the fuselage. Not that Buchanan could feel the rumble. His body continued to have absolutely no sensation. The cabin's presumably hard floor might as well have been a feathered mattress. Neither hard nor soft, hot nor cold, sharp nor blunt had any significance. All was the same: numb.

In compensation, his senses of hearing and sight intensified tremendously. Every sound in the cabin, especially Holly's agonized wheezing, was amplified. Beyond a window of the cabin, the sky was an almost unbearably brilliant turquoise. He feared that he would have gone blind from the radiance if not for merciful flicks of his eyelids, which—like his heart and lungs—weren't part of the system controlled by the drug.

Indeed his heart was nauseatingly stimulated, pounding wildly, no doubt at least in part from fear. But if he vomited (assuming that his stomach, too, wasn't paralyzed), he would surely gag and die. He had to concentrate on controlling his fear. He didn't dare lose his discipline. The faster his heart pounded, the more his lungs wanted air. But his chest muscles wouldn't cooperate, and the panic of involuntary, smothering hyperventilation almost overcame him.

Concentrate, he thought. Concentrate.

He struggled to fill his mind with a calming mantra. He strove for a single all-consuming thought that would give him purpose. Juana, he thought. Juana. Juana. Have to survive to help her. Have to survive to find her. Have to survive to save her. Have to . . .

His frenzied heart kept speeding. His panicked lungs kept insisting. No. The mantra wasn't working. Juana? She was a distant memory, years away—in Buchanan's case, literally lifetimes away. He'd been so many people in the meanwhile. Searching for her, as determined as he'd been to find her, he'd really been searching for himself, and as a new all-consuming, all-purposeful thought filled his mind—

—it was unwilled, spontaneous—

—Holly—

—listening to her struggle to breathe—

—need to help Holly, need to save Holly—

—he suddenly knew that he finally had a purpose. Not for Peter Lang. Not for any of his other assumed identities. But for Brendan Buchanan. And that realization gave him an urge to look forward rather than behind, something he hadn't felt since he'd killed his brother so long ago. Brendan Buchanan had a purpose, and it had nothing to do with himself. It was simply, absolutely, to do everything in his power to make sure that Holly survived this. Not because he wanted her to be with him. But because he wanted her to live. Trapped in himself, he had found himself.

While his heart continued to speed, he sensed—from a change in pressure behind his ears—that the helicopter was descending. He couldn't move his head to notice where Delgado sat next to Raymond, but he could hear them talking.

"I don't see why it was necessary for me to come along."

"It was an order that Mr. Drummond radioed to me as I was flying to Cuernavaca. He wants you to see the progress at the site."

"Risky," Delgado said. "I might be associated with the project."

"I suspect that was Mr. Drummond's idea. It's time for you to pay off your debt."

"That ruthless son of a bitch."

"Mr. Drummond would consider it a compliment to be called ruthless. Look down there. You can see it now."

"My God."

The helicopter continued descending, the pressure behind Buchanan's ears more painful.

Painful? Buchanan suddenly realized that he was feeling something. He had never expected to welcome pain, but now he did—joyously. His feet tingled. His hands seemed pricked by needles. The stitches in his knife wound began to itch. His nearly healed bullet wound throbbed. His skull felt swollen, his excruciating headache returning. These sensations didn't occur all at one time. They came separately, gradually. Each gave him hope. He knew that if he tried to move, he'd be able to, but he didn't dare. He had to keep still. He had to make sure that his limbs were fully functional. He had to wait for the ideal moment to . . .

"Just about now, the drug should be wearing off," Raymond said.

A strong grip seized Buchanan's left wrist and snapped a handcuff onto it. Then the left wrist was tugged behind Buchanan's back, and with force, a handcuff was snapped onto his right wrist.

"Comfortable?" Raymond's tone suggested that he might have been speaking to a lover.

Buchanan didn't answer, continuing to pretend that he couldn't move. Meanwhile the clink and scrape of metal told him that Holly was being handcuffed as well.

The helicopter's roar diminished, the pitch of its rotor blades changing, as it settled onto the ground. The pilot shut off the controls, the blades spinning with less velocity, the turbine's roar turning into a whine.

When the hatch was opened, Buchanan expected his eyes to be assaulted by a blaze of sunlight. Instead, a shadow blanketed him. A haze. He'd noticed that the sky had become less brilliantly blue as the helicopter descended, but with so much else to think about, he hadn't paid the lack of clarity much attention. Now the haze swirled into the cabin, and the odor was so acrid that he coughed reflexively. Smoke! Nearby something was on fire.

Buchanan kept coughing.

"The drug temporarily stops your saliva glands from working," Raymond said, dragging Buchanan from the cabin, dumping him onto the ground. "That makes your throat dry. In fact, your throat'll feel irritated for quite some time." Raymond's tone suggested that he enjoyed the thought of Buchanan's discomfort.

Holly coughed as well, then groaned as Raymond dragged her from the cabin and dumped her next to Buchanan. Smoke drifted past them.

"Why are you burning so many trees?" Delgado sounded alarmed.

"To make as wide a perimeter as possible. To keep the natives away."

"But won't the flames ignite the—?"

"Mr. Drummond knows what he's doing. Everything's been calculated."

Raymond kicked Buchanan's side.

Buchanan gasped, making himself sound more in pain than he was, thankful that Raymond hadn't kicked him in the side where he'd been stabbed.

"Get up," Raymond said. "Our men have better things to do than carry you. I know you can do it. If you don't, I'll kick you all the way to the office."

To prove his point, Raymond kicked Buchanan again, this time harder.

Buchanan struggled to his knees, wavered, and managed to stand. His mind swirled, imitating the smoke that forced him to cough once more.

Holly staggered upright, almost falling, then gaining her balance. She looked at Buchanan in terror. He tried to communicate an expression of reassurance.

It didn't work. Raymond shoved both of them, nearly knocking them down before their momentum jerked them upright and forward. They were being herded toward a wide log building that was partially obscured by smoke.

But what captured Buchanan's attention was the welter of activity around him, workmen rushing, bulldozers and trucks laboring past, cranes lifting girders and pipes. Amid the din of machinery, Buchanan thought he heard a shot, and then he saw stone blocks scattered before him, hieroglyphs on them, obviously from ruins. Here and there, he saw the stunted remains of ancient temples. At once, as the smoke cleared temporarily, he had a brief view of a pyramid. But the pyramid wasn't ancient, and it wasn't composed of stone blocks.

This one, tall and wide, was built of steel. Buchanan had never seen anything like it. The structure was like a gigantic tripod, its legs splayed, unfamiliar reinforcements linking them. Even though he'd never seen anything like it, he knew intuitively what it was, what it resembled. An oil derrick. Is that what Drummond wants down here? he wondered. But why does the derrick have such an unusual design?

At the smoke-hazed log building, Raymond shoved the door, then thrust Buchanan and Holly through the opening.

Buchanan almost fell into the shadowy, musty interior, his eyes needing time to adjust to the dim, generator-powered overhead light bulbs. He staggered to a halt, straightened, felt Holly stumble next to him, and found himself blinking upward at Alistair Drummond.

6

None of the photographs in the biography and the newspaper stories Buchanan had read communicated how fiercely Drummond dominated a room. Behind thick spectacles, the old man's eyes were deep in their sockets and radiated an unnerving, penetrating gaze. Even the age in his voice worked to his advantage, powerful despite its brittleness.

"Mr. Buchanan," Drummond said.

The reference was startling. How did he find out my name? Buchanan thought.

Drummond squinted, then turned his attention to Holly. "Ms. McCoy, I trust that Raymond made you comfortable on the flight. Señor Delgado, I'm pleased that you could join me."

"The way it was put to me, I didn't feel I had a choice."

"Of course you have a choice," Drummond said. "You can

go to jail or become the next president of Mexico. Which would you prefer?''

Raymond had shut the door after they entered. Now it was bumped open, the cacophony of the construction equipment intruding. A woman in dusty jeans and a sweaty work shirt came in holding long tubes of thick paper that Buchanan thought might have been charts.

"Not now, goddamn it," Drummond said.

The woman looked startled. Smoke drifted behind her as she backed awkwardly from the building and shut the door.

Drummond returned his attention to Delgado. "We're much further along than I anticipated. By tomorrow morning, we ought to be able to start pumping. When you get back to Mexico City, I want you to make the necessary arrangements. Tell your people that everything's in place. I don't want any trouble. The payments have been made. I expect everyone to cooperate.''

"You brought me here to tell me what I already knew?"

"I brought you here to see what you sold your soul for," Drummond said. "It's not good to keep a distance from the price of your sins. Otherwise, you might be tempted to forget the bargain you made. To remind you, I want you to see what happens to my two guests." With a fluid motion amazing for his age, he turned toward Buchanan and Holly. "How much do you know?"

"I found this in their camera bag," Raymond said. He placed a videotape on a table.

"My, my," Drummond said.

"I played it at Delgado's."

"And?"

"The copy's a little grainy, but Delgado's performance is as enthralling as ever. It holds my attention every time," Raymond said.

"Then you know more than you should," Drummond told Buchanan and Holly.

"Look, this isn't any of our business," Buchanan said.

"You're right about that."

"I'm not interested in oil, and I don't care about whatever you're doing to punish Delgado," Buchanan said. "All I'm trying to do is find Juana Mendez."

Drummond raised his dense white eyebrows. "Well, in that you're not alone."

They stared at each other, and Buchanan suddenly realized what must have happened. Juana had agreed to work for Drummond and impersonate Maria Tomez. But after several months, Juana had felt either trapped or threatened, or possibly she'd just been disgusted by Drummond. Whatever her motive, she'd broken her agreement and fled. Along the way, unable to risk a phone call to Buchanan's superiors, needing to contact Buchanan but without allowing any outsider to understand her message, she'd mailed the cryptic postcard that only Buchanan could decipher. Meanwhile, Drummond's people had frantically searched for her, staking out her home and her parent's home and anywhere else they suspected she might go. They had to guarantee her silence. If the truth about Maria Tomez was revealed, Drummond would no longer have control of Delgado. Without Delgado, Drummond wouldn't have the political means to sustain this project. The oil industry in Mexico had been nationalized back in the thirties. Foreigners weren't allowed to have the influence in it that Drummond evidently wanted. That this was an archaeological site made the political problem all the more enormous, although from the looks of things, Drummond had solved the archaeological problem simply and obscenely by destroying the ruins. When Delgado became president of Mexico, he could use his power with appropriate politicians. A back-door arrangement could be made with Drummond. For discovering and developing the site, Drummond would secretly be paid the huge profits that foreign oil companies used to earn before the days of nationalization. But that wasn't all of it, Buchanan sensed. There was something more, a further implication, although he was too preoccupied with saving his life to analyze what it was.

"Do you know where Juana Mendez is?" Drummond asked.

"For all I know, she's working on that oil rig out there."

Drummond chuckled. "Such bravado. You're a credit to Special Forces."

The reference surprised Buchanan. Then it didn't. "The car I rented in New Orleans and drove to San Antonio."

Drummond nodded. "You used your own credit card to rent it."

"I didn't have an alternative. It was the only card I had."

"But it gave me a slight advantage," Drummond said. "When my people saw you arrive at the Mendez house in San Antonio, they were able to use the car's license number to find out who had rented the car and then to research your identity."

Identity, Buchanan thought. After so many years of surviving as other people, I'm probably going to die because of my own identity. He felt totally exhausted. His wounds ached. His skull throbbed with greater ferocity. He didn't have any more resources.

Then he looked at Holly, at the terror in her eyes, and the mantra again filled his mind. Have to survive to help Holly. Have to save Holly.

"You're an instructor in tactical maneuvers," Drummond said.

Buchanan tensed. Instructor? Then Drummond hadn't penetrated his cover.

Drummond continued, "Did you know Juana Mendez at Fort Bragg?"

Desperate, Buchanan tried to find a role to play, an angle with which to defend himself. "Yes."

"How? She was in Army Intelligence. What does that have to do with—?"

Abruptly, a role came to mind. Buchanan decided to play the most daring part of his life. Himself.

"Look, I'm not a field instructor, and Juana's Army Intelligence status was only a cover."

Drummond looked surprised.

"I'm looking for Juana Mendez because she sent me a postcard, telling me in code that she was in trouble. It had to be in code because I'm not supposed to exist. Juana used to belong and I still do belong to a Special Operations unit that's so covert it might as well be run by ghosts. We look after our own: past members as well as present. When I got the SOS, my unit sent me to find out what was going on. I've been reporting on a regular basis. My unit still has no idea where Juana Mendez is. But they know I was in Cuernavaca. They know I was headed toward Delgado, and after him, they know I was headed toward you. They won't be able to track me here, not right away, not without questioning Delgado. But they will question him, and they will come to you, and believe me, these men care only about sacrifice and loyalty. If they do not find me, they will destroy you. Take my word—at the moment, Holly McCoy and I are your most valuable assets.''

Drummond sighed. From outside the building, amid the muffled roar of the construction equipment, Buchanan thought he heard another gunshot.

"For something you invented on the spur of the moment, that's an excellent negotiating posture,'' Drummond said. ''I'm a collector, did you know that? That's how I came to be here. Journalists''—he nodded toward Holly—''have always wondered what motivates me. What do *you* think, Ms. McCoy?''

Despite her evident fear, Holly managed to say, ''Power.''

''Partially correct. But only in a simplistic way. What keeps me going, what gives me drive, is the desire to be unique. To own unique things, to be in unique situations, to control unique people. I became interested in the Yucatán because of my collection. Three years ago, an individual came to me with an object of great price. The ancient Maya had their own version of books. They were long strips of thin bark that were folded again and again until they resembled small accordions. Historians call them codices. When the Spaniards invaded this area in the 1500s, they were determined to destroy the native culture and replace it with their own. In their zeal, they set fire to the Mayan libraries. Only three authenticated codices are known to have survived. A fourth may be a forgery. But a fifth exists. It is authentic, and I own it. It is absolutely unique because, unlike the others, which are lists, mine has substantial information. Of course, I didn't know that at the time. I bought it because I had the means to and because I didn't want anyone else to own it. Naturally, I wanted to know what the hieroglyphs signified, so I hired the world's greatest experts in Mayan symbols. You might say I owned those experts. And I eventually discovered that the text described the presence of a massive oil field in this area. The Maya called it the god of darkness, the god of black water, the god that seeps from the ground. At first, I thought they were using metaphors. Then it came to me that they were being literally descriptive. The text emphasized that the god was held in control by temples and a great pyramid, but the location described in the text didn't match any known ruins. Early this year, *these* ruins were discovered, thanks to photographs taken from a space shuttle. Because I controlled Delgado, I was able to control this site, to bring in my own people, to seal off the area, to search.''

''And in the process, destroy the ruins,'' Buchanan said.

''An unavoidable necessity.'' Drummond raised his shoulders. ''Besides, *I'd* seen the ruins. Why should I care if anyone else does? I didn't want to start drilling until I was certain. It turned out that the oil seepage was exactly where the text said it would be. Beneath the pyramid. The pyramid rested on it, capped it, kept the god in control. But the uniqueness doesn't end there. Oil in the Yucatán means nothing if you can't get to it. This area is so unstable that conventional equipment is useless here. That's why no one else took the trouble to explore for oil in this region. Periodic earthquakes would have destroyed their derricks. But *my* equipment is one of a kind. It's designed to be flexible, to withstand quakes. Because of it, from now on geologists can look for oil in areas that they previously ignored because there wasn't any way to develop the site. Of course, they'll have to pay a considerable amount to get permission to use my equipment. I doubt they'll ever find an oil field as immense as this one is, however. It's of Kuwaiti proportions, far beyond my expectations. And that's what finally makes this situation truly unique. When the field is fully developed, the oil will not be used.''

Buchanan must have looked surprised, for in response, Drummond's eyes gleamed. ''Yes. It won't be used. To put so much oil on the market would cause the price of oil to plummet. It would be an economic disaster to the oil-producing nations. When Delgado becomes president, he'll allow me to negotiate with the other oil-producing nations for them to pay Mexico *not* to put its oil on the market. And there's no limit to what they will pay us. As a consequence, less oil will be used. In that sense, you could say I'm a humanitarian.'' Drummond smirked.

''Or maybe you just want to collect the world,'' Buchanan said.

''What we're discussing is whether your argument is persuasive enough to make me want to collect *you*.'' Drummond squinted toward Raymond. "Find out if he's lying about this covert Special Operations group."

7

The sun was low, adding to the gloom of the acrid smoke that drifted across the area. Buchanan coughed again as he and Holly were shoved through the haze toward the only part of the ruins that Drummond had allowed to remain intact.

"The ball court," Drummond said.

The haze lifted enough for Buchanan to see a flat stone playing surface one hundred feet long and twenty-five feet wide. On each side was a wall, fifteen feet high, the top of which was a terrace from which spectators could watch. Drummond climbed steps to the terrace, followed by Delgado and guards flanking Holly. She looked sick from fear. Her handcuffs had been removed. She nervously rubbed her wrists.

Buchanan did the same, trying to increase the flow of blood to his numb hands. Anxiety surged through him as he studied the walls of the court, noting the hieroglyphs and the drawings engraved on the stone.

"The acoustics of the ball court are amazing." Drummond spoke from the terrace, peering down at Buchanan. "I'm using a normal voice, and yet it sounds as if I have a microphone."

Despite the roar of construction equipment in the background, despite the closer crackle of flames and the occasional bark of a gunshot, Buchanan heard Drummond with remarkable clarity. The crusty voice seemed to echo from and be amplified by all points of the court.

"The game was called *pok-a-tok*," Drummond said. "If you study the engravings on the stone wall below me, you can see images of the ancient Maya playing the game. They used a latex rubber ball roughly the size and weight of a medicine ball. The intention was to hurl the ball through the vertical stone circle projecting from the middle of this side of the court. A second stone circle projects from the other side of the court. Presumably, that was the goal for the opposite team. The ancient Maya considered *pok-a-tok* more than mere recreation.

To them, it had enormous political and religious significance. In their mythology, the two gods who founded their race did so by winning this game in a contest with other gods. There is evidence that commoners were never allowed to witness the game. Only nobles, priests, and royalty. There is further evidence that the game was a prelude to human sacrifice and that it was played most often with warriors captured from other tribes.''

''The stakes were life and death.'' Raymond's voice came suddenly from behind Buchanan, making him whirl.

8

What Buchanan saw stunned him. Threw his mind off balance. Assaulted his sanity. For a moment, he told himself that he had to be hallucinating, that fatigue combined with his concussion had distorted his perceptions.

But as Raymond stepped through the haze of smoke, tinted crimson by the lowering sun, Buchanan forced himself to accept that what confronted him, however grotesque, was definitely, dismayingly real.

Raymond was partially naked. He wore thick leather pads around his waist and groin. Similar armor was strapped to his shoulders, elbows, and knees. Otherwise, his body was bare, his nipples showing. His exposed muscles implied the strength and tone that could have come only from hours of daily exercise.

Buchanan, who had been in excellent condition before he began his assignment in Mexico, had been on the move for so long and been so wearied by his various injuries that he hadn't had time for exercise and wasn't in peak condition.

Raymond's leather armor looked grotesque enough. But what added to the dismaying sense of the surreal was a helmet he wore, from which long feathers of numerous brilliant colors were swept back, creating the illusion that a Mayan warrior had stepped not only through smoke but through time. In addition, he carried a large ball that he dropped to the stone court. As it struck and rolled, it caused a thunking echo that communi-

cated how solid and heavy it was. He threw leather pads at
Buchanan's feet. "Undress and put them on."

"Like hell," Buchanan said.

Raymond picked up the ball and hurled it at Buchanan, who
dodged, but not soon enough, the drug still affecting him. The
glancing impact of the ball against his left arm was startlingly
painful.

"Undress and put on the armor, or you won't last thirty
seconds in the game," Raymond said.

Buchanan slowly complied, gaining time, calculating.
Above him, Holly looked even more terrified. Buchanan
strained to think of a way for the two of them to escape, but
no plan was adequate against the guard next to Holly and the
automatic weapon in his hands. The guard would shoot before
Buchanan could climb the wall and get to them.

As Buchanan's naked skin felt prickly cold despite the sweat
dripping from him, he strapped on the rough, thick leather
armor.

"I designed these myself," Raymond said, "based on the
drawings on these walls." He pointed to Buchanan's left, just
below the vertical stone hoop that projected from the top of the
wall. "That engraving, in particular, interests me."

Buchanan frowned in that direction, and for a moment, the
image—a warrior in armor, with a feathered headdress—
looked disturbingly like Raymond.

"When I first stepped onto this ball court," Raymond said,
"I felt as if I'd come home. I felt as if I'd been here, as if I'd
played here. Long, long ago."

Buchanan kept staring at the image. Appalled, he realized
that the warrior was clutching a severed human head, blood
dripping from the neck as the warrior raised the skull by its
hair.

"That's what I meant about life and death," Raymond said.
"You see, the penalty for the losers was execution. And the
winner? He not only got to stay alive. He got to be the execu-
tioner."

"What are we talking about here?" Buchanan demanded.
"Are you telling me that if I win, I go free?"

Except for the din of construction equipment in the background, the ball court became silent.

"That's what I thought," Buchanan said. "For me, it's a no-win situation."

"It may have been for the ancient Maya as well," Drummond interrupted, his voice filled with phlegm.

"What's that supposed to mean?"

"There's a theory among a few historians of Mayan culture that it wasn't the losers who were executed but, rather, the winners."

"That's absurd," Buchanan said. "Who on earth would want to play?"

"Raymond agrees with you," the old man said. "But the theory is that winning was such an honor, it put you on a level with the gods. The next logical step was for you to be sacrificed so that you could take your place among the gods."

"It sounds to me like the only true winners were those who watched."

"Yes," Drummond said. "As I told you, I pursue the unique. I'm about to be privileged to witness a rarity. For the first time in five hundred years, a game of *pok-a-tok* is going to be played. For me."

"And how is this supposed to prove whether I'm telling the truth about the Special Ops unit that'll come here looking for me? Am I supposed to confess so I won't have my head cut off?"

"Oh, I think as the game progresses, you'll have many painful inducements to tell the truth," Drummond said. "But it's not you I'm concerned about. My interest is in Ms. McCoy. I suspect that what she sees will make her more than willing to tell the truth. In exchange for ending what's being done to you."

"It won't do you any good," Buchanan said. "She doesn't know anything about my unit."

"Perhaps. I'll soon find out. Raymond, if you're ready."

9

The ball struck Buchanan's back with such force that he was knocked to the stone floor, his chin scraping on one of the slabs. If not for the padded leather armor, he suspected that the ball would have broken some of his ribs. Gasping, ignoring his pain, he scrambled to his feet and charged toward the ball. Raymond got there at the same time he did.

Buchanan rammed his padded elbow against the side of Raymond's head, knocking him sideways. Before Raymond could recover, Buchanan lifted the ball, its weight surprising him, and hurled it at Raymond, who grunted and lurched back as the ball struck his thigh, bouncing off his leather armor, thudding onto the court.

"No, no, no," Drummond said from the platform. "This won't do at all. The point of the game is to throw the ball through the stone hoop, not at your opponent."

"Why didn't you tell that to Raymond when he threw it at me to begin with? What the hell was he doing?"

"Getting your attention," Raymond said.

"How many points does it take to win?"

"Well, that's a problem."

"Yeah, I thought so."

"No, you don't understand," Drummond said. "You see, *no one* knows how many points are required in order to win. That information hasn't survived the centuries. We'll have to improvise."

"Ten." Raymond smiled.

"Ten what?" Buchanan asked in fury. "Do you mean I have to win by ten points? For Christ sake, what are you saying?"

"The best of ten. Whoever gets to ten first."

"And then what?"

"It depends on the answers I receive from you and Ms. McCoy," Drummond said.

Without warning, Buchanan dodged toward the ball, picked it up, and lunged toward the vertical hoop. As he aimed to throw, Raymond battered his padded shoulder against Buchanan's arm, jolting him sideways, slamming him against the stone wall.

Buchanan groaned, spun, and struck Raymond's chest with the ball. Continuing to grip the ball, Buchanan kept spinning as Raymond stumbled backward. Braced beneath the stone hoop, Buchanan hurled the ball and felt his heartbeat surge when he saw the ball arc through the vertical circle.

Raymond's hands struck Buchanan's back, knocking him forward and down, Buchanan's chin again scraping on the court.

Jesus, Buchanan said. Not my head. I can't let anything happen to my head. Another concussion would . . .

He scrambled to his feet, wiped blood from his chin, and glared at Raymond.

"*No, no, no,*" Drummond repeated. "*You're not playing by the rules.*"

"Tell that to Raymond!" Buchanan shouted. "*I'm* the one who got the ball through the hoop."

"But you didn't get the ball through legally!"

"*What are you talking about?*"

"You're not allowed to use your hands!"

"Not allowed to—?"

"We don't know much about the game." Drummond gestured forcefully. "But we do know this. Presumably except for picking up the ball, you were not allowed to use your hands. The ball was kept in motion by thrusting it with your forearms, your shoulders, your hips, your knees, and your head."

The idea of hitting the ball with his head made Buchanan inwardly flinch. It would probably kill him.

"For breaking the rules, you have to be given a penalty. One point demerit. Now you have to score eleven, while Raymond needs only ten. Unless of course he breaks a rule."

"Sure. But somehow I get the feeling he'll make up the rules as he goes along and I'll keep breaking rules that haven't been invented yet."

"Just play the game," Raymond said.

Before Buchanan could react, Raymond scurried toward the ball, picked it up with his hands, threw it into the air, caught it with his forearms, and hurled it toward the hoop, the ball flying neatly through.

Thunking, the ball landed at Buchanan's feet.

"Raymond, I get the feeling you've been practicing."

"Good sport," Drummond said. "I like a man who loses a point graciously."

"But I'll bet you like winners more," Buchanan said.

"Then make me like you better," Drummond said. "Win."

Buchanan managed to grab the ball. At once he felt his legs kicked out from under him as Raymond leapt, hitting with his feet.

Buchanan fell backward, the weight of the ball against his chest. He struck the court hard, grateful for the leather armor on his shoulders. Even so, his impact sent a spasm through the shoulder that was still healing from where he'd been shot in Cancún. The weight of the ball took his breath away.

Raymond jerked the ball from his hands, threw it into the air again, caught it with his forearms again, and hurled it toward the vertical hoop, scoring another point.

"Yes, you've definitely been practicing." As Buchanan came to his feet, he felt his body begin to stiffen.

"This isn't amusing at all. You're going to have to try harder," Drummond said.

Sooner than anticipated, Buchanan scooped up the ball, grasped it with his forearms, pretended to lunge toward the hoop, but actually watched for Raymond to attack, and as Raymond darted to slam against him, Buchanan spun. Clutching the ball to his chest, avoiding Raymond, Buchanan jabbed with his elbow as Raymond went past, and Raymond lurched, doubling over, holding his side from the pain in his left kidney. Instantly Buchanan ran toward the hoop, stood with his back to it, cautiously watched Raymond, then risked a glance upward, judged his distance from the hoop, and threw the ball up behind him, exhaling with satisfaction when the ball hurtled through.

"Excellent coordination," Drummond said. "You look like you've had experience with basketball. But this game has aspects of volleyball and soccer as well. How were you at those?"

Distracted, Buchanan felt the wind knocked out of him as Raymond attacked headfirst, plowing his skull into Buchanan's stomach, knocking him over.

Buchanan writhed, struggling to breathe. Meanwhile Raymond scooped up the ball and scored another point.

"What's the name of your Special Operations unit?" Drummond asked. "This mythical unit that's supposed to come and rescue you or else punish me if I harm you."

Buchanan wavered upright, wiped blood from his chin, and squinted toward Raymond.

"I asked you a question," Drummond demanded. "What is the name of your unit?"

Buchanan pretended to dart toward the ball. Raymond lunged to intercept him. Buchanan zigzagged, coming toward Raymond from the opposite side, once more ramming his padded elbow into Raymond's left kidney.

The repeated damage to the area made Raymond groan, faltering with his hands on the ball. Buchanan yanked it away, wedged it between his forearms, and started to throw. Pain blurred his vision as Raymond tackled him from behind at his midsection.

Falling, Buchanan was terribly conscious of the ball beneath him, of Raymond's weight on top of him. When he hit the court, he felt as if the ball were a wedge against which the top and bottom of his body were being split in opposite directions. Raymond's plummeting body shoved the ball against Buchanan's stomach. For a terrifying moment, Buchanan couldn't breathe. He felt smothered.

Then Raymond scrambled free, and Buchanan rolled off the ball, gasping, knowing that his abdomen had been bruised—worse, that the stitches in his knife wound had been torn open beneath the leather armor that girded his right side.

Raymond picked up the ball with his forearms and, without any visible strain, threw it, scoring another point.

The court echoed with the powerful thunk of the ball as it landed. Construction equipment kept roaring in the background. The fires kept crackling. A gunshot reverberated from the forest. Smoke, tinted crimson by the sunset, drifted over the court.

Drummond coughed.

He kept coughing. Phlegm rattled in his throat. He spat and finally managed to say, "You'll have to try harder. *What is the name of your Special Operations unit?*"

Stiff, weary, in pain, Buchanan stood. If he and Holly were going to get out of this alive, he had to convince Drummond that the old man couldn't afford the consequence of killing his hostages.

"Name, rank, and serial number," Buchanan said. "But I'll go to hell before I give you classified information."

"You don't know what hell can be," Drummond said. "*What is the name of your Special Operations unit?*"

Buchanan grabbed for the ball. Although his movements were an excruciating effort, he had to keep trying. He had to ignore the sticky wetness beneath the leather pad on his right side. He had to overcome his pain.

Raymond sprinted to intercept him, stooping to grab the ball.

Buchanan increased speed, getting to Raymond much sooner than expected, kicking, his right shin striking the unprotected area between Raymond's shoulders and his abdomen.

Bent over, Raymond took the kick so hard that he was lifted off the court. He tilted in midair, landed on his side, rolled onto his back, kept rolling, came to his feet, and whacked his forearm across Buchanan's face so hard that Buchanan's teeth snapped together.

For a moment, Buchanan was blind, jolted backward.

Raymond struck him again, knocking him farther backward. Blood flew. Dazed, Buchanan prepared for a third blow, shielding his face, ducking to the left, unable to see clearly.

"*What is the name of your unit?*" Drummond demanded.

Raymond struck again, smashing Buchanan's lips.

Then suddenly Buchanan had nowhere to go. He was thrust against the wall of the court. Through blurred vision, he saw Raymond drawing back his arm to strike yet again.

"*The name of your unit?*" Drummond shouted.

"Yellow Fruit!" Holly blurted.

"Yellow . . . ?" Drummond sounded confused.

"You want the unit's name! That's it!" Holly's voice was unsteady from terror. "Stop. My God, look at the blood. Can't you see how hurt he is?"

"That's the general idea." Raymond struck Buchanan again.

Buchanan slumped to his knees.

Keep going, Holly. Buchanan strained to clear his vision. Damn it, keep on. Hook them.

Yellow Fruit! She hadn't told Drummond about Scotch and Soda. Instead, she'd used the name for a unit that was no longer operative. She was following what Buchanan had taught her during their search. When you're absolutely stuck, tell the truth, but only that portion of the truth that's useful. Never expose your core identity.

"And what exactly is Yellow Fruit?" Drummond demanded.

"It's a covert Army unit that supplies security and intelligence to Special Operations units." Holly's voice continued to shake.

"And how do you know this? A while ago, Buchanan assured me that your knowledge was limited."

"Because of a story I've been working on. I've tracked down leads for a year. Buchanan's one of them. I wouldn't be here if I hadn't tried to get close to him and hope he'd say more than he meant to."

"Did he?"

"Not enough to satisfy you. Damn it, I've got nothing to do with this. I want out of this. Jesus, tell him what he wants, Buchanan. Maybe he'll let us go."

"Yes," Drummond said, "take her advice and tell me everything I want."

Buchanan was kneeling, his head bowed. Wiping blood from his mouth, he nodded. Abruptly he struck Raymond in his solar plexus, doubling Raymond over, striking again, this time with an uppercut that made Raymond's eyes cross and sent him reeling back, collapsing on the court. Raymond's feathered helmet rolled away.

Buchanan struggled to his feet. If he'd been allowed to use his Special Forces hand-to-hand-combat skills, he would not have had so much trouble dealing with Raymond. But winning in hand-to-hand combat wasn't the point. Winning the game was. Otherwise, Drummond might become so outraged that he'd order Buchanan and Holly to be executed. And Buchanan doubted that the rules of *pok-a-tok* included karate.

As it was, the damage that he had inflicted on Raymond was sufficient to leave Raymond sprawled on the court. Wavering, Buchanan picked up the ball between his forearms. He studied the vertical hoop, tried to clear his blurred vision, and threw the ball underhanded. His stomach turned cold when the ball struck the edge of the ring and thunked back toward him.

Shit, he thought. He wiped sweat from his eyes, whirled to make certain that Raymond was still on his back, then glared up at Holly.

"You bitch!" he shouted. "You were just leading me on! All I meant to you was a story!"

"Damned right!" she shouted back. "Did you figure you were so wonderful I'd fall hopelessly in love with you? Get real, and look in the mirror! I don't intend to get killed because of you! For God's sake, tell him what he wants!"

Buchanan turned toward the ring, threw the ball underhanded again, and this time the ball went through.

"Tell him what he wants?" Buchanan glared harder. "I'll tell him, bitch. Just enough to save my life. *You're* the threat to him, not me. You're the damned reporter! I'm a soldier! I can be trusted to keep my mouth shut!"

Buchanan threw the ball yet again. It arced through the ring. "And I'll win this fucking game."

"Just enough to save *your* life?" Holly turned paler than she already was. "Hey, we're in this together!"

"Wrong."

Buchanan threw the ball.

And cursed when it struck the edge of the ring.

"And *you're* wrong as well," Raymond said unexpectedly.

Buchanan turned to look behind him.

Raymond had stood. Blood streamed from his mouth, dripping onto his leather armor. "You're not going to win, after all."

Raymond scrambled toward the ball.

Buchanan lunged after him.

And slipped.

He'd been standing too long in one place. The blood from the opened stitches in his side had seeped from beneath his armor. It had trickled down his leg and formed a slippery pool where he stood.

Although he didn't fall, the strenuous effort of regaining his balance lost him sufficient time that Raymond was able to throw the ball through the ring.

Without pause, Raymond darted toward it again. But as he scooped it up, Buchanan swept his right forearm beneath the ball, freeing it from Raymond's grip. Using his other forearm,

Buchanan thrust the ball against Raymond's left shoulder. The ball's impact made Raymond groan. It rebounded, and as Raymond staggered back, Buchanan caught the ball with upraised forearms. Hurling it, seeing it touch the ring, he felt elated.

Then his chest cramped. The ball did not go through. It bounced off the edge and fell back. Jesus. Running forward, Buchanan leapt. But he didn't get there soon enough. He didn't raise his arms quickly enough. In midair, he had to strike the ball with his padded left shoulder. It flew back toward the ring.

And bounced yet again. But this time, Buchanan was ready. As he completed his leap and landed on the court, he raised his forearms, caught the ball, threw, and scored a point.

"Bravo," Drummond yelled. "Yes, that's how the game is played! Shoulders! Angles! Rebounds!"

"Bitch, watch me win!" Buchanan yelled at Holly. "You're the one who's going to lose! You're the one who's going to die! You'll wish you'd never met me! You'll wish you'd never led me on!"

At once Buchanan felt his breath taken away as hands slammed his back, propelling him against the side of the court. In a daze, Buchanan raised his padded forearms to cushion the impact against the stone wall. He spun and was slammed again, this time by Raymond's right padded shoulder, a full blow to the chest. Then Buchanan's back struck the wall, and a sharp pain made him fear that one of his ribs had been broken.

"Argue with her later," Raymond said. "*How do you contact your unit?*"

"Exactly," Drummond said. He coughed again, violently. More smoke swirled over him. The construction equipment continued roaring. Increasing gunshots reverberated, closer.

"Not until we have a deal!" Buchanan winced from the pain in his chest. Another pool of blood formed at his feet. He felt light-headed and fought to concentrate. He had to keep Holly and himself alive. Play your role, Holly. Play your role.

"What kind of deal?" Drummond asked.

"I tell you what you need, and I get to walk away," Buchanan said. "In exchange for calling off my unit, I stay alive. But this bitch gets what she deserves."

"You'd believe any bargain I made with you?" Drummond asked.

"Hey, your problem hasn't changed! If anything happens to me, my unit comes after you!" Buchanan held his chest, the sharp pain restricting his breath.

"And what about Juana Mendez? Do you expect me to believe you won't stop looking for her? Or maybe *she* no longer matters to you, either."

"No." Buchanan sweated. "She's the reason I'm in this. I'll keep looking. I'll convince her this is none of her business. I want her left alone. The same as me."

"She must be very special to you."

"Years ago, I should have married her."

"Buchanan, don't do this to me," Holly said. "Don't sell me out."

"Shut up. Anybody who uses me the way you did *deserves* to be sold out."

"All right," Drummond said. "Deal with the woman as you like. How do you contact your unit?"

Buchanan told them a radio frequency. "If you're using a telephone, the number is . . ." He told them that as well.

"That's a lie," Holly said.

Good, Buchanan thought. Keep going, Holly. Take my cue. Play the role. Buy us time.

"A lie?" Drummond asked.

"I don't know about the radio frequency, but the telephone number isn't the one I saw him use several times when he reported in. *That* number was . . ." She gave a different one.

"Ah," Drummond said. "It seems you haven't been perfectly honest," he told Buchanan.

"*She's* the one who's lying," Buchanan said. "I have to call my people by midnight. Let me use your radio and—"

"This is bullshit," Raymond said.

He picked up the ball and hurled it through the ring.

He did so again.

And again.

"You're stalling," Raymond said. "The two of you are pretending to fight with each other until you hope we're so confused that we'll keep you alive a little longer."

Raymond threw the ball and scored another point. "That's nine." He stared at Buchanan. "I don't believe either of you. One more point, and you're dead."

As Raymond prepared to throw the ball a final time, Buchanan lunged. He felt a tremor. The court seemed to ripple. His legs became wobbly.

Nonetheless, he kept charging. When Raymond threw, the ball struck the side of the rim. Buchanan intercepted it in midair, bounced it off his padded forearms, and knocked it through the ring.

But as he landed, his legs buckled. He was suddenly aware that the roar of the construction equipment had stopped. By contrast, the crackle of flames and the rattle of gunshots became louder. Men screamed.

He wavered.

"One more," Raymond said.

He picked up the ball. "One more."

He glared at Buchanan. "And the loser pays the penalty."

He threw the ball.

Buchanan didn't even bother to see if it went through the ring. He was too busy struggling to remain upright, preparing to defend himself.

Above him, he heard a commotion. Scuffling. A shout. Someone falling.

"Buchanan!" Holly screamed. "Behind you!"

Risking the distraction, he glanced quickly backward and saw that the guard had fallen from the terrace.

No! he realized. He was wrong. The guard hadn't fallen. He'd been pushed! By Holly.

The fifteen-foot drop had dazed the man. He lay, holding his leg as if it might be broken. The man had lost his grip on his automatic weapon.

Buchanan scurried off balance toward it and was knocked to the side by the startling heavy impact of the ball against his back.

My head! It almost hit my head! I'll die if it hits my head!

Buchanan heard more gunshots, more screams, but all he cared about was Raymond stalking toward him.

"You lost," Raymond said. His blue eyes glinted with anticipation. His boyish smile was stiff and cruel. It made him look devoid of all sanity. "I'm going to kill you with this." He picked up the weighty ball. "It's going to take a long time. Finally, I'm going to use the ball to smash your head like an eggshell."

Dizzy, Buchanan stumbled unwillingly back. He slipped on his blood. His brain felt swollen, his skull in terrible pain. He feinted toward the right, then dove toward the left, grabbing the fallen guard's automatic weapon.

Raymond stood over him, swaying, the ball raised over his head, preparing to hurl it down with all his strength.

Buchanan aimed the Uzi and pulled the trigger.

But nothing happened.

The weapon had jammed.

Buchanan's bowels felt as if they were suddenly filled with boiling water.

With a laugh, Raymond compacted his muscles to propel the ball down toward Buchanan's face.

10

And froze, his body eerily motionless. His blue eyes seemed more empty than ever, glassy. His grotesque smile seemed even more rigid.

At once the ball fell from his hands, dropping behind him, thunking on the court.

But his arms remained upstretched.

Blood trickled from his mouth.

He toppled forward, Buchanan scrambling to get out of the way.

As Raymond's face struck the court, Buchanan saw a mass of arrows embedded in Raymond's back.

He stared forward, in the direction from which the arrows must have come, but all he saw was smoke. Hearing a noise to his right, he spun. The guard, having adjusted to the shock of his fall from the terrace, was drawing a pistol. Buchanan pulled back the arming lever on his Uzi, freed the shell that had jammed, chambered a fresh round, and pulled the trigger, hitting the guard with a short, controlled burst that jolted him backward and down, blood flying.

"Holly!" Buchanan yelled. The terrace above him was deserted. "Holly! Where—?"

"Up here!"

He still couldn't see her.

"On my stomach!"

"Are you all right?"

"Scared!"

"*Can you climb down? Where are Drummond and—?*"

"Ran!" She raised her head. "When they saw . . . My God." She pointed past Buchanan.

Whirling, crouching, aiming the Uzi, Buchanan squinted toward the smoke at the end of the court. Any moment, he feared that more arrows would be launched.

He saw movement.

He tightened his finger on the trigger.

Shadows, then figures, emerged from the smoke.

Buchanan felt a chill surge through him. Earlier, when Raymond had arrived with his leather armor and his feathered helmet, Buchanan had experienced an uncanny sense that Raymond was stepping not only through smoke but time.

Now Buchanan had that skin-prickling sensation again, but in this case, the figures striding toward him from the smoke were indeed Maya, short and thin, with straight black hair, dark brown skin, round heads, wide faces, and almond-shaped eyes. Like Raymond, they wore leather armor and feathered helmets, and for a dismaying instant, his mind swirling, Buchanan felt as if he'd been sucked back a thousand years.

The Maya carried spears, machetes, and bows and arrows. A dozen men. Their leader kept his stern gaze on Buchanan all the while he approached, and Buchanan slowly lowered the Uzi, holding it with his left hand parallel to his leg, pointing the weapon down toward the ball court.

The Maya stopped before him, their leader assessing Buchanan. In the background, only the crackle of flames could be heard. The gunshots had stopped, and Buchanan thought he knew why: This wasn't the only group of Maya who, outraged by the desecration of their ancestors' temples, had finally rebelled instead of allowing themselves to be hunted.

The Mayan chieftain narrowed his gaze with fierce emotion and raised his machete.

Buchanan didn't know if he was being tested. It took all his control not to raise the Uzi and fire.

The chieftain whirled toward Raymond's body, striking with the machete, chopping off Raymond's head.

With contempt, the chieftain raised the head by its hair.

As blood drained from the neck, Buchanan couldn't help being reminded of the engraving on the wall of the ball court that Raymond had singled out at the start of the game.

The chieftain pivoted and hurled the skull toward the stone ring. It whunked against the rim, spun, then hurtled through and landed on the court, spattering blood, rolling, making the sound of an overripe pumpkin.

Raymond, you were wrong, Buchanan thought. It wasn't the loser but the *winner* who got sacrificed.

The chieftain scowled toward Buchanan and raised his machete a second time. Buchanan needed all of his discipline not to defend himself. He didn't flinch. He didn't blink. The chieftain nodded, made a forward gesture with the machete, and led his companions past Buchanan, as if he didn't exist, as if he and not they were a ghost.

Buchanan felt paralyzed for a moment, watching them stride forward into the smoke, disappearing as if they had never been, and then his legs felt wobbly. He glanced down, appalled by the amount of blood at his feet, *his* blood, the blood from his reopened knife wound.

"Holly!"

"Next to you."

He spun. Her features strained with fright, she seemed to have appeared from nowhere.

"Lie down," she said.

"No. Can't. Help me. This won't be over"—he swallowed, his mouth dry—"until we find Drummond and Delgado."

Ahead, through the smoke, men shrieked.

Dizzy, Buchanan put his arm around Holly and stumbled forward, ready with his Uzi. They entered the smoke. Briefly, nothing could be seen. Then they emerged into what seemed a different world. The ball court had been left behind. So had hundreds of years. They faced the obscene pyramid-shaped oil rig that stood where a pyramid of stone, a temple, a holy place, had once stood, focusing the energy of the universe.

Except for the crackle of flames, the place was unnervingly silent. The bodies of construction workers lay all around.

"Dear God," Holly murmured.

Abruptly, Buchanan heard a metallic whine. An increasing *whump-whump-whump*. An engine's roar.

The helicopter, Buchanan realized. Drummond and Delgado had reached it. He strained to peer up, squinting in pain past the flames that whooshed up from trees ahead of him. There. He saw the blue helicopter rising.

But something was wrong. It wobbled. It had trouble gaining altitude. As Buchanan struggled to clear his vision, he saw the cluster of men that clung to its landing skids, desperate to be carried away. Inside the crowded chopper, someone had opened a hatch, kicking at the men, trying to knock them off the struts.

The helicopter wavered, fought for altitude.

And plummeted into the blazing trees. An instant later, a walloping explosion burst from the flames, scattering bodies and wreckage in all directions. The blast reverberated across the site and into the jungle.

Buchanan and Holly were jolted back, horrified, smoke drifting over them. Coughing, wiping sweat and grime from their faces, they surveyed the wreckage. The steel pyramid had been struck by a huge spinning chunk from the helicopter. A support beam had been severed. The derrick listed, drooped, and toppled, metal screeching. Construction equipment was buried by twisted metal. Only the remnants of once-great monuments, the ruins of the ruins that Drummond had allowed to remain, seemed permanent.

A man groaned, "Help."

Buchanan glanced around, hobbling, following the voice through the smoke.

"Here. Oh, God, please help."

Buchanan recognized the voice before he saw him. Delgado. The man lay on his back, a spear projecting from his chest. His face was ashen.

"Help." He gestured weakly toward the spear. "Can't move. Pull it out."

"Out? Are you sure?"

"Yes."

"If that's what you want," Buchanan said. Knowing what would happen, he gripped the spear and tugged.

Delgado screamed. At once his scream became a gurgle as the force of the spear's removal caused him to hemorrhage internally. Blood erupted from his mouth.

"For what you did to Maria Tomez," Buchanan said, "you deserve a whole lot worse."

Holly clung to him, just as he clung to Holly. The sun was setting. The crimson-tinted, smoke-obscured area seemed completely deserted.

"Dear Christ," Holly said, "did *all* of them die? Everybody?"

"The Maya. I don't see them," Buchanan said. "Where are they?"

The bump of a falling log disturbed the illusion. Buchanan stared toward the right.

And bristled, finding another survivor.

Alistair Drummond staggered from a leaning, smoking remnant of the log building that had been the camp's office.

At last, he showed his age. Even more than his age. Stooped, shriveled, his cheeks gaunt, his eyes sunken, he seemed the oldest man Buchanan had ever seen.

Noticing Buchanan, the old man shuddered, then hobbled to try to get away.

Weakness forced Buchanan to hobble in imitation. Several times, Drummond fell. So did Buchanan. But relentless, Buchanan persisted, passing hieroglyph-covered blocks of stone that stood next to fallen clumps of twisted girders.

Drummond faltered from something before him. Turning, he tried to stand proudly, failing miserably as Buchanan stumbled up to him.

"I thought you died on the helicopter," Buchanan said.

"They wouldn't let me on." Drummond's white hair had been singed by flames. His scalp had been seared. He was almost bald. "Can you believe it?" Drummond's voice wavered. "They were all so eager to escape that they wouldn't let me on."

"Tell me," Buchanan said. "What made you ever think you could get away with this?"

"Think? I *know*. As old as I am, as powerful as I am, what can anybody do to punish me? Never forget I'm so very rich."

"What you are is a bastard."

Buchanan reached out and pushed him with his right index finger. The minuscule force was enough to throw the old man off balance. His gangly arms flailed. He listed. He screamed. He fell.

What had stopped him from continuing to hobble away from Buchanan was a deep, wide pit above which the ancient Maya had built their stone pyramid to hide and control the god of darkness, the god of black water, the god that seeped from the earth. The steel pyramid with which Drummond had replaced the original pyramid had collapsed into the pit, and at the bottom, oil rippled thickly, its petroleum smell nauseating.

Drummond struck the surface of the oil.

And was swallowed.

"He wanted that oil so damned bad. Now he's got it," Buchanan said.

He sank to the ground. His mind swirled.

11

Holly's blurred face hovered over him.

The Mayan chieftain, who'd confronted him in the ball court, seemed to hover next to her, the colorful feathers of his head-dress radiant in the crimson sunset. Other warriors appeared, gripping blood-covered spears and machetes. Holly seemed not to realize her danger.

Buchanan tried to raise a hand to point and warn her. He couldn't move the hand. He tried to open his mouth and tell her. His mouth wouldn't move. The words wouldn't come. He felt as if the earth spun beneath him, tugging him into a vortex.

The Mayan chieftain stooped, his broad round face distorting the closer it came to Buchanan.

In his delirium, Buchanan felt himself being lifted and placed upon a litter. He had a floating sensation. Although his eyelids were closed, he saw images. A towering pyramid. Statues that depicted gigantic snake heads. Evocative hieroglyphics. Magnificent palaces and temples.

Then the jungle rose before him, and he was carried through a clearing in the trees and bushes, a clearing that went on and on, his litter bearers proceeding along a wide pathway made of gray stone, higher than the forest floor. It seemed to him that everywhere, except on the pathway, snakes made the ground ripple.

Night settled over them. Nonetheless they continued, Holly staying close to his litter, the Mayan chieftain guided by moonlight, leading the way.

This is how it was a thousand years ago, Buchanan thought.

They came to a village, where through a gate, beyond a head-high wooden stockade, torches flickered, revealing huts. The walls of the huts were made from woven saplings, the roofs from palm fronds. Pigs and chickens, wakened by the procession, scattered noisily. Villagers waited, short, round-faced, dark-haired, almond-eyed, the women wearing ghostly white dresses.

Buchanan was taken into one of the huts. He was placed on a hammock. So the snakes can't get at me, he thought. Women undressed him. In the light from a fire, the chieftain peered at his wounds.

Holly shrieked and tried to stop him, but the villagers restrained her, and after the chieftain sewed Buchanan's knife wound shut, after he applied a compress to Buchanan's almost-healed bullet wound, after he put salve on Buchanan's cuts and bruises, he examined Buchanan's bulging eyes, used a knife to shave the hair from one side of Buchanan's head.

And raised a pulley-driven wooden drill to Buchanan's aching skull.

The sharp point was excruciating.

As if a huge boil had been lanced, Buchanan fainted from the ecstasy of tremendous release.

12

"How long have I been unconscious?" Buchanan managed to ask. His mind was clouded. His body felt unrelated to him. Words were like stones in his mouth.

"Two weeks."

That so surprised him his thoughts were jolted, forced to be less murky. He raised his right hand toward the bandage around his skull.

"Don't touch it," Holly said.

"What happened to my—? How did—?"

Holly didn't answer. She soaked a clean cloth in rainwater that she'd collected in half a hollowed-out coconut shell. While Buchanan lay partially naked on a hammock outside a hut, the late-afternoon sunlight comfortably warm against his wounds, she bathed him.

"Tell me." He licked his dry, swollen lips.

"You almost died. You'd lost a lot of blood, but the medicine man was able to stop it."

"My head. What about my—?"

"You were raving. Convulsing. Your eyes were so huge, I was afraid they'd pop out of your head. Obviously there was pressure behind them. He operated."

"What?"

"On your head. He drilled a hole in your skull. Blood spurted across the hut as if . . ."

Buchanan's strength waned. His eyelids drooped. He licked again at his dry lips.

Holly raised another hollowed-out half of a coconut and gave him rainwater to drink.

It dribbled down his chin, but he kept trying and was able to swallow most of it, luxuriating in its cool sweetness.

"Drilled a hole in . . ." he murmured.

"Primitive surgery. From a thousand years ago. It's like this place is suspended in time. No electricity. Everything they need, they get from the forest. Their clothes are handmade. Their soap is . . . They burn corncobs to boil water. Then they put the ashes from corncobs into the water and use it to scour dirty clothes. Then they take the clothes out and rinse the ashes from the clothes in other boiling pots. The clothes are incredibly clean. Then they pour the water on their crops so the corncob ashes can be a fertilizer."

Buchanan had trouble concentrating. His eyelids kept drooping.

"Primitive surgery," he said in muted dismay.

That was two days later, the next time he wakened.

Holly told him that she'd managed to get him to swallow

liquids—water and chicken broth—while he was unconscious, but although he was hydrated, he'd lost an alarming amount of weight and would have to try to eat soon, regardless of whether his stomach felt up to it.

"I'm ready," Buchanan said.

She dipped a wooden spoon into a clay bowl, tested the squash soup to make sure it wasn't too hot, and placed it into his mouth.

"Delicious."

"Don't give me credit. I didn't make it. There's a woman who comes with food. She gestures to tell me what to do about you."

"And the medicine man?"

"He comes twice a day to give you a spoonful of a thick, sweet-smelling syrup. It might be the reason you didn't get an infection. I wish I understood their language. I tried the little Spanish I know, but they don't seem to recognize it. We communicate with sign language."

"Why did they go to so much trouble?" Buchanan wondered. "Why did they let us live?"

"I don't know," Holly said. "They treat you as if you're a hero. I don't understand."

"Something to do with the game," Buchanan said. "Fighting against Raymond. Being obvious enemies with Drummond. The natives decided we're on their side." Buchanan brooded. "I lost the game, and yet . . . In the old days, it could be the Maya felt so sorry for the loser that they took care of him."

"Why would they feel sorry for him?"

"Because the winner was sacrificed and got to be with the gods."

"Raymond isn't with the gods."

"No. Nor is Drummond. He's in hell, where he deserves to be," Buchanan said. "He reminds me of the colonel."

"The colonel?"

Buchanan hesitated. "What happened at the drilling site is yours. Write about it. Just leave me out of it. But what I'm going to tell you now is off the record."

"Hey, if you don't know enough to trust me by now . . ."

Buchanan hesitated again, then made a decision. "Maybe trust is another part of what it means to be human. I certainly trusted you back there in the ball court. You were convincing, and yet I believed you were acting when you said that you'd stayed with me just because of the story.''

"And I trusted you, even when you told Drummond that you didn't care if I died. All I did was believe you were acting and follow your lead, but I didn't know where we were going. What did you hope to accomplish?''

"Raymond had part of it right. I wanted them to be so confused that they'd have to keep us alive until they figured out which one of us was telling the truth. Eventually, they'd have been tempted to try those telephone numbers we gave them, and the automatic trace would have led the colonel's hit team in this direction. With luck, we'd have still been alive.''

"Chancy.''

"No kidding. In that kind of situation, there aren't any long-term plans. But you and I sure made a good team.''

"Well, l had a good teacher,'' Holly said.

"I was telling you about my commanding officer. The colonel and Drummond are very much alike. The colonel has a goal, and nothing matters except achieving it.''

"But that's standard military discipline.''

"No. The military has ethics. Politicians don't. It's politicians who give soldiers immoral goals. But sometimes a soldier like the colonel comes along and . . .'' Buchanan's fragile strength waned. Only his angry thoughts kept him going. ''I'm beginning to think that it was the colonel who had Jack and Cindy Doyle killed. And Bailey. Because of the photographs you took of me with the colonel. Because he was afraid he'd be identified as the director of Scotch and Soda and his career would be ruined. Also, I think it was the colonel who arranged to have me knifed in New Orleans. So you wouldn't have anybody to question. So the story would die with me. He turned against his own to protect himself. Maybe he's getting kickbacks from the drug deals that Scotch and Soda is making in Latin America. Who the hell knows? But one day, I'll find out. And one day, the colonel will have to justify himself to me.''

"What about Juana?''

"Drummond's men will stop looking for her now that he's dead and they're not being paid. Knowing how skilled she became at disguising her appearance, I don't think I can ever find her."

"But do you intend to keep trying?"

"You mean, does she still matter to me?"

Holly nodded.

"Yes," Buchanan said.

Holly lowered her eyes.

"But not the way *you* matter," Buchanan said.

Holly looked up.

"She's a friend who needed help, and for too long in my life, I wasn't able to help friends I'd known under other identities. I need to find out that she's safe. My guess is, once she learns that Drummond and Delgado are dead, she'll gradually come into the open. I look forward to seeing her again." Buchanan touched her arm. "But I swear to you, she's not your rival."

Holly felt overwhelmed by emotion. "What happens to us now?"

"One thing's certain. The colonel will never find us here."

"True. That's certainly looking on the bright side."

"Is it so bad here?"

"With you. No," Holly said. "Strange. As beat up as you look, there's something about . . . your eyes. Even though you're angry about the colonel, you seem at peace."

"I'm myself."

Holly frowned in confusion.

"Something's missing from me," Buchanan said. "Maybe it's because of everything we've been through. Or maybe it's because of you. Or . . . When the medicine man drilled into my skull, I think he took out more than blood. I think he took out whatever was in my head that tortured me for so long. I've come to terms with the past. I want to move on. With you. What matters now isn't the past but the present." Buchanan squeezed Holly's hand. "And the future. No more trying to run from myself. No more assumed identities."

"It'll be a pleasure getting to know you," Holly said.

"I'm kind of curious about it myself."

"Yes." Holly kissed him. "It's what I've been waiting for."